PAT OF SILVER BUSH
&
MISTRESS PAT

BY

L. M. MONTGOMERY

Author of
"Anne of Green Gables,"
"Anne of Avonlea,"
"Kilmeny of the Orchard," etc.

Pat of Silver Bush first published 1933
Mistress Pat first published 1935
This edition published by Read Books Ltd.
Copyright © 2017 Read Books Ltd.

British Library Cataloguing-in-Publication Data
A catalogue record for this book is available
from the British Library

CONTENTS

———

Lucy Maud Montgomery

Lucy Maud Montgomery was born on 30th November 1874, on Prince Edward Island, Canada. Her mother, Clara Woolner (Macneil), died before Lucy reached the age of two and so she was raised by her maternal grandparents in a family of wealthy Scottish immigrants. The Family were deeply rooted in the development of the island, having arrived there in the 1770's, and both Lucy's grandfather and great grandfather had been figures in the province's governance.

As a young girl, Montgomery had a very privileged upbringing. Due to the families wealth, she had access to a greater number of books than was usual in this era. These resources, coupled with the family's Scottish traditions of oral storytelling, gave her a taste for literature.

Montgomery took a teacher's degree at Charlottetown's Prince of Wales College before beginning work at a rural school to raise funds for and additional year at Dalhousie University. She continued to teach for a couple of years until her income from writing enabled her to become a full-time author. She then moved back home to live with her grandmother. In 1908, Montgomery produced her first full-length novel, titled *Anne of Green Gables*. It was an instant success and, following it up with several sequels, Montgomery became a regular on the best-seller list and an international household name.

In 1911 she married Ewan Macdonald, a Presbyterian minister, following the death of her grandmother. They had two sons together but the marriage was fraught with difficulties. Ewan had a severe mental disorder that frequently left him incapacitated, seriously hampering his career and eventually forcing him to resign from the ministry in 1935. The couple retired to Toronto and resided there together until Montgomery's death on 24th April 1942.

PAT OF SILVER BUSH

1

INTRODUCES PAT

1

"Oh, oh, and I think I'll soon have to be doing some rooting in the parsley bed," said Judy Plum, as she began to cut Winnie's red crepe dress into strips suitable for "hooking." She was very much pleased with herself because she had succeeded in browbeating Mrs. Gardiner into letting her have it. Mrs. Gardiner thought Winnie might have got another summer's wear out of it. Red crepe dresses were not picked up in parsley beds, whatever else might be.

But Judy had set her heart on that dress. It was exactly the shade she wanted for the inner petals of the fat, "raised" roses in the fine new rug she was hooking for Aunt Hazel ... a rug with golden-brown "scrolls" around its edges and, in the centre, clusters of red and purple roses such as never grew on any earthly rose-bush.

Judy Plum "had her name up," as she expressed it, for hooked rugs, and she meant that this should be a masterpiece. It was to be a wedding gift for Aunt Hazel, if that young lady really got married this summer, as, in Judy's opinion, it was high time she should, after all her picking and choosing.

Pat, who was greatly interested in the rug's progress, knew nothing except that it was for Aunt Hazel. Also, there was another event impending at Silver Bush of which she was ignorant and Judy thought it was high time she was warned. When one has been the "baby" of a family for almost seven years just how is one going to take a supplanter? Judy, who loved everybody at Silver Bush in reason, loved Pat out of reason and was worried over this beyond all measure. Pat was always after taking things a bit too seriously. As Judy put it, she "loved too hard." What a scene she had been after making that very morning because Judy wanted her old purple sweater for the roses. It was far too tight for her and more holy than righteous, if ye plaze, but Pat wouldn't hear of giving it up. She loved that old sweater and she meant to wear it another year. She fought so tigerishly about it that Judy . . . of course . . . gave in. Pat was always like that about her clothes. She wore them until they simply wouldn't look at her because they were so dear to her she couldn't bear to give them up. She hated her new duds until she had worn them for a few weeks. Then she turned around and loved them fiercely, too.

"A quare child, if ye'll belave me," Judy used to say, shaking her grizzled head. But she would have put the black sign on any one else who called Pat a queer child.

"What makes her queer?" Sidney had asked once, a little belligerently. Sidney loved Pat and didn't like to hear her called queer.

"Sure, a leprachaun touched her the day she was born wid a liddle green rose-thorn," answered Judy mysteriously.

Judy knew all about leprachauns and banshees and water-kelpies and fascinating beings like that.

"So she can't ever be just like other folks. But it isn't all to the bad. She'll be after having things other folks can't have."

"What things?" Sidney was curious.

"She'll love folks . . . and things . . . better than most . . . and that'll give her the great delight. But they'll hurt her more, too. 'Tis the way of the fairy gift and ye have to take the bad wid the good."

"If that's all the leppern did for her I don't think he amounts to much," said young Sidney scornfully.

"S . . . sh!" Judy was scandalised. "Liddle ye know what may be listening to ye. And I'm not after saying it was all. She'll *see* things. Hundreds av witches flying be night over the woods and steeples on broomsticks, wid their black cats perched behind them. How wud ye like that?"

"Aunt Hazel says there aren't any such things as witches, 'specially in Prince Edward Island," said Sidney.

"If ye don't be belaving innything what fun are ye going to get out av life?" asked Judy unanswerably. "There may niver be a witch in P. E. Island but there's minny a one in ould Ireland even yet. The grandmother av me was one."

"Are *you* a witch?" demanded Sidney daringly. He had always wanted to ask Judy that.

"I might be having a liddle av it in me, though I'm not be way av being a full witch," said Judy significantly.

"And are you sure the leppern pricked Pat?"

"Sure? Who cud be sure av what a fairy might be doing? Maybe it's only the mixed blood in her makes her quare. Frinch and English and Irish and Scotch and Quaker . . . 'tis a tarrible mixture, I'm telling ye."

"But that's all so long ago," argued Sidney. "Uncle Tom says it's just Canadian now."

"Oh, oh," said Judy, highly offended, "if yer Uncle Tom do be knowing more about it than meself whativer are ye here plaguing me to death wid yer questions for? Scoot, scat, and scamper, or I'll warm your liddle behind for ye."

"I don't believe there's either witches or fairies," cried Sid, just to make her madder. It was always fun to make Judy Plum mad.

"Oh, oh, indade! Well, I knew a man in ould Ireland said the same thing. Said it as bould as brass, he did. And he met some one night, whin he was walking home from where he'd no business to be. Oh, oh, what they did to him!"

"What . . . what?" demanded Sid eagerly.

"Niver ye be minding what it was. 'Tis better for ye niver to know. He was niver the same again and he held his tongue about the Good Folk after that, belave me. Only I'm advising ye to be a bit careful what ye say out loud whin ye think ye're all alone, me bould young lad."

2

Judy was hooking her rug in her own bedroom, just over the kitchen . . . a fascinating room, so the Silver Bush children thought. It was not plastered. The walls and ceiling were finished with smooth bare boards which Judy kept beautifully whitewashed. The bed was an enormous one with a fat chaff tick. Judy scorned feathers and mattresses were, she believed, a modern invention of the Bad Man Below. It had pillowslips trimmed with crocheted "pineapple" lace, and was covered with a huge "autograph quilt" which some local society had made years before and which Judy had bought.

"Sure and I likes to lie there a bit when I wakes and looks at all the names av people that are snug underground and me still hearty and kicking," she would say.

The Silver Bush children all liked to sleep a night now and then with Judy, until they grew too big for it, and listen to her tales of the folks whose names were on the quilt. Old forgotten fables . . . ancient romances . . . Judy knew them all, or made them up if she didn't. She had a marvellous memory and a knack of dramatic word-painting. Judy's tales were not always so harmless as that. She had an endless store of weird yarns of ghosts and "rale nice murders," and it was a wonder she did not scare the children out of a year's growth. But they were only deliciously goosefleshed. They knew Judy's stories were "lies," but no matter. They were absorbing and interesting lies. Judy had a delightful habit of carrying a tale on night after night, with a trick of stopping at just the right breathless place which any writer of serial stories would have envied her. Pat's favourite one was a horrible tale of a murdered man who was found in pieces about the house . . . an arm in the garret . . . a head in the cellar . . . a hambone in a pot in the pantry. "It gives me such a lovely shudder, Judy."

Beside the bed was a small table covered with a crocheted tidy, whereon lay a beaded, heart-shaped pin-cushion and a shell-covered box in which Judy kept the first tooth of all the children and a lock of their hair. Also a razor-fish shell from Australia and a bit of beeswax that she used to make her thread smooth and which was seamed with innumerable fine, criss-cross wrinkles like old Great-great-aunt Hannah's face at the Bay Shore. Judy's Bible lay there, too, and a fat little brown book of "Useful Knowledge" out of which Judy constantly fished amazing information. It was the only book Judy ever read. Folks, she said, did be more interesting than books.

Bunches of dried tansy and yarrow and garden herbs hung from the ceiling everywhere and looked gloriously spooky on moonlight nights. Judy's big blue chest which she had brought out with her from the Old Country thirty years ago stood against the wall and when Judy was in especial good humour she would show the children the things in it . .

. an odd and interesting *mélange,* for Judy had been about the world a bit in her time. Born in Ireland she had "worked out" in her teens . . . in a "castle" no less, as the Silver Bush children heard with amazed eyes. Then she had gone to England and worked there until a roving brother took a notion to go to Australia and Judy went with him. Australia not being to his liking he next tried Canada and settled down on a P. E. Island farm for a few years. Judy went to work at Silver Bush in the days of Pat's grandparents, and, when her brother announced his determination to pull up stakes and go to the Klondike, Judy coolly told him he could go alone. She liked "the Island." It was more like the Ould Country than any place she'd struck. She liked Silver Bush and she loved the Gardiners.

Judy had been at Silver Bush ever since. She had been there when "Long Alec" Gardiner brought his young bride home. She had been there when each of the children was born. She belonged there. It was impossible to think of Silver Bush without her. With her flair for picking up tales and legends she knew more of the family history than any of the Gardiners themselves did.

She never had had any notion of marrying.

"I niver had but the one beau," she told Pat once. "He seranaded me under me windy one night and I poured a jug av suds over him. Maybe it discouraged him. Innyway, he niver got any forrarder."

"Were you sorry?" asked Pat.

"Niver a bit, me jewel. He hadn't the sinse God gave geese innyhow."

"Do you think you'll ever marry now, Judy?" asked Pat anxiously. It would be so terrible if Judy married and went away.

"Oh, oh, at me age! And me as grey as a cat!"

"How old are you, Judy Plum?"

"'Tis hardly a civil question that, but ye're too young to know it. I do be as old as me tongue and a liddle older than me teeth. Don't be fretting yer liddle gizzard about me marrying. Marrying's a trouble and not marrying's a trouble and I sticks to the trouble I knows."

"I'm never going to marry either, Judy," said Pat. "Because if I got married I'd have to go away from Silver Bush, and I couldn't bear that. We're going to stay here always . . . Sid and me . . . and you'll stay with us, won't you, Judy? And teach me how to make cheeses."

"Oh, oh, cheeses, is it? Thim cheese factories do be making all the cheeses now. There isn't a farm on the Island but Silver Bush that does

11

be making thim. And this is the last summer I'll be doing thim I'm thinking."

"Oh, Judy Plum, you *mustn't* give up making cheeses. You must make them forever. *Please*, Judy Plum?"

"Well, maybe I'll be making two or three for the family," conceded Judy. "Yer dad do be always saying the factory ones haven't the taste av the home-made ones. How could they, I'm asking ye? Run be the min! What do min be knowing about making cheeses? Oh, oh, the changes since I first come to the Island!"

"I *hate* changes," cried Pat, almost in tears.

It had been so terrible to think of Judy never making any more cheeses. The mysterious mixing in of something she called "rennet" . . . the beautiful white curds next morning . . . the packing of it in the hoops . . . the stowing it away under the old "press" by the church barn with the round grey stone for a weight. Then the long drying and mellowing of the big golden moons in the attic . . . all big save one dear tiny one made in a special hoop for Pat. Pat knew everybody in North Glen thought the Gardiners terribly old-fashioned because they still made their own cheeses, but who cared for that? Hooked rugs were old-fashioned, too, but summer visitors and tourists raved over them and would have bought all Judy Plum made. But Judy would never sell one. They were for the house at Silver Bush and no other.

3

Judy was hooking furiously, trying to finish her rose before the "dim," as she always called the twilights of morning and evening. Pat liked that. It sounded so lovely and strange. She was sitting on a little stool on the landing of the kitchen stairs, just outside Judy's open door, her elbows on her thin knees, her square chin cupped in her hands. Her little laughing face, that always seemed to be laughing even when she was sad or mad or bad, was ivory white in winter but was already beginning to pick up its summer tan. Her hair was ginger-brown and straight . . . and long. Nobody at Silver Bush, except Aunt Hazel, had yet dared to wear bobbed hair. Judy raised such a riot about it that mother hadn't ventured to cut Winnie's or Pat's. The funny thing was that Judy had bobbed hair herself and so was in the very height of the fashion she disdained. Judy had always worn her grizzled hair short. Hadn't time to be fussing with hairpins she declared.

Gentleman Tom sat beside Pat, on the one step from the landing into Judy's room, blinking at her with insolent green eyes, whose very expression would have sent Judy to the stake a few hundred years ago. A big, lanky cat who always looked as if he had a great many secret troubles; continually thin in spite of Judy's partial coddling; a black cat . . . "the blackest black cat I iver did be seeing." For a time he had been nameless. Judy held it wasn't lucky to name a baste that had just "come." Who knew what might be offended? So the black grimalkin was called Judy's Cat, with a capital, until one day Sid referred to it as "Gentleman Tom," and Gentleman Tom he was from that time forth, even Judy surrendering. Pat was fond of all cats, but her fondness for Gentleman Tom was tempered with awe. He had come from nowhere apparently, not even having been born like other kittens, and attached himself to Judy. He slept on the foot of her bed, walked beside her, with his ramrod of a tail straight up in the air, wherever she went and had never been heard to purr. It couldn't be said that he was a sociable cat. Even Judy, who would allow no faults in him, admitted he was "a bit particular who he spoke to."

"Sure and he isn't what ye might call a talkative cat but he do be grand company in his way."

2

INTRODUCES SILVER BUSH

1

Pat's brook-brown eyes had been staring through the little round window in the wall above the landing until Judy had made her mysterious remark about the parsley bed. It was her favourite window, opening outward like the port-hole of a ship. She never went up to Judy's room without stopping to look from it. Dear little fitful breezes came to that window that never came anywhere else and you saw such lovely things out of it. The big grove of white birch on the hill behind it which gave Silver Bush its name and which was full of dear little screech owls that hardly ever screeched but purred and laughed. Beyond it all the dells and slopes and fields of the old farm, some of them fenced in with the barbed wire Pat hated, others still surrounded by the snake fences of silvery-grey "longers," with golden-rod and aster thick in their angles.

Pat loved every field on the farm. She and Sidney had explored every one of them together. To her they were not just fields . . . they were persons. The big hill field that was in wheat this spring and was now like a huge green carpet; the field of the Pool which had in its very centre a dimple of water, as if some giantess when earth was young had pressed the tip of her finger down into the soft ground: it was framed all summer in daisies and blue flags and she and Sid bathed their hot tired little feet there on sultry days. The Mince Pie field, which was a triangle of land running up into the spruce bush: the swampy Buttercup field where all the buttercups in the world bloomed; the field of Farewell Summers which in September would be dotted all over with clumps of purple asters; the Secret Field away at the back, which you couldn't see at all and would never suspect was there until you had gone through the woods, as she and Sid had daringly done one day, and come upon it suddenly, completely surrounded by maple and fir woods, basking in a pool of sunshine, scented by the breath of the spice ferns that grew in golden clumps around it. Its feathery bent grasses were starred with the red of wild strawberry leaves; and there were some piles of large stones here and there, with bracken growing in their crevices and clusters of long-stemmed strawberries all around their bases. That was the first time Pat had ever picked a "bouquet" of strawberries.

In the corner by which they entered were two dear little spruces, one just a hand's-breadth taller than the other . . . brother and sister, just like Sidney and her. Wood Queen and Fern Princess, they had named them instantly. Or rather Pat did. She loved to name things. It made them just like people . . . people you loved.

They loved the Secret Field better than all the other fields. It seemed somehow to belong to them as if they had been the first to discover it; it was so different from the poor, bleak, little stony field behind the barn that nobody loved . . . nobody except Pat. She loved it because it was a

Silver Bush field. That was enough for Pat.

But the fields were not all that could be seen from that charming window on this delightful spring evening when the sky in the west was all golden and soft pink, and Judy's "dim" was creeping down out of the silver bush. There was the Hill of the Mist to the east, a little higher than the hill of the silver bush, with three lombardies on its very top, like grim, black, faithful watchmen. Pat loved that hill dreadfully hard, although it wasn't on Silver Bush land . . . quite a mile away in fact, and she didn't know to whom it belonged; in one sense, that is: in another she knew it was hers because she loved it so much. Every morning she waved a hand of greeting to it from her window. Once, when she was only five, she remembered going to spend the day with the Great-aunts at the Bay Shore farm and how frightened she had been lest the Hill of the Mist might be moved while she was away. What a joy it had been to come home and find it still in its place, with its three poplars untouched, reaching up to a great full moon above them. She was now, at nearly seven, so old and wise that she knew the Hill of the Mist would never be moved. It would always be there, go where she would, return when she might. This was comforting in a world which Pat was already beginning to suspect was full of a terrible thing called change . . . and another terrible thing which she was not yet old enough to know was disillusionment. She only knew that whereas a year ago she had firmly believed that if she could climb to the top of the Hill of the Mist she might be able to touch that beautiful shining sky, perhaps . . . oh, rapture! . . . pick a trembling star from it, she knew now that nothing of the sort was possible. Sidney had told her this and she had to believe Sid who, being a year older than herself, knew so much more than she did. Pat thought nobody knew as much as Sidney . . . except, of course, Judy Plum who knew everything. It was Judy who knew that the wind spirits lived on the Hill of the Mist. It was the highest hill for miles around and the wind spirits did always be liking high points. Pat knew what they looked like, though nobody had ever told her . . . not even Judy who thought it safer not to be after describing the craturs. Pat knew the north wind was a cold, glittering spirit and the east wind a grey shadowy one; but the spirit of the west wind was a thing of laughter and the south wind was a thing of song.

The kitchen garden was just below the window, with Judy's mysterious parsley bed in one corner, and beautiful orderly rows of onions and beans and peas. The well was beside the gate . . . the old-fashioned open well with a handle and roller and a long rope with a bucket at its end, which the Gardiners kept to please Judy who simply wouldn't hear of any new-fangled pump being put in. Sure and the water would never be the same again. Pat was glad Judy wouldn't let them change the old well. It was beautiful, with great ferns growing out all the way down its sides from the crevices of the stones that lined it, almost hiding from sight the deep clear water fifty feet below, which always mirrored a bit of blue sky and her own little face looking up at her from those always untroubled depths. Even in winter the ferns were there, long and green, and always the mirrored Patricia looked up at her from a world where tempests never blew. A big maple grew over the well . . . a maple that reached with green arms to the house, every year a little nearer.

Pat could see the orchard, too . . . a most extraordinary orchard with spruce trees and apple trees delightfully mixed up together . . . in the Old Part, at least. The New Part was trim and cultivated and not half so interesting. In the Old Part were trees that Great-grandfather Gardiner had planted and trees that had never been planted at all but just *grew*, with delightful little paths criss-crossing all over it. At the far end was a corner full of young spruces with a tiny sunny glade in the midst of them, where several beloved cats lay buried and where Pat went when she wanted to "think things out." Things sometimes have to be thought out even at nearly seven.

2

At one side of the orchard was the grave-yard. Yes, truly, a grave-yard. Where Great-great-grandfather, Nehemiah Gardiner, who had come out to P. E. Island in 1780, was buried, and likewise his wife, Marie Bonnet, a French Huguenot lady. Great-grandfather, Thomas Gardiner, was there, too, with his Quaker bride, Jane Wilson. They had been buried there when the nearest grave-yard was across the Island at Charlottetown, only to be reached by a bridle path through the woods. Jane Wilson was a demure little lady who always wore Quaker grey and a prim, plain cap. One of her caps was still in a box in the Silver Bush attic. She it was who had fought off the big black bear trying to get in at the window of their log cabin by pouring scalding hot mush on its face. Pat loved to hear Judy tell that story and describe how the bear had torn away through the stumps back of the cabin, pausing every once in so long for a frantic attempt to scrape the mush off its face. Those must have been exciting days in P. E. Island, when the woods were alive with bears and they would come and put their paws on the banking of the houses and look in at the windows. What a pity that could never happen now because there were no bears left! Pat always felt sorry for the last bear. How lonesome he must have been!

Great-uncle Richard was there . . . "Wild Dick Gardiner" who had been a sailor and had fought with sharks, and was reputed to have once eaten human flesh. He had sworn he would never rest on land. When he lay dying of measles . . . of all things for a dare-devil sailor to die of . . . he had wanted his brother Thomas to promise to take him out in a boat and bury him under the waters of the Gulf. But scandalised Thomas would do nothing of the sort and buried Dick in the family plot. As a result, whenever any kind of misfortune was going to fall on the Gardiners, Wild Dick used to rise and sit on the fence and sing his rake-helly songs until his sober, God-fearing kinsfolk had to come out of their graves and join him in the chorus. At least, this was one of Judy Plum's most thrilling yarns. Pat never believed it but she wished she could. Weeping Willy's grave was there, too . . . Nehemiah's brother who, when he first came to P. E. Island and saw all the huge trees that had to be cleared away, had sat down and cried. It was never forgotten. Weeping Willy he was to his death and after, and no girl could be found willing to be Mrs. Weeping Willy. So he lived his eighty years out in sour old bachelorhood and . . . so Judy said . . . when good fortune was to befall his race Weeping Willy sat on his flat tombstone and wept. And Pat couldn't believe that either. But she wished Weeping Willy *could* come back and see what was in the place of the lonely forest that had frightened him. If he could see Silver Bush *now!*

Then there was the "mystery grave." On the tombstone the inscription, *"To my own dear Emily and our little Lilian."* Nothing more, not even a date. Who was Emily? Not one of the Gardiners, that was known. Perhaps some neighbour had asked the privilege of burying his dear dead near him in the Gardiner plot where she might have company in the lone new land. And how old was the little Lilian? Pat thought if any of the Silver Bush ghosts did "walk" she wished it might be Lilian. She wouldn't be the least afraid of *her*.

There were many children buried there . . . nobody knew how many because there was no stone for any of them. The Great-greats had horizontal slabs of red sandstone from the shore propped on four legs, over them, with all their names and virtues inscribed thereon. The grass grew about them thick and long and was never disturbed. On summer afternoons the sandstone slabs were always hot and Gentleman Tom loved to lie there, beautifully folded up in slumber. A paling fence, which Judy Plum whitewashed scrupulously every spring, surrounded the plot. And the apples that fell into the grave-yard from overhanging boughs were never eaten. "It wudn't be rispictful," explained Judy. They were gathered up and given to the pigs. Pat could never understand why, if it wasn't "rispictful" to eat those apples, it was any more "rispictful" to feed them to the pigs.

She was very proud of the grave-yard and very sorry the Gardiners had given up being buried there. It would be so nice, Pat thought, to be buried right at home, so to speak, where you could hear the voices of your own folks every day and all the nice sounds of home . . . nice sounds such as Pat could hear now through the little round window. The whir of the grindstone as father sharpened an axe under the sweetapple-tree . . . a dog barking his head off somewhere over at Uncle Tom's . . . the west wind rustling in the trembling poplar leaves . . . the saw-wheats calling in the silver bush—Judy said they were calling for rain . . . Judy's big white gobbler lording it about the yard . . . Uncle Tom's geese talking back and forth to the Silver Bush geese . . . the pigs squealing in their pens . . . even that was pleasant because they were Silver Bush pigs: the Thursday kitten mewing to be let into the granary . . . somebody laughing . . . Winnie, of course. What a pretty laugh Winnie had; and Joe whistling around the barns . . . Joe did whistle so beautifully and half the time didn't know he was whistling. Hadn't he once started to whistle in church? But that was a story for Judy Plum to tell. Judy, take her own word for it, had never been the same again.

The barns where Joe was whistling were near the orchard, with only the Whispering Lane that led to Uncle Tom's between them. The little barn stood close to the big barn like a child . . . such an odd little barn with gables and a tower and oriel windows like a church. Which was exactly what it was. When the new Presbyterian church had been built in South Glen Grandfather Gardiner had bought the old one and hauled it home for a barn. It was the only thing he had ever done of which Judy Plum hadn't approved. It was only what she expected when he had a stroke five years later at the age of seventy-five, and was never the same again though he lived to be eighty. And say what you might there hadn't been the same luck among the Silver Bush pigs after the sty was shifted to the old church. They became subject to rheumatism.

3

The sun had set. Pat always liked to watch its western glory reflected in the windows of Uncle Tom's house beyond the Whispering Lane. It was the hour she liked best of all the hours on the farm. The poplar leaves were rustling silkily in the afterlight; the yard below was suddenly full of dear, round, fat, furry pussy-cats, bent on making the most of the cat's light. Silver Bush always overflowed with kittens. Nobody ever had the heart to drown them. Pat especially was fond of them. It was a story Judy loved to tell . . . how the minister had told Pat, aged four, that she could ask him any question she liked. Pat had said sadly, "Why don't Gentleman Tom have kittens?" The poor man did be resigning at the next Presbytery. He had a tendency to laughing and he said he couldn't preach wid liddle Pat Gardiner looking at him from her pew, so solemn-like and reproachful.

In the yard were black Sunday, spotted Monday, Maltese Tuesday, yellow Wednesday, calico Friday, Saturday who was just the colour of the twilight. Only striped Thursday continued to wail heart-brokenly at the granary door. Thursday had always been an unsociable kitten, walking by himself like Kipling's cat in Joe's story book. The old gobbler, with his coral-red wattles, had gone to roost on the orchard fence. Bats were swooping about . . . fairies rode on bats, Judy said. Lights were springing up suddenly to east and west . . . at Ned Baker's and Kenneth Robinson's and Duncan Gardiner's and James Adams'. Pat loved to watch them and wonder what was going on in the rooms where they bloomed. But there was one house in which there was never any light . . . an old white house among thick firs on the top of a hill to the south-west, two farms away from Silver Bush. It was a long, rather low house . . . Pat called it the Long Lonely House. It hadn't been lived in for years. Pat always felt so sorry for it, especially in the "dim" when the lights sprang up in all the other houses over the country side. It must feel lonely and neglected. Somehow she resented the fact that it didn't have all that other houses had.

"It wants to be lived in, Judy," she would say wistfully.

There was the evening star in a pale silvery field of sky just over the tall fir tree that shot up in the very centre of the silver bush. The first star always gave her a thrill. Wouldn't it be lovely if she could fly up to that dark swaying fir-top between the evening star and the darkness?

3

CONCERNING PARSLEY BEDS

1

The red rose was nearly finished and Pat suddenly remembered that Judy had said something about rooting in the parsley bed.

"Judy Plum," she said, "what do you think you'll find in the parsley bed?"

"What wud ye be after thinking if I told ye I'd find a tiny wee new baby there?" asked Judy, watching her sharply.

Pat looked for a moment as if she had rather had the wind knocked out of her. Then . . .

"Do you think, Judy, that we really need another baby here?"

"Oh, oh, as to that, a body might have her own opinion. But wudn't it be nice now? A house widout a baby do be a lonesome sort av place I'm thinking."

"Would you . . . would you like a baby better than me, Judy Plum?"

There was a tremble in Pat's voice.

"That I wudn't, me jewel. Ye're Judy's girl and Judy's girl ye'll be forever if I was finding a dozen babies in the parsley bed. It do be yer mother I'm thinking av. The fact is, she's got an unaccountable notion for another baby, Patsy, and I'm thinking we must be humouring her a bit, seeing as she isn't extry strong. So there's the truth av the matter for ye."

"Of course, if mother wants a baby I don't mind," conceded Pat. "Only," she added wistfully, "we're such a nice little family now, Judy . . . just mother and daddy and Aunt Hazel and you and Winnie and Joe and Sid and me. I wish we could just stay like that forever."

"I'm not saying it wudn't be best. These afterthoughts do be a bit upsetting whin ye've been thinking a family's finished. But there it is . . . nothing'll do yer mother but a baby. So it's poor Judy Plum must get down on her stiff ould marrow-bones and see what's to be found in the parsley bed."

"Are babies really found in parsley beds, Judy? Jen Foster says the doctor brings them in a black bag. And Ellen Price says a stork brings them. And Polly Gardiner says old Granny Garland from the bridge brings them in her basket."

"The things youngsters do be talking av nowadays," ejaculated Judy. "Ye've seen Dr. Bentley whin he was here be times. Did ye iver see him wid inny black bag?"

"No . . . o . . . o."

"And do there be inny storks on P. E. Island?"

Pat had never heard of any.

"As for Granny Garland, I'm not saying she hasn't a baby or two stowed away in her basket now and again. But if she has ye may rist contint she found it in her own parsley bed. What av that? She doesn't pick the babies for the quality. Ye wudn't want a baby av Granny Garland's choosing, wud ye, now?"

"Oh, no, no. But couldn't I help you look for it, Judy?"

"Listen at her. It's liddle ye know what ye do be talking about, child dear. It's only some one wid a drop av witch blood in her like meself can see the liddle craturs at all. And it's all alone I must go at the rise av the moon, in company wid me cat. 'Tis a solemn performance, I'm telling ye, this finding av babies, and not to be lightly undertaken."

Pat yielded with a sigh of disappointment.

"You'll pick a pretty baby, won't you, Judy? A Silver Bush baby *must* be pretty."

"Oh, oh, I'll do me best. Ye must remimber that none av thim are much to look at in the beginning. All crinkled and wrinkled just like the parsley leaves. And I'm telling ye another thing . . . it's mostly the pretty babies that grow up to be the ugly girls. Whin *I* was a baby . . ."

21

"Were *you* ever a baby, Judy?" Pat found it hard to believe. It was preposterous to think of Judy Plum ever having been a baby. And could there ever have been a time when there was *no* Judy Plum?

"I was that. And I was so handsome that the neighbours borryed me to pass off as their own whin company come. And look at me now! Just remimber that if you don't think the baby I'll be finding is as good-looking as ye'd want. Of course I had the jandies whin I was a slip av a girleen. It turned me as yellow as a brass cint. Me complexion was niver the same agin."

"But, Judy, you're not ugly."

"Maybe it's not so bad as that," said Judy cautiously, "but I wudn't have picked *this* face if I cud have had the picking. There now, I've finished me rose and a beauty it is and I must be off to me milking. Ye'd better go and let that Thursday cratur into the granary afore it breaks its heart. And don't be saying a word to inny one about this business av the parsley bed."

"I won't. But, Judy . . . I've a kind of awful feeling in my stomach . . ."

Judy laughed.

"The cliverness av the cratur! I know what ye do be hinting at. Well, after I'm finished wid me cows ye might slip into the kitchen and I'll be frying ye an egg."

"In butter, Judy?"

"Sure in butter. Lashings av it . . . enough to sop yer bits av bread in it the way ye like. And I'm not saying but what there might be a cinnymon bun left over from supper."

Judy, who never wore an apron, turned up her drugget skirt around her waist, showing her striped petticoat, and stalked downstairs, talking to herself as was her habit. Gentleman Tom followed her like a dark familiar. Pat uncoiled herself and went down to let Thursday into the granary. She still had a queer feeling though she could not decide whether it was really in her stomach or not. The world all at once seemed a bit too big. This new baby was an upsetting sort of an idea. The parsley bed had suddenly become a sinister sort of place. For a moment Pat was tempted to go to it and deliberately tear it all up by the roots. Judy wouldn't be able to find a baby in it then. But mother . . . mother wanted a baby. It would never do to disappoint mother.

"But I'll hate it," thought Pat passionately. "An *outsider* like that!"

If she could only talk it over with Sid it would be a comfort. But she had promised Judy not to say a word to anybody about it. It was the first time she had ever had a secret from Sid and it made her feel uncomfortable. Everything seemed to have changed a little in some strange fashion . . . and Pat hated change.

2

Half an hour later she had put the thought of it out of her mind and was in the garden, bidding the flowers goodnight. Pat never omitted this ceremony. She was sure they would miss her if she forgot it. It was so beautiful in the garden, in the late twilight, with a silvery hint of moonrise over the Hill of the Mist. The trees around it . . . old maples that Grandmother Gardiner had planted when she came as a bride to Silver Bush . . . were talking to each other as they always did at night. Three little birch trees that lived together in one corner were whispering secrets. The big crimson peonies were blots of darkness in the shadows. The blue-bells along the path trembled with fairy laughter. Some late June lilies starred the grass at the foot of the garden: the columbines danced: the white lilac at the gate flung passing breaths of fragrance on the dewy air: the southernwood . . . Judy called it "lad's love" . . . which the little Quaker Great-grand had brought with her from the old land a hundred years ago, was still slyly aromatic.

Pat ran about from plot to plot and kissed everything. Tuesday ran with her and writhed in furry ecstasy on the walks before her . . . walks that Judy had picked off with big stones from the shore, dazzlingly whitewashed.

When Pat had kissed all her flowers good-night she stood for a little while looking at the house. How beautiful it was, nestled against its wooden hill, as if it had grown out of it . . . a house all white and green, just like its own silver birches, and now patterned over charmingly with tree shadows cast by a moon that was floating over the Hill of the Mist. She always loved to stand outside of Silver Bush after dark and look at its lighted windows. There was a light in the kitchen where Sid was at his lessons . . . a light in the parlor where Winnie was practising her music . . . a light up in mother's room. A light for a moment flashed in the hall, as somebody went upstairs, bringing out the fan window over the front door.

"Oh, I've got such a *lovely* home," breathed Pat, clasping her hands. "It's such a nice *friendly* house. Nobody . . . nobody . . . has such a lovely home. I'd just like to *hug* it."

Pat had her eggs in the kitchen with plenty of butter gravy, and then there was the final ceremony of putting a saucer of milk for the fairies on the well platform. Judy never omitted it.

"There's no knowing what bad luck we might be having if we forgot it. Sure and we know how to trate fairies at Silver Bush."

The fairies came by night and drank it up. This was one of the things Pat was strongly inclined to believe. Hadn't Judy herself seen fairies dancing in a ring one night when she was a girleen in Ould Ireland?

"But Joe says there are no fairies in P. E. Island," she said wistfully.

"The things Joe do be saying make me sometimes think the b'y don't be all there," said Judy indignantly. "Wasn't there folks coming out to P.E.I, from the Ould Country for a hundred years, me jewel? And don't ye be belaving there'd always be a fairy or two, wid a taste for a bit av adventure, wud stow himself away among their belongings and come too, and thim niver a bit the wiser? And isn't the milk always gone be morning, I'm asking ye?"

Yes, it was. You couldn't get away from *that*.

"You're sure the cats don't drink it, Judy?"

"Oh, oh, cats, is it? There don't be much a cat wudn't do if it tuk it into its head, I'm granting ye, but the bouldest that iver lived wudn't be daring to lap up the milk that was left for a fairy. That's the one thing no cat'd ever do . . . be disrespictful to a fairy—and it'd be well for mortal craturs to folly his example."

"Couldn't we stay up some night, Judy, and watch? I'd love to see a fairy."

"Oh, oh, see, is it? Me jewel, ye can't see the fairies unless ye have the seeing eye. Ye'd see nothing at all, only just the milk drying up slow, as it were. Now be off to bed wid ye and mind ye don't forget yer prayers or maybe ye'll wake up and find Something sitting on your bed in the night."

"I never do forget my prayers," said Pat with dignity.

"All the better for ye. I knew a liddle girl that forgot one night and a banshee got hold av her. Oh, oh, she was niver the same agin."

"What did the banshee do to her, Judy?"

"Do to her, is it? It put a curse on her, that it did. Ivery time she tried

24

to laugh she cried and ivery time she tried to cry she laughed. Oh, oh, 'twas a bitter punishment. Now, what's after plaguing ye? I can tell be the liddle face av ye ye're not aisy."

"Judy, I keep thinking about that baby in the parsley bed. Don't you think . . . they've no baby over at Uncle Tom's. Couldn't you give it to them? Mother could see it as often as she wanted to. We're four of a family now."

"Oh, oh, do ye be thinking four is innything av a family to brag av? Why, yer great-great-grandmother, Old Mrs. Nehemiah, had seventeen afore she called it a day. And four av thim died in one night wid the black cholera."

"Oh, Judy, how could she ever bear *that*?"

"Sure and hadn't she thirteen left, me jewel? But they do say as she was niver the same agin. And now it's not telling ye agin to go to bed I'll be doing . . . oh, no, it's not *telling*."

3

Pat tiptoed upstairs, past the old grandfather clock on the landing that wouldn't go . . . hadn't gone for forty years. The "dead clock" she and Sid called it. But Judy always insisted that it told the right time twice a day. Then down the hall to her room, with a wistful glance at the close-shut spare-room door as she passed it . . . the Poet's room, as it was called, because a poet who had been a guest at Silver Bush had slept there for a night. Pat had a firm belief that if you could only open the door of any shut room quickly enough you would catch all the furniture in strange situations. The chairs crowded together talking, the table lifting its white muslin skirts to show its pink sateen petticoat, the fire shovel and tongs dancing a fandango by themselves. But then you never could. Some sound always warned them and they were back in their places as demure as you please.

Pat said her prayers . . . *Now I Lay me*, and the Lord's Prayer, and then her own prayer. This was always the most interesting part because she made it up herself. She could not understand people who didn't like to pray. May Binnie, now. May had told her last Sunday in Sunday School that she never prayed unless she was scared about something. Fancy that!

Pat prayed for everybody in the family and for Judy Plum and Uncle Tom and Aunt Edith and Aunt Barbara . . . and for Sailor Uncle Horace at sea . . . and everybody else's sailor uncle at sea . . . and all the cats and Gentleman Tom and Joe's dog . . . "little black Snicklefritz with his curly tail," so that God wouldn't get mixed up between Joe's dog and Uncle Tom's dog who was big and black with a straight tail . . . and any fairies that might be hanging round and any poor ghosts that might be sitting on the tombstones . . . and for Silver Bush itself . . . dear Silver Bush.

"Please keep it always the same, dear God," begged Pat, "and don't let any more trees blow down."

Pat rose from her knees and stood there a bit rebelliously. Surely she had prayed for everybody and everything she could really be expected to pray for. Of course on stormy nights she always prayed for people who might be out in the storm. But this was a lovely spring night.

Finally she plumped down on her knees again.

"Please, dear God, if there is a baby out there in that parsley bed, keep it warm to-night. Dad says there may be a little frost."

4

SUNDAY'S CHILD

1

It was only a few evenings later that there was a commotion in the house at Silver Bush . . . pale faces . . . mysterious comings and goings. Aunt Barbara came over with a new white apron on, as if she were going to work instead of visit. Judy stalked about, muttering to herself. Father, who had been hanging round the house all day rather lazily for him, came down from mother's room and telephoned with the dining-room door shut. Half an hour afterwards Aunt Frances came over from the Bay Shore and whisked Winnie and Joe off on an unlooked-for week-end.

Pat was sitting on Weeping Willy's tombstone. She was on her dignity for she felt that she was being kept out of things somehow and she resented it. There was no resorting to mother who had kept her room all the afternoon. So Pat betook herself to the grave-yard and the society of her family ghosts until Judy Plum came along . . . a portentously solemn Judy Plum, looking wiser than any mortal woman could possibly be.

"Pat, me jewel, wud ye be liking to spend the night over at yer Uncle Tom's for a bit av a change? Siddy will be going along wid ye."

"Why?" demanded Pat distantly.

"Yer mother do be having a tarrible headache and the house has got to be that still. The doctor's coming . . ."

"Is mother bad enough to want a doctor?" cried Pat in quick alarm. Mary May's mother had had the doctor a week before . . . and died!

"Oh, oh, be aisy now, darlint. A doctor's just a handy thing to have round whin a body has one of thim headaches. I'm ixpecting yer mother to be fine and dandy be the morning if the house is nice and quiet to-night. So just you and Siddy run over to Swallowfield like good children. And since the moon do be at its full at last I'm thinking it's high time for the parsley bed. No telling what ye'll be seeing here to-morrow."

"That baby, I suppose," said Pat, a little contemptuously. "I should think, Judy Plum, if mother has such a bad headache it's a poor time to bother her with a new baby."

"She's been waiting for it so long I'm looking for it to iffect a miraculous cure," said Judy. "Innyhow, it's tonight or niver wid that moon. It was be way av being just such a night whin I found *you* in the parsley bed."

Pat looked at the moon disapprovingly. It didn't look like a proper moon . . . so queer and close and red and lanterny. But it was all of a piece with this odd night.

"Come, skip along . . . here's yer liddle nighty in the black satchel."

"I want to wait for Sid."

"Siddy's hunting me turkeys. He'll be over whin he finds them. Sure, ye're not afraid to go alone? It's only a cat's walk over there and the moon's lit up."

"You know very well, Judy Plum, that I'm not afraid. But things are . . . queer . . . to-night."

Judy chuckled.

"They do take spells av being that and far be it from me to deny it. Likely the woods are full av witches to-night but they won't be bothering ye if ye mind yer own business. Here's a handful av raisins for ye, same as ye git on Sundays, and niver be bothering yer head wid things ye can't understand."

Pat went over to Swallowfield rather unwillingly, although it was a second home to her . . . the adjoining farm where Uncle Tom and Aunt Edith and Aunt Barbara lived. Judy Plum approved of Aunt Barbara, had an old vendetta with Aunt Edith, and had no opinion of old bachelors. A man should be married. If he wasn't he had cheated some poor woman out of a husband. But Pat was very found of big, jolly Uncle Tom, with his nice, growly way of speaking, who was the only man in North Glen still wearing a beard . . . a beautiful, long, crinkly black beard. She liked Aunt Barbara, who was round and rosy and jolly, but she was always a little afraid of Aunt Edith, who was thin and sallow and laughterless, and had a standing feud with Judy Plum.

"Born unmarried, that one," Judy had been heard to mutter spitefully.

Pat went to Swallowfield by the Whispering Lane, which was fringed with birches, also planted by some long-dead bride. The brides of Silver Bush seemed to have made a hobby of planting trees. The path was picked out by big stones which Judy Plum whitewashed as far as the gate; from the gate Aunt Edith did it, because Uncle Tom and Aunt Barbara wouldn't be bothered and she wasn't going to let Judy Plum crow over her. The lane was crossed half way by the gate and beyond it were no birches but dear fence corners full of bracken and lady fern and wild violets and caraway. Pat loved the Whispering Lane. When she was four she had asked Judy Plum if it wasn't the "way of life" the minister had talked about in church; and somehow ever since it had seemed to her that some beautiful secret hid behind the birches and whispered in the nodding lace of its caraway blossoms.

She skipped along the lane, light-hearted again, eating her raisins. It was full of dancing, inviting shadows . . . friendly shadows out for a playmate. Once a shy grey rabbit hopped from bracken clump to bracken clump. Beyond the lane were dim, windy pastures of twilight. The air smelled deliciously. The trees wanted to be friends with her. All the little grass stems swayed towards her in the low breezes. Uncle

Tom's barn field was full of woolly-faced lambs at their evening games and three dear wee Jersey calves, with soft, sweet eyes, looked at her over the fence. Pat loved Jersey calves and Uncle Tom was the only man in North Glen who kept Jerseys.

Beyond, in the yard, Uncle Tom's buildings were like a little town by themselves. He had so many of them . . . pig houses and hen houses and sheep houses and boiler houses and goose houses and turnip houses . . . even an apple house which Pat thought was a delightful name. North Glen people said that Tom Gardiner put up some kind of a new building every year. Pat thought they all huddled around the big barn like chickens around their mother. Uncle Tom's house was an old one, with two wide, low windows that looked like eyes on either side of a balcony that was like a nose. It was a prim and dignified house but all its primness couldn't resist its own red front door which was just like an impish tongue sticking out of its face. Pat always felt as if the house was chuckling to itself over some joke nobody but itself knew, and she liked the mystery. She wouldn't have liked Silver Bush to be like that: Silver Bush mustn't have secrets from *her*: but it was all right in Swallowfield.

2

If it had not been for mother's headache and the doctor coming and Judy Plum's parsley bed Pat would have thought it romantic and delightful to have spent a night at Swallowfield. She had never been there for a night before . . . it was too near home. But that was part of its charm . . . to be so near home and yet not quite home . . . to look out of the window of the gable room and *see* home . . . see its roof over the trees and all its windows lighted up. Pat was a bit lonely. Sid was far away at the other end of the house. Uncle Tom had made speeches about doctors and black bags until Aunt Edith had shut him up . . . or Pat. Perhaps it was Pat.

"If you mean, Uncle Tom," Pat had said proudly, "that Dr. Bentley is bringing us a baby in a black bag you're very much mistaken. *We grow our own babies.* Judy Plum is looking for *ours* in the parsley bed at this very minute."

"Well . . . I'm . . . dashed," said Uncle Tom. And he looked as if he *were* dashed. Aunt Edith had given Pat a pin-wheel cookie and hustled her off to bed in a very pretty room where the curtains and chair covers were of creamy chintz with purple violets scattered over it and where the bed had a pink quilt. All very splendid. But it looked big and lonesome.

Aunt Edith turned the bedclothes and saw Pat cuddled down before she left. But she did not kiss her as Aunt Barbara would have done. And there would be no Judy Plum to tiptoe in when she thought you were asleep and whisper, "God bless and kape ye through the night, me jewel." Judy never missed doing that. But to-night she would be hunting through the parsley bed, likely never thinking of her "jewel" at all. Pat's lips trembled. The tears were very near now . . . and then she thought of Weeping Willy. One disgrace like that was enough in a family. *She* would not be Weeping Pat.

But she could not sleep. She lay watching the chimneys of Silver Bush through the window and wishing Sid's room were only near hers. Suddenly a light flashed from the garret window of Silver Bush . . . flashed a second and disappeared. It was as if the house had winked at her . . . called to her. In a moment Pat was out of bed and at the window. She curled up in the big flounced and ruffled wing chair. It was no use to try to sleep so she would just cuddle here and watch dear Silver Bush. It was like a beautiful picture . . . the milk-white house against its dark wooded hill, framed in an almost perfectly round opening in the boughs of the trees. Besides . . . who knew? . . . maybe Ellen Price was right after all and the storks did bring the babies. It was a nicer idea than any of the others. Perhaps if she watched she might see a silvery bird, flying from some far land beyond the blue gulf's rim and lighting on the roof of Silver Bush.

The boughs of the old fir tree outside tapped on the house. Dogs seemed to be barking everywhere over North Glen. Now and then a big June-bug thudded against the window. The water in the Field of the Pool glimmered mysteriously. Away up on the hill the moonlight glinting on one of the windows of the Long Lonely House gave it a strange, momentary appearance of being lighted up. Pat had a thrill. A tree-top behind the house looked like a witch crouched on its roof, just alighted from her broomstick. Pat's flesh crawled deliriously. Maybe there really were witches. Maybe they flew on a broomstick over the harbour at nights. What a jolly way of getting about! Maybe they

30

brought the babies. But no, no. They didn't want anything at Silver Bush that witches brought. Better the parsley bed than that. It was a lovely night for a baby to come. Was that a great white bird sailing over the trees? No, only a silvery cloud. Another June-bug . . . swoop went the wind around Uncle Tom's apple house . . . tap-tap went the fir boughs . . . Pat was fast asleep in the big chair and there Sidney found her when he slipped cautiously in at dawn before any one else at Swallowfield was up.

"Oh, Siddy!" Pat threw her arms about him and held him close to her in the chair. "Isn't it funny . . . I've been here all night. The bed was so big and lonesome. Oh, Sid, do you think Judy has found it yet?"

"Found what?"

"Why . . . the baby." Surely it was all right to tell Sid now. It was such a relief not to have a guilty secret from him any longer. "Judy went hunting for it in the parsley bed last night . . . for mother, you know."

Sid looked very wise . . . or as wise as a boy could look who had two big, round, funny brown eyes under fuzzy golden-brown curls. *He* was a year older than Pat . . . *he* had been to school . . . *he* knew just what that parsley bed yarn amounted to. But it was just as well for a girl like Pat to believe it.

"Let's go home and see," he suggested.

Pat got quickly into her clothes and they crept noiselessly downstairs and out of doors into a land pale in the morning twilight. The dew-wet earth was faintly fragrant. Pat had no memory of ever having been up before sunrise in her life. How lovely it was to be walking hand in hand with Sid along the Whispering Lane before the day had really begun!

"I hope this new kid will be a girl," said Sid. "Two boys are enough in a family but nobody cares how many girls there are. And I hope it'll be good-looking."

For the first time in her life Pat felt a dreadful stab of jealousy. But she was loyal, too.

"Of course it will. But you won't like it better than me, will you . . . oh, *please* Siddy?"

"Silly! Of course I won't like it better than you. I don't expect to like it at all," said Sid disdainfully.

"Oh, you *must* like it a little, because of mother. And oh, Sid, please promise that you'll never like *any* girl better than me."

"Sure I won't." Sid was very fond of Pat and didn't care who knew it.

31

At the gate he put his chubby arms about her and kissed her.

"You won't ever *marry* another girl, Sid?"

"Not much. I'm going to be a bachelor like Uncle Tom. He says he likes a quiet life and I do, too."

"And we'll always live at Silver Bush and I'll keep house for you," said Pat eagerly.

"Sure. Unless I go west; lots of boys do."

"Oh!" A cold wind blew across Pat's happiness. "Oh, you must never go west, Sid . . . you *couldn't* leave Silver Bush. You couldn't find any nicer place."

"Well, we can't *all* stay here, you know, when we grow up," said Sid reasonably.

"Oh, why can't we?" cried Pat, on the point of tears again. The lovely morning was spoiled for her.

"Oh, well, we'll be here for years yet," said Sid soothingly. "Come along. There's Judy giving Friday and Monday their milk."

"Oh, Judy," gasped Pat, "did you find it?"

"Sure and didn't I that? The prettiest baby ye iver set eyes on and swate beyond iverything. I'm thinking I must be putting on me dress-up dress whin I get the work done be way av cilebrating."

"Oh, I'm so glad it's pretty because it belongs to our family," said Pat. "Can we see it right away?"

"Indade and ye can't, me jewel. It's up in yer mother's room and she's sound aslape and not to be disturbed. She had a wakeful night av it. I was a tarrible long time finding that baby. Me eyesight isn't what it was I'm grieving to say. I'm thinking that's the last baby I'll iver be able to find in the parsley bed."

3

Judy gave Pat and Sid their breakfast in the kitchen. Nobody else was up. It was such fun to have breakfast there with Judy and have the milk poured over their porridge out of her "cream cow" . . . that little old brown jug in the shape of a cow, with her tail curled up in a most un-cowlike fashion for a handle and her mouth for a spout. Judy had brought the cream cow from Ireland with her and prized it beyond all saying. She had promised to leave it to Pat when she died. Pat hated to hear Judy talk of dying, but, as she had also promised to live a hundred years . . . *D. V.* . . . . that was nothing to worry about yet awhile.

The kitchen was a cheery place and was as tidy and spotless as if Silver Bush had not just been passing through a night of suspense and birth. The walls were whitewashed snowily: the stove shone: Judy's blue and white jugs on the scoured dresser sparkled in the rays of the rising sun. Judy's geraniums bloomed in the windows. The space between stove and table was covered by a big, dark-red rug with three black cats hooked in it. The cats had eyes of yellow wool which were still quite bright and catty in spite of the fact that they had been trodden over for many years. Judy's living black cat sat on the bench and thought hard. Two fat kittens were sleeping in a patch of sunlight on the floor. And, as if that were not enough in the cat line, there were three marvellous kittens in a picture on the wall . . . Judy's picture, likewise brought out from Ireland. Three white kittens with blue eyes, playing with a ball of silk thread gloriously entangled. Cats and kittens might come and go at Silver Bush, but Judy's kittens were eternally young and frisky. This was a comfort to Pat who, when she was *very* young, was afraid they might grow up and change, too. It always broke her heart when some beloved kitten turned overnight into a lanky half-grown cat.

There were other pictures . . . Queen Victoria at her coronation and King William riding his white horse over the Boyne: a marble cross, poised on a dark rock in a raging ocean, lavishly garlanded with flowers, having a huge open Bible on a purple cushion at its foot: the Burial of the Pet Bird: mottoes worked in wool . . . *Home Sweet Home* . . . *Upwards and Onwards.* These had all been judged at successive spring cleanings to be unworthy of the other rooms but Judy wouldn't have them burned. Pat wouldn't have liked them anywhere else but she liked them on the walls of Judy's kitchen. It wouldn't have been quite the same without them.

It was lovely, Pat thought as she ate her toast, that everything was just the same. She had had a secret, dreadful fear that she would find everything changed and different and heart-breaking.

Dad came in just as they finished and Pat flew to him. He looked tired but he caught her up with a smile.

"Has Judy told you that you have a new sister?"

"Yes. I'm glad. I think it will be an improvement," said Pat, gravely and staunchly.

Dad laughed.

"That's right. Some folks have been afraid you mightn't like it . . . might think your nose was out of joint."

"My nose is all right," said Pat. "Feel it."

"Av course her nose is all right. Don't ye be after putting inny such notions in her head, Long Alec Gardiner," said Judy, who had bossed little Long Alec about when he was a child and continued to do so now that he was big Long Alec with a family of his own. "And ye naden't have been thinking that child wud be jealous . . . she hasn't a jealous bone in her body, the darlint. Jealous, indade!" Judy's grey-green eyes flashed quite fiercely. Nobody need be thinking the new baby was more important than Pat or that more was going to be made of it.

4

It was well on in the forenoon when they were allowed upstairs. Judy marshalled them up, very imposing in her blue silk dress, of a day when it was a recommendation for silk that it could stand alone. She had had it for fifteen years, having got it in honour of the bride young Long Alec was bringing to Silver Bush, and she put it on only for very special occasions. It had been donned for every new baby and the last time it had been worn was six years ago at Grandmother Gardiner's funeral. Fashions had changed considerably but what cared Judy? A silk dress was a silk dress. She was so splendid in it that the children were half in awe of her. They liked her much better in her old drugget but Judy tasted her day of state.

A nurse in white cap and apron was queening it in mother's room. Mother was lying on her pillows, white and spent after that dreadful headache, with her dark wings of hair around her face and her sweet, dreamy, golden-brown eyes shining with happiness. Aunt Barbara was rocking a quaint old black cradle, brought down from the garret . . . a cradle a hundred years old which Great-great-Grandfather Nehemiah had made with his own hands. Every Silver Bush baby had been rocked in it. The nurse did not approve of either cradles or rocking but she was powerless against Aunt Barbara and Judy combined.

"Not have a cradle for it, do ye be saying?" the scandalised Judy ejaculated. "Ye'll not be intinding to put the swate wee cratur in a

34

basket? Oh, oh, did inny one iver be hearing the like av it? It's niver a baby at Silver Bush that'll be brought up in your baskets, as if it was no better than a kitten, and that I'm telling ye. Here's the cradle that I've polished wid me own hands and into that same cradle she'll be going."

Pat, after a rapturous kiss for mother, tip-toed over to the cradle, trembling with excitement. Judy lifted the baby out and held it so that the children could see it.

"Oh, Judy, isn't she sweet?" whispered Pat in ecstasy. "Can't I hold her for just the tiniest moment?"

"That ye can, darlint," . . . and Judy put the baby into Pat's arms before either nurse or Aunt Barbara could prevent her. Oh, oh, that was one in the eye for the nurse!

Pat stood holding the fragrant thing as knackily as if she had been doing it all her life. What tiny, darling legs it had! What dear, wee, crumpled paddies! What little pink nails like perfect shells!

"What colour are its eyes, Judy?"

"Blue," said Judy, "big and blue like violets wid dew on them, just like Winnie's. And it's certain I am that she do be having dimples in her chakes. Sure a woman wid a baby like that naden't call the quane her cousin."

> "'The child that is born on the Sabbath day
> Will be bonny and blithe and good and gay,'"

said Aunt Barbara.

"Of course she will," said Pat. "She would, no matter what day she was born on. Isn't she *our* baby?"

"Oh, oh, there's the right spirit for ye," said Judy.

"The baby must really be put back in the cradle now," said the nurse by way of reasserting her authority.

Pat relinquished it reluctantly. Only a few minutes ago she had been thinking of the baby as an interloper, only to be tolerated for mother's sake. But now it was one of the family and it seemed as if it had always been at Silver Bush. No matter how it had come, from stork or black bag or parsley bed, it was *there* and it was *theirs*.

5

"WHAT'S IN A NAME?"

1

The new baby at Silver Bush did not get its name until three weeks later when mother was able to come down stairs and the nurse had gone home, much to Judy's satisfaction. She approved of Miss Martin as little as Miss Martin approved of her.

"Oh, oh, legs and lipstick!" she would say contemptuously, when Miss Martin doffed her regalia and went out to take the air. Which was unjust to Miss Martin, who had no more legs than other women of the fashion and used her lipstick very discreetly. Judy watched her down the lane with a malevolent eye.

"Oh, oh, but I'd like to be putting a tin ear on that one. Wanting to call the wee treasure Greta! Oh, oh, *Greta!* And her with a grandfather that died and come back to life, that he did!"

"Did he really, Judy Plum?"

"He did that. Old Jimmy Martin was dead as a dorenail for two days. The doctors said it. Thin he come back to life . . . just to spite his family I'm telling ye. But, as ye might ixpect, he was niver the same agin. His relations were rale ashamed av him. Miss Martin naden't be holding that rid head av hers so high."

"But why, Judy?" asked Sid. "Why were they ashamed of him?"

"Oh, oh, whin ye're dead it's only dacent to *stay* dead," retorted Judy. "Ye'd think she'd remimber that whin she was trying to boss folks who looked after babies afore she was born or thought av, the plum-faced thing! But she's gone now, good riddance, and we won't have her stravaging about the house with a puss on her mouth inny more. Too minny bushels for a small canoe . . . it do be that that's the trouble wid *her.*"

"She can't help her grandfather, Judy," said Pat.

"Oh, oh, I'm not saying she could, me jewel. We none of us can hilp our ancistors. Wasn't me own grandmother something av a witch? But it's sure we've all got some and it ought to kape us humble."

Pat was glad Miss Martin was gone, not because she didn't like her but because she knew she would be able to hold the baby oftener now. Pat adored the baby. How in the world had Silver Bush ever got on without her? Silver Bush without the baby was quite unthinkable to Pat now. When Uncle Tom asked her gravely if they had decided yet whether to keep or drown the baby she was horrified and alarmed.

"Sure, me jewel, he was only tazing ye," comforted Judy, with her great, broad, jolly laugh. "'Tis just an ould bachelor's idea av a joke."

They had put off naming the baby until Miss Martin had gone, because nobody really wanted to call the baby Greta but didn't want to hurt her feelings. The very afternoon she left they attended to the matter . . . or tried to.

But it was no easy thing to pick a name. Mother wanted to call it Doris after her own mother and father wanted Rachel after his mother. Winnie, who was romantic, wanted Elaine, and Joe thought Dulcie would be nice. Pat had secretly called it Miranda for a week and Sidney thought such a blue-eyed baby ought to be named Violet. Aunt Hazel thought Kathleen just the name for it, and Judy, who must have her say with the rest, thought Emmerillus was a rale classy name. The Silver Bush people thought Judy must mean Amaryllis but were never sure of it.

In the end father suggested that each of them plant a named seed in the garden and see whose came up first. That person should have the privilege of naming the baby.

"If we find more than one up at once the winners must plant over again," he said.

This was a sporting chance and the children were excited. The seeds were planted and tagged and watched every day: but it was Pat who thought of getting up early in the mornings to keep tabs on the bed. Judy said things came up in the night. There was nothing at dark . . . and in the morning there you were. And there Pat was on the eighth morning, just as the sun was rising, up before any one but Judy. You would have to get up before you went to bed if you meant to get ahead of Judy.

And Pat's seed was up! For just one moment she exulted. Then she grew sober and her long-lashed amber eyes filled with troubled wonder. Of course Miranda was a lovely name for a baby. But father wanted Rachel. Mother had named her and Sidney, Uncle Tom had named Joe, Hazel had named Winnie, surely it was father's turn. He hadn't said much . . . father never said much . . . but Pat knew somehow that he wanted very badly to name the baby Rachel. In her secret heart Pat had hoped that father's seed would be first.

She looked around her. No living creature in sight except Gentleman Tom, sitting darkly on the cheese stone. The next moment her seed was yanked out and flung into the burdock patch behind the hen-house. Dad had a chance yet.

But luck seemed against poor dad. Next morning Win's and mother's seeds were up. Pat ruthlessly uprooted them, too. Win didn't count and mother had named two children already. That was plenty for her. Joe's met the same fate next morning. Then up popped Sid's and Judy's. Pat was quite hardened in rascality now and they went. Anyhow, no child ought *ever* to be called Emmerillus.

The next day there was none up and Pat began to be worried. Every one was wondering why none of the seeds were up yet. Judy darkly insinuated that they had been planted the wrong time of the moon. And perhaps father's wouldn't come up at all. Pat prayed very desperately that night that it might be up the next morning.

It was.

Pat looked about her in triumph, quite untroubled as yet by her duplicity. She had won the victory for father. Oh, how lovely everything was! Gossamer clouds of pale gold floated over the Hill of the Mist. The wind had fallen asleep among the silver birches. The tall firs among them quivered with some kind of dark laughter. The fields were all around her like great gracious arms. The popples, as Judy called them, were whispering around the granary. The world was just a big, smiling greenness, with a vast, alluring blueness seawards. There was a clear, pale, silvery sky over her and everything in the garden seemed to have burst into bloom overnight. Judy's big clump of bleeding-heart by the kitchen door was hung with ruby jewels. The country was sprinkled with white houses in the sunrise. A stealthy kitten crept through the orchard. Thursday was licking his sleek little chops on the window sill of his beloved granary. A red squirrel chattered at him from a bough of the maple tree over the well. Judy came out to draw a bucket of water.

"Oh, Judy, father's seed is up," cried Pat. She wouldn't say up *first* because *that* wasn't true.

"Oh, oh!" Judy accepted the "sign" with good grace. "Well, it do be yer dad's turn for a fact, and Rachel is a better name than Greta inny day. Greta! The impidence av it!"

2

Rachel it was in fact and Rachel it became in law one Sunday six weeks later when the baby was baptised at church in a wondrous heirloom christening robe of eyelet embroidery that Grandmother Gardiner had made for her first baby. All the Silver Bush children had been christened in it. Long robes for babies had gone out of fashion but Judy Plum would not have thought the christening lawful if the baby had not been at least five feet long. They tacked Doris on to the name, too, by way of letting mother down easy, but it was dad's day of triumph.

Pat was not sorry for what she had done but her conscience had begun to trouble her a bit and that night when Judy Plum came in to leave her nightly blessing, Pat, who was wide-awake, sat up in bed and flung her arms around Judy's neck.

"Oh, Judy . . . I did something . . . I s'spose it was bad. I . . . I wanted father to name the baby . . . and I pulled up the seeds as fast as they came up in the mornings. Was it very bad, Judy?"

"Oh, oh, shocking," said Judy, with a contradictory twinkle in her eyes. "If Joe knew he'd put a tin ear on ye. But I'll not be telling. More be token as I wanted yer dad to have his way. He do be put upon be the women in this house and that's a fact."

"His seed was the last one to come up," said Pat, "and Aunt Hazel's never came up at all."

"Oh, oh, didn't it now?" giggled Judy. "It was up the morning afore yer dad's and I pulled it out meself."

6

WHAT PRICE WEDDINGS?

1

Late in August of that summer Pat began to go to school. The first day was very dreadful . . . almost as dreadful as that day the year before when she had watched Sidney start to school without her. They had never been separated before. She had stood despairingly at the garden gate and watched him out of sight down the lane until she could see him no longer for tears.

"He'll be back in the evening, me jewel. Think av the fun av watching for him to come home," comforted Judy.

"The evening is so far away," sobbed Pat. It seemed to her the day would never end: but half past four came and Pat went flying down the lane to greet Sid. Really, it was so splendid to have him back that it almost atoned for seeing him go.

Pat didn't want to go to school. To be away from Silver Bush for eight hours five days out of every week was a tragedy to her. Judy put her up a delicious lunch, filled her satchel with her favourite little red apples and kissed her good-bye encouragingly.

"Now, darlint, remember it's goin' to get an eddication ye are. Oh, oh, and eddication is a great thing and it's meself do be after knowing it because I never had one."

"Why, Judy, you know more than anybody else in the world," said Pat wonderingly.

"Oh, oh, to be sure I do, but an eddication isn't just knowing things," said Judy wisely. "Don't ye be worrying a bit. Ye'll get on fine. Ye know yer primer so ye've got a good start. Now run along, girleen, and mind ye're rale mannerly to yer tacher. It's the credit av Silver Bush ye must be kaping up, ye know."

It was this thought that braced Pat sufficiently to enable her to get through the day. It kept the tears back as she turned, at the end of the lane, clinging to Sid's hand, to wave back to Judy who was waving encouragingly from the garden gate. It bore her up under the scrutiny of dozens of strange eyes and her interview with the teacher. It gave her back-bone through the long day as she sat alone at her little desk and made pot-hooks . . . or looked through the window down into the school bush which she liked much better. It was an ever-present help in recesses and dinner hour, when Winnie was off with the big girls and Sid and Joe with the boys and she was alone with the first and second primers.

When school came out at last Pat reviewed the day and proudly concluded that she had not disgraced Silver Bush.

And then the glorious home-coming! Judy and mother to welcome her back as if she had been away for a year . . . the baby smiling and cooing at her . . . Thursday running to meet her . . . all the flowers in the garden nodding a greeting.

"I *know* everything's glad to see me back," she cried.

Really, it was enough to make one willing to go away just to have the delight of coming back. And then the fun of telling Judy all that had happened in school!

"I liked all the girls except May Binnie. She said there wasn't any moss in the cracks of *her* garden walk. I said I *liked* moss in the cracks of a garden walk. And she said our house was old-fashioned and needed painting. And she said the wall-paper in our spare-room was stained."

"Oh, oh, and well you know it is," said Judy. "There's that lake be the chimney that Long Alec has niver been able to fix, try as he will. But if ye start out be listening to what a Binnie says ye'll have an earful. What did ye say to me fine Miss May Binnie, darlint?"

"I said Silver Bush didn't need to be painted as often as other people's houses because it wasn't ugly."

Judy chuckled.

"Oh, oh, that was one in the eye for me fine May. The Binnie house is one av the ugliest I've iver seen for all av its yaller paint. And what did she say to *that*."

"Oh, Judy, she said the pink curtains in the Big Parlour were faded and shabby. And that *crushed* me. Because they *are* . . . and everybody else in North Glen has such nice lace curtains in their parlours."

41

2

But this was all three weeks ago and already going to school was a commonplace and Pat had even begun to like it. And then one afternoon Judy casually remarked, out of a clear sky so to speak,

"I s'pose ye know that yer Aunt Hazel is going to be married the last wake in September?"

At first Pat wouldn't believe it . . . simply couldn't. Aunt Hazel *couldn't* be married and go away from Silver Bush. When she had to believe it she cried night after night for a week. Not even Judy could console her . . . not even the memory of Weeping Willy shame her.

"Sure and it's time yer Aunt Hazel was married if she don't be intinding to be an ould maid."

"Aunt Barbara and Aunt Edith are old maids and they're happy," sobbed Pat.

"Oh, oh, two ould maids is enough for one family. And yer Aunt Hazel is right to be married. Sure and it's a kind av hard world for women at the bist. I'm not saying but what we'll miss her. She's always had a liddle knack av making people happy. But it's time she made her ch'ice. She's niver been man-crazy . . . oh, oh, her worst inimy couldn't say that av her. But she's been a bit av a flirt in her day and there's been a time or two I was afraid she was going to take up wid a crooked stick. 'Judy,' she wud a'way be saying to me, 'I want to try just a few more beaus afore I settle down.' It's a bit av good luck that she's made up her mind for Robert Madison. He's a rale steady feller. Ye'll like yer new uncle, darlint."

"I won't," said Pat obstinately, determined to hate him forever. "Do *you* like him, Judy?"

"To be sure I do. He's got more in his head than the comb'll iver take out I warrrant ye. And a store-kaper he is, which is a bit asier than farming for the wife."

"Do you think he's good-looking enough for Aunt Hazel, Judy?"

"Oh, oh, I've seen worse. Maybe there's a bit too much av him turned up for fate and there's no denying he has flying jibs like all that family. They tuk it from the Callenders. Niver did inny one see such ears as old Hinry Callender had. If ye hadn't been seeing innything but his head ye cudn't have told whether he was a man or a bat. Oh, oh, but it's the lucky thing they've got pared down a bit be the Madison mixture! Robert's got a rale nice face and I'm after telling ye we're all well satisfied wid yer Aunt Hazel's match. We've had our worries I can be telling ye now. There was Gordon Rhodes back a bit . . . but I niver belaved she'd take a scut like him. Too crooked to lie straight in bed like all the Rhodeses. And Will Owen . . . to be sure Long Alec liked him but the man had no more to say for himself than a bump on a log. If the Good Man Above had struck him dumb we'd niver av known it. For me own part I like thim a bit more flippant. At one time we did be thinking she'd take Siddy Taylor. But whin she tould him one night that she cudn't abide his taste in neck-ties he went off mad and niver come back. Small blame to him for that. If ye do be wanting a man iver, Pat, don't be after criticising his neck-ties until ye've landed him afore the minister. And yer mother kind av liked Cal Gibson. Sure and he was the ladylike cratur. But he was one av the Summerside Gibsons and I was afraid he'd always look down on yer Aunt Hazel's people. Barring the fact that he was as quare-looking as a cross-eyed cat . . . . But this Robert Madison, he kept a-coming and a-coming, always bobbing up whiniver one of the other lads got the mitten on the wrong hand. Whin the Madisons do be wanting a thing they have the habit av getting it in the long run. Rob's Uncle Jim now . . . didn't I iver tell ye the story av how he pickled his brother in rum and brought him home to be buried?"

"*Pickled* him, Judy?"

"I'm telling ye. Ned Madison died on board Jim's ship back in 1850 whin they were in the middle av the Indian Ocean. Iverybody said he must be buried at say. But Jim Madison swore till all turned blue that Ned shud be tuk home and buried in the fam'ly plot on the Island. So he got the ship's carpenter to make a lead coffin and he clapped young Ned in it and filled it up wid rum. And Ned come home fresh as a daisy. I'm not saying that Jim was iver the same man agin though, mind ye. And that's the Madison for ye. Oh, oh, it's all for the bist as it is and we must have a rale fine widding for the honour av the fam'ly."

Pat found it hard to be reconciled to it. She had always been so fond of Aunt Hazel . . . far fonder than of Aunt Edith or even Aunt Barbara. Aunt Hazel was so jolly and pretty. Her face was as brown as a nut, her eyes and hair were brown, her lips and cheeks scarlet. Aunt Hazel looked her name. Some people didn't. Lily Wheatley was as black as a crow and Ruby Rhodes was pale and washed out.

The rest of the Silver Bush children took it more philosophically. Sidney thought it would be rather exciting to have a wedding in the family. Winnie thought it must be rather good fun to be married.

"I don't see the fun of it," said Pat bitterly.

"Why, everybody has to be married," said Winnie. "You'll be married yourself some day."

Pat rushed to mother in anguish.

"Mother, tell me . . . I don't have to get married ever . . . do I?"

"Not unless you want to," assured mother.

"Oh, that's all right," said relieved Pat. "Because I'll never want to."

"The girls all talk that way," said Judy, winking at Mrs. Gardiner over Pat's head. "There's no jidging the minute I might take the notion meself. Sure and didn't I have the fine proposal the other night. Old Tom Drinkwine shuffled up here and asked me to be his fourth missus, so he did. Sure and I all but dropped the new tay-pot whin he come out wid it. It's the long time I've waited to be axed but me chanct has come at last."

"Oh, Judy, you wouldn't marry him?"

"Oh, oh, and why shudn't I now?"

"And leave us?"

"Oh, oh, there's the rub," remarked Judy, who had sent old Tom off to what she called "the tune the ould cow died on."

"'Twud be more than the quarter av inny man that'd tempt me to do that same."

But a *whole* man might tempt Judy some day and Pat was uneasy. Oh, change was terrible! What a pity people had to get married!

3

"The widding's to be the last wake av September, *D. V.*" Judy told her one day.

Pat winced. She knew it must be but to have announced in this indifferent fashion was anguish.

"What does *D. V.* mean, Judy?"

"Oh, oh, it means if the Good Man Above is willing."

"And what if He isn't willing, Judy?"

"Thin it wud niver happen, me jewel."

Pat wondered if she prayed to God *not* to be willing if it would do any good.

"What would happen if you prayed for . . . for a *wicked* thing, Judy?"

"Oh, oh, you might get it," said Judy so eerily that Pat was terrified and decided that it was wiser to take no risks.

Eventually she became resigned to it. She found herself quite important in school because her aunt was going to be married. And there was a pleasant air of excitement about Silver Bush, which deepened as the days went by. Little was talked of but the wedding preparations. The old barn cat had what Judy called a "clutch" of kittens and nobody was excited over it except Pat. But it was nice to have a bit of a secret. Only she and the barn cat knew where the kittens were. She would not tell until they were too old to drown. Somehow, most of the spring kittens had vanished in some mysterious fashion which Pat never could fathom. Only Tuesday and Thursday were left and Tuesday was promised to Aunt Hazel. So the new kittens were warmly welcomed, but finding names for them had to be left until the wedding was over because Pat couldn't get any one interested in it just now.

The Poet's room was re-papered, much to her joy . . . though she was sorry to see the old paper torn off . . . and when mother brought home new, cobwebby lace curtains for the Big Parlour Pat began to think a wedding had its good points. But she was very rebellious when her room was re-papered, too. She loved the old paper, with its red and green parrots that had been there ever since she could remember. She had never been without a secret hope that they might come alive sometime.

"I don't see why my room has to be papered, even if Aunt Hazel is going to be married," she sobbed.

"Listen to rason now, darlint," argued Judy. "Sure and on the widding day the place'll be full av quality. All yer grand relations from town and Novy Scotia will be here and the Madisons from New Brunswick . . . millionaires, they do be saying. And some av thim will have to be putting their wraps in yer room. Ye wudn't want thim to be seeing old, faded wall-paper, wud ye now?"

No . . . o . . . o, Pat wouldn't want that.

"And I've tould yer mother ye must be allowed to pick the new paper yerself . . . sure and there do be a pattern of blue-bells at the store that you'd love. So cheer up and help me wid the silver polishing. Ivery piece in the house must be rubbed up for the grand ivent. Sure and we haven't had a widding at Silver Bush for twinty years. It do be too much like heaven that, wid nather marrying nor giving in marriage. The last was whin yer Aunt Christine got her man. Sure and I hope yer Aunt Hazel won't have the mischance to her widding veil that poor liddle Chrissy had."

"Why, what happened to it, Judy?"

"Oh, oh, what happened to it, sez she. It had a cap av rose point that yer great-great-grandmother brought from the Ould Country wid her. Oh, oh, 'twas the illigant thing! And they had it lying in state on the bed in the Poet's room. But whin they wint in to get it, me jewel, . . . well, there was a liddle dog here at Silver Bush thin and the liddle spalpane had got into the room unbeknownst and he had chewed and slobbered the veil and the lace cap till ye cudn't tell where one left off and the other begun. Poor liddle Chrissie cried that pitiful . . . small blame to her."

"Oh, Judy, what did they do?"

"Do, is it? Sure they cud do nothing and they did it. Poor Chrissy had to be married widout her veil, sobbing all troo the cirrimony. A great scandal it made I'm telling ye. It's meself that will kape the key av the Poet's room this time and if I catch that Snicklefritz prowling about the house it's meself that'll put a tin ear on that dog, if Joe takes a fit over it. And now, whin we've finished this lot av silver, ye'll come out to the ould part and help me pick the damsons. Sure and I'm going to do up a big crock av baked damsons for yer Aunt Hazel. Hasn't she always said there was nobody cud bake damsons like ould Judy Plum . . . more be token of me name perhaps."

"Oh, hurry with the silver, Judy."

Pat loved picking damsons with Judy . . . and the green gages and the golden gages and the big purple-red egg plums.

"Oh, oh, I'm niver in a hurry, me jewel. There's all the time in the world and after that there's eternity. There's loads and lashins av work if yer Aunt Hazel is to have the proper widding but it'll all be done dacently and in order."

4

Pat couldn't help feeling pleasantly excited when she found that she was to be Aunt Hazel's flower girl. But she felt so sorry for Winnie who was too old to be a flower girl and not old enough to be a bridesmaid, that it almost spoilt her own pleasure. Aunt Hazel was to have two bridesmaids and all were to be dressed in green, much to Judy's horror, who declared green was unlucky for weddings.

"Oh, oh, there was a widding once in the Ould Country and the bridesmaids wore grane. And the fairies were that mad they put a curse on the house, that they did."

"How did they curse it, Judy?"

"I'm telling ye. There was niver to be inny more laughter in that house . . . niver agin. Oh, oh, that's a tarrible curse. Think av a house wid no laughter in it."

"And wasn't there ever any, Judy?"

"Niver a bit. Plinty of waping but no laughing. Oh, oh, 'twas a sorryful place!"

Pat felt a little uneasy. What if there never were to be any more laughter at Silver Bush . . . father's gentle chuckles and Uncle Tom's hearty booms . . . Winnie's silvery trills . . . Judy's broad mirth? But her dress was so pretty . . . a misty, spring-green crepe with smocked yoke and a cluster of dear pink rosebuds on the shoulder. And a shirred green hat with roses on the brim. Pat had to revel in it, curse or no curse. She did not realise . . . as Judy did . . . that the green made her pale, tanned little face paler and browner. Pat as yet had no spark of vanity. The dress itself was everything.

The wedding was to be in the afternoon and the "nuptial cemetery," as Winnie, who was a ten-year-old Mrs. Malaprop . . . called it, was to be in the old grey stone church at South Glen which all the Gardiners had attended from time immemorial. Judy thought this a modern innovation.

"Sure and in the ould days at Silver Bush they used to be married in the avening and dance the night away. But they didn't go stravaging off on these fine honeymoon trips then. Oh, oh, they wint home and settled down to their business. 'Tis the times that have changed and not for the better I do be thinking. It used to be only the Episcopalians was married in church. Sure and it's niver been a Presbytarian custom at all, at all."

"Are you a Presbyterian, Judy?"

Pat was suddenly curious. She had never thought about Judy's religion. Judy went to the South Glen church with them on Sundays but would never sit in the Gardiner pew . . . always up in the gallery, where she could see everything, Uncle Tom said.

"Oh, oh, I'm Presbytarian as much as an Irish body can be," said Judy cautiously. "Sure and I cud niver be a rale Presbytarian not being Scotch. But innyhow I'm praying that all will go well and that yer Aunt Hazel'll have better luck than yer grand-dad's secound cousin had whin she was married."

"What happened to grand-dad's second cousin, Judy?"

"Oh, oh, did ye niver hear av it? Sure and it seems nobody'd iver tell ye yer fam'ly history if ould Judy didn't. She died, poor liddle soul, of the pewmonia, the day before the widding and was buried in her widding dress. 'Twas a sad thing for she'd been long in landing her man . . . she was thirty if she was a day . . . and it was hard to be disap'inted at the last moment like that. Now, niver be crying, me jewel, over what happened fifty years ago. She'd likely be dead innyhow be this time and maybe she was spared a lot av trouble, for the groom was a wild felly enough and was only taking her for her bit av money, folks said. Here, give me a spell stirring this cake and don't be picking the plums out av it to ate."

5

During the last week the excitement was tremendous. Pat was allowed to stay home from school, partly because every one wanted her to run errands, partly because she would probably have died if she hadn't been allowed. Judy spent most of her time in the kitchen, concocting and baking, looking rather like an old witch hanging over some unholy brew. Aunt Barbara came over and helped but Aunt Edith did her share of the baking at home because no kitchen was big enough to hold her and Judy Plum. Aunt Hazel made the creams and mother the sparkling red jellies. That was all mother was allowed to do. It was thought she had enough work looking after Cuddles . . . as the baby was called by every one in spite of all the pother about her name. Mother, so Judy Plum told Pat, had never been quite the same since that bad headache the night Cuddles was found in the parsley bed, and they must be taking care of her.

Pat beat eggs and stirred innumerable cakes, taking turns with Sid in eating the savory scrapings from the bowls. The house was full of delicious smells from morning till night. And everywhere it was "Pat, come here," and "Pat, run there," till she was fairly bewildered.

"Aisy now," remonstrated Judy. "Make yer head save yer heels, darlint. 'Tis a great lesson to learn. Iverything'll sort itsilf out in God's good time. They do be imposing on ye a bit but Judy'll see yer not put upon too much. Sure and I don't see how we'd iver get yer Aunt Hazel married widout ye."

They wouldn't have got the wedding butter without her, that was certain. Judy had kept the blue cow's milk back for a week from the factory and the day before the wedding she started to churn it in the old-fashioned crank churn which she would never surrender for anything more modern. Judy churned and churned until Pat, going down into the cool, cobwebby cellar in mid-forenoon, found her "clane distracted."

"The crame's bewitched," said Judy in despair. "Me arms are fit to drop off at the roots and niver a sign av butter yet."

It was not to be thought of that mother should churn and Aunt Hazel was busy with a hundred things. Dad was sent for from the barn and agreed to have a whirl at it. But after churning briskly for half an hour he gave it up as a bad job.

"You may as well give the cream to the pigs, Judy," he said. "We'll have to buy the butter at the store."

This was absolute disgrace for Judy. To buy the butter from the store and only the Good Man Above knowing who made it! She went to get the dinner, feeling that the green wedding was at the bottom of it.

Pat slipped off the apple barrel where she had been squatted, and began to churn. It was great fun. She had always wanted to churn and Judy would never let her because if the cream were churned too slow or too fast the butter would be too hard or too soft. But now it didn't matter and she could churn to her heart's content. Splash . . . splash . . . splash! Flop . . . flop . . . flop! Thud . . . thud . . . thud! Swish . . . swish . . . swish! The business of turning the crank had grown gradually harder and Pat had just decided that for once in her life she had got all the churning she wanted when it suddenly grew lighter and Judy came down to call her to dinner.

"I've churned till I'm all in a sweat, Judy."

Judy was horrified.

"A sweat, is it? Niver be using such a word, girleen. Remimber the Binnies may *sweat* but the Gardiners *perspire*. And now I s'pose I'll have to be giving the crame to the pigs. 'Tis a burning shame, that it is . . . the blue cow's crame and all . . . and bought butter for a Silver Bush widding! But what wud ye ixpect wid grane dresses? I'm asking ye. Inny one might av known . . ."

Judy had lifted the cover from the churn and her eyes nearly popped out of her head.

"If the darlint hasn't brought the butter! Here it is, floating round in the buttermilk, as good butter as was iver churned. And wid her liddle siven-year-old arms, whin nather meself nor Long Alec cud come be it. Oh, oh, just let me be after telling the whole fam'ly av it!"

Probably Pat never had such another moment of triumph in her whole life.

7

HERE COMES THE BRIDE

1

The wedding day came at last.

Pat had been counting dismally towards it for a week. Only four more days to have Aunt Hazel at Silver Bush . . . only three . . . only two—only one. Pat had the good fortune to sleep with Judy the night before, because her bedroom was needed for the guests who came from afar. So she wakened with Judy before sunrise and slipped down anxiously to see what kind of a day it was going to be.

"Quane's weather!" said Judy in a tone of satisfaction. "I was a bit afraid last night we'd have rain, bekase there was a ring around the moon and it's ill-luck for the bride the rain falls on, niver to mintion all the mud and dirt tracked in. Now I'll just slip out and tell the sun to come up and thin I'll polish off the heft av the milking afore yer dad gets down. The poor man's worn to the bone wid all the ruckus."

"Wouldn't the sun come up if you didn't tell it, Judy?"

"I'm taking no chances on a widding day, me jewel."

While Judy was out milking Pat prowled about Silver Bush. How queer a house was in the early morning before people were up! Just as if it were watching for something. Of course all the rooms had an unfamiliar look on account of the wedding. The Big Parlour had been filled with a flame of autumn leaves and chrysanthemums. The new curtains were so lovely that Pat felt a fierce regret the Binnies were not to be among the guests at the house. Just fancy May's face if she saw them! The Little Parlour was half full of wedding presents. The table had been laid in the dining-room the night before. How pretty it looked, with its sparkling glass and its silver candlesticks and tall slender candles like moonbeams and the beautiful colours of the jellies.

Pat ran outside. The sun, obedient to Judy's mandate, was just coming up. The air was the amber honey of autumn. Every birch and poplar in the silver bush had become a golden maiden. The garden was tired of growing and had sat down to rest but the gorgeous hollyhocks were flaunting over the old stone dyke. A faint, lovely morning haze hung over the Hill of the Mist and trembled away before the sun. What a lovely world to be alive in!

Then Pat turned and saw a lank, marauding, half-eared cat . . . an alien to Silver Bush . . . lapping up the milk in the saucer that had been left for the fairies. So that was how it went! She had always suspected it but to *know* it was bitter. Was there no real magic left in the world?

"Judy," . . . Pat was almost tearful when Judy came to the well with her pails of milk . . . "the fairies *don't* drink the milk. It's a cat . . . just as Sidney always said."

"Oh, oh, and if the fairies didn't nade it last night why shudn't a poor cat have it, I'm asking. Hasn't he got to live? I niver said they come ivery night. They've other pickings no doubt."

"Judy, did you ever really *see* a fairy drinking the milk? Cross your heart?"

"Oh, oh, what if I didn't? Sure the grandmother of me did. Minny's the time I've heard her tell it. A leprachaun wid the liddle ears av him wriggling as he lapped it up. And she had her leg bruk nixt day, that she had. Ye may be thankful if ye niver see any av the Grane Folk. They don't be liking it and that I'm tellin ye."

2

It was a day curiously compounded of pain and pleasure for Pat. Silver Bush buzzed with excitement, especially when Snicklefritz got stung on the eyelid by a wasp and had to be shut up in the church barn. And then everybody was getting dressed. Oh, weddings *were* exciting things . . . Sid was right. Mother wore the loveliest new dress, the colour of a golden-brown chrysanthemum, and Pat was so proud of her it hurt.

"It's so nice to have a pretty mother," she exclaimed rapturously.

She was proud of all her family. Of father, who had had a terrible time finding his necktie and who, in his excitement, had put his left boot on his right foot and laced it up before he discovered his mistake, but now looked every inch a Gardiner. Of darling wee Cuddles with her silk stockings rolled down to show her dear, bare, chubby legs. Of Winnie, who in her yellow dress looked like a great golden pansy. Of Sid and Joe in new suits and white collars. Even of Judy Plum who had blossomed out in truly regal state. The dress-up dress had come out of the brown chest, likewise a rather rusty lace shawl and bonnet of quilted blue satin of the vintage of last century. Judy would have scorned to be seen in public without a bonnet. No giddy hats for her. Also what she called a "paireen" of glossy, patent leather slippers with high heels. Thus fearsomely arrayed Judy minced about, keeping a watchful eye on everything and greeting arriving friends in what she called her "company voice" and the most perfect English pronunciation you ever heard.

Aunt Hazel and her bridesmaids were as yet invisible in the Poet's room. Mother dressed Pat in her pretty green dress and hat. Pat loved it . . . but she ran upstairs to her closet to tell her old blue voile that she still loved it the best. Then the aunts came over, Aunt Barbara very weddingish in a dress and coat of beige lace which Aunt Edith thought far too young for her. Nobody could call Aunt Edith's dress young but it was very handsome and Pat nearly burst with pride in her whole clan.

Uncle Brian from Summerside was going to take the bride and her maids to the church in his new car and it was a wonderful moment when they came floating down the stairs. Pat's eyes smarted a wee bit. Was this mysterious creature in white satin and misty veil, with the great shower bouquet of roses and lilies of the valley, her dear, jolly Aunt Hazel? Pat felt as if she were already lost to them. But Aunt Hazel lingered to whisper.

"I've slipped the pansies you picked for me into my bouquet, darling . . . they're the 'something blue' the bride must wear, and thanks ever so much."

And all was well again for a while.

Father took mother and Winnie and Judy and Joe in the Silver Bush Lizzie but Pat and Sid went in Uncle Tom's "span." No Lizzie or any other such lady for Uncle Tom. He drove a great roomy, double-seated "phaeton" drawn by two satin bay horses with white stars on their foreheads and Pat liked it far better than any car. But why was Uncle Tom so slow in coming? "We'll be late. There's a million buggies and cars gone past already," worried Pat.

"Oh, oh, don't be exaggerating, girleen."

"Well, there was five anyway," cried Pat indignantly.

"There he's coming now," said Judy. "Mind yer manners," she added in a fierce whisper. "No monkey-didoes whin things get a bit solemn, mind ye that."

Pat and Sid and Aunt Barbara sat in the back seat. Pat felt tremendously important and bridled notably when May Binnie looked out enviously from a car that honked past them. Generally she and Sid walked to church by a short cut across the fields and along a brook scarfed with farewell summers. But the road was lovely, too, with the sunny, golden stubble fields, the glossy black crows sitting on the fences, the loaded apple boughs dragging on the grass of the orchards, the pastures spangled with asters, and the sea far out looking so blue and happy, with great fleets of cloudland sailing over it.

Then there was the crowded church among its maples and spruces— the arrangement of the procession—the people standing up—Aunt Hazel trailing down the aisle on father's arm—Jean Madison and Sally Gardiner behind her—Pat bringing up the rear gallantly with her basket of roses in her brown paws—the sudden hush—the minister's solemn voice—the prayer—the lovely colours that fell on the people through the stained glass windows, turning them from prosaic folks into miracles. At first Pat was too bewildered to analyse her small sensations. She saw a little quivering ruby of light fall on Aunt Hazel's white veil . . . she saw Rob Madison's flying jibs . . . she saw Sally Gardiner's night-black hair under her green hat . . . she saw the ferns and flowers . . . and suddenly she heard Aunt Hazel saying, "I will," and saw her looking up at her groom.

A dreadful thing happened to Pat. She turned frantically to Judy Plum who was sitting just behind her at the end of the front pew.

"Judy, lend me your hanky. I'm going to cry," she whispered in a panic.

Judy fairly came out in gooseflesh. She realised that a desperate situation must be handled desperately. Her hanky was a huge white one which would engulf Pat. Moreover the Binnies were at the back of the church. She bent forward.

"If there do be one tear out av ye to disgrace Silver Bush I'll niver fry ye an egg in butter agin as long as I live."

Pat took a brace. Perhaps it was the thought of Silver Bush or the fried egg or both combined. She gave a desperate gulp and swallowed the lump in her throat. Savage winking prevented the fall of a single tear. The ceremony was over . . . nobody had noticed the little by-play . . . and everybody thought Pat had behaved beautifully. The Silver Bush people were much relieved. They had all been more or less afraid that Pat would break down at the last, just as Cora Gardiner had done at her sister's wedding, erupting into hysterical howls right in the middle of the prayer and having to be walked out by a humiliated mother.

"Ye carried yerself off well, darlint," whispered Judy proudly.

Pat contrived to get through the reception and the supper but she found she couldn't eat, not even a chicken slice or the lovely "lily salad" mother had made. She was very near crying again when somebody said to Aunt Hazel,

"What is it like to be Hazel Madison? Do you realise that you *are* Hazel Madison now?"

Hazel Gardiner no longer! Oh, it was just too much!

8

AFTERMATH

1

And then the going away! For the first time in her life Pat found out what it was like to say good-bye to some one who was not coming back. But she could cry then because everybody cried, even Judy, who seldom cried.

"When I feels like crying," Judy was accustomed to say, "I just do be sitting down and having a good laugh."

She would not let Pat stand too long, looking after Aunt Hazel, tranced in her childish tears.

"It's unlucky to watch a parting friend out av sight," she told her.

Pat turned away and wandered dismally through the empty rooms. With everything so upset and disarranged upstairs and down Silver Bush wasn't like home at all. Even the new lace curtains seemed part of the strangeness. The table, that had been so pretty, looked terrible . . . untidy . . . crumby . . . messy . . . with Aunt Hazel's chair pushed rakily aside just as she had risen from it. Pat's brown eyes were drowned again.

"Come along wid me, darlint, and help me out a bit," Judy . . . wise Judy . . . was saying. "Sure and yer mother has gone to bed, rale played out wid all the ruckus, and small wonder. And Winnie's tying hersilf into kinks wid the stomachache and that's no puzzle ather wid the way she was after stuffing hersilf. So there's nobody but us two to look after things. We'll lave the dining-room as it is till the morning but we'll straighten up the parlours and the bedrooms. Sure and the poor house do be looking tired."

Judy had doffed her silk and high heels and company voice and was in her comfortable old drugget and brogans . . . and brogue . . . again. Pat was glad. Judy seemed much more homelike and companionable so.

"Can we put all the furniture back in its right place?" she said eagerly. Somehow it would be a comfort to have the sideboard and the old parlour rocker that had been put out of sight as too shabby, and the vases of pampas grass that had been condemned as old-fashioned, back again where they belonged.

"Oh, oh, we'll do that. And lave off looking as doleful as if yer Aunt Hazel had been buried instid av being married."

"I don't feel much like smiling, Judy."

"There's rason in that. Sure and I've been grinning that much to-day I fale as if I'd been turned into a chessy-cat. But it's been one grand widding, so it has, and the like av it Jen Binnie will never see for all av her city beau. As for the supper, Government House itsilf cudn't bate it. And the cirrimony was that solemn it wud av scared me out av the notion av getting married if I iver had inny."

"I would have cried and spoiled it all if it hadn't been for you, Judy dear," said Pat gratefully.

"Oh, oh, I wasn't blaming ye. I knew a big, handsome bridesmaid onct and she burst out waping right in the middle av the cirrimony. And the things people did be saying . . . such as she was crying bekase she wasn't getting married hersilf, whin it was just her full heart. At that it was better than the bridesmaid that was laughing in the middle av things at Rosella Gardiner's widding. No one iver did be knowing what she laughed at . . . she wud niver tell . . . but the groom thought it was at him, and he niver wud spake to her again. It started a ruckus in the fam'ly that lasted for forty years. Oh, oh, the liddle things that do be having a big inding!"

Pat didn't think that for the bridesmaid to laugh in the middle of the ceremony was a little thing. She was very glad nothing like that had happened to make Aunt Hazel's wedding ridiculous.

"Come now and we'll swape up all this confetti stuff first. The ould days av rice were better I'm thinking. The hins got a good fade innyhow. Oh, oh, this table do be looking like the relics of ould dacency, doesn't it now? I'm seeing one av the good silver crame jugs has got a dint in it. But whin all's said and done it don't be looking much like the table did after yer Great-aunt Margaret's widding over at the Bay Shore farm. Oh, oh, that was a tommyshaw!"

"What happened, Judy?"

"Happened, is it? Ye may well ask. They had a fringed cloth on the table be way av extry style and whin the groom's cousin . . . ould Jim Milroy he is now . . . Jim wid the beard he was called thin . . . oh, oh, he had the magnificent beard. Sure and 'twas a shame to shave it off just bekase it wint out av fashion . . . well, where was I at? He wint to get up from the table in a hurry as he always did and didn't one av his buttons catch in the fringe and away wint fringe and cloth and dishes and all. Niver did inny one see such a smash. I was down to the Bay Shore to hilp thim out a bit and me and yer Aunt Frances claned up the mess, her crying and lamenting all the time and small blame to her. All the illigant dishes smashed and the carpet plastered wid the stuff that was spilled, niver to spake av the poor bride's dress as was clane ruined be a great cup av tay tipped over in her lap. Oh, oh, I was a young skellup av a thing thin and I thought it a great joke but the Bay Shore people were niver the same agin. Now, run up to yer room, and put off yer finery and we'll get to work. I belave we're after having a rainy night av it. The wind's rising and it's dark as a squaw's pocket already."

It was such a comfort to put things back in their places. When the job was finished Silver Bush looked like home again. Darkness had fallen and rain was beginning to splash against the windows.

"Let's go into the kitchen now and I'll get ye a tasty liddle bite afore I do be setting the bread. I noticed ye didn't ate innything av their fine spread. I've a pot of hot pay soup I brewed up for mesilf kaping warm on the back av the stove and there's some chicken lift over I'm thinking."

"I don't feel like eating with Aunt Hazel gone," said Pat, rather mistily again. That thought *would* keep coming back.

"Oh, oh, fat sorrow is better than lean sorrow, me jewel. Here now, ain't this snug as two kittens in a basket? We'll shut out the dark. And here's a liddle cat wid an illigant grey suit and a white shirt, be the name av Thursday, wid his small heart breaking for a word after all the neglict av the day."

A fierce yowl sounded outside. Gentleman Tom was demanding entrance.

"Let me let him in, Judy," said Pat eagerly. She did so love to let things in out of the cold. Pat held the door open for a moment. It was a wild night after the lovely day. The rain was streaming down. The wind was thrashing the silver bush mercilessly. Snicklefritz was howling dolefully in the church barn since Joe was not yet back from the station to comfort him.

Pat turned away with a shiver. The peace of the old kitchen was in delightful contrast to the storm outside. The stove was glowing clear red in the dusk. Thursday was coiled up under it, thinking this was how things should be. It was so nice to be in this bright, warm room, supping Judy's hot pea soup and watching the reflection of the kitchen outside through the window. Pat loved to do that. It looked so uncanny and witchlike . . . so real yet so unreal . . . with Judy apparently calmly setting bread under the thrashing maple by the well.

2

Pat loved to watch Judy set bread and listen to her talking to herself as she always did while kneading and thumping. To-night Judy was reviewing the church wedding.

"Oh, oh, she was dressed very gay outside but I'm wondering what was undernath. Sure and it's well if it was no worse than patches . . . Bertha Holmes is the pert one. Only fifteen and she do be making eyes at the b'ys already. I remember her at her own aunt's widding whin she was about the age av Pat here. She was after throwing hersilf on the floor and kicking and scraming. Oh, oh, wudn't I like to have had the spanking av her! Simon Gardiner was be way av being rale groomed up to-day. Sure and whin I saw him, so starched and proper in his pew, looking as if he was doing the world a big favour be living, it was hard to belave the last time I saw him he was so drunk he thought the table was follying him round, and crying like a baby he was bekase it wud be sure to catch him, having four legs to his two. It tickled me ribs, that. Oh, oh, it's liddle folks know what other folks do be thinking av thim in church. And wud ye listen to Ould Man Taylor calling his wife sugar-pie and him married thirty years, the ould softy. Though maybe it's better than George Harvey and his 'ould woman.' There was ould Elmer Davidson stumbling in late whin the cirrimony had begun and sp'iling the solemnity. He'll be late for the resurrection, that one. Mary Jarvis and her yilping whin they were signing the papers! Thim that likes can call it singing. Singing, indade! The Great-aunts av the Bay Shore farm were after being a bit more stately than common . . . be way of showing their contimpt for both Gardiners and Madisons I'm thinking. Sure and it's a wonder they condescend to come at all. Oh, oh, but the supper wud give thim one in the eye. It's a long day since they've set down to such a spread I'm thinking. Oh, oh, but I got square wid Ould Maid Sands. Sez I to her, sly-like, 'While there's life there's hope.' *She* knew well what I was maning, so she did."

Judy was shaking with silent laughter as she patted her bread. Then she grew sober.

"Oh, oh, there was one at the widding that'll be to none other. Kate MacKenzie has got the sign."

"What sign, Judy?" asked Pat drowsily.

"Oh, oh, I forgot liddle pitchers have the long ears, darlint. 'Tis the death sign I mint. But it do be life. There's always the birth and the death and the bridal mixed up togither. And a nice cheerful widding it was in spite av all."

Pat was almost asleep. The down-trodden black cats were beginning to trot around the rug under her very eyes.

"Wake up, me jewel, and go to bed properly. Listen at that wind. There'll be apples to pick up to-morrow."

Pat looked up, yawning and comforted. After all, life at dear Silver Bush was going on. The world hadn't come to an end just because Aunt Hazel was gone.

"Judy, tell me again about the man you saw hanged in Ireland before I go to bed."

"Oh, oh, that do be a tarrible story for bed-time. It wud make yer hair stand on end."

"I *like* having my hair stand on end. Please, Judy."

Judy picked Pat up on her knee.

"Hug me close, Judy, and tell me."

The harrowing tale was told and Pat, who had heard it a dozen times before, thrilled just as deliciously as at the first. There was no doubt about it . . . she enjoyed "tarrible" things.

"Sure and I shudn't be telling ye all these tales av bad people," said Judy, a bit uncomfortably, looking at Pat's dilated eyes.

"Of course, Judy, I like to *live* with good people better than bad, but I like *hearing* about bad people better than good."

"Well, I do be thinking it wud be a dull world if nobody iver did anything he oughtn't. What wud we find to talk about?" asked Judy unanswerably. "Innyway, it's to bed ye must be going. And say a prayer for all poor ghosts. If Wild Dick or Waping Willy or ather or both av thim are on the fence to-night 'tis a wet time they'll be having av it."

"Maybe I won't be so lonesome if I say my prayers twice," thought Pat. She said them twice and even contrived to pray for her new uncle. Perhaps as a reward for this she fell asleep instantly. Once in the night she wakened and a flood of desolation poured over her. But in the darkness she heard a melodious purring and felt the beautiful touch of a velvet cat. Pat swallowed hard. The rain was still sobbing around the eaves. Aunt Hazel was gone. But Silver Bush held her in its heart. To lie in this dear house, sheltered from the storm, with Thursday purring under her hand . . . apples to be picked to-morrow . . . oh, life to beckon once more. Pat fell asleep comforted.

9

A DAY TO SPEND

1

Again it was September at Silver Bush . . . a whole year since Aunt Hazel was married: and now it seemed to Pat that Aunt Hazel had always been married. She and Uncle Bob often came "home" for a visit and Pat was very fond of Uncle Bob now, and even thought his flying jibs were nice. The last time, too, Aunt Hazel had had a darling, tiny baby, with amber-brown eyes like Pat's own. Cuddles wasn't a baby any longer. She was toddling round on her own chubby legs and was really a sister to be proud of. She had been through all her teething at eleven months. It was beautiful to watch her waking up and beautiful to bend over her while she was asleep. She seemed to know you were there and would smile delightedly. A spirit of her own, too. When she was eight months old she had bitten Uncle Tom when he poked a finger into her mouth to find out if she had any teeth. He found out.

And now had come the invitation for Pat to spend a Saturday at the

Bay Shore farm, with Great-aunt Frances Selby and Great-aunt Honor Atkins . . . not to mention "Cousin" Dan Gowdy and a still greater aunt, who was mother's great-aunt. Pat's head was usually dizzy when she got this far and small wonder, as Judy would say.

Pat loved the sound of "a day to spend." It sounded so gloriously lavish to "spend" a whole day, letting its moments slip one by one through your fingers like beads of gold.

But she was not enthusiastic over spending it at the Bay Shore. When she and Sid had been very small they had called the Bay Shore the Don't-touch-it House guiltily, to themselves. Everybody was so old there. Two years ago, when she had been there with mother, she remembered how Aunt Frances frowned because when they were walking in the orchard, she, Pat, had picked a lovely, juicy, red plum from a laden tree. And Aunt Honor, a tall lady with snow-white hair and eyes as black as her dress, had asked her to repeat some Bible verses and had been coldly astonished when Pat made mistakes in them. The great-aunts always asked you to repeat Bible verses . . . so said Winnie and Joe who had been there often . . . and you never could tell what they would give when you got through . . . a dime or a cooky or a tap on the head.

But to go *alone* to the Bay Shore! Sidney had been asked, too, but Sidney had gone to visit Uncle Brian's while his teeth were attended to. Perhaps it was just as well because Sidney was not in high favour at the Bay Shore, having fallen asleep at the supper table and tumbled ingloriously off his chair to the floor, with an heirloom goblet in his hand, the last time he was there.

Pat talked it over with Judy Friday evening, sitting on the sandstone steps at the kitchen door and working her sums to be all ready for Monday. Pat was a year older and an inch taller, by the marks Judy kept on the old pantry door where she measured every child on its birthday. She was well on in subtraction and Judy was helping her. Judy could add and subtract. When her head was clear she could multiply. Division she never attempted.

The kitchen behind them was full of the spicy smell of Judy's kettle of pickles. Gentleman Tom was sitting on the well platform, keeping an eye on Snicklefritz, who was dozing on the cellar door, keeping an eye on Gentleman Tom. In the corner of the yard was a splendid pile of cut hardwood which Pat and Sid had stacked neatly up in the

PAT OF SILVER BUSH

summer evenings after school. Pat gloated over it. It was so prophetic
of cosy, cheerful winter evenings when the wind would growl and snarl
because it couldn't get into Silver Bush. Pat would have been perfectly
happy if it had not been for the morrow's visit.

"The aunts are so . . . so stately," she confided to Judy. She would
never have dared criticise them to mother who had been a Selby and
was very proud of her people.

"The grandmother av thim was a Chidlaw," said Judy as if that
explained everything. "I'm not saying but they're a bit grim but they've
had a tarrible lot av funerals at the Bay Shore. Yer Aunt Frances lost
her man afore she married him and yer Aunt Honor lost hers after she
married him and they've niver settled which got the worst av it. They're
a bit near, too, it must be confessed, and thim wid lashings of money.
But they do be rale kind at heart and they think a lot av all yer mother's
children."

"I don't mind Aunt Frances or Aunt Honor, but I'm a *little* afraid of
Great-great-aunt Hannah and Cousin Dan," confessed Pat.

"Oh, oh, ye nadn't be. Maybe ye'll not be seeing the ould leddy at all.
She hasn't left her own room for sixteen years and she's ninety-three
be the clock, so she is, and there don't be minny seeing her. And ould
Danny is harmless. He fell aslape at the top av the stairs and rolled
down thim whin he was a lad. He was niver the same agin. But some
do be saying he saw the ghost."

"Oh, Judy, is there a ghost at Bay Shore?"

"Not now. But long ago there was. Oh, oh, they were tarrible
ashamed av it."

"Why?"

"Ye know they thought it was kind av a disgraceful thing to have a
ghost in the house. Some folks do be thinking it an honour but there
ye are. I'm not denying the Bay Shore ghost was a troublesome cratur.
Sure and he was a nice, frindly, sociable ghost and hadn't any rale dog-
sense about the proper time for appearing. He was a bit lonesome it
wud seem. He wud sit round on the foot-boards av their beds and look
at thim mournful like, as if to say, 'Why the divil won't ye throw a civil
word to a felly?' And whin company come and they were all enjying
thimselves they'd hear a dape sigh and there me fine ghost was. It was
be way av being tarrible monotonous after a while. But the ghost was
niver seen agin after yer great-great-uncle died and yer Great-aunt

62

Honor tuk to running things. I'm thinking she was a bit too near, aven for a ghost, that one. So ye nadn't be afraid av seeing him but ye'd better not be looking too close at the vase that makes the faces."

"A vase . . . that makes faces!"

"Sure, me jewel. It's on the parlour mantel and it made a face once at Sarah Jenkins as was hired there whin she was dusting it. She was nather to hold nor bind wid fright."

This was delightful. But after all, Pat thought Judy was a little too contemptuous of the Bay Shore people.

"Their furniture is very grand, Judy."

"Grand, is it?" Judy knew very well she had been snubbed. "Oh, oh, ye can't be telling *me* innything about grandeur. Didn't I work in Castle McDermott whin I was a slip av a girleen? Grandeur, is it? Lace and sating bed-quilts, I'm telling ye. And a white marble staircase wid a golden bannister. Dinner sets av solid gold and gold vases full av champagne. And thiry servants if there was one. Sure and they kipt servants to wait on the other servants there. The ould lord wud pass round plates wid gold sovereigns at the Christmas dinner and hilp yerself. Oh, oh, what's yer Bay Shore farm to that, I'm asking. And now just rin over thim verses ye larnt last Sunday, in case yer Aunt Honor wants ye to say some."

"I can say them without a mistake to you, Judy. But it will be so different with Aunt Honor."

"Sure and ye'd better just shut yer eyes and purtind she's a cabbage-head, darlint. Though old Jed Cattermole didn't be thinking her that whin she put him in his place at the revival meetings."

"What did she do, Judy?"

"Do, is it? I'm telling ye. Old Jed thought he was extry cliver bekase he didn't belave in God. Just be way av showing off one night he wint to one av the revival matings ould Mr. Campbell was having whin he was minister at South Glen. And after all the tistimonies me bould Jed gets up and sez, sez he, 'I'm not belaving there's inny God but if there is He do be a cruel, unrasonable ould tyrant. And now,' sez Jed, swelling up all over wid consate, like an ould tom turkey, 'if there is a God why doesn't he strike me dead for what I've said. I dare Him to do it,' sez ould Jed, feeling bigger than iver. Iverybody was so shocked ye cud have heard a pin fall. And yer Aunt Honor turns round and sez she, cool-like, 'Do you really think ye're av that much importance to God,

63

Jedediah Cattermole?' Iverybody laughed. Did ye iver be seeing one av .thim big rid balloons whin ye've stuck a pin in it? Oh, oh, that was me proud Jed. He was niver the same agin. Now yer sums are done and me pickles are done, so we'll just have a bit av fun roasting some crab apples wid cloves stuck in thim for scint."

"I wish Sid was here," sighed Pat. "He does love clove apples so. Will he be back Sunday night, do you think, Judy? I *can't* live another week without him."

"Ye set yer heart too much on Siddy, me jewel. What'll ye be after doing whin ye grow up and have to part?"

"Oh, that'll never be, Judy. Sid and I are never going to part. We'll neither of us marry but just live on here at Silver Bush and take care of everything. We have it all settled."

Judy sighed.

"I wish ye wudn't be so set on him. Why don't ye be after getting yersilf a chum in school like the other liddle girls? Winnie has lashings av thim."

"I don't want anybody but Sid. The girls in school are nice but I don't love any of them. I don't *want* to love any one or anything but my own family and Silver Bush."

2

Since Pat had to go to the Bay Shore farm she was glad it was this particular Saturday because father was going to replace the old board fence around the orchard with a new one. Pat hated to see the old fence torn down. It was covered with such pretty lichens, and vines had grown over its posts and there was a wave of caraway all along it as high as your waist.

Judy had a reason for being glad, too. The ukase had gone forth that the big poplar in the corner of the yard must be cut down because its core was rotten and the next wind might send it crashing down on the hen-house. Judy had plotted with Long Alec to cut it down the day Pat was away for she knew every blow of the axe would go to the darlint's heart.

Joe ran Pat down to the Bay Shore in the car. She bent from it as it whirled out of the lane to wave good-bye to Silver Bush. Cuddles' dear little rompers on the line behind the house were plumped out with wind and looked comically like three small Cuddles swinging from the line. Pat sighed and then resolved to make the best of things. The day was lovely, full of blue, sweet autumn hazes. The road to the Bay Shore was mostly down hill, running for part of the way through spruce "barrens," its banks edged with ferns, sweet-smelling bay bushes, and clusters of scarlet pigeon-berries. There was a blue, waiting sea at the end and an old grey house fronting the sunset, so close to the purring waves that in storms their spray dashed over its very doorstep . . . a wise old house that knew many things, as Pat always felt. Mother's old home and therefore to be loved, whether one could love the people in it or not.

It still made quite a sensation at Bay Shore when any one arrived in a car. The aunts came out and gave a prim welcome and Cousin Dan waved from a near field where he was turning over the sod into beautiful red furrows, so even and smooth. Cousin Dan was very proud of his ploughing.

Joe whirled away, leaving Pat to endure her ordeal of welcome and examination. The great-aunts were as stiff as the starched white petticoats that were still worn at Bay Shore. To tell truth, the great-aunts were really frightfully at a loss what to say to this long-legged, sunburned child whom they thought it a family duty to invite to Bay Shore once in so long. Then Pat was taken up to the Great-great's room for a few minutes. She went reluctantly. Great-great-aunt Hannah was so mysteriously old . . . a tiny, shrunken, wrinkled creature peering at her out of a mound of quilts in a huge, curtained bed.

"So this is Mary's little girl," said a piping voice.

"No. I am Patricia Gardiner," said Pat, who hated to be called anybody's little girl, even mother's.

Great-great-aunt Hannah put a claw-like hand on Pat's arm and drew her close to the bed, peering at her with old, old blue eyes, so old that sight had come back to them.

"Nae beauty . . . nae beauty," she muttered.

"She may grow up better-looking than you expect," said Aunt Frances, as one determinedly looking on the bright side. "She is terribly sunburned now."

Pat's little brown face, with its fine satiny skin, flushed mutinously. She did not care if she were "no beauty" but she disliked being criticised to her face like this. Judy would have said it wasn't manners. And then when they went downstairs Aunt Honor said in a tone of horror,

"There's a rip in your dress, child."

Pat wished they wouldn't call her "child." She would have loved to stick her tongue out at Aunt Honor but that wouldn't be manners either. She stood very stiff while Aunt Honor brought needle and thread and sewed it up.

"Of course Mary can't attend to everything and Judy Plum wouldn't care if they were all in rags," said Aunt Frances condoningly.

"Judy *would* care," cried Pat. "She's *very* particular about our clothes and our manners. That shoulder ripped on the way over. So there."

In spite of this rather unpropitious beginning the day was not so bad. Pat said her verses correctly and Aunt Honor gave her a cooky . . . and watched her eat it. Pat was in agonies of thirst but was too shy to ask for a glass of water. When dinner time came, however, there was plenty of milk . . . Judy would have said "skim" milk. But it was served in a lovely old gold-green glass pitcher that made the skimmiest of milk look like Jersey cream. The table was something of the leanest, according to Silver Bush standards. Pat's portion of the viands was none too lavish, but she ate it off a plate with a coloured border of autumn leaves . . . one of the famous Selby plates, a hundred years old. Pat felt honoured and tried not to feel hungry. For dessert she had three of the tabooed red plums.

After dinner Aunt Frances said she had a headache and was going to lie down. Cousin Dan suggested aspirin but Aunt Frances crushed him with a look.

"It is not God's will that we should take aspirin for relief from the pain He sends," she said loftily, and stalked off, with her red glass, silver-stoppered vinaigrette held to her nose.

Aunt Honor turned Pat loose in the parlour and told her to amuse herself. This Pat proceeded to do. Everything was of interest and now she was alone she could have a good time. She had been wondering how she could live through the afternoon if she had to sit it out with the aunts. Both she and Aunt Honor were mutually relieved to be rid of each other.

3

The parlour furniture *was* grand and splendid. There was a big, polished brass door-handle in which she saw herself reflected with such a funny face. The china door-plate had roses painted on it. The blinds were pulled down and she loved the cool, green light which filled the room . . . it made her feel like a mermaid in a shimmering sea-pool. She loved the little procession of six white ivory elephants marching along the black mantel. She loved the big spotted shells on the what-not which murmured of the sea when she held them to her ear. And there was the famous vase, full of peacock feathers, that had made a face at Sarah Jenkins. It was of white glass and had curious markings on its side that did resemble a face. But it did not grimace at Pat though she wished it would. There was a brilliant red-and-yellow china hen sitting on a yellow nest on a corner table that was very wonderful. And there were deep Battenburg lace scallops on the window shades. Surely even Castle McDermott couldn't beat that.

Pat would have liked to see all the hidden things in the house. Not its furniture or its carpets but the letters in old boxes upstairs and the clothes in old trunks. But this was impossible. She dared not leave the parlour. The aunts would die of horror if they caught her prowling.

When everything in the room had been examined Pat curled herself up on the sofa and spent an absorbed hour looking at the pictures in old albums with faded blue and red plush bindings and in hinged leather frames that opened and shut like a book. What funny old pictures in full skirts and big sleeves and huge hats high up on the head! There was one of Aunt Frances in the eighties, in a flounced dress and a little "sacque" with its sloping shoulders and square scallops . . . *and* a frilled parasol. Oh, you could just see how proud she was of that parasol! It seemed funny to think of Aunt Frances as a little girl with a frivolous parasol.

There was a picture of father . . . a young man without a moustache. Pat giggled over that. One of mother, too . . . a round, plump face, with "bangs" and a big bow of ribbon in her hair. And one of Great-uncle Burton who went away and was "never heard of again." What fascination was in the phrase! Even dead people were heard of again. They had funerals and head-stones.

And here was Aunt Honor as a baby. Looking like Cuddles! Oh, would Cuddles *ever* look like Aunt Honor? It was unthinkable. How terribly people changed! Pat sighed.

10

A MAIDEN ALL FORLORN

1

At dusk there was the question of how Pat was to get home. Aunt Frances, who was the horsewoman of Bay Shore, was to have driven her. But Aunt Frances was still enduring God's will in her bedroom and Aunt Honor hadn't driven a horse for years. As for Cousin Dan, he couldn't be trusted away from home with a team. Aunt Honor finally telephoned to the nearest neighbour.

"Morton MacLeod is going to town. I thought he would, since it is Saturday night. He says he'll take you and drop you off at Silver Bush. You don't mind going as far as the MacLeod place alone, do you? You will be there before dark."

Pat didn't mind anything except the prospect of staying at the Bay Shore overnight. And she was never in the least afraid of the dark. She had often been alone in it. The other children at her age had been afraid of the dark and ran in when it came. But Pat never did. They said at Silver Bush that she was "her father's child" for that. Long Alec always liked to wander around alone at night . . . "enjoying the beauty of the darkness," he said. There was a family legend that Pat at the age of four had slept out in the caraway in the orchard all one night, nobody missing her until Judy, who had been sitting up with a sick neighbour, came home at sunrise and raised a riot. Pat dimly remembered the family rapture when she was found and joy washing like a rosy wave over mother's pale, distracted face.

She said her good-byes politely and made her way up to the MacLeod place where bad news met her. Morton's car was "acting up" and he had given up the idea of going to town.

"So you'll have to run back to the Bay Shore," his mother told her kindly.

Pat went slowly down the lane and when she was screened from sight of the house by a spruce grove she stopped to think. She did not want to go back to the Bay Shore. The very thought of spending the night in the big spare room, with its bed that looked far too grand to be slept in, was unbearable. No, she would just walk home. It was only three miles . . . she walked that every day going to school and back.

Pat started off briskly and gaily, feeling very independent and daring and grown-up. How Judy would stare when she sauntered into the kitchen and announced carelessly that she had walked home from the Bay Shore all alone in the dark. "Oh, oh, and ain't ye the bould one?" Judy would say admiringly.

And then . . . the dark chilly night seemed suddenly to be coming to meet her . . . and when the road forked she wasn't sure which fork to take . . . the left one? . . . oh, it must be the left one . . . Pat ran along it with sheer panic creeping into her heart.

It was dark now . . . quite dark. And Pat suddenly discovered that to be alone on a strange road two miles from home in a very dark darkness was an entirely different thing from prowling in the orchard or running along the Whispering Lane or wandering about the Field of the Pool with the homelights of Silver Bush always in sight.

The woods and groves around her, that had seemed so friendly on the golden September day were strangers now. The far, dark spruce hills seemed to draw nearer threateningly. *Was this the right road?* There were no homelights anywhere. Had she taken the wrong turn and was this the "line" road that ran along the backs of the farms between the two townships? Would she ever get home? Would she ever see Sid again . . . hear Winnie's laugh and Cuddles' dear little squeals of welcome? Last Sunday in church the choir had sung, *"The night is dark and I am far from home."* She knew what that meant now as she broke into a desperate little run. The white birches along the roadside seemed to be trying to catch her with ghostly hands. The wind wailed through the spruces. At Silver Bush you never quite knew how the wind would come at you . . . from behind the church barn like a cat pouncing . . . down from the Hill of the Mist like a soft bird flying . . . through the orchard like a playmate . . . but it always came as a friend. This wind was no friend. Was that it crying in the spruces? Or was it the Green

Harper of Judy's tale who harped people away to Fairyland whether they would or no? All Judy's stories, enjoyed and disbelieved at home, became fearfully true here. Those strange little shadows, dark amid the darkness, under the ferns . . . suppose they *were* fairies. Judy said if you met a fairy you were never the same again. No threat could have been more terrible to Pat. To be changed . . . to be not yourself!

That wild, far-away note . . . was it the Peter Branaghan of another of Judy's tales, out on the hills piping to his ghostly sheep? And still no light . . . she *must* be on the wrong road.

All at once she was wild with terror of the chill night and the eerie wind and the huge, dark pathless world around her. She stopped short and uttered a bitter little cry of desolation.

"Can I help you?" said a voice.

Some one had just come around the turn of the road. A boy . . . not much taller than herself . . . with something queer about his eyes . . . with a little blot of shadow behind him that looked like a dog. That was all Pat could see. But suddenly she felt safe . . . protected. He had such a nice voice.

"I . . . think I'm lost," she gasped. "I'm Pat Gardiner . . . and I took the wrong road."

"You're on the line road," said the boy. "But it turns and goes down past Silver Bush. Only it's a little longer. I'll take you home. I'm Hilary Gordon . . . but everybody calls me Jingle."

Pat knew at once who he was and felt well acquainted. She had heard Judy talk about the Gordons who had bought the little old Adams farm that marched with Silver Bush. They had no family of their own but an orphan nephew was living with them and Judy said it was likely he had poor pickings of it. He did not go to the North Glen school for the old Adams place was in the South Glen school district, but they were really next-door neighbours.

2

They walked on. They did not talk much but Pat felt happy now as she trotted along. The moon rose and in its light she looked at him curiously. He had dark-coloured, horn-rimmed glasses . . . that was what was the matter with his eyes. And he wore trousers of which one leg came to the knee and the other half way between knee and ankle, which Pat thought rather dreadful.

"I belong to Silver Bush, you know," she said.

"I don't belong anywhere," said Jingle forlornly.

Pat wanted to comfort him for something she did not understand. She slipped her little hand into his . . . he had a warm pleasant hand. They walked home together so. The wind . . . the night . . . were friendly again. The dark boughs of the trees, tossing against the silver moonlit sky, were beautiful . . . the spicy, woodsy smells along the road delightful.

"Where does that road go?" asked Pat once as they passed an inviting path barred by moonlight and shadow.

"I don't know but we'll go and see some day," said Jingle.

They were just like old, old friends.

And then the dear light of Silver Bush shining across the fields . . . the dear house overflowing with welcoming light. Pat could have cried with joy to see it again. Even if nobody would be very glad to see her back the house would.

"Thank you so much for coming home with me," she said shyly at the gate of the kitchen yard. "I was so frightened."

Then she added boldly . . . because she had heard Judy say a girl ought always to give a dacent feller a bite whin he had seen her home and Pat, for the credit of Silver Bush, wanted to do the proper thing . . .

"I wish you'd come and have dinner with us Monday. We're going to have chickens because it's Labour Day. Judy says she labours that day just the same as any day but she always celebrates it with a chicken dinner. Please come."

"I'd like to," said Jingle. "And I'm glad McGinty and I happened along when you were scared."

"Is McGinty the name of your dog?" asked Pat, looking at it a little timidly. Snicklefritz and Uncle Tom's old Bruno were all the dogs she was acquainted with.

"Yes. He's the only friend I've got in the world," said Jingle.

"Except me," said Pat.

Jingle suddenly smiled. Even in the moonlight she saw that he had a nice smile.

"Except you," he agreed.

Judy appeared at the open kitchen door, peering out.

"I must run," said Pat hastily. "Monday then. Don't forget. And bring McGinty, too. There'll be some bones."

"Now who was ye colloguing wid out there?" asked Judy curiously. "Sure and ye might av brought yer beau in and let's give him the once-over. Not but that ye're beginning a trifle young."

"That wasn't a beau, Judy," cried Pat, scandalised at the bare idea. "That was just Jingle."

"Hear at her. And who may Jingle be, if it's not asking too much?"

"Hilary Gordon . . . and I was coming home alone . . . and I got lost . . . I was a *little* frightened, Judy . . . and he's coming to dinner on Monday."

"Oh, oh, it's the fast worker ye are," chuckled Judy, delighted that she had got something to tease Pat about . . . Pat who had never thought there was any boy in the world but Sidney.

But Pat was too happy to mind. She was home, in the bright kitchen of Silver Bush. The horror of that lonely road had ceased to be . . . had never been. It was really beautiful to come home at night . . . to step out of darkness into the light and warmth of home.

"Did ye save a piece of pie for me, Judy?"

"Oh, oh, that I did. Don't I know the skimp males of the Bay Shore? Sure and it's niver cut and come agin there. It's more than a bit av pie I have for ye. What wud ye say now to a sausage and a baked pittaty?"

Over the supper Pat told Judy all about the day and her walk home.

"Think av the pluck av her, starting out alone like that on Shank's mare," said Judy, just as Pat had expected. That was the beauty of Judy. "Though I'm not saying it isn't a good thing that Jingle-lad happened along whin he did. Mind ye ask the cratur over for a liddle bite now and agin. I knew ould Larry Gordon whin he lived on the Taylor farm beyant the store. He's a skim milk man, that he is."

Judy had several classifications of people who were not lavish. You were "saving" . . . which was commendable. You were "close" . . . which was on the border line. You were "near" . . . which was over it. You were "skim milk" . . . which was beyond the pale. But Judy could not resist giving Pat a sly dig.

"I s'pose me poor kitchen is very tame after the splendours av the Bay Shore farm?"

"Silver Bush kitchen is better than the Bay Shore parlour," declared Pat: but she declared it drowsily. It had been a pretty full and strenuous day for eight years.

"Niver rub yer eyes wid innything but yer elbows, me jewel," cautioned Judy, as she convoyed Pat upstairs.

Mother, who had been singing Cuddles to sleep, slipped in to ask Pat if she had had a good time.

"The Bay Shore farm is such a lovely place," said Pat truthfully. It *was* a lovely *place*. And Pat wouldn't hurt mother's feelings for the world by confessing that her visit to mother's old home had not been altogether pleasant. Mother loved Bay Shore almost as well as she, Pat, loved Silver Bush. Dear Silver Bush! Pat felt as if its arms were around her protectingly as she drifted into dreamland.

11

DINNER IS SERVED

1

Pat had a bad Sunday of it.

When she found that the old poplar had been cut down she mourned and would not be comforted.

"Look, me jewel, what a pretty bit av scenery ye can see between the hin-house and the church barn," entreated Judy. "That bit av the South river, ye cud niver see it from here afore. Sure and here's yer Sunday raisins for ye. Be ating thim now and stop fretting after an ould tree that wud better av been down tin years ago."

Judy always gave every Silver Bush child a handful of raisins as a special treat for Sundays. Pat ate hers between sobs but it was not until evening that she would admit the newly revealed view was pretty. Then she sat at the round window and watched the silver loop of the river and another far blue hill, so far away that it must be on the very edge of the world. But still she missed the great, friendly, rustling greenness that had always filled that gap.

"I'll never see the kittens chasing each other up that tree again,

Judy," she mourned. "They had such fun . . . they'd run out on that big bough and drop to the hen-house roof. Oh, Judy, I didn't think trees *ever* got old."

Monday morning she remembered that she had asked Jingle to dinner. Remembered it rather dubiously. Suppose he came in those awful trousers with part of one leg missing? She dared not, for fear of being teased, ask Judy to put anything extra on the table. But she was glad when she saw Judy putting on the silver knives and forks and the second best silver cream jug.

"Why all this splendour?" demanded Joe.

"Sure and isn't Pat's beau coming to dinner?" said Judy. "We must be after putting our best foot forward for the credit av the fam'ly."

"Judy!" cried Pat furiously. Neither then nor in the years to come could she endure having any one call Jingle her beau. "He isn't my beau! I'm never going to have a beau."

"Niver's a long day," said Judy philosophically. "Ye'd better be shutting Snicklefritz up, Joe, for I understand the young man's bringing his dog and we don't want inny difference av opinion atween them."

Presently Jingle and McGinty were discerned, hanging about the yard gate, too shy to venture further. Pat ran out to welcome him. To her relief he wore a rather shabby but quite respectable suit, with legs of equal length. He was bare-legged, to be sure, but what of that. All the boys in North Glen went barefooted in summer . . . although not when asked out to dinner, perhaps. Somebody had given his brown hair a terrible cut. His eyes were invisible behind blue glasses, he had a pale face and an over-long mouth. Certainly he was not handsome but Pat still liked him. Also McGinty, who now revealed himself as a very young dog just starting out to see life.

"Doesn't that stuffing smell good?" asked Pat, as she convoyed him into the kitchen. "And Judy's made one of her apple-cakes for dessert. They're delicious. Judy, this is Jingle . . . and McGinty."

The Silver Bush family accepted Jingle calmly . . . Judy had probably warned them all. Dad gravely asked him if he would have white or dark meat and mother asked him if he took cream and sugar. You could always depend on father and mother, Pat felt. Even Winnie was lovely and made him take a second helping of apple-cake. What a family!

As for McGinty, Judy had set a big platter of meat and bones for him on the cellar hatch.

74

"Go to it, Mister Dog," she told him. "I'll warrant it's a long day since ye saw the like av that at Maria Gordon's."

After dinner Jingle said shyly,

"Listen . . . I saw some lovely rice lilies in our back field across the brook yesterday. Let's go and get some."

Pat had always longed to explore the brook that ran between Silver Bush and the old Adams place for a field's length and then branched across Adams territory. None of the Silver Bush children had ever been allowed to cross the boundary line. It was well known that old Mr. Adams wouldn't "have young ones stravaging over his fields."

"Do you think your uncle will mind?" asked Pat.

It turned out that neither uncle nor aunt was home. They had gone to spend Labour Day with friends.

"What would you have done for dinner if you hadn't come here?" exclaimed Pat.

"Oh, they left out some bread and molasses for me," said Jingle.

Bread and molasses on a holiday! This was skim milk with a vengeance.

"Mind ye don't poison yerselves wid mushrooms," warned Judy, handing them a bag of cinnamon buns. "I knew a b'y and girl onct as et a lot av toadstools in the woods by mistake."

"And I suppose they were never the same again?" said Joe teasingly.

"They've been dead iver since, if that's what ye mane be niver being the same agin," retorted Judy in a huff.

Once out of sight of the house Jingle's shyness dropped away from him and Pat found him a delightful companion . . . so delightful that she had a horrible sense of disloyalty to Sid. She could only square matters by reminding herself that she was just terribly sorry for Jingle, who had no friends.

It was Jingle who proposed that they should name the brook Jordan because it "rolled between."

"Between our farm and yours," said Pat delightedly. Here was a pal who liked to name places just as she did.

"And let's build a bridge of stones over it, so that we can cross easy whenever we want to," proposed Jingle, who evidently took it for granted that there would be plenty of crossing.

That was fun; and when the bridge was made . . . well and solidly, for Jingle would tolerate no jerry-building . . . they had an afternoon of prowling and rambling. They followed Jordan to its source at the very back of the old Adams place by fields that seemed made of sunshine and silence, over fences guarded by gay companies of golden-rod, through woods dappled with shadows, along little twisted paths that never did what you expected them to do. There was no end of lovely kinks and tiny cascades in the brook and the mosses on its banks were emerald and gold.

McGinty was in raptures. To roam like this was the joy of a little dog's life. He would race madly far ahead of them, then sit on his haunches waiting for them to come up with him, with his little red tongue lolling from his jaws. Pat loved McGinty; she was afraid she loved him better than curly, black Snicklefritz who, when all was said and done, was a one-man dog and a bit snappish with anybody but Joe. McGinty was such a dear little dog . . . so wistful . . . so anxious to be loved: with his little white cheeks and his golden-brown back and ears . . . pointed ears that stuck straight up when he was happy and dropped a bit when he was mournful: and tail all ready to wag whenever any one wanted it to wag.

2

In the end they found a beauty spot . . . a deep, still, woodland pool out of which the brook flowed, fed by a diamond trickle of water over the stones of a little hill. Around it grew lichened spruces and whispering maples, with little "cradle hills" under them; and just beyond a breezy slope with a few mossy, grass-grown sticks scattered here and there, and a bluebird perched on the point of a picket. It was all so lovely that it hurt. Why, Pat wondered, did lovely things so often hurt?

"This is the prettiest spot I've ever seen," cried Pat . . . "almost" . . . remembering the Secret Field.

"Isn't it?" said Jingle happily. "I don't think any one knows of it. Let's keep it a secret."

"Let's," agreed Pat.

"It always makes me think of a piece of poetry I learned at school . . . *The Haunted Spring* . . . ever hear it?"

Jingle recited it for her. He must be clever, Pat thought. Even Sid couldn't recite a long piece of poetry off by heart like that. And some of the lines thrilled her like a chord of music . . . *"gaily in the mountain glen,"* . . . *"distant bugles faintly ring."* But what did *"wakes the peasants' evening fears,"* mean? What *was* a peasant? Oh, just a farmer . . . *"wakes the farmer's evening fears . . ."* no, that was too funny. Better leave it peasant. She and Jingle had one of those chummy laughs that ripen friendship.

They sat on the hill, in the sweet, grass-scented air, and ate their cinnamon buns. Far down over the fields and groves they could see the blue plain of the gulf.

"There's a fairy diamond," cried Pat, pointing . . . that dazzling point of light sometimes seen for a moment in a distant field where a plough has turned up a bit of broken glass.

Jingle taught her how to suck honey out of clover horns. They found five little yellow flowers like stars by a flat lichened old stone and Jingle gloated over them through his absurd glasses. Pat was glad Jingle liked flowers. Hardly any boys did. Joe and Sid thought they were all right . . . for girls.

McGinty lay with his head on Jingle's legs and his tail across Pat's bare knees. And then Jingle took a bit of birch bark from a fallen tree near them and, with the aid of a few timothy stems, made under her very eyes the most wonderful little house . . . rooms, porch, windows, chimneys, all complete. It was like magic.

"Oh, how do you do it?" breathed Pat.

"I'm always building houses," said Jingle dreamily, rolling McGinty over and clasping his hands around his sunburned knees. "In my head, I mean. I call them my dream-houses. Some day when I'm grown up I'm going to build them really. I'll build one for *you,* Pat."

"Oh, will you really, Jingle?"

"Yes, I thought it out last Saturday night after I went to bed. And I'll think of lots more things about it. It will be the loveliest house you ever saw, Pat, by the time I get it finished."

"It couldn't be lovelier than Silver Bush," cried Pat jealously.

"Silver Bush *is* lovely," admitted Jingle. "It satisfies me when I look at it. Hardly any other house does. When I look at a house I nearly always want to tear it down and build it right. But I wouldn't change Silver Bush a bit."

Canny Jingle! Pat never dreamed of doubting his opinions of houses after that.

McGinty turned over on his back and entreated some one to tickle his stomach.

"I wish Aunt Maria liked McGinty better," said Jingle. "She doesn't like him at all. I was afraid the day he chewed up one of her good table napkins she was going to send him away. But Uncle Lawrence said he could stay. Uncle Lawrence doesn't mind McGinty but he laughs at him and McGinty can't bear to be laughed at."

"Dogs don't," said Pat knowingly, out of her extensive acquaintance of three dogs.

"McGinty has to sleep in the straw shed at nights. He howled so the other night I went out and slept with him. *Mother* would let him sleep indoors and bring his bones in."

Pat's eyes grew big with surprise. Jingle's mother! Judy had called him an orphan. And hadn't he himself said he hadn't a friend in the world except McGinty?

"I thought your mother was . . . dead."

Jingle selected a timothy stalk and began to chew it with an affectation of indifference.

"No, my dad is dead. He died when I was a baby. Mother married again. They live in Honolulu."

"Don't you ever see her?" exclaimed Pat, to whom Honolulu meant simply nothing at all. But something in Jingle's tone made her feel as if it must be very far away.

"Not often," said Jingle, who could not bear to admit that he had no recollection of ever seeing his mother. "You see, her husband's health is bad and he can't stand the Canadian climate. But of course I write to her—every Sunday."

He did not tell Pat that the letters were never sent but kept in a careful bundle in a box under his bed. Perhaps some day he could give them to mother.

"Of course," agreed Pat, who had already accepted the situation with the unquestioning philosophy of eight. "What does she look like?"

"She's . . . she's very pretty," said Jingle stoutly. "She . . . she has pale gold hair . . . and big blue, shining eyes . . . eyes as blue as that water out there."

"Like Winnie's," said Pat, understandingly.

"I wish she didn't have to live so far away," said Jingle chokingly. He choked so valiantly that he choked something down. When you were a big boy of ten you simply mustn't cry . . . anyway, not before a girl.

Pat said nothing. She just put her skinny little paw on his and squeezed it. Pat, even at eight, had all the wisdom of the world.

They sat there until the air grew cool and faint blue shadows fell over far-away hills beyond which neither of them had ever been, and little shivers ran over the silver-green water of the Haunted Spring. To other people this might just be Larry Gordon's back field. To Pat and Jingle it was, from that day, forever fairyland.

"Let's name this place, too," said Jingle. "Let's call it Happiness. And let's keep it a secret."

"I love secrets," said Pat. "It's nice to have them. This has been a lovely afternoon."

3

They were late for supper when they got back, but Judy fed them with fried ham and corn-cake in the kitchen. After Jingle and McGinty had gone Judy asked Pat how she and her boy-friend had got on. Boy-friend was not so insulting as beau. Pat, hauling in a big word to impress Judy, condescended to remark haughtily,

"We entertained each other very well."

"Oh, oh, I'm not doubting it. Sure and ye've picked a pretty good one for yer first. Ye can see there's brading behind him."

Judy was always so strong on breeding.

"He's dreadful awkward, Judy." Pat thought if she criticised him she might convince Judy there was nothing in this beau business. "Didn't you see how he run into the door when he was coming out of the dining-room and begged its pardon?"

"Oh, oh, that's why I'm saying he's a gintleman. Wud inny one else have begged a dure's pardon?"

"But he was so stupid he thought it was a person he'd run into."

"Oh, oh, he isn't that stupid. No, no, me jewel, he's nobody's fool, that lad. And he's rale mannerly. He et his broth widout trying to swally the spoon and it's meself has niver been able to tache Siddy that yet."

"But he's not a bit nice-looking, Judy . . . not like Sid."

"Oh, oh, I'm owning thim glasses av his do be giving him a quare look. And a shears-and-basin cut av hair niver improved inny one.

But did ye be noticing how nice his ears were set aginst his head? And handsome is as handsome does. Remimber that, Miss Pat, whin ye be come to picking a man in earnest. He's a bit thin and gangling but thim kind fills out whin they get older. Ye can tell be the look av him that he doesn't be getting half enough to ate. Be sure ye ask him in for a male whiniver ye dacently can. They do be saying his mother neglicts him tarrible, she's so taken up wid her fine new man."

"Did you ever see her, Judy?"

"Niver . . . and no one else round here. Jim Gordon married her out av Novy Scotia and they lived there. He did be dying just after the baby was born and his lady widow didn't be wearing her weeds long. She married her second whin this Jingle-lad was no more'n two and wint away to foreign parts and left the baby wid his uncle Larry. Jim Gordon was as nice a feller as iver stepped, aven if he did be always trying to make soup in a sieve. I'm thinking he'd turn over in his grave if he knew that Larry had the bringing-up av his b'y. Larry do be taking after his mother. His father was the gay lad wid a flattering tongue. He cudn't spake widout paying ye a compliment. But he was whispered to death."

"*Whispered* to death, Judy?"

"I'm telling ye. He bruk a poor girl's heart and she died. But her voice was always at his ear after that . . . she whispered him to death for all av his fine new bride. Ye shud av seen him in church wid his head hanging down, hearing something that all the praching and singing cudn't drown. Oh, oh, 'tis an ould story now and better forgotten. There do be few fam'lies that haven't a skiliton in some av their closets. There was Solomon Gardiner over at South Glen . . . the man who swore at God."

"What happened to him?"

"Nothing."

"Nothing?"

"Just that. Nothing iver happened to him agin. The Good Man Above just left him alone. Oh, oh, but it was hard on the family. Come and hilp me wid the turkeys now. But what's troubling ye, darlint?"

"I'm afraid, Judy . . . perhaps Jingle has a flattering tongue, too. He said . . . he said . . ."

"Out wid it."

"He said I had the prettiest eyes he ever saw."

Judy chuckled.

"Sure and there's no great flattery in that. And to think av him that shy at dinner ye wud be thinking he cudn't say bo to a goose. There's a bit av Irish in the Gordons be token of their old lady grandmother."

"Do *you* think I have pretty eyes, Judy?" It was the first time Pat had ever thought about her eyes.

"Ye have the Selby eyes and Winnie has the Gardiner eyes and they'll both pass wid a shove. But niver be minding yer eyes for minny a year yet and don't be belaving all the b'ys say to ye, me jewel. Remimber compliments cost thim nothing."

When Judy's fine flock of white turkeys had been shooed off the grave-yard fence and into their house Sid had arrived home in Uncle Brian's car. He had to be told about Jingle but took it quite easily . . . to Pat's relief and something that was not relief. She almost wished he had taken it a little harder. Didn't he *care?*

"He needs a friend so much," she explained. "I've got three brothers now. But of course I'll always love you best, Siddy."

"You'd better, old girl," said Sid. "If you don't I'll like May Binnie better'n you."

"Of course I couldn't love anybody better than my own family," said Pat, still wistfully.

But Sid ran in to coax a snack out of Judy Plum. He was in high spirits for he had just discovered a new wart on his left hand. That meant he was ahead of Sam Binnie at last. They had been ties for quite a time.

Pat crept a bit lonesomely up the back stairs and sat down by the round window. The little pearly pool over in the field was mirroring black spruce trees against a red sunset. For a moment the windows of the Long Lonely House were ablaze . . . then went sorrowfully out. There was not even a kitten to be seen in the yard. Oh, if Sid had just been a *little* jealous of Jingle! She knew how *she* would feel if he had made a chum of any girl but her. Suppose he should ever like May Binnie better . . . hateful May Binnie with her bold black eyes. For a moment she almost hated herself for liking Jingle.

Then she thought of Happiness and the water laughing down the stones in that secret place.

"Jingle likes my eyes," thought Pat. "Friends *are* nice."

12

BLACK MAGIC

1

It was in the last week of October that McGinty disappeared. Pat was just as heartbroken as Jingle. It seemed now that Jingle and McGinty had been always part of her life . . . as if there could never have been a time when they did not come over Jordan every Saturday afternoon or slip into Judy's kitchen in the chill "dims" for an evening of fun and laughter. To Jingle, who had never known a real home, these evenings were wonderful . . . little glimpses into another world.

The only fly in Pat's ointment was that Sid and Jingle didn't hit it off very well. Not that they disliked each other; they simply did not speak the same language. Had they been older they might have said they bored each other. Sid thought Jingle a queer, moony fellow with his dream houses and his dark glasses and his ragged clothes, and said so. Jingle thought Sid had a bit too high an opinion of himself, even for a Gardiner of Silver Bush, and did not say so. Thus it came about that Pat and Sid played and prowled together after school, but Saturday afternoons, when Sid wanted to be off with Joe at the farm work, she gave to Jingle. For the most part they spent them in Happiness and Jingle built no end of houses and had a new idea every week for the house he was going to build for Pat. Pat was interested in it although of course she would never live anywhere but at Silver Bush. They explored woodland and barrens and stream but Pat never took Jingle to the Secret Field. *That* was her and Sid's secret just as Happiness was hers and Jingle's. Pat hugged herself in delight. Secrets were such lovely things. She used to sit in church and pity the people who didn't know anything about the Secret Field and Happiness.

McGinty went everywhere with them and was the happiest little dog in the world. And then . . . there was no McGinty.

Pat found Jingle in Happiness one afternoon, face downwards amid the frosted ferns, sobbing as if his heart would break. Pat herself had been feeling a good deal like crying. For one thing, that hateful May Binnie had given Sid an apple in school the day before . . . a wonderful apple with Sid's initials and her own . . . such cheek! . . . in pale green on its red side. May had pasted the letters over the apple weeks before and this was the result. Sid was quite tickled over it but Pat would have hurled the apple into the stove if she had dared. Sid put it on the dining-room mantel and she had to look at it during every meal. Then, too, Sid had been cross with her that morning because it had rained the day before.

"You prayed for rain Thursday night . . . I heard you," he reproached her. "And you *knew* I wanted Friday to be fine."

"No, I didn't, Siddy," wailed Pat. "I heard dad saying the springs were so low . . . and the one in Hap . . . the one that Jordan comes from is. That was why I prayed for rain. I'm sorry, Siddy."

"Don't call me Siddy," retorted Sid, who seemed full of grievances just then. "You know I hate it."

"I won't, ever again," promised Pat. "Please don't be mad at me, Siddy . . . Sid, I mean. I just can't bear it."

"Well, don't be a baby then. You're worse than Cuddles," said Sid. But he gave her a careless hug and Pat was partially comforted. Only partially. She set off for Happiness rather dolefully but the sight of Jingle's distress drove all thoughts of her own troubles from her mind.

"Oh, Jingle, what's the matter?"

"McGinty's gone," said Jingle, sitting up.

"Gone?"

"Gone . . . or lost. He went with me to the store at Silverbridge last night and he . . . he disappeared. I couldn't find him anywhere. Oh, Pat!"

Jingle's head went down again. He didn't care who saw him cry. Pat mingled her tears with his but assured him that McGinty would be found . . . must be found.

Followed a terrible week. No trace of McGinty could be discovered. Judy was of opinion that the dog had been stolen. Jingle put up a notice in the stores offering a reward of twenty-five cents . . . all he had in the world . . . for the recovery of McGinty. Pat wanted to make it forty-five cents . . . she had a dime and was sure she could borrow another from Judy. But Jingle wouldn't let her. Pat prayed every bed-time that McGinty might be found and sat up in the middle of the night to pray again.

"Dear God, please bring McGinty back to Jingle. *Please*, dear God. You know he's all Jingle's got with his mother so far away."

And everything was in vain. There was no trace of McGinty. Jingle went home every night with no little golden-brown comrade running through the yard to meet him. He could not sleep, picturing a little lost dog alone in the world on a bleak autumn night. Where was McGinty? Was he cold and lonely? Maybe he wasn't getting enough . . . or anything . . . to eat.

"Judy, can't you do something?" begged Pat desperately. "You've always said there was a bit of a witch in you. You said once your grandmother could turn herself into a cat whenever she wanted to. Can't you find McGinty?"

Judy—who had, however, decided that something must be done before Pat worried herself to death . . . shook her head.

"I've been trying, me jewel, but I know whin I'm bate. If I had me grandmother's magic book I might manage it. But there it is. My advice to ye is to go and see Mary Ann McClenahan on the Silverbridge road. She's a witch in good standing I belave, though I'm telling the world she do be a bit hefty for a broomstick. If she can't hilp ye I don't know av inny that can."

Pat had been compelled to give up believing in fairies but she still had an open mind towards witches. They had certainly existed once. The Bible said so. And you couldn't get away from the fact that Judy's grandmother had been one.

"Are you sure Mary Ann McClenahan is a witch, Judy?"

"Oh, oh, she always knows what ye do be thinking av. That shows she's a witch."

Pat ran to tell Jingle. She found him standing on the stone bridge over Jordan, scowling viciously at the sky and shaking his fist at it.

"Jingle . . . you're not . . . praying that way?"

"No, I was just telling God what I thought of the whole business," said Jingle despairingly.

But he agreed to go the next evening to Mary Ann McClenahan's. They asked Sid to go, too . . . the more the safer . . . but Sid was training a young owl he had caught in the silver bush and declined to have any truck with witches. They started off staunchly, although Joe, going off to plough the Mince Pie field, with a delightful jingle of chains about his horses, solemnly warned them to watch out.

"Old Mary Ann signed her name in the devil's book you know. *I'd* jump out of my skin if she looked cross-wise at me."

Pat was not easily frightened and remained in her skin. If God, seemingly, wouldn't pay any attention to your desperate little prayers could you be blamed if you resorted to a witch?

"Mind ye're home afore dark," cautioned Judy. "Sure and 'tis Hollow Eve this blessed night and all the dead folks will be walking. Ye just do be telling Mary Ann yer story straight out and do as she bids ye."

Jingle and Pat went down the lane where the wind blew the shadows of bare birches about and waves of dead leaves lay along under the spruce hedges. The late autumn sunshine flowed goldenly about them. The Hill of the Mist wore a faint purple scarf. Pat had on her new scarlet tam and was pleasantly conscious of it, amid all her anxieties about McGinty. Jingle strode along, his hands in his ragged pockets, and his still raggeder trousers flapping about his bare legs. Pat had never been out on the main road with him in broad daylight before. In Happiness and along the kinks of Jordan it did not matter how he was dressed. But here . . . well, she hoped none of the Binnies would be abroad, that was all.

2

Mrs. McClenahan's little, white-washed house with its bright blue door was a good two miles from Silver Bush, along the Silverbridge road. A huge willow, from which a few forlorn, pale-yellow leaves were fluttering down on the grey roof, overshadowed it, and there was a quaint little dormer window over the door.

"Oh, Pat, look at that window," whispered Jingle, forgetting even McGinty in his momentary ecstasy. "I never saw such a lovely window. I'll put one like that in *your* house."

The window might be all right but the paling was very ragged and the yard it enclosed was a jungle of burdocks. Pat reflected that being a witch didn't seem like a very profitable business after all. She thought shrewdly that if *she* had ever signed her name in the devil's book she would have made a better bargain than that.

Jingle knocked on the blue door. Presently steps sounded inside. A prickly sensation went over Pat. Perhaps after all it was not right to tamper with the powers of darkness. Then the door opened and Mary Ann McClenahan stood on the threshold, looking down at them out of tiny black eyes, surrounded by cushions of fat. Her untidy hair was black too, coal-black, although she must be as old as Judy. Altogether she looked much too plump and jolly for a witch and Pat's terror passed away.

"Now who may ye be and what might ye be wanting wid me," said Mrs. McClenahan with an accent three times as strong as Judy's.

Pat had the Selby trick of never wasting words or breath or time.

"Hilary Gordon here has lost his dog and Judy said if we came to you perhaps you could find it for him. That is, if you really are a witch. Are you?"

Mary Ann McClenahan's look at once grew secretive and mysterious.

"Whisht, child . . . don't be talking av witches in the open daylight like this. Little ye know what might happen. And finding a lost cratur isn't something to be done on a dure-step. Come inside . . . and at that ye'd better come up to the loft where I can go on wid me waving. I'm waving a tablecloth for the fairies up there. All the witches in P. E. Island promised to do one apiece for thim. The poor liddle shiftless craturs left all ther tablecloths out in the frost last Tuesday night and 'twas the ruination av thim."

They went up the narrow stairs to a cluttered loft where Mrs. McClenahan's loom stood by the window that had caught Jingle's eye. On the sill a perfectly clean black cat was licking himself all over to make himself cleaner. His big, yellow, black-rimmed eyes shone rather uncannily in the gloom of the loft. In spite of his being a witch's cat Pat liked the look of him. What she would have felt like had she known that he was her lost and deplored Sunday, given to Mary Ann McClenahan by Judy a year before I cannot tell you. Luckily Sunday had grown out of all recognition.

Mrs. McClenahan pushed a stool and a rickety chair towards the children and went back to her weaving.

"Sure and I can't be wasting a moment. It's the quane's own cloth I'm waving and sour enough her Majesty'll look if it's not finished on time."

Pat knew very well it was only a flannel blanket Mary Ann was weaving but she was not going to contradict a witch. Besides . . . perhaps Mary Ann *did* turn it into a gossamer web when she had finished it . . . one of those things of jewelled mist and loveliness you saw on the grass and on the fern beds along the woods on a summer morning.

"So ye've come to get me to find the b'y's McGinty," said Mary Ann. "Oh, I know the name . . . I'm after knowing all about it. Yer Aunt Edith's cat was telling mine the whole story at the last dance we had. Yer Aunt Edith do be too grand for the likes av us but it's liddle she thinks where her cat do be going be spells. It's lucky ye come in the right time av the moon. I cudn't have done a thing for ye nixt wake. But now there's maybe just a chanct. Why doesn't that fine lady mother av yours iver be coming to see ye, young Hilary Gordon?"

Jingle thought witches were rather impertinent. However, if you dealt with them . . .

"My mother lives too far away to come often," he explained politely.

Mary Ann McClenahan shrugged her fat shoulders.

"Ye're in the right to make excuses for her, young Hilary, but I've me own opinion av her and ye nadn't get mad at me for saying so bekase a witch doesn't have to care who gets mad. And now that I've got that off me chist I'll be thinking av yer dog. It'll take a bit av conniving."

Mrs. McClenahan leaned over and extracted two handfuls of raisins from a paper bag on a shelf.

"Here, stow these away in yer liddle insides whilst I do a bit av thinking."

There was silence for awhile. The children devoted themselves to the business of eating and watching Mrs. McClenahan's shuttle fly back and forth. Pat eyed her wonderingly. Had she really signed her name in the devil's big black book, as Joe said?

Presently Mrs. McClenahan caught her eye and nodded.

"Ye've got a liddle mole on yer neck. Sure and 'tis the witch's mark. Come now, child dear, wudn't ye like to be a witch? Think av the fun av riding on a broomstick."

Pat *had* thought of it. The idea had a charm. Though she would have preferred to fly on a swallow's back, skimming over the steeples and dark spruce woods at night. But . . .

"Must I sign my name in the devil's book?" she whispered.

Mrs. McClenahan nodded solemnly.

"I'd pick out a rale nice shiny black divil for ye . . . though mind ye, it's the fact that aven divils are not what they used to be."

"I think I'm too young to be a witch, thank you," said Pat decidedly. Mrs. McClenahan chuckled.

"Sure and it's the young witches that do be having the power, child dear. No sinse in waiting till ye're grey as an owl. Think it over . . . 'tisn't ivery one can be a witch . . . we're that exclusive ye'd niver belave. As for this McGinty cratur. Whin ye lave here folly yer noses up the hill and turn yerselves around free times, north, south, east and west. Then go down the hill to Silverbridge. There's a house just foreninst the bridge wid a rid door like yer Uncle Tom's, only faded like. Turn yerselves about free times again and knock twict on the door. And if inny one comes . . . mind I'm not saying inny one will . . . cross yer fingers and ask, 'Is McGinty here?' Thin, if ye get McGinty . . . mind I'm not saying ye will . . . make a good use av yer legs and ask no questions. That's all I can be doing for ye."

"And what is your charge for the advice?" asked Jingle gravely, producing his quarter.

"Sure and we can't charge folks wid moles innything. It's clane aginst our rules."

"Thank you very much, Mrs. McClenahan," said Pat. "We're very much obliged to you."

"You do be a pair av mannerly children at that," said Mrs. McClenahan. "If you hadn't been it wudn't be Mary Ann McClenahan that wud have hilped ye to a dog. I'm that fed up wid the sass and impidence av most av the fry around here. It was diffrunt whin I was young. Now hurry along . . . sure and wise folks will be indures afore moonrise on Hollow Eve. Don't forget the turning round part or ye may look for yer McGinty till the eyes fall out av yer heads."

Mrs. McClenahan stood on her doorstep and watched them out of sight. Then she said a queer thing for a witch. She said,

"God bless the liddle craturs."

Whereat Mary Ann McClenahan waddled over to Mr. Alexander's across the road and asked if she might use their phone to call up a frind at the bridge, plaze and thank ye.

3

The October day was burning low behind the dark hills when Pat and Jingle left Mrs. McClenahan's. When they reached the top of the hill they turned themselves around three times and bowed gravely to north, south, east and west. When they paused before the red-doored house at Silverbridge they turned three times again. If there were no McGinty at the end of the quest it should be through no failure of theirs to perform Witch McClenahan's ritual scrupulously.

When Jingle knocked twice the door was opened with uncanny suddenness and the doorway filled by a giant of a man in sock feet, with a bushy red head and a week's growth of red whisker. A very strong whiff floated out, reminding Pat of something Judy took out of a black bottle now and again in winter for a cold.

They both crossed their fingers and Jingle said hoarsely,

"Is McGinty here?"

The man turned and opened a mean little door at his right. Inside, on a rickety chair, sat McGinty. The look of misery in the poor dog's eyes changed to rapture. With one bound he was in Jingle's arms.

"He come here one night about a wake ago," said the man. "That cold and hungry he was . . . and we tuk him in."

"That was real good of you," said Pat, since Jingle was temporarily bereft of speech.

"Wasn't it that now?" said the man with a grin.

Something about him made Pat remember Witch McClenahan's advice to make friends of their legs.

"Thank you very much," she said, and pulled the tranced Jingle by the arm.

The red door was shut . . . the red moon was staring at them just over a hill between two tall firs . . . and they had a dog that was nearly dying of happiness in their arms. What a walk home that was! The whole world was touched with wonder. They went straight over the fields in a cross-country cut, with their long shadows running before them. Jingle walked in a kind of dreamy rapture, hugging McGinty, but Pat had eyes for all the charm of bare, lonely stubble fields, woods where boughs darkled against a sky washed white in moonlight and of a wind that had been only a whisper when they had left home but was now wild, cold, and rustly, sweeping up from the sea. They passed through Happiness where all the little cradle hills were sound asleep and along Jordan. Then down through the silver bush on a path that wound through moonlit birches to the backyard of home, where Sid had decorated the gateposts with wonderful turnip lanterns and Judy had set her little copper candlestick, saucer-shaped with a curly handle, on the window-sill for welcome, and they had smelt her salt pork frying half way through the bush. Then the warm kitchen, full of delicious smells, and Judy's delight and welcome, and the supper of fried salt pork and potatoes baked in their jackets. Just the three of them. Sidney and Joe were doing the barn chores. Winnie was off with a chum, mother was upstairs with Cuddles, and dad was snoozing on the dining-room lounge.

After supper Pat and Jingle went down into the big, mysterious cellar, spooky with giant shadows, for apples, and then they all sat around the stove that was as good as a fireplace, with its doors that slid so far back, and talked things over. It was lovely to sit there, so cosy and warm, with that eerie wind moaning without . . . full of the voices of ghosts, Judy said, for this was Hallow E'en. McGinty sprawled out on the black cat rug, his eyes fixed on Jingle, evidently afraid to go to sleep for fear he might waken to find this all a dream. Thursday, who had been missing for a day or two, had turned up, a fat and flourishing prodigal, and Gentleman Tom sat on the bench, thinking. Like Puck of Pook's Hill, Gentleman Tom could have sat a century, just thinking.

"I'm so glad it's got cold enough to have a fire in the evenings," said Pat. "And in winter it'll be even nicer. One can be so *cosy* in winter."

Jingle said nothing. His idea of winter evenings was very different. A cold, dirty kitchen . . . a smoking coal oil lamp . . . a bed in the unfinished loft. But just now he had his dog back and he was perfectly happy. To sit here and munch apples with Pat while Judy thumped and kneaded her bread was all he asked.

"Oh, oh, she isn't called a witch for nothing, that one," said Judy, when she had heard the whole tale. "I used to be after knowing the McClenahans rale well years ago. Tom McClenahan was a dacent soul although he'd talk the hind-leg off a cat whin he got started. A tarrible talker, I'm tellin ye. Onct he got mad whin Mary Ann twitted him wid his good going tongue, and swore he wudn't spake a word for a month. He kept the vow two days but he was niver the same man agin. The strain was too much for him. Mary Ann always belaved it was why he dropped dead in about a year's time. He was a fine fiddler in his day and he had a fiddle that cud make iverybody dance."

"*Make* them dance, Judy?"

"I'm telling ye. Whin folks heard it they *had* to dance. It was an ould fiddle his dad brought out from Ireland. Sure and he tried it on a minister onct, the spalpane."

"Did the minister dance?"

"Didn't he that? It made a tarrible scandal. They had him up afore Presbytery. Tom offered to go and fiddle to the whole lot av thim to prove poor Mr. MacPhee cudn't hilp it, but they wudn't have him. A pity now. Think what a sight it wud av been . . . a dozen or more long-tailed ministers all dancing to Tom McClenahan's fiddle. Oh, oh! But they let Mr. MacPhee off and hushed the whole thing up. Is it going ye are, Jingle? Well, say a prayer for all poor ghosts and have as liddle truck wid witches as ye can after this. All very well for onct in a while but not to make a habit av it."

Jingle slipped away, meaning to spend the night in the Gordon hayloft with McGinty, and sleepy Pat went happily to bed.

"Why do you fill those children up with all that nonsense about witches, Judy?" called Long Alec, half laughing, half rebuking, from the dining room. He had been rated that day by Edith for allowing Judy Plum to stuff his children with such lies as she did and felt it was time for one of his spasmodic attempts to regulate her. Judy chuckled.

"Rest ye aisy, Alec Gardiner. They only half belave it and they do be getting a big kick out av it. I'll warrant Mary Ann had her fun wid them."

"What made you think of sending them to her?"

"Sure now I'd an idea she'd know where McGinty was. She's in wid that gang at Silverbridge that stole Rob Clark's collie and all Mrs. Taylor's barred rocks wake afore last and thim all ready for market. Mary Ann's be way av being an aunt be marriage to Tom Cudahy av the rid door. But she's that kind-hearted, the cratur, and rale soft about children and I thought she might hilp. She's got a bit av money saved up and the Cudahys pipe whin she calls the tune. So all's well that inds well and niver be bothering if the children do be having a liddle fun thinking she's a witch. Sure and didn't I bring all of yes up on witches and are ye inny the worse av it? I'm asking ye."

13

COMPANY MANNERS

1

Winter that year, at least in its early months, was a mild affair, and Pat and Jingle, or Pat and Sid, as the case might be, but seldom the three together, roamed far afield at will, exploring new haunts and re-loving old ones, running through winter birches that wore stars in their hair on early falling dusks, coming in from their frosty rambles with cheeks like "liddle rid apples," to be fed and cossetted and sometimes scolded by Judy. At least, she scolded Sid and Pat when she thought they needed it for their souls' good, but she never scolded Jingle. He wished she would. He thought it would be nice if some one cared enough about you to scold . . . in Judy's way, with sly laughter lurking behind every word and apples and cinnamon buns to bind up your bruised feelings immediately afterwards. Even his aunt did not scold him . . . she merely ignored him as if he had no existence for her at all. Jingle used to go home after one of Judy's tirades feeling very lonely and wondering what it would be like to be important to somebody.

Though snowless, it was cold enough to freeze the Pool solid. Sid taught Pat to skate and Jingle learned for himself, with a pair of old skates Judy dug out of the attic for him. Jingle skating, his long legs clad as usual in ragged trousers, his lanky body encased in an old "yallery-green" sweater whose sleeves his aunt had darned with red, his ill-cut hair sticking out from under an old cap of his uncle's, was rather an odd object.

"Isn't he a sight?" laughed Sid.

"He can't help his looks," said Pat loyally.

"Oh, oh, that b'y will be having the fine figure whin he's filled out a bit and he's got more brains in his liddle finger than ye have in yer whole carcase, Sid, me handsome lad," said Judy.

And then unreasonable Pat was furious with Judy for maligning Sid.

"Sure and it's the hard life I have among ye all," sighed Judy. "Be times I'm thinking I'd better have taken ould Tom. Well, they tell me he's single yet."

Whereupon Pat dissolved in tears and begged Judy to forgive her and never, never leave them.

Although once in a while a few delicate white flakes flew against your face in the late afternoons, it was December before the first real snow came, just in time to make a white world for Christmas, much to Judy's relief, since a green Christmas meant a fat grave-yard, she said. Pat sat curled up at her round window and watched gardens and fields and hills grow white under the mysterious veil of the falling snow, and the little empty nests in the maple by the well fill up with it. Every time she looked out the world had grown whiter.

"I love a snowstorm," she said rapturously to Judy.

"Oh, oh, is there innything ye don't love, me jewel?"

"It's nice to love things, Judy."

"If ye don't be loving thim too hard. If ye do . . . they hurt ye too much in the ind."

"Not Silver Bush. Silver Bush will never hurt me, Judy."

"What about whin ye have to lave it?"

"You know I'm never going to leave Silver Bush, Judy . . . never. Oh, Judy, see how white the Hill of the Mist is. And how lonesome the Long Lonely House looks. I wish I could go and build a fire in it sometimes and warm it up. It would feel better."

"Oh, oh, ye're not thinking houses raly fale, are ye now?"

"Oh, Judy, I'm *sure* they do. Jingle says so, too. I know Silver Bush does. It's glad when we are and sorry when we are. And if it was left without any one to live in it it would break its heart. I know Silver Bush has always been a little ashamed of me because I could never get up in school Friday afternoons and say a piece like the others. And then last Friday I did. I learned the *Haunted Spring* from Jingle and I got up on the floor . . . oh, Judy, it was awful. My legs shook so . . . May Binnie giggled . . . and I couldn't get a word out. I was just going to run back to my seat . . . and I thought of Silver Bush and how could I come home and face it if I was such a coward. And I just up and said my piece right out and Miss Derry said, 'Well done, Patricia,' and the scholars all clapped. And when I came home I'm sure Silver Bush smiled at me."

"Ye're a quare child enough yet," said Judy. "But I'm glad ye didn't let May Binnie triumph over ye. That's a liddle girl I'm not liking much and I don't care who knows it."

"Sid likes her," said Pat, a bit forlornly.

2

Soon Silver Bush became a house full of secrets. Mystery lurked everywhere and Judy went about looking like a bobbed Sphinx. Pat helped her make the pudding and helped Winnie and mother decorate the dining room and wreathe the banisters with greenery from the woods around the Secret Field. And she helped Sid pick his presents in the Silverbridge store for every one but her. She did not feel hurt when he slipped off upstairs in the store to the room where the dishes were kept and she did not ask him what the bulging parcel in his pocket was as they went home. She only wondered a bit dismally whether it was for her or May Binnie.

It was such fun wading home from the mail-box with armfuls of brown parcels that were not to be opened until Christmas morning and then revealed lovely boxes of silver paper tied with gold ribbons. Christmas itself was a wonderful day. Jingle and McGinty came for dinner. They had had a narrow escape from not coming. Pat was so mad because Judy told her to be sure and ask her beau that she wouldn't say a word to Jingle about it until the very "dim" of Christmas Eve. Then she suddenly relented and tore off to the garret to set a candle in the window. There was no telephone at the Gordon place and she and Jingle had agreed that when she wanted him specially she was to set a light in the garret window. Jingle arrived speedily and so got his Christmas invitation by the skin of his teeth.

It was the first time in his life that Jingle had had a real Christmas and McGinty nearly died of the dinner he ate. Everybody got presents . . . even Jingle. Judy gave him a pair of mittens and Pat gave him a little white china dog with blue eyes and a pink china ribbon around its neck . . . the best she could afford after all the family had been remembered out of her small hoard. Nobody knew what earthly use it could be to Jingle but he slept with it under his pillow that night and got more warmth from it than from Judy's mittens. His mother had not sent him anything . . . not even a letter. It took all the comfort Jingle got out of the blue-eyed dog to keep back the tears when he remembered this. He tried to make excuses for her. Perhaps in Honolulu, that land of eternal summer, they didn't have Christmases.

Sidney gave Pat a jug with a golden lining . . . a little fat brown jug that seemed somehow to have grown fat from laughing. Pat loved it but she thought Jingle's present the most wonderful thing she got. A doll's house which he had made himself and which was really a much more wonderful bit of work than Pat had any idea of. Long Alec whistled when he saw it and Uncle Tom said, "By ginger!"

"I hadn't any money to buy you a present," said Jingle, who had spent his solitary, long-saved quarter on a Christmas card for his mother, "so I made this."

"I like something that's made better than something that's bought," said Pat. "Oh, what chimneys . . . and real windows that *open.*"

"That's nothing to the house I'll build for you some day, Pat."

Christmas Day was just like all the pleasant Christmases at Silver Bush. The only exciting thing was a terrible fight all over the kitchen between Gentleman Tom and Snooks, the pet owl. Snooks was quite a family pet by now. He endured and was endured by Thursday and Snicklefritz but he and Gentleman Tom had declared war on each other at sight. Gentleman Tom was licked and fled into ignominious retreat under the stove: but there were a good many feathers strewn over the kitchen floor first.

One night the following week Pat excitedly called out to Judy,

"Oh, Judy . . . Judy . . . I've got a growing pain!"

She had never had growing pains and both she and Judy were afraid she wouldn't grow properly. Long Alec talked worriedly of rheumatism but Judy laughed at him and sat up half the night rubbing Pat's legs joyously.

"Ye'll be taking a start this spring and growing like a weed after this," she promised Pat. "Sure and it's a rale relief to me mind, I'm telling ye. I'm not wanting inny sawed-off girls at Silver Bush."

3

After Christmas the snow went away and the January winds whined over cold, hard-frozen pastures and through grey, cold trees. Only the red edges of the furrows in the Mince Pie field had little feathers of white on them and a persistent wreath lay along the north side of the Hill of the Mist.

January evenings were pleasant at Silver Bush. Uncle Tom would come over and he and dad would sit by Judy's stove and talk, while Pat and Jingle and Sidney listened and Winnie and Joe studied their lessons in the dining room. They would talk of politics and pigs and finally drift into family histories and community tales. The white-washed walls of the old kitchen re-echoed to their laughter. Sometimes Uncle Tom got mad and the shadow of his big beard would quiver with indignation on the wall. But Uncle Tom's rages never lasted long. One thump of his fist on the table and all was well again.

Sometimes mother would come in with Cuddles and sit for awhile just looking beautiful. Mother never talked much. Perhaps she couldn't get a chance, what with Judy and dad and Uncle Tom. But sometimes she looked at Pat and Sidney and little Cuddles with eyes that made a lump come into Jingle's throat. To have a mother look at you like that!

"Judy," Pat said after one of these evenings, when she was sleeping with Judy because Winnie had a chum in. "I don't see how heaven could be any better than this."

"Oh, oh, will ye listen at her?" said the scandalised Judy. "Sure and do ye be thinking there'll be a biting wind like that wailing around the windy in heaven?"

"Oh, I like that wind, Judy. It makes it seem cosier . . . to cuddle here snug and warm and think it can't get at you. Listen to it tearing down through the silver bush, Judy. Now please, Judy, tell me a ghost story. It's so long since I've slept with you . . . please, Judy. Something that'll just make the flesh creep on my bones."

"Did I iver tell ye about how Janet McGuigan come back for her widding ring the night after she was buried, her man having tuk it off her finger afore they coffined her, thinking it might come in handy for his second? Oh, oh, the McGuigans do be that far-seeing."

"How did they know she came back for it?"

"I'm telling ye. The ring wasn't in Tom McGuigan's cash-box the nixt morning. But six years afterwards whin he tuk a plot in the new grave-yard they tuk up her coffin to shift it and it bruk open . . . being an economical kind av coffin, ye see . . . and there on her hand was the ring. Oh, oh, me saving Tom was niver the same agin."

February and still no snow. Judy began to talk of getting ready to hook a big crumb-cloth for the dining room, a bigger one than Aunt Edith's of which she was so proud. "Oh, oh, I'll be taking the pride av her down a peg or two," vowed Judy. Her dye-pot was always on the stove. She was an expert in home-made dyes. No "bought" dyes for Judy. They faded in a year, she averred. Crottle and lichens and barks . . . elderberries that gave purple dyes . . . the inner bark of birch trees for brown . . . green dye from willow stems . . . yellow from Lombardy poplars. Judy knew them all and she and the children tramped far afield searching for them.

And then came March, with its mad, galloping winds, and the anniversary of father's and mother's wedding day. The Gardiners always celebrated birthdays and wedding days by a little family gathering of some kind. This year Uncle Brian's family and Aunt Helen Taylor were the guests. They were to come in the afternoon and have dinner at night . . . an innovation that made Judy's head whirl.

"Oh, oh, this having company isn't what it's cracked up to be," she muttered discontentedly.

Pat was in her element, although she was not looking forward to the party quite as joyously as usual. Uncle Brian was no friend of hers because whenever he came to Silver Bush he was always saying to father, "If I were you I'd make some changes here." And Aunt Helen was coming . . . rich Aunt Helen, dad's sister but so much older that she seemed more like his aunt than his sister. And Aunt Helen, Judy said, was coming to take either Winnie or Pat back to Summerside for a visit.

Pat hoped and prayed Aunt Helen wouldn't take her. She didn't want to leave Silver Bush . . . why, she had never slept out of it a night in her life. It would be terrible. But how happy it made her to do little, homely services for the dear house. To dust and polish and bake and run errands. To help get out mother's wedding set of fluted china with the gold pansy on the side of the cups and in the centre of the plates. She and Winnie were allowed to fix up the Poet's Room and make the bed a thing of beauty with a lace spread and cushions like flowers.

Judy concocted and baked, and Cuddles tasted everything that came her way, including a frosty latch. After which she tasted no more of anything for a time but lived on malted milk.

When the feast day came Pat was careful to put on her blue georgette dress. She didn't like it as well as her red one but it was its turn and it mustn't be neglected. How she hoped Aunt Helen wouldn't choose her! It took all the fun out of the party for Pat. Suppose she pretended to be sick? No, Judy might give her castor oil, as she had done the last time Pat had a cold.

"Why don't you give me something out of your black bottle, Judy?" Pat had protested. "That smells nicer than castor oil."

"Oh, oh." Judy looked very sly. "'Tis too strong entirely for the likes av ye. . . ."

"*What* is in that bottle, Judy?"

"Oh, oh, 'tis only last wake I was burying a cat that died av curiosity," retorted Judy. "Not another skelp out av ye and swally this tay-spoon at once."

Even Aunt Helen would be better than castor oil. But perhaps she would be sick and not able to come. Would it be wrong, Pat wondered, to pray that somebody might be sick . . . not very sick . . . just a little sick . . . just enough to make them not want to come out on a cold, blustery March day?

Pat wound a blue scarf around her head and she and Jingle climbed up into the hayloft of the church barn where they could watch for the arrivals through the oriel window, while McGinty hunted imaginary rats over the mow or lay before them and pretended to be dead when he thought himself neglected. Every car or buggy that drove up or down the road made Pat squirm with fear that it was Aunt Helen. She *did* come . . . in Uncle Brian's car and waddled up through the garden.

"She looks just like a jug," said Pat resentfully.

And Uncle Brian's Norma was with them. Pat had hoped Norma wouldn't come either. She didn't like her because Norma was reputed prettier than Winnie.

"I don't think she's half as pretty," she said.

"*You* look awful nice in that blue scarf, Pat," said Jingle admiringly.

Which would have been all right if he had stopped there. But he went on and said the thing that spoiled it all.

"Pat . . . when we grow up . . . with you be *my* girl?"

Pat, not at all realising that at nine she had just had what was practically her first proposal, went scarlet with anger.

"If you ever say anything like that to me again, Hilary Gordon, I'll never speak to you as long as I live," she stormed.

"Oh, all right, I didn't mean to make you mad," said Jingle abjectly. "Don't you like me?"

"Of course I like you. But I'm *never* going to be *anybody's* girl."

Jingle looked so woebegone that it made Pat madder still . . . and cruel.

"If I was anybody's girl," she said distinctly, "he'd have to be good-looking."

Jingle took off his spectacles.

"Ain't I better looking now?" he demanded.

He *was*. Pat had never seen his eyes before. They were large and grey and steady with a twinkle somewhere behind their steadiness. But Pat was in no mood to admire.

"Not a great deal. Your hair is all raggedy and your mouth is too wide. Sid says it would take a foot-rule to measure it."

And Pat shook the dust of the hayloft from her feet and departed indignantly.

"Maybe she'll change her mind," said McGinty.

"She'll have to," said Jingle.

4

But the day continued to go criss-cross for Pat. She fell foul of Norma as soon as she went in. Norma was going about, tossing her famous red-gold curls, with her nose cocked up and her greenish-brown eyes full of contempt. "So *this* is Silver Bush," she said. "It's an awful old-fashioned place."

Again Pat crimsoned with wrath.

"Shutters give a house an *air*," she said.

"Oh, I don't mean the shutters. We've got shutters on our house, too . . . ever so much greener than yours. You should just see *our* house. You haven't a verandah . . . or even a garage."

"No. But we've got a grave-yard," said Pat triumphantly.

Norma was a bit floored. She couldn't deny the graveyard.

"And you haven't got a Poet's room or a round window," went on Pat still more tauntingly. The mention of the window gave Norma an inspiration.

"You haven't *one* bay window," she cried. "Not one. We've got three . . . two in the living room and one in the dining room. A house without any bay window is just *funny*."

To hear Silver Bush called funny! Pat simply couldn't stand it. She slapped Norma's pink-and-white face . . . slapped it hard.

Then there was what Judy called a tommyshaw. Norma screamed and burst into tears. Mother was horrified . . . dad was shocked . . . or pretended to be. Judy came in and frog-marched Pat to the kitchen.

"A nice show ye've made av yerself!"

"I don't care . . . I don't care . . . I *won't* let her make fun of Silver Bush," sobbed Pat. "I'm glad I slapped her. You can scold me all you like. I'm *glad*."

"The timper av her!" said Judy. And then went up to her room and sat on her blue chest and laughed till she cried.

"Oh, oh, didn't me fine Miss Norma get her comeuppance for onct, wid her airs and graces and her slams about the house her father was brought up in!"

Pat was not allowed to have dinner in the dining room. For punishment she must eat in the kitchen. To be punished because she had stood up for Silver Bush. It was too much.

"I'd *rather* eat here with you, Judy, any time," she sobbed. "But it's my *feelings* that are hurt."

There was balm in Gilead. Aunt Helen was so shocked at Pat's behaviour that there was no question of inviting her to Summerside. Winnie went with her. Pat made her peace with the family . . . none of whom cared much for the spoiled Norma . . . and she and Sid and Judy picked the bones of the sacrificial turkeys before they went to bed, while Judy told them all about Norma's grandmother on the mother's side.

"Oh, oh, it's the quare one she was and the foolish things she wud be saying. Her poor husband was long in dying and she did be after grudging him ivery breath he drew. 'If he lives too long I'll niver get another man,' she sez to me, time and time again, mournful like. And nather she did. He hung on till he spiled her chances and it wasn't Judy Plum that was sorry for her, I'm telling ye."

14

THE SHADOW OF FEAR

1

No sooner had Winnie gone than winter came in a day. Pat's round window was thick furred with snow; the Whispering Lane was filled with huge drifts through which dad and Uncle Tom shovelled a fascinating narrow path until they met at the gate. The piles of stones in the Old Part of the orchard were marble pyramids. The Hill of the Mist shone like silver. The hill field was a dazzling white sheet. Even the stony field was beautiful. Pat remembered that the Secret Field must be lovely, with Wood Queen and Fern Princess standing guard.

The grave-yard was filled almost to the level of the paling.

"Sure and aven Wild Dick wud find it hard to get out av that," said Judy, busy providing comforts for cold little creatures . . . cats and dogs and chickens and children.

Pat liked a big storm. Especially did she love to snuggle in warm, fluffy blankets and defy the great, dark, wintry night outside her cosy room, hugging her hot water bottle. A hot water bottle was such a nice thing. You kneaded your toes in it; when your feet were warm as warm could be you held it close in your arms: and finally you put it against the cold spot in your back. And the first thing you knew it was morning and the sun was shining through the drift . . . and the hot water bag was unpleasantly like a clammy dead rat just behind you.

It was rather nice, too, to have one's room all to oneself; still, she missed Winnie terribly . . . the blue laughter of her eyes . . . the silver music of her voice.

"Just two more weeks and Winnie'll be home," she counted exultantly.

It was in school that she heard it. Of course it was May Binnie who told her.

PAT OF SILVER BUSH

"So your Aunt Helen is going to adopt Winnie."

Pat stared at her.

"She isn't."

May giggled.

"Fancy your not knowing. Of course she is. It's a great thing for Winnie, ma says. And it might have been you if you hadn't slapped Norma's face."

Pat stood staring at May. Something had fallen over her spirit like the cold grey light that swept over the world before a snow squall in November. She was too chilled to resent the fact that Sid must have told May about her slapping Norma. There was no room for any but the one terrible thought. It was only afternoon recess but Pat rushed to the porch, snatched her hat and coat, and started home, stumbling wildly along the deep-rutted, drifted road. Oh, to get home to mother . . . mother now, not Judy. Judy did for little griefs but for this, only mother . . . to tell her this ghastly thing was not true . . . that nobody had ever thought of such a thing as Winnie going to live with Aunt Helen.

"Oh, oh, and what's bringing ye home so early?" cried Judy, as Pat stumbled, half-frozen, into the kitchen. "Ye've niver walked all that way in thim roads . . . and yer Uncle Tom was going for ye all in his fine new pung."

"Where's mother?" gasped Pat.

"Mother, is it? Sure yer dad and her is gone over to the Bay Shore. They phoned over that yer Aunt Frances was down with pewmony. Whativer is it that's the matter wid the child?"

But for the first time Pat had nothing to say to Judy. The question she had to ask could not be asked of Judy. Judy, rather huffed, let her alone, and Pat ranged the deserted house like a restless ghost. Oh, how empty it was! Nobody there . . . neither mother nor father nor Cuddles. Nor Winnie! And perhaps Winnie would never be back. Suppose her laugh would never be heard again at Silver Bush!

"Something's been happening in school," reflected Judy uneasily. "I'm hoping she didn't get into a ruckus wid her lady tacher. I niver cud be knowing what the trustees mint be hiring ould Arthur Saint's girl for a tacher, wid her hair the colour av a rid brick."

Pat could eat no supper. Bed-time came and still father and mother were not back. Pat cried herself to sleep. But she awoke in the night . . . sat up . . . remembered sickeningly. Everything was quiet. The wind

102

had gone down and Silver Bush was cracking in the frost. Through her window she could see the faint light of stars over the dark fir trees that grew along the dyke between the Silver Bush and Swallowfield pastures. Pat found just then that things always seem worse in the dark. She felt she could not live another minute without knowing the truth.

Resolutely she got out of bed and lighted her candle. Resolutely the small white figure marched down the silent hall, past Joe's room and the Poet's room to father's and mother's room. Yes, they were home, sound asleep. A fragrant adorable Cuddles was curled up in her little crib but for the first time Pat did not gloat over her.

Long Alec and his tired wife, just fallen soundly asleep after a cold drive over vile roads, were wakened to see a desperate little face bending over them.

"Child, what's the matter? Are you sick?"

"Oh, dad, Aunt Helen isn't going to adopt Winnie? She isn't, is she, dad?"

"Look here, Pat." Dad was stern. "Have you come here and wakened your mother and me just to ask that?"

"Oh, dad, I *had* to know."

Mother understandingly put a slender hand on Pat's shaking arm.

"Darling, she's not going to adopt her . . . but she may keep her for awhile and send her to school. It would really be a great thing for Winnie."

"Do you mean . . . Winnie wouldn't come back *here*?"

"It isn't settled yet. Aunt Helen only threw out a hint. Of course Winnie'll be home *often*. . . ."

2

The following week of dark, tortured days was the hardest Pat had ever known in her life. She could not eat and the sight of Winnie's vacant place at meals reduced her to tears. Her family found it rather hard to make excuses for what they thought was her unreasonable behaviour.

"Just humour her a liddle," pleaded Judy. "She's that worked up and miserable she doesn't know which ind of her is up. A bird cudn't be living on what she ates."

"You spoil her, Judy," said Long Alec severely. He was out of patience with Pat's moping.

"Iverybody do be the better for a bit av sp'iling now and thin," said Judy loyally. But she tried to bring Pat into a more reasonable frame of mind.

"Don't ye want Winnie to get an eddication?"

"She could get an education at home," sobbed Pat.

"Not much av a one. Oh, oh, I'd have ye know the Gardiners don't be like the Binnies. 'We're not going to eddicate Suzanne,' sez me Madam Binnie. 'Soon as she'd get through Quane's she'd marry and the money'd be wasted.' No, no, me jewel, the Gardiners are a differunt brade av cats. Winnie's thirteen. Sure and she'll soon be wanting to study for her intrance and who's ould Arthur Saint's daughter for that I'm asking ye? Ye'll niver convince me she knows a word av the Lating and French."

"English is good enough for anybody," protested Pat.

"Ye'll find it isn't good enough for Quane's," retorted Judy. "Winnie'd be able to go to the Summerside schools and yer Aunt Helen cud do more for her than yer dad iver can, wid his one small farm and the five av ye ating it up. Now, stop fretting, me jewel, and come and cut rags for me while I do a bit av hooking."

Then came the letter from Aunt Helen for dad. Pat, her hands locked behind her so that no one should see them trembling, stood mutely by while Long Alec deliberately tried on two pairs of spectacles, scrutinised the stamp, remarked that Helen had always been a pretty writer, hunted up a knife to slit the envelope . . . took out the letter. Outside in the yard somebody was laughing. How dared anybody laugh at such a moment?

"Helen says Brian is bringing Winnie home Saturday," he announced casually. "So I guess she's given up the notion of keeping her. I always thought she would. So that's that."

"Oh, I *must* be flying," thought Pat as she ran to tell Judy. Judy admitted satisfaction.

"It do be just as well I'm thinking. Helen was always a bit of a crank. And I'm not thinking it's a wise-like thing to break up a family inny sooner than nade be."

"Isn't a family one of the loveliest things in the world, Judy?" cried Pat. "And oh, look at Gentleman Tom. Isn't he sitting cute?"

"Oh, oh, it's the different looking girl ye are from the morning. Iverything plazes ye to-night, aven the way a poor cat arranges his hams," chuckled Judy, who was overjoyed to see her darling happy again.

Pat ran out in the twilight to tell the good news to the silver bush and the leafless maples. She looked with eyes of love at the old, snow-roofed house drawing its cloak of trees around it in the still mild winter evening. Even in winter Silver Bush was lovely because of what it sheltered and hoped for.

Then she ran back in and up to the garret to set a light for Jingle. Jingle had been her only comfort during the past dreadful week. Even Sid hadn't seemed to worry much whether Winnie came home or not. He hoped she would, of course, but he didn't lose sleep over it. Jingle had always assured Pat she would. Who, he thought, wouldn't come back to Silver Bush if she could? So now he came to share in Pat's joy. The two of them waded back along Jordan to Happiness; it was buried in snow but the Haunted Spring was still running freshly, hung about with jewels. How lovely the silvery world was . . . how lovely the white hills of snow! They did not get home till nearly eight and Judy scolded.

"I'm not having ye roaming off wid any Jingle if ye can't be home and to bed at the proper time."

"What is the proper time for going to bed, Judy?" laughed Pat. Every word was a laugh with Pat to-night. And oh, how good supper tasted!

"Sure now and ye're asking a question that's niver been answered," chuckled Judy.

Saturday came with more March wind and snow. Oh, it shouldn't storm the day Winnie was coming home. Perhaps Uncle Brian wouldn't bring her if it stormed. But in the late afternoon the sun came out below the storm cloud and made a dazzling fair world. The rooms of Silver Bush were all filled with a golden light from the clearing western sky. All the gardens and yards and orchards were pranked out with the exquisite shadows of leafless trees.

And then they came, right out of the heart of the wild winter sunset. Winnie was very glad Aunt Helen had decided not to keep her.

"She said I laughed too much and it got on her nerves," Winnie told Pat. "Besides, I put pepper in the potatoes instead of salt the day her maid was away . . . oh, by mistake of course. That settled it. She said I had the makings of a sloppy housekeeper."

"Silver Bush is *glad* to hear you laugh," whispered Pat, hugging her savagely.

The storm came up again in the night. Pat woke up and heard it . . . remembered that everything was all right and sank happily to sleep again. What difference now how much it stormed? All her dear ones were near her, safe under the same kindly roof. Dad and mother and little Cuddles . . . Joe and Sidney . . . Judy in her own eyrie, with her black Gentleman Tom curled up at her feet . . . Thursday and Snicklefritz behind the kitchen stove. And Winnie was home . . . home to stay!

15

ELIZABETH HAPPENS

1

"I smell spring!" Pat cried rapturously, sniffing the air one day . . . the day she discovered the first tiny feathery green sprays of caraway along the borders of the Whispering Lane. That same night the frogs had begun to sing in the Field of the Pool. She and Jingle heard them when they were coming home in the "dim" from Happiness.

"I love frogs," said Pat.

Jingle wasn't sure he liked frogs. Their music was so sad and silver and far away it always made him think of his mother.

Never, Pat reflected, looking back over her long life of almost nine years, had there been such a lovely spring. Never had the long, rolling fields around Silver Bush been so green: never had the gay trills of song in the maple by the well been so sweet: never had there been such wonderful evenings full of the scent of lilacs: and never had there been anything so beautiful as the young wild cherry tree in Happiness or the little wild plum that hung over the fence in the Secret Field. She and Sid went back to pay a call on their field one Sunday afternoon, to see how it had got through the winter. It was always spring there before it was spring anywhere else. Their spruces tossed them an airy welcome and the wild plum was another lovely secret to be shared.

Everything was so *clean* in spring, Pat thought. No weeds . . . no long grass . . . no fallen leaves. And all over the house the wholesome smell of newly-cleaned rooms. For Judy and mother had been papering and scrubbing and washing and ironing and polishing for weeks. Pat and Winnie helped them in the evenings after school. It was lovely to make Silver Bush as beautiful as it could be made.

"Sure and I do be getting spring fever in me bones," said Judy one night. The next day she was down with flu; it ran through the whole family . . . lightly, with one exception. Pat had it hard . . . "as she do be having iverything, the poor darlint," thought Judy . . . and did not pick up rapidly. Aunt Helen came down unexpectedly one day and decreed that Pat needed a change. In the twinkling of an eye it was decided that Pat was to go to Elmwood for three weeks.

Pat didn't want to go. She had never been away from Silver Bush overnight and three weeks of nights seemed an eternity. But nobody paid any heed to her protestations and the dread morning came when father was to take her to Summerside. Jingle was over and they ate breakfast together, sitting on the sandstone steps, with the sun rising redly over the Hill of the Mist and the cherry trees along the dyke throwing sprays of pearly blossoms against the blue sky. . . .

Pat was more resigned, having begun to thrill a little to the excitement about her. After all, it was nice to be quite important. Sid was blue . . . or envious . . . and Jingle was undoubtedly blue. Cuddles was crying because she had got it into her small golden head that something was going to happen to Pat. And Judy was warning her not to forget to write. Forget! Was it likely?

"And you must write me, Judy," said Pat anxiously.

"Oh, oh, I don't be much av a hand at writing letters," said Judy dubiously. The truth being that Judy hadn't written any kind of a letter for over twenty years. "I'm thinking ye'll have to depind on the rest av the folks for letters but sind me a scrape av the pin now and agin for all that."

Pat had put her three favourite dolls to bed in her doll house and got Judy to put it away for her in the blue chest. She had bid tearful farewells to every room in the house and every tree within calling distance and to her own face in the water of the well. Snicklefritz and McGinty and Thursday had been hugged and wept over. Then came the

107

awful ordeal of saying good-bye to everybody. Judy's last glimpse of Pat was a rather tragic little face peering out of the back window of the car.

"Sure and this is going to be the lonesome place till she comes back," sighed Judy.

2

Pat had no sooner arrived at Elmwood than she wrote mother a pitiful letter entreating to be taken home. That first night at Elmwood was a rather dreadful one. The big, old-fashioned bed, with its tent canopy hung with yellowed net, was so huge she felt lost in it. And at home mother or Judy would be standing at the kitchen door calling everybody in out of the dark. "O . . . w!" Pat gave a smothered yelp of anguish at the thought. But . . .

"This is just a visit. I'll soon be home again . . . in just twenty-one days," she reminded herself bravely.

Her next letter to Judy was more cheerful. Pat had discovered that there were some pleasant things about visiting. Uncle Brian's house was quite near and Aunt Helen was surprisingly kind and nice in her own home. It was quite exciting to be taken down town every day and see all the entrancing things in the store windows. Sometimes Norma and Amy took her down Saturday evenings when the windows were lighted up and looked like fairyland, especially the druggist's, where there were such beautiful coloured bottles of blue and ruby and purple.

"Aunt Helen's house is very fine," wrote Pat, beginning also to discover that she liked writing letters. "It is much more splendid than the Bay Shore house. And Uncle Brian's is finer still. But I wouldn't let on to Norma that I thought it fine because she has always bragged so about it. She said to me, 'Isn't it handsomer than Silver Bush?' and I said, 'Yes, much handsomer but not half so lovely.'

"I like Uncle Brian better now. He shook hands with me just as if I was grown up. Norma is as stuck-up as ever but Amy is nice. Aunt Helen has a plaster Paris dog on the dining-room mantel that looks just like Sam Binnie. Aunt Helen says all Amasa Taylor's apple trees were nawed to death by mice last winter. Oh, Judy, I hope our apple trees will never be nawed by mice. Please tell father not to name the new red calf till I come home. It won't be long now . . . only fourteen more days.

Don't forget to give Thursday his milk every night, Judy, and please put a little cream in it. Are the columbines and the bleeding-heart out yet? I hope Cuddles won't grow too much before I get back.

"Aunt Helen gave me a new dress. She says it is a sensible dress. I don't like sensible dresses much. And there are no Sunday raisins here.

"Aunt Helen is a perfect housekeeper. The neighbours say you could eat your porridge off her floor but she never puts enough salt in her porridge so I don't like to eat it anywhere.

"Uncle Brian says Jim Hartley will come to a bad end. Jim lives next door and it is exciting to look at him and wonder what the end will be. Do you think he may be hung, Judy?

"Aunt Helen lets me drink tea. She says it is all nonsense the way they bring up children nowadays not to drink tea.

"Old cousin George Gardiner told me I didn't look much like my mother. He said mother had been a beauty in her day. It made me feel he was disappointed in me. He praised Norma and Amy for their good looks. I don't mind how much he praises their looks but I can't bear to hear their house praised. I think bay windows are *horrid*.

"Oh, Judy, I do hope everything will stay just the same at Silver Bush till I get back."

It was wildly exciting to get letters from home . . . *"Miss Patricia Gardiner, Elmwood, Summerside."* Jingle wrote the nicest letters because he told her things no one else thought of telling her . . . how the Silver Bush folks were pestered with squirrels in the garret and Judy was clean wild . . . how the sheep laurel was out in Happiness . . . what apple trees had the most bloom . . . how Joe had cut off Gentleman Tom's whiskers but Judy said they would grow in all right again . . . how the barn cat had kittens . . . and, most wonderful of all, how the farm with the Long Lonely House had been sold to some strange man who was coming there to live. Pat was thrilled over this: but it was terrible to think of these things happening and she not there to see them.

"Only ten days more," said Pat, looking at the calendar. "Only ten days more and I'll be home."

Judy did not write but she sent messages in everybody's letters. "Tell her the house do be that lonely for her," was the one Pat liked best, and "that skinny beau of yours do be looking as if he was sent for and couldn't go," was the one she liked least.

Pat found Aunt Jessie's afternoon tea, which she was giving for a visiting friend, very tiresome. Norma and Amy were too much taken up with their own doings to bother with her, her head ached with the crowd and the lights and the chatter . . . "they sound just like Uncle Tom's geese when they all start chattering at once," thought Pat unkindly. She slipped away upstairs to seek a quiet spot where she could sit and dream of Silver Bush and found it in Uncle Brian's snuggery at the end of the hall. But when she pulled aside the curtain to creep into the window seat it was already occupied. A little girl of about her own age was curled up in the corner . . . a girl who had been crying but who now looked up at Pat with half appealing, half defiant eyes . . . beautiful eyes . . . large, dreamy, grey eyes . . . the loveliest eyes Pat had ever seen, with long lashes quilling darkly around them. And there was something besides beauty in the eyes . . . Pat could not have told what it was . . . only it gave her a queer feeling that she had known this girl always. Perhaps the stranger felt something of the same when she looked into Pat's eyes. Or perhaps it was Pat's smile . . . already "little Pat Gardiner's smile" was, unknown to Pat, becoming a clan tradition. At all events she suddenly shook back her thick brown curls, drew her feet under her, and pointed to the opposite corner of the seat with a welcoming smile on her small, flower-like face. They were good friends before they spoke a word to each other.

Pat hopped in and squirmed down. The heavy blue velvet curtain swung behind her, cutting them off from the world. Outside, the boughs of a pine tree screened the window. They were alone together. They looked at each other and smiled again.

"I'm Patricia Gardiner of Silver Bush," said Pat.

"I'm Elizabeth Wilcox . . . but they call me Bets," said the girl.

"Why, that's the name of the man who has bought the Long Lonely House Farm at North Glen," cried Pat.

Bets nodded.

"Yes, that's dad. And that's why I've been crying. I . . . don't want to go away down there . . . so far from everybody."

"It's not far from me," said Pat eagerly.

Bets seemed to find comfort in this.

"Isn't it . . . really?"

"Just a cat's walk, as Judy says. Right up a hill from Silver Bush. And it's a lovely old house. I'm so fond of it. I've always wanted to see a light in it. Oh, I'm glad you're coming to it, Bets."

Bets blinked the last tears out of her eyes and thought she might be glad, too. They sat there together and talked until there was a hue and cry through the house for them and Bets was dragged away by the aunt who had brought her to the party. But by this time she and Pat knew all that was worth while knowing about each other's pasts.

3

"Oh, Judy," Pat wrote that night, "I've found the dearest friend. Her name is Bets Wilcox and she is coming to live at the Long Lonely House. It will soon have a light in its windows now. Her full name is Elizabeth Gertrude and she is so pretty, far prettier than Norma, and we've promised each other that we'll always be faithful till death us do part. Just think, Judy, this time yesterday I didn't know there was such a person in the world. Aunt Helen says she is very delicate and that is why her father has sold his farm which is kind of low and marshy and he thinks the Long House farm will be healthier.

"I never thought I could like any one outside my own family as much as I like Bets. It was Norma found us in the window seat and I guess she was jealous because she sniffed and said, 'Birds of a feather, I suppose,' and when I said yes she said to Bets, 'You mustn't cut her out with Hilary Gordon. She's his girl you know.' I said . . . very dignified, Judy . . . 'I am not his girl. We are just good friends.' I told Bets all about Jingle and she said we ought to try to make his life happier and she thinks it's awful silly to talk about a boy being your beau when he is just a friend and she says we can't think about beaus for at least seven years yet. I said I was never going to think of them but Bets said they might be nice to have when you grew up.

"But oh, Judy, I haven't told you the strangest thing. Bets and I were born on the same day. That makes us a kind of twins, doesn't it? And we both love poetry *passionately*. Bets says that Mr. George Palmer, who lives on the farm next to them, found out his son was writing poetry and whipped him for it. Bets is going to lend me a fairy story called *The Honey Stew of the Countess Bertha*. She says there is a lovely ghost in it.

"Oh, Judy, day after to-morrow I'll be home. It seems too good to be true."

111

4

"The best part of a visit is getting home," said Pat.

Uncle Brian drove her down to Silver Bush one evening. To Uncle Brian it meant a pleasant half-hour's run after a tiresome day in the office. To Pat it meant a breath-taking return from exile. It was dark and she could see only the lights of the North Glen farmsteads but she knew them all. Mr. French's light and the Floyd light, Jimmy Card's light and the lights of Silverbridge away off to the right; the Robinsons' light . . . the Robinsons had been away for months but they must be home again. How nice to see their light in its old place! The dark roads were strange but it was their own strangeness . . . a strangeness she knew. And then the home lane . . . wasn't that Joe's whistle? . . . and the friendly old trees waving their hands at her . . . and the house with all its windows alight to welcome her . . . Gentleman Tom sitting on the gate-post and all the family to run out and meet her . . . except dad who had to go to a political meeting at Silverbridge. And Cuddles, who was two years old and hadn't said a word yet, to the secret worry of everybody, suddenly crowed out, "Pat," clearly and distinctly. Jingle and McGinty were there, too, and supper in the kitchen with crisp, golden-brown rolls and fried brook trout Jingle had caught in Jordan for her. Judy wore a new drugget dress and the broadest of smiles. Nothing was changed. Pat had been secretly afraid they might have moved some of the furniture about . . . that the kittens in the picture might have grown up or King William and his white horse got across the Boyne. It was beautiful to see the moon rising over her own fields. She loved to hear the North Glen dogs barking from farm to farm.

"Did Joe really cut off Gentleman Tom's whiskers, Judy?"

"Sure he did that same, the spalpane, and a funnier looking baste ye niver saw, but they're growing in agin fine."

"I'll have to get acquainted with everything all over again," said Pat joyfully. "Won't dad be home before I go to bed, Judy?"

"It's not likely," said Judy . . . who had her own reasons for wanting Pat to get a good night's rest before she saw Long Alec.

Her own dear room . . . such a quiet pleasant happy little room . . . and her own dear bed waiting for her. Then the fun of getting up in the morning and seeing everything by daylight. The garden had grown beyond belief but it knew her . . . oh, it knew her. She flew about and kissed all the trees, even the cross little spruce tree at the gate she had never really liked, it was so grumpy. She flung a kiss to Pat in the well. Life was *too* sweet.

And then she saw father coming from the barn!

They got her comforted after awhile though for a time Judy thought she had them beat. Long Alec had to promise he would let his moustache grow again immediately before she would stop crying.

"Sure and I told ye what a shock it wud be to her," Judy said reproachfully to Long Alec. "Ye know how hard she takes inny change and ye shud av waited until she had her fun out av coming home afore ye shaved it off."

It was a subdued Pat who went along the Whispering Lane to see the folks at Swallowfield and be rejoiced over by an uncle and aunts who had missed her sadly. But still it was lovely to be back home. And thank goodness Uncle Tom hadn't shaved *his* whiskers off!

16

THE RESCUE OF PEPPER

1

As a matter of fact Long Alec never let his moustache grow again after all. When he asked Pat gravely about it, Pat, having got used to seeing him without it, decided she rather liked the look of him as he was. Besides, as she candidly told Judy, it was nicer for kissing. She had another cry on the day when Winnie's famous golden curls were bobbed at last . . . and a shingle bob at that. And yet, when Winnie had been bobbed for a week, it seemed as if she had been bobbed always.

Judy's disapproval lasted longer.

"Making a b'y out av her," sniffed Judy, as she put the shorn curls tenderly away in her glory box. "Oh, oh, it's not meself that do be knowing what the girls av to-day are coming to. Trying to make themselves into min and not succading very well at that. Sure and they'll all be bald as nuts be the time they're fifty and that's one comfort."

Worse than the bobbing as far as Pat was concerned was the notion Winnie took one day in Sunday School that she would be a missionary when she grew up and go to India. Pat worried for weeks over it, despite Judy's philosophy.

"Oh, oh, don't borry trouble so far ahead, Patsy dear. She cudn't go for all av tin years yet at the laste and a big lot av water will have run down yer Jordan be that time. So just sit ye down and have a liddle bite av me bishop's bread and niver be minding Winnie's romantic notions av religion."

"I suppose it's very wicked of me not to want her to be a missionary," sighed Pat. "But India is so far away. Do you think, Judy, it would be wrong for me to pray that Winnie will change her mind before she grows up?"

"Oh, oh, I wudn't be meddling much wid that kind of praying," said Judy, looking very wise. "Ye niver can tell how it will be turning out, Patsy dear. I've known minny a quare answer in me time. Just trust to the chanct that Winnie'll change her mind av her own accord. It's a safe bet wid inny girl."

Pat ate her bishop's bread . . . made from a recipe Judy had brought from Australia and would never give to any one. She had promised to will it to Pat, however.

The latter still had a grievance.

"Mr. James Robinson has gone and cut down that row of spruce trees along the fence in his cow-pasture. I just can't forgive him."

"Listen at her. Sure and hadn't the man a right to do what he liked wid his own? Though ye wudn't catch inny Robinson planting a tree be chanct. Not they. It's aisier to cut down and destroy."

"They weren't his trees half as much as they were mine," said Pat stubbornly. "He didn't love them and I did. I used to watch the red sunrise behind them in the mornings when I woke up. They were so lovely and clear and dark against it. And don't you remember them in the silver thaw last winter, Judy . . . how they just looked like a row of funny old women that had got caught in a shower without umbrellas walking along one behind the other?"

It was a great day for Pat when the Wilcoxes moved to the Long House farm and for the first time in her recollection a light shone down from its windows that night. It gave Pat such delightful little thrills of comradeship to help Bets get settled. Mr. and Mrs. Wilcox were quiet folks who adored Bets and gave her her own way in everything. This might have spoiled some children but Bets was too sweet and wholesome by nature to be easily spoiled. She was allowed to pick the wall-paper for her own room and Pat went to Silverbridge with her to help choose it. They both liked the same one . . . a pale green with rose sprays on it. Pat could see it already on the walls of that long room, dim with fir shadows, which had been assigned to Bets.

"Oh, isn't this house glad to have people living in it again," she exulted. "It will always be the Long House but it won't be lonely any more."

Judy was secretly well pleased that Pat had a girl friend of her own age at last. Judy had always felt worried over the fact that Pat had none. Winnie had half a dozen chums, but Pat, although she got on well enough with the girls at school, had never been closely drawn to any of them.

"Bets is the prettiest girl in school now," she told Judy proudly. "May Binnie can't hold a candle to her . . . and oh, doesn't May hate her! But every one else loves her. I love her *dreadfully*, Judy."

"I wudn't be after loving her too much," warned Judy. "Not too much, Patsy dear."

"As if any one could be loved too much!" scoffed Pat. But Judy shook her head.

"She'll never comb grey hairs, that one. Sure and that liddle face av hers do be having a bloom that's not av earth," she muttered to herself, thinking of Bets' too brilliant roses and the strange look that went and came in her eyes, as if she had some secret source of happiness no one else knew. Perhaps Bets' charm lay in that look. For charm she had. Every one felt it, old and young.

"Some of the girls in school are jealous because Bets is *my* chum," Pat told Judy. "They've tried and tried to get her away. But Bets and I just hang together. We're twins really, Judy. And every day I find out something new about her. Sometimes we call each other Gertrude and Margaret. We are so sorry for out middle names because they are never used. We think they feel bad about it. But that is one of our secrets. I like *nice* secrets. May Binnie told me a secret last week and it was a horrid one. Oh, Judy, aren't you glad the Wilcoxes have come to the Long House?"

"I am that. It's a trate to have good neighbours. And George Wilcox do be a quiet inoffensive man enough. But his dad, old Geordie, was a terror to snakes in his time. Whin he got in one av his fine rages I've seen him grab the pudding from the pot and throw it out av the door. And that stubborn he was. Whin they voted in church to set for prayers d'ye think me fine Geordie wud do it? Not be a jugful. Stiff as a ramrod wud he stand up, wid his back to the minister, and his legs a yard apart and glare over the congregation. Oh, oh, he's in heaven now, poor man, and I hope he lets the angels have a bit av their own way."

"What funny things you do remember about people, Judy," giggled Pat.

"Remimber, is it? Sure thin and it isn't a funny thing I remimber about Geordie's cousin, Matt Wilcox. *He* was be way av having a rat or two in his garret. Thought he was haunted by a divil."

"Haunted by a devil?" Pat had a real thrill.

"I'm telling ye. But his fam'ly didn't be worrying much over until he tuk to liking to hear the cratur's talk. Said its conversation was rale interesting. They tuk him to the asylum thin but sorra a bit did he care, for his divil went wid him. He lived there for years, rale happy and continted as long as they'd just let him sit quiet and listen. Thin one day they found him crying fit to break his heart. 'Sure,' sez he, 'me divil has gone back to his own place and what I'm to do now for a bit av entertainment I don't know.' They tuk him home quite cured but he always said there niver was inny rale flavour in innything folks said to him the rist av his life. He said he missed the tang av . . . oh, oh, av a place I'll not be mintioning to ye, Patsy dear."

"I suppose you mean hell," said Pat coolly, much to Judy's horror. "I'm sure I hear it often enough. Uncle Tom's man is always telling things to go there. Uncle Tom says he just can't help it."

"Oh, oh, maybe he can't at that. He's ould Andy Taylor's grandson and ould Andy had a great gift av swearing. He was the only man in South Glen that ever did be swearing. Sure and nobody else had the heart to try whin they'd heard what ould Andy cud do. Swearing and laughing he always was, the ould scallywag. 'As long as I can laugh at things I'll get along widout God,' sez he. 'Whin I can't laugh I'll turn to him,' sez he. Whin his own son died he laughed and sez, 'Poor b'y, he's been saved a lot av trouble,' sez he. Whin his wife died he sez, 'There's one mistake corrected,' sez he. But whin ould Soapy John, that he'd hated and quarrelled wid all his life, fell out av his buggy and bruk his neck he sez, 'This is too funny to laugh at,' sez he, 'I'll have to be going to church and getting religion,' sez he. And niver a Sunday he missed from that to the day av his death."

2

Pat had never had such a happy summer. It was lovely to have some one to walk to and from school with. Sid was drifting more and more to the companionship of the other boys, although he and Pat still had their beautiful hours of prowling in the fields or hunting eggs in the barn or looking for strayed turkeys in the dims.

Sometimes Bets would come down to Silver Bush where she and Pat had a playhouse among the birches. Time and again Judy let them have their suppers in it. It was so romantic and adventurous to have meals out of doors, finishing up with a dessert of ruby red currants eaten off a lettuce leaf. Or they sat in the moonlight at the kitchen door and listened to Judy's stories of ghosts and fairies and ancestors and "grey people" that haunted apple orchards in the dusks of eve and morn. No wonder that Pat had to go clear up to the Long House with Bets afterwards. Pat was so pickled in Judy's stories that they only gave her thrills. Bets had the thrills, too, but if her father and mother had known the extent of Judy's repertoire they might not have been so complacent over Bets' visits to Silver Bush.

They helped Judy makes her cheeses . . . for the last time. The decree had gone forth that henceforth all the milk must be sent to the factory and the cheese bought there.

"Oh, Judy, I *wish* things didn't have to change."

"But they do, Patsy dear. That do be life. And yer dad nades all the money he can be getting for his milk. But there'll niver be a bit av dacent flavoured cheese at Silver Bush agin. Factory cheese indade!" sniffed Judy rebelliously.

Sometimes Pat would go up to the Long House . . . by a fascinating path up the hill fields . . . a path you always felt happy on, as if the fairies had traced it. She found something new to love every time she traversed it . . . some sunny fern corner or mossy log or baby tree. You went along the Whispering Lane and across the end of Uncle Tom's garden and there was your path. The first outpost of this land of fairy was a big clump of spruce trees where Pat generally lingered to pick a "chew" of gum. Then there was a brook . . . a tiny thread of a brook that ran into Jordan . . . with a lady silver birch hanging over the log bridge. Beyond it a meadow cross-cut enticed you in daisies with an old pine at the top that always seemed to be waiting for something, Pat thought. Then it ran along an upland dyke where you could pick bouquets of long-stemmed strawberries in the crevices and look down far over the lowlands and groves to the sea. Sometimes Bets would come to meet her here . . . or again she would be waving at her from one of her windows as Pat came through the spruces on the hill. Then Silver Bush and the world Pat knew dropped out of sight and before them were the bush-dotted fields of the Long House farm and the shining loops of the Silverbridge river. And it was wonderful just to be alive.

The tragedy of that summer was Thursday's death. Poor Thursday was missing for a couple of days and was found lying stiff and stark on the well platform one morning, having dragged himself home to die.

"Judy, it's dreadful that cats can't live as long as we do," sighed Pat. "You just have time to get so fond of them . . . and they die. Judy, do you think it hurt poor Thursday very much to die?"

Pat took it pretty hard but Thursday had been away a good deal all summer, sometimes for weeks at a time, and Pepper and Salt, two adorable kittens, one smoky grey, one grey and white, with a pansy face, had crept into Pat's heart for her consolation. They had an affecting funeral at which Sid and Jingle were pallbearers and Salt and Pepper reluctant mourners with huge black bows around their necks. Pat and Bets made wreaths of wild flowers for the dead pussy. Pat wanted to bury him in the grave-yard, between Weeping Willy and Wild Dick, because he seemed so much like one of the family. But Judy was horrified at the idea; so they buried Thursday in the little glade among the spruces where the other Silver Bush cats slept the sleep that knows no waking. Clever Bets wrote an epitaph in verse for him and Jingle burnt it on a board. Thursday's funeral was always remembered in Silver Bush annals because Cuddles inadvertently sat down on a Scotch thistle after it and only Pat could comfort her. Cuddles always turned to Pat in her woes.

"At least I suppose I can put flowers on Thursday's grave," said Pat a little defiantly. She found it hard to forgive Judy for refusing Thursday the grave-yard.

3

There was a terrible time one soft, golden end of a rainy day when Pepper fell into the well. Pepper had a knack of getting into trouble. It was only the preceding Sunday night that he had walked up Judy's back and danced on her shoulders when they were all at family prayers in the Little Parlour. Sid had disgraced himself by laughing out and dad had been very angry.

Pepper was missing one evening when Pat put his saucer of milk on the well platform and when Pat called him lamentable shrieks were heard from somewhere. But from *where?* Pat and Bets hunted everywhere a cat could possibly be but no Pepper. Only those piteous cries that seemed to come now from the sky, now from the silver bush, now from the grave-yard.

"Sure and the cratur's bewitched," cried Judy. "He can't be far off but I'm bate to say where."

Bets finally solved the mystery.

"He's in the well," she cried.

Pat ran to it with a shriek of despair. Nothing could be seen in the dim depths but there was no doubt that Pepper was down there somewhere. As they looked down the shrieks redoubled.

"The water's calm as a clock," said Judy. "Where has the baste got to? Oh, oh, I'm seeing. Look at the eyes av him blazing. He must have fell in the water but me brave Pepper has climbed out on that liddle shelf av rock between the stones and the water. Listen at him. He'll split his throat. And well may he wail for I'm blist if I can be seeing how we're to get him up, what wid yer dad and the b'ys away to the Bay Shore and not likely back till midnight. This do be a tommyshaw."

"We *can't* leave him there all night," cried Pat in agony. She flew to the garret to set the signal light. If only Jingle would see it! Jingle had been spending most of his evenings grubbing young spruces out of a big field Mr. Gordon wanted to clean up, but he saw Pat's light as he tramped home and in a few minutes he and McGinty were in the Silver Bush yard. McGinty, when he found out what was the trouble, sat down and howled antiphonally to Pepper's yells. It was a doleful duet.

119

"Oh, Jingle, can't *you* save Pepper?" implored Pat.

Jingle was a rather comical knight-errant, to be sure, with his frayed trousers and dark glasses and "raggedy hair," but he came promptly and practically to the help of lady fair. The three of them, aided by Judy, dragged a ladder from the barn and contrived, goodness knew how, to get it down the well. Down went Jingle, while Pat and Bets prevented McGinty from a suicidal leap after him. Terrible moments of suspense. Up came Jingle, grasping a forlorn, dripping kitten who promptly expressed his gratitude by giving his rescuer a ferocious bite on the wrist.

"Oh, oh," groaned Judy, "but I'm faling as if I'd been pulled through a key-hole. It's been the tarrible day, what wid Cuddles catching her liddle fingers in the wringer and Snicklefritz ating up one av yer dad's boots and Siddy's owl gone the Good Man Above only knows where. And now," she concluded in a tone of despair, "we'll have to be dragging water up from yer Jordan till we can get the well claned. And nobody knowing how minny lizards we'll have to be drinking in that same."

"Lizards!"

"I'm telling ye. Didn't ould Mr. Adams' grandfather swally a lizard one day whin he tuk a drink of the brook water? Sure and he was niver the same again . . . he wud always fale it wriggling about in his insides whin his stomach was impty."

Pat reflected with a grue that she and Jingle had often drunk of Jordan water . . . though it was generally from the rock spring up in Happiness. She immediately felt something wrong with *her* stomach. But maybe that was only because it was empty. They shut Pepper up in the granary to dry off and went in to a supper of hot meat pie in Judy's kitchen. After so much excitement one really needed a little nourishment. . . .

But that night Pat had a dreadful dream that she had swallowed a frog!

4

Pat found a new delight in life . . . going up to stay all night with Bets. The first time was in early December when Judy was glad to pack her off to the Long House as soon as she came from school, because

Long Alec was killing the pigs and Pat was neither to hold nor bind when they killed the pigs. Not, as Judy sarcastically pointed out to her, that it prevented her later on from enjoying the sausages and fried ham that were among the products of the late lamented.

Pat went up to the Long House over a silver road of new-fallen snow. Every time she turned to look down on home the world was a little whiter. Bets, who had not been in school that day, was waiting for her under the pine. Just above them the Long House, amid its fir trees, was like a little dark island in a sea of snow.

There was something about the long, low-eaved house, with the dormer windows in its roof, that pleased Pat. And Bets' room was a delightful one with two dormers along its side and one at each end. It was very grand, Pat told Judy, with a real "set of furniture" and a long mirror in which the delighted girls could see themselves from top to toe. The west window was covered with vines, leafless now but a green dappled curtain in summer, and the east looked right out into a big apple tree. Pat and Bets sat by the little stove and ate apples until any one might have expected them to burst. Then they crept into bed and cuddled down for one of those talks dear to the hearts of small school-girls from time immemorial.

"It's so much easier to be confidential in the dark," Pat had told Judy. "I can tell Bets *everything* then."

"Oh, oh, I wudn't tell *iverything* to innybody," warned Judy. "Not iverything, me jewel."

"Not to anybody but Bets," agreed Pat. "Bets is different."

"Too different," sighed Judy. But she did not let Pat hear it.

To lie there, with the soft swish of the fir trees sounding just outside, and talk "secrets" with Bets . . . lovely secrets, not like May Binnie's . . . was delightful. Bets had recently been to some wedding in the Wilcox clan and Pat had to hear all about it . . . the mysterious pearl-white bride, the bridesmaids' lovely dresses, the flowers, the feast.

"Do you suppose *we* will ever get married?" whispered Bets.

"*I* won't," said Pat. "I couldn't ever go away from Silver Bush."

"But you wouldn't like to be an old maid, would you?" said Bets. "Besides, you could get him to come and live with you at Silver Bush, couldn't you?"

This was a new idea for Pat. It seemed quite attractive. Somehow, when you were with Bets, everything seemed possible. Perhaps that was another part of her charm.

"We were born on the same day," went on Bets, "so if we're ever married we must try to be married the same day."

"And die the same day. Oh, wouldn't that be romantic?" breathed Pat in ecstasy.

Pat woke in the night with just a little pang of homesickness. Was Silver Bush all right? She slipped out of bed and stole across to the nearest dormer window. She breathed on its frosty stars until she had made clear a space to peer through . . . then caught her breath with delight. The snow had ceased and a big moon was shining down on the cold, snowy hills. The powdered fir trees seemed to be covered with flowers spun from moonshine, the apple trees seemed picked out in silver filigree. The open space of the lawn was sparkling with enormous diamonds. How beautiful Silver Bush looked when you gazed down on it on a moonlit winter night! Was darling Cuddles covered up warm? She *did* kick the clothes off so. Was mother's headache better? Away over beyond Silver Bush was the poor, lean, ugly Gordon house which nobody had ever loved. Jingle would be sleeping in his kitchen loft now. All summer he had slept in the hay-mow with McGinty. Poor Jingle, whose mother never wrote to him! How could a mother be like that? Pat almost hated to go back to sleep again and lose so much beauty. It had always seemed a shame to sleep through a moonlit night. Somehow those far hills looked so different in moonlight. A verse she and Bets had learned "off by heart," in school that day came to her mind:

> "Come, for the night is cold,
> And the frosty moonlight fills
> Hollow and rift and fold
> Of the eerie Ardise hills."

She repeated it to herself with a strange, deep exquisite thrill of delight, such as she had never felt before . . . something that went deeper than body or brain and touched some inner sanctum of being of which the child had never been conscious. Perhaps that moment was for Patricia Gardiner the "soul's awakening" of the old picture. All her life she was to look back to it as a sort of milestone . . . that brief, silvery vigil at the dormer window of the Long House.

17

JUDY PUTS HER FOOT DOWN

1

"Just as naked as the day she was born," concluded Aunt Edith . . . and said no more. She felt . . . everybody felt . . . that there was no more to be said.

Mother looked horrified and ashamed. Uncles Tom and Brian looked horrified and amused. Aunt Jessie looked horrified and contemptuous. Norma and Amy looked horrified and smug. Winnie looked horrified and annoyed. Dad and Joe and Sid looked just plain horrified.

Pat stood before this family court, with Aunt Edith's hand on her shoulder, struggling unsuccessfully to keep back her tears. Well might she cry, thought the family; but her tears were not of shame or fear, as they supposed, but of regret over something marvellously beautiful which Aunt Edith had destroyed . . . something which could never be replaced. This was why Pat was crying; the realisation of her enormity hadn't yet come home to her.

For a week Pat had been a lonely soul. Bets was away for a visit. Jingle and Sid were busy with hay-making; and Judy, of all things unthinkable, was away. Judy had never been away from Silver Bush in Pat's recollection. Vacations were unknown in Judy's calendar.

"Sure and I'd niver work if I cud find innything else to do," she would say, "but the puzzle av it is I niver can."

There was trouble at the Bay Shore. Cousin Danny had broken his leg and Aunt Frances was ill, so Bay Shore borrowed Judy from Silver Bush to tide over the emergency. Pat found this especially dreadful. She missed Judy at every turn. The house had never seemed so full of her as when she was away, and even the delight of having mother in the kitchen most of the time and helping her in all household doings did not quite compensate. Besides, Gentleman Tom was gone, too. He had disappeared the very day Judy had been whirled away to Bay Shore; and the back yard and kitchen without Gentleman Tom were lonesome places. And what would Judy say when she came home and found her cat was gone? Perhaps she would think Pat had forgotten to feed him.

Pat consoled herself by working feverishly over the garden, determined that Judy should be satisfied with it on her return. Evening after evening Pat carried pails of water to it. She liked drawing the water up. It was fun to watch the bucket going down. Over that oval of blue sky with her own face framed in it at the bottom of the well. And then, as the bucket struck the water, to see it all blotted out, as if a mirror had been shattered. When the last bucketful had been drawn up Pat hung over the curb and watched the water grow slowly calm again and Pat of the Well coming back, at first very shiveringly, then more clearly, then clear and distinct once more, with just an occasional quiver when a drop of water fell from a fern.

Pat loved watering the garden . . . giving thirsty things drink after a hot day. First of all she always watered Judy's pets . . . the row of garden violets under the kitchen window which Judy called "Pink-o'-my-Johns" . . . such a delightful name! . . . and a clump of mauve and white "sops-in-wine" by the turkey house and the "pinies" by the gate. Then all the other flowers . . . and the roses last of all because she liked to linger over them, especially the white roses with the dream of gold in their hearts and the plot of pansies in a far corner that seemed to bloom for her alone.

On this particular evening Pat had been at loose ends. It had rained so heavily the night before that the garden did not need watering and when the "dim" came there was nothing to do and nobody to talk to. But it was a summer evening of glamour and enchantment and mystery and Pat was full of it, as she ran, with her hair streaming behind her, through the silver birches at moonrising, until she came out on the southern side in a little glade misted over with white daisies, lying amid its bracken like a cool pool of frosty moonlight.

She paused there to drink in the loveliness of the scene before her. More and more that summer of her tenth year, Pat had found herself responsive to the beauty of the world around her. It was becoming a passion with her.

The moon was rising over the Hill of the Mist . . . the moon that Pat had thought, when she was a tiny tot, must be a beautiful world where all was happiness. Little pools of shadow lay here and there all over the farm, among the shorn hayfields. There was one big field of hay that hadn't been touched yet; wind waves went over it in that misty light. Beyond it a field where happy calves were in buttercups to their shoulders . . . the only living creatures in sight if you were sure those shadows along the edge of the silver bush *were* shadows and not little rabbits dancing.

A warm brooding night . . . a night that surely belonged to the fairies. For the moment Pat could believe in them wholeheartedly again. Some strange bewitchment entered into her and crept along her veins. She remembered a Judy-story of an enchanted princess who had to dance naked in the moonlight every night of full moon in a woodland glen, and a sudden craving possessed her to dance thus in moonlight, too. Why not? There was nobody to see. It would be beautiful . . . beautiful.

Pat disrobed. There was not much to do . . . she was already bare-legged. Her pale-blue cotton frock and two small undies were cast aside and she stood among the shadows, a small, unashamed dryad, quivering with a strange, hitherto unknown ecstasy as the moon's pale fingers touched her through the trees.

She stepped out among the daisies and began the little dance Bets had taught her. A breeze blew on her through the aisles of the shining birches. If she held up her hands to it wouldn't it take hold of them? A faint, delicious perfume arose from the dew-wet ferns she danced on; somewhere far away laughter was drifting across the night . . . faint, fairy laughter which seemed to come from the Haunted Spring. She felt as light of being as if she were really made of moonlight. Oh, never had there been such a moment as this! She paused on tip-toe among the daisies and held out her arms to let the cool fire of that dear and lovely moon bathe her slim child-body.

"Pat!" said Aunt Edith, with forty exclamation points in her voice.

Pat came back to earth with a shudder. Her exquisite dream was over. The horror in Aunt Edith's voice enrobed her like a garment of shame. She could not even find a word to say.

"Put on your clothes," said Aunt Edith icily. Not for her to deal with the situation. That was Long Alec's job. Pat dumbly put on her clothes and followed Aunt Edith down through the silver bush and into the Little Parlour where the rest of the Silver Bushites were entertaining the Brianites who had run down for a call. Of course, thought Pat miserably, Norma and Amy, who never misbehaved, would have to be there to see her humiliation.

"How *could* you, Pat?" asked mother reproachfully.

"I . . . I wanted to bathe in the moonlight," sobbed Pat. "I didn't think it was any harm. I didn't think any one would see me."

"I never heard of any decent child wanting to bathe in moonlight," said Aunt Jessie.

And then Uncle Tom laughed uproariously.

2

The punishment of Pat, which the Silver Bush family thought was a very light one, considering the enormity of her offence, was to Pat the most terrible thing they could have devised. She was "sent to Coventry." For a week she was to speak to nobody at Silver Bush and nobody was to speak to her, except when it was absolutely necessary.

Pat lived . . . she could never tell how . . . through three days of it. It seemed like an eternity. To think that *Sid* wouldn't speak to her! Why, Sid had been the most furious of them all. Mother and father seemed sorry for her but firm. As for Winnie . . .

"She looks at me as if I was a stranger," thought poor Pat.

She was not allowed to play with Jingle who came over unsuspectingly the next evening. Jingle was very indignant and Pat snubbed him for it.

"My family have the right to correct me," she told him haughtily.

But she cried herself to sleep every night. On the third night she went to bed sadly, after kissing all her flowers and her two little cats good-night. Below stairs the house was full of light and laughter for Uncle Tom and dad were roaring in the kitchen and Winnie was practising her singing lesson in the Little Parlour and Joe and Sid were playing "grab" in the dining room, and Cuddles was chuckling and gurgling with mother on the front porch. Only she, Pat, had no part or lot with them. She was outcast.

Pat woke up in the darkness . . . and smelled ham frying! She sat up in bed. The Little Parlour clock was striking twelve. Who on earth could be frying ham at midnight in Silver Bush? Nobody but Judy . . . Judy must be home!

Pat slipped noiselessly out of bed, so as not to wake Winnie . . .

Winnie who would not even *ask* what she was doing if she did. Sniffing that delectable odour Pat crept down through the silent house. She hoped that Judy would not send her to Coventry; and she thought her heart might stop aching for a little while if she could feel Judy's arms around her.

Softly she opened the kitchen door. Beautiful sight! There was dear old Judy frying herself a snack of ham, her jolly old shadow flying in all directions over the kitchen walls and ceiling as she darted about.

And . . . was it believable? . . . there was Gentleman Tom, sitting inscrutably on the bench, watching her. How peaceful and home-y and comforting it all was!

There had been anything but a peaceful scene in the kitchen two hours before when Judy had arrived home and demanded if all was well with the children. When she was told Pat was in disgrace and why Judy, as she expressed it, tore up the turf. Such a "ruckus" had never been known at Silver Bush. Everybody caught it.

"Suppose she had been *seen*, Judy?" protested mother.

"Oh, oh, but they didn't see her, did they?" demanded Judy scornfully.

"Nobody but Aunt Edith . . ."

"Oh, oh, is it *Aunt* Edith?" sniffed Judy. "And it was me fine *Edith* that dragged her in and blew it all afore Brian and his fine lady wife, ye're telling me? Sure it was like her. It's a pity a liddle thing like that cudn't av been hushed up in the fam'ly. And to punish the tinder-hearted cratur so cruel! Ye rale ly ain't wise, Long Alec. A bit av a tongue-lashing might av been all right but to kape on torturing the poor jewel for a wake and her that fond av ye all! It's telling ye to yer face, I am Long Alec, ye don't deserve such a daughter."

"Well, well," said Long Alec, quite cowed, "I don't think it's done her much harm. We'll let her off the rest of the week."

"I don't know what possessed the child to do such a thing," said mother.

"Oh, oh, it's a bit av that ould Frinch leddy coming out in her, I warrant ye," suggested Judy.

"Certainly it didn't come from the Quaker side," chuckled Uncle Tom.

"Judy!"

Pat was in Judy's arms, laughing, crying. It was a glorious five minutes. Even Gentleman Tom betrayed a trifle of sympathy.

Finally Judy held Pat off and pretended to look stern.

"I don't want to be hard on ye, Patsy, but what monkey-didoes have ye been cutting up? It's a fine yarn yer dad has been spinning me av ye dancing in the bush widout inny clothes on."

"Oh, Judy, I never saw such a moon . . . and I was pretending I was a bewitched princess . . . and Uncle Tom *laughed* at me. That spoiled it worst of all, Judy . . . and it *was* so beautiful before Aunt Edith came."

There was some wild strain of poetry in Judy that made her understand. She hugged Pat with a fierce tenderness.

"Oh, oh, I've rid the riot act to thim, I'm telling ye. Whin I get me dander up I'm a terror to snakes. There'll be no more visiting in Coventry for ye, me jewel. But ye'd better not be doing any more quare things for awhile."

"The trouble is, *I* don't think the things I do are queer," said Pat gravely. "They seem quite reasonable to me. And Aunt Edith was just . . . ridiculous."

"Ye niver spoke a truer word. Oh, oh, what a shock it must av been to the poor sowl. She's forgotten she has inny legs, that one. But ye'd better be a bit careful, Patsy, and if ye fale inny more hankering for such bathing just ye tell me and I'll get a pitcherful av moonlight and pour it over ye. And now just sit down and have a liddle bit av ham wid me and tell me all that's happened. Sure and it's good to be home agin."

"Oh, Judy, where did Gentleman Tom come from? He's never been seen here since you went away."

"Are ye telling me? Sure and he was sitting on the dure-step when I got out av the Bay Shore rig, looking as if he wasn't knowing where his nixt mouse was coming from. *I'm* not asking him where he's been. I mightn't be liking the answer. Innyway, here he is and here I am . . . and there's a beautiful pink dress av eyelet embroidery in me grip that yer Aunt Honor sint ye. It'll be one in the eye for Norma whin she sees ye in it."

"I'm going to sleep the rest of the night with you, Judy," said Pat resolutely.

18

UNDER A CLOUD

1

When in mid-September Long Alec suddenly announced to his family that, harvest being over, he meant to take a trip out west to visit a brother who had settled there years ago Pat took it more calmly than they had feared. It was rather dreadful, of course, to think of dad being away for a whole month, but, as he said himself, if he didn't go away he couldn't come back again. There would be his home-coming to expect and plan for, and meanwhile life was very pleasant at Silver Bush. She liked the fall nights because the fires were lighted. Jingle was building an elegant bird-house for her to be put up in the maple by the well when finished; and Mr. Wilcox was going to take Bets and her to the Exhibition in Charlottetown. Pat had never been to one yet. To the small denizens of North Glen a visit to the Exhibition loomed up with as much of excitement and delight as a trip to Europe or "the coast" might to older folks. Socially you were not in the swim unless you had been to the Exhibition. There were the weeks of delightful anticipation . . . the Exhibition itself . . . then weeks of just as delightful reminiscence. All things considered, Pat was quite cheerful about dad's absence. It was Judy who seemed to view it most gloomily . . . Pat couldn't understand why. For the week preceding Long Alec's departure Judy had done an extra deal of talking to and arguing with herself. Disjointed sentences reached Pat's ears every now and again.

"I'm not knowing what gets into the min be times. It do be saming as if they had to have a crazy spell once in so long" . . . "a bit av Wild Dick coming out in him I'm telling ye" . . . "'tis the curse av the wandering foot" . . . "oh, oh, it's too aisy to get about now. Sure and that's what's the matter wid the world."

But when Pat asked what the trouble was Judy's only reply was a curt:

"Ax me no questions and I'll be telling ye no lies."

Dad went away one windy, cloudy September morning. Uncle Tom and the aunts came along the Whispering Lane to say good-bye. Everybody was a little sober. The "west" was a long way off . . . the good-byes a bit tremulous.

"May the Good Man Above give us all good health," muttered Judy, as she dashed back into the kitchen and began to rattle the stove lids fiercely. Pat hopped into the car and went as far as the road with dad. She stood and watched the car out of sight and then turned towards home with a choking sensation. At that moment the sun broke through a black cloud and poured a flood of radiance over Silver Bush. Pat realised afresh how beautiful home was, nestling under its misty blue hill with its background of golden trees.

"Oh, how lovely you are!" she cried, holding out her arms to it. The tears that filled her eyes were not caused by dad's going. She was pierced by the swift exquisite pang which beauty always gave her . . . always would give her. It was almost anguish while it lasted . . . but the pain was heavenly.

It was well that Pat had her trip to the Exhibition over before she heard the terrible thing. She did have it . . . two glorious days with Bets . . . and, as the gods themselves cannot recall their gifts, she always had it, although for a time it seemed as if she had nothing . . . would have nothing for evermore . . . but pain and fear.

Again it was May Binnie who told her . . . that dad meant to buy a farm out west and settle there!

A strange icy ripple, such as she had never felt before, ran over Pat.

"That isn't true," she cried.

May laughed.

"It is. Everybody knows it. Winnie knows it. I s'pose they were afraid to tell you for fear you'd make a scene."

Pat looked passionately into May's bold black eyes.

"I wouldn't have hated you for telling me this, May Binnie, if you hadn't *liked* telling it. But I am going to *tell God about you to-night*."

May laughed again . . . a little uncomfortably. What she called Pat Gardiner's "rages" always made her uncomfortable. And who knew what Pat might tell God about her?

Pat went home sick and cold with agony to the very depth of her being.

"Mother, it isn't true . . . it isn't . . . say it isn't!"

Mother looked compassionately into Pat's tortured young eyes. They had tried to keep this from Pat, hoping she might never have to be told. Dad might not like the west. But if he did, go they must. When easy-going Long Alec did make up his mind there was no budging it, as everybody at Silver Bush knew.

"We don't know, dear. Father is thinking of it. He had a hankering to go when Allan went, years ago, but he couldn't leave his parents then. Now . . . I don't know. Be brave, Pat, dear. We'll all be together . . . the west is a splendid country . . . more chances for the boys perhaps . . ."

She stopped. Better not say more just now.

"So ye've heard?" was all Judy said, when Pat came, white-faced, into the kitchen.

"Judy, it can't happen . . . it just can't. Judy, God wouldn't let such a thing happen."

Judy shook her head.

"Long Alec will settle that, laving God out av the question, Patsy, me jewel. Oh, oh, it's a man's world, so it is, and we women must just be putting up wid it."

"It will be the end of everything, Judy."

"I'm fearing it will be worse than that," muttered Judy. "I'm fearing it will be the beginning av a lot av new things. Sure, the heart av me will be bruk."

She did not say this aloud. Pat must not know until it became necessary that Judy would not be going west with them. To Judy, the idea of leaving Silver Bush was as dreadful as it was to Pat; but she could not leave the Island. Judy had a secret conviction that if the Gardiners went west she would end her days at the Bay Shore farm, taking Danny's part and waiting on the ould leddy who would live forever . . . and eating her soul out with longing and loneliness for her own.

"Oh, oh, they do be all I've got," she mourned. "And all I axed was to be let go on working for thim as long as I was on the hoof. To the divil wid Long Alec and his notions and his stubbornness . . . him that ye wudn't think cud stand up aginst a moonbame. But 'tis in the blood to be set that way whin they think they want innything. His ould Great-uncle Alec was the same but he had a bit av sinse in his pate and whin he onct tuk a notion he wanted to go somewhere he was knowing he shudn't didn't he go and shave his head complate and thin he cudn't go till the hair grew in and be that time the danger was over. Minny's the time I've heard ould Grandfather Gardiner tell av it. 'Twas be way av being a fam'ly joke."

"When will we *know,* Judy?"

"That I can't tell ye, darlint. Long Alec said he'd write as soon as he made up his mind. God hasten the day! There's nothing we can be doing but wait."

Pat shivered. The words were so terrible and so true. How could one wait? To-morrow would be more cruel than to-day.

2

In the weeks that followed Pat felt as if her heart were bleeding drop by drop. She seemed to be alone in her anguish. Sid rather hoped dad wouldn't go west but was not terribly cut up about it. Joe frankly hoped he *would* go. Winnie thought it might be fun. Mother *seemed* quite indifferent to it, in her usual calm, gentle fashion. Even Judy was fiercely silent and would give tongue to neither regrets nor hopes. Bets and Jingle were both in despair but Pat found she could not talk the matter over with them. It went too deep.

She got through the days in school somehow and then wandered about Silver Bush like an unhappy little ghost. She could not read. The books she had loved were no more than printed words. She and Bets had been half way through *The Wind In The Willows,* reading it under the Watching Pine on the hill-top, but now it lay neglected in the bookcase at the Long House. She could not play with Bets or Jingle . . . she could not bear it when she might soon have to leave them forever. She could not play with Sid because Sid *could* play and showed thereby that he was not feeling as badly as he should be. She could not play with Salt and Pepper because they were too cheerful. McGinty was the only animal that seemed to realise the situation. He and Jingle were a gloomy pair.

Pat slept badly and ate next to nothing.

"That thin she do be getting," worried Judy to Mrs. Gardiner. "Sure there isn't a pick on her bones. It's me belafe that if Long Alec drags that child out west it'll be killing her. She can't live away from Silver Bush. Sure and she do be loving ivery inch av it."

"I wish she didn't love it so much," sighed mother. "But she is young . . . she will forget. We older ones . . ." Mother stopped quickly. That was like mother. Mother never showed what she felt. That had been a Bay Shore tradition. The more emotional and expressive Gardiners sometimes thought she had no "feelings."

Pat was having plenty and very dreadful ones they were. Everything she looked at hurt her. It hurt her to be in the house . . . to think of those dear rooms being cold . . . perhaps nobody even bothering to light a fire in them. Perhaps there would be no light in the windows at night . . . in the house that had always overflowed with light: no plumes of homely smoke going up from its chimneys: nobody looking on beauty from the round window. And if there were people in it . . . she hated that thought, too. Who would be sleeping in her room . . . who would be ruling in Judy's kitchen?

It was worse outside. The garden would be so lonely. No one there to love or welcome the flowers. The daffodils and the columbines would come up in the spring but she would not be there to see. The bees would hum in the Canterbury bells and she not there to listen. The poplars would whisper but she would not hear them whispering. The tiny, pointed, crimson buds would come on the wild rose-bushes in the lane, not for her gathering. Perhaps the people who would come to Silver Bush would root up the old garden entirely. Pat had heard Uncle Brian say once it was really only an old jungle and Alec should clear it out. They would change and tear up. Oh, she could not bear it!

And yet, somehow, it could never be theirs. In after years Pat said of this time, "I knew they could never have the soul of Silver Bush. *That* would always be mine."

But she would not be there. There would be no more jolly meals in the old kitchen . . . no more chronicles of Judy on the sandstone steps . . . no more kitten hunts in the old barns . . . no more delightful days and nights at the Long House . . . no more pilgrimages over Jordan . . . no Happiness . . . no Secret Field . . . no Hill of the Mist. There wouldn't be any hills at all on the prairie.

This *must* be a dream. Oh, if she could only wake up!

So many poisonous things were said in school. The girls talked so casually of the Gardiners going west . . . some a little enviously as if they would like to go, too. Jean Robinson said she only wished she could get away from this dull old hole.

And then one day May Binnie said that her father had decided to buy Silver Bush!

"If he does we'll fix it up a bit, I can tell you," she said to Pat. "Pa says he'll cut down that old part of the orchard and plough it up and sow it with beans. We'll build a sun-porch of course. And pa says he'll cut down all them birch trees. He says too many trees aren't healthy."

Only sheer malice could have made her say *that*. Pat dragged herself home.

"The Binnies will cut down all our birches, Judy."

"Oh, oh, the Good Man Above may have something to say to *that*," said Judy darkly. But her faithful old heart was heavy. She knew Mac Binnie already looked on Silver Bush as his and was telling everybody about the "improvements" he meant to make.

"Improvements, is it?" Judy had demanded. "Sure he'd better be making some improvements in the manners av himsilf and his daughters, if it's improvements he do be wanting, the ould wind-bag. Mrs. Binnie hersilf cud do wid a few. Fancy her in me kitchen and her looking like a haystack, niver to mintion her presiding at the dining room table where a Selby from Bay Shore has been sitting. Oh, oh, 'tis a topsy-turvy world, so it is, and getting no better fast."

"I was so happy just a little while ago, Judy. And now I'll never be happy again."

"Oh, oh, niver's a long day, me jewel."

"I hate May Binnie, Judy . . . I *hate* her!"

"Sure, Patsy dear, hating do be something that's always bist done yesterday. Life do be too short to waste inny av it hating. Though, if a body *did* have a liddle more time . . . but thim Binnie craturs do be clane benath hating."

"If there was anything we could do to prevent it," sobbed Pat.

Judy shook her head.

"But there isn't . . . not in Canady innyhow. That's the worst av a new land where nather God nor the divil have had time to be getting much av a hold on things. Now, if there was a wishing well here like there was in me home in ould Ireland sure and ye cud make it all right in the twinkle av a fairy's eye. All ye'd have to do is go to it at moonrise and ye'd get yer wish."

Pat went to Happiness that night and wished over the Haunted Spring. Who knew?

It was horrible to live with fear . . . and suspense. Dad's first letter came when Pat was in school and Judy told her first thing that there was no news yet. Long Alec thought the west a grand country. Allan had done well. But he hadn't decided yet . . . he was looking about . . . he would be able to tell them next letter.

"So kape up yer pecker, Patsy darlint. There's hope yet."

"I'm afraid to hope, Judy," said Pat drearily. "It *hurts* too much to hope. It would be so much worse when you had to stop hoping."

"Oh, oh, but ye're too young to be larning *that*," muttered Judy. She pounded and thumped and battered her bread, wishing it were Long Alec. Oh, oh, but wudn't she knead some sinse into him! Him wid the good Island farm and a fine growing fam'ly to be draming av pulling up stakes and going to a new country at his age!

3

The next letter came. It was Saturday and Pat had wakened to a grey dawn. The rain against the windows was very dreary. Everybody at Silver Bush expected dad's letter that day though nobody said anything about it, and Pat felt that the rain was a bad omen.

"Oh, oh, cheer up, Patsy darlint," said Judy. "Sure and I remimber a bit av poetry I larned whin I was a girleen . . . '*a dark and dreary morning often brings a pleasant day.*' Often have I seen it mesilf."

It stopped raining at noon, although the clouds still hung dark and heavy over the silver bush. Pat was watching from the garden as the old postman drove up to the mail box. He was a little bent old man with a fringe of white beard, driving a crazy buggy behind a lean old sorrel horse. It seemed incredible that her destiny was in his bag. She went slowly down the lane, a pale moth of a girl, hardly knowing whether she wanted to see a letter or not. It would be so terrible to wait for its opening but at least they would *know*.

The letter was there. Pat took it out and looked at it . . . "*Mrs. Alex. B. Gardiner, Silver Bush, North Glen, P. E. Island.*" All her life after a letter seemed to Pat a terrible intriguing, devilish thing. What might

. . . or might not . . . be in it? She remembered that when she had been very small she had been horribly frightened of a "dead" letter she had carried home. She had thought it had come from a dead person. But this was even worse.

She walked back up the lane. Half way up she paused in a little bay of the fence which was full of the white-gold of the "life everlasting" that blooms in September. Her knees were shaking.

"Oh, dear God, please don't let there be any bad news in this letter," she whispered. And then desperately . . . because old Alec Gardiner in South Glen had a daughter Patricia, middle-aged and married, and there must be no mistake . . . "Dear God, it's Long Alec's Pat of Silver Bush speaking, not just Alec's Pat."

Somehow everybody was in the kitchen when Pat entered. Judy sat down on a chair rather suddenly. Bets was just arriving, having torn breathlessly down the hill when she saw the postman. Jingle and McGinty were hanging around the doorstep. McGinty had his ears turned down. Mother, her eyes very bright and with an unusual little red spot on either cheek, took the letter and looked around at all the tense, waiting faces . . . except Pat's. She could not bear to look at Pat's.

It was a thousand fold worse than when the letter had come about Winnie.

"We must all be as brave as possible if father says we must go," she said gently.

She opened the letter steadily and glanced over it. It seemed as if the very trees outside stopped to listen.

"Thank God," she said in a whisper.

"Mother . . ."

"Father is coming back. He doesn't like the west as well as the Island. He says, 'I'll be very happy to be home again.'"

And at that very moment, as if waiting for the signal, the sun broke out of the clouds above the Silver Bush and the kitchen was flooded with dancing lights and elfin leaf shadows.

"So that's that," said Joe, a bit glumly. He whistled to Snicklefritz and went out.

Pat and Bets were weeping wildly in each other's arms. Judy got up with a grunt.

"Oh, oh, and what's all the tears for, I'm asking ye? I thought ye'd be dancing for joy."

"You're crying yourself, Judy." Pat laughed through her tears.

"Sure and it's the tinder heart av me. I cud niver see inny one crying that I didn't jine in. Haven't I wept the quarts at the funerals av people who didn't be mattering a hoot to me? I'm that uplifted I wudn't call the quane me cousin. Oh, oh, and it's me limon pies that are burned as black as a cinder in me oven. Well, well, I'll just be making another batch. We've had minny a good bite here and plaze the Good Man Above we'll have minny another. It's been a hard wake av it but iverything do be coming to an ind sometime if only ye do be living to see it."

Pat had put on gladness like a garment. She wondered if anybody had ever died of happiness.

"I just couldn't have borne it, Pat, if you went away," sobbed Bets.

Jingle had said nothing. He had sniffed desperately, determined not to let any one see *him* cry. He was at that moment lying face downwards in the mint along Jordan and McGinty could have told you what he was doing. But McGinty wasn't worried. His ears stuck up for he knew somehow that, in spite of shaking shoulders, his chum was happy.

4

Pat came dancing down the hill that night on feet that hardly seemed to touch the earth. She halted under the Watching Pine to gloat over Silver Bush, all her love for it glowing like a rose in her face. It had never looked so beautiful and beloved. How nice to see the smoke curling up from its chimney! How jolly and comfortable the fat, bursting old barns looked, where hundreds of kittens yet unborn would frisk! The wind was singing everywhere in the trees. Over her was a soft, deep, loving sky. Every field she looked on was a friend. The asters along the path were letters of the poem in her heart. She seemed to move and breathe in a trance of happiness. She was a reed in a moonlit pool . . . she was a wind in a wild garden . . . she was the stars and the lights of home . . . she was . . . she was Pat Gardiner of Silver Bush!

"Oh, dear God, this is such a lovely world," she whispered.

"A nice hour to be coming in for yer supper," said Judy.

"I was so happy I forgot all about supper. Oh, Judy, I'll always love this day. I'm so happy I'm a little frightened . . . as if it couldn't be *right* to feel so happy."

"Oh, oh, drink all the happiness ye can, me darlint, whin the cup is held to yer lips," said Judy wisely. "Now be after ating yer liddle bite and thin to bed. I packed yer mother off whin Cuddles wint. *She* hasn't been slaping much of late ather I'm telling ye, though the Selbys kape their falings to thimselves. Oh, oh, and so Madam Binnie won't be bossing things here for a while yet. And what may ye be thinking av that, me Gintleman Tom?"

"I don't know if I'll be able to sleep much even to-night, Judy. It's lovely to be so happy you can't sleep."

But Pat was sound as a bell when Judy crept in to see if the little sisters had the extra blanket for the chill September night.

"Oh, oh, she'll niver be quite that young agin," whispered Judy. "It's such a time as she's had that makes even the liddle craturs old in their sowls. If one cud be after spanking Long Alec now as I did whin he was a b'y!".

19

"AM I SO UGLY JUDY?"

1

For the first time Pat was getting ready to go to a party . . . a real, evening party which Aunt Hazel was giving for two of her husband's nieces who were visiting her. It was what Uncle Tom called a "double-barrelled party" . . . girls and boys of Winnie's and Joe's age for Elma Madison and young fry from ten to twelve for Kathleen. Sid pretended to hate the whole thing and vowed he wouldn't go till the last minute when he suddenly changed his mind . . . perhaps because Winnie twitted him with sulking because May Binnie wasn't invited.

"Sure and ye wudn't be expicting she wud be," said Judy loftily. "Since whin have the Binnies set themselves up for the aquals av the Gardiners . . . or aven av the Madisons I'm asking ye."

Pat was very glad when Sid decided to go for Bets was laid up with a sore throat and Jingle, though invited, couldn't or wouldn't go because his only decent suit of clothes had become absurdly tight for him. He had hoped that his mother might send him money for a new suit at Christmas but Christmas had passed as usual without present or letter.

"It's lovely to be nearly eleven," Pat was exulting to Judy. "I'm almost one of the big girls now."

"That ye are," said Judy with a sigh.

It was exciting to be dressing for a real party. Winnie had already gone to several and it was one of the dear delights of Pat's life to sit on the bed and watch her getting ready. But to be dressing yourself!

"Yellow's yer colour, me jewel," said Judy, as Pat slipped into her little party frock of primrose voile. "Sure and whin yer mother talked av getting the Nile grane I put me foot down. 'One grane dress is enough in a life-time,' sez I to her. 'Don't ye be remimbering all the bad luck she had in the one ye got her for the widding? Niver once did she put it on but something happened her or it.'"

"That was true, Judy, now that I come to think of it. I had it on when I broke mother's Crown Derby plate . . . and quarrelled with Sid . . . we'd never done that before . . . and found the hole in my stocking leg at church . . . and put too much pepper in the turnips the day Aunt Frances was here to dinner. . . ."

"'And innyhow,' sez I, clinching the matter like, 'grane doesn't be suiting her complexion.' So the yellow it is and ye'll look like a dancing buttercup in it."

"But I won't be dancing, Judy. I'm not old enough. We'll just play games. I do hope they won't play Clap in and Clap out. They do that so often at school and I hate it . . . because . . . because, Judy, none of the boys ever pick me out to sit beside. I'm not pretty, you know."

Pat said it without bitterness. Her lack of beauty had never worried her. But Judy tossed her head.

"They'd better wait till ye come into yer full looks afore they say that, I'm thinking. Now, here's a trifle av scint for yer hanky . . ."

"Put a little bit behind my ears, too . . . please, Judy."

"That I won't. Scint behind the ears is no place for dacency. A drop on yer hanky and maybe a dab on yer frill. Here's yer bit av blue fox for yer neck . . . though I'm not seeing where the blue comes in. But it sets ye. Now hold yer head up wid the best of thim and don't be forgetting ye're a Gardiner. Ye're to recite I'm hearing?"

"Yes. Aunt Hazel asked me to. I've been practising to the little spruce bushes behind the hen-house. Bets was to sing if she hadn't got a bad throat. It's just too mean she's sick. It would have been so wonderful to go to our first party together. I know I'll be lonesome. I don't know many of the Silverbridge girls. And I'll miss Bets so. She's lovely, Judy. They say Kathie Madison is pretty but I'm sure she isn't prettier than Bets."

Joe and Winnie and Sid and Pat all piled into the cutter to drive to Silverbridge through the fine blue crystal of the early winter evening, along roads where slender, lacy trees hung darkly against the rose and gold of the sky. That was fun . . . and at first the party was fun, too. Kathleen Madison *was* pretty . . . the prettiest girl Pat had ever seen in her life. A girl with close-cut curls of dark glossy gold, a skin of milk and roses, a dimpled bud of a mouth, and brilliant bluish-green eyes. Pat heard Chet Taylor of South Glen say she was worth walking three miles to see.

Well and good. It did not bother Pat. The evening went with a swing. The Silverbridge girls were all nice and friendly. They *did* play Clap in and Clap out but Mark Madison asked Pat to sit with him so it did not matter if half a dozen other boys were jealously trying for Kathie. Oh, parties *were* fun!

Then, in an evil moment Pat's hair bow fell off and she ran upstairs to put it on. Kathie Madison was in the room, too, pinning together a rent in the lace of her frock. As Pat stood before the looking-glass Kathie came and stood beside her. There was no particular malice in Kathie. She liked Pat Gardiner, as almost every girl did. But unluckily Mark Madison was the one boy Kathie had wanted for Clap in and Clap out. So she came and stood by Pat.

"It's a lovely party, isn't it?" she said. "Your dress is real pretty. Only . . . do you think yellow goes well with such a brown skin?"

Something happened to Pat, as she looked at herself and Kathie in the mirror . . . something that had never happened before. It was not jealousy . . . it was a sudden, dreadful despair. *She was ugly!* Standing beside this fairy girl she was ugly. Pale hair . . . a brown face . . . a mouth like a straight line and a much too long straight line . . . Pat shuddered.

"What's the matter?" asked Kathie.

"Nothing. I just hit my funny bone," said Pat valiantly. But everything had burst like a bubble. There was no more fun for her that evening. She even hated Mark Madison. He must have asked her to sit with him only out of pity . . . or because Aunt Hazel had ordered him to do it. She could not eat Aunt Hazel's wonderful supper and her recitation fell flat because as Uncle Robert said, she did not put any pep in it. Pep! Pat felt that she would never have pep again. She only wished she could get away home and cry. She did cry, quietly, as they drove home through the sparkling night of windless frost, over shadow-barred moonlit roads, between black velvet trees. All the beauty of the night was wasted on Pat who could see nothing but herself and Kathie side by side in the glass.

When she got home she slipped into the Poet's room to have another look at herself. Yes, there was no doubt about it. She was ugly. One did not mind not being very pretty. When Uncle Brian the last time he had been down, had said to her on leaving, "Try to be better looking when I come back," Pat had laughed with the others . . . all except Judy, who had sent a very black look after Brian.

But to be ugly. The tears welled up in Pat's eyes. She had never thought she was ugly until she had seen herself beside Kathie. Now she *knew*. What a way for a lovely party to end! Talk about green being unlucky! Nothing worse than this could have happened to her in green. It was she who was unlucky. Nobody would ever love her . . . . Bets couldn't really care for an ugly friend . . . Jingle must just have been making fun of her when he told her she had a cute nose and lovely eyes. Eyes . . . just between yellow and brown . . . they had looked just like a cat's beside Kathie's enormous blue orbs. And her lashes!

"Even if mine were long I couldn't flicker them like she does," thought Pat disconsolately, forgetting that Kathie had "flickered" them in vain at Mark Madison.

Pat's bed was by the window where she could see the sunrise . . . if she woke early enough. She woke early enough the next morning but the wild red sunrise through the trees and its light falling over the white snow-fields did not thrill her. She had very little to say at breakfast. She told Judy dully that the party had been "very nice." She went to school, blind to the aerial colouring of the opal winter day and the dance of loose snow over the meadows. She kept aloof from all the girls who had also been at the party. They were raving over Kathleen's looks. Pat simply couldn't bear it.

141

She had never been jealous of a girl's looks before. Bets was pretty and Pat was proud of her. To be sure she had always hated Norma but that was because Norma was said to be prettier than Winnie. She wondered if Jingle thought her *very* ugly. She remembered the coloured chromo of the pretty little girl in the Gordon parlour which she knew Jingle adored. She did not know he adored it because he had heard some one say it looked like his mother. As Pat remembered it it looked like Kathie. Pat writhed.

Did everybody think her ugly? The old man who called around once a week selling fish always addressed her as "Pretty." But then he called everybody pretty. She had never thought she was pretty . . . she had never thought much about her looks at all. And now she could think of nothing else. She was ugly . . . nobody would ever like her . . . Sid and Joe would be ashamed of their ugly sister. . . .

"Patricia, have you finished your composition?"

Patricia hadn't. How could you write compositions when the heart of you was broken?

2

There was company for supper at Silver Bush that night and Judy was too busy to pay any attention to Pat, although she watched her out of the tail of her eye. Pat had to wash the supper dishes. Ordinarily she made a saga of doing it. She liked to wash pretty dishes. Pat loved everything about the house but she loved the dishes particularly. It was such fun to make them clean and shining in the hot soapy water. She always washed her favourites first. The dishes she didn't like had just to wait until she was good and ready for them and it was fun to picture their dumb, glowering wrath as they waited *and* waited and saw the others preferred before them. That hideous old brown plate with the chipped edges . . . how furious it got! "It's *my* turn now . . . I'm an old family plate . . . I won't be treated like this . . . I've been at Silver Bush for fifty years . . . that stuck-up thing with the forget-me-nots on the rim has only been here for a year." But it always had to wait until the very last in spite of its howls. To-night Pat washed it first. Poor thing, it couldn't help being ugly.

She was glad of bedtime and crept off in mingled moonlight and twilight, while the purple shadows gathered along the lee of the snowdrifts behind the well and the west wind in the silver bush was twisting the birches mercilessly.

And then Judy, who had been out milking, invaded the room with a resolute air.

"What do be ailing ye, Pat? Sure and if ye're faling the way ye've been looking all day there's something sarious the matter. Wandering around widout a word to throw to a dog and peering into the looking-glass be times as if ye was after seeing if the wrinkles was coming. Make a clane breast av it, darlint."

Pat sat up.

"Oh, Judy, it's such a terrible thing to be ugly, isn't it, Judy? *Am* I so very ugly, Judy?"

"So *that's* it? Oh, oh, and who's been telling ye ye was ugly if a body may ask?"

"Nobody. But at the party Kathie Madison stood beside me in front of the glass . . . and I saw it for myself."

"Oh, oh, there's not minny girls but wud look a bit plainer than common beside me fine Kathleen. I'm not denying she's handsome. And so was her mother afore her. But she wasn't after getting any more husbands than her homely sister for all av that . . . only one and that one no great shakes I'm telling ye. Wid all her looks she tuk her pigs to a poor market. It isn't the beauties that make the good marriages as a rule, Patsy darlint. There was Cora Davidson now at the Bay Shore. She was that good-looking the min were said to be crazy over her. But it's the fact, Patsy darlint, and her own mother it was that tould me, there niver was but one axed her to marry him. He axed her on Widnesday and on Thursday they took him to a lunatic asylum. Oh, I'm telling ye. And have ye iver heard what happened at her sister Annie's widding supper? They had the cake made in Charlottetown a wake before be way of being more stylish than their neighbours and whin the bride made a jab at it to cut it didn't a bunch av mice rin out and scamper all over the table? Oh, oh, the scraming and jumping! More like a wake than a widding! The Davidsons niver hilt up their heads agin for minny a long day I'm telling you."

It was no use. Pat was not to be side-tracked by any of Judy's tales to-night.

"Oh, Judy, I hate to think I'm so ugly my family will be ashamed of me . . . people will call me 'that plain Gardiner girl.' Last week at the pie social at Silverbridge nobody would buy Minnie Fraser's pie because she was so ugly . . ."

Pat's voice broke on a sob. Judy perceived that skilful handling was required. She sat down on Pat's bed and looked very lovingly at her. The dear liddle thing wid her wide, frindly smile, as if she did be imbracing all the world, and the golden-brown swateness of her eyes! Thinking she was ugly! Setting off in such high cockalorum for her first liddle party and coming home wid her bit av a heart half bruk in two!

"I'm not saying ye're handsome, Patsy, but I *am* saying it's distinguished looking ye are. Ye haven't come into yer looks yet. Wait ye a few years till ye've outgrown yer arms and legs. Wid yer eyes and a bit av luck ye'll get a finer husband than minny av thim."

"Oh, Judy, it's not husbands I'm thinking of," sobbed Pat impatiently. "And I don't want to be terribly handsome. Bets and I read a story last week about a girl who was so beautiful crowds rushed out to see her and a king died for love of her. I wouldn't want that. I just want to be pretty enough so that people wouldn't mind looking at me."

"And who's been minding looking at ye, I'd like to know," said Judy fiercely. "If that stuck-up puss av a Kathie Madison said innything to hurt yer liddle falings . . ."

"It wasn't what she said, Judy, so much as the way she said it. 'Such a brown skin' . . . as if I was an Indian. Oh, Judy, I can't outgrow my skin, can I?"

"There's thim that thinks a brown skin handsomer than all yer Miss Pink-and-whites. She'll freckle in summer, that one."

"And I'm not even clever, Judy. I can only love people . . . and things."

"Oh, oh, 'tis a great gift that . . . and it's not ivery one that has it, me jewel. Now, we'll just be seeing where ye are for looks, rale calm and judicial like. Ye've got the fine eyes, as Jingle told ye . . ."

"And a cute nose, he said, Judy. *Have* I?"

"Ye have that . . . and the dainty liddle eye-brows . . . oh, oh, but ye've got no ind av good p'ints . . . and the nice ears like liddle pink shells. I warrant ye that Kathie one hasn't much to brag av in ears . . . not if she's a Madison."

"Her hair hid them mostly but I got a glimpse of one . . . It *did* stick out," confessed Pat.

"I'm telling ye! Yer mouth may be a bit wide but ye're not seeing the way it curls up at the corners whin ye laugh, darlint. Oh, oh, ye've got a way av laughing, Patsy. And the 'ristocratic ankles av ye! I'll be bound that Kathie one has a bit too much beef on hers."

"Yes, Kathie *has* fat ankles," Pat recalled to her comforting. "But she has such lovely hair. Look at mine . . . straight as a string and just the colour of ginger."

"Yer hair will be getting darker all the time, me jewel. Sure and the wonder is ye girls have inny skin or hair at all, running round in sun and wind bare-headed as ye do. Yer mother and her leddy sisters all wore sunbonnets I'm telling ye."

"Oh, Judy, that would be horrid. I *love* the sun and wind."

"Oh, oh, thin don't be howling bekase yer skin is brown and yer hair all faded. Ye can't ate yer cake and have it, too. I'm guessing it's healthier."

"Winnie has such lovely curls. I don't see why I haven't any."

"Winnie do be Selby and ye do be Gardiner. Yer mother now . . . oh, oh, but she had the rale permanent, so she had, that yer Aunt Jessie cudn't have if she had her head boiled and baked for a year. But ye've got a flavour av yer own and a tongue as swate as violets whin ye begin blarneying . . . and whin ye smile yer eyes twinkle like yer Grandmother Gardiner's . . . and she was the prettiest ould leddy I iver laid me eyes on. And ye've got a way av looking at a body and dropping yer eyes and thin looking agin that's going to play havoc some day. I've seen me lad Jingle's face whin ye looked at him so."

"Judy . . . have I really?"

"Oh, oh, maybe I shudn't be telling ye av it . . . not but what ye'd find it out sooner or later. I'm telling ye, Patsy darlint, a look like that is worth all the blue eyes and liddle red mouths in the world. Yer mother had it. Oh, oh, *she* knew all the tricks in her day."

"Father says mother was a great belle when she was a girl, Judy."

"Well may he say it for the hard time he had to get her! Ivery one thought she wud take Fred Taylor. Oh, oh, but he had the silver tongue. He cud wheedle the legs off an iron pot. But whin it came to the last ditch sure and she laped it wid yer dad. Minny was the sore heart at her widding."

"But she was pretty, Judy."

"Her own sister . . . yer Aunt Doris . . . wasn't pretty I'm telling ye, and she had more beaus than yer mother aven. Sure and I think it was bekase she always looked so slapy the min wanted to wake her up. She was the lazy one av the Bay Shore girls but ivery one liked her nixt to yer mother. Yer Aunt Evelyn had the prettiest arms and shoulders av the lot . . . as ye'll have yersilf some day, darlint, whin ye get a liddle more mate on yer bones. Yer Aunt Flora now . . . *she* was the flirt. She tried to flirt wid ivery one in sight. Now there's niver no sinse in that, Patsy dear. A few like to kape yer hand in . . . but not ivery one. Remimber that whin yer time comes."

"Kathie told me that Jim Madison climbed to the top of the biggest tree at Silverbridge to see if he could pick a star for her."

"Oh, oh, but did he get the star, darlint? There's inny number av ways av showing off. Now just ye be going to slape wid a good heart. Ye've got a liddle better opinion of yersilf I be thinking?"

"A whole lot better, Judy. I guess I've been pretty silly. But I did look so brown . . ."

"Sure and I'll tell ye an ould beauty secret, Patsy dear. Whin the spring comes just ye run out ivery morning and wash yer face in morning dew. I'm not saying it'll make ye pink and white like Kathleen but it'll make yer skin like satin."

"Really, Judy?"

"Sure and isn't it in me book av Useful Knowledge? I'll be showing it to ye to-morrow."

"Why haven't *you* done that, Judy?"

"Oh, oh, nothing cud make inny diffrunce to me old elephant's hide. Ye've got to begin it young. Georgie Shortreed made a rigular beauty av hersilf that way, so she did, and made a good match in a fam'ly that was as full av ould maids as a pudding av plums. Was I iver telling ye how her sister Kitty lost her one chanct? Sure and didn't she throw a pan av dish-water over her beau one night, accidental like, whin he was standing on the kitchen dure-step, trying to get up enough spunk to knock . . . him being a bould young lad av fifty wid a taste for ugly girls and not used to sparking. Away he wint and niver come back, small wonder, for wasn't his bist suit ruint entirely wid grase? The Shortreeds all had that lazy trick av opening the dure and letting the dish-water fly right and lift widout looking. Was I iver telling ye how their ould dad, Dick Shortreed, quarrelled wid his marching neighbour, Ab Bollinger, over a hin?"

"No." Pat snuggled down on her pillow, happy again and ready to taste Judy's yarns.

"They fought over the hin for three years and wint to law about it . . . to the magistrate innyway . . . and 'twas the joke av the country side. And after they had spint more money than wud buy a hundred hins this same Ab Bollinger's daughter up and married ould Dick Shortreed's son and the ould folks made up their quarrel and killed the hin for the widding supper. 'Twas a tough bite I'm thinking be that time."

After Judy went out Pat slipped out of bed to the window where the moonlight was glittering on the frosted panes. Winnie had not come up yet and the night was very still. Pat could see the fields of crystal snow, the shadows in the Whispering Lane, and the silver fringe of icicles on the church barn. A light was shining in Bets' dormer up at the Long House. She was good friends with the world again. What did it matter if she had no great beauty herself? She had the beauty of shining meadows . . . of moon secrets in field and grove . . . of beloved Silver Bush.

Still, it was a comfort as she crept to bed again to remember that Kathie had the Madison ears.

20

SHORES OF ROMANCE

1

"Sure and it'll rain afore night," said Judy at noon. "Look how clare ye can see yer Hill av the Mist."

Pat hoped it wouldn't rain. She and Jingle had planned a walk to the shore. This was by way of being a treat to Pat for although you could, from Silver Bush, see the great gulf to the north and the shimmering blue curve of the harbour to the east, it was a mile and a half to the shore itself and the Silver Bush children did not often get down. Pat felt that she needed something to cheer her up. Buttons, the dearest kitten that had ever been at Silver Bush . . . to be sure, every kitten was that . . . had died that morning without rhyme or reason. All his delights were over . . . frisking in the "dim" . . . flying up trees . . . catching small mice in the jungle of the Old Part . . . basking on the tombstones. Pat had tearfully buried this little dead thing that only yester-night had been so beautiful.

Besides, she was "out" with Sid over his frog. Pat was always so sorry for imprisoned things and Sid had had that poor frog in a pail in the yard for a week. Every time Pat looked at it it seemed to look at her appealingly. Perhaps it had a father or mother or husband or wife in the pool. Or even just a dear friend to whom it longed to be reunited. So Pat carried it away to the Field of the Pool and Sid hadn't spoken to her for two days.

All the afternoon the heat waves shimmered over the Buttercup Field and the sun "drew water" . . . as if some far-off Weaver in the west were spinning shining threads of rain between sky and sea. But it was still a lovely evening when Jingle and Pat . . . and McGinty . . . started for the shore, although far down on the lowlands was a smudge of fog here and there, with little fir trees sticking spectrally up out of it.

"Don't ye go and get drownded now," warned Judy, as she always did when anybody went to the shore. "And mind ye don't fall over the capes or get caught be the tide or run over by an auty afore ye get to the shore road or . . ." but they were out of hearing before Judy could think up any more "ors."

Pat loved that long red road that wandered on until it reached the sea, twisting unexpectedly just because it wanted to, among the spruce "barrens," where purple sheep laurel bordered the path and meadow-sweet and blue-eyed grass grew along the fences. "Kiss-me-quicks," Judy called the blue-eyed grasses. Pat liked this name best but you couldn't call it that to a boy. They rambled happily on, sucking honey-filled horns of red clover, a mad, happy little dog tearing along before them with his tongue out. Sometimes they talked and sometimes they didn't. That was what Pat liked about Jingle. You didn't have to talk to him unless you wanted to.

Half way to the shore they had to call at Mr. Hughes', where Jingle had an errand for his uncle. The Hughes house was a rather tumbledown one but it had some funny twinkly windows that Jingle liked. Jingle was always on the lookout for windows. They had a peculiar fascination for him. He averred that the windows of a house made or marred it.

"Will I put windows like that in your house, Pat?"

Pat giggled. Jingle had put all kinds of windows in that imaginary house of hers already.

She would rather have waited outside and looked at the windows, even if more than one of the panes was broken and stuffed with rags, while Jingle did his errand but he dragged her in. Jingle knew that there were three Hughes girls there and face them alone he would not.

Mr. Hughes was out but they were asked to sit down and wait until he came in. Neither felt at home. The Hughes kitchen was in what Judy would have called a "tarrible kilter" and a black swarm of flies had settled on the dirty dishes of the supper table. Sally and Bess and Cora Hughes sat in a row behind the table and grinned at the callers . . . a malicious grin not in the least likely to put shy or sensitive people at their ease. Pat knew them only slightly but she had heard of them.

"Which of us girls," said Bess to Jingle with an impish, green-eyed smile, "are you going to marry when you grow up?"

Jingle's face turned a dark, uncomfortable red. He shuffled his bare feet but did not answer.

"Oh, ain't you the bashful one?" giggled Sally. "Just look how he's blushing, girls."

"I'm going to get ma's tape and measure his mouth," said Cora, sticking her tongue out at Jingle.

Jingle looked hunted and desperate but still would not speak . . . could not, probably. Pat was furious. These girls were making fun of Jingle. She recalled a word she had heard the minister use in his sermon last Sunday. Pat had no idea what it meant but she liked the sound of it. It was dignified.

"Don't mind them, Jingle. They are nothing but protoplasms," she said scornfully.

For a moment it worked. Then the Hughes temper broke.

"Skinny!" cried Bess.

"Shrimp!" cried Cora.

"Moon-face!" cried Sally.

and,

"*You* needn't get your Scotch up, Pat Gardiner," they all cried together.

"Oh, I'm not angry, if that's what you mean," said Pat icily. "I'm only sorry for you."

This got under the Hughes skins.

"Sorry for us?" Bess laughed nastily. "Better be sorry for your old Witch Judy. She's going straight to the Bad Place when she dies. Witches do."

There was an end to all dignity. Pat tossed her head.

"Judy isn't a witch. I think your father is a cousin of Mary Ann McClenahan's, isn't he?"

There was no denying this. But Sally got even.

"Why doesn't your mother ever come to see you," she asked Jingle.

"I don't think that is any business of yours," said Pat.

"I wasn't addressing you, *Miss* Gardiner," retorted Sally. "Better hang *your* tongue out to cool."

"Now, now, what's all this fuss about?"

Mrs. Hughes waddled into the room with an old felt hat of her husband's atop of her rough hair. She subsided into a mangy old plush chair and looked reproachfully at everybody.

"Who's been slapping your face, Jingle? You girls been teasing him I s'pose. I declare I don't see why you can't try and act as if you'd been *raised*. You mustn't mind their nonsense, Jingle. They're a bit too fond of their fun."

Fun! If it was fun to insult callers! But Mr. Hughes came in at last. Jingle delivered his uncle's message and they got away. McGinty had long since fled and was waiting for them on the shore road.

"Let's forget all about it," said Pat. "We won't spoil our walk by thinking about them."

"It's not *them*," said Jingle, too miserable to care whether he was ungrammatical or not. "It's what they said about . . . about mother."

2

It was so lovely at the shore that they soon forgot the Hughes episode. They passed by the old, wind-beaten spruces of Tiny Cove and ran down to where the wind and shore were calling each other. Fishing boats went past, wraith-like. Far-off was the thunder of waves on the bar but here the sea crouched and purred. They raced along the shore with the sting of the blowing sand in their faces. They waded in the pools among the rocks. They built "sea-palaces" with shells and driftwood. Finally they sat them down on a red rock in a little curve below the red "capes" and looked far out in the soft fading purple of the longshore twilight to some magic shore beyond the world's rim.

"Would you like to go away 'way out there, Pat?"

"No." Pat shivered. "It would be too far from home."

"I think *I* would," said Jingle dreamily. "There's so much in the world I want to see . . . the great palaces and cathedrals men have built. I want to learn how to build them, too. But . . ."

Jingle stopped. He knew it was no use to hope for such a thing. He must, as far as he could see, spend his life picking up stones and grubbing out young spruce trees on his uncle's farm.

"Joe used to say he would like to be a sailor like Uncle Horace," said Pat. "He said he hated farming, but he hasn't said anything about it lately. Father wouldn't listen to him."

"School will begin next week," said Jingle. "I hate to go. Miss Chidlaw will want me to join the entrance class . . . and what's the use? I can't get to Queen's . . . ever."

"You want to go, Jingle?"

"Of course I want to go. It's the first step. But . . . I can't."

"Next year they'll want *me* to join the entrance but I'm not going to," said Pat resolutely. "I don't want to go to college. I'm just going to stay at Silver Bush and help Judy. Oh, isn't the salt tang in the air here lovely, Jingle? I wish we could come to the shore oftener."

"The mists down by the harbour look like ghosts, don't they? And look at that little, lonely ship away over there . . . it looks as if it was drifting over the edge of the world. There's a fog coming in from sea. I guess maybe we'd better be going, Pat."

There was only one objection to their going. While they had sat there the tide had come in. It was almost at their feet now. The rocks at the cape points were already under water. They looked at each other with suddenly whitened faces.

"We . . . we can't get around the capes," gasped Pat.

Jingle looked at the rocks above them. Could they climb them? No, not here. They overhung too much.

"Will we . . . be drowned, Jingle?" whispered Pat, clutching him.

Jingle put his arm around her. He must be brave and cool for Pat's sake.

"No, of course not. See that little cave in the cape? We can climb up to it. I'm almost sure the tide never rises as high as that."

"Oh, you can't be sure," said Pat. "Remember Judy's stories of people being caught by the tide and drowned."

"That was in Ireland. I never heard of it happening here. Come . . . quick."

Jingle caught up McGinty and they raced through the water which was by now almost to their knees. Two rather badly scared children scrambled up into the little cave. As a matter of fact they need not have been scared. The cave was well above high tide mark. But neither of them was quite sure of that. They sat huddled together with McGinty between them. McGinty at least was quite easy in his mind. Indian plains and Lapland snows were all the same to McGinty when the two people he loved were with him.

Pat's panic subsided after a few minutes. She always felt safe with Jingle. And it wasn't likely the tide rose this high. But how long would it be before they could escape? The folks at home would be wild with fright. If they had only remembered Judy's warning!

But, in spite of everything, the romance of it appealed to Pat. Marooned in a cave by the tide was romantic if ever anything was. As for Jingle, if he had been sure that they were quite safe, he would have been perfectly happy. He had Pat all to himself . . . something that didn't happen very often since Bets had come to the Long House. Not but what he liked Bets. But Pat was the only girl with whom Jingle never felt shy.

"If those horrid Hughes girls could see us now wouldn't they laugh," giggled Pat. "But I'm sorry I let them make me mad. Judy says you must never lower yourself to be mad with *scum*."

"I wasn't mad," said Jingle, "but what they said about mother hurt. Because . . . it's *true*."

Pat squeezed his hand sympathetically.

"I'm sure she'll come some day, Jingle."

"I've given up hoping it," said Jingle bitterly. "She . . . she never sent me a card last Christmas at all."

"Doesn't she answer your letters, Jingle . . . ever?"

"I . . . I never send the letters, Pat," said Jingle miserably. "I've never sent any of them. I write them every Sunday but I just keep them in a box in an old chest. She never answered the first one I sent . . . so I never sent any more."

Pat just couldn't help it. She felt so sorry for Jingle . . . writing those letters Sunday after Sunday and never sending them. Impulsively she put her arm around his neck and kissed his cheek.

"There's no one like you in all the world, Pat," said Jingle comforted.

"Hear, hear," said the thuds of McGinty's tail.

Far-away shores were now only dim grey lands. The dark shadows of the oncoming night were all around them.

"Let's pretend things to pass the time," suggested Pat. "Let's pretend the rocks dance . . ."

"Let's pretend things about that old house up there," said Jingle.

The old house was on the top of the right cape. It was not one of the fish-houses that sprinkled the shore. Two generations ago it had been built by an eccentric Englishman who had brought his family out from England and lived there mysteriously. He seemed to have plenty of money and there were gay doings in the house until his wife died. Then he had left the Island as suddenly as he had come. Nobody would buy a house in such a place and it had sunk into a ruin. Its windows were broken . . . its chimneys had toppled down. The wind and the mist were the only guests now in rooms that had once echoed to music and laughter and dancing feet. In the gathering shadows the old house had the look of fate which even a commonplace building assumes beneath the falling night . . . as if it brooded over dark secrets . . . grim deeds whereof history has no record.

"I wonder if anybody was ever murdered in that house," whispered Pat, with a delicious creepy thrill.

They peopled the old house with the forms of those who had once lived there. They invented the most grewsome things. The Englishman had killed his wife . . . had thrown her over the cape . . . had buried her under the house . . . her ghost walked there on nights like this. On stormy nights the house resounded with weeping and wailing . . . on moonlit nights it was full of *shadows* . . . restless, uneasy shadows. They scared themselves nearly to death and McGinty, excited by their tragic voices, howled dismally.

All at once they were too scared to go on pretending. It was dark . . . too dark to see the gulf although they could hear it. The bar moaned. An occasional bitter splash of rain blew into their cave. The little waves sobbed on the lonely shore. The very wind seemed full of the voices of the ghosts they had created. It was an eerie place . . . Pat snuggled close to Jingle.

"Oh, I wish somebody would come," she whispered.

Wishes don't often come true on the dot but Pat's did. A dim bobbing light came into sight out on the water . . . it drew nearer . . . there was a boat with a grizzled old fisherman in it. Jingle yelled wildly and the boat pulled in to the cape. Andrew Morgan lifted a lantern and peered at them.

"I-golly, if it isn't the Gordon boy and the Gardiner girl! Whatever are ye doing there? Caught by the tide, hey? Well, it's a bit of luck for ye that I took the notion to row down to Tiny Cove for a bag of salt. I heered that dog yelping and thought I'd better see where he was. Climb down now . . . a bit careful . . . ay, that's the trick. And where do ye want to go?"

3

Two thankful children were duly landed in the cove and lost no time in scampering home. A lovely clean rain was pelting down but they did not mind it. They burst into Judy's kitchen joyfully . . . out of the wind and rain and dark into the light of home. Why, the house was holding out its arms to them!

Judy was scandalised.

"Chilled to the bone ye are! Pewmony'll be the last of it."

"No, really, Judy, we kept warm running. Don't scold, Judy. And don't tell any one. Mother would worry so if we ever went to the shore again. I'll slip into a dry dress and Jingle can put on a shirt of Sid's. And you'll give us a snack, won't you, Judy? We're hungry as bears."

"Oh, oh, and ye might have been drowned . . . or if ould Andy Morgan hadn't come along . . . sure and for onct in his life the ould ninny was in the right place . . . ye'd av had to stay there till the tide turned . . . a nice scandal."

"The Hughes girls would have made one out of it anyway," laughed Pat.

"That tribe!" said Judy contemptuously, when she heard the story. "Sure and that Sally-thing is glib since she got her tongue righted. Charmed be a snake she was whin she was three years ould and cudn't talk plain agin for years."

"Charmed by a snake?"

"I'm telling ye. Curled upon the dure-step me fine snake was and Sally a-staring into its eyes. Her mother fetched it a swipe wid a billet av wood and Sally yelled as if she'd been hit herself. Old Man Hughes told me the tale himsilf so I lave ye to guess how much truth was in it. Maybe they was ashamed av the way she lisped . . . but there's no being up to snakes and one thing is certain . . . Sally had the cratur's hiss in her v'ice till she was six. Mary Ann McClenahan was be way av saying she was a changeling. Oh, oh, ye did well to give them a bar about Mary Ann. They ain't proud av the connection I'm telling ye. But . . . me memory's getting that poor . . . what was it ye was after calling them now?"

"Protoplasms," said Pat proudly.

"Oh, oh, that sounds exactly like thim, whin I come to think av it," nodded Judy. "Now sit ye down and ate yer liddle bite. I sint yer mother off to bed, niver letting on to her where ye'd gone and don't let me see ye coming home agin wid such didoes to yer credit."

"You know it would be dull if nothing out of the common ever happened, Judy. And if we never have any adventures we'll have nothing to remember when we get old."

"The sinse av her," said Judy admiringly.

21

WHAT WOULD JUDY THINK OF IT?

1

When Pat went to Silverbridge in September to spend a few days with Aunt Hazel she went willingly, for a brief exile from Silver Bush was not so terrible as it used to be and Aunt Hazel's home was a jolly place to visit. But when, just as the visit was nearly ended, word came that Cuddles and Sid were down with measles and that Pat must not come home until all danger of catching them was past, it was rather a cat of another colour. However, what with one thing and another, Pat contrived to enjoy herself tolerably well and consoled herself in her spasms of homesickness by writing letters to everybody.

(The letter to Bets. With a border of dinky little black cats inked in all around it.)

"Sweetheart Elizabeth:—

"I think 'sweetheart' is a *tenderer* word than darling, don't you? This is my birthday and your birthday and isn't it a shame we can't spend it together? But even if we couldn't be together I've been thinking of you all day and loving you. Aren't you glad our birthday is in September? I think it is one of the nicest things that ever happened me because September is my favourite month in the year. It's such a friendly month and it seems as if the year had stopped being in a hurry and had time to think about you.

"Bets, just think of it. We're twelve. It seems such a short time since I was a child. And just think, our next birthday we'll be in our teens. Uncle Robert's Maiden Aunt says once you are in your teens the years just whirl by and first thing you know you're old. I can't believe we'll ever be old, Bets . . . can you?

"I like it pretty well here. Aunt Hazel's place is lovely but everything would be prettier if you could share it with me. The window in my room looks out on the orchard and off to the left is a dear little valley all full of young spruces and shadows. I mean the spruces are young not the shadows. I think shadows are always *old*. They are lovely but I think I am always a little bit afraid of them because they are so very old. Aunt Hazel laughed when I said this and said notions like that were what came of Judy Plum stuffing us all with her yarns about fairies but I don't think that has anything to do with it. It's just that shadows always seem to me to be *alive*, especially when moonlight and twilight are mixing.

"I go over the road to Uncle Robert's brother's house quite often to play with Sylvia Cyrilla Madison. I like that name. It has a nice, ripply, gurgly sound like a brook. She is a nice girl but I can never like any one as well as you, Bets. I *like* Sylvia Cyrilla but I *love* you. Sylvia Cyrilla thinks Sid is very handsome. Somehow I don't like to hear her praise him. When her grown-up sister Mattie said the same thing I was *proud*. But I hated to hear Sylvia Cyrilla say it. Why?

PAT OF SILVER BUSH

"Sylvia Cyrilla's big brother, Bert, told her I was a cute little skeesicks. But probably he only said it out of politeness.

"Aunt Hazel is teaching me to make fudge and hemstitch. I like doing things like that but Sylvia Cyrilla says it's old-fashioned. She says girls have to have a career now. She is going to have one. But I'm sure I don't want one. Somebody has to make fudge and I notice Sylvia Cyrilla likes to eat it as well as any one.

"Jen Campbell is Sylvia Cyrilla's dearest friend. She is good fun but she doesn't like to be beaten in anything. When I said Sid and Cuddles had the measles she said proudly, 'I had mumps and measles and scarlet fever and middle ear in one year and now I have to get my tonsils out.' It made me feel very inexperienced.

"Jen says she wishes she had been born a boy. I don't, do you? I think it is just lovely to be a girl.

"I am writing this up in Aunt Hazel's garret and it's raining. I love to be in a garret when it's raining, don't you? I love a sweet, rainy darkness like there is outside. The rain seems so friendly when it's gentle. Uncle Rob says I'm a regular garret cat but the reason I like to be up here is because I can see the harbour from one window and Silver Bush from another. From here it just looks like a little white spot against the birch bush. I can't see your house but I can see the Hill of the Mist, only it is north of me now instead of being east. That gives me a queer, Alice-in-the-looking-glass feeling.

"To-night there are windy shadows flying over the harbour under the rain . . . like great long misty wings. It gives me a strange feeling when I look at them . . . it almost hurts me and yet I love them. Oh, Bets, darling, isn't it lovely to be alive and see things like that?

"I am going to tell you a secret. I wouldn't tell it to any one in the world but you. I know you won't laugh and I can't bear to have secrets from *you*.

"I think I fell in love last Sunday night at eight o'clock. Aunt Hazel took me to a sacred concert in Silverbridge given by three blind men. One played the piano and one played the violin and one sang. His singing was just *heavenly*, Bets, and he was so handsome. He had dark hair and a beautiful nose and the loveliest blue eyes although he was blind. When he began to sing I had such a queer sinking feeling at the pit of my stomach. I thought I must be getting religion, as Judy says, and then in a flash I knew what had happened to me because my knees were shaking. I asked Judy once how you cold tell when you fell in love and she said, 'Ye'll find yer legs trimbling a bit.'

"Oh, how I wished I could only do some splendid thing to make him notice me, or die for him. I was glad Aunt Hazel had scented my hands with toilet water before I left and that I had on my blue dress and my little blue necklace even if he couldn't see it. It would have been awful to fall in love if you had your old clothes on or if you had a cold in the head like poor Sylvia Cyrilla. She was sniffing and blowing her nose all the evening.

"Oh, I shall never forget it, Bets. But the trouble is it didn't last. It was all over by Monday morning. That seemed terrible because Sunday night I thought it would last to all eternity as it says in books. I don't feel a bit like that about him now, though it makes me a little dizzy just to remember it. Am I fickle? I'd hate to be fickle.

"Won't it be lovely when I can go home and we can be together again? I'm crossing every day off on the calendar and I pray every night that nobody else at Silver Bush will take measles. Please don't read any poetry under the Watching Pine until I get back. I can't bear to think of you being there without me.

"I must go to bed now and get my 'beauty sleep' as Uncle Rob says. I like the words 'beauty sleep.' Just suppose one *could* fall asleep ugly and wake up beautiful. That wouldn't seem so wonderful to you, darling, because you *are* beautiful, but poor me!

"It would be rather nice to have a blind husband because he wouldn't care if you weren't pretty. But I don't suppose I'll ever see him again.

"Think of me every moment you can.

"Your own,

"Patricia.

"P.S. Aunt Hazel says I ought to get my hair bobbed. But what would Judy say?"

2

(The letter to mother)

"My Own Sweetest Mother:—

"I'm just making believe you're *here*, mother, and that I'm feeling your arm around me. I'm just starving for you all. There is something pleasant about most of the days here but you seem so far away at night. Do you miss me? And does Silver Bush miss me? Dear Silver Bush. When I came up to the garret to-night and looked to where it was all was dead and dark. Then it just came to life with lights in all its windows and I thought I could see you all there, and Judy and Gentleman Tom, and I guess I cried a little.

"I was so glad to hear Sid and Cuddles were getting on all right. I hope Cuddles won't forget me. I'm glad you baked your letter in the oven so I wouldn't get germs in it, because it would be dreadful if just when I was ready to go home I'd come down with measles here. Mother dearest, I hope you don't have any of your bad headaches while I am away.

"I read my chapter in the Bible every night, mother, and say my prayers. Miss Martha Madison is here for a long visit. Uncle Robert calls her his Maiden Aunt behind her back and you can just see the capitals. Every night she comes in and asks me if I've said my prayers. I don't like strangers meddling with my prayers. It will soon be a year since dad came home from the west but still every night I thank God for it. I just can't thank Him enough. Jen says she has cousins out there and it is a splendid country. Likely it is . . . but it isn't Silver Bush.

"There's one thing I do like here, mother. The sheepskin rug by my bed. It's so nice to hop out of bed and dig your toes into a sheepskin rug, ever so much nicer than cold oilcloth or even a hooked mat. Can I have a sheepskin rug, mother? That is, if it won't hurt Judy's feelings.

"I had a lovely letter from Bets to-day. Mother, I do love Bets. I'm so glad that I have such a beautiful friend. There is something about her voice makes me think of the wind blowing through the Silver Bush. And her eyes are like *yours,* always looking as if she knew something lovely.

"You are just the loveliest mother. I like writing letters because it is easier to write things like that than say them.

"Mother, can my new winter dress be red? I love soft glowing colours like red. Sylvia Cyrilla says she would like to have a new dress every month but I wouldn't. I like to wear my clothes long enough to get fond of them. I hate to think that my last year's brown has got too small for me. I've had so many good times in that dear old dress. Mind you don't let Judy have any of my old things for hooking until I come home. I know she's got her eye on my yellow middy blouse but you can lengthen the sleeves, can't you, mother?

"There's a lovely moon rising over the harbour to-night although the wind sounds a little sad around the garret. Judy says that when I saw the full moon one night when I was three years old I said, 'Oh, see the man carrying a lantern in the sky.' Did I really?

"The Maiden Aunt says she likes lavender among sheets. When I said we always put sweet clover between ours she sniffed. Aunt Hazel said yesterday I could make the Brown Betty for dinner but I couldn't do it right with the Maiden Aunt looking on and watching for mistakes. So it wasn't good and I felt *humiliated* but anyhow I think Brown Betty sounds too cannibalish.

"I think Sylvia Cyrilla's mother just worships her parlour. She keeps it locked up and the blind down and only very special visitors ever get into it. I'm glad *we* live all over our house, mother.

"The Maiden Aunt says there will be a frost to-night. Oh, I hope not. I don't want the flowers to be nipped before I get back. But I noticed to-day that the yellow leaves have begun to fall from the poplars so the summer is over.

"I've just thrown a kiss out to the wind to carry to you. And I'm putting lots of kisses in this letter, a kiss for everybody and everything and a special kiss for father and Cuddles. Isn't it lucky love doesn't make a letter weigh any heavier? If it did this letter would be so heavy I couldn't afford the postage.

"Aunt Hazel's new baby is very sweet but not so pretty as Cuddles was. Oh, mother, there really isn't anybody like the Silver Bush people, is there? I think we're *such* a nice family! And you are the nicest person in it.

"Your devoted daughter,

"Pat.

"P.S. Aunt Hazel says I ought to have my hair bobbed. Do you think Judy would mind now? Sylvia Cyrilla says her mother cried for a week when she had hers bobbed but she likes it now.

"P.G."

3

(Letter to Sid)

"Dearest Sid:—

"I'm so glad to hear you are getting better and able to eat. The Maiden Aunt says you shouldn't be let eat much when you are getting over measles but I guess Judy knows better than a Maiden Aunt. I hated to think you were sick and me not there to fan your fevered brow or do a single thing for you. But I knew Judy would look after you if mother couldn't spare time from Cuddles.

"I like it here. It is a nice friendly house and Aunt Hazel lets me stay up till half past nine. But I will be glad when I can go home. I hope I won't take the measles but I think it would be real exciting to be sick. They would make such a fuss over me then. When you get well we must go back to our Secret Field and see how our spruces are.

"Sylvia Cyrilla says that Fred Davidson and his sister Muriel used to be devoted to each other just like you and me but they quarrelled and now they never speak. Oh, Sid, don't let us *ever* quarrel. I couldn't bear it.

"Of course they are only Davidsons.

"Sylvia Cyrilla says the South Glen Petersons got a bad scare last week. They thought Myrtle Peterson had eloped. But it turned out she was only drowned. And Sylvia says May Binnie is your girl. She isn't, is she, Sid? You'd never have a Binnie for a girl. They are not in our class.

"I wish you would marry Bets when you grow up. I wouldn't mind *her* coming to Silver Bush. She would love it as much as I do and I'm sure she'd make you a lovely wife. And she wouldn't mind my living with you I know.

"If the grey and white barn-cat has kittens tell Joe to save one for me.

"It will soon be ploughing time. I'll be home in time to help pick the apples. Bert Madison is teaching me how to tie a sailor's knot and I'll show you but you won't show May Binnie, will you, Sid?

"Your own dear sister,

"Pat.

"P.S. Aunt Hazel says I ought to have my hair bobbed. Do you think it would improve me? But what would Judy say?"

4

(Letter to Jingle)
"Dear Jingle:—

"It was ripping of you to write me so often. I'm glad you missed me. Nobody at Silver Bush have *said* they missed me. I supposed Sid and Cuddles were too sick to, and Winnie and Joe are so big now I guess I don't matter much to them.

"I'm up in the garret. I like to sit here and watch the trees in the spruce valley getting black and listen to the wind moaning round the chimneys. To-night it's the kind that Judy calls the ghost wind. It makes me think of that piece of poetry you read the last day we were in Happiness.

> "*The midnight wind came wild and dread*
> *Swelled with the voices of the dead.*

"Those lines always give me a lovely creepy shudder, Jingle, and I'm glad you feel it, too. Sid thinks it's all bosh. He laughs at me when I wonder what is the meaning of the things the trees are always saying and what some of the winds are always so sorry for. But you never laugh at me, Jingle. Every night here, before I go to sleep I lie still and think I can hear the water falling over the mossy rock in dear Happiness.

"How is McGinty? Give him a hug for me. The Maiden Aunt has a dog but I'm sorry for it. She never lets it out of her sight and the poor thing has nothing but a rubber rat to play with. They have several dogs at Sylvia Cyrilla's, Bert's dog and Myrtle's dog and the family dog, but none of these are as nice as McGinty. Uncle Rob's father down the road has a dog but he is not an exciting dog. Uncle Rob says he is always so tired he has to lean against a fence to bark. Speaking of dogs, I found such a lovely poem in Aunt Hazel's scrapbook called *The Little Dog Angel*. I cried when I read it because I thought of you and McGinty. I could just *see* McGinty slipping out of heaven's gates between St. Peter's legs to 'bark a welcome to you in the shivering dark.' Oh, Jingle, I'm sure dear little dogs like McGinty *must* have souls.

"I wonder what you'd think of Aunt Hazel's house. I think you'd say it was too tall. But it's really very nice inside. Only there are no back steps to sit on and no round window and no dead clock.

"What do you think, Jingle? Old Mr. Peter Morgan from the harbour told me he was a pirate in his young days and buried a treasure worth millions on a West Indies island and never could find the place again. If he had told me that four years ago I would have believed him but he has left it too late. I wish it was as easy to believe things as it used to be.

"The fence back of Uncle Robert's house is the line between Queen's and Prince county. It's perfectly thrilling, Jingle, to think you can go into another county just by climbing over a fence. Somehow you expect everything to be different. I climb over it every day just to get the nice adventure feeling. Aunt Hazel says it doesn't take much to give me a thrill but I think it is lucky. What would life be without a few thrills? And what would life be without Betses and Jingles and Sids and Judys and Silver Bushes?

"Chum Pat.

"P.S. Aunt Hazel says she thinks I ought to have my hair bobbed. Would you like me bobbed, Jingle?"

5

(Letter to Judy with Judy's comments)

"My Own Dear Judy:—

"It just seems ages since I left home and I've been so lonesome for you all and the dear old kitchen. Aunt Hazel's kitchen is very up to date but it isn't as cosy as ours, Judy. When I get homesick at nights I go up to the garret and watch the lights of Silver Bush and picture out what every one is doing and I see you setting bread in the kitchen, talking to yourself, *(fancy that now.)* And Gentleman Tom thinking away on his bench. *(Sure and it's the grand thinker ye are, Tom. I'm after telling the world ye can think more in a day than most folks can in a wake.)* They have no cats here because Uncle Robert's Maiden Aunt visits so often and so long and she doesn't like them. I don't like the Maiden Aunt very well. *(Oh, oh, small blame to ye for that, Patsy.)* She is very homely. I know I'm not much to look at myself but I haven't a nose like hers. Everything, even her hair, seems to be frightened of it and trying to get away from it. *(Sure and there's observation for ye.)* And yet I'm a little sorry for her, Judy, *(oh, oh, the tinder heart av her now)*, because she is really lonely. She hasn't anybody or any place to love. That must be dreadful.

"Aunt Hazel has the loveliest blue quilt, quilted in fans, on her spare bed. And she has the rose mat you hooked for her on her living room floor. She is very proud of it and points it out to every one. *(Oh, oh, so I'm getting me name up, it sames.)* She hasn't a parlour or she would have put it there. It isn't fashionable to have parlours now, Sylvia Cyrilla says. I don't know what she'd say if she knew we have *two. (Sure and who cares what she'd say? A parlour sounds far grander than a living room inny day.)*

"Mother says I can have a new red dress this winter, Judy. And I hope she'll let me get a little red hat to go with it. *(Oh, oh, but that would be rale chick.)* Jen Davidson says she is going to have two new hats. She says the Davidsons always do. Well, you can't wear more than one hat at a time, can you, Judy? *(The philosophy av her.)* The Maiden Aunt sniffs when I talk of clothes but Aunt Hazel says that is because she can't afford them herself and if Uncle Robert didn't help her out every year she wouldn't have a stitch to her back. *(Sure and folks don't be wanting minny stiches to their backs nowadays, jidging be the fashion books I've been seeing.)*

"Oh, Judy dear, the Maiden Aunt say it isn't right to tell fairy tales, not even that there is a Santa Claus. *(Set her up wid it.)* But I'm going to keep on believing in fairy rings and horseshoes over the door and witches on broomsticks. It makes life so thrilling to believe in things. If you believe in a thing it doesn't matter whether it exists or not. *(Sure and she cud argy a Philadelphy lawyer down, the darlint.)*

"We don't have any eating between meals here, Judy. I guess it's healthier but when bed-time comes I *do* think of your eggs and butter. I think a snack at bed-time is healthy. *(Sure and all sinsible people do be thinking the same.)* But Aunt Hazel is a good cook. She can make the loveliest ribbon cake. I wish you would learn to make ribbon cake, Judy. *(Oh, oh, yer ribbon cake, is it? I'm too old a dog to be larning yer new millinery tricks.)* But her cranberry pies aren't as nice as yours, Judy. They're too sweet. *(Oh, oh, the blarney of the cratur! She's after wanting to put me in the good humour.)* Sylvia Cyrilla's mother can make lovely Devonshire cream. *(Devonshire crame, is it? I cud make Devonshire crame afore she was born or thought of. But will ye be telling me where the crame is to come from wid ivery drop of milk sint off to the cheese factory?)* But she isn't a good cook in other ways. Her things *look* all right but something always *tastes* wrong. Not enough salt or too much, or no flavouring or something like that. *(No gumption, me jewel, that's the trouble. No gumption.)*

"Sylvia Cyrilla's father's cousin in Charlottetown tried to cut his throat last week but Sylvia Cyrilla says he didn't succeed and they took him to the hospital and sewed him up. *(Alvin Sutton that wud be. Sure and none av the Suttons iver made a good job av innything they undertook.)*

"Aunt Hazel's father-in-law and mother-in-law live up the road a piece, Mr. and Mrs. James Madison. I often go up on errands. Mr. James has no use for me because I can't eat a plate of porridge. He says it is a dish for a king. But I'm not a king. *(Porridge, is it? Sure and I'm not running down porridge but skinny ould Jim Madison isn't after being much av an advertisement for it.)* They are very proud of their oldest daughter, Mary. She is an M. A. and won some great scholarships and is a teacher in a college. I suppose it is nice to be so clever, Judy. *(Oh, oh, but I'm not hearing av her getting a man, though.)* Mr. James likes to tease his wife. When Sylvia Cyrilla's father asked him if he would get married over again he laughed and said yes, but not to the same woman. Mrs. James didn't laugh though. *(Oh, oh, she was after knowing it might be half fun and whole earnest.)* They say Mr. James was very wild when he was young but he says if he hadn't been there'd have been no stories to tell about him now . . . he'd be nothing but a dull old grandfather.

"I've been collecting stories ever since I've been here, Judy, so that I'll have lots to tell when I'm old like you. There is one about a ghost on a farm belonging to Sylvia Cyrilla's uncle who has whiskers. I mean the ghost has whiskers. Isn't that funny? Can you imagine a ghost with whiskers? *(Sure and I knew a ghost in ould Ireland wid a bald head. There's no accounting for the freaks av the craturs.)* And Jen Davidson had a cousin who always cried when he was drunk. I thought it was because he was sorry he was drunk but Jen says it was because he couldn't get drunk oftener. Old Mr. McAllister from the bridge was up to see Mr. James last Monday and said he would have been up Sunday only he was wrestling with Satan all day. Do you suppose he really was, Judy, or was he just speaking poetically. *(Oh, oh, I'm guessing he must av been trying to keep on good terms wid his wife. She'd quarrel wid a feather bed, that one. Sure and he only married her be accident.*

Whin he proposed to her he was expicting her to say no and whin she said yes poor Johnny McAllister got the surprise av his life.) His brother was a dreadful man and died shaking his fist at God. *(Ye cudn't be ixpicting a McAllister to have inny manners, aven on his death-bed, Patsy darlint.)* The Maltby brothers have made up their quarrel after never speaking for thirty years. I don't think they're half as interesting now. Uncle Rob says they've made up because they've forgotten what they quarrelled about but if anybody could remember it they'd start all over again. And Mr. Gordon Keys at the bridge keeps his wife in order by crocheting lace whenever she won't do as he says. She hates to see him do it and so she gives in.

"The funniest story I've collected so far is this. Several years ago old Sam McKenzie was very sick in Charlottetown and everybody thought he was going to die. He was very rich and prominent, so Mr. Trotter, the undertaker, knew the family would want a fine coffin for him and he imported an extra fine one right off to have it ready because it was a very cold winter and he was afraid the strait might freeze over any day. And then old Sam went and got better and poor Mr. Trotter was left with that expensive coffin on his hands, and nobody likely to buy it. But he kept quiet and one day a few months afterwards old Tom Ramsay, who was rich and prominent, too, dropped dead when nobody expected him to. And Mr. Trotter told the family he had just one coffin on hand that was good enough and they took it and so old Tom Ramsay was buried in Sam McKenzie's coffin. The secret leaked out after awhile and the Ramsays were furious but they couldn't unbury him.

"That is my funniest story but the nicest is about old Mr. George McFadyen who died four years ago and went to heaven. At first he couldn't find any Islanders but after awhile he found out there were lots of them, only they had to be kept locked up for fear they would try to get back to the Island. Mr. James Madison told me that but he wouldn't explain how he found out about Mr. McFadyen's experience. Anyway I'm sure I'd feel like that, Judy. If I went to heaven I'd want to get back to Silver Bush.

"I was afraid when it blew so hard last night some of our trees would blow down. If Joe saves a kitten for me be sure you give it some cream, Judy. Jen Davidson has an aunt that has been married four times. *(Oh, oh, the lies she must av been after telling the min, that one!)* Jen seems proud of her but Uncle Rob says she ought to be more economical with husbands when there isn't enough to go round. I think he said that to tease the Maiden Aunt. Madge Davidson is going to marry Crofter Carter. *(Sure and she's a bit shopworn or she wudn't be after looking at him. I've seen the day a Davidson wudn't walk on the same side av the road as a Carter.)* Ross Halliday and Marinda Bailey at Silverbridge are married. They were engaged for fifteen years. I suppose they got tired of it. *(Sure and Marinda Bailey always said she wudn't marry till she got used to the thought av it. She was always a bit soft in the head, that one. But the min same to like that sort I'm telling ye. She niver had inny looks but kissing goes be favour and if Ross is the happy man at last it isn't Judy Plum that'll grudge it to him.)* Mrs. Samuel Carter is dead and the funeral is Friday. They've had a terrible lot of funerals there, Sylvia Cyrilla says, but Mr. Carter says funerals are not as expensive as weddings when all is said and done. *(And that's no drame whin ye have to support yer son-in-laws as Sam Carter has. I'm telling ye.)*

"I hope you won't be tired reading this long letter, Judy. I've written some of it every day for a week and just put down everything that came into my head. I'll soon be home now and we can talk everything over. Don't let anybody change any of the furniture about when I'm away. If this letter is bulgy it's just because I've put so many hugs in it for you.

"Your loving

"Patsy.

"P.S. Aunt Hazel says she thinks my hair would grow darker if it was bobbed. Do you think it would, Judy?

"P."

(Sure and it's the good latter she does be writing. It's the lonesome place around here widout the liddle dancing fate and the dear laugh av her. That way she has av smiling at ye as if there was some nice liddle joke atween ye'll carry her far. But nixt year will be lashings av time to talk av bobbing. Sure and I must be putting this letter in me glory box.)

22

THREE DAUGHTERS OF ONE RACE

1

If the years did not exactly whirl past after you were twelve, as the Maiden Aunt had so dolefully predicted, they really did seem to go faster. Pat and Bets could hardly believe that their thirteenth birthday was so near when mother told Pat that Joan and Dorothy were coming over from St. John for a visit and it would be nice to have a little party for them.

"You can have it on your birthday. That is Bets' birthday, too, and you will kill three birds with one stone," said mother gaily.

Pat was not very keen about parties . . . not as keen as Judy would have liked her to be. Neither was she especially excited over the visit of Joan and Dorothy Selby, although she was rather curious. She had heard a good deal at one time or another about the beauty of Dorothy. Both Joan and Dorothy had had their pictures in a society paper as "the lovely little daughters of Mr. and Mrs. Albert Selby of Linden Lodge." One would just like to see for oneself if Dorothy were as pretty as family gossip reported.

"I don't believe she's a bit prettier than Winnie."

"Oh, oh, 'tis likely not, if Winnie was dressed up like her . . . sure and it's sometimes the fine feathers that make the fine birds. But yer Uncle Albert was the fine-looking b'y and they say Dorothy takes after him. He's niver been home much. He got a gay young wife that thought things dull here."

"Joan and Dorothy are being educated at a convent boarding school," said Pat. "I suppose they'll be frightfully clever."

Judy sniffed.

"Oh, oh, cliverness can't be put in wid a spoon aven at yer convints. We do be having *some* brains at Silver Bush. Don't let thim overcrow ye, Pat, wid their fine city ways and convint brading. Howsomiver, I ixpect they're nice liddle girls and seeing as they're yer only cousins on the spindle side I'm hoping ye'll take to thim."

Joan and Dorothy had not been at Silver Bush twenty-four hours before Pat had secretly made up her mind that she was not going to "take" to them. Perhaps, although she would never have owned it, she was a little jealous of Dorothy who certainly lived up to her reputation for beauty. She *was* prettier than Winnie . . . though Pat never could be got to admit that she was prettier than Bets. Her hair was a dark, nutty brown, dipping down prettily over her forehead, and it made Pat's look even more gingery and faded by contrast. She had velvety brown eyes that made Pat's amber-hued ones look almost yellow. She had beautiful hands . . . which she put up to her face very often and which made everybody else's look sunburned and skinny. Joan, who was the brainy one and made no great claims to beauty, was very proud of Dorothy's looks and bragged a little about them.

"Dorothy is the prettiest girl in St. John," she told Pat.

"She *is* very pretty," admitted Pat. "Almost as pretty as Winnie and Bets Wilcox."

"Oh, Winnie!" Joan looked amused. "Winnie *is* quite nice-looking, of course. You would be, too, if your hair wasn't so long and terribly straight. It's so Victorian."

Probably Joan hadn't any very clear idea what Victorian meant but had heard somebody say it and thought it would impress this rather independent country cousin.

"Judy doesn't want me to bob my hair," said Pat coldly.

"Judy? Oh, that quaint old servant of yours. Do you really let her run you like that?"

"Judy isn't a servant," cried Pat hotly.

"Not a servant? What is she then?"

"She's one of the family."

"Don't you pay her wages?"

Pat had really never thought about it.

"I . . . I suppose so."

"She *is* a servant then. Of course it's awfully sweet of you to love her as you do but mother says it doesn't do to make too much of servants. It makes them forget their place. Judy isn't very respectful I notice. But of course it's different in the country. Oh, *look* at Dorothy over there by the lilies. Doesn't she look like an angel?"

Pat permitted herself an impertinence.

"I've heard that pretty girls hardly ever make pretty women. Do you think it's true, Joan?"

"Mother was a pretty girl and she is a pretty woman. Mother was a Charlottetown Hilton," said Joan loftily.

Pat knew nothing about Charlottetown Hiltons but she understood Joan was putting on airs, as Judy would say.

This was when they had been several days at Silver Bush. They had been very polite the first day. Silver Bush was such a *charming* spot . . . the garden was so "quaint" . . . the well was so "quaint" . . . the church barn was so "quaint" . . . the grave-yard was "priceless." What was the matter? Pat knew in a flash. They were patronising the garden and the well and the barn. And the grave-yard!

"You drink water out of a tap, I suppose," she said scornfully.

"Oh, you are the *funniest* darling," said Dorothy, hugging her.

But after they did not condescend quite so much. They had all sized each other up and formed opinions that would last for some time. Pat liked Dorothy well enough but Joan was a "blow."

"I wish you could see *our* mums," she said when Pat showed her the garden. "Dad always takes all the prizes at the Horticultural Show with them. Why doesn't Uncle Alec cut that old spruce down? It shades the corner too much."

"That tree is a friend of the family," said Pat.

"I wouldn't have violets in that corner," suggested Dorothy. "I'd have them over at the west side."

"But the violets have always been in that corner," said Pat.

"How this gate creaks!" said Joan with a shudder. "Why don't you oil it?"

"It has *always* creaked," said Pat.

"Your garden is quaint but rather jungly. It ought to be cleared out," said Dorothy as they left it.

Pat had learned a few things since the day she had slapped Norma. For the honour of Silver Bush no guest must be insulted. Otherwise there is no knowing what she might have done to Dorothy.

It was just as bad inside the house. Joan was all for changing the furniture about if it had been *her* house.

"Do you know what I'd do? I'd put the piano in *that* corner . . ."

"But it *belongs* in this corner," said Pat.

"The room would look so much better, darling, if you just changed it a little," said Joan.

"The room would *hate* you if you changed it," cried Pat.

Joan and Dorothy exchanged amused glances behind her back. And Pat knew they did. But she forgave them because they praised Bets. Bets, they said, was lovely, with such sweet ways.

"Oh, oh, she has the good heart, av course she has the good manners," said Judy.

Pat warmed to Joan when Joan admired the bird-house Jingle had given her. Jingle had a knack of making delightful bird-houses. But when the girls met Jingle Joan lost grace again. Dorothy was sweet to him . . . perhaps a little too sweet . . . but Joan saw only the badly cut hair and the nondescript clothes. And Dorothy enraged Pat by saying afterwards,

"It's awfully sweet of you to be nice to that poor boy."

Patronising! That was the word for it. She had patronised Jingle, too. And yet Jingle liked to hear Dorothy play on the piano. It couldn't be denied she could do it. Winnie's performance was nothing beside hers. Both the Selby girls were musical . . . Joan practised night and day on her guitar and Dorothy "showed off" her pretty little paws on the piano.

"Ye'd be thinking she mint to tear the kays out be the roots," muttered Judy, who did not like to see Winnie so eclipsed.

2

So the visit was not a great success although the older folk . . . all but Judy . . . thought the girls got on beautifully. Pat found it a bit hard to keep Joan and Dorothy amused . . . and they had to be amused all the time. They could not hunt their fun for themselves as she and Bets could. Pat showed them the grave-yard and introduced them to all the fields by name, to the Old Part and the Whispering Lane. She even tried not to mind when Sid took Dorothy back and showed her the Secret Field. But it did hurt horribly.

She knew the family thought Sid was "sweet" on Dorothy. Perhaps that was better than being sweet on May Binnie. But Pat did not want

Sid to be sweet on anybody.

"You're just jealous of Dorothy because Cuddles has taken such a fancy to her," jeered Sid.

"I'm not . . . I'm not," cried Pat. "Only . . . that was *our* secret."

"We're getting too big to have secret fields and all that nonsense," said Sid in a grown-up manner.

"I hate growing up," sobbed Pat. "Oh, Sid, I don't mind you liking Dorothy . . . I'm glad you like her . . . but *she* didn't care about that field."

"No, she didn't," admitted Sid. "She said what on earth did we see in it to make a secret of. And what *did* we see, Pat, if it comes to that?"

"Oh!" Pat felt helpless. If Sid couldn't *see* what they had seen he couldn't be made to.

Joan and Dorothy did not care for the play-house in the birch bush; they did not care for hunting kittens in the barn: two fluffy-tailed orange ones left them cold, although Dorothy did distracting things with them when any boys were around. She cuddled them under her lovely chin and even kissed the sunwarm tops of their round, velvety heads . . . "Just," as Judy muttered to herself, "to be making the b'ys wish they were kittens."

They knew nothing about "pretending adventures." They did not like fishing in Jordan with long fat worms; they could not sit for hours on a fence or boulder or apple-tree bough and talk over the things they saw, as Pat and Bets could. They found nothing delightful in sitting on Weeping Willy's tombstone and looking for the first star. Joe took them driving in the evenings and the party was a bit of excitement. They wore dresses the like of which had never been seen in North Glen before and were remembered for years by the girls who saw them. But they were bored, though they tried politely to hide it.

One thing they did like, however . . . sitting in the kitchen or on the back door-steps in the September twilights, when the sky was all full of a soft brightness of a sun that had dropped behind the dark hills and the birchen boughs in the big bush waved as if tossing kisses to the world, listening to Judy's stories while they ate red, nut-sweet apples. It was the one time when Pat and her cousins really liked each other. Nor . . . though Dorothy thought it so "quaint" to eat in the kitchen . . . did they despise Judy's "liddle bites" after the story telling. Pat caught them exchanging amused glances over Judy's fried eggs and codfish cakes but they praised her bishop's bread and doughnuts so warmly that Judy's heart softened to them a bit. Judy felt rather self-reproachful because she did not like these girls better herself after having been so anxious that Pat should like them. Gentleman Tom, who had never noticed any one but Judy, seemed to take a fancy to Joan and followed her about. Pat thought Judy would be jealous but not a bit of it . . . apparently.

"He knows she nades watching, that one," sniffed Judy.

"It is nice here in summer," admitted Joan on one of these evenings, "but it must be frightfully dull in winter."

"It isn't. Winter here is lovely. One can be so cosy in winter," retorted Pat.

"You haven't even a furnace," said Joan. "How in the world do you keep from freezing to death?"

"We've stoves in every room," said Pat proudly. "And heaps of good firewood . . . look at the pile over there. We can *see* our fires . . . we don't have to sit up to a hole in the floor to get warm."

Joan laughed.

"We have steam radiators, silly . . . and open fireplaces. You *are* funny, Pat . . . you're so touchy about Silver Bush. One would think you thought it was the only place in the world."

"It is . . . for me," said Pat.

"Joe doesn't think so," said Joan. "I've had talks with Joe when we were out driving. He isn't contented here, Pat."

Pat stared.

"Did Joe tell you that?"

"Oh, not in so many words but I could see. I don't think any of you here really understand Joe. He doesn't like farming . . . he wants to be a sailor. Joe is a boy with very deep feelings, Pat, but he doesn't like showing them."

"The idea of her explaining Joe to me," sobbed Pat to Judy, after the girls had gone to their bed in the Poet's room. "I know Joe has some silly ideas about sailing, just as well as she does, but father says he'll soon have more sense. I'm sure Joe would never want to go away from Silver Bush."

"Ye can't all be staying here foriver, darlint," warned Judy.

"But we needn't think of that for years yet, Judy. Joe is only nineteen. And Joan to be putting on airs about 'understanding' him!"

"Oh, oh, that's where the shoe pinches," chuckled Judy.

"And Joan asked me to-day if I didn't think Dorothy had a lovely laugh. She said Dorothy was noted for her laugh. I agreed, just to be polite, Judy . . ."

"Oh, oh, if one hadn't to be polite! But thin . . . one has."

"But I don't think Dorothy's laugh is half as pretty as Winnie's, Judy."

"Sure and they've both got the Selby laugh and ye can't be telling which av thim is laughing if ye don't see her. But I'm knowing nather ye nor Joan cud be convinced av that. The trouble is, me jewel, that ye and Joan are a bit too much alike in a good minny things iver to be hitting it off very well."

Pat did not tell Judy everything that had stung her. Joan had said, "After all, that Jingle of yours has a lovely smile."

"He's not *my* Jingle," said Pat shortly. And what difference did it make to Joan whether Jingle had a lovely smile or not? Hadn't she made fun of his hair and his glasses and his frayed trousers? And she had also laughed at Uncle Tom's beard and Judy's book of Useful Knowledge. One was "Victorian" and the other was "outmoded." They condescended to Aunt Edith and Aunt Barbara, too . . . they were "such quaint old darlings." Pat had never been so conscious of the leak stain on the dining-room ceiling and the worn places in the Little Parlour carpet until she saw Joan looking at them, and she had not noticed how mossy the shingles of the kitchen roof were growing until Joan said amiably that she rather liked old houses.

"*Our* house is really rather too new. It's of white stucco with a red-tiled roof . . . a bit glaring. Father says it will mellow with time."

"I never like new houses," said Pat. "They haven't any ghosts."

"Ghosts? But you don't believe in ghosts, do you, Pat?"

"I didn't mean ghosts . . . exactly."

"What did you mean then?"

"Oh . . . just that . . . when a house has been lived in for years and years . . . *something* of the people who have lived in it *stays* in it."

"You quaint darling!" said Dorothy.

3

Pat exulted in the freedom and silence of home after they had gone. It was altogether delightful to be alone again. The books that had been strewn everywhere were back in their places; the Poet's room was no longer cluttered up with alien dresses and shoes and brushes and necklaces.

"Isn't it nice just to be here by ourselves and no outsiders?" she said to Judy as they sat on the steps. A night of dim silver was brooding over the bush and the pale, perfect gold of the trembling aspen leaves had faded into shadow. The still air was full of far, muted surf thunder. Gentleman Tom had arranged himself beautifully on the well platform and the two orange kittens were blinking their jewel eyes and purring their small hearts out on Pat's lap.

"Mother says she is so sorry I didn't love my cousins. I *do* love them, Judy, but I don't *like* them."

"Oh, oh, but three's a crowd," said Judy. "Two girls can be getting on very well but whin there's three av ye and all high-steppers, some one's bound to get rubbed the wrong way. Often have I been seeing it."

"I liked Joan in spots . . . but she made me feel *unimportant,* Judy. She snubbed me."

"Sure and she'd snub the moon, that one. But she's the cliver one for all."

"And she bragged . . . she *did.*"

"The Hiltons always did be liking to make a bit av a splash. And didn't ye do a bit av snubbing and bragging now yersilf, Patsy darlint? Thought I'm not saying ye didn't be having the aggravation. There don't be minny families that haven't their own liddle kinks. Even the Selbys now, niver to mintion the Gardiners. Ye have to be making allowances. I'm thinking ye'd av been liking the girls better if it wasn't for yer liddle jealousy, Patsy . . ."

"I wasn't jealous, Judy!"

"Oh, oh, be honest now, me jewel. Ye was jealous of Joan because Joe liked her and ye was jealous of Dorothy because Sid and Cuddles liked her. Ye have yer liddle faults, Patsy, just as they have."

"I don't tell fibs anyway. They told mother when they went away they had had a perfectly lovely time. They hadn't. That was a lie, Judy."

"Oh, oh . . . a polite lie maybe . . . and maybe not all a lie. They had it in spots as ye say, I'm thinking."

"Anyway there's one word I never want to hear again as long as I live, Judy, and that's 'quaint.'"

"Quaint, is it? Sure and whin Joan called Gintleman Tom quaint I'll be swearing the baste winked at me. I cud av been telling Miss Joan her own grandfather was quaint the night he got up to be making a spach at a Tory meeting and his wife, who was born a Tolman and be the same token a Grit, laned over from the sate behind and pulled him down be his coat-tails. Ye cud hear the thud all over the hall. Not a word wud she let him be saying. Oh, oh, quaint!"

"Sometimes, Judy, they made me awful mad . . . *inside*."

"But ye kept it inside. That shows ye're getting on. It's what we all have to be larning, me jewel, if we want to be living wid folks paceable. Mad inside, is it? Sure and I was mad inside ivery day they was here whin they began showing off in me own kitchen. And that Joan one talking about kaping 'abreast av the times.' Sure, thinks I to mesilf, if chasing around in circles after yer own tail is kaping up wid the times ye're the lady that can be doing it. And thin I wud be thinking that yer Aunts at the Bay Shore were just the same whin they were liddle girls and thinks I, fam'lies must be standing be each other and life will be curing us all av a lot av foolishness. I wudn't wonder if ye'd be mating the girls some time agin whin ye've all got a bit riper and finding ye like thim very well."

Pat received this prediction in sceptical silence. She looked up to the Long House where the light in Bets' window was glowing like a friendly star on a dark hill.

"Anyway I'm glad Bets and I can be alone again. Bets is the only girl I want for a friend."

"What will ye be doing whin she grows up and goes away?"

"Oh, but she never will, Judy. Even if she gets married she will go on living at the Long House because she is the only child. And I'll always be here and we'll always be together. We have it all arranged."

Judy sighed and nudged.

"Don't be after saying thim things out loud, Patsy . . . not out loud, darlint. Sure and ye niver can tell who might be listening to ye."

23

MOCK SUNSHINE

1

"Pat, can you meet me in Happiness right away?" phoned Jingle.

The Gordons had had a telephone put in at last and Jingle and Pat generally kept the wire from rusting.

Pat knew from Jingle's voice that something exciting had happened . . . exciting and pleasant. What could it be? Exciting and pleasant things were so rare in Jingle's life, poor fellow. She went to Happiness so speedily that she was there before Jingle, waiting for him in a ferny hollow among the cradle hills. Jingle lingered for a moment behind a screen of young spruces to watch her . . . her wonderful golden-brown eyes fixed dreamily on the sky . . . a provoking smile over hidden thoughts lingering around her mouth . . . just enough of a smile to give it that dear little kissable quirk at the corner that was beginning to make Jingle's heart act queerly whenever he saw it. What was she thinking of? What *did* girls think of? Jingle found himself wishing he knew more about them in general.

Pat looked away from her clouds to see a Jingle she had never seen before with eyes so bright that their radiance shone through even the dark quenching glasses.

"Jingle, you look as if . . . as if everything had come true."

"It has . . . for me." Jingle flung himself down on the grass and propped his face on his thin sunburned hands. "Pat . . . mother's coming . . . to-morrow!"

Pat gasped.

"Oh, Jingle! At last! How wonderful!"

"The telegram came last night. I phoned right over to Silver Bush but Judy said you were away. Then this morning I had to leave at five to take a load of factory cheese to town. I've just got back . . . I wanted you to be the first to know."

"Jingle . . . I'm so glad!"

"I am, too . . . only, Pat . . . I wish she'd written she was coming instead of wiring it."

"Likely she hadn't time. Where was she?"

"In St. John. Oh, Pat, think of it . . . I'm fifteen and I've never seen my mother . . . not to remember her. Not even a picture of her . . . I haven't the least idea what she really looks like. Long ago . . . you remember, Pat . . . the day we found Happiness? . . . I told you she had blue eyes and golden hair. But I just imagined that because I heard Aunt Maria say once that she was 'fair.' Perhaps she isn't like that at all."

"I'm sure she'll be lovely whatever kind of eyes and hair she has," assured Pat.

"Ever since I saw that Madonna of the Clouds in your little parlour I've been imagining mother looked like that. Of course she must be older . . . mother is really thirty-five. I couldn't sleep last night for thinking about her coming. I don't see how I can wait till to-morrow. Last night I thought I couldn't wait for *two* morrows."

Jingle's thin, delicately-cut face was dreamy and remote. Pat gazed at him, thrilling with sympathy. She knew what this meant to him.

"I know. Judy says when I was small and promised anything 'to-morrow' I'd keep plaguing her, 'Where is tomorrow now, Judy?' *Your* to-morrow is somewhere, Jingle . . . right this very minute it must be somewhere. Isn't that nice to think?"

"All day to-day I've just been in a dream, Pat. It didn't seem real. I've taken out and read the telegram a hundred times just to be sure. If it had only been a letter, Pat . . . a letter she had written . . . *touched*."

"You'll have her, herself, to-morrow and that will be better than any letter. How long will she stay?"

"I don't know. She doesn't say anything but that she'll be here. I hope for *weeks*."

"Perhaps . . . perhaps she'll take you away with her, Jingle."

Pat was a little breathless. The idea had gone through her like lightning. It was a very unwelcome one. Jingle gone? Jordan and no Jingle! Happiness and no Jingle! A queer chill seemed to begin somewhere inside of her and spread all over her body.

Jingle shook his head.

"I don't think so . . . some way I . . . I don't think I'd even want to go. But to see her . . . to feel her arms around me just once! To tell her everything. I'm going to give her all the letters, Pat. I got them out of the box last night and read them over. The first ones, when I just had to print the letters, were so funny. But a mother wouldn't think them funny, would she? A mother would like them, don't you think?"

"I'm sure she'll just love them. She couldn't help it."

Jingle gave a sigh of satisfaction.

"You know so much more about a mother than I do, Pat. You've had one all your life."

Pat winked her eyes savagely. It would be absurd to cry. But she was twisted with a sudden fierce pity for Jingle . . . whose mother had never come to see him . . . who had *years* of letters that he had never sent. She was sorry for the mother who had missed them.

But everything would be all right after this.

"You must come over and see mother, Pat."

"Oh, but, Jingle, I don't like to. You'll want to be alone together."

"Most of the time, I suppose. But I want you to see her . . . and I want her to see you. And we'll bring her up here and show her Happiness, won't we, Pat? You won't mind?"

"Of course not. And of course she'll want to see it because it's a place you love."

"I haven't had time to make anything for her. . . ."

"You can get a lovely bouquet ready for her, Jingle. She'll just love that."

"But we haven't any nice flowers at our place."

"Come over early in the morning and get some from our garden. I'll make the bouquet up for you . . . there's some lovely baby's breath out now. You can choose the flowers and I'll arrange them. Judy says I have a knack with flowers. Jingle, what is your mother's name?"

"Mrs. Garrison," said Jingle bitterly. It was a hateful thing to him that his mother's name was not his. "Her first name is Doreen. That is a pretty name, isn't it?"

"So Jim's fine widdy is coming to see her b'y at last?" said Judy when she heard the news. "Well, it's not afore the time. I'm thinking Larry Gordon wrote her a bit av a letter. I've heard him say it was time he knew what her plans for the b'y was if she had inny. The tacher up at South Glen has been at him to take up the branches this year but Larry says what wud the use be. They can't ixpect *him* to foot the bills for

Quane's, what wid him being barely able to scrape up his interest ivery year."

"Then . . . you think . . . you don't think Jingle's mother is coming just because she wanted to see him?" said Pat slowly.

"I'm not saying she isn't. But ye do be knowing she's niver wanted to see him for over a dozen years. Howsomiver, maybe she's had a change av heart and let's hope it hard, Patsy, for I'm thinking that poor Jingle-lad is all set up over her coming."

"He is . . . oh, Judy, it just means everything to him. Maybe . . . when she *sees* him . . ."

"Maybe," agreed Judy dubiously.

2

Jingle was over bright and early to get the bouquet for his mother. He had put on his poor best suit, which was too short for him and had been too short for a year. His aunt had cut his hair and made rather a worse job than usual of it. But his face was flushed with excitement and for the first time it occurred to Pat that Jingle wasn't such a bad-looking boy. If it were not for those awful glasses!

"Jingle, take them off before your mother comes. It couldn't hurt your eyes for a little while."

"Aunt Maria wouldn't like it. She paid for my glasses, you know, and she says I've got to wear them all the time or it would be wasted money. She . . . she knows I hate them, I think . . . and that's really why she gets so cross if I leave them off. When we get mother away by ourselves . . . when we go to Happiness . . . I'll take them off. Pat, think of mother . . . my own mother . . . in Happiness!"

They spent a long time over the bouquet. Jingle was hard to please. Only absolutely perfect flowers must go into it . . . and no delphiniums.

"Delphiniums are so haughty," said Jingle. "And they've no perfume. Just sweet-smelling flowers, Pat. And a bit of southern wood. You know Judy calls it 'lad's love.' So it ought to go in mother's bouquet."

Jingle laughed a bit consciously. But he did not mind if Pat thought him sentimental.

"We'll put in some of the leaves of the old sweet-briar . . . they've such a lovely apple scent. I wish there were more roses out. It's too early for them . . . but these little pink buds are darling . . . and those white ones with the pink hearts. There was one lovely copper rose out last night . . . just one on father's new bush. He told me we could have it. But it rained last night and it was all beaten and ruined this morning. I almost cried. But here's one long red bud from Winnie's bush and I'll put it in your coat, Jingle."

"Just two hours more," said Jingle. "Pat, I want you to come over right after dinner, before she comes. Will you?"

"Oh, Jingle . . . wouldn't you want to be alone when you see her first?"

"If I *could* be alone . . . but Uncle Lawrence and Aunt Maria will be there . . . and, somehow . . . I don't know . . . I just feel as if I wanted you there, too, Pat."

In the end Pat went, thrilling from head to foot with excitement . . . and considerable curiosity. She had put her hair in curlers the night before, to look her best before Jingle's mother, but the result was rather bushy and rampant. "It would look all right if it was bobbed, Judy," she muttered rebelliously.

"Standing out round yer head like a hello," said Judy sarcastically.

Pat braided it in tightly and put on the new blue pullover Judy had knitted for her, over her cornflower blue skirt. Would Jingle's mother think her just a crude little country girl with a head like a fuzz-bush?

"I don't suppose she'll ever think of me at all," Pat comforted herself. "She'll be so taken up with Jingle."

Jingle was waiting with his bouquet, his lips set tightly to hide their quivering. Larry Gordon's old car clattered in at the gate.

"Here she comes," said Pat . . . magic, breathless words.

She came. They saw her get out of the car and drift up the stone walk. Jingle had meant to run to meet her. But he found he couldn't move. He stood there stupidly, his breath coming quickly, his bouquet quivering in his hands. Was this his mother . . . this?

Pat saw her more clearly than Jingle did. Tall, slender, graceful as a flower, in a soft fluttering chiffon dress like blue mist; pale, silvery-golden hair sleeked down all over her head like a cap under a little tilted hat of smooth blue feathers: bluish-green eyes that never seemed to see you, even when they looked at you, under eyebrows as thin as a line drawn in soot; a mouth that spoiled everything, so vividly red and arched was it. She might have stepped off a magazine cover. Beautiful .

. . oh, yes, very beautiful! But not . . . somehow . . . like a mother!

"I like a mother who *looks* like a mother," was the thought that whisked through Pat's head. This woman looked . . . at first . . . like a girl.

Doreen Garrison came up the walk, looking rather curiously at the two standing by the door. Jingle spoke first. "Mother!" he said. It was the first time he had ever said it. It sounded like a prayer.

A flash of amazement flickered in Doreen Garrison's restless eyes . . . . a little tinkling laugh rippled over her carmine lips.

"You don't mean to say *you* are my Jingle-baby? Why . . . why . . . you're almost grown up, darling."

She stooped and dropped a light kiss, as cold as snow, on his cheek.

She hadn't known him! Pat, looking at Jingle, thought it was dreadful to see happiness wiped out of a human face like that.

"This is for you . . . mother." Jingle poked the bouquet out to her stiffly. She glanced at it . . . took it . . . again the little rippling insincere laugh . . . that was *not,* Pat thought, laughter . . . came. Jingle flinched as if she had boxed his ears.

"Angel-boy, what can I do with such an enormous thing? How did you ever get so many flowers into it? It must weigh a ton. Just put it somewhere, honey, and I'll take a bud out of it when I go. I haven't much time . . . I have to catch the evening boat and I must have a long talk with your Uncle Lawrence. I had no idea how you had grown."

She laid one of her very long, very slender, ivory-white hands, with its tinted, polished nails, on his shoulder and looked him over in a cool appraising manner.

"You're a bit weedy, aren't you, angel? Do you eat enough? But I suppose you're at the weedy age. Take off those terrible glasses. Do you really need them? Have you had your eyes tested lately?"

"No," said Jingle. He did not add "mother" this time. "This is Pat Gardiner," he finished awkwardly.

Mrs. Garrison flicked an eye over Pat, who had an instant conviction that her stockings were on crooked and her hair like a Fiji islander's. Somehow, they all found themselves sitting in the Gordon parlour. Nobody knew what to say, but Mrs. Garrison talked lightly, saying sweet, insincere things in her silvery voice to Mr. and Mrs. Gordon, making such play with her hands that you had to look at them to see how lovely they were. Pat thought of her own mother's hands . . . a little thin, a little knotted, the palms seamed and hardened a bit with years of work. But hands you liked to have touch you. She couldn't imagine any one liking the touch of Mrs. Garrison's hands.

Jingle stared at the carpet but Pat, her first shyness gone, looked Mrs. Garrison over very coolly. Lovely . . . very lovely . . . but what was wrong with her face? In after years Pat found a word for it . . . a *cheated* face. In after years Pat knew that this woman had worked so hard remaining young and beautiful for a husband whose fancy strayed lightly to every beautiful woman he met that she had spent herself. She was like a shadow . . . beautiful . . . elusive . . . not real. And this was Jingle's mother . . . who called everybody, even Larry Gordon, "darling" and now and then flung a word to her son as one might throw a bone to a hungry dog. Pat could not fathom the depth of the embarrassment Doreen Garrison was feeling in the presence of this forgotten, unloved boy. But she knew that Jingle's mother would not stay here one moment longer than she had to.

"What an ugly little dog!" laughed Doreen as McGinty dashed in to Jingle. McGinty had been shut up in the stable but had found his way out. He knew he was needed.

"Do you really like dogs, Jingle-baby? I'll send you a nice one."

"McGinty is a nice dog, thank you. I don't want another dog," said Jingle, his face flushing a dark red.

Pat got up and went home. Jingle followed her to the door.

"She . . . she's pretty, isn't she?" he asked wistfully.

"The prettiest woman I've ever seen," agreed Pat heartily.

When she looked at Jingle's face she couldn't help remembering the copper rose, so beautiful in the evening, so broken and battered the next morning. She hated Doreen Garrison . . . hated her for years . . . until she had learned to pity her.

"You'll come back as soon as you can, Pat? You know . . . I want to show her Happiness. And it's as much yours as mine."

Pat promised. She knew that Jingle knew that his mother would not care about seeing Happiness, and she knew he didn't want to be alone with his mother. But Pat learned that day that you may know a great many things you must never put in words.

3

She went back in mid-afternoon to find Doreen Garrison ready to leave.

"But . . . mother . . ." Jingle seemed forcing himself to speak the word . . . "Pat and I want to show you Happiness. It's such a pretty place."

"Happiness? Why in the world do you call it that, you funny darlings?"

"Because it is such a lovely spot we pretend nobody could ever be unhappy there," said Pat.

Amusement flickered into Doreen Garrison's eyes . . . the eyes Jingle had once pretended were as blue as a starlit sky.

"How wonderful to know nothing about life and so be able to imagine everything," she said lightly. "I can't visit your Happiness, Jingle-baby . . . how could heels like these travel over fields and stumps? Besides, I must not risk losing the boat. If I did it would mean missing the steamer at San Francisco. Jingle-baby, you're standing incorrectly . . . so . . . that's better. And you *do* look so much better without those glasses. *Never* put them on again, honey-boy. I've told your uncle to take you to a good oculist and if you really need glasses to have you equipped with proper ones. He's to get you some decent clothes, too, and take you to the barber at Silverbridge . . . there's the car . . . well . . ."

She looked a little uncertainly at Jingle, as if she supposed she ought to kiss him again. But there was something about Jingle just then that did not encourage kissing. Doreen Garrison felt relieved. It had really been a dreadful day . . . one felt so awkward . . . so ill at ease with this great half-grown hobbledehoy with his preposterous hair and clothes, who couldn't even talk. How had her lovely Jingle-baby ever turned into such a creature? But her duty was done . . . his future was arranged for . . . Lawrence would see to it.

She patted him lightly on the head.

"Bye, honey-boy. So sorry I haven't longer to stay. Don't grow *quite* so much in the next twelve years, please, angel. Good-bye . . . Nora, is it?"

"Good-bye," said Pat haughtily, with the disconcerting conviction that Doreen Garrison did not even notice that she was being haughty.

She flitted down the stone walk like a bird glad to escape its cage, leaving a trace of some exotic perfume behind her. Jingle stood on the step and watched her go . . . this tarnished, discrowned queen who had so long sat on the secret throne of his heart. Would she look back and wave to him? No, she was gone. His bouquet was lying on the hall table. She had not even remembered to take the bud. The southernwood in it was limp and faded.

"Well, how did you like your mother?" asked Aunt Maria.

Jingle winced. His aunt's harsh, disagreeable voice jarred horribly on his sensitive nerves.

"I . . . I thought she was lovely," he said. It was ghastly to have to lie about your mother.

Aunt Maria shrugged her bony shoulders.

"Well, she's settled things for you anyhow. You're to go in the entrance class next year and after that to college. She says you can be anything you like and she'll foot the bills. As for clothes . . . she found as much fault with yours as if she'd paid for them. You're to have two new suits . . . *tailored.* No hand-me-downs for *her* son! Humph!"

Aunt Maria disappeared indignantly into the kitchen.

Jingle looked at Pat with dead lustreless eyes. Something caught at her throat.

"Will you come to Happiness after supper?" he said quietly. "There's something I want you to do for me."

24

ASHES TO ASHES

1

Jingle was lying face downwards among the ferns in Happiness when Pat got there. A little dog with a big heart was sitting beside him, apparently mounting guard over a brown paper parcel on the grass.

Pat squatted down beside him, saying nothing. She was beginning to learn how full of silent little tragedies life is. She wished wildly that she could help Jingle in some way. Judy was fond of telling a story of long long ago when Pat had been four years old and was being trained to say "please." One day she could not remember it. "What is the word that makes things happen, Judy?" she had asked. Oh, for such a magic word now . . . some word which would make everything right for Jingle.

It was very lovely in Happiness that evening. There was a clear, pale, silvery-blue sky, feathered with tiny, blossom-like clouds, over them. The scent of clover was in the air. A corner of Happiness lay in the shadow of the woods, the rest of it was flooded with wine-red sunset. There was the elfin laugh of the hidden brook and there was the beauty of pale star-flowers along its banks. The only thing in sight that was not beautiful was the huge gash in the woods on the hill where Larry Gordon had got out his winter fuel. It was terrible to see the empty places where the trees had been cut. Trees *had* to be cut . . . people had to have firewood . . . but Pat could never see the resultant ugliness without a heartache. Of course time would beautify it again. Great clumps of ferns would grow by the hacked stumps . . . the crooks of the bracken would unfold along its desecrated paths . . . slender birches and poplars would spring up as years went by. Perhaps the wounds and scars in human lives would be like that, too.

"I wish," said Jingle suddenly, twisting himself around until his head lay in Pat's lap, "I wish my dream hadn't come true, Pat. It was so much more beautiful when it wasn't true."

"I know," said Pat softly. She patted the rough head with brown hands that were tender and gentle and wise. Their touch unloosed the floods of Jingle's bitterness.

"She . . . she gave me ten dollars, Pat. It burned my fingers when I took it. And I'm to go to college. But she wasn't interested in my plans. I showed her the house I'd drawn for her . . . she only laughed."

"Jingle, I think your mother was so . . . so surprised to find you so big that she felt . . . she didn't feel . . . she felt you were a stranger. Next time she comes it may be very different."

"Whose fault is it if I am like a stranger to her? And there will never be a next time . . . I knew that when she went away. She doesn't love me . . . she never has loved me. I know that now. I might have known it always if I hadn't been a fool."

Pat couldn't endure the desolation in his tone. She patted his head again.

"*I* love you anyhow, Jingle . . . almost . . . *just* as well as I love Sid."

Jingle caught the caressing hand and held it tight against his tear wet cheek.

"Thank you, Pat. And . . . Pat, will you do me a favour? Will you call me 'Hilary' after this? I . . . I . . . somehow, Jingle is such a silly nickname for a big boy."

Pat knew his mother had spoiled the name for him. It had been her pet name for him once. Surely she must have loved him then.

"I'll try . . . only you mustn't mind if I call you Jingle sometimes before I get the new habit."

In her heart she was saying, "I'll *call* him Hilary to his face but I'll always think of him as Jingle."

"I told you there was something I wanted you to do for me, Pat," Jingle went on, still with that strange, new bitterness. "I . . . I didn't give her those letters. I'll light a fire over there on that rock . . . and will you burn them for me?"

Pat assented. She knew there was nothing else to be done with those letters now. Jingle built the fire and Pat opened the parcel and fed them to the hungry little flames . . . a burnt offering of a boy's wasted love and faith and hope. Pat hated to burn them. It seemed a terrible thing to do. The tiny scraps of letters written when he was a little boy and paper was hard to come by . . . on a flyleaf torn from an old school-book or the back of a discarded circular . . . sometimes even on a carefully cut and folded piece of wrapping paper. A mother should have treasured them as jewels. But Doreen Garrison would never read them. The pity of it! Now and then a white line came out for a moment on the quivering black ash . . . Pat couldn't help seeing them . . . *"My own darling mother"* . . . *"perhaps you will come to see me soon, dearest"* . . . *"I was head of my class all the week, mother dearest. Aren't you glad?"* . . . Pat ground her little white teeth in a futile rage against fate.

After the last letter was burned Pat gathered up the little pile of ashes and scattered them in the brook.

"There, that's done." Hilary stood up; he looked older: there was a stern set to his jaw, a new ring in his voice, as of one who had put away childish things. "And now . . . well, I'm going to college . . . and I'm going to be an architect . . . and I'm going to succeed."

They walked back in silence along the ferny windings of Jordan. The moon was rising and the bats were out. An owl was calling eerily from the spruce hill beyond Happiness. A great golden star hung over Silver

187

Bush. They parted on the bridge. Pat lifted her eyes to his.

"Good-night, Jingle dear . . . I mean Hilary."

"Good-night, Pat. You've been a brick. Pat . . . your eyes are lovely . . . lovely."

"Oh, that's just the moonlight," said Pat.

2

Pat helped Judy wash the milk pails and get all the fluffy little golden chicks into their coops while she told her about Doreen Garrison.

"Oh, Judy, she was . . . she was . . ."

"Sort of supercilious like," suggested Judy.

"No, no, not that . . . she was as polite to us as if we were strangers . . . but . . . just as if she didn't believe we were there at all. I couldn't have believed there was a mother like that in the world, Judy."

"Oh, oh, ye do be liddle knowing what some mothers are like, more shame to them. And you can't be putting into thim the things the Good Man Above left out, so why be worrying over it? Just be saying a prayer for all poor orphans and be thankful ye've got a mother that has roots."

"Roots?"

"Sure and that's what's the matter wid yer Doreen Garrison. She hasn't a root to her. Nothing to anchor her down and hold aginst the winds. Sure and she may be one av thim things they do be calling a modern mother, I've been hearing av thim."

"I just felt, Judy, as if she had remembered him against her will and would forget him again as soon as he was out of her sight."

"I'm telling ye. Maria Gordon did be saying once that Jim's widdy was the best hand at forgetting things she didn't want to remimber she was iver knowing. I'm rale sorry for yer Jingle. Ye'd better ask him over to dinner tomorrow and give him a liddle bite av blackberry roly-poly. Sure and I'll be making it on purpose for him."

"He wants to be called Hilary after this, Judy. And . . . it's a funny coincidence . . . last week Bets and I decided that after this we would call each other Elizabeth and Patricia. But of course," added Pat hastily, "we don't expect other people to call us that."

"Oh, oh, and that same is just as well, me jewel, because ye're Pat to me and niver innything but Pat ye'll be."

"Pat of Silver Bush," said Pat happily. It was beautiful to have home and love and family ties. Bold-and-Bad, the kitten of the summer, came flying across the yard to her. Pat picked him up and squeezed some purrs out of him. No matter what dreadful things happened at least there were still cats in the world.

In the moonlight she went along the Whispering Lane and down the field path and up the hill. She made a tryst with Bets to tell her about Jingle's mother . . . at least as much as Jingle would wish told. Bets must know the state of things so that she would not hurt Jingle's feelings.

Pat reached the Watching Pine first and stood under it, her face against its rough old trunk as she waited. At first the moon was veiled in a misty cloud and Pat thrilled to a dim sense of magic and wonder that came with the glimpse of that cloudy moon through the pine. It was a wonderful night . . . a night when she might see the Little People perhaps. She had believed in them long ago and this was one of the moments she still believed in them. Wasn't that some tiny moonshine creature in a peaked cap with little bells on it sitting on a fence panel? No, only a vibrating strip of dried bark. The soft sweet air blew to her from the secret meadows at the back of the farms. Then the moon came out from her cloud and the little fir trees scattered along the fences were splashes of ink-black shadows in mystic shapes. Below were houses sleeping in moonlit gardens. Far out there was a trail of moonlight on the sea like a lady's silken dress. Pat felt herself a sister to all the loveliness of the world. If only everybody could feel this secret, satisfying rapture! Poor Jingle would be curled up in the hay-loft with McGinty, trying to forget his broken heart. It seemed cruel to be happy when he was miserable but it was no use trying not to be, when the night was full of wonder and Silver Bush with its love was below you, and you could hear Joe's delightful whistle and Snicklefritz's bark even at this distance. And when you were waiting for the dearest friend any girl ever had to join you. There, lilting along the path came Bets, part of the beauty of the night.

"We must love him all the more to make it up to him," said Bets when she had heard the tale . . . all except the burned letters which Pat knew must be a secret always between herself and . . . Hilary.

25

HIS WAY IS ON THE SEA

1

There was a family council at Silver Bush when school opened in September. It was decreed that Pat must join the entrance class and prepare herself for the Queen's Academy examinations the next year. Pat protested . . . but father was inexorable. He had let Winnie off, realising that Winnie's golden curls thatched a brain that could never be brought to distinguish between a participle and an infinitive: but Pat's record in school, although never brilliant, had been above the average: so to Queen's she must go and study for a teacher's licence.

"You'll get the North Glen school and board at home," said dad . . . which was the only gleam of hope Pat saw in the whole dismal prospect. She flew to the kitchen and poured out her discontent and rebellion to Judy.

"Oh, oh, and don't ye want to be eddicated, Patsy darling?"

To be educated was all right . . . but to go away from home was all wrong.

"I don't seem to be like other girls, Judy. They all want to go to college and have a career. I don't . . . I just want to stay at Silver Bush and help you and mother. There's work for me here, Judy . . . you know there is. Mother isn't strong. As for being educated . . . I *shall* be well educated . . . love educates, Judy."

"Oh, oh, and ye're not so far out there, girleen. But there's minny a thing to be considered besides. Money doesn't be growing on bushes, darlint."

"What fun if it did!" For a moment Pat was side-tracked by a vision of little gold dollars hanging from the ends of branches like golden blossoms.

"Yer dad isn't rich . . . and a fam'ly like this is ixpinsive whin they're growing up and nading the pretty clothes. You'll have to get ready to help him out a bit until some av ye are married or gone away."

"I don't want any of us to get married or go away."

"Ye're clane unrasonable, darlint."

Pat was beginning to suspect that she was unreasonable . . . that these things would have to be faced some time. For instance, Winnie had a beau. Not "beaus" . . . she had had beaus for over a year and Pat had grown used to their coming and going and Winnie's resultant chatter about "dates" . . . but "a" beau. Frank Russell of the Bay Shore Russells seemed to have scattered all the others and Winnie was beginning to blush painfully when Joe teased her about him. Pat hated Frank so bitterly that she could hardly be civil to him. Judy got quite out of patience with her.

"Ye ought to be having a liddle bit av sinse, Pat. Young Frank is be way av being a rale good match. The Russells do be all knowing how to make one hand wash the other. An only son and his mother dead and all the Bay Shore girls trying to nab him. Winnie'd just be stepping into that grand ould Russell place at the Bay Shore and be quane, wid niver a mother-in-law to look black at her if she moved a sofy. And that near home and all."

"Winnie's too young to *think* of being married," protested Pat.

"Sure and the darlint is eighteen. There's no question av being married yet awhile . . . she must have her courting time as is proper. But a Russell always means business and young Frank has the glint in his eye. I'm telling ye. He knows where to be coming for a good wife."

"He isn't very intelligent," snapped Pat.

"Will ye listen at her? He ain't much for rading poetry or building fancy houses, like yer Jingle, I'm supposing, but he's got a rale grip on politics, as Long Alec was quick to see, and I'm clane missing me guess if he don't be in Parliamint be the time he's a bit bald. Ye're not nading inny great intilligence for that. Winnie's no rale scholard hersilf, the darlint, but there isn't the like av her for the light biscuit on the Island. She'll be the grand housekeeper for that fine house. I'm telling ye."

Pat didn't want telling. The thought of Winnie ever leaving home, no matter how long the courting days were, remained intolerable. She continued to hate Frank but she resigned herself to the entrance class and even took up the work with a certain grim determination to do well for the sake of Silver Bush. She knew people thought the Silver

Bush family was lacking in ambition. Joe had stubbornly refused to go to school after he was fifteen; Winnie had always been "dumb" when it came to lessons; Sid was determined to know farming and nothing else. So it was up to her to re-establish the Gardiner credit in the halls of learning.

"I'm so thankful Bets is in the entrance class, too, Judy. I was afraid for a long while she couldn't be . . . her father thought she wasn't strong enough. But Bets coaxed so hard he has given in. If Bets is with me when I go to Queen's it won't be so bad . . . supposing I ever get there."

"Supposing, is it? Sure and there isn't much doubt but ye'll get there, cliver and all as ye are whin ye give yer mind to it. Whin I watch ye working out them queer al*geb*ra things it makes me have wheels in me head. As for yer jawmetry stuff, Gintleman Tom himsilf cudn't be seeing through it."

"Geometry is my favourite class, Judy. Bets doesn't like it . . . but she loves everything else that I love. We have planned to study together each night about all through the winter. We'll study hard for two hours and then we'll talk."

"I belave ye. The liddle tongues av ye do be always clacking."

"Yes, but, Judy, there are times when we don't talk at all. We just sit and think. Sometimes we don't even think . . . we just *sit*. It's enough just to be together. And oh, Judy, Bets and I . . ."

"I did be hearing ye was calling each other Elizabeth and Patricia."

Pat laughed.

"We did try to. But it didn't work. Elizabeth and Patricia sounded like strangers . . . we didn't know ourselves. As I was saying . . . Bets and I have begun to read the Bible right through. We're not going to skip a single chapter, not even those awful names in Chronicles. You've no idea how interesting the Bible is, Judy, when you read it just as a story."

"Oh, oh, haven't I now? Sure and wasn't I rading me Bible afore ye were born or thought av? But I *did* be skipping the names. There was too minny jaw-breakers among thim for me. I do be wondering if there niver was inny nicknames in thim days. D'ye think now, Patsy dear, that ivery time Jehosaphat's mother called him to his liddle dinner she said the whole name?"

2

The autumn drifted by: maple fires were kindled around the Secret Field: bracken and lady fern turned brown in Happiness: Jordan ran to the sea between borders of purple asters: golden harvest moons looked down over the Hill of the Mist. A gracious September and a mellow October were succeeded by a soft and sad November, when long silken lines of rain slanted across the sere hillsides.

And then one day, without any warning, came the first break in the family at Silver Bush.

They had all, except Joe, been spending Saturday afternoon and evening at the Bay Shore farm . . . where nothing had changed in Pat's remembrance. It was "a world where all things seemed the same." She was beginning to love the Bay Shore for that very changelessness . . . . it seemed the one place you could depend on in a changing world. Aunt Frances and Aunt Honor were just as "stately" as ever, though they had given up asking her to say Bible verses and tapping her on the head when they disapproved of her. They still disapproved of her in many things but Pat liked even the disapproval because anything else would have been change. Cousin Danny still wore his elvish grin. The Great-great was still alive . . . at ninety-eight . . . and not a day older apparently, nor any more complimentary. Every time she saw Pat she said "Nae beauty," in the same peevish tone, as if Pat were entirely to blame for it. The vase that had made the face at Sarah Jenkins still stood on the same bracket and the polished door-knobs still brightly reflected your face. The white ivory elephants had never finished marching across the mantel and the red and yellow china hen had evidently never succeeded in hatching out her eggs.

Bets was with them and this added to the pleasure of the day. It was such fun to show Bets everything. The aunts liked her . . . but who could help liking Bets? Even the Great-great peered at her with admiration in her bright old eyes and for once forgot to tell Pat she was no beauty.

When they came back to Silver Bush Pat must walk up the hill with Bets: it had turned colder and the first snowfall was whitening down over the twilight world when Pat came into the kitchen. At once she saw that something must be wrong . . . terribly wrong. Mother was looking as white as if she had been struck . . . Winnie was crying . . . and Judy, of all people, had been crying. Sid looked as if he were trying not to cry.

Father stood by the table holding a letter in his hand. Snicklefritz sat by him, looking up with mute, imploring eyes. Gentleman Tom had an air of not liking things. Even Bold-and-Bad, whom ordinarily nothing could subdue, crouched with an apologetic air under the stove.

Pat looked around. Everybody was there . . .except . . . except . . .

"Where's Joe?" she cried.

For a moment nobody spoke. Then Winnie sobbed, "He's gone."

"Gone! Where?"

"To sea. He went to the harbour to-night and sailed in Pierce Morgan's vessel for the West Indies."

"And me niver suspicting it, the gomeril I am," wailed Judy. "Not aven whin he come in, all queer like, and said he wud be taking a run to Silverbridge. Sure and if I'd known what was in his head I'd have hung on to him till after the tide set . . ."

"That wouldn't have done any good," said Long Alec, rousing himself from his abstraction. "He was bound to go sooner or later. I've known that for some time. But he was so young . . . and to go off like this without a word to one of us . . . it was cruel of him. There, there, Mary."

For mother had turned and buried her face on his shoulder with a little, broken cry. Father led her out of the kitchen. Winnie and Cuddles followed. Sid went out and Pat was weeping wildly in Judy's arms.

"Judy, I can't bear it . . . I can't bear it! Joe to go . . . and like that."

"Sure and it do be cruel, as Long Alec said. The young fry do be cruel be times . . . they don't know . . . they don't know. Now, don't be breaking yer liddle heart, darlint. Remimber it's harder for yer mother than for inny av the rest av ye. Joe'll be back some time . . ."

"But never to *stay*, Judy . . . never to stay. Oh, I'll always hate this day . . . always."

"Oh, oh, don't be cynical now," said Judy, who picked up words as the children studied their lessons but not always the exact meaning. "Where's the sinse av hating the poor day? Ye must just be looking this in the face. It's Wild Dick and yer Uncle Horace over again . . . sure and Joe had always been more like Horace than his own dad. He knew if he tried to say good-bye Long Alec wud be trying to put him off. Now kape up yer pecker, Patsy, for the sake av yer mother. Siddy's here to carry on and it's the smart lad he is. His heart's in the farm as Joe's niver was, and he can aven drive the autymobile which the Good

Man Above niver intinded innybody to do. Joe's gone but he hasn't taken Silver Bush wid him. Did ye be after seeing the liddle note he lift on Long Alec's desk . . . no? There was a missage for ye in it . . . 'tell Pat to be good to Snicklefritz' . . . and there was one for me, too, be way av a joke. Joe always had a joke, the darlint. 'Tell Judy to see that those blamed kittens in her picture are grown up be the time I come back.' Sure and wasn't he always laughing at thim same kittens."

But Pat could not laugh again for a long time. She was the last one at Silver Bush to resign herself to the inevitable. Eventually she found herself doing it, with a sense of shame that it could be so. But the raw rainy winter was half over before she ceased to have sleepless nights when it stormed and began looking forward with pleasure to Joe's letters, with bewitching foreign stamps on them which Cuddles proudly collected. They were full of the glamour of strange ports and distant lands, of the lure of adventure and white-winged ships, to which Pat thrilled in spite of herself. Somehow, although she hadn't believed it possible, Silver Bush got on without him. Sid had stepped manfully into his place . . . in truth Sid was glad of an excuse to leave school . . . mother began to smile again, Frank Russell consoled Winnie, everybody ceased to listen for the gay whistle that had echoed so often through the twilights around the old barns. Even Snicklefritz stopped wearing a sorrowful cast of countenance and listening mournfully to every footstep on the stone walk.

Change . . . and worse than change, forgetfulness! It seemed dreadful to Pat that things could be forgotten. Why, they were just as bad as the family at Silverbridge that had one son in California and one in Australia, one in India and one in Petrograd and didn't seem to mind it at all.

"Oh, oh, how cud we be living if we didn't forget, me jewel?" said Judy.

"But Christmas was so terrible," sighed Pat. "The first time we weren't all here. I couldn't help thinking of something I heard you say once . . . that once one of a family was away for Christmas it was likely they would never be all together again. I just couldn't eat . . . and I didn't see how any one else could."

"But do ye be remimbering how ye slipped into the kitchen at bedtime and we had a faste on the bones?" said Judy slyly.

195

3

Everything passes. Winter was spring before they knew it. Everybody was looking forward with delight to Joe's homecoming. March brought a saddening letter from him. He was not coming home in Pierce Morgan's vessel. He had shipped for a voyage to China. Well, that was a disappointment . . . but meanwhile March was April, with sap astir and frogs tuning up the field of the Pool, and all the apple boughs that had fallen in winter storms to be gathered up and burned. Sid and Pat did that and they and Bets and Hilary had a glorious bonfire at night: and after it was over Pat couldn't walk home with Bets because Sid did. Pat didn't mind . . . she was too happy because Sid seemed to be having quite a crush on Bets this spring.

"He's all out with May Binnie, Judy. Won't it be lovely if he marries Bets some day?"

"Oh, oh, go aisy wid yer match-making," said Judy sarcastically.

Besides, it was nice to sit with Hilary on Weeping Willy's tombstone, in the glow from the smouldering embers in the orchard, and talk about things. Pat had learned to call him Hilary . . . she was even beginning to think of him as Hilary, though in moments of excitement the old name popped out. Judy never could bring her tongue to call him anything else. To her he would always be Jingle.

"The darlints," she would say to Gentleman Tom, looking out of her kitchen window at them. "I do be wondering what's afore thim in life. And how much longer is it they have to be young and light-hearted."

Gentleman Tom would not tell her.

April was May, with a white fire of wild cherry in Happiness and young daffodils dancing all over the garden and little green cones shooting up in the iris beds. Every day Pat made some new discovery.

"One forgets all through the year how lovely spring really is and so it comes as a surprise every time," she said.

And finally May was June, with a fairy wild plum hanging out in the Whispering Lane and purple waves of lilac breaking along the yard fence and Judy's beds of white pansies all ablow . . . big white, velvety pansies . . . and everywhere all the different shades of green in the young spring woods on the hills.

"Spring is nicer at Silver Bush than anywhere else, Judy. Just look what a lovely iris . . . frosty white with a ripple of blue fringing every petal. It's Joe's iris . . . he planted it last spring . . . and now where is he?"

"On the other side av the world belike. Tell me, Patsy dear, do you be understanding how it is they don't fall off down there? I've niver been able to get the hang of it into me mind somehow."

Pat tried to explain but Judy still shook her grey bob in a maze of uncertainty.

"Oh, oh, it's me own stupidity I'm knowing."

"No, it's my fault, Judy. I've a headache to-night."

"Sure and it's studying too hard ye are. That al*geb*ra now, it's mesilf do be thinking it isn't fit for girls to be larning. Morning, noon and night at it as ye are."

"I *must* study, Judy . . . the Entrance comes in another month and I *must* pass. Father and mother will feel dreadfully if I don't. I'm not afraid of the mathematics; I've always been fond of arithmetic especially. Only . . . do you remember how dreadfully sorry I used to be for poor A and B and C because they had to work so hard. D appeared to have things easier."

"Sure and I do remimber how pitiful ye used to look up and say, 'Doesn't A *iver* have a holiday, Judy?' It's the grand marks ye'll be making in iverything I'm ixpecting."

"No, I'm such a dub in history, Judy. I can't remember dates."

"Dates, is it? And who care about dates? What difference does it make whin things happened as long as they did happen?"

"The examiners think it makes some difference, Judy. The only two dates I'm positively sure of are that Julius Caesar landed in Britain 55 B.C. and that the battle of Waterloo was fought in 1815. Outside of those everything is in a fog."

"Me own Great-grandfather fell at the battle av Waterloo," said Judy. "And left me Great-grandmother a widdy with nine small children. But what's a widdy more or less in the world now after the Great War? Do ye be remimbering anything av it, Pat?"

"I was five when the armistice was signed. I remember the fireworks at the bridge . . . and, dimly, people talking of it before that. It seems like a dream. *You* never talk of it, Judy."

"Sure and I was ashamed all through it bekase I had none of me own to go . . . and thankful that Siddy and Joe were children. Yer mother and yer Aunt Hazel and mesilf just knit socks for the soldiers and sat tight. It's a time I don't like to be thinking av, wid ivery one ranting at the Kaiser and yer Uncle Tom and yer dad moaning bekase they was too old to go, and us lying awake at night worrying for fear they'd find a loop-hole in spite av the Fam'ly Bible. And yet all av us a bit ashamed in our hearts that we didn't have inny maple leaves in the windies. Not but what there was a bit av fun about it, wid all the girls that proud to be walking wid the boys in khaki and yer Uncle Tom singing a hymn av hate in the back yard at Swallyfield ivery morning afore breakfast. Sure and if I didn't hear him shouting, 'I'd rather die in the trenches than live under German rule,' while I was milking I'd be running over to see if he'd got lumbago. He was that ixcited whin the election for the Union Government was on . . . sure and I did be fearing he'd burst a blood vessel. Whin he found yer Aunt Edith praying that it might go in he was rale indignant. 'Elections ain't won be prayers,' sez he, and he marched her down to vote and her protesting all the way it was unwomanly. Ye niver saw such a tommyshaw. Sandy Taylor at the Bay Shore called his first b'y John Jellico Douglas Haig Lloyd George Bonar Law Kitchener. Ye shud av seen the look av the minister whin he was christened. And after it all the b'ys has just called him Slats all his life, him being so thin. They did be saying that Ralph Morgan married Jane Fisher just to escape inlisting. Sure and I'm no jidge av things matrimonial, Patsy, and niver pretinded to be but it did seem to me that I'd rather be facing the Kaiser and all his angels than marry a Fisher. Maybe Ralph come round to the same way av thinking. Whin we had the memorial service for the boys as had been killed he heaves a big sigh and sez to me, 'Ah, Judy, *they're at peace*,' sez he. Oh, oh, it's all over now and I'm hoping the world will have more sinse than iver to get in a mess like the same agin, more be token that the women can be voting."

"Old Billy Smithson at Silverbridge doesn't agree with you, Judy. He says women are fools and things will soon be in a worse mess than ever."

"Oh, oh, and are ye thinking that possible now?" said Judy sarcastically. "Old Billy shudn't be after jidging all women be his own. Well do I remimber the first time I was iver voting. I wore me blue silk and me high-heeled boots whin I wint to the polls and I was that ixcited I cud niver tell where I put the cross on me ballot. From what I culd ixplain to him yer dad always thought I'd put it in the wrong place. But innyway me man wint in so it was no great matter if I did.

PAT OF SILVER BUSH

I've niver been voting since bekase it always happens I've been canning tomaties or some special job like that whiniver there's an election."

"Uncle Tom says every one ought to exercise her franchise . . . that it's solemn duty."

"Listen at that. Don't it be sounding fine? But wud I be letting me tomaties or me baked damsons spoil bekase I had to traipse off to Silverbridge to be voting? Sure, Patsy dear, governmints may go in and governmints may go out but the jam pots av Silver Bush do have to be filled."

26

GENTLEMAN TOM SITS ON THE STAIRS

1

Pat need not have worried about her history paper. She was not fated to write it that year. The headache she complained of had not disappeared by next morning and it was further complicated by a sore throat. Mother advised her to stay in bed and Pat agreed so meekly that Judy was alarmed. Early next morning she tip-toed anxiously in to see her.

"How's the morning wid ye, me jewel?"

Pat looked at her with burning eyes above a flushed face.

"The dead clock out in the hall has begun ticking, Judy. Please stop it. Every tick hurts my head so."

Judy ran out, roused Mrs. Gardiner, and telephoned for Dr. Bentley. Pat had scarlet fever.

At first nobody was much alarmed. Joe and Winnie had had scarlet fever in childhood and had not been especially ill. But as the days wore on anxiety settled down over Silver Bush like an ever deepening cloud. Dr. Bentley looked grave and talked of "complications." Mother, who had never had scarlet fever herself, was debarred from the sick room and Judy and Winnie waited on Pat. Judy would not hear of a trained

199

nurse. She had never got over Miss Martin and her "Greta." Nobody ever knew when she slept or if she slept at all. All night she sat by Pat's bed in the bandy-legged Queen Anne chair, with its faded red damask seat, which Pat had rescued from the garret because she loved it . . . never dozing or nodding, ready with cooling drink and tender touch. Dr. Bentley afterwards spoke of her as "one of those born nurses who seem to know by instinct what it takes most women years of training to learn."

When Pat became delirious she would do nothing and take nothing for anybody but Judy.

And Pat was very delirious. Delusion after delusion chased each other through her fevered brain. Weeping Willy had carried off the wooden button on the pantry door. *"I'm sure God will think that so funny,"* said Pat, vainly searching for it before God could find out. The cracks in the ceiling wouldn't stay in place but crawled all over. She was on a lonely road, where the dark was waiting to pounce on her, calling to Jingle who was walking away unconcernedly with Emily-and-Lilian's tombstone under his arm. She was at the bottom of the well where Wild Dick had thrown her. She was searching for the Secret Field which Dorothy had taken away. She heard Joe's whistle but could never see Joe. Somebody had changed all the furniture in Silver Bush and Pat was vainly trying to get it back in place. The minister had said in church last Sunday that God held the world in the hollow of his hand. *Suppose He got tired and dropped it, Judy?*

"Sure and that's one thing He'll niver be doing, Patsy, rest ye aisy."

The wind blew and would never stop . . . *it must be so tired, Judy. Please make it stop.* She was on a road at the head of a long procession of rolling cheeses . . . all the cheeses that had ever been made at Silver Bush . . . she *had* to keep ahead of them. Faces were looking in at the window . . . pressed against the pane . . . or leering in a row along the footboard of the bed like the Bay Shore ghost. Hideous faces, cruel, crafty, terrifying faces. *Please, Judy, drive them away . . . please . . . please.* She had long fierce arguments between Pat and Patricia. Time was running by her like the dark river of the hymn. She couldn't catch up with it. *If we stopped all the clocks couldn't we stop time, Judy? Please!* And who, oh, who would give poor Bold-and-Bad his meals?

"Sure and I will, Patsy darlint. Ye nadn't be fretting over Bold-and-Bad. He's living up to his name ivery minute of the day, slaping on the

Poet's bed and getting rolled up in me shate of fly-paper. Sure and ye niver saw a madder cat. It's Gintleman Tom that's doing the worrying. He do be setting on the landing ivery moment he can spare from his own lawful concerns."

Then came two or three dreadful days when Pat's life hung in the balance. Dr. Bentley shook his head. The family gave her up. But Judy never quailed. She hadn't got the "sign" and as for Gentleman Tom he never budged off the landing, although sometimes he bristled and spat.

"Sure and whativer is after Pat will have the hard time to get past that baste," Judy said confidently.

But the third night, in the wee sma' hours, when Silver Bush was holding its wakeful breath, wondering despairingly what the morrow would bring, Gentleman Tom arose, shook himself, and walked gravely downstairs to his own cushion in the kitchen.

"He was knowing there wasn't inny more nade av sitting there," said Judy at sunrise. "Pat had got the turn. I met him coming down whin I was coming up and he was after giving me a look. Whin I wint in the darlint's room I was ixpecting to see a difference and I did. Look at her there, slaping as paceful as a lamb. Sure and this is a joyful day for Silver Bush. Ye can be watching her, Winnie, the while I brew me a jug av tay. I nade a bit av a stimulant, what wid me knees shaking and me poor head going round in circles."

2

Pat's convalescence was a long one. It was five weeks before she could even sit up in bed and drink her broth out of the dear little yellow bowl with blue roses in it . . . a Bay Shore heirloom . . . which Aunt Honor had sent over for her. She had a little gold cushion that was like a small sun behind her head . . . Aunt Hazel had sent *it* up . . . and wore a lovely jacket of primrose silk which Aunt Edith had brought over for her. Everybody was so good to her. The banished Bets sent her up leaves full of wild strawberries and Hilary brought brook trout for her. When Hilary sprained his ankle so badly that he had to keep the house for a week Judy herself, armed with a can of worms and Sid's hook and line stalked up and down the banks of Jordan to cater to Pat's slowly-reviving appetite. Mother came to the door and looked in with happy eyes. Sometimes Cuddles' darling anxious little face peered through the stair railings, not permitted to come any nearer.

It was seven weeks before Pat was allowed out of bed, despite her pleadings.

"I'm getting so tired of the bed, Judy. I'm sure it wouldn't hurt me to get up for a little and sit in a chair by the window. I want to see *outside* so much. You don't know how tired I am of looking at the blue-bells on the wallpaper. That cluster of them over the wash-stand looks just like a little pot-bellied elf with a bonnet on and it grins at me. Now, don't look terrified, Judy dear. I'm not out of my head again. You can see it for yourself."

"I'm not denying there's a resimblance. But ye'll not be out av bed for two days more. Thim's the doctor's orders and I'll folly them."

"Well, prop me up on the pillows, Judy, so that I can at least see something out of the window."

That was nice. She could see the slender fir-tops against the blue sky at the bottom of the garden . . . the cloud-castles that came and went . . . the swallow-haunted gable end of the barn . . . the smoke from Uncle Tom's chimney making magic against the hills. Pat lived on this for two days more and then Judy let her sit on a chair by the window for half an hour. Pat managed to walk to the chair although she admitted she felt very like a bowl of jelly that would all fall apart if violently shaken. But her eyes and ears made the most of that half hour. At first it was a shock to see how the summer had gone while she had been sick. But what beautiful colours the world was showing. How wonderful to see again the blue shoulders of the hills across the harbour and the ecstasy of farewell summers in the field of that ilk . . . the silky wind ripples going over the grass on the lawn and all her own intimate, beloved trees. The breeze whispering from hill to hill and blowing in the scent of flowers to her. The honeysuckle over the grave-yard paling with Judy's ducks squattering around the well. Bold-and-Bad on the window sill of the church barn and a curly black dog, with a white heart on his breast, on the granary steps.

And . . . could it be? . . . Bets! A slim lovely girl in a lilac dress, her arms full of peonies, waving to her from the Whispering Lane. Bets had *grown*.

"Judy sent me word I could just look at you from here if I was right on the dot. Oh, Pat, darling, it's just heavenly to see you again. If you knew what I've been through! I wanted to send Hilary word . . . he's just been frantic . . . but Judy thought both of us would be too much excitement for you. He'll be here to-morrow."

Every day Pat was allowed to sit up a little longer, until she could spend the whole afternoon at her window. Hilary and Bets were allowed in the garden now and could shout things up at her, though Judy wouldn't allow her to talk much in return. But it was enough just to be there, looking out on the beautiful moods of the fields, that sometimes twinkled in summer rain and sometimes basked in sunshine. One evening Judy let her stay up after supper. It was lovely to see the "dim" come stealing over the garden again. She recalled the last story she and Bets had read together, of an old enchanted garden in which flowers could talk. Just suppose her own flowers talked at night. That red rose in the corner became a passionate lover and whispered compliments to the white rose. That swaggering tiger lily told tales of incredible adventures. The nodding sleepy poppies gave away all their secrets. But the Madonna lilies only said their prayers.

She hadn't seen the stars for so long. And to watch the moon rise! Bets and she had read a poem once about the moon rising over Hymettus. But it couldn't be more beautiful than the moon rising over the Hill of the Mist with the harbour beyond. The tree shadows were lovely. The tall lilies looked like white saints in the moon-glow.

Judy coming in was quite horrified to find that Pat had not yet returned to bed.

"Ye haven't been slaping, have ye now?" she queried anxiously. "Not slaping in the moonlight, child dear?"

"No. But I'd love to. Why shouldn't I?"

"Listen at her. Don't ye iver go slaping in moonlight. It's liable ye are to go mad. Sure and I knew a man once . . . he slipt out in the moonlight one night and he was niver the same again."

Pat sighed. She hated to leave that delicious silver bath of moonlight but she *was* tired. It was nice to feel tired again and drift off to sleep so easily.

Ten weeks from the day she took sick Pat came downstairs, feeling a glad freedom. What a day that was! Such a triumphant Judy! All the poppies dancing to do her honour! Comfortably hungry for her dinner once more. Such a delightful meal with everybody exchanging happy looks. Even Gentleman Tom made a fuss over her.

"Sure and the house do be glad to see you round it again," gloated Judy.

"It was nice to see everything in the same place. She had been afraid something would be changed. The garden *had* changed a great deal. And even Bets and Jingle seemed changed . . . older, some way. Jingle had certainly grown taller. Oh, why did things have to change? The old sad question.

"Maybe there's a bit av change in yersilf, darlint," said Judy, a little sadly. Pat *was* changed . . . she looked older in some unmistakeable way.

"Sure and ye can't be going quite so near the gate av death widout it changing ye," whispered Judy to herself. "She isn't the child inny more. She'll never be the same again."

The others thought it was just her pallor and thinness. Uncle Tom told her she had a lovely suit of bones.

"I'll soon fatten up on your cooking, Judy. Life tastes good to-day."

"Sure and life do be having a taste, don't it, Patsy? I'm only a poor ould maid as has worked out all her days for a living and yet I'm declaring life has a taste. Sure and I smack me lips over it."

"Hilary has brought me a jolly book to read . . . Bets is sweeter than ever. On the whole, it's a pretty nice world in spite of change and it's wonderful to be back in it again."

"I'm telling ye. But, Patsy darlint, ye must be going careful. There's to be no running all over for a while yet. Just sit ye still and listen to yer hair growing."

3

Pat found it was more likely she would have to listen to her hair falling out. It began to fall out alarmingly. Judy assured her that it was only to be expected but even Judy was scared. Pat wept and would not be comforted.

"I'm bald, Judy . . . actually bald. I suppose it's a judgement on me for hating my ginger hair. Judy, what if it never comes in again?"

"But av coorse it will," said Judy . . . who was by no means as sure of it as she would have liked to be. She made Pat a cap of lace and silk to wear but there were some bad weeks. Some prophesied dire things.

Aunt Edith had known a girl whose hair had come out like that.

"It grew in again *white,*" said Aunt Edith.

Then the hair *did* begin to grow in . . . a dark fuzz at first. Pat was relieved to find it was not white at any rate. Then longer . . . thicker . . .

"I do be belaving it's going to be curly," whispered Judy in a kind of awed rapture.

For the first time in weeks Pat wanted a mirror. The hair *was* curly. Not too curly but just lovely natural waves. And *dark* . . . dark brown. Pat thought she would die of happiness. Her hair was "bobbed" now and at no cost to Judy who was only too glad to see her darling with hair at all.

"So you've made up your mind to be a beauty after all," said Uncle Tom, the first time he saw her without a cap.

"Hardly that," decided Pat, as she scrutinised herself in the mirror that night. "But it *is* an improvement."

"Innyway, ye'll niver be nading a permanent," said Judy, "and that's be way av being a blessing. Sure and Dr. Bentley's wife do be having a permanent, they tell me, and her scalp was burned so bad the hair do be all coming out in patches. I'm thinking she'll be wishing she'd left the Good Man's work alone."

Altogether Pat was well satisfied with her bout of scarlet fever. She had got dark wavy hair out of it and escaped Queen's for another year.

27

GLAMOUR OF YOUTH

1

Bets had passed her entrance but refused to go to Queen's until Pat could go, too. Pat, having missed her exams, must wait until next year.

A nice thing had happened. Hilary had failed to pass his entrance . . . that was not the nice thing . . . owing to the fact that the teacher at the South Glen school had been a poor one. Larry Gordon took Hilary away and sent him to the North Glen school. Consequently every morning Hilary and Bets and Pat walked gaily to school together and found life good. Sid went no longer. He was father's right-hand man now. But Cuddles was going. She started blithely off one September morning and Pat, recalling the day she had "started school," felt very motherly and protective and sentimental as she watched dear Cuddles trotting along before them, hand in hand with another small, gleeful mite from the Robinson family. How little they knew of life, poor wee souls! How very aged and experienced Pat felt herself!

"Can you believe *we* were ever as young as that?" she asked of Bets incredulously.

Bets couldn't and sighed. Yet both of them tripped along the road as if they had been born, like Beatrice, under a dancing star. It was lovely to be old enough to remember childhood with a sigh. It was lovely to have before them a road filled with soft amethyst mist. It was lovely to see dark young fir trees edging harvest meadows. It was lovely to take a short cut through the little wood lane in Herbert Taylor's woods. It was lovely to be together. For it all came back to that. Nothing would have had just the same flavour if it had not been shared with each other.

Joe had never been home. Letters came from him from spicy tropic lands and Arctic wastes and Mediterranean ports, and were great events at Silver Bush. After everybody had read them they were sent over to Swallowfield and from there to the Bay Shore and then back for mother's "glory box," as they called it in imitation of Judy's glory box. Pat had a glory box of her own now in which she kept all kinds of "souvenirs," labelled somewhat systematically . . . "a flower from Bets' garden" . . . "new plan for 'my house,' drawn by Hilary Gordon" . . . "letters from my brother, Joseph A. Gardiner" . . . "a snap-shot of Bets and me under the Watching Pine" . . . "a packet of notes from my beloved friend, Elizabeth Gertrude Wilcox" . . . "the pencil I wrote my first letter to H.H. with."

For "H.H." was Harris J. Hynes . . . and Pat was over head and ears in love with him! Absolutely sunk, Winnie said. It had happened in church, one dull November day, when the moan of an eerie wind sounded around the tower and Pat was feeling sad for no earthly reason than that it pleased her to feel so. She had not felt sad when she had left Silver Bush for she had on her new scarlet hat under which her amber eyes glowed like jewels. Her skin, which had looked sallow with ginger

206

hair, looked creamy with dark brown. Her lips were as red as her hat.

"Oh, oh, and isn't that chick now!" said Judy admiringly. "I niver saw innything chicker. Oh, oh, Patsy darlint" . . . Judy sighed . . . "the beaus will soon be coming."

Pat tossed her head.

"I don't want beaus, Judy."

"Oh, oh, ivery girl shud have a few beaus, Patsy. Sure and it's her right and so I do be telling ould Tillie Taylor last wake whin she was saying she didn't hold wid beaus. 'Ather they manes nothing or they manes too much,' sez she but what she was maning hersilf the Good Man Above only knows and maybe He'd be puzzled."

"Anyway they don't call them beaus now, Judy. That's old fashioned. It's boy-friends now."

"Boy-friends, is it? Oh, oh, Patsy me jewel, some day ye'll be finding the difference atween a frind and a beau."

Pat and Bets were both pleased to be a bit sorrowful during that walk to church. They confessed they felt old. November was such a dreary month.

"Oh, Bets, the years will just go round like this . . . and changes will come . . . you'll marry some one and go away from me. Bets, when I think of it I couldn't suffer any more if I was dying. Bets, I just couldn't bear it."

"I couldn't either," said Bets in a broken voice. Then they both felt better. It was so wonderful to be young and sad together.

2

Pat's mood lasted until the second hymn. Then everything was changed in the twinkling of an eye.

He had come in with some other boys. He was standing just across the aisle from her. He was looking right at her over his hymn book. Looking admiringly. It was the first time Pat had ever noticed a boy looking at her admiringly. She suddenly felt that she was beautiful. And . . . also for the first time she blushed devastatingly and dropped her eyes. There had never been a boy she couldn't look squarely at before.

She knew what had happened to her . . . just what had happened years ago at the blind men's concert . . . and by the same sign. Her legs were trembling.

But *this* was real.

"I wonder if I dare look at him," she thought . . . and dared.

The hymn was over now. They were all sitting down. He appeared to find his boots interesting. Pat had a good chance to look at him.

He was handsome. Wonderful crinkly golden-brown hair . . . clear-cut features—all the heroes in stories had clear-cut features . . . great brown eyes. For he lifted his eyes at that moment and looked at her again. Thousands of electric thrills went over Pat.

She heard not one word of the sermon, not even the text, much to Long Alec's indignation, for it was one of his rules that every one in his family must be able to tell the text at the dinner table on Sundays. But if Pat could not remember the text she would always remember the anthem. *"Joy to the world,"* sang the choir. Could anything be more appropriate? She never glanced his way again but when they left the church she passed him in the porch and again their eyes met. It was quite terrible and Pat was breathless as she went down the steps.

Everything was changed. Even November had its points. The clouds were gone. The wood-path was beaded with pale sunlight. Quiet grey trees on all sides treasured some secret of loveliness.

"Did you see Harris Hynes?" asked Bets.

"Who is Harris Hynes?" asked Pat, knowing quite well, although she had never heard the name before.

"The new boy. His people have bought the Calder place. He sat just across from us."

"Oh, that boy? Yes, I noticed him," said Pat casually. She felt horribly disloyal. It was the first time she had kept anything from Bets.

"He would be rather handsome if it wasn't for his nose," said Bets.

"His nose? I didn't see anything wrong with his nose," said Pat, rather coldly.

"Oh, it's crooked. Of course you only notice it in profile. But he has gorgeous hair. They say he goes with Myra Lockley at Silverbridge."

A dreadful sinking feeling engulfed Pat. Joy to the world, indeed! Where had the sunlight gone? November was a horrid month.

But that look in his eyes.

3

The invitation to Edna Robinson's party came the next day. Would he be there? She thought of nothing else for two days. When Wednesday night came it was an exquisite night of moonlight and frost but because Harris Hynes might be at Edna's dance she was blind to its beauty. It was sweet agony to decide which of two dresses she should wear . . . the red was the smartest but the blue and silver made her look more grown up . . . a slender swaying thing of moonshine and twilight. She put it on—she put little dabs of perfume on her hair and throat . . . she even borrowed a pair of Winnie's milky pearl ear-drops for her ears. It was wonderful to dress for him . . . to wonder if he would notice what she wore. For the first time she made a little ritual of dressing.

Then she went down to show herself to Judy who was making sausage meat in the kitchen. Judy knew there was something in the wind the moment she sniffed the perfume, but she said only,

"Ye're looking lovely, darlint."

Would *he* think her lovely? That was the question. But she pretended to be interested only in the sausage meat. Judy mustn't forget to put nutmeg in. Father liked nutmeg. Judy shook with laughter when the door closed behind Pat.

"It isn't sausage meat the darlint is thinking av. Oh, oh, I do be knowing the signs."

How dreadful to think he mightn't be there! How thrilling to look at that dark hill against the sunset, just behind which was the Calder place, now the Hynes place. *He* lived there. If he were at the party and she met him what would she say? Suppose she talked too much . . . or not enough? Would his people . . . his mother . . . like her? She heard not a word that Sid and Bets said. But when May Binnie, seeing the blue and silver dress for the first time in the Robinson guest room, said,

"That's the new shade they call twilight, isn't it? It would be a lovely colour on some people. But don't you think you're too sallow for such a trying blue, Pat?" it worried her. Not that she cared what May Binnie thought . . . but would *he* think her sallow? She seemed to remember Myra Lockley had a lovely complexion.

She knew the minute he came in . . . her heart beat suffocatingly when she heard his laugh in the hall. She had never heard it before but there was only one person in the world who could laugh like that. It was wonderful to see him enter the room with the other boys . . . with them but not of them . . . set apart . . . a young Greek god.

Oh, Pat had it very bad.

She was dancing with Paul Robinson when Harris cut in. Then she was dancing with him. It was like a miracle. They hadn't even been introduced. But then they didn't need any introduction. They knew each other . . . they had known each other for ages. It seemed as if they danced in silence for an eternity. Then . . .

"Won't you look at me, wonder-girl?" he was saying softly.

Pat lifted her face and looked at him. After that it was all over with her. But she was not Pat Gardiner for nothing. Judy's training stood her in good stead. She made her eyes mocking . . . challenging. He was not going to know . . . not just yet. Now that *she* knew what *his* eyes had told. Knowledge *was* power.

"So this is Patricia?" he said. The way he pronounced her name was enchanting. Never, so his tone said, had there been such a beautiful name. "Have you been thinking about me?"

"Now, why in the world should I have been thinking about you?" said Pat airily. Nobody could have dreamed that she had been thinking about nothing else. Nobody would have dreamed how exultant she was at this proof that Sunday had meant to him what it had meant to her.

"Indeed, I don't know why," he agreed with a masterly sigh. "I only know that I want you to be very, very nice to me."

He walked home with her. Sid and Bets faded away into the blue crystal of the night and they were alone. To walk with Harris over the hills, with the dark woods behind and a starry sky above and the cool white birches along the meadow fences, was something never to be forgotten. Pat was afraid everything she said was stupid. But Harris didn't seem to think so. Not that she said a great deal. Harris was the talker. She listened breathlessly while he described his recent trip in an aeroplane. He was going to be a bird-man. No tame career for *him*.

"What a dull old party," yawned Winnie, as she scrambled into bed. Frank had not been there.

And to Pat it had been cataclysmic. She held her pretty dress caressingly to her face before she hung it in her closet. *He* had liked it. She would keep that dress forever. Judy should never have *it* for her hooked rugs. She put the flowery paper serviette *he* had spread over her knee at supper in her glory box, smoothing and folding it with reverent fingers. She lay awake until the pale golden dawn came in, recalling all he had said and saying it over again to herself. She worried for fear she had been too stiff. Perhaps he wouldn't understand. Judy always said to give them the fun of a chase . . . but Judy was old-fashioned. When she wakened to find the sunshine raining all over her bed she wondered how any one could be unhappy in such a world. She could never feel sad again.

She went about in a dream all day haunted by the ghostly echoes of the violins . . . by *his* voice . . . and by lines of romantic poetry that came and went like beautiful wraiths in her memory. *Read life's meaning in each other's eyes.* Bets had a poem with that line in it in *her* glory box and Pat had once thought it silly. Oh, *this* was life. She knew its meaning now.

"Let me be seeing yer tongue," said Judy anxiously at night. "I'm thinking ye're after catching cold at that dance. Ather that or . . . is it a beau, Patsy darlint? Won't ye be telling ould Judy if it's a beau?"

"Judy, you're too ridiculous."

No matter how hard she tried Pat couldn't hide her secrets from her family. Soon they all knew that Pat "had a crush" on Harris Hynes and got no end of fun out of it. Nobody, to Pat's indignation, took it very seriously . . . except Judy and Bets. She told Bets all about it the first night she spent at the Long House. Every once in so long she and Bets simply *had* to sleep together and talk things over. Bets was quite enthralled to find herself the confidante of a real love affair. She got almost as many thrills out of it as Pat.

28

EVEN AS YOU AND I

1

For Pat life had become a serial of excitement. The curves of the dullest road were intriguing because she might meet Harris J. Hynes around them. The prosiest sermon good old Mr. Paxton might preach became eloquent when her eyes exchanged messages with Harris' across the aisle. She blushed furiously when he entered a room unexpectedly or when he handed her a book from the Sunday School library or held a door open for her to pass through. His manners were so courtly!

She marked a little ring around the date in the calendar in her glory box on which he first called her "dear." He had given her the calendar . . . a calendar in the shape of a pink rose with gilt greetings on its petal months. "To mark your happy days on," he told her. "Frightfully sentimental," jeered Winnie. But Judy was quite enraptured with it.

"I do be kind av liking a sentimental beau, Patsy. They do mostly seem to be too hard-boiled nowadays."

Pat had one of her moments of beauty when he told her he had been watching her window light half the night. (It was really Judy's light but neither Harris nor Pat ever knew that.) It was thrilling to discover that he liked cats and was not in the least annoyed when Bold-and-Bad rubbed against his best trousers and haired them. Really, his temper must be angelic! Pat would not have been surprised to find he had wings under his navy blue coat.

And it was the delight of all delights to go to the movies at Silverbridge with him.

A theatre had been started in the shabby old community hall in Silverbridge and pictures were shown Wednesday and Saturday nights. Judy was persuaded to go once but never again. She said it was too upsetting. Pat was sure she could never forget the first time Harris took her.

"Has any one ever told you how lovely you were?" he whispered, as he helped her on with her coat in the Silver Bush kitchen.

"Lots of people," laughed Pat mendaciously, with an impish light in her eyes.

("Oh, oh, that's the way to answer thim," exulted Judy to herself in the pantry. "You won't be finding the Silver Bush girls too aisy, *Mr. Hynes*.")

Pat felt as sparkling as the night. They went to Silverbridge by a short cut up the hill, past the Long House and down over the fields to the river. The white sorcery of winter was all around them and her arm was tucked warmly in the curve of Harris' arm. Just a little ahead were Sid and Bets. Sid was really having quite a case on Bets, much to

Pat's delight.

"I couldn't dream of anything more perfect," she told Judy.

"Oh, oh, Bets'll be having a dozen other beaus yet afore she settles down . . . like yerself," retorted Judy. Whereat Pat went off in high dudgeon. Well, old folks couldn't understand.

"I wonder who was the first person to think the new moon beautiful," said Pat dreamily.

"I've no eyes for the moon to-night," said Harris significantly.

Pat felt faintly chilled. The implication of Harris' remark was complimentary . . . but that slim crescent hanging over the snowy spruces that were like silver palms was so exquisite that Pat wanted Harris to share its loveliness with her. Hilary would have. Then she was horrified at such a thought.

She forgot her momentary disloyalty in the theatre. It *was* so wonderful . . . Pat would have worked that word to death that winter if she had not given it an occasional rest by using "marvellous." Crowds were around them but they were alone in the scented darkness. Once Harris took her hand and held it. When she tried to pull it away . . . "say please," whispered Harris. Pat did not say please.

The only fly in her ointment was the beauty of the screen sirens. Did they ever sneeze . . . have cold sores . . . swallow a crumb the wrong way? How could any boy sit and look at them a whole evening and then see *anything* in ordinary, everyday girls? It was almost worse than last Sunday in church when Myra Lockley had been there, the guest of Dell Robinson. Pat couldn't keep her eyes off Myra's dazzling complexion . . . all her own, too. You could tell that. Pat was sure Myra spent the whole service gazing at the navy blue back of Harris Hynes who had taken a notion that day to sit in his family pew up front. She tried to tease Harris a little about Myra the next evening when they were skating on the moonlight pool. Harris had just laughed and said, "There *was* a Myra."

At first Pat was pleased. Then she wondered if the day would ever come when he would say, "There was a Patricia."

2

Her first love letter was another "wonderful" thing. Harris had gone to visit a friend in town and Pat had never expected him to write her. But he did. Pat found the letter behind Judy's clock when she came home from school.

"Sure and I tucked it out of sight so that me bould Siddy shudn't be seeing it," whispered Judy.

Pat was put to it to find a place wherein to read the sacred missive. At that moment there was somebody in every room of the house, even the Poet's room, because Aunt Helen was at Silver Bush for a visit. To read it in the kitchen where Judy was "dressing" a brace of fat hens, was unthinkable.

Pat had an inspiration. She got her snowshoes and was away through the Silver Bush, across the hill field, and through the woods. Soon she found the Secret Field, an untrodden level of spirit-blue snow, where the Wood Queen and the Fern Princess were slender saplings now. The very spot for love-letters. Seated on a grey "longer" under the maples Pat read her letter. *Little Queen* . . . she had always wondered, ever since she and Bets had read Ella Wheeler Wilcox's poems together if any one would ever call *her* "little queen." *I can see you at this very moment, wonderful Patricia . . . I wish I could write you with a rose instead of a pen* . . . and he was *hers unalterably, Harris J. Hynes.*

What *did* the J stand for? He would never tell any one. But he had said,

"I'll tell *you* what it is some day," in a tone implying that it was some beautiful secret that would affect their entire lives.

"Oh, oh, and how minny kisses was there in your billy-doo?" said Judy, when Pat came home, her cheeks crimson from something more than her tramp in the frosty night. It was no use being angry with Judy.

"They don't call them billets-doux now, Judy," she said, gravely. "They call them mash notes."

"They would that. The uglier the better nowadays. There's something rale romantic in the sound av billy-doo. Now, Patsy darlint, ye'll be writing back to him but don't be forgetting that the written words do be lasting."

Pat had mislaid her fountain pen and the family ink-bottle was dry so she hunted up her very prettiest pencil to answer it, the one

Sid had given her on her birthday, all gold and blue, with a big, silk, flame-coloured tassel. Judy need not have worried over what Pat would write back. Her letter was really full of a dainty mockery that made the devoted Harris more "unalterably hers," than ever.

And, having written her letter, she wrapped the pencil in tissue paper and put it away in her glory box, vowing solemnly that it should never be used to write anything else . . . unless another letter to Harris. And she lay awake for hours with Harris' letter under her pillow . . . she did not want to waste this happy night sleeping.

"But what," said Judy very slyly one day, "does Jingle be thinking av all this?"

Pat winced. Hilary's attitude had been a secret thorn in her side all winter. She knew he hated Harris by the fact that he always was dourly silent when Harris was about. One evening when Harris had been bragging a bit what several noted relatives of his had done . . . Judy could have told you all the Hynes bragged . . . Hilary had said quite nastily,

"But what are *you* going to do?"

Harris had been fine. He had just flung up his splendid crest and laughed kindly at Hilary: and when Hilary had turned away Harris had whispered to Pat,

"I'm going to win the most wonderful girl in P.E. Island . . . something no other Hynes has ever done."

Still, Pat hated to feel the little chill of alienation between her and Hilary. They never went to Happiness now. Of course, they hardly ever had gone in winter and Hilary was studying very hard so that he had few foot-loose evenings to spend in Judy's kitchen. Harris, of course, never spent his evenings in the kitchen. He was entertained in the Little Parlour, where he was supposed to help Pat with her French and Latin. Sometimes Pat thought it would have been much jollier in the kitchen. There were times when, Latin and French being exhausted, she found herself with little to say. Though that didn't matter much. Harris had plenty for both.

But, when the beautiful copper beech at the top of the hill field blew down in a terrific March gale, it was Hilary who understood her grief and comforted her. Harris couldn't understand at all. Why such a fuss over an old tree? He laughed at her kindly as at an unreasonable child.

"Snap out of it, Pat. Aren't there any number of trees left in the world yet?"

"There are any number of people left in the world when some one dies, but that doesn't mend the grief of those who love him," said Hilary.

Harris laughed. He always laughed when Hilary said anything. "The moonstruck house-builder" he called him . . . though never in Pat's hearing. Just at this moment Pat found herself thinking that Harris' eyes were really *too* brown and glossy. Strange she had never noticed it before. But Hilary understood. Darling Hilary. A wave of affection for him seemed to flood her being. Even when it ebbed it seemed to have swept something away with it that had been there. She went to the picture with Harris that night but it was a little . . . flat. And Harris was really too possessive. He had his brother's cutter and he was absurdly solicitous about the robes.

"I'm not quite senile yet," said Pat.

Harris laughed.

"So it can scratch."

Why could he never take anything seriously?

When he lifted her out at the gate Pat looked at Silver Bush. It seemed to look back at her reproachfully. It struck her that she had been thinking more about Harris Hynes that winter than of dear Silver Bush. She was suddenly repentant.

"Aren't you ever going to kiss me, Pat?" Harris was whispering.

"Perhaps . . . when you grow up," said Pat . . . and laughed too.

Harris had driven angrily away but Pat slept soundly, albeit it was their first tiff. Harris did not show himself at Silver Bush for a week and Sid and Winnie tormented her mercilessly about it. Pat wasn't worried although Judy thought she might be.

"Boys do be like that now and then, Patsy. They take the quare notions. He'll be along some av these long-come-shorts, darlint."

"I haven't a doubt of it," said Pat with a shrug. "Meanwhile, I'll get a little real studying done."

3

Harris came back and everything was as before. Or was it? Where had the glamour gone? Pat felt a little disgusted with herself . . . and with Harris . . . and with the world in general. And then Harris went into Mr. Taylor's store in Silverbridge! There was no reason why a clerk in a dry-goods store shouldn't be as romantic as anybody else. But it seemed such a terrible come down after all his bird-man talk! Pat felt as if he were a stranger.

"Mr. H. Jemuel Hynes has taken a position with Mr. Taylor of Silverbridge" . . . so ran one of the locals in the next paper . . . perhaps inspired by no friend of Hynes.

"Jemuel! So that is what the J stood for. No wonder he wouldn't tell it," Pat giggled, as Judy read it out to her.

Judy talked to herself as she kneaded her bread that night in a quiet kitchen. For everybody was out except Pat, who was studying in the Little Parlour.

"Sure and the ind's near whin she do be laughing at him. I'm not knowing why he shud be ashamed av a good Bible name. Well, it's been a liddle experience like for her. She'll know better how to handle the nixt one."

There was one final flare-up of romance the night she and Harris walked down the hill from Bets' party. Harris had been very nice that evening; and he really would have been very handsome if his nose hadn't that frightful kink in it. His hair *was* wonderful and he was a wonderful dancer. And it was a wonderful night. After all, there was no use, as Judy said, in expecting too much of any boy. They all had their liddle failings.

"It's cold . . . hurry," she said impatiently.

If Judy had heard that she would have known that the end was nearer still.

They went through the Whispering Lane and Harris paused by the garden gate and drew her to him. Pat was looking at the garden, all sparkle and snow in the moonshine. How sweet it was, with its hidden secrets!

"Look, Harris," she said . . . and her voice rippled through a verse she loved.

> *"So white with frost my garden lies,*
> *So still, so white my garden is,*
> *Full sure the fields of Paradise*
> *Are not more fair than this.*

The streets of pearl, the gates of gold,
Are they indeed more peace possessed,
Than this white pleasaunce pure and cold
Against the amber west?"

"Don't let's talk about the weather," Harris was saying. "I want you only to think of me."

The light went out of Pat's face as if some one had blown it out.

"Hilary would have loved that."

She hadn't meant to say it aloud . . . but it seemed to say itself.

Harris laughed. Harris certainly had a frightful knack of laughing at the wrong time.

"That sissy! I suppose he *would* moon over gardens and trees."

Something clicked inside Pat's brain.

"He isn't a sissy," she cried. "The idea of *you* calling him a sissy . . . *you with your curls and your great soft cowey eyes,"* she finished, but in thought.

Harris tightened his arm.

"It mustn't be cross," he said fatally.

Pat stepped back and removed his arm.

"I don't want to see you again, Harris Jemuel Hynes," she said clearly and distinctly.

Harris found out eventually that she meant it.

"You're as fickle-minded as a breeze," were his bitter parting words.

Pat was not worried over her fickleness but she was rather worried over the conviction that Harris had always taken a bit too much for granted from the start. He was what horrid May Binnie called horridly, "a fast worker." And she, Pat Gardiner of Silver Bush, had fallen for it.

Judy used a dreadful phrase sometimes of certain girls . . . "a bit too willing."

"Have I been too willing?" Pat asked herself solemnly.

When it became manifest that Pat's case with Harris Hynes was off she was tormented a good deal. Bets was very sweet and understanding and comforting, but Pat did not feel entirely easy until she had talked the matter over with Judy.

"Oh, Judy, it was very exciting while it lasted. But it didn't last."

"Oh, oh, darlint, I niver thought it wud come to innything. Ye're too young for the sarious side. He was just a bit of an excursion like for ye.

I wudn't be after criticising him as long as ye'd a liking for him, Pat, but wasn't he a bit too free and aisy now? I do be liking the shy ones better that don't be calling the cows be their first name at the second visit. And he do be standing wid his legs too far apart for real illigance. Now did ye iver notice the way Jingle stands? Like a soldier. He do be such a diffrunt looking b'y since he do be wearing better clo'se and having his hair cut at Silverbridge, niver to mintion his stylish glasses."

It was strange but rather nice just to feel quietly happy again, without thrills and chills and semi-demi-quavers.

"Sid and Hilary are better than all the beaus in the world, Judy. I'm never going to fall in love again."

"Not before the nixt time innyway, Patsy."

"There won't be any next time."

"Oh, oh, it's much more comfortable not to be in love, I'm agreed. And wud ye be wanting that blue dress av yours much longer, darlint? It's all gone under the arms and it do be just the shade for that bit av blue scroll in me mat."

"Oh, you can have it," said Pat indifferently. She burned the letter just as indifferently. Nevertheless, years after, when she came across a little tasselled pencil in an old box in the attic she smiled and sighed.

Hilary came in with his lean brown hands filled with the first mayflowers for her and they went off on a ramble to Happiness.

"Sure and it's the happy b'y that Jingle is this blessed night," chuckled Judy.

"Friendship is much more satisfactory than love," Pat reflected, before she went to sleep.

29

APRIL MAGIC

1

One dim wet evening in early spring, when a shabby old world was trying to wash the winter grime from its face before it must welcome April, there was wild music among the birches and Pat listened to it as she chatted with Judy in the kitchen. Mother was tired and had been packed off to bed early. Somehow, everybody at Silver Bush, without saying anything about it, was becoming very careful of mother.

Cuddles was singing to herself in the Little Parlour . . . Cuddles had such a sweet voice, Pat reflected lovingly. Judy was mixing her bread with Gentleman Tom on one side of her and Bold-and-Bad on the other. Snicklefritz was curled up by the stove, snoring. Snicklefritz was getting old, as nobody would admit.

And then . . . there was the sound of footsteps on the stone walk. Dad or Sid coming in from the barn, thought Pat. But Snicklefritz knew better. In an instant he was awake and had hurled himself at the door in a frenzy of barks and scratches.

"Now, whativer's got into the dog?" said Judy. "Sure and it's long wakes since he bothered his liddle old head about inny stranger . . . and it's the quare dream I had last night . . . and, hivenly day, am I draming still?"

For the door was open and a bronzed young man was on the stop . . . and Snicklefritz was speechless in ecstasy . . . and Pat had flown to his arms, wet as he was. Sid and dad were rushing in from the barn . . . and mother, who had been disobedient and hadn't gone to bed after all, was flying down stairs . . . and Bold-and-Bad was spitting and bristling at all this fuss over a stranger. And everybody was a little crazy because Joe had come home . . . Joe so changed and yet the same Joe . . . hugging mother and the girls and Judy and laughing at the antics of Bold-and-

Bad and pretending to be in a fury because the white kittens in Judy's picture hadn't grown up after all.

They had a gay fortnight at Silver Bush. Snicklefritz simply refused to be parted one moment from Joe and insisted on sleeping on his bed at night. And every night Judy crept in to see if Joe was warm and ask the Good Man Above to bless him, as she had done when he was a child.

There were tales to tell of far lands and strange faces and everybody was happy. Pat was *too* happy, Judy thought, with several wise shakes of her head.

"The Ould Ones don't be giving ye a gift like that for nothing, as me grandmother used to say. No, no, you would have to be paying."

And then Joe was gone again. And this time those he left knew that Joe would never belong to Silver Bush again. He would be home for a visit once in a while . . . with longer intervals between each visit . . . but his path was on the sea and his way on the great waters. To Pat came bitterly the realisation that Joe was an outsider. The life of Silver Bush closed over his going with hardly a ripple.

"Judy, it seems a little terrible. I was so broken-hearted when Joe went away the first time . . . I felt sure I couldn't live without him. And now . . . I love him just as much as ever . . . and it was queer and lonely without him for a few days . . . but now it's as if he'd always been away. If . . . if he had *wanted* to stay home . . . it doesn't seem as if there was any real place for him. His old place seems to have grown over. And *that* hurts me, Judy."

"It do be life, Patsy darlint. They come and they go. But there do be one liddle heart that can't find comfort. Do ye be looking at the eyes av that poor Snicklefritz. He's too old to be standing such another parting."

Judy was right. The next morning Snicklefritz was found on Joe's bed, with his head on Joe's pillow. And Snicklefritz would waken no more to wail or weep. Pat and Sid and Hilary and Bets and Cuddles buried him in a corner of the old grave-yard. Judy made no objections to this although she would never let a cat be buried there.

"I thought you liked cats better than dogs, Judy," said Cuddles.

"I do that same, but a cat do be having no right in a grave-yard," was all Judy's explanation.

Cuddles prayed that night that Snicklefritz wouldn't be lonesome.

Pat knew he wouldn't. He slept with his own. What more could an old dog ask? And perhaps on the nights when Wild Dick sang and Willy wept a jolly little ghost dog would come out of his grave and bark.

2

Pat and Bets were lingering by the little green gate at the top of the hill path, making plans. They were full of plans that spring . . . plans for the summer . . . plans for college in the fall . . . plans for life beyond. They were going to camp out for a week this summer . . . they were going to room together at Queen's . . . and in a few years' time they were going to take a trip to Europe. They had been planning imaginary journeys through all their years of comradeship but this one was going to be real . . . some day.

"Isn't it fun to make plans?" Pat would say happily.

They had spent the afternoon together at the Long House. Pat loved the Long House next to Silver Bush. It was a house that always invited you to enter . . . a house, Pat often thought, that always said, "So glad you've come." Open doors . . . geraniums in the windows . . . wide, shallow, well-trodden steps up to the porch. Inside, to take off the chill of the early spring, glowing fires. They had read poetry, together savouring the wealth of beauty found in linked words; they had discussed their grievances. Bets' mother wouldn't let her wear pyjamas but insisted on nightdresses. And Bets did so crave a lovely pair of yellow ones like Sara Robinson had. So up to date. They did a great deal of laughing, pouncing on their jokes like frolicsome young kittens. And at the end Bets walked to the green gate with Pat and stood there talking for another hour. They just couldn't get talked out. And anyway Pat was going the next day to the Bay Shore for a visit and there were so many things to say. It was, they agreed, just tragic to be parted so long.

It was the first mild evening of that late, cold spring. Beyond the lowlands the sea was silver grey, save just at the horizon where there was a long line of shining gold. Far, far away a bell was ringing . . . some bell of lost Atlantis perhaps. A green, mystical twilight was screening all the bare, ugly fields from sight. Faint, enchanted star-fire shone over the spruces behind them. Down below them Uncle Tom was burning brush. Was there anything more fascinating than a fire in the open after night? And somewhere beyond those chilly skies was the real spring of blossom and the summer of roses. They gazed out over the world with all the old hill rapture no dweller in the valley ever knows. Oh, life was sweet together!

"Couldn't we have our tent back in the Secret Field the nights we sleep out?" said Bets. Bets knew about the Secret Field now. Sid had told her and Pat was glad. She couldn't have told herself, after her pact with Sid, but she hated to have Bets shut out of any of her secrets.

"Think of it," she breathed. "Sleeping there . . . with the woods all around us . . . and the silver birches in the moonlight . . . we must arrange for a moon, of course. Bets, can't you *see* it?"

Bets could. Her cherry-blossom face, wrapped in a scarlet scarf, reflected Pat's enthusiasm. That scarf became Bets, Pat reflected. But then everything did. Her clothes always seemed to love her. She could wear the simplest dress like a queen. She was so pretty . . . and yet you always thought more of the sweetness than the prettiness of her face.

"Sid says we'd be scared to death back there," she said. "But we won't. Not even if the wee green folks of the hills Judy talks about came to our tent door and peeped in."

Suddenly the night laid its finger on their lips. Something uncanny . . . something fairy-like was abroad. The spruces on the hill against the pale sunset were all at once a company of old crones. They seemed to be listening to something. Then they would shake with scornful laughter. The near-by bushes rustled as if a faun had slipped through them. Pat and Bets instinctively put their arms around each other. At that moment they were elfin-hearted things themselves, akin to the shadows and the silences. They could have knelt down on the dear earth and kissed its clods for very gladness in it.

Did it last for a moment or a century? They could never have told. A light flashing out in the kitchen of Silver Bush recalled Pat to reality.

"I must go. Sid is going to run me over to the Bay Shore when the chores are done."

"Tell them hello for me," said Bets lightly.

"I wish you were going with me. Nothing has the same flavour without you, Bets." Pat leaned over the gate and dropped a kiss on Bets' cool cheek. Life had as yet touched them both so lightly that parting was still "sweet sorrow."

Pat ran lightly down the path, turning her back, although she knew it not, on her years of unshadowed happiness.

A flock of geese flying over in the April night . . . a grey cat pouncing out from the ferns in the Whispering Lane . . . lantern shadows in the barn-yard . . . a girl half-drunk with the sweet, heady wine of spring.

"Oh, Judy, life is so beautiful . . . and spring is so beautiful. Judy, how can you help dancing?"

"Dancing, is it?" Judy sat down with a grunt. She was tired and she did not like it because it meant that she was growing old. Judy had just one dread in life . . . that she might grow too old to be of use to Silver Bush. "Whin ye come to my years, Patsy darlint, dancing don't be coming so aisy. But dance while ye can . . . oh, oh, dance while ye can. And rap a bit av wood."

30

ONE SHALL BE TAKEN

1

Pat was to have stayed two weeks at the Bay Shore farm. She did not mind . . . much. She had learned how to get along with the aunts and they thought her "much improved." A good bit of Selby in her after all. The Great-great had "passed away" a year ago but nothing else had changed at the Bay Shore. Pat liked this . . . it gave her a nice sensation of having cheated Time.

But at the end of a week Long Alec came for her one evening. And his face . . .

"Dad, is anything wrong? Mother . . ."

No, not mother. Bets. Bets had flu pneumonia.

Pat felt an icy finger touch . . . just touch . . . her heart.

"Why wasn't I sent for before?" she said very quietly.

"They didn't think she was in danger until this evening. She asked for you. I think we'll be in time."

Bets "in danger" . . . "in time," . . . the phrases made a meaningless jumble in Pat's head. The drive home was like a nightmare. Nothing was real. It couldn't be real. Things like this simply didn't happen. God wouldn't let them. Of course she would waken soon. Meanwhile . . . one must keep very quiet. If one said a word too much . . . one might have to go on dreaming. She had such a queer feeling that her heart was a stone . . . sinking, sinking, sinking . . . ever since that finger had touched it.

They drove up to Silver Bush. Pat would go up the hill path. It was quicker so because the lane of the Long House ran to the Silverbridge road. Judy caught Pat in her arms as she stumbled from the car.

"Judy . . . Bets . . ." but no, one must be quiet. One mustn't ask questions. One dared not.

"I'll walk up the hill with you, Pat."

It was Hilary . . . a pale, set-lipped Hilary. Judy . . . wise Judy . . . whispered to him,

"No, let her be going alone, Jingle. It'll be . . . kinder."

"Don't you think there's a little hope, Judy?" asked Hilary huskily.

Judy shook her head.

"I do be getting the sign, Jingle. It's a bit hard to understand. Ivery one loved her so. Sure and hiven must be nading some laughter."

Pat didn't know whether she was alone or not. She ran breathlessly along the Whispering Lane and down the field and up the hill. The Watching Pine watched . . . *what was it watching for?* A grim red sun with a black bar of cloud across it was setting behind a dark hill as she reached the green gate. She turned for a moment . . . just a moment before one had to . . . know. As long as one didn't *know* one could live. The black sea of a cold grey April twilight was far below her. That faraway bell was still ringing. It was only a week since she and Bets had listened to it and made their plans for the summer. A thing like this couldn't come in a week . . . it would need years and years. How foolish she was to be . . . afraid. One *must* waken soon.

May Binnie was in the Long House kitchen when Pat went in . . . . always pushing herself in where she wasn't wanted, Pat reflected detachedly. Then the room where she and Bets had slept and whispered and laughed . . . and Bets lying on the bed, pale and sweet . . . always sweet . . . breathing too quickly. There were others there . . . Mr. and Mrs. Wilcox . . . the nurse . . . but Pat saw only Bets.

"Dearest Pat . . . I'm so glad you've come," Bets whispered.

"Darling . . . how are you?"

"Better, Pat . . . much better . . . only a little tired."

Of course she was better. One had known she must be.

Why, then, didn't one waken?

Some one put a chair by the bed for Pat and she sat down. Bets put out a cold hand . . . how very thin it had grown . . . and Pat took it. The nurse came up with a hypodermic. Bets opened her eyes.

"Let Pat do that for me, please. Let Pat do everything for me now."

The nurse hesitated. Then some one else . . . Dr. Bentley . . . came up.

"There is no use in giving any more hypodermics," he said. "She has ceased to react to them. Let her . . . rest."

Pat heard Mrs. Wilcox break into dreadful sobbing and Mr. Wilcox led her from the room. The doctor went, too. The nurse adjusted the shade of the light. Pat sat movelessly. She would not speak . . . no word must disturb Bets' rest. Bets must be better if she were resting. Now and then she felt Bets' fingers give a gentle little pressure against her own. Very gently Pat squeezed backed. In a few days she and Bets would be laughing over this . . . next summer when they would be sleeping in their tent in the moonlit Secret Field it would be such a joke to recall . . .

"My breath . . . is getting . . . very short," said Bets.

She did not speak again. At sunrise a little change came over her face . . . such a little terrible change.

"Bets," cried Pat imploringly. Bets had always answered when she called before. Now she did not even lift the heavy white lids of her beautiful eyes. But she was smiling.

"It's . . . over," said the nurse softly.

Pat heard some one . . . Bets' mother . . . give a piteous moan. She went over to the window and looked out. The sky in the east was splendid. Below in the valley the silver birches seemed afloat in morning mists. Far-off the harbour lighthouse stood up, golden-white against the sunrise. Smoke was curling up from the roofs of Swallowfield and Silver Bush.

Pat wished sickly that she could get back into last year. There were no nightmares there.

The room was so dreadfully still after all the agony. Pat wished some one would make a noise. Why was the nurse tiptoeing about like that? Nothing could disturb Bets now . . . Bets who was lying there with the dawn of some eternal day on her face.

Pat went over and looked at her quite calmly. Bets looked like some one with a lovely secret. Bets had always looked like that . . . only now one knew she would never tell it. Pat dimly recalled some text she had heard ages ago . . . last Sunday in the Bay Shore church. *I am come into deep waters where the floods overflow me.* If one could only wake!

"I think if I could cry my throat wouldn't ache so much," she thought dully.

2

Home . . . mother's silent hand-clasp of sympathy . . . Winnie's kind blue eyes . . . Judy's anxious, "Patsy darlint, ye've had no breakfast. Can't ye be ating a liddle bite? Ye must be kaping up yer strength. Don't grieve, me jewel. Sure and they tell me she died smiling . . . she's gone on a glad journey."

Pat was not grieving. Death was still incredible. Her family wondered at her calm.

"There's something in her isn't belaving it yet," said Judy shrewdly.

The days were still a dream. There was the funeral. Pat walked calmly up to the Long House by the hill path. She would not have been surprised to see Bets coming dancing through the green gate to meet her. She glanced up at the window that used to frame Bets' laughing face . . . surely she must be there.

The Long House was full of people. May Binnie was there . . . May Binnie was crying . . . May Binnie who had always hated Bets. And her mother was trying to comfort her! That was *funny*. If only Bets could share in her amusement over it!

But Bets only lay smiling with that white, sweet peace on her waxen face and Hilary's cluster of pussywillows from the tree in Happiness between her fingers. There were flowers everywhere. The Sunday School had sent a cross with the motto, *Gone Home*, on it. Pat would have laughed at that, only she knew she was never going to laugh again. Home! *This* was Bets' home . . . the Long House and the garden she had loved and planned for. Bets was *not* gone home . . . she had only gone on an uncompanioned journey from which she must presently return.

May Binnie almost had hysterics when the casket was closed. Many

227

people thought Pat Gardiner was very unfeeling. Only a discerning few thought that fierce, rebellious young face more piteous than many tears.

If only she could get away by herself! Somewhere where people could not look at her. But, if one persisted in dreaming, one must go to the grave-yard. She went with Uncle Tom, because Sid and Hilary, who were pall-bearers, had taken the car. Spring still refused to come and it was a bleak, dull day. A few snowflakes were falling on the gray fields. The sea was black and grim. The cold road was hard as iron. And so they came to the little burying-ground on a western hill that had been flooded with many hundreds of sunsets, where there was a heap of red clay and an empty grave. The boys Bets had played around with carried her to it over a path heaped with the sodden leaves of a vanished year; and Pat listened unflinchingly to the most dreadful sound in the world . . . the sound of the clods falling on the coffin of the beloved.

"She is in a Better Place, my dear," Mrs. Binnie was saying to the sobbing May behind her. Pat turned.

"Do you think there is a better place than Silver Bush and the Long House farm?" she said. "I don't . . . and I don't think Bets did either!"

"That awful girl," Mrs. Binnie always said when she told of it. "She talked like a perfect heathen."

Pat wakened from her dream that evening. The sun set. Then came darkness . . . and the hills and trees drawing nearer . . . no light in Bets' window.

Pat had never really believed that any one she loved could die. Now she had learned the bitter lesson that it is possible . . . that it does happen.

"Let me be alone to-night, Winnie," she said; and Winnie sympathetically went away to the Poet's room.

Pat undressed and crept into bed, shivering. The wind at the window was no longer a friend . . . it was a malignant thing. She was so lonely . . . it was impossible to endure such loneliness. If she could only sleep . . . sleep! But then there would be such a dreadful awakening and remembering.

Bets was . . . dead. She, who loved everything beautiful, was now lying in that cold, damp grave on the hill with the long grasses and withered leaves blowing drearily around it. Pat buried her face in her pillow and the long-denied tears came in a flood.

"Darlint . . . darlint . . . don't be mourning like this."

Judy had crept in . . . dear, tender old Judy. She was kneeling by the bed and her arms were about the tortured creature.

"Oh, Judy, I didn't know life could ever hurt like this. I can't bear it, Judy."

"Dear heart, we do all be thinking that at first."

"I can never forgive God for taking her from me," gasped Pat between her racking sobs.

"Child dear, whoiver heard av not forgiving God," said the horrified Judy who did not know her Omar. "But He won't be holding it aginst ye."

"Life has all gone to pieces, Judy. And yet I have to go on living. How can I?"

"Sure and ye've only got to live one day at a time, darlint. One can always be living just one more day."

"She was such a dear, Judy . . . we had so many plans . . . I *can't* go to Queen's without her. Oh, Judy, our friendship was so beautiful. Why didn't God let it go on? Doesn't He like beautiful things?"

"Sure and we can't be telling what He has in mind but we can be belaving it's nothing but good. Maybe He was wanting to *kape* your friendship beautiful, Patsy darlint."

31

LOST FRAGRANCE

1

When Bets had been dead for a week it seemed to Pat she had been dead for years, so long is pain. The days passed like ghosts. Pat went for long walks over hills and fields in the evenings . . . trying to face her sorrow . . . seeing the loveliness of the crescent spring around her. She only *saw* it . . . she could not *feel* it. *Where was Bets who had walked with her last spring?*

Everything had ended. And everything had to begin anew. That was the worst of it. How was one to begin anew when the heart had gone out of life?

"I wish I could forget her, Judy . . . I wish I could forget her. It hurts to remember," she cried wildly once. "If I could drink some cup of forgetfulness like that in your old story, Judy . . ."

"But wud ye be after doing it if ye could, darlint? Ye'd forget all the gladness along with the pain . . . all the fun and happiness ye had wid yer liddle chum. Wud ye be wanting *that*?"

No, she would not want that. She hugged her sweet memories to her heart. But how to go on living . . .

"Ye don't be remembering one day whin ye was a liddle dot av four, Patsy? Ye wint to the door and all the sky was clouded over thick and dark. Ye was frightened to death. Ye did be running to yer mother, crying, 'Oh, mother, where is the blue sky gone to . . . oh, mother!' Ye wudn't be belaving us whin we tould ye it wud come back. But the nixt morning there it was smiling at ye."

Pat still couldn't believe that her blue sky would ever come back . . . couldn't believe that there would come a time when she would be happy again. Why, it would be terrible to be happy without Bets, even if it were possible . . . disloyal to Bets . . . disloyal to love. She despised herself when she had to admit that she felt hungry once more!

Silver Bush was all her comfort now. Her love for it seemed the only solid thing under her feet. Insensibly she drew comfort and strength from its old, patient, familiar acres. Spring passed. The daffodils and spirea and bleeding-heart and columbines bloomed. Bets had loved the columbines so, she should be here to see them. The pansies they had planted together, because, for some mysterious reason, pansies would not grow up on the hill, bloomed at Silver Bush, but no slim girl figure ever came down the hill to pick them in a sunset garden. The big apple tree at the Long House bloomed as it had bloomed for two generations but she and Bets could not sit on the long bough and read poetry. Pat couldn't bear to open the books she had read with Bets . . . to see the lines and paragraphs they had marked. Bets seemed to die afresh every time there was something Pat wanted to share with her and could not.

Summer came. The honeysuckle was thick over the graveyard paling. To think that the scent of honeysuckles meant nothing to Bets now . . . or the soft stars of evening . . . or the moon on white roses. The little path up the hill field grew over with grass. Nobody ever walked on it now. The Wilcoxes had sold the Long House farm and moved to town . . . Stranger lights were in it but Bets' room was always dark. Sundays were terrible. She and Bets had always spent the afternoon and evening together. Sid wouldn't talk of Bets . . . Sid in his secret boyish way had been hard hit by her death . . . but Hilary would.

"I could never have lived through this summer if it hadn't been for Hilary," Pat thought.

Yet, undeniably life began to beckon once more. The immortal spirit of beauty again held aloft its torch for her. Pat hated herself because she could enjoy anything with no Bets in the world.

"Judy, I feel as if I oughtn't to be even a little bit happy. And yet, to-day, back in the Secret Field I *was* happy. I forgot Bets for a little while . . . and then . . . oh, Judy . . . I *remembered*. It seemed sad to think I *could* forget her. And the Secret Field was changed somehow . . . more beautiful than ever but still . . . not just the same, Judy."

Judy recalled an old line in a poem she had learned in far-away school days . . . a poem by a forgotten, outmoded author who yet had the secret of touching the heart. *"Ye have looked on death since ye saw me last,"* she whispered to herself. But aloud . . .

"Ye naden't be worrying over being happy, darlint. Bets would be glad av it."

"You know, Judy, at first it hurt me to think of Bets . . . I couldn't bear it. But now . . . it's a comfort. I can think of her in all our old haunts. To-night, when the moon came up I thought, 'She is standing in it under the Watching Pine, waiting for me.' And it was sweet . . . for a little while . . . just to pretend it. But I'll never have another chum, Judy . . . and I wouldn't if I could. It hurts too much to lose them."

"Ye're young to have larned that, darlint, but we all have to sooner or later. And as for another . . . oh, oh, oh, that's all as it's ordered. I've talked to ye as wise as inny av thim, Patsy, about choosing frinds but ye don't be choosing frinds after all. They *come* to ye . . . or they don't. Just that. Ye get the ones meant for you, be they minny or few, in the time app'inted for their coming."

Summer passed. The old days were once more lovely in remembrance. The root of white perennial phlox Bets had given her bloomed for the first time. The gold and bronze dahlias flamed against the green spruce hedge. The pageant of autumn woods began. Bets had gone "rose-crowned into the darkness" . . . Joe had forsaken them . . . but the Hill of the Mist was still amethyst and mysterious on September mornings . . . the Secret Field held all its old allure . . . Silver Bush, dear Silver Bush . . . was still her own, beautiful and beloved. Pat's laughter once more echoed in Judy's kitchen . . . once more she bandied jokes with Uncle Tom . . . once more she spent long hours in Happiness with Hilary, talking over college plans. The world *was* sweet again.

> *"Yet in the purple shadow*
> *And in the warm grey rain*
> *What hints of ancient sorrow*
> *And unremembered pain!"*

No, not "unremembered." She would always remember it. She had had Bets for nine wonderful years and nothing could take them from her. Judy had been right as she always was. One would not drink of the cup of forgetfulness if one could.

32

EXILE

1

When the pass lists came out in August Hilary led and Pat had a very respectable showing. So it was Queen's in September for both and Pat thought she might like it if she could survive an absence from Silver Bush for two-thirds of the year. She had always had a sneaking sympathy for Lot's wife. Was she really to be blamed so much for lingering to look back at her home? Pat's only comfort was that Hilary would be at Queen's too, and they would be coming home every weekend.

"You wouldn't think a house could be so nice as Silver Bush is in so many different ways, Judy. And the pieces of furniture in it don't seem like furniture. They're persons, Judy. That old chair that was Great-grandfather Nehemiah's . . . when I sit in it it just puts its arms around me, Judy. I feel it. And all the chairs just *want* to be sat in."

"Sure and iverything in the house has been loved and took care av and used be so minny human beings, Patsy. It stands to rason they do be more than just furniture."

"I guess I'm hopelessly Victorian, Judy. Norma says I am. I really don't want to do anything in the world but stay on here at Silver Bush and love it and take care of the things in it and plan for it. If I do really get through the licence exams next year and get a school I'm going to shingle the roof with my first quarter's salary. Those new red and green shingles, Judy. Think how lovely they'd look against the silver birches in winter. And we must have a new rug for the Little Parlour. And oh, Judy, don't forget to see that the delphiniums are divided in October, will you? They must be this year . . . and I'm afraid nobody will remember it when I'm not here."

There was some excitement in getting her outfit ready . . . and secret sorrow, remembering how much fun it would have been to talk things over with Bets. Pat couldn't have a great deal . . . crops had been poor that year. But the necessary things were managed and Uncle Tom gave her a beautiful coat with a huge fluffy fur collar and Aunt Barbara gave her a smart little hat of brown velvet, tipped over one eye, and the aunts at the Bay Shore gave her an evening dress. Judy knit her two lovely pullovers and Aunt Edith would have given her silk undies if it had not been for the pyjama question. Silver Bush was rocked to its foundation over that. Aunt Edith, who thought even coloured silk nighties immoral, declared pyjamas were immodest and brazen faced. Pat was set on pyjamas. Even Judy favoured them simply because Aunt Edith hated them.

"How," said Aunt Edith solemnly, "would you like to die in your sleep and go before your Maker in pyjamas, Patricia?"

Mother gave the casting vote . . . as she had a trick of doing—and Pat got her pyjamas.

When the last day came Pat went to the Secret Field to say good-bye and on her return lingered long at the top of the hill field. Autumn was here . . . the air was full of its muted music. The old farm lay before her in the golden light of the mellow September evening. She knew every kink and curve of it. Every field was an intimate friend. The Pool glimmered mysteriously. The round window winked at her. The trees she had grown up with waved to her. The garden was afoam with starry white cosmos backed by the stately phalanx of the Prince's Feather. Dear Silver Bush! Never had she felt so close to it . . . so one with it.

Since the Silver Bush treasury was so very lean Pat had to put up with a rather cheap boarding house that always seemed full of stale cooking smells. It was a square, bare house on a treeless lot, on a street that was quiet only for a little while at night . . . a street where the wind could only creep in a narrow space like a cringing, fettered thing, instead of sweeping grandly over wide fields and great salt wastes of sea. But at least it was not exactly like the other houses on the street. Pat felt that she couldn't have borne to live on a street where the houses were all exactly alike. And it had a little park next to it, with a few trees.

When Pat stood alone in her room that night, with its mustard coloured ingrain carpet and its dreadful maroon walls and the arrogance of its pert alarm clock, loneliness rolled over her like a wave. Judy had sent her off that morning with "gobs av good luck to ye," but at this moment Pat was sure there was no good luck in the world for her away from Silver Bush.

She ran to the window. Below the street the western train was puffing and chugging. If she could only step on it and go home! Far beyond was cold moonlight on alien hills.

She shut her eyes and imagined she could see Silver Bush. The moon would be shining down on the Secret Field now. The little rabbits would be sitting on the paths among the birches. She heard the gulf wind sighing in the old firs and the maples whispering on the hills of home. She saw the silvery poplar leaves drifting down through the blue "dim." She thought of the old doorstep listening for her footfall . . . of her room missing her. She saw Judy in the kitchen knitting, with Gentleman Tom beside her and Bold-and-Bad in her lap . . . Cuddles perched thoughtfully somewhere about as was her dear habit . . . as *she*, Pat, had perched long years ago.

She was overcome with homesickness . . . submerged in it. She cast herself on her hard little bed and wept.

2

Pat lived through the pangs of homesickness. She was finding out how many things can be lived through. Eventually she was homesick only on rainy evenings when she could imagine the rain splashing on the back doorstones and running down the windows of a kitchen crowded with cats defiant of the weather.

She liked Queen's fairly well. She liked all the professors except the one who always seemed looking with amused tolerance at every one and everything. She imagined him looking just so at Silver Bush. As for studies she contrived to get along with a good average. The only marked talent she had was for loving things very greatly and that did not help you much with Greek verbs and dates. It helped you a bit socially, though. Pat was popular at Queen's, in spite of the fact that the other students always felt she was a little detached and aloof . . . among them but not of them. She was early elected to membership in the Saturday Satellites and by New Year's she was a star in the Dramatic Club. She was voted "not exactly pretty but charming." A bit proud . . . you knew her a street off by the way she carried her head. A bit reserved . . . she had no chums among the girls. A bit odd . . . she would rather sit in that shabby little park by her boarding house in the evenings than go to a movie.

Pat liked to sit there in the twilight and watch the lights spring up in the houses along the street and in the valley and over on the other hill. Commonplace-looking houses, most of them, but who knew what might be going on inside of them? Sometimes Hilary sat there with her. Hilary was the only boy in the world with whom she could be at the same time taciturn and comfortable. They knew how to be silent together.

Pat took Hilary for granted and did not think about his looks at all, other than to see that he did not wear weird neck-ties. But quite a number of Queen's girls thought Hilary a charming fellow, although everybody knew that he had eyes only for Pat Gardiner who did not care a hoot about him. Hilary was first and foremost a student and cared little for social doings although he had outgrown all his old awkwardness and shyness. The week-end trip home with Pat was all the diversion he sought or desired.

Those week-ends were always delightful. They went on the train to

Silverbridge and then walked home. First along the road. Up one long, spruce-walled hill . . . down into a green valley . . . another hill . . . another valley . . . twists and turns . . .

"I hate a straight road or a flat one," said Pat. "This is a road I love . . . all curves and dips. It's *my* road. Oh, it may belong nominally to the township but it's *mine*. I love it all, even that dark little glen Judy calls Suicide Hollow. She used to tell me the loveliest creepy story about it years ago."

Then they left the road and went straight home over country . . . past the eerie misty marsh and across the Secret Field and through the woods by little paths that had never been made but just happened. Perhaps there would be northern lights and a hazy new moon; or perhaps just a soft blue darkness. Cool running waters . . . aeolian harps in the spruces. The very stars were neighbours.

If only Bets could have been with them! Pat never took that walk home without thinking of Bets . . . Bets whose grave on the hillside was covered with a loose drift of autumn leaves.

And then Silver Bush! It came on you so suddenly and beautifully as you stepped over the crest of the hill field. It welcomed you like a friend with all its windows astar . . . Judy saw to that. Though once they caught her napping when she was late getting in from the barn and mother had gone to bed with a headache. There wasn't a light in Silver Bush and Pat thought she almost loved it best in the dark . . . so brooding and motherly.

The same dear old creak to the gate . . . and the happiest dog in the world throwing himself at Hilary. McGinty always came as far as Silver Bush to meet Hilary. Never a Friday night did he miss. Then Judy's kitchen and welcome. Hilary always stayed to supper and Judy invariably had hot pea soup to begin with, just to warm them up a liddle mite after their cold walk. And a juicy bone for McGinty.

The wind snoring round the house . . . all the news to hear . . . all the mad, bad, sad deeds Bold-and-Bad had done . . . three balls of velvet fluff with tiny whiskered faces tumbling about on the floor. Silver Bush was, as Aunt Edith scornfully said, always infested with kittens. As for Bold-and-Bad, he was ceasing to be a cat and was on the way to becoming a family habit.

Judy always gave them a box of eats to take back Monday morning.

"As long as one can get a liddle bite one can kape up," she would say.

Pat wondered how Queen's students who got home only once in a blue moon, survived. But then their homes were not Silver Bush!

33

FANCY'S FOOL

1

Pat met him for the first time at the Dramatic Club's exclusive dance in the Queen's auditorium, by which they celebrated the successful presentation of their play *Ladies in Waiting*. Pat had been one of the ladies and had been voted exceptionally good, although in certain vivid scenes she could never look "passionate" enough to satisfy an exacting director.

"*How* can any one look passionate with a cute nose?" she would ask him pathetically. In the end she looked impish and elusive which seemed to take just as well with the audience.

He came up to her and told her that he was going to dance with her. He never asked a girl to dance or drive with him . . . he simply told her that she was going to do it. That, said the Queen's girls, was his "line." It seemed to be a popular one, though the girls he didn't notice talked contemptuously of cave man stuff.

"I've been wondering all the evening who you were," he told her.

"Couldn't you have found out?" asked Pat.

"Perhaps. But I wanted to find out from yourself alone. We are going to the sun-porch presently to see if the moon is rising properly and then we can discover who we are."

Pat discovered that he was Lester Conway and that he was in his third year at Queen's, but had just come back to college after an absence caused by pneumonia. She also discovered that his home was in Summerside.

"I know you're thinking just what I'm thinking," he said gravely. "That we have been living ten miles apart all our lives and have never met till now."

His tone implied that all their lives had been terribly wasted. But then, everything he said seemed to have some special significance. And he had a way of leaning towards you that shut out all the rest of the world.

"What an escape I've had. I was so bored with the whole affair that I was just going to go when . . . you happened. I saw you coming downstairs and ever since that moment I've been afraid to look away for fear you'd disappear."

"Do you say that to every girl half an hour after you've met her?" demanded Pat, hoping that the sound of her voice would keep him from hearing how her heart was thumping.

"I've never said it to any girl before and I think you know that. And I think you've been waiting for me, haven't you?"

Pat was of the opinion that she had but she had enough Silver Bush sense to keep her from saying so. A lovely colour was staining her cheeks. Her French-English-Scotch-Irish-Quaker blood was running like quicksilver through her veins. Yes, *this* was love. No nonsense this time about your knees shaking . . . no emotional thrills. Just a deep, quiet conviction that you had met your fate . . . some one you could follow to the world's end . . . *"beyond its utmost purple rim"* . . . *"deep into the dying day"* . . .

He told her he was going to drive her home and did, through a night drenched with moonlight. He told her that he was going to see her soon again.

"This wonderful day has come and gone but there will be another to-morrow," he said, dropping his voice and whispering the final word confidentially as he announced this remarkable fact.

Pat thought she was getting very sensible because she slept quite well that night . . . after she once got to sleep.

It was speedily an item of college gossip that Lester Conway and Pat Gardiner had a terrible "case" on each other. It was a matter of speculation what particular brand of magic she had used, for Lester Conway had never really fallen for any girl before though he had played around with several.

He was a dark lover . . . Pat felt that she could never bear a fair man again, remembering Harris Jemuel's golden locks. He was not especially good-looking but Pat knew she had got far beyond the stage of admiring movie stars. He was distinguished-looking . . . with that faint, mysterious scowl. Lester thought he looked more interesting when he was scowling . . . like *Lara* and those fellows. His psychology was sound. Whenever a girl met him she wondered what he looked like when he smiled . . . and tried to find out.

He was appallingly clever. There was nothing he couldn't do. He danced and skated and footballed and hockeyed and tennised and sang and acted and played the ukulele and drew. He had designed the last cover for *The Lantern*. Very futuristic, that drawing was. And in the February number he had a poem, *To a Wild Blue Violet*, containing some daring lines in spite of its Victorian title. It was unsigned and speculation was rife as to who had written it and who the wild blue violet was. Pat knew. It speaks volumes for her condition of heart and mind that she didn't see anything comical in being called a blue violet. If she had been sane she would have known that a brown-and-orange marigold was more in her line. She was, in spite of her infatuation, a bit surprised to find that Lester could write poetry. She had faintly and reluctantly suspected that he wouldn't know poetry when he saw it. But *A Wild Blue Violet* was "free verse." Everything else, Lester told her, was outmoded. The tyranny of rhyme was ended forever. She would never have dared let him know after that that she had bought a second-hand volume called *Poems of Passion* and underlined half of them. *I shall be dust when my heart forgets,* she underlined twice.

She was horribly afraid she wasn't half clever enough for him. He completely flabbergasted her one evening by a casual reference to the Einstein theory . . . looking at her sidewise to see if she were properly impressed. Pat didn't know anything about the Einstein theory. She did not suspect that neither did he and spent much of the night writhing over her ignorance. What must he think of her? She went to the public library and tried to read up about it but it made her head ache and she was unhappy until the next evening when Lester told her she was as wonderful as a new-mooned April evening.

"I'd like to know if you said that because it just came into your head or if you made it up last night," said Pat. Her tongue was always her own, whatever her heart might be. But she was happy again in spite of Einstein. Lester really did not pay many compliments, so one prized it when he did. Not like Harris Hynes whose "line" had evidently been to say something flattering whenever he opened his mouth. Judy had always said *he* must have kissed the Blarney stone. How wraith-like Harris seemed now, beside Lester's scowls and commands. To think she had ever fancied she cared for him! Mere school-girl infatuation . . . calf love. He had so little appreciation of the beautiful, poor fellow. She recalled pointing out the Hill of the Mist to him one moonlit winter night and he had said admiringly that it looked like a frosted cake. Poor Harris!

And poor Hilary! *He* had had to retire into his corner again. No more evenings in the park . . . no more rambles together. Even the week-end walks did not often come his way now. The car roads held and Lester drove her home in his little red roadster. He was the only boy at Queen's who had his own car. There was no pea soup in Judy's kitchen for *him*. And Pat almost prayed that he wouldn't notice the terrible crack in the dining-room ceiling.

2

It worried Pat a little that Judy didn't have much of a mind to him. Not that she ever said so. It was what she *didn't* say. And her tone when Pat told her he was one of the Summerside Conways . . . Lester B. Conway.

"Oh, oh, it do be a noble name. And is it any secret what the B. do be standing for? Not Bartholomew be inny chance?"

"B. stands for Branchley," said Pat shortly. "His mother was one of the Homeburn Branchleys."

"Sure I do be knowing thim all. Conways *and* Branchleys. His mother used to visit here before ould Conway made his pile. She was rale humble thin. Minny's the time I've wiped yer Lester's liddle nose for him whin he was knee high to a toad. Howsomiver," concluded Judy loftily, "it's likely the matter is too high for me. Money makes the mare go and it's the cute one ye are, I'm thinking."

Judy was really impossible. To insinuate that she, Patricia Gardiner, had picked out Lester Conway because he had money.

"She should know me better," thought Pat indignantly.

But she felt the lack of Judy. If darling Bets were only alive! She would have understood. What a comfort it would have been to talk over her problems with Bets. For there *were* problems. For instance,

Lester had told her she was to marry him right away as soon as college closed. There was no sense in waiting. He was going right into business with his dad.

This was simply ridiculous. Of course, some day . . . but she wasn't going to even think of getting married for years yet. She must teach school and help them at home . . . reshingle and repaint Silver Bush . . . get a hardwood floor in the dining-room . . . a brass knocker for the front door . . . pay for Cuddles' music lessons.

Lester just laughed at this the night of the Saturday Satellites' Easter dance.

"You are too lovely, Pat, to be wasted any longer on a shabby, obscure old farm like Silver Bush," he said.

A little madness came over Pat. The very soul of her was aflame.

"Don't ever speak to me again, Lester Conway," she said, each word falling like a tinkling drop of icy water on a cold stone.

"Why, what have I done?" said Lester in genuine amazement.

That made it worse, if anything could make it worse. He didn't realise at all what he had done. Pat turned her back on him and flew upstairs. To get her wraps was the work of a minute . . . to slip down the back-stairs and through the side-hall, another minute. Then out . . . and back to Linden Avenue. The bite and tang of the cold air seemed to increase her anger. Patricia Gardiner of Silver Bush had never in all her life been so furious.

Lester came down the next evening, looking more Lara-like than ever. He ignored the incident . . . he thought that would be the best policy . . . and told her she was going with him to the Easter Prom.

"Thank you, I'm not," said Pat, "and please don't waste any more of those charming scowls on me. When I tell anybody I'm through with him I'm *through*."

When Pat said anything in a certain way she was believed.

"Of all the fickle girls," said Lester. Just like Harris. Men were so tiresomely alike.

"I was born in moonlight, they tell me," said Pat coolly. "So I'm naturally changeable. No one can insult Silver Bush in my hearing. And I'm tired . . . very tired . . . of taking orders from you."

The Conway temper . . . Judy could have told you a few things about *it* . . . flared up.

"Oh . . . well . . . if you're going off the deep end about it!" he said nastily. "Anyway, I just began going about with you to put a spoke in Hilary Gordon's wheel."

She was glad he had said that. He had set her free. She had been hating him so bitterly that her hate had made her as much of a prisoner as love had. Now he had simply ceased to exist.

"I've heard Judy use a phrase," said Pat to herself after he had flung away, scowling for once in real earnest, "'fancy's fool.' Well, I've been fancy's fool. And that is that."

3

It was a good while before she could talk the whole thing over with Judy. *Now* Judy sympathised and understood.

"Oh, oh, Patsy dear, I niver did be liking yer taking up wid a Conway, not aven if his pockets were lined wid gold. Gintleman Tom didn't like him . . . there was something in that cat's eye whiniver he saw him. And he was always a bit too lordly for me taste, Patsy. A man shud be a bit humble like whin he's courting for if he isn't whin will he be? I'm asking ye."

"I can never forgive him for making fun of Silver Bush, Judy."

"Making fun av Silver Bush, was he? Oh, oh, if ye'd seen the liddle shack his father was raised in, wid the stove-pipe sticking out av its roof. Sure and the Conways were the scrapings av the pot in thim days. And the timper av the ould man. One time he wasn't after liking the colour av a new petticoat his wife did be buying . . . it was grane whin he wanted purple. He did be taking it up to the attic av his grand house in Summerside and firing it out av the windy. It caught on the top av a big popple at the back av the house and there it did be hanging all the rist av the summer. Whin the wind filled it out 'twas a proper sight now. The folks did be calling it the Conway flag. Ould Conway cudn't get it down bekase the popple was ralely in Ned Orley's lot and Ned and him were bad frinds and Ned wudn't be letting inny one get at the tree. He said he was a better Irishman than ould Conway and liked a bit av rale Paddy grane in his landscape."

"Lester admits his father was a self-made man, Judy."

"Oh, oh, that wud be a very pretty story if it was the true one. Ould Conway didn't be making himsilf. The Good Man Above attinded to that. And he made his pile out av a grane and feed store. But I'm saying for him he wasn't skim milk . . . like his brother Jim. *He* was the miser, now. 'Take out the lamp,' sez he whin he was dying. 'A candle do be good enough to die by.' Oh, oh, there do be some quare people in the world," conceded Judy. "As for me poor Lester, they tell me he's rale down-hearted now that his temper fit do be over. I'm afraid it's ye that do be the deluthering cratur, Patsy. He did be thinking ye were rale fond av him."

"Of course I admit I was a perfect idiot, Judy. But I'm cured. I'll never fall in love again . . . if I can help it," she added candidly.

"Oh, oh, why not, me jewel?" laughed Judy. "As yer Aunt Hazel used to say it's a bit av fun in a dull life. Only don't be carrying it too far and breaking hearts, aven av the Conways. There do be big difference atween falling in love and loving, Patsy."

"How do you know all this, Judy? Were *you* ever in love?" said Pat impudently.

Judy chuckled.

"One can be larning a lot be observation," she remarked.

"But, Judy, how can one *tell* the difference between loving and being in love?"

"It do be taking some experience," acknowledged Judy.

Pat burned *Poems of Passion* but when she came across the line . . . *"spilt water from a broken shard,"* in one of Carman's poems she underlined it. That was all love really was, anyway.

She went to the Easter Prom with Hilary.

"Poor Jingle!" said Judy to Gentleman Tom. "That does be *twicet*. If she gets over the third time . . ."

34

"LET'S PRETEND"

1

"Let us see the handsome houses where the wealthy nobles dwell," quoted Hilary. "In other words let us take a stroll along Abegweit Avenue. There's one of the new houses there I want to show you. I won't tell you which one it is . . . I want you to guess it. If you're the lass I take you to be, Pat, you'll spot it at sight."

It was a Saturday afternoon in spring with sudden-sweeping April winds. The world seemed so friendly on a day like this, Pat thought. She wore her crimson jersey and tam and knew she looked well in them and that Lester Conway, scowling by in his roadster, knew it, too. But let Lester scowl on. Hilary's quizzical smile was much pleasanter in a companion and Hilary looked brown and wholesome in the spring sunshine. Not much like the ragged little lad who had met her on that dark, lonely road of long ago. But the same at heart. Dear old Hilary! Faithful, dependable Hilary. Such a friend was better than a thousand of Judy's "beaus."

They had not gone home for this week-end, since the Satellites were having a wind-up jamboree that night. Pat could by now survive staying a week-end in town. Yet she felt that she always missed something when she did. Today, for instance, the wild violets would be out in Happiness . . . the white ones . . . and they not there to find them.

Abegweit Avenue was the finest residential street in town and at the end it ran out into the country, with a vision of distant emerald hills beyond. It always compelled Pat to admit that there were a few satisfying houses in the world beside Silver Bush. All kinds of houses were built on it—from Victorian monstrosities with towers and cupolas, to the newest thing in bungalows. Pat and Hilary loved to walk along it, talking when they felt like it, holding their tongues when they didn't, discussing and criticising the houses, making changes in most of them, putting in a window here and slicing one off there, lifting or lowering roofs . . . "a low roof gives a house a friendly air," said Hilary.

Some houses thrilled them, some charmed them, some annoyed them. Some were attractive, some repellent . . . "I'd like to smash a few of your windows," was Pat's reaction to one. Even the doors were fascinating. What went on behind them? Did they let you out . . . or in?

Then they had to settle which house they would accept as a gift, supposing they were simply compelled to take one.

"I think I'd take that gentle house on the corner," said Pat. "It has an attic . . . I must have an attic. And it looks as if it had been loved for years. I knew *that* the first time I ever saw it. It would like me, too. And that funny little window away off by itself has a joke it wants to tell me."

"I'm choosing one of the new houses this time," said Hilary. "I like a new house better than an old one when all is said and done. I would feel that *I* owned a new house. An old house would own *me*."

Pat had kept a keen look-out for Hilary's house. She had thought several of the new ones might be it. But when she saw it she knew it. A little house nestled in a hollow half way up a little hill. Its upper windows looked right out on the top of the hill. Its very chimneys smacked of romance. A tremendous maple tree bent over it. The tree was so enormous and the house so small. It looked like a toy house the big tree had picked up to play with and got fond of it. It had a little garden by its side, with violets in a corner and in the centre a pool with a border of flat stones, edged with daffodils.

"Oh!" Pat drew a long breath. "I'm so glad I didn't miss that. Yes, if they give you that house, Hilary, take it. It's so . . . so *right,* isn't it?"

"That tree in the front should be cut down though," said Hilary thoughtfully. "It breaks the line . . . and spoils the view."

"It doesn't . . . it simply guards it as a treasure. You wouldn't cut that lovely birch down, Hilary."

"I'd cut any tree down if it wasn't in the right place," persisted Hilary stubbornly.

"A tree is always in the right place," said Pat just as stubbornly.

"Well, I won't cut it down yet awhile," conceded Hilary. "But I'll tell you what I am going to do some dark night, Pat. I'm going to sneak up here and carry off that cast-iron deer next door and sink it in the bay fathoms deep."

"Would it be worth while? The whole place is so awful. You couldn't carry off that enormous portico. The house looks like a sanitarium. Did you ever suppose any place could be so hideous?"

"The house next to it isn't hideous . . . exactly. But it has a cruel, secretive look. I don't like it. A house shouldn't be so sly and reserved. And there's a house I'd like to buy and groom it up. It's so out at elbows. The shingles are curling up and the verandah roof is sagging."

"But at least it isn't self-satisfied. The next one *is* . . . positively smug. And *that* one . . . they say it cost a fortune and it's as gloomy as a tomb."

"Shutters on those stark windows would make an amazing difference," said Hilary reflectively. "It's really wonderful, Pat, how much a little thing can do to make or mar a house. But I don't think there's any place for dreaming in that house . . . or for ghosts. There must be a place for dreams and ghosts in every house I'll design."

"There's that unfinished house, Hilary . . . it always makes my heart ache. Why don't they finish it?"

"I've found out why. A man began to build that house just to please his wife and she died when it was only half done. He hadn't the heart to finish it. That white place is a house for the witch of the snow. It's positively dazzling."

"What is the matter with that house in the middle of the block, Hilary? It's very splendid but . . ."

"It hasn't enough restraint. It bulges like . . . like . . ."

"Like a fat woman without corsets," laughed Pat. "Like Mary Ann McClenahan. Poor Mary Ann died last week. Do you remember how we thought she was a witch, Hilary?"

One house was as yet only a hole in the ground, with men setting pipes and running wires in it. Who was waiting for that house? Perhaps a bride-to-be. Or perhaps some tired old body who never in her life had a house to her liking and meant to have one before she died. There was a house that wanted to be wakened up. And there was one with Dr. Ames coming away from it. He looked grave. Perhaps some one was dying in that house. He wouldn't be looking like that if a baby had come.

"I would like to see all the houses in the world . . . all the beautiful ones at least," said Hilary. "And I've got a new idea for your house to-day."

He was always getting new ideas for it but nowadays he never told her what they were. Everything was to be a surprise.

They walked back in silence. Hilary was dreaming. All men dream. His dream was of building beautiful homes for love to dwell in . . . houses to keep people from the biting wind and the fierce sun and the loneliness of dark night. It must be a fascinating thing to build a house . . . to create beauty that would last for generations and be shelter and protection and friendliness as well as beauty. And some day he *would* build a house for Pat . . . and she *must* live in it.

Pat was thinking again how nice it was to walk with Hilary. With Harris and Lester she had felt that she must be always bright and witty and sparkling lest they might think her "dumb." Hilary was restful. And he never said embarrassing things. To be sure his looks sometimes said many things his tongue never did. But who could quarrel with looks?

35

SHADOW AND SUNSHINE

1

Care sat visibly on Patricia's brow.

"My vision cannot pierce beyond the darkness of next week, Judy. It is completely bounded by the gloomy shade of licence exams. Judy, what if I don't pass?"

"Oh, oh, but ye will, darlint. Haven't ye been studying all the term like a Trojan? Excipt maybe thim few wakes whin me bould Lester was ordering ye about. So don't be worrying yer head about it. Just take a bit av a walk through the birches and fale thankful that spring do never be forgetting to come. And thin, maybe, ye'll be making Siddy's fav'rite pancakes for supper. It's mesilf can't give thim the turn at the right moment like ye can."

"Judy, you old flatterer! You know nobody can make pancakes like yours."

"Oh, oh, but the pastry now, Patsy, I niver had the light hand wid it that ye do be having. Sure that pie ye was after making last wake-ind . . . it did be looking as if it had just stipped out av the pages av that magazine Winnie takes."

"Sure and that'll divart her a bit," thought Judy. But it didn't.

"I can't help worrying, Judy. It will be dreadful if I don't pass . . . it will hurt mother so. And she *mustn't* be hurt."

For everybody at Silver Bush had become very careful of mother without saying much about it. Nobody ever heard her complain but all winter she had been taking little bitter strychnine tablets for the heart and a "rest" in the afternoons. The shadow had crept towards Silver Bush so stealthily that even yet they hardly realised its grim presence. Father was looking grey and worried. Although none of the children knew it the doctor was advising an operation and Judy and Aunt Edith were, for the first, last, and only time in their lives of the same opinion about it.

"They'll just cut her up for an experiment," said Aunt Edith wrathfully. "*I* know them."

"Indade and I wudn't put it by thim," agreed Judy bitterly.

Mother herself would not hear of an operation. She felt that it couldn't be afforded: but she didn't tell Long Alec that. She merely said that she was frightened of it. Long Alec rather marvelled at this. He had never associated fear of any kind with his wife. But then neither had he ever associated that strange languor and willingness to lie quietly and let other people do the work. Mother had never hurried through life; she had walked leisurely . . . Judy was wont to say she had never known any one who made so little noise moving round a house . . . but she got a surprising amount of work done.

Pat got through the exams eventually and even dared to hope she had done fairly well. She left Queen's with a good deal of regret and grimy Linden Avenue with none at all. Home again to dear Silver Bush, never more to leave it . . . for the home school was promised her and Pat had already in imagination spent a year's salary on Silver Bush. Several years', in fact . . . there were so many things she wanted to do for it. How she loved it! The house and everything about it were linked inextricably with her life and thought. There was one verse in the Bible she could never understand. *Forget also thine own people and thy father's house.* It always made her shiver. How could anybody do *that*?

She fell in love with life all over again on those spring evenings when she walked over the hill or by Jordan or in the secret paths of her enchanted birches. Winds . . . delicate dawns . . . starry nights . . . shore fields blurred by a silvery fog . . . the cool wet greenness of the spring rains . . . all had a message for her and all made her think of Bets . . . even yet Pat's voice quivered when she pronounced that name.

Where was Bets?

> *"In what ethereal dances,*
> *By what eternal streams"*

did her footsteps wind?

"I wonder if Bets isn't homesick in heaven for *this*?" Pat pointed to the white lilac over the garden fence. "And she must miss the sunsets. This is just such a night as she loved, Judy. Oh, Judy, last spring she was *here*. All winter at Queen's, where she had never been, it wasn't so hard. But here . . . everything seems to speak of her. To-night, when I smell that white lilac it seems to me that she must be near. She doesn't seem dead any more. She just seems around the corner somewhere, still dear and loving. But oh, I want her so!"

"Pat," came Cuddles' voice, clear and insistent at her elbow, "do you think I have It?"

"We'll be having our hands full wid that same young Cuddles," Judy had confided to Pat that very day. "In a few years that is, whin she grows into her eyes. Yer Uncle Tom sees it. Wasn't it only yisterday he sez to me, sez he, 'Ye'll be finding her a handful.' Oh, oh, she'll dance through life, that one."

Pat could not realize that Cuddles was by way of getting to be a big girl. It was only yesterday she had been an adorable baby, with dimpled arms and cheeks, whose very look said "come and love me." And now she was eleven . . . with one teasing, unruly curl hanging down the middle of her forehead and a nose that even at eleven was not the smudge of other elevens. And her eyes! No wonder Cuddles was spoiled. When she looked up sorrowfully and appealingly, she was never punished severely. You couldn't punish a young saint gone astray. Cuddles' eyes were always asking for something and always getting it. Unlike Pat, Cuddles revelled in chums and Silver Bush was over-run with them . . . "chattering like crows," said Judy indulgently. Judy was proud of Cuddles' popularity. As for the opposite sex . . . well, if tributes of sticky candies and moist apples, and stickier and moister dabs of kisses meant anything Cuddles certainly had "It."

"When *I* was eleven," said Pat with the tone of eighty, "I wasn't thinking of such things, Miss Rachel."

"Oh, but I'm a modern child," said Cuddles serenely. "And Trix Binnie says you've got to have It or the boys won't look at you."

Judy shook her grey head solemnly, as if to remark, "If they say these things in the green tree what will they say in the dry?" But Cuddles persisted.

"You might tell me what it is, Pat, and if you think I've got It. After all" . . . Cuddles was very serious . . . . "I'd rather get information from my own family than from the Binnies."

"The sinse av her now!" said Judy.

Pat took Cuddles off into the grave-yard and, sitting on Wild Dick's tombstone, tried to give her some "information." She felt that she must fill mother's place with darling Cuddles now. Mother must not be bothered.

2

And then the shadow, which had been creeping nearer and nearer, pounced.

Mother was ill . . . mother was very, very ill.

Mother was dying.

Nobody said it but everybody knew it. Except Judy who stubbornly refused to believe it. Judy wouldn't give up hope. She hadn't got "the sign."

"And I'll not be belaving it till I do," she said.

Pat wouldn't believe it either.

"Mother can't die," she said desperately, "not *our* mother."

They had always taken mother so for granted. She had always been there . . . she always would be there. How was it possible to picture anything else?

Pat had not even Hilary to help her through those weeks. Hilary was up west, helping another uncle build a house. The task delighted

Hilary. It had an ideal quality for him. Besides, before he could design houses he wanted to know all about building them, from the ground up.

"Bets last year . . . and now mother," thought Pat.

Then came a torturing hope. The specialist who was called in advised an operation. With it, he conceded, there was a chance. Without it, none.

Judy, when she heard there was to be an operation, gave up hope at once, sign or no sign.

"Oh, oh, it's mesilf shud be dying instid av her," she muttered. "I don't be knowing what the Good Man Above means, so I don't."

Gentleman Tom winked inscrutably.

"Ye can't be doing innything, cat dear. Ye wudn't let what was after Patsy that time get her. But ye can't be guarding Mrs. Long Alec . . . not if they take her to that hospital to be cut up. And her a Selby av the Bay Shore!"

Pat was up in mother's room. A new Pat . . . older . . . graver. But more hopeful. As long as one had a little hope!

Mother had asked to be propped up in bed, so that she might see the green fields she loved. Her hands lay on the counterpane. It was strange to see mother's hands so white and idle.

She was to be taken to the hospital the next day. Mother was very fine and simple and brave about it. But when had mother ever been anything else? Mother had never been excitable like the Gardiners. Her *spirit* was always at rest, so that any one who came into her presence was always conscious of a great calm. Her eyes were still the asking eyes of a girl and yet there was something maternal about her bosom that made you want to lay your head on it if you were tired or troubled.

"The apple blossoms are out. I'm glad I've seen them once more. I was a girl under them once, Pat, like you . . . and your father . . ."

Mother's voice trailed off into some hinterland of happy remembrance.

"You'll see the apple blossoms for many more springs, mother darling. You'll come back from the hospital cured and well . . . and I've ordered a lovely day for you to go on."

Mother smiled.

"I hope so. I've never given myself up yet, Pat. But I'd like to talk to you a little about some things . . . supposing I don't come back. We must look that in the face, dearest. Winnie will be marrying Frank . . . and you will have to take my place, you know."

"I . . . I know," choked Pat. "And I'll never, never marry, mother, I promise that. I'll stay here and keep a home for dad and Sid and Cuddles. Sid won't want to marry ever, when he has me."

Again mother smiled.

"I don't ask you to promise that, dear. I'd like to think you'll marry some day. I want you to be a happy wife and a joyful mother of children. Like I've been. I've been so happy here, Patsy. I was only twenty when I came here. A spoiled child, too . . . and as for housekeeping, I didn't know the difference between simmering and boiling. Judy taught me . . . wonderful old Judy. Be good to her, Pat . . . if I don't come back. But I needn't tell you that. Judy was so good to me. She was even quite fierce about my working . . . she hated to see my hands spoiled. I *had* pretty hands, Pat. But I didn't mind spoiling them for Silver Bush. I've loved it as you do. Every room in it has always been a friend of mine . . . had a life of its own for me. How I loved to wake up in the night and feel that my husband and my children were well and safe and warm, sleeping peacefully. Life hasn't anything better to offer a woman than that, Patsy."

Mother didn't say this all at one. There were long pauses when she lay very still . . . little gasps for breath. Sometimes terrible lances of fear pierced Pat's new armour of hope. When father came in to take her place as watcher Pat went down and out to the dark garden. Every one else was in bed, even Judy. She could not go to bed . . . she could not sleep. The night was warm and kind. It put its arms around her like a mother. The white iris seemed to shine hopefully in the dark. Bold-and-Bad came padding along the walk and curled up in her lap. There were times when even Bold-and-Bad could behave like a Christian. He knew that Pat needed comfort and he did his best to give it.

Pat sat on the garden bench until dawn came over the Hill of the Mist and Bold-and-Bad ran away for a glorious mouse hunt in the grave-yard. The day had begun in a pale windless morning . . . the day on which mother was to go. *Would she ever return?*

That old hynm she had hated . . . *"change and decay in all around I see."*

Change was what she had always dreaded.

"Oh, Thou who changest not abide with me."

It was not a hateful hymn after all . . . it was a hymn to be loved. How wonderful to feel that there *was* something that never changed . . . a Power under and above and around on which you could depend. Peace seemed to flow into her.

"Child dear, whativer got ye up so early?"

"I wasn't in bed at all. I've been in the garden, Judy . . . just praying."

"Oh, oh, it's all inny av us can be doing now," said Judy despairingly.

Cuddles had not been allowed to know the worst but she heard it in school that day and Pat had hard work to comfort her that evening.

"And what do you think Trix Binnie said?" she sobbed. "She said she *envied* me . . . it was so exciting to have a death in the house."

"You go down on yer liddle marrow bones this night and thank the Good Man Above he didn't be making ye a Binnie," said Judy solemnly.

Even that day was lived through. At night dad telephoned from town that the operation was successfully over and that mother was coming out of the anesthetic nicely. The Silver Bush folk slept that night; but there was still a long week of suspense to be lived through before they dared really hope. Then dad came home, with a light in his tired eyes that had not shone there for many a day. Mother would live: never very strong perhaps . . . never just the woman she had been. But she would live.

"Oh, oh, and didn't I be always telling ye so?" said Judy triumphantly, forgetting all her gloomy dreads of "cutting up." "There niver was no sign. Gintleman Tom did be knowing it. That cat niver worried himsilf at all, at all."

3

Mother could not come home for six weeks, and during those weeks Pat and Judy ran Silver Bush, for both the aunts at the Bay Shore were ill and Winnie had to go the rescue. Pat was in the seventh heaven. She loved everything about the house more than ever. The fine hemstitched tablecloths . . . Judy's hooked rugs . . . the monogrammed sheets . . . the cedar chest full of blankets . . . the embroidered centerpieces . . . the lace doilies . . . the dear old blue willow-ware plates . . . Grandmother Selby's silver tea service, the old mirrors that had stolen a bit of loveliness from every fair face that had ever looked into them. All had a new meaning for her. Every window was loved for some special bit of beauty to be seen from it. She loved her own because she could see the Hill of the Mist . . . she loved the Poet's window because there was a far-away glimpse of the bay . . . she loved the round window because it looked right into the silver bush . . . she loved the front hall window because it looked squarely on the garden. As for its attic windows, one saw everything in the world worth seeing from them and sometimes Pat would go up the attic for no earthly reason except to look out of them.

She and Judy didn't make slaves of themselves. Every once in so long Pat would say,

"Now, let's stop thinking housework, Judy, and think wild strawberries," . . . or ferns . . . or June-bells as the case might be, and off they would go for a ramble. And in the "dims" they would sit on the back-door steps as of old and Judy would tell funny tales and Pat would laugh until she took kinks.

"Oh, oh, ye do be knowing how to work, Patsy darlint . . . stopping for a bit av a laugh once in so long. There's few people do be knowing the sacret. Yer aunts at the Bay Shore . . . they niver do be laughing and it's the rason they do be taking sick spells so often."

"Uncle Brian and Aunt Jessie are coming for the weekend, Judy. I must cut some iris for the Poet's room. I do love fixing up that room for a guest. And we must have an apple tart with whipped cream. That's Uncle Brian's favourite dessert."

Pat always remembered what a guest liked to eat. And she was, as Judy declared, "a cook be the grace av God." She loved to cook, feeling delightedly that in this one thing at least she was akin to the women of all lands and all ages. Almost all her letters to mother and Hilary and college correspondents began, "I've just put something in the oven." The pantry was never without its box of spicy cookies and the fluffy perfection of her cakes left Judy speechless. As for the fruit cake she proudly concocted and baked one day all on her own, take Judy's word for it, there never had been a fruit cake to match it at Silver Bush.

"I was niver no great hand at fruit cake, darlint," she said sadly. "Yer Aunt Edith always do be saying it takes a born lady to make a rale fruit cake and maybe she is right. But I might av been larning the trick if it hadn't been for a bit av discouragement I was having just after I came to Silver Bush. I thought one day I'd be making a fruit cake and at it I wint, wid more zale than jidgement. Yer Uncle Horace was home thin

. . . and a young imp he was . . . hanging round to see what he could see and mebbe get a licking av the bowl. 'What do ye be putting in a fruit cake, Judy Plum,' he sez, curious like. 'A liddle bit av iverything,' sez I short like. And whin I turns me back to line the pan what did the young divil do but impty the ink-bottle on the clock shelf into me cake . . . and me niver knowing it. Sure and yer Aunt Edith do be saying a good fruit cake shud be black. Mine was black enough to plaze her, Patsy darlint."

Pat exulted in finding a new recipe and serving it before anybody else when the Ladies' Aid met at Silver Bush. She loved to pore over the advertisement pictures in the magazines . . . the lovely cookies and fruits and vegetables . . . dear little white and red radishes . . . curly lettuce . . . crimson beets . . . golden asparagus with little green tips. She loved going to town to shop. There were certain things in the stores there, *hers*, though she had not yet bought them. She liked to browbeat the butcher and bulldoze the grocer delicately . . . to resist temptation and yield to it . . . to save and spend. She loved to think of weary and lonely people coming to Silver Bush for rest and food and love.

And under everything a sense of deep satisfaction in doing the thing she was meant to do. She tasted it to the full in the beautiful silences which occasionally fell over Silver Bush when every one was quietly busy and the cats basked on the window sills.

And then to prepare for mother's home-coming!

36

BALM IN GILEAD

1

"Father walks slow to what he used to do," said Winnie with a sigh, as she and Pat shelled peas on the kitchen steps in the sultry August afternoon, with Bold-and-Bad sitting between them. An occasional breeze set the leaves of the young aspen by the door shaking wildly.

Pat loved that aspen. It had grown up unregarded in a few summers . . . Judy always threatening to cut it down . . . and then over night it had turned from a shrub into a tree. And then dad had declared it must come down but Pat had interceded successfully.

"In a year or two it will shade the steps so nicely. Think of the moonlight falling through it on summer nights, dad."

Dad shrugged and let her have her way. Everybody knew Pat couldn't bear to have a tree cut down. No use having the child cry her golden-brown eyes out.

Over in the field of the Pool Sid was building an oat-stack. Sid, it was said, could build the best oat-stack in P.E. Island.

Pat looked after dad wistfully as he crossed the yard and went over to the field of the Pool. He did walk slower; he was more stooped. Yet how she hated to admit it.

"Is it any wonder? After those dreadful weeks when we didn't know whether mother would live or die. And I don't think he ever really got over Joe's going." Winnie sighed again. Pat looked keenly at her. Winnie had been very remote and dreamy for some days past. Pat suddenly remembered that she had not heard Winnie laughing . . . since when? Since the last night Frank Russell had been over. And he had not been over for a week.

It had been a suspected thing all through the year that Winnie and Frank would be married in the fall. All through the winter Judy had hooked rugs "like mad." Pat did not warm to the thought but it had to be faced and accepted.

"Winnie, what is the trouble, darling?"

"There's no trouble," said Winnie impatiently. "Don't be silly, Pat."

"I'm not silly. You've been . . . funny . . . for a week. Have you quarrelled with your Frank?"

"No," said Winnie slowly. Then her face went white and her eyes filled with tears. She *must* tell somebody and mother mustn't be bothered now. Pat wasn't old enough to understand, of course . . . Winnie still persisted in thinking of Pat as a mere child . . . but she was better than nobody at all.

"It's only . . . he was a little angry when I told him we couldn't be married this fall after all . . . perhaps not for years."

"But . . . Winnie . . . *why?* I thought it was all settled."

"So it was. Before mother took ill. But you know perfectly well, Pat, that everything is changed now. We simply have to look facts in the face. Mother may be spared to us for many years but she'll always be an invalid. You will be teaching and Judy isn't as young as she once was. She can't do all the work that has to be done here, even with your help after school. And it would break her heart to get any one in to help her, even if dad could afford it, which he can't. So I must give up all thoughts of being married just now. Of course Frank doesn't like it, but he'll just have to reconcile himself to it. If he doesn't . . . well, there are plenty of other girls ready to keep house for him."

In spite of herself Winnie's voice faltered. The thought of all those willing girls was very bitter. And Frank had been very . . . difficult. The Russells did not like to be kept waiting. She knew he wouldn't wait for years. And if he did . . . they would be old and tired and all the first blossom of life would be withered and scentless. Just like poor Sophie Wright. She and Gordon Dodds had waited for fifteen years until her paralysed father died; and Sophie had never seemed like a bride. Just a faded little woman who no longer cared greatly whether she was married or not. Yet Winnie did not falter in her decision. There was good stuff in the Silver Bush girls. They put duty first always, even in a world which was clamouring that the word was outmoded and the thing to do was to grab what you wanted when you wanted it and let everything else go hang.

For just a moment a wild thrill of joy swept over Pat. Winnie wouldn't marry Frank after all. There wouldn't be any more changes at Silver Bush. She and Winnie and Sid would just go on living there, taking care of father and mother, loving Silver Bush and each other, recking nothing of the changing world outside. It would be heavenly.

But Winnie's eyes! They looked like blue violets that somebody had stepped on and bruised horribly.

Pat had never been able to understand how Winnie *could* love Frank as she did. Frank . . . if you didn't hate him because he was stealing your sister . . . was a nice enough fellow, with a wholesome pink face and steady grey-blue eyes. But nothing romantic about him . . . no smart compliments, no Lara-like glooms . . . nothing to induce such a riot of feeling as Winnie evidently experienced whenever she heard his step at the door.

What did Winnie see in him? Pat gave it up.

All the lawless joy died out of Pat when she saw Winnie's eyes. It was simply ridiculous to think of Winnie's eyes looking so . . . just ridiculous, that was all. And quite unnecessary. Because she, Pat, had everything nicely planned out already.

"Winnie, do you know you're just talking nonsense? Of course you're going to marry Frank. I am not going to take the school. I decided that as soon as mother came home. I'll be here to help Judy."

"Pat, you can't do that. It wouldn't be fair to ask you to give up your school after you studied so hard at Queen's to get your licence . . . you *ought* to have your chance . . ."

Pat laughed.

"My chance! That's just it. I've got my chance . . . the chance I've been aching for. The chance to stay at Silver Bush and care for it. I've hated the thought of teaching school. Who knows even if I'd get on well in the home school? I might have to go away another year . . . and *that* . . . but we needn't go into that. Of course I'd rather have mother well and strong than anything else even if I had to go to the ends of the earth. But since she can't be . . . well, I have the consolation of knowing I can stay home anyhow."

"What will dad say?"

"Dad knows. Why, Win, he was relieved. He never thought but that you'd be getting married and he didn't know just how things could be managed here. Because he didn't want me disappointed either in having to give up my school. *Disappointed!*" Pat howled again. "Win, parents aren't the selfish creatures so many horrid stories make them out. They *don't* want their children to sacrifice and give up for them. They want them to be happy."

"All but the cranks," said Judy, who had brought her little spinning wheel out to the platform and thought herself at liberty to butt into any conversation. "There do always be a few cranks aven among parents. Oh, oh, but not among the Gardiners."

"I think," said Winnie in a rather unsteady tone, "if you don't mind finishing the peas, Pat . . . I'll go upstairs for a little while."

Pat grinned. Winnie would go upstairs and write to Frank.

"Likely Winnie will be marrying Frank this fall, Judy," Pat said with a gulp. It seemed to make a thing so irrevocable to *say* it.

"Oh, oh, and why not, the darlint? She can cook and she can sew. She can get along widout things. She do be knowing whin to laugh and whin not to. Oh, oh, she's fit to be married. It do be eliven years since we had a wedding at Silver Bush. Sure and that's a liddle bit too much like heaven, wid nather marrying nor giving in marriage."

"George Nicholson is going to be married to Mary Baker," announced Cuddles, who had wandered along with a little spotted barn cat she affected in her arms. "I wish he would wait till I grow up. I believe he would like me better than Mary because there is no fun in her. There's a good deal in me when my conscience doesn't bother me. O . . . h, look at Bold-and-Bad."

Bold-and-Bad had met his match since Cuddles had been bringing the barn cat to the house. The barn cat was scrawny and ugly but she was taking impudence from nobody. Bold-and-Bad was ludicrously afraid of her. It was a sight of fun to see that whiffet of a cat attack and put to flight an animal who should have been able to demolish her with a blow of his paw. Bold-and-Bad fled over the yard and through the grave-yard and across the Mince Pie field with yowls of terror.

"Look at Gintleman Tom enjoying av it," chuckled Judy.

"We have nice cats at Silver Bush," said Cuddles complacently. "Interesting cats. And they have an *air*. They walk so proud and hold their tails up. Other cats *slink*. Trix Binnie laughed when I said that and said, 'You're getting just as crazy as Pat over your old Silver Bush, thinking there's nothing like it.' 'Well, there isn't,' I told her. And I was right, wasn't I, Pat?"

"You were," said Pat fervently. "But there comes your barn cat back and you'd best take her to the barn before dad sees her. You know he doesn't want the barn cats encouraged to the house. He says he puts up with Gentleman Tom and Bold-and-Bad because they're old established customs."

"How old is Gentleman Tom, Judy?"

"Oh, oh, old, is it? The Good Man Above do be knowing that. All *I* do be knowing is that he come here twelve years ago, looking as old as he does this blessed minute. Maybe there isn't inny age about him," concluded Judy mysteriously. "Ye can't iver be thinking av him as a kitten, can ye now?"

"I'm sure he could tell some queer tales, Judy. It's a pity cats can't talk."

"Talk is it? Whoiver told ye they cudn't talk, Cuddles darling? The grandfather of me heard two cats talking onct but he niver cud be got to tell what they said . . . No, no, he didn't want to be getting in wrong wid the tribe. As I was telling Siddy last Sunday whin he was raving mad because Bold-and-Bad had gone to slape on his Sunday pants and they was kivered wid cat hairs, 'Think whativer ye like av a cat, Siddy darlint,' sez I to him, 'but don't be *saying* innything. If the King av the cats heard ye now!"

"And what would have happened if the King of the cats had heard him, Judy?"

"Oh, oh, let's lave that tale for a rale wild stormy winter night, Cuddles, whin ye're slaping wid old Judy snug and cosy. Thin I'll be telling ye what happened to a man in ould Ireland that did be saying things av cats a liddle too loud and careless like. It's no tale for a summer afternoon wid a widding looming up."

2

Winnie was to be married in late September and Silver Bush settled down to six weeks of steady preparation. Judy had a new swing shelf put up in the cellar to fill with rows on rows of ruby jam-pots for Winnie. The wood-work in the Poet's room was to be painted all over in robin's egg blue and then there was the excitement of choosing paper to harmonise with it. Though Pat hated to tear the old paper off. It had been on so long. And she resented having the chairs in the Big Parlour recovered. There was a sort of harmony about the old room as it was. New things jarred. But Silver Bush must look its best, for Winnie was to have a big wedding.

"The clan do be liking a bit av a show," said Judy delightedly.

"It means a great deal of work," said Aunt Edith rather disapprovingly.

"Work, is it? Ye do be right. It's busy as a hin wid one chick we all are. I do be kaping just one jump ahead. But I'm not liking yer sneaking widdings as if they was ashamed av it. We'll be having one to be proud av, wid ivery relative on both sides and lots av prisents and two bridesmaids and a flower girl . . . Oh, oh, and Winnie's trosso now! The like av it has niver been seen at Silver Bush. All her liddle undies made be hand. 'An inch av hand-work do be worth a machine mile,' sez I to Mrs. Binnie whin she do be saying her cousin's daughter had two dozen av ivery kind. It do be a comfort to me whin I climb up to me loft at night, faling as if I'd been pulled through a kay-hole."

"Oh, Judy, you and I are getting to be old women," sighed Aunt Barbara.

Judy looked scandalised.

"Yes, yes, but whisht . . . don't be spaking av it, woman dear," she whispered apprehensively.

Winnie had a dream of a wedding dress . . . the sort of dress every girl would like to have. Everybody loved it except Aunt Edith, who was horrified at its brevity. Dresses were at their shortest when Winnie was married. Aunt Edith had been praying for years that women's skirts might be longer but apparently in vain.

"It's a condition that can't be affected by prayer," Uncle Tom told her gravely.

Winnie moved through all the bustle of preparation with a glory in her eyes, smiling dreamily over thoughts of her own. Frank haunted Silver Bush to such an extent that Judy was a trifle peeved at him.

"He do be all right in his place but I'm not liking him spread over everything," she grumbled.

"Frank is devoted to Winnie," said Pat rather distantly. "I think it is beautiful." She had finally accepted Frank as one of the family and he had straightway become a person to be defended, even from Judy.

"I wonder how Frank proposed to Winnie," remarked Cuddles, as she helped Pat adorn a cake with pale green slivers of angelica and crimson cherries. "I suppose he would be very romantic. Do you think he went on his knees?"

Sid, in for a drink of water, roared.

"We don't do that nowadays, Cuds. Frank just said to Winnie, 'How about it, kid?' I heard him," Sid salved his conscience by winking at Judy behind Cuddles' back.

"When I grow up and anybody proposes to me he'll have to be a good deal more flowery and eloquent than that. I can tell you, if he wants me to listen to him," she said.

"The frog went a-courting," remarked Judy cryptically.

37

_____

WINNIE'S WEDDING

1

The engagement was announced in the papers . . . a new-fangled notion which met with Judy's disapproval.

"Oh, oh, there do be minny a slip 'twixt the cup and the lip," she muttered. "Sure and we'd be in the pretty scrape if innything but good happened Frank in the nixt three wakes. There was Maggie Nicholson now . . . her beau did be going clane out av his head a wake before the day itsilf and it's in the asylum he's been iver since. Wudn't thim Binnies have the laugh on us if the widding didn't come off after all."

Only three weeks to the wedding day . . . Winnie's wedding day when she would leave Silver Bush forever. There were moments when Pat felt she couldn't endure it. When Vernon Gardiner said jokingly to Winnie,

"Next time we meet I'll have to call you Mrs. Russell," Pat went upstairs and cried. To think of Winnie being Mrs. Russell. It sounded so terribly changed and different and far away. Her Winnie!

Tears didn't stop the days from flying by. The wedding was to be in the church. Pat wanted Winnie to be married at home under the copper beech on the lawn. Mother couldn't go to the church. But Frank wanted the church. The Russells were Anglicans and had always been married in church. Frank got his way . . . "of course," as Pat scornfully remarked to the air.

Pat and Judy were up to their eyes in baking and favourite recipes were hunted up . . . recipes that had not been used for years because they took so many eggs. The traditional Silver Bush bride-cake alone required three dozen.

The Bay Shore aunts and the Swallowfield aunts sent over baskets of delicious confections. Aunt Barbara's basket was full of different kinds of cookies . . . orange cookies and date cookies and vanilla crisps and walnut bars and the Good Man Above knew how many more.

"Oh, oh, it won't be much like Lorna Binnie's wedding table," exulted Judy. "Sure and poor Mrs. Binnie thought if she did be cutting her cookies in a dozen different shapes it wud be giving thim a different flavour. Now, Patsy darlint, just ye be kaping an eye on thim chickens while I do be getting me yard posts whitewashed."

At first dawn Bold-and-Bad was shouting all over Silver Bush that he had found a mouse and Judy's footsteps sounded on the kitchen stairs. The morning hush was already broken by the stir of last-minute preparations. It had rained in the night but now it was a fine and a new, lovely world with its face washed and blinking its innocent eyes at the sun.

"Sure and the day was ordered," said Judy as she raked the lawn where robins were pulling out long fat worms.

Pat couldn't eat a mouthful of breakfast. It was a shock to see Winnie eating so heartily. Pat was sure that if *she* were going to be married she couldn't eat for a week beforehand. Of course she wouldn't want Winnie to be like that silly Lena Taylor, who, it was said, cried for a month before she was married. But when you were going away from Silver Bush that day how could you have an appetite?

The forenoon was like a whirlwind. The table had to be set . . . *oh, why did families have to be broken up like this?* Among salads, jellies and cakes Pat moved as to the manor born. *This time to-morrow Winnie would belong to another family.* Everybody's place was settled; Pat had a knack of dovetailing people rather cleverly . . . *only herself and Siddy and Cuddles left at Silver Bush.* The rooms bloomed under her hands. The little alcove Uncle Tom called Cuddle Corner was a nest of round golden pillows like small suns . . . *It was dreadful to find pleasure in these things when Winnie was going away.*

Flowers must be cut. As a rule Pat didn't like to cut the flowers. She always felt such a vivid crimson delight in her splendid blossoms . . . a feeling that made the thought of cutting them hurt her. But now she slashed at them savagely.

The table looked beautiful. It would be such a shame to spoil it . . . turn it into an after-dinner mess. But, as Judy said, that was life.

"Anyhow, Silver Bush looks perfectly lovely," thought Pat in a momentary rapture.

In a way it was all like an echo of Aunt Hazel's long-ago wedding day. The same confusion when everybody was dressing. Gentleman Tom was the only calm creature in the house. Judy was distracted because Bold-and-Bad had been seen dashing through the hall with a very large, very dead mouse and the Good Man Above only knew what he had done with it. That vain Cuddles, who had been trying all the mirrors in the house to see which was the most becoming, was in trouble over the hang of her flowered chiffon dress. It had been a bitter pill to Cuddles that she was too old to be Winnie's flower girl. Aunt Hazel's six-year-old Emmy was cast for that part and Cuddles was secretly determined to look prettier than she did.

"What does my nose look like, Pat? Do you think it is too big?"

Cuddles' nose had always worried her. How would it turn out?

"If it is I don't see how you can remedy it," laughed Pat. "Never mind your nose, Cuddles darling. You look very sweet."

"Can't I put a dab of powder on it, Pat? Please. I'm eleven."

"That would only draw attention to it," warned Pat.

Cuddles saw this. She cast a satisfied look at herself in the glass.

"I have decided," she remarked in a matter-of-fact tone, "that I will get married when I am twenty and have three children. Pat, do I have to kiss Frank?"

"I'm not going to," said Pat savagely.

Judy, who was set on "witnessing the nuptials," as she expressed it, had again laid aside her drugget dress and her Irish brogue. Out came the dress-up dress and the English pronunciation as good as ever. Only the former was a bit tight. Pat had a terrible time getting Judy hooked into it.

"Sure and I had a waist whin this was made," mourned Judy. "Do you be thinking it's a trifle old-fashioned like, Pat?"

Pat got some lace and did wonders with it. Judy felt real "chick."

Mother was dressed, sitting in state in the Big Parlour with her grey hair and her soft blue eyes. Pat realised with a swift pang that mother had got very grey in the year. But she looked like a picture in her pretty dress of silver-grey and rose, with the necklace dad had given her when she came out of the hospital . . . an amber string like drops of golden dew. Father was not going to the church after all. At the last moment he had decided that he simply could not leave mother alone. Uncle Tom must give the bride away. Winnie was not very well pleased over this. That fierce, immense black beard of his was so old-fashioned. But Winnie was too happy to mind anything much. In her bridal array she was an exquisite, shimmering young thing with face and eyes that were love and rapture incarnate. Pat's throat swelled as she looked at her. Frank Russell suddenly became the man who could make Winnie look like this. She forgave him the offence of becoming her brother-in-law.

The kitchen clock was ten to, the parlour clock was five past, the dining-room clock was striking the hour. Which meant that it was a quarter past and time to go.

2

Sitting in the crowded church, with its decorations of tawny tiger lilies and lemon-hued gladioli . . . the C. G. I. T. girls had done it for Winnie . . . Pat thought busily to keep herself from crying. Winnie had warned her solemnly . . . "Pat, don't you *dare* cry when I'm getting married." She had been so near crying at Aunt Hazel's wedding long ago but this was tenfold worse.

It was odd to see the groom so pale . . . he was always so pink and chubby. But he looked well. She was glad he was nice-looking. If Silver Bush had to have in-laws it should have handsome ones. Uncle Tom's magnificent beard looked purple in the light that fell on it through the stained glass window . . . like some old Assyrian king's. Winnie had said, "I do." How solemn! Just a word uttered or unuttered and a whole life was changed . . . perhaps even the course of history. If Napoleon's mother had said "No," in place of "Yes?" Why, it was over . . . it was over . . . Winnie was Mrs. Frank Russell . . . the bridal party was going into the vestry . . . Uncle Brian's Norma was singing the bridal anthem . . . Pat recalled that long-ago day when she had slapped Norma's face.

What was that dreadful old Cousin Sam Gardiner whispering to her over the top of the pew? "I wunner how many husbands and wives in this church would like a change." How many, indeed? Perhaps old Malcolm Madison, who was said to have laughed only three times in his life. Perhaps Gerald Black, whose wife had such a passion for swatting flies that she had bent forward in church one day and swatted one on Jackson Russell's bald head. Or Mrs. Henry Green, whose husband, Pat reflected wildly, looked like his own tombstone. She wondered if the story Judy told of him was true . . . that he had been whipped in school one day because the master caught him writing a love-letter on his slate to Lura Perry who was half gipsy. It couldn't be . . . not with that Scotch-Presbyterian-elder mouth. Old Uncle John Gardiner was improving the wait by snatching a nap. Wasn't there a story about his wooden leg catching fire one day when he dozed by the fire? There was Mrs. James Morgan who had never forgiven her daughter for marrying Carl Porter and had never entered her house. How *could* families act like that?

Mrs. Albert Cody . . . Sarah Malone that was. Judy had a story about her. "Oh, oh, she had one of thim aisy-going fellers . . . wint around wid her for years and years and niver got no forrader. Sarah wint away for a visit to her Aunt in Halifax and writ back great yarns av her beaus and fine times. That scared him and he writ for her to come home and be married. Sure and there hadn't been a word av truth in what Sarah had tould him. Her aunt was that sick and cranky she niver wint out av the house."

Sarah Cody was a Sunday School teacher and looked very meek and devout beside her easy-going Abner. Very likely Judy had made it all up.

(What was that horrid Mrs. Stephen Russell whispering . . . "made the mistake of choosing a prettier bridesmaid than herself." It wasn't true . . . it wasn't . . . Allie Russell wasn't half as pretty as Winnie.) Old Grant Madison, who had told dad once that he had read too many dreadful things in old histories ever to believe in God. How dreadful not to believe in God. How could one live? Mrs. Scott Gardiner had ironed out her wrinkles in some way . . . "beauty tricks," said Judy contemptuously. Why in the world didn't Winnie come back? But there was no Winnie now . . . only a mysterious stranger known as Mrs. Frank Russell. What was darling Cuddles thinking of as she gazed dreamily up at the tinted window, nimbused in its blue and gold. She was really a delightful little thing. Pat recalled in amazement that she hadn't wanted Cuddles to be born.

3

Home again. Hand-shakings and congratulations and kisses. Pat even kissed Frank. But she hugged Winnie fiercely.

"Here's a whole heartful of good wishes for you, dear one," she whispered.

Then she must fly for her ruffled organdy apron. The chilled cocktails must be got out of the ice-house, the creamed chicken put in the patties, the wedding gifts placed with just the right emphasis. Children ran about the grounds like small roses. The house was full. Every Gardiner and half-Gardiner, every Selby, every Russell was there. "This looks like the Day of Judgment," said old Cousin Ralph Russell. He caught Pat by the arm as she flew by him.

"Long Alec's girl. I hear you've got to be a beauty, hey? Let me look at you. No, no, not a beauty . . . and you've no great brains they tell me . . . but you've got a way with you. You'll get a man."

How people did harp on getting married! It was disgusting. Even oldish Ellery Madison, who still congratulated himself on escaping traps, called Pat "Ducky" and told her he'd take her if she liked.

"If you wait till we're both grown-up I might think of it," retorted Pat.

"Oh, oh, but that's the way to talk to them," Judy told her as they lighted the candles. "'Twas mesilf that shut him up quick whin he sez to me, sez he, 'It's time *you* were married, Judy.' 'How the min do be hating a woman that's dared to do widout thim,' sez I. Sure and I've been snubbing the craturs right and left. They've no more sinse than to be cluttering up me kitchen and ruining the rugs. Ould Jerry Russell sez to me, sez he, 'Miss Plum, do ye be thinking God is God or just a great first cause?' And Mark Russell sez, wid a face as grave as a jidge's, 'What is yer opinion av the governmint bringing on an election this fall, Miss Plum?' Sure and didn't I know they was pulling me leg? I sez to thim, sez I, 'Ye haven't the sinse ye was born wid,' sez I, 'if ye don't know a widding is no place to be talking av God or politics. And I'll thank ye to stop Miss Plumming me,' sez I, and that finished thim. Sure and wasn't the cirrimony grand, Patsy dear? Jake Russell sez to me, 'She's the prettiest bride ye've iver had at Silver Bush,' and I sez to him, sez I, 'For once in yer life ye've said a mouthful.' But that platinum ring now, do ye be thinking it's rale legal? I'm thinking Winnie'd fale a bit safer wid an old-fashioned gold one.”

“Judy, how can I *bear* to see Winnie go away?”

“Ye must sind her away wid a smile, Patsy darlint. Whativer comes after, sind her away wid a smile.”

38

LAUGHTER AND TEARS

1

It was all over. Winnie had gone.

“Pat darling,” she whispered, with her eyes softly full of farewell, “everything was lovely. I’ve really enjoyed my own wedding. You and Judy were wonderful.”

Pat managed to smile as Judy had exhorted, but when Judy found her looking at the deserted festal board she said,

“Judy, isn’t it nice to be . . . able to . . . stop smiling? I . . . I hope there won’t be another wedding at Silver Bush for a hundred years.”

“Why, I wish we could have a wedding every day,” said Cuddles. “I suppose the next one here will be your own. And then it will be my turn. That is,” she added reflectively, “if I can get any one to have me. I don’t want to be an old maid.”

“Sure and don’t be hurting my falings,” said Judy. “I’m an ould maid.”

“I always forget that,” said Cuddles contritely. “You aren’t a bit like an old maid, Judy. You’re . . . you’re just *Judy*.”

“Mr. Ronald Russell of St. John told me mother was the most beautiful woman he had ever seen,” said Pat.

“And ye’ll be loving Mr. Ronald Russell foriver bekase av it. But I’m thinking he’s right. Did ye hear him saying to Winnie, ‘Are ye going to be making a Prisbytarian av him?’ . . . maning Frank. And Winnie sez, sez she, Prisbytarians don’t be made, they’re born,’ sez she. Oh, oh, wasn’t that the answer to me smart gintleman? St. John can’t be getting far ahead av Silver Bush I'm thinking. He had his appetite wid him, that one. But I do be liking a man who enj'ys his vittles."

"He's a member of Parliament," said Pat, "and they say he'll be Premier some day."

"And him ould Short-and-dirty Russell's son! A fat chanct!" said Judy scornfully.

"I hope the pictures will turn out well," said Cuddles. "I was in them all."

"Innyway, Winnie wasn't photygraphed wid her arm round her groom like Jean Madison was. Ondacint I call it. And now, Patsy darlint, will we start claning up or lave it till the morning?"

"Whatever you like, Judy."

"Oh, oh, it's ye are the mistress here now, wid Winnie gone and yer mother niver to be troubled. It's for ye to give orders and for me to obey them."

"Nonsense, Judy. Fancy me giving you orders!"

"I'd rather it that way, Patsy darlint," said Judy firmly.

Pat hesitated. Then quietly accepted the sovereignty of Silver Bush.

"Very well, Judy. We'll leave things just as they are tonight. We're all tired. Do you remember the night after Aunt Hazel's wedding when we did the dining room?"

"It's the darlint ye was, working like a liddle slave to kape from crying."

"And you told me funny stories: Judy, let's have a bit of a fire . . . there's a chill in the air and the first fire is such a delightful thing. And we'll sit by it and you'll tell stories."

"Ye must av been hearing all me stories a million times over, Patsy. Though I do be thinking whin I saw the Joe Kellers to-day—he did be marrying his wife bekase a liddle girl he was swate on jilted him and she married him bekase Sam Miller av the Bay Shore jilted her. So what wud ye ixpect?"

"That they wouldn't be very happy, Judy."

"Oh, oh, and that's where ye wud be wrong, me jewel. The marriage was be way av being a big success. That do be life, ye know."

"Life *is* queer, Judy. Winnie and her Frank now . . . she doesn't seem to have a fear or doubt. I'd be frightened . . . I could never be *sure* I loved any one *enough* to marry him. And then to-day . . . away down in my heart I was just *sick* over Winnie going . . . and yet on the surface I was enjoying the excitement, too."

"There do be always something to take the edge off things," said Judy shrewdly. "That do be why nothing is iver as hard as ye think it's going to be."

Hilary came in after having driven some of the guests to the station and joined them. Bold-and-Bad, who had been sulking all day because nobody had admired him, lay down on the rug, gathered his feet and nose and tail into a snug circle, and forgave the world. Old Aunt Louisa, who had seen so much come and go, looked down on them from the wall. The white kittens still gambolled in immortal youth. King William still rode proudly across the Boyne. It was . . . rather nice to have a feeling of leisure and tranquillity again. And yet Pat was afraid that upstairs there was a dreadful stillness and silence after all the fuss was over that would pounce on her when she went to bed. She kept Hilary as long as she could and was so nice to him that when he said good-night to her on the poplar-patterned doorstep he was bold enough to ask her to kiss him.

"Of course I'll kiss you," said Pat graciously. "I've been kissing so many friends to-day one more or less doesn't matter."

"I don't want a friendly kiss," said Hilary . . . and went off on that note.

"Oh, oh, and ye might av give him his kiss," said Judy, who was always hearing what she had no business to. "He'll be going away far enough all too soon, poor b'y."

"I . . . I . . . was perfectly willing to kiss him," cried Pat chokily. "And don't . . . *don't* . . . talk of his going away. I can't bear it to-night."

2

Pat was very lonely when she went up to bed. The house seemed so strangely empty now that Winnie's laugh had gone out of it. Here was the mirror that had reflected her face. That little vacant chair where she had always sat was very eloquent. Her little discarded slippers that could have danced by themselves the whole night through, so often had Winnie's feet danced in them, comforted each other under the bed. They looked as if her feet had just stepped out of them. Her fragrance still lingered in the room. It was all terrible.

Pat leaned out of the window to drink in the cold, delicious air. The wind sounded eerie in the bushes. A dog was barking over at Swallowfield. Pat had rather thought that when she found herself alone she would cast herself on the bed in an abandonment of anguish. But there was still moonlight in the world . . . still owls in the silver bush. The old loyalties of home were still potent . . . it *would* be nice to have a room of one's very own.

A house always looks very pathetic and unfriended on a dawn after a festivity. Pat found happiness and comfort in restoring it all from cellar to garret. The presents were packed and sent to the Bay Shore. It *was* fun to read the account of the wedding in the papers.

"*The bride before her marriage was Winifred Alma, daughter of Mr. and Mrs. Alec Gardiner.*" That hurt Pat. Wasn't Winnie *still* their daughter? "*The bridesmaids wore dresses of pink Georgette crêpe with pink mohair hats and bouquets of sweet peas. Little Emmy Madison made a charming flower girl in a smocked frock of pink voile.*" Fancy little Emmy having her name and dress in the papers! *Miss Patricia Gardiner, sister of the bride, was charming in marigold voile.* And oh, oh . . . "*Miss Judy Plum wore blue silk with corsage of roses.*" It must have been that rogue of a Jen Russell who had put that in. Judy was tremendously pleased. Her name right there with all the quality, bracketed with the groom's aunt, the haughty Mrs. Ronald Russell in her black satin with mauve orchids! Though Judy was a bit dubious about "corsage." It sounded . . . well . . . a liddle quare.

Then there were visits to the Bay Shore to help Winnie get settled in her big white house with its background of sapphire water, where there was a coloured, fir-scented garden, full of wind music and bee song, that dipped in terraces to the harbour shore and was always filled with the sound of "perilous seas forlorn." Pat would have been quite happy if she could have forgotten that Hilary was going away.

39

THE CHATELAINE OF SILVER BUSH

1

Pat was feeling older than she would probably feel at fifty. Life had all at once grown bare and chilly. Hilary was going to Toronto to take the five-year course in architecture.

His mother had arranged it, he told Pat briefly. Since that bitter day, when Doreen Garrison had finally turned her back on her Jingle-baby Hilary had never spoken of his mother. Pat knew he never heard from her except for some brief note containing a check for his college expenses.

Pat was glad for Hilary's sake. He was on the way to realise all his dreams and ambitions. But on her own account she was very bleak. Nobody to prowl with . . . nobody to tell things to . . . it was always so easy to tell things to Hilary. Nobody to joke with.

"We've always laughed at the same things, Judy."

"Oh, oh, and that's why ye do be such good frinds, Patsy. It's the rale test. It's sorry I am mesilf that Jingle is going. A fine gintleman he's got to be, that tall and straight standing. And ye tell me he's to be an arkytict. Oh, oh, I'm hoping he won't be like the one I heard of in ould Ireland. He did be buying the plan av a fine house from the Bad Man Below. And the price he had to be paying was his swateheart's soul. 'Twas a grand house I'm telling ye but there was few iver wanted to live in it."

"I don't think Hilary will spend souls buying plans from the devil," said Pat, with a forlorn smile. "He can design plenty himself. But, Judy, it seems to me I just can't bear it. Bets dead . . . Winnie gone . . . and now Hilary."

"It's mesilf that's noticed how things do be going in threes like that, Patsy. It do be likely nothing but good'll happen to ye for a long time now."

"But life will be so . . . so empty, Judy."

"He'll be coming back some fine day."

Pat shook her head. Talk of Hilary's return was empty and meaningless. She knew he would never come back, unless for a vacation month or two. Their days of happy comradeship were over . . . their hours in Happiness . . . their rambles by field and shore. Childhood was gone. The "first fine rapture" of youth was gone.

"What's to become av McGinty? Oh, oh, there'll be one poor broken-hearted liddle dog."

"Hilary is giving McGinty to me. I know he *will* be broken-hearted. But if love can help him . . ."

Pat choked. She was seeing McGinty's eyes when the morrow brought no Hilary.

"Oh, oh, but I'm glad to hear that. I'm not liking a dogless house. Cats do be int'resting craturs, as Cuddles says, but there's *something* about a dog, now. Sure and there'll be some fun saving bones again."

Pat knew Hilary was waiting for her in Happiness. They had agreed to have their parting tryst there, before Hilary left to catch the night train. Slowly she went to keep it. The air was full of colour; there was just the faintest hint of frost in its sweet mildness; the evening sunshine was exceedingly mellow on grey old barns; as she went over Jordan she noticed the two dark, remote, pointed firs among the golden maples in the corner of the field. Hilary loved those firs. He said they were the twin spires of some mystic cathedral of sunset.

2

Hilary was waiting in Happiness, sitting on an old mossy stone by the spring that the years had never touched. Beside him sat a gay little dog with a hint of wistfulness behind his gaiety. McGinty felt something coming to him . . . something formless and chill. But as long as he was with his dear master what did it matter?

Hilary drew a quick breath: his eyes lit up slowly from within as was their way. She was coming to him over the field . . . a slip of a girl in a gold and orange sweater, the autumnal sunshine burnishing her dark-brown hair and glinting in her amber eyes; her face glowing with warm, ripe, *kissable* tints, her body like a young sapling never to be broken, however it might bend.

> *"Trusty, dusky, vivid, true,*
> *With eyes of gold and bramble dew."*

Why couldn't he have said that instead of Stevenson? It was truer of Pat than it could be of anybody else. Why couldn't he say to her all the burning and eloquent things he thought of in the night but could never utter the next day?

Pat sat down on the stone beside Hilary. They talked only a little and that in rather jerky sentences.

"I'll never come to Happiness again," said Pat.

"Why not? I'd like to think of you sitting here sometimes . . . with McGinty."

"Poor little dorglums!" Pat absently caressed McGinty's willing head with one of her slender brown hands . . . her *dear* hands, thought Hilary. "No, I couldn't bear to come here without you, Hilary. We've been here so often . . . we've been chums for so many years."

"Can't we . . . can't we . . . sometime . . . be more than chums, Pat?" blurted Hilary desperately.

Pat instantly became just a little aloof, although her face had flushed to a sudden warm rose. Hilary was such a nice friend . . . chum . . . brother . . . but never a lover. Pat was very positive on that point.

"We've always been wonderful friends, Hilary. Don't spoil it now. Why, we've been chums ever since that night you saved me from heaven knows what on the Line road. Ten years."

"They've been very good years." Hilary seemed to have taken his repulse more philosophically than she had feared. "What will the years to come be, I wonder?"

"They'll be marvellous years for you, Hilary. You'll succeed . . . you'll reach the top. And then all your old friends here . . . 'specially little old maid Pat of Silver Bush, will brag about having once known you."

"I *will* succeed," Hilary set his teeth together. "With your . . . friendship . . . I can do anything. I want to tell you . . . if I can . . . what your friendship and the life I've shared with you at Silver Bush have meant to me. It's kept me from growing up hateful and cynical. You've all been so sure that life is good that I've never been able to disbelieve it . . . never will be able to. You'll write me often, won't you, Pat? It will be . . . lonely . . . at first. I don't know a soul in Toronto."

"Of course I will. And don't forget, Hilary," . . . Pat laughed teasingly . . . "you're to build a house for me some day. I'll live in it when Sid gets married and turns me out of Silver Bush. And you'll come to see me in it . . . I'll be a nice old lady with silver hair . . . and I'll give you a cup of tea out of Grandmother Selby's pot . . . and we'll talk over our lives and . . . and . . . pretend it's all been a dream . . . and that we're just Pat and Jingle home once more."

"Wherever *you* are, Pat, will always be home to me."

There he went again. If it were not that they must presently say a long good-bye she would be angry with him. But she couldn't be angry to-night. He would soon forget this nonsense. Hundreds of beautiful clever girls in Toronto. But they would always be friends . . . the very best of friends . . . she couldn't imagine *not* being friends with Hilary.

They went back, following the curves of Jordan, talking of old days. It was lovely to remember things together. There were asters along their way. Hilary wanted to pick a rarely dark-blue cluster for her but she would not let him.

"No. Don't pick them because they would fade and that would be my last memory of them. Let's just leave them here and we can always remember them as we saw them together . . . beautiful and unfaded."

That was the real Pat touch. Hilary remembered that she had never really liked to pick flowers. He never forgot her, as she stood there gloating over them, herself, to him, as beautiful and mysterious as the autumn twilight. Dear . . . desirable!

The brook was prattling away and crooning to itself. Tall firs, that had been mere saplings when they first explored it, stretched their protecting arms over it: the mosses were green on its banks. In its ripple and murmur the voices of their childhood sounded . . . all the long-unheard notes were there, blended with the sweet sorrow inseparable from bygones. Hilary at twenty and Pat at eighteen felt themselves to be aged travellers wistfully recalling youth.

They paused on the stone bridge across Jordan. Pat held out her hands. She wanted to cry on his shoulder and knew she must not. If she did . . . he would take her in his arms. That would be nice . . . but . . .

She wanted to tell him that she loved him dearly. She did love him so much . . . better than Joe now . . . almost better than Sidney. She wanted to kiss him . . . but Hilary did not want friendly kisses. Yet they *couldn't* part like this.

"I'm not going to say good-bye half a dozen times before I'm really gone . . . like old Aunty Sarah Gordon," said Hilary, pretending to laugh. "Good-bye, Pat."

But he seemed to have forgotten to let go her hands. This simply couldn't be endured any longer.

"Good-bye, Jingle." The old name came impulsively to her lips. She pulled her hands away from his warm, pleasant grip and ran up the path against the moon.

Hilary stood and looked after her. McGinty huddled shivering against his leg. McGinty knew things were all wrong somehow.

Hilary was thinking of the house he would build for Pat. He could see it . . . he could almost see its lights gleaming through the dusk of some land "beyond the hills and far away." More beautiful than even Silver Bush. For a moment he almost hated Silver Bush. It was the only rival he feared. Then he set his teeth.

"I'll have you yet, Pat."

3

Pat stumbled up the path and across the field blindly and brought up against the garden gate. Then the denied tears came. She simply couldn't bear it. Everything gone! Who *could* bear it?

Rays of the rising moon touched the Hill of the Mist with delicate silver fingers. The night was a blue pearl seaward. The low continual thunder of the gulf tides in the harbour bar filled the air. The dreaming peace of the orchard seemed to beckon. The old barns, that must be alive with the ghosts of all the kittens that had frolicked in them, were huddled together companionably. Silver Bush was full of friendly lights. Pat brushed the tears from her eyes and looked at it.

It was such a loyal old house . . . always faithful to those who loved it. You felt it was your friend as soon as you stepped into it. It was full of dear yesterdays and beautiful old years. It had been assimilating beauty and loveliness . . . which is not quite the same thing . . . for generations. There had been so many things in this house and it had not forgotten one of them. Love and sorrow . . . tragedies . . . comedies. Babies had been born . . . brides had dreamed . . . all sorts of fashions had come and gone before the old mirrors. Its very walls seemed to hold laughter.

The house remembered her whole life. *It* had always been the same . . . *it* had never changed . . . not really. Only little surface changes. How she loved it! She loved it in morning rose and sunset amber, and best of all in the darkness of night, when it loomed palely through the gloom and was all her own. This beauty was hers . . . all hers. Life could never be empty at Silver Bush. Somebody had pitied her once . . . "so out of the world." Pat laughed. Out of the world? Nay, she was *in* the world here . . . *her* world. *"I dwell among my own people."* Wise Shulamite!

A mysterious content flooded her. This was home.

THE END

MISTRESS PAT

THE FIRST YEAR

1

There were hundreds of trees, big and little, on the Silver Bush farm and every tree was a personal friend of Pat's. It was anguish to her when one of them, even some gnarled old spruce in the woods at the back, was cut down. Nobody had ever been able to convince Pat that it was not murder to cut a tree down . . . justifiable homicide perhaps, since there had to be fires and lumber, but homicide nevertheless.

And no tree was ever cut in the grove of white birches behind the house. *That* would have been sacrilege. Occasionally one blew down in an autumn storm and was mourned by Pat until time turned it into a beautiful mossy log with ferns growing thickly all along it.

Everybody at Silver Bush loved the birch grove, though to none of them did it mean what it meant to Pat. For her it *lived*. She not only knew the birches but they knew her: the fern-sweet solitudes, threaded with shadows, knew her: the wind in the boughs always made her a glad salutation. From the first beginnings of memory she had played in it and wandered in it and dreamed in it. She could not remember the time it had not held her imagination in thrall and dominated her life. In childhood it had been peopled by the leprechauns and green folk of Judy Plum's stories: and now that those dear and lovely beliefs had drifted away from her like faint and beckoning wraiths their old magic still haunted the silver bush. It could never be to Pat just the ordinary grove of white-skinned trees and ferny hollows it was to other people. But then, Pat, so her family always said, was just a little different from other people, too. She had been different when she was a big-eyed child . . . different when she was a brown, skinny little imp in her early teens . . . and still different, now that she was twenty and ought, so Judy Plum felt, to be having beaus.

There *had* been a boy or two in Pat's past but Judy considered them mere experiments. Pat, however, did not seem to want beaus, in spite of Judy's sly hints. All she really wanted, or seemed to want, was to "run" Silver Bush and take care of mother . . . who was a bit of an invalid . . . and see that as few changes as possible came into existence there. If she could have been granted a fairy wish it would be that she might wave a wand and make everything remain exactly the same for at least a hundred years.

She loved her home with a passion. She was deeply loyal to it . . . to its faults as well as its virtues . . . though she would never admit it had any faults. Every small thing about it gave her the keenest joy. If she went away for a visit she was homesick until she could return to it.

"Silver Bush isn't her house . . . it's her religion," Uncle Brian had once said teasingly.

Every room in it meant something . . . had some vital message for her. It had the look that houses wear when they have been loved for years. It was a house where nobody ever seemed to be in a hurry . . . a house from which nobody ever went away without feeling better in some way . . . a house in which there was always laughter. There had been so much laughter at Silver Bush that the very walls seemed soaked in it. It was a house where you felt welcome the moment you stepped into it. It took you in . . . rested you. The very chairs clamoured to be sat upon, so hospitable was it. And it was overrun by beautiful cats . . . fat, fluffy fellows basking on the window sills or huddles of silk-soft kittens sleeping on the warm sandstone slabs in the old family graveyard beyond the orchard. People came from all over the Island to get a Silver Bush cat. Pat hated to give them away but of course something had to be done, since the kitten crop never failed.

"Tom Baker was here for a kitten to-day," said Judy.

"'What brade is it?' sez he, solemn-like. That fam'ly av Bakers never did be having too much sinse. 'Oh, oh, no brade at all,' sez I. 'Our cats do be just common or garden cats,' sez I. 'But we give them a good home and talk to thim now and thin as inny self-respicting cat likes to be talked to,' sez I, 'wid a bit av a compliment thrown in once in a while. And so they do their bist for us in the matter av kittens as well as all ilse. Sure and I do be forgetting what a rat looks like,' sez I. I was faling a bit unwilling to give him the kitten. They'll trate it well, I'm having no manner av doubt, but they'll niver remimber to pass the time av day wid it."

"Our cats own us anyway," said Cuddles lazily. "Aunt Edith says it's absurd the way we spoil them. She says there are lots of poor Christians don't have the life our cats have and she thinks it awful that we let them sleep at the foot of our beds."

"Oh, oh, see there now, ye've sint Gintleman Tom off mad," said Judy reprovingly. "Cats always do be knowing what ye're saying av thim. And Gintleman Tom's that sensitive."

Cuddles idly watched Gentleman Tom . . . Judy's lank, black cat who was so old that he had forgotten to die, Sid said . . . stalk indignantly off through the ferns of the path. She and Pat and Judy were spending the hours of the late summer afternoon in the silver bush. They had fallen into the habit of doing their odd jobs there, where bird music occasionally dripped through the leafy silence or a squirrel chattered or wood winds wove their murmurous spells. Pat went there to write her letters and Cuddles studied her lessons. Often mother brought her knitting and sewing. It was a lovely place to work in . . . though Cuddles seldom worked while there. She generally left that to Pat and Judy. The latter was sitting on a mossy log, stoning cherries for preserving and the former was making new apple-green curtains for the dining room. Cuddles, observing that it was a poor place that couldn't support one lady, put her hands on the grass behind her and leaned back on them, looking up at the opal-hued sky between the tree-tops.

"Bold-and-Bad won't leave us," she said. "*He* isn't so touchy."

"Oh, oh, ye cudn't be hurting that cat's falings, by rason that he hasn't got inny," said Judy, with a somewhat scornful glance at the big grey cat sitting on the log by Pat, blinking eyes of pale jade with a black line down their centre at a dog with a sleek, golden-brown back who was happily gnawing a rather malodorous bone behind the log, occasionally pausing to gaze up in Pat's face adoringly and wistfully. Then Pat would stroke his head and pull his pointed ears, whereat Bold-and-Bad would look more remote than ever. Bold-and-Bad always considered "the dog McGinty," as Judy called him, an interloper. Hilary Gordon had left him with Pat nearly two years ago, when he went away to college in Toronto. At first McGinty had nearly broken his heart but he knew Pat loved him and eventually he perked up a bit and gave Bold-and-Bad as good as he sent. An armed truce existed between them, for Bold-and-Bad had not forgotten what Pat did to him the day he scratched McGinty's nose. McGinty would always have been friends but Bold-and-Bad was simply not having any.

"Oh, oh, what wid all these cherries to be stoned afore supper I do be wishing we had a ghost like they had at Castle McDermott in the ould days," said Judy, with an exaggerated sigh. "That was a ghost now . . . a rale useful, industrious cratur. The odd jobs he'd do ye wudn't be belaving . . . stirring the porridge and peeling the pittaties and scouring the brasses . . . he wasn't above turning his hand to innything. Sorra the day the ould lord lift a bit av money on the kitchen dresser for him, saying the labourer was worthy av his hire. He niver come again . . . his falings having been hurt be the same. Oh, oh, it cost the McDermott the kape av another maid. Ye niver know where ye are whin ye're dealing wid the craturs. Sure and that's the disadvantage av ghosts. Some wud have been offinded if they hadn't been thanked. But a ghost like that wud be rale handy once in a while at Silver Bush, wudn't it now, Cuddles, darlint?"

Luckily Judy did not see Pat and Cuddles exchanging smiles. They had begun to share with each other their amused delight in Judy's stories, which had replaced the credulity of early childhood. There had been a time when both Pat and Cuddles would have believed implicity in the industrious McDermott ghost.

"Judy, if that yarn is a gentle hint for me to get busy and help you stone those cherries I'm not going to take it," said Cuddles with a grin. "I hate sewing and preserving. Pat is the domestic type . . . I'm not. When I'm here I just like to squat on the grass and listen to you talking. I've got my blue dress on and cherry juice stains. Besides, I've got pains in my stomach . . . I really have . . . every now and then."

"If ye *will* ate liddle grane apples ye must put up wid pains in yer stomach," said Judy, as remorselessly as cause and effect. "Though whin I was a girleen it wasn't thought rale good manners to talk av yer insides so plain, Cuddles."

"You keep on calling me Cuddles," said Cuddles sulkily. "I've asked you all to stop it and not one of you will. Away from home I'm Rae . . . I like that, but here at Silver Bush everybody 'Cuddles' me. It's so . . . so babyish . . . now that I'm thirteen."

"So it is, Cuddles dear," agreed Judy. "But I'm too old to be larning new names. I'm guessing ye'll always be Cuddles to me. And such a tommyshaw as we had finding a name for ye at that! Do ye be minding, Pat? And how upset ye was bekase I wint hunting in the parsley bed for a new baby the night Cuddles was born? Oh, oh, that was the tarrible night at Silver Bush! We niver thought yer mother wud live through it, Patsy dear. To think it do be thirteen years ago!"

"I remember how big and red the moon was that night, rising over the Hill of the Mist," said Pat dreamily. "Oh, Judy, did you know that the lightning struck the middle lombardy on the Hill of the Mist last week? It killed it and it has to be cut down. I don't see how I can stand it. I've always loved those three trees so. They've been there ever since I can remember. Now, McGinty, don't do it. I know it's a temptation when his tail hangs down so . . . that's right, Bold-and-Bad, tuck it up. And while I think about it, Bold-and-Bad, you needn't . . . you really needn't . . . bring any more mice to my bedside in the early morning hours, I'll take your word for it that you caught them."

"The yells av him whin he's carrying one upstairs!" said Judy. "It'd break his heart if he cudn't be showing it off to somebody."

"I thought you said a moment ago he hadn't any feelings," giggled Cuddles.

Judy ignored her and turned to Pat.

"Will we be having a cherry pudding to-morrow, Patsy?"

"Yes, I think so. Oh, do you remember how Joe loved cherry puddings?"

"Oh, oh, there's not much I do be forgetting about Joe, Patsy dear. Was it Shanghai his last letter was from? I'm not belaving thim yellow Chinese know innything about making cherry puddings. Or plum puddings ather. We'll have one av thim for Christmas when Joe will be home."

"I wonder if he really will," sighed Pat. "He has never been home for Christmas since he went away. He's always planned to come but something always prevents."

"Trix Binnie says Joe has had his nose tattooed and that's the reason he doesn't come home," said Cuddles. "She says Captain Dave Binnie saw him last year in Buenos Ayres and didn't know him, he looked so awful. Do you think there's any truth in it?"

"Not if a Binnie do be telling it," said Judy contemptuously. "Don't be worrying, Cuddles."

"Oh, I'm not. I rather hoped it was. It would be so interesting. If he *is* tattooed I'm going to get him to do me when he comes home."

There was simply nothing to be said to this. Judy turned again to Pat.

"He's to be captain by Christmas, didn't he say? Oh, oh, but that b'y has got on! He'll be a year younger than yer Uncle Horace was whin he got his ship. I do be minding the time *he* come home that summer and brought his monkey wid him."

"A monkey?"

"I'm telling ye. The baste took possession. Yer liddle grandmother was nearly out av her wits. And poor ould Jim Appleby . . . he was niver known to be sober . . . just a bit less drunk than common was all ye cud be saying at the bist av times . . . he come down to Silver Bush to buy some pigs and yer Uncle Horace's monkey was skipping along the top av the pig-pen fince quite careless-like. Yer grandfather said ould Jim turned white . . . all but his nose . . . and he sez, sez he, 'I've got 'em! Ma always said I'd git 'em and I have. But I'll niver be touching a drop again.' He kipt his word for two months but he was that cross and cantankerous his family were rale glad whin he forgot about the monkey. Mrs. Jim did be saying she wished Horace Gardiner wud kape his minagerie widin bounds. If Jim comes it's a rale reunion we'll have, Patsy."

"Yes. Winnie and Frank will be over and we'll all be together again. We must plan it all out some of these days. I do love planning things."

"Aunt Edith says it's no use making plans because something always happens to upset them," said Cuddles gloomily.

"Niver ye be belaving it, me jewel. And innyhow what if they do be upset? Ye've had the fun av planning. Don't be letting yer Aunt Edith make a . . . a . . . what did Siddy be calling it now?"

"A pessimist."

"Oh, oh, doesn't that sound just like her! Innyway, don't be letting her make ye that. Aven if Joe doesn't get home, the darlint, there'll be Winnie and Frank and yer Aunt Hazel's liddle gang, and the turkeys we'll be having for dinner are roosting on the fence behind the church barn this blessed minute growing as hard as they kin. And Pat there is saving up all the resates and menoos in the magazines. Oh, oh, there'll be the great preparations I'm thinking and me fine Edith won't be spiling it wid her sighs and sorrows. She do be having a grudge at life, that one. Patsy, do ye be minding the time ye were dancing naked here by the light av the moon and me lady Edith nabbed ye?"

"Dancing naked? And you won't even let me wear shorts round home," moaned Cuddles.

"And they broke my heart by sending me to Coventry," went on Pat, as if Cuddles had not spoken. "They never knew how cruel they were. And the night you came home, Judy, and I smelt the ham frying!"

"Sure, minny's the good liddle bite we've had in the ould days, Patsy. But there's as minny ahead as behind I'm hoping. And maybe, Miss Cuddles . . . as I shud be after calling Rachel . . . if ye won't be stoning inny cherries will ye be above making some blueberry muffins for supper? Patsy is wanting to finish her hemstitching and Siddy's that fond av thim."

"I'll do that," agreed Cuddles. "I like blueberry things. Oh, and I'm going up to the Bay Shore next week to pick blueberries with Winnie. She says I can sleep out in a tent right down by the shore. I want to sleep out some night here in Silver Bush. We could have a hammock swung between those two big trees there. It would be heavenly. Judy, did Uncle Tom ever have any love affairs when he was young?"

"Oh, oh, the way ye do be jumping from one thing to another!" protested Judy. "No doubt he had his fun girling like the rest av the b'ys. I'm not knowing why it niver turned serious. What put him into yer head?"

"He's asked me to mail a letter for him at Silverbridge three times this summer. He said they were too nosy at the North Glen post office. It was addressed to a lady."

Pat and Judy exchanged knowing glances. Judy repressed her excitement and spoke with careful carelessness.

"Did ye be noticing the name av the lady, Cuddles darlint?"

"Oh, Mrs. Something-or-other," said Cuddles with a yawn. "I forget the name. Uncle Tom looked so red and sheepish when he asked me I just wondered what he was up to."

"Yer Uncle Tom must be close on sixty," reflected Judy. "It do be the time some min take a second silly spell about the wimmen. But wid Edith to kape him straight he can't go far. Sure and I do be minding how crazy he was to go to the Klondike whin the big gold rush was on . . . nather to hold nor bind. But me lady Edith nipped that in the bud and I'm thinking he's niver ralely forgiven her for it. Oh, oh, we've all had our bits av drames that niver come true. If I cud just have a run over to the Ould Country now and see if Castle McDermott is as grand as it used to be. But it'll niver come to pass."

"'Each mortal has his Carcassonne,'" quoted Pat dreamily, recalling a poem Hilary Gordon had marked for her once.

But Cuddles, always the more practical, said coolly, "And why can't it, Judy? You could take a couple of months off any summer, now that I'm old enough to help Pat. The fare second class wouldn't be too much and you could see all your relatives there and have a gorgeous time."

Judy blinked as if somebody had struck her. "Oh, oh, Cuddles darlint, it sounds rale reasonable whin ye put it that way. It's a wonder I niver thought av it. But I'm not so young as I once was . . . I do be getting a bit ould for gallivanting round."

"You're not too old, Judy. Just you go next summer. All you have to do is to make up your mind."

"Oh, oh, make up yer mind, sez she. That takes a bit av doing, Cuddles dear . . . as well as a bit av thinking av."

"Don't think about it . . . just go," said Cuddles, rolling over on her stomach and pulling McGinty's ears. "If you think too much about it you'll never do it."

"Oh, oh, whin I was thirteen I was be way av being nearly as wise as you are. I've larned foolishness since," said Judy sarcastically. "It's not running off to Ireland I'll be as if it was a jaunt to Silverbridge. And me frinds there have grown ould . . . I doubt if they'd know me, grey as an owl that I am. There do be a new McDermott at the castle, I'm ixpicting, talking rale English. The ould lord had a brogue so thick ye cud stir it."

"It's perfectly thrilling to think you ever lived in a castle, Judy . . . and waited on a lord. It's even more exciting than remembering that mother's fourth cousin married into the English nobility. I wonder if we'll ever see her. Pat, let's you and I go over some day and call on our titled friend."

"I'm afraid she's not even aware of our existence," grinned Pat. "A fourth cousin is pretty far removed and she went to England to live with her aunt when she was a little girl. Mother saw her once, though."

"Oh, oh, that she did," said Judy. "She visited at the Bay Shore whin she was tin and they all come over here one day to play wid the young fry here. They had a day av it. She's a barrownite's wife now . . . Sir Charles Gresham . . . and his aunt do be married to an earl."

"Is he a belted earl?" demanded Cuddles. "A belted earl sounds so much more earlish than an unbelted one."

"Oh, oh, he's iverything an earl shud be. I do be forgetting what he was earl of but it was a rale aristocratic name. It was all in the papers whin yer cousin was married. Lady Gresham wasn't young but she made a good market be waiting. Oh, oh, niver shall I be forgetting the aunts at the Bay Shore whin the news come. They cudn't be inny prouder than they always were, so they got rale humble. 'It's nothing to us av coorse,' sez yer Great-aunt Frances. 'She's a great leddy now and she wudn't be acknowledging inny kin to common people like us.' Oh, oh, to be hearing Frances Selby calling herself common people!"

"Trix Binnie says she doesn't believe that Lady Gresham is any relation at all to us," said Cuddles, picking up a yellow kitten, with a face like a golden pansy, that came skittering through the ferns, and tucking it under her chin.

"She wudn't! But yer fourth cousin she is and it was her uncle the Bishop they did be blaming for staling the silver at the Bay Shore the night he slipt there."

"Stealing the silver, Judy?" Pat had never heard of this though Judy had been recounting her family legends to her all her life.

"I'm telling ye. Ye know that illigant silver hair-brush and comb in the spare room at the Bay Shore, to say nothing av the liddle looking glass and the two scent bottles. That proud av it they was. They niver did be putting it out for common people but a Bishop was a Bishop and whin he wint up to bed there it was all spread out gorgeous-like on the bury top. Oh, oh, but it wasn't there the nixt morning, though. Yer Great-great-Aunt Hannah was on the hoof thin . . . it was long afore she got bed-rid . . . and she was just about wild. She just set down and wrote and asked the Bishop what he'd done wid it. Back he wrote, 'I am poor but honest. The silver is in the box av blankets. It was too luxurious for a humble praste like mesilf to use and I was afraid some av me medicine might fall on it.' Oh, oh, the silver was on top av the blankets all right enough and yer poor Great-great-Aunt was niver the same agin, after as much as accusing the Bishop av staling it. Patsy darlint, spaking av letters, was there inny news in the one ye got from Jingle this morning if a body may ask?"

"A very special bit of news," said Pat. "I saved it to tell you this afternoon when we'd be out here. Hilary sent in the design for a window to some big competition . . . and it won the prize. Against a hundred and sixty competitors."

"It's the cliver lad Jingle is . . . and it'll be the lucky girl that do be getting him."

Pat ignored this. She didn't want Hilary Gordon for anything but a friend but she did not exactly warm to the idea of that "lucky girl" whoever she was.

"Hilary always had a liking for windows. Whenever he saw one that stood out from the ordinary run he went into raptures over it. That little dormer one in old Mary McClenahan's house . . . Judy, do you remember the time you sent us to her to witch McGinty back?"

"And she did, didn't she now?"

"She knew where he was to be found anyhow," Pat sighed. "Judy, life was really more fun when I believed she was a witch."

"I'm telling ye." Judy nodded her clipped grey head mysteriously. "The less ye do be belaving the colder life do be. This bush now . . . it was nicer whin it was packed full av fairies, wasn't it?"

"Yes . . . in a way. But their magic still hangs round it, though the fairies are gone."

"Oh, oh, ye belaved in thim once, that's why. If ye don't belave in fairies they can't exist. That do be why grown folks can niver be seeing thim," said Judy sagely. "It's pitying the children I am that niver have the chanct to belave in fairies. They'll be the poorer all their lives bekase av it."

"I remember one story you told me . . . of the little girl who was playing in a bush like this and was lured away to fairyland by exquisite music. I used to tiptoe through here in the 'dim' and listen for it. But I don't think I really wanted to hear it . . . I was afraid that if I went to fairyland I'd never come back. And no fairy country could ever satisfy me after Silver Bush."

The look came into Pat's brook-brown eyes which always made people feel she was remembering something very lovely. Pat was not the beauty of the Gardiner family but there was magic in her face when that look came. She rose and folded up her sewing and went down to the house, followed by McGinty. The robins were beginning to whistle and the clouds over the bush were turning to a faint rose. The ferns and long grasses of the path were gold in the light of the westering sun. Away to the right long shadows were creeping over the hill pasture. And down beyond the low fields was the blue mist that was an August sea.

Sid was in the yard trying to make an obstinate calf drink. Cuddles' two pet white ducks were lying by the well. They were to be offered up for Thanksgiving dinner but Judy had not dared to hint this to Cuddles as yet. Father was mowing the early oats. Mother, her nap over, was down in the garden among the velvety Sweet Williams. A squirrel was running saucily over the kitchen roof. It was going to be a dear quiet evening, such as she loved best, with every one and everything at Silver Bush happy. Pat loved to see things and people happy; and she herself had the gift, than which there is none more enviable, of finding great pleasure in little things. The bats would be coming out at the rising of the moon and the great, green spaciousness of the farm would be all around the house that always seemed to her more a person than a house.

"Pat's just as crazy as ever about Silver Bush, isn't she?" said Cuddles. "I think she'd die if she had to leave it. I don't believe she'll ever get married, Judy, just because of that. I love Silver Bush, too, but I don't want to live here *all* my life. I want to go away . . . and have adventures . . . and see the world."

"Sure and it wudn't do if iverybody wanted to stay at home," agreed Judy. "But Patsy has always had Silver Bush in her heart . . . right at the very core av it. Whin she was no more than five she was asking yer mother one fine day where God was. And yer mother sez gentle-like, 'He is iverywhere, Patsy.' 'Iverywhere?' sez Pat, her eyes that pitiful. 'Hasn't He got inny home? Oh, mother, I'm so sorry for Him.' Did ye iver hear av such a thing as being sorry for God! Well, that was me liddle Pat. Cuddles dear" . . . Judy lowered her voice like a conspirator, although Pat was well out of sight and hearing . . . "Jem Robinson has been hanging round a bit, hasn't he now? He's a rale nice lad and only one year more to go at college. Do ye be thinking Pat has inny notion av him?"

"I'm sure she hasn't, Judy. Though she says the only thing she has against him is that his face needs side-whiskers and he was born a generation too late. I heard her say that to Sid. What did she mean, Judy?"

"The Good Man Above do alone be knowing," groaned Judy. "Sure, Cuddles darling, it's all right to be a bit particular-like. The Silver Bush girls have niver been like the Binnies. 'Olive has a beau for ivery night in the wake,' sez Mrs. Binnie to me onct, boastful-like. 'So she do be for going in for quantity afore quality,' sez I. But what if ye're too particular? I'm asking ye."

"I'm not old enough to have beaus yet," said Cuddles, "but just you wait till I am. It must be thrilling, Judy, to have some one tell you he loves you."

"Ould Tom Drinkwine did be telling me that onct upon a time but niver a thrill did I be faling," said Judy reflectively.

2

"All the months are friends of mine but apple month is the dearest," chanted Pat.

It was October at Silver Bush and she and Cuddles and Judy picked apples in the New Part of the orchard every afternoon . . . which wasn't so very new now, since it was all of twenty years old. But the Old Part was very much older and the apples in it were mostly sweet and fed to the pigs. Sometimes Long Alec Gardiner thought it would be far better to cut it down and get some real good out of the land but Pat couldn't be made to hear reason about it. She loved the Old Part far better than the New. It had been planted by Great-grandfather Gardiner and was shadowy and mysterious, with as many old spruce trees as apple trees in it, and one special corner where generations of beloved cats and kittens had been buried. Besides, as Pat pointed out, if you cleared away the Old Part it would leave the graveyard open to all the world, since the Old Part surrounded it on three sides. This argument had weight with Long Alec. He was proud, in his way, of the old family burial plot, where nobody was ever buried now but where so many greats and grands of every degree slept . . . for the Gardiners of Silver Bush came of old P.E. Island pioneer stock. So the Old Part was spared and in spring it was as beautiful as the New Part, when the gnarled trees were young and bridal again for a brief space in the sweet spring days and the cool spring nights.

It was such a mellow and dreamy afternoon and Silver Bush seemed mellow and dreamy, too. Pat thought the old farm had a mood for every day in the year and every hour in the day. Now it would be gay . . . now melancholy . . . now friendly . . . now austere . . . now grey . . . now golden. To-day it was golden. The Hill of the Mist had wrapped a scarf of blue haze about its brown shoulders and was mysteriously lovely still, in spite of the missing Lombardy. Behind it a great castle of white cloud, with mauve shadows, towered up. There had been a delicate, ghostly rain the night before and the scent of the little hollow in the graveyard, full of frosted ferns, was distilled on the air. How green the pastures were for autumn! The kitchen yard was full of the pale gold of aspens and the turkey house was almost lost in a blaze of crimson sumacs. The white birches which some forgotten bride had planted along the Whispering Lane, that led from Silver Bush to Swallowfield, were amber, and the huge maple over the well was a flame. When Pat paused every few minutes just to look at it she whispered,

> "'The scarlet of the maples can shake me like a cry
> Of bugles going by.'"

"What might ye be whispering to yersilf, Patsy? Sure and ye might be telling us if it's inny joke. It seems to be delighting ye."

Pat lifted eyebrows like little slender wings.

"It was just a bit of poetry, Judy, and you don't care much for poetry."

"Oh, oh, po'try do be all right in its place but it won't be kaping the apples if there's a hard frost some av these nights. We're a bit behind wid the picking as it is. And more work than iver to look forward to, now that yer dad has bought the ould Adams place for pasture and going into the live stock business."

"But he's going to have a hired man to help him, Judy."

"Oh, oh, and who will be looking after the hired man I'm asking ye. He'll be nading a bite to ate, I'm thinking, and mebbe a bit av washing and minding done. Not that I'm complaining av the work, mind ye. But ye can niver tell about an outsider. It's been minny a long day since we had inny av the brade at Silver Bush and it'll be a bit av a change, as ye say yersilf."

"I don't mind changes that mean things *coming* as much as changes that means things *going*," said Pat, pausing to aim a wormy apple at two kittens who were chasing each other up the tree trunks. "And I'm so glad dad has bought the old Adams place. The little stone bridge Hilary and I built over Jordan and the Haunted Spring will belong to us now . . . and Happiness."

"Oh, oh, to think av buying happiness now!" chuckled Judy. "I wasn't after thinking it cud be done, Patsy."

"Judy, don't you remember that Hilary and I called the little hill by the Haunted Spring Happiness? We used to have such lovely times there."

"Oh, I'm minding. It was just me liddle joke, Patsy dear. Sure and it tickled me ribs to think av inny one being able to buy happiness. Oh, oh, there do be a few things God kapes to Himsilf and that do be one av thim. Though I did be knowing a man in ould Ireland that tried to buy off Death."

"He couldn't do that, Judy," sighed Pat, recalling with a shiver the dark day when Bets, the lovely and beloved friend of her childhood, had died and left a blank in her life that had never been filled.

"But he *did*. And thin, whin he wanted death and prayed for him Death wudn't come. 'No, no,' sez Death, 'a bargain is a bargain.' But this hired man now . . . where is he going to slape? That's been bothering me a bit. Wud yer dad be wanting me to give up me snug kitchen chamber for him and moving somewhere up the front stairs?"

Judy couldn't keep the anxiety out of her voice. Pat shook her slim brown hands, that talked quite as eloquently as her lips, at Judy reassuringly.

"No, indeed, Judy. Dad knows that kitchen chamber is your kingdom. He's going to fit up that nice little loft over the granary for him. Put a stove and a bed and a bit of furniture in it and it will be very comfortable. He can spend his evenings there when he's home, don't you think? What's been worrying *me,* Judy, was that he might want to hang around the kitchen and spoil our jolly evenings."

"Oh, oh, we'll manage." Judy was suddenly in good cheer. She would have surrendered her kitchen chamber without a word of protest had Long Alec so decreed but the thought had lain heavy on her heart. She had slept so cosily in that chamber for over forty years. "All I'm hoping is that yer dad won't be hiring Sim Ledbury. He's been after the place I hear."

"Oh, surely dad wouldn't want a Ledbury round," said Cuddles.

"Ye can't pick and choose, Cuddles dear. That do be the trouble. Hired hilp is be way av being scarce and yer dad must be having a man that understands cows. Sim do be thinking he does. But a Ledbury wid the freedom av me kitchen will be a hard pill to swallow and him wid a face like a tombstone and born hating cats. Gintleman Tom took just the one look at him the day he was here and thin made himsilf scarce. If we can be getting a man who'll be good company for the cats ye'll niver hear a word av complaint from me about him, as long as he's willing to do a bit av work for his wages. Yer dad has got his name up for niver being put out at innything so he cud be imposed upon something shameful. But we'll all be seeing what we'll see and now we've finished wid this tree I'm going in to bake me damsons."

"I'm going to stay out till the sunshine fails me. I think, Judy, when I grow *very* old I'll just sit and bask in the sunshine all the time . . . I love it so. Cuddles, what about a run back to the Secret Field before sunset?"

Cuddles shook a golden-brown head.

"I'd love to go but you know I twisted my foot this morning and it hurts me yet. I'm going over to sit on Weeping Willy's slab in the graveyard for a while and just dream. I feel shimmery to-day . . . as if I was made of sunbeams."

When Cuddles said things like that Pat had a vague feeling that Cuddles was clever and ought to be educated if it could be managed. But it had to be admitted that so far Cuddles seemed to share the family indifference to education. She went in unashamedly for "a good time" and pounced on life like a cat on a mouse.

Pat slipped away for one of her dear pilgrimages to the Secret Field . . . that little tree-encircled spot at the very back of the farm, which she and Sid had discovered so long ago and which she, at least, had loved ever since. Almost every Sunday evening, when they walked over the farm, talking and planning . . . for Sid was developing into an enthusiastic farmer . . . they ended up with the Secret Field, which was always in grass and always bore a wonderful crop of wild strawberries. Sid had promised her he would never plough it up. It was really too small to be worthwhile cultivating anyhow. And if it were ploughed up there might never be any more of Judy's famous wild strawberry shortcakes or those still more delicious things Pat made and which she called strawberry cream pies.

It was nice to go there with Sid but it was even nicer to go alone. There was nothing then to come between her and the silent, rapt communion she seemed to hold with it. It was the loneliest and loveliest spot on the farm. Its very silence was friendly and seemed to come out of the woods around it like a real presence. No wind ever blew there and rain and snow fell lightly. In summer it was a pool of sunlight, in winter a pool of frost . . . now in autumn a pool of colour. Musky, spicy shadows seemed to hover around its grey old fences. Pat always felt that the field knew it was beautiful and was happy in its knowledge. She lingered in it until the sun set and then went slowly back home, savouring every moment of the gathering dusk. What a lovely phrase "gathering dusk" was . . . almost as lovely as Judy's "dim", though the latter had a certain eerie quality that always gave Pat a rapture.

At the top of the hill field she paused, as always, to gloat over Silver Bush. The light shone out from the door and windows of the kitchen where Judy would be preparing supper, with the cats watching for a "liddle bite" and McGinty cocking a pointed ear for Pat's footstep. Would it be as nice when that unknown creature, the all-too-necessary hired man, would be hanging round, waiting for his supper? Of course it wouldn't. He would be a stranger and an alien. Pat fiercely resented the thought of him.

They would have supper by lamplight now. For a while she always hated to have to light the lamp for supper . . . it meant that the wind had blown the summer away and that winter nights were closing in. Then she liked it . . . it was so cosy and companionable and Silver Bushish, with Judy's "dim" looking in through the crimson vines around the window.

The colour of home on an autumn dusk was an exquisite thing. The trees all around it seemed to love it. The house belonged to them and to the garden and the green hill and the orchard and they to it. You couldn't separate them, Pat felt. She always wondered how any one could live in a house where there were no trees. It seemed an indecency, like a too naked body. Trees . . . to veil and caress and beshadow . . . trees to warn you back and beckon you on. Lombardies for statelines . . . birches for maiden grace . . . maples for friendliness . . . spruce and fir for mystery . . . poplars to whisper secrets. Only they never really did. You thought you understood as long as you listened . . . but when you left them you realized they had just been laughing at you . . . thin, rustling, silky laughter. All the trees kept some secret. Who knew but that all those white birches, which stood so primly all day, when night and moonlight came, might step daintily out of the earth and pirouette over the meadows, while the young spruces around the Mince Pie field danced a saraband? Laughing at her fancy, Pat ran into the light and good cheer of Judy's white-washed kitchen with life singing in her heart.

294

3

"Tillytuck! Did ye iver be hearing the like av that for a name?" said Judy, quite flabbergasted for once. "Niver have I heard such a name on the Island before."

"He's been working on the south shore for years but he really belongs to Nova Scotia, dad says," said Cuddles.

"Oh, oh, that ixplains it. Minny a quare name I've known coming out av Novy Scoshy. And what will we be after calling him? If he's a young chap we can be calling him be his given name if he do be having one but if he's a bit oldish it'll have to be Mr. Tillytuck, since hired hilp is getting so uppish these days, and it'll be the death av me if I do have to be saying 'Mr. Tillytuck' ivery time I open me mouth. *Mister* Tillytuck!"

Judy savoured the absurdity of it.

"He's quite old, dad says. Over fifty," remarked Cuddles.

"And dad says, too, that he's a bit peculiar."

"Peculiar, is it, thin? Oh, oh, people do be saying that I'm a bit that way mesilf, so there'll be a pair av us. Is he peculiar in being worth his salt in the way av work? That do be the question."

"He comes well recommended and dad was almost in despair of getting any one half suitable."

"And is *Mister* Tillytuck married, I'm asking. *Mistress* Tillytuck! Oh, oh."

"Dad didn't say. But he's to be here to-morrow so we'll find out all about him. Judy, what *have* you got in that pot?"

"A bit av soup lift over from dinner. I did be thinking we'd like a liddle sup av it be bed-time. And lave a drop in the pot for Siddy. He's gone gallivanting and it's a cold night and mebbe a long drive home."

There was no trace of disdain in Judy's "gallivanting." Judy thought gallivanting one of the lawful delights of youth.

It was a wild wet November evening, with an occasional vicious swish of rain on the windows. But the fire glowed brightly: Gentleman Tom was curled up on his own prescriptive chair and McGinty slumbered on the rug; Bold-and-Bad on one side of the stove, and Squedunk, a half-grown, striped cat on his promotion, on the other, kept up a lovely chorus of purrs: and Cuddles had a cherry-red dress on that brought out the young sheen of her hair. Cuddles had such lovely hair, Pat thought proudly. Nothing so pallid and washed out as gold, like Dot Robinson's . . . no, a warm golden brown.

Judy's soup had a very tempting aroma. Judy was past-mistress of the art of soup-making. Long Alec always said all she had to do was wave her hand over the pot. Mother was mending by the table. Mother had never been strong since her operation and Pat, who watched her with a jealous love, thought she ought to be resting. But mother always liked to do the mending.

"It will be the last thing I'll give up, Pat. Most women don't like mending. I always did. The little worn garments . . . when you were children . . . they seemed so much a part of you. And now your bits of silk things. It doesn't hurt me really. I like to think I'm a little use still."

"Mother! Don't you dare say anything like that again! You're the very heart and soul of Silver Bush . . . you know you are. We couldn't do without you for a day."

Mother smiled . . . that little slow, sweet, mysterious smile of mother's . . . the smile of a woman very wise and very loving. But then everything about mother was wise and loving. When shrieks of laughter rang out she looked as if she were laughing, too, though mother never did laugh . . . not really.

"Let's have a jolly evening," Cuddles had said. "If this Tillytuck creature doesn't like staying in the granary loft in the evenings this may be the last evening we'll have the kitchen to ourselves, so let's make the most of it. Tell us some stories, Judy . . . and I'll roast some clove apples."

"'Pile high the logs, the wind blows chill,'" quoted Pat. "At least put a few more sticks in the stove. That doesn't sound half as romantic as piling high the logs, does it?"

"I'm thinking it might be more comfortable if it isn't be way av being romantic," said Judy, sitting down to her knitting in a corner whence she could give the soup pot an occasional magic stir. "They did be piling the logs in Castle McDermott minny the time and we'd have our faces frying and the backs av us frazing. Oh, oh, give me the modern ways ivery time."

"It seems funny to think of fires in heaven," ruminated Pat, curling up Turk-fashion on the old hooked rug before the stove, with its pattern of three rather threadbare black cats. "But I want a fire there once in a while . . . and a nice howly, windy night like this to point the contrast. And now for your ghost story, Judy."

"I'm clane run out av ghosts," complained Judy . . . who had been saying the same thing for years. But she always produced or invented a new one, telling it with such verisimilitude of detail that even Pat and Cuddles were . . . sometimes . . . convinced. You could no longer believe in fairies of course, but the world hadn't quite given up all faith in ghosts. "Howsiver, whin I come to think av it, I may niver have told ye av the night me own great-uncle saw the Ould Ould McDermott . . . the grandfather of the Ould McDermott av me own time . . . a-sitting on his own grave and talking away to himsilf, angry-like. Did I now?"

"No . . . no . . . go on," said Cuddles eagerly.

But the ghost story of the Ould Ould McDermott was fated never to be told for at that moment there came a resounding treble knock upon the kitchen door. Before one of the paralysed trio could stir the door was opened and Tillytuck walked into the room . . . and, though nobody just then realised it, into the life and heart of Silver Bush. They knew he was Tillytuck because he could be nobody else in the world.

Tillytuck came in and shut the door behind him but not before a lank, smooth-haired black dog had slipped in beside him. McGinty sat up and looked at him and the strange dog sat down and looked at McGinty. But the Silver Bush trio had no eyes just then for anybody but Tillytuck. They stared at him as if hypnotised.

Tillytuck was short and almost as broad as he was long. His red face was almost square, made squarer, if possible, by a pair of old-fashioned mutton-chop whiskers of a faded ginger hue. His mouth was nothing but a wide slit and his nose the merest round button of a nose. His hair could not be seen for it was concealed under a mangy old fur cap. His body was encased in a faded overcoat and a rather gorgeous tartan scarf was wrapped around his neck. In one hand he carried a huge, bulging old Gladstone bag and in the other what was evidently a fiddle done up in a flannel case.

Tillytuck stood and looked at the three wimmen critters out of twinkling little black eyes almost buried in cushions of fat.

"How pleased ye look to see me!" he said. "Only sorter paralysed as it were. Well, I can't help being good-looking."

He went into what seemed an internal convulsion of silent chuckles. Pat jerked herself out of her trance. Mother had gone upstairs . . . somebody must do . . . say . . . something. Judy, probably for the first time in her life, seemed incapable of speech or movement.

297

Pat scrambled up from the rug and went forward.

"Mr . . . Mr. Tillytuck, is it?"

"The same, at your service . . . Christian name, Josiah," said the newcomer, with a bow that might have been courtly if he had had any neck to speak of. It was not till afterwards that Pat thought what a nice voice he had. "Age, fifty-five . . . in politics, Liberal . . . religion, fundamentalist . . . gentleman-at-large, symbolically speaking. And an Orangeman," he added, looking at a large picture of King William on a white horse, crossing the Boyne, that hung upon the wall.

"Won't you . . . take off your coat . . . and sit down?" said Pat rather stupidly. "You see . . . we didn't expect you tonight. Father told us you would be here to-morrow."

"I got a chance up on a truck to Silverbridge so I thought I'd better take it," rumbled Mr. Tillytuck. He hung his cap up on a nail, revealing a head thatched with thick pepper-and-salt curls. He took off his scarf and coat and the cause of a mysterious bulge at one side was explained . . . a huge, stuffed, white Arctic owl which he proudly set up on the clock shelf. He put his bag in one corner with his fiddle on top of it. Then, with unerring discrimination, he selected the most comfortable chair in the kitchen . . . Great-grandfather Nehemiah Gardiner's old glossy wooden armchair with its red cushions . . . sank into it and produced a stubby black pipe from his pocket.

"Any objections?" he rumbled. "I never smoke if ladies object."

"We don't," said Pat. "We're used to Uncle Tom smoking."

Mr. Tillytuck deliberately loaded and lighted his pipe. Ten minutes before no one in the room had ever seen him. And now he seemed to belong there . . . to have been always there. It was impossible to think of him as a stranger or a change. Even Judy, who, as a rule, didn't care what any man thought of her clothes, was thanking her stars that she had on her new drugget dress and a white apron. McGinty had sniffed once at him approvingly and then gone to sleep again, ignoring the new dog entirely. The two grey cats went on purring. Only Gentleman Tom hadn't yet made up his mind and continued to stare at him suspiciously.

Mr. Tillytuck's body was almost as square as his face and was encased in a faded and rather ragged old grey sweater, revealing glimpses of a red flannel shirt which brought a sudden peculiar gleam into Judy's eyes. It was so exactly the shade she would be wanting for the red rosebuds in the rug she meant to hook coming on spring.

298

"If ye've no objection to the pipe have ye any to the dog?" went on Mr. Tillytuck. "If ye haven't maybe ye wouldn't mind him lying down in that corner over there."

Judy decided that it was time she asserted herself. After all, this was *her* kitchen, not *Mister* Tillytuck's.

"Oh, oh, and is it a well-behaved dog he is, *Mister* Tillytuck, I'm asking ye."

"He is," replied Tillytuck solemnly. "But he's been an unfortunate kind of dog . . . born to ill-luck as the sparks fly upward. Ye may not believe me, Miss . . . Miss . . ."

"Plum," said Judy shortly.

"Miss Plum, that dog has had a hard life of it. He's had mange and distemper once each and worms continual. He got run over by a truck last summer and poisoned by strychnine the summer before that."

"He must have as many lives as a cat," giggled Cuddles.

"He's in good health now," assured Mr. Tillytuck. "He's a bit lame from cutting his foot with a sliver of broken glass last week but he'll soon be over it. And he throws a fit once in a while . . . epileptic. Foams at the mouth. Staggers. Falls. In ten minutes gets up and trots away as good as new. So ye need never be worrying about him if ye see him take one. He's really a broth of a dog, only kind of sensitive, and fine with the cows. I have a great respect for dogs . . . always touch my cap when I meet one."

"What is his name?" asked Pat.

"I call him just Dog," responded Mr. Tillytuck. And Just Dog he remained during his entire sojourn at Silver Bush.

"A bit too glib wid yer tongue, *Mister* Tillytuck," thought Judy. But she only said,

"And what may yer mind be in regard to cats?"

"Oh," said Mr. Tillytuck, who seemed quite contented with a whiff of his pipe between speeches, "I have a feeling for cats, Miss Plum. When I wandered in here the other morning I thought I'd like the people here because there was a cat on the window sill. It's a kind of instink with me. So thinks I to myself, 'This place has got a flavour. I could do with a job here.' And how right I was!"

"Where might your last place be?"

"On a fox farm down South Shore way. No names mentioned. I've been there three years. Got on well . . . liked it well . . . till the old missus died and the boss married again. I couldn't pull with the new one at all. Everything on the table bought and only enough to keep the worms quiet at that. A terrible tetchie old woman. Ye couldn't mention the weather to her but she'd quarrel with ye over it. Seemed to take it as a personal insult if you didn't like the day. Then she picked on Dog right along. 'Even a dog has some rights, woman,' I told her. 'You and me ain't going to click,' I told her. 'I'm rather finnicky as to the company I keep,' I told her. 'My dog is better company than a contentious woman,' I told her. 'I'm nobody's slave,' I told her . . . and give notice. When I can't stay in a place without quarrelling with the folks I just mosey along. Likely I'll be here quite a while. Looks like a snug harbour to me. This arm-chair just fits my kinks. I've had my ups and downs. Escaped from the *Titanic* for one thing."

"Oh!" Cuddles and Pat were all eyes and ears. This *was* exciting. Judy gave her soup a vicious swirl. Was she to have a rival in the story telling art?

"Yes, I escaped," said Mr. Tillytuck, "by not sailing in her." He put his pipe back into his mouth and emitted a rumble which they were to learn he called laughter.

"Oh, oh, so that do be your idea of a joke," thought Judy. "I'm getting yer measure, *Mister* Tillytuck."

"Not but what I've had my traggedies," resumed Mr. Tillytuck. He rolled up his sweater sleeve and showed a long white scar on his sinewy arm. "A leopard gave me that when I was a tamer in a circus in the States in my young days. Ah, that was the exciting life. I have a peculiar power over animals. No animal," said Mr. Tillytuck impressively, "can look me in the eye."

"Oh, oh, and are ye married?" persisted Judy remorselessly.

"Not by a jugful!" exclaimed Mr. Tillytuck, so explosively that every one jumped, even Gentleman Tom. Then he subsided into mildness again. "No, I've neither wife nor progeny, Miss Plum. I've often tried to get married but something always prevented. Sometimes every one was willing but the girl herself. Sometimes nobody was willing. Sometimes I couldn't get the question out. If I hadn't been such a temperance man I might have been married many a time. Needed something to loosen my tongue."

Mr. Tillytuck winked at Pat and Pat had a horrible urge to wink back at him. Really, some people did have a queer effect on you.

"I've always thought nobody understood me quite as well as I understood myself," resumed Mr. Tillytuck. "It isn't likely I'll ever marry now. But while there's life there's hope." This time it was at Judy he winked and Judy felt that she was not half as "mad" as she should be. She gave her soup a final stir and stood up briskly.

"Wud ye be jining us in a sup av soup, *Mister* Tillytuck?"

"Ah, some small refreshment will not be amiss," responded Mr. Tillytuck in a gratified tone. "I am not above the pleasures of the palate in moderation. And ever since I entered this dwelling I've been saying to myself whenever you stirred that pot, 'Of all the smells that I ever did smell I never smelled a smell that smelled half as good as that smell smells.'"

Pat and Cuddles proceeded to set the table. Mr. Tillytuck watched them with approbation.

"A pair of high-steppers," he remarked presently in a hoarse aside to Judy. "Some class to *them*. The little one has the wrist of an aristycrat."

"Oh, oh, and so ye've noticed that now?" said Judy, highly gratified.

"Naturally. I'm an expert in regard to weemen. 'There's elegance for you,' I said to myself the moment I opened the door. Some difference from the girls at the fox farm. Just between friends, Miss Plum, they looked like dried apples on a string. One of them was as thin as a weasel and living on lettuce to get thinner. But these two now . . . Cupid will be busy I reckon. No doubt you've a terrible time with the boys hanging round, Miss Plum?"

"Oh, oh, we're not altogether overlooked," said Judy complacently. "And now, *Mister* Tillytuck, will ye be sitting in?"

Mr. Tillytuck slid into a chair.

"I wonder if you'd mind leaving out the 'mister,'" he said. "I'm not used to it and it makes me feel like a pilgrim and sojourner. Josiah, now . . . if you wouldn't mind."

"Oh, oh, but I wud," said Judy decidedly. "Sure and Josiah has always been a name I cudn't bear iver since old Josiah Miller down at South Glen murdered his wife."

"I was well acquainted with Josiah Miller," remarked Mr. Tillytuck, taking up his spoon. "First he choked his wife, then he hanged her, then he dropped her in the river with a stone tied to her. Taking no chances. Ah, I knew him well. In fact, I may say he was a particular friend of mine at one time. But after that happened of course I had to drop him."

"Did they hang him?" demanded Cuddles with ghoulish interest.

"No. They couldn't prove it although everybody knew he did it. They kind of sympathised with him. There's an odd woman that *has* to be murdered. He died a natural death but his ghost walked. I met it once on a time."

"Oh!" Cuddles didn't notice Judy's evident disapproval of this poaching on her preserves. "Really, Mr. Tillytuck?"

"No mistake, Miss Gardiner. Most ghosts is nothing but rats. But this was a genuwine phantom."

"Did he . . . did he speak to you?"

Mr. Tillytuck nodded.

"'I see you're out for a walk like myself,' says he. But I made no reply. I have discovered it is better not to monkey with spooks, miss. Interesting things, but dangerous. So irresponsible, speaking romantically. So, as Friend Josiah was right in the road and I couldn't get past him I just walked through him. Never saw him again. Miss Plum, this *is* soup."

Judy had spent the evening swinging from approval to disapproval of Mr. Tillytuck . . . which continued to be the case during his whole sojourn at Silver Bush. His appreciation of her soup got him another bowlful. Pat was wishing father would come home from Swallowfield. Perhaps Mr. Tillytuck didn't know he had to sleep in the granary. But Mr. Tillytuck said, as he got up from the table,

"I understand my quarters is in the granary . . . so if you'll be kind enough to tell me where it is . . ."

"*Miss Rachel* will be taking the flashlight and showing ye the way," said Judy. "There do be plinty av good blankets on the bed but I'm afraid ye'll find it cold. There do be no fire since we didn't be knowing ye were coming."

"I'll kindle one in a jiffy."

"Oh, oh, thin ye'll be smoked out. That fire has to be lit for an hour afore it'll give over smoking. There do be something out av kilter wid the chimney. Long . . . Mr. Gardiner is maning to have it fixed."

"I'll fix it myself. I worked with a mason for years. Down at the fox farm they had a bad chimney and I built it over in fine shape."

"Did it draw?" asked Judy sceptically.

"Draw! Miss Plum, that chimney drew the cat clean up it one night. The poor animal was never seen again."

Judy subsided. Mr. Tillytuck possessed himself of his bag and his violin and his owl and his dog.

"I'm ready, Miss Gardiner. And as for the matter of names, Miss Plum, the Prince of Wales called me Josiah the whole summer I worked on his ranch in Alberta. A very democratic young man. But if you can't bring yourself to it plain Tillytuck will do for me. And if you've warts or anything like that on your hands" . . . Cuddles guiltily put a hand behind her . . . "I can cure them in a jiffy."

Judy primmed her mouth and took a high tone.

"Thank ye kindly but we do be knowing a few things at Silver Bush. Me grandmother did be taching me a charm for warts whin I was a girleen and it works rale well. Goodnight, *Mister* Tillytuck. I'm hoping ye'll be warm and slape well."

"I'll be in the arms of old Murphy in short order," assured Mr. Tillytuck.

They heard Cuddles' laughter floating back through the rain all the way to the granary. Evidently Mr. Tillytuck was amusing her.

"Certainly he is peculiar," said Pat. "But peculiar people give colour to life, don't they, Judy?"

Cuddles ran in, her face sparkling and radiant from wind and rain.

"Isn't he a darling? He told me he belonged to one of the best families in Nova Scotia."

"Av which statement I have me doubts," said Judy. "I'm thinking he was spaking symbolically, as he sez himsilf. And it didn't use to be manners, taking yer story right out av yer mouth as ye heard him do to mesilf. But he sames a good-natured simple sort av cratur and likely we can put up wid him as long as our family animals can."

"He thinks you're wonderful, Judy. And he wishes you *would* call him Josiah."

"That I'll not thin. But I'm not saying I won't be laving off the Mister after a day or two. It's too much of a strain. Cuddles dear, to-morry I'll be fixing up a bit av a charm for that liddle wart av yours. I'm knowing it shud av been attinded to long ago but what wid all these comings and goings and hirings it wint out av me head. Oh, oh, I'll not be having any *Mister* Tillytuck wid a side-whisker casting up the fam'ly warts to me!"

"I must write Hilary all about him," laughed Pat. "He would delight in him. Oh, Judy, if Hilary could only drop in some of these November evenings as he used to do things would be perfect. It's over two years now since he went away and it seems like a hundred. Is there any soup left for Sid, Judy?"

"Loads and lashings av it. Was it to the dance at South Glen he was going?"

"Wherever he went he took Madge Robinson," said Cuddles. "He's giving her quite a rush now. All summer it was Sara Russell. I believe Sid is a dreadful flirt."

Pat smiled contentedly. There was safety in numbers. After all, Sid had never seemed really to have a serious notion of any girl since Bets had died. It pleased Pat to think he would be faithful to her sweet memory all his life . . . as she, Pat, would be. She would never have another intimate girl friend. She liked to think of herself as a happy old maid and Sid a happy old bachelor, living gaily together all their lives, loving and caring for Silver Bush, with Winnie and Cuddles and Joe coming home for long visits with their families, and McGinty and the cats living forever and Judy telling stories in the kitchen. One couldn't think of Silver Bush without Judy. She had always been there and of course she always would be.

"Judy," said Cuddles solemnly, turning back in the hall doorway on her way to bed, "Judy, mind you don't go and fall in love with Josiah. I saw him winking at you."

Judy's only reply was a snort.

4

The days of that late autumn seemed to Pat to slip by like a golden river of happiness, even after the last cricket song had been sung. Mother was keeping well . . . father was jubilant over the good harvest . . . Cuddles was taking more interest in her lessons . . . the surplus kittens of the summer's crop had all found excellent homes . . . and there was enough of dances and beaus to satisfy Pat's not very passionate love of social life. Almost any time she would have preferred to roast apples and bandy lovely ghost stories in Judy's kitchen to going to a party. Cuddles could not understand this: *she* was longing for the day when she would be old enough to go to dances and have "boyfriends."

"I mean to have a great deal of *attention*," she told Judy gravely. "A few flirtations . . . *nice* ones, Judy . . . and then I'll fall in love *sensibly*."

"Oh, oh," said Judy with a twinkle, "I'm thinking that can't be done,

Cuddles darlint. A sinsible love affair now . . . it do be sounding a bit dull to me."

"Pat says she's never going to fall in love with anybody. I really believe she does want to be an old maid, Judy."

"I've been hearing girls talk that way afore now," scoffed Judy. But she was secretly uneasy. The Silver Bush girls in any generation had never been flirts but she would have liked Pat to show a little more interest in the young men who came and went at Silver Bush and took her to dances and pictures and corn-roasts and skating parties and moonlight snowshoe tramps. Pat had any number of "boy-friends" but friends were all they were or seemed likely to be. Judy was quite elated when Milton Taylor of South Glen began haunting Silver Bush and taking Pat out when she would go. But Pat would not go often enough to please Judy.

"Oh, oh, Patsy dear, he'll have the finest farm in South Glen some day and the nice boy he is! It's the affectionate husband he'd be making ye."

"'An affectionate husband,'" giggled Pat. "Oh, Judy, you're so Victorian. Affectionate husbands are out of date. We like the cave men, don't we, Cuddles?"

Cuddles and Pat exchanged grins. In spite of the difference in their ages they were great chums and Pat had a dreadful habit of telling Cuddles all about her beaus, what they did and what they said. Pat had a nippy tongue when she chose and the youths in question would not have been exactly delighted if they could have overheard her.

"But don't you intend to get married sometime, Pat?" Cuddles asked once.

Pat shook her brown head impatiently.

"Oh . . . sometime perhaps . . . when I have to . . . but not for years and years. Why, Silver Bush couldn't spare me."

"But if Sid brings a wife in sometime . . ."

"Sid won't do that," cried Pat passionately. "I don't believe Sid will ever marry. You know he was in love with Bets, Cuddles. I believe he will always be faithful to her memory."

"Judy says men aren't like that. And every one says May Binnie is making a dead set at him."

"Sid will never marry May Binnie . . . that's one thing I'm sure of," said Pat. The very thought made her feel cold. She and May Binnie had always hated each other.

Tillytuck was almost as much interested in Pat's affairs as was Judy. Every young man who came to Silver Bush got a severe scrutiny, though he knew it not, from Tillytuck's little black eyes. It delighted him to listen to Pat's badinage.

"Gosh, but she knows how to handle the men!" he exclaimed admiringly one night, when the door closed behind Pat and Milton Taylor. "She'll make a fine wife for some one. I admit that I admire her deportment, Judy."

"Oh, oh, we all do know how to be handling the men at Silver Bush, Tillytuck," said Judy loftily.

For it was "Judy" and "Tillytuck" now. Judy would none of Josiah and "mister" was too formal to keep up for long. They were excellent friends after a fashion. It seemed to Judy, as to everybody, that Tillytuck must have always been at Silver Bush. It was impossible to believe that it was only six weeks since he had dropped in with his owl and his fiddle and Just Dog. The very cats purred louder when he came into the house. To be sure, Gentleman Tom never quite approved of him. But then Gentleman Tom had always been a reserved, taciturn cat who never really took up with any one but Judy.

Tillytuck had his prescriptive corner and chair in the kitchen and he was always slipping in to ask Judy to make a cup of tea for him. The fun of it, to Pat and Cuddles, was that Judy always made it, without a word of complaint. She soon discovered that Tillytuck had a sweet tooth where pies and cake were concerned and when she was in a good humour with him there was usually a triangle of one or a slice of the other waiting for him, to the amusement of the girls who affected to believe that Judy was "sweet" on Tillytuck, much to her scorn. Sometimes she would even sit down on the other side of the stove and drink a cup of tea with him. When she felt compelled to scold him he always soothed her with a compliment.

"See how I can manage the weemen," he would whisper complacently to Pat. "Ain't it the pity I'm not a marrying man?"

"Perhaps you may marry yet," responded Pat with a grave face, dropping a dot of red jelly like a gleaming ruby in the pale yellow centre of her lemon tarts.

"Maybe . . . when I make up my mind whether I want to take pity on Judy or not," Tillytuck answered with a wink. "There's times when

I think she'd suit me. She's fond of talking and I'm fond of listening."

Judy ignored nonsense of this kind. She had, so she informed the girls, taken Tillytuck's measure once and for all.

She was, however, very bitter because he never went to church. Judy thought all hired men ought to go to church. It was only respectable. If they did not go who knew but that censorious neighbours would claim it was because they were so overworked at Silver Bush during the week that they did not be having the strength to go to church on Sundays. But Tillytuck was adamantine to her arguments.

"I don't approve of human hymns," he said firmly. "Nothing should be sung in churches but the psalms of David . . . with maybe an occasional paraphrase on special occasions. Them's my principles and I sticks to them. I always sing a psalm before I go to bed and every Sunday morning I read a chapter in my testament."

"And on Waping Willy's tombstone," muttered Judy, who, for some mysterious reason resented Tillytuck's habit of going into the graveyard to read the said chapter.

And then . . . Christmas was drawing near and Great Preparations were being made. You could hear the capitals in Tillytuck's voice when he referred to them. They were going to have a real "re-union." Winnie and Frank would come and Uncle Tom and Aunt Edith and Aunt Barbara from Swallowfield and Aunt Hazel and Uncle Rob Madison and their five children and the Bay Shore Great-aunts if their rheumatism let them. In fact, it was to be what Judy called "a regular tommyshaw" and Pat was brimful of happiness and expectation over it all. It would be the first "real" Christmas since she had become the virtual mistress of Silver Bush. The previous one Frank had had bronchitis, so he and Winnie couldn't come, and the one before that Aunt Hazel's family had measles and Hilary was not there for the first time in years, and it hadn't been a Christmassy Christmas at all. But everything would be different this year. And Joe expected to be home for the first Christmas since he went away. Judy's turkeys were fat as fat could be and there was to be a goose because dad liked goose and a couple of ducks because Uncle Tom liked ducks. As for the rest of the bill of fare, Pat was poring over cookbooks most of her spare time. Many and old were the cookbooks of Silver Bush, full of clan recipes that had stood the test of time. Most of them had nice names linked up with all kinds of people who had invented the recipes . . . many of them people who were dead or in far lands. It gave Pat a thrill to thumb them over . . . Grandmother Selby's jellied cabbage salad . . . Aunt Hazel's ginger cookies . . . Cousin Miranda's beefsteak pie . . . the Bay Shore pudding . . . Great-grandmother Gardiner's fruit cake . . . Old Joe Pingle's mince pie . . . Uncle Horace's raisin gravy. Pat never could find out who Old Joe Pingle was. Nobody, not even Judy, seemed to know. But Uncle Horace had brought the recipe for raisin gravy home from his first voyage and told Judy he had killed a man for it . . . though nobody believed him.

Judy was planning to get a new "dress-up dress" for the occasion. Her old one, a blue garment of very ancient vintage, was ralely a liddle old-fashioned.

"And besides, Patsy dear, I'd be nading it if I took a run over to ould Ireland some av these long-come-shorts. I can't be getting the thought out av me head iver since Cuddles put it in. Sure and if I wint I'd want to make a rale good apparance afore me ould frinds, not to spake av a visit to Castle McDermott. What wud ye think av a nice wine-colour, Patsy? They tell me it's rale fashionable, this fall. And mebbe sating as a bit av a change from silk."

Pat, although the thought of Judy going to Ireland, even if only for a visit, gave her a nasty sensation, entered heartily into the question of the new dress and went to town with Judy to help in the selection and bully the dressmaker into making it exactly as Judy wanted it. Uncle Tom was in town that day and they saw him dodging out of a jeweller's shop, trying hastily to secrete a small, ornately wrapped parcel in his pocket before he encountered them. Not succeeding, he muttered something about having to see a man and shot down a side street.

"Uncle Tom is awfully mysterious about something these days," said Pat. "What do you suppose he has been buying in that shop? I'm sure it couldn't have been anything for Aunt Edith or Aunt Barbara."

"Oh, oh, Patsy dear, I'm belaving yer Uncle Tom has a notion av getting married. I know the signs."

Pat experienced another disagreeable sensation. Change at Swallowfield was almost as bad as change at Silver Bush. Uncle Tom and the aunts had *always* lived there . . . always would. Pat couldn't fit an Aunt Tom into the picture at all. "Oh, Judy, I can't think he would be so foolish. At his age! Why, he's sixty!"

"Wid me own eyes, Patsy, I saw him rading a letter one day and stuffing it into his pocket like mad whin he caught me eye on him. And blushing! Whin a man av his age do be blushing there's something quare in the wind. Do ye be minding back in the summer Cuddles telling us she was after mailing letters from him to a lady?"

Pat sighed and put the disagreeable matter out of her mind. She wasn't going to have the afternoon spoiled. There were many things to buy besides Judy's satin dress. Pat loved shopping. It was so fascinating to go into the big department store and pick things to buy . . . pretty things that just wanted to be taken away from all the glitter and too-muchness to be made part of a real home. They had to have some new overdrapes for the dining-room and new covers for the Big Parlour cushions and a set of little glass dishes to serve the chilled fruit cocktails Pat had decided on for the first course of the Christmas dinner. Judy was a little dubious about trying to put on too much style . . . "cocktails" had a quare sound whin all was said and done and Silver Bush had always been a great timperance place . . .

"Oh, Judy darling, it isn't that kind of cocktails at all. Just bits of fruit . . . and juice . . . and a red maraschino cherry on top. You'll love them."

Judy surrendered. If Patsy wanted quality dishes she must have them. Anyhow, Judy was sure the Binnies never opened a dinner with cocktails and it was always well to be a few frills ahead of them. Judy enjoyed every minute of her excursion to town and brought home a wine-coloured satin of a lustre to dazzle even Castle McDermott. It dazzled Tillytuck to whom Judy proudly displayed it that night.

"A bit too voluptuous" was all he would say. And got no pie that night. Tillytuck confessed to himself as he took his way to the granary that this was one of the times he had failed in tact. If he has known that Judy had in the pantry a cold roast duck and a dish of browned potato which she had intended to share with him by way of a "liddle bite" he would have had still poorer opinion of his tact. As it was, Cuddles discovered it and she and Pat and Judy did justice to it before they went to bed, Sid coming in at the last to pick the bones and listen to Judy's story about a lost diamond ring that had been found in a turkey's crop cut open by accident.

"And that do be minding me . . . did I iver be telling ye av the first time yer Aunt Hazel dressed a turkey for dinner whin she was a slip av a girleen? Oh, oh, there niver was such a disgrace at Silver Bush. It tuk us years to live it down."

"What happened, Judy?"

"Ye'll niver be telling her I told ye? Well, thin, she tuk a great notion to be dressing and stuffing the turkey for dinner one time and nobody was to interfere wid it. We didn't be ixpicting any company that day, just having the turkey for ourselves we were, not being Binnies as sells ivery blessed thing off the farm they can and living on potatoes and point. But unixpicted company come . . . quality folks from town no less . . . a mimber of Parlymint and his lady wife. I did be thanking me stars we had the turkey but oh, oh, what happened whin yer dad cut a slice off the brist, maning to give all white mate to the lady visitor!"

"Judy, what *did* happen? Don't be so mysterious."

"Mysterious, is it? Well, it's hating to tell it av Silver Bush I am. Not but what yer dad laughed till he was sick afterwards. Well, thin, to tell the worst, yer Aunt Hazel had niver taken out the turkey's crop and whin yer dad carved off that slice kernels av whate and a bunch av oats fell down all over the plate. I wasn't there av coorse . . . I niver wud be setting at the table whin there was quality company . . . and it did be well I wasn't for niver wud I have been the same agin. It was bad enough to hear yer grandmother telling av it. She niver hilt up her head quite so high agin, poor ould leddy. Oh, oh, it's only something to be laughing over now, though we did be thinking it was a tragedy thin."

Cuddles screamed over the tale but Pat felt a little troubled. It *was* a dreadful thing to have happened at Silver Bush even if it had been a quarter of a century before. Nothing worse could have been told of the Binnies.

"I do hope nothing disgraceful will happen at our Christmas dinner," she said anxiously.

"Niver worry, Patsy dear. There do be no paycock's feathers in the house now. Sure and I burned thim all the day after *that*. Yer Uncle Horace said I was a superstitious ould woman and was rale peeved bekase he had brought thim home. So there'll be nothing to bring us bad luck but still I'll be thankful whin it's all well over. As Tillytuck was remarking yisterday, there do be a certain amount av nervous strain over it all."

"Tillytuck told me to-day that his grandfather was a pirate," said Cuddles. "Also that he was through the Halifax horror when that ship loaded with munitions blew up in the days of the war. Do you really think, Judy, that Tillytuck has had all the adventures that he says he has?"

Judy's only reply was a sardonic laugh.

5

Christmas was drawing nearer and there was so much to be done. Pat and Cuddles worked like beavers and Judy flew about, or tried to, in three directions at once. A big box of goodies had to be packed and sent to Hilary . . . poor Hilary who must spend his Christmas in a dreary Toronto boarding house. Mince meat and Christmas cake must be concocted. Judy had to go for fittings of the new dress and nearly died of them. The silver and brasses had to be cleaned: everything must be made spick and span.

"The things in this house *are* nice," said Cuddles, as she rubbed at the spoons. "I wonder why. They're not really so handsome but they're *nice.*"

"They're loved, that's why," said Pat softly. "They've been loved and cared for for years. I love everything in this house *terribly,* Cuddles."

"I believe you love them too much, Pat. I love them, too, but you seem to worship them."

"I can't help it. Silver Bush means everything to me and it seems to mean more every year of my life. I do want this Christmas to go off well . . . everything just right . . . all the folks enjoying themselves. Judy, do you think six mince pies will be enough? It would be disgraceful if we didn't have enough of everything."

"Loads and lashings," assured Judy. "Mrs. Tom Robinson do be thinking we're tarrible extravagant. 'A fat kitchen makes a lean will,' she did be sighing to me the other day whin she was in, borrying the quilt clamps off av me. 'Oh, oh,' sez I, 'we're not like the Birtwhistles at the bridge,' sez I. 'After they do be having a bit av company,' sez I, 'not a dab av butter will be et in that house till all the extry bills are made up,' sez I. She tuk it wid her chin up but she was faling it all right. Ould Mrs. Birtwhistle was her mother's cousin. Oh, oh, I'm knowing too much about all the folks in these parts for inny av thim to be giving me digs in me own kitchen. A lean will indade! Plaze the Good Man Above it'll be a long time afore there's inny nade to talk av wills at Silver Bush."

"But Aunt Edith says we do live too high at Silver Bush," said

Cuddles. "She says we really ought to be more frugal."

"Frugal! I hate that word," said Pat. "It sounds so . . . so porridgy. I do hope Joe will get home in time. We must give a party for him if he does, some night between Christmas and New Year's. I love to give parties. It's so nice to see people coming to Silver Bush in pretty dresses, all smiling and happy. I hope everybody will have a good appetite Christmas Day. I love to feed hungry people."

"Oh, oh, and what are women for if it's not to fade the world?" said Judy complacently. "Sure and it do be giving me pleasure just to see a cat lapping his milk. It's glad I am you girls do be having the rale Silver Bush notions av hospitality. I'm minding the fuss yer Aunt Jessie did be making once bekase company came unixpicted like and she had nothing to give them to ate. Niver was Silver Bush in inny such predicament I'm telling ye."

"There ain't so much fun here as at the Jebbs' though," said Tillytuck, who was sandpapering an axe-handle in his corner and thought Judy needed taking down a bit. "They were always quarrelling there. Two would start and then all the rest would join in. It was interesting. You folks here never quarrel. I never saw such a harmonious family."

"I should think we wouldn't quarrel," said Pat indignantly. "It would be terrible to have quarrels at Silver Bush. I hope we never, never will have."

"You'll be a fortunate family then," said Tillytuck. "There ain't many families but have a ruction once in a while."

"I think I would *die* if any of us quarrelled," said Pat. "We leave that to people like the Binnies."

Hope died hard in the matter of Joe but the days passed without any word of him or his ship. It was over three years since Joe had been home and Pat always knew, when she surprised a certain look in mother's eyes, that she was longing for her sailor boy. It would shadow mother's Christmas a bit if Joe didn't get home in time for it.

Pat had hoped for a fine Christmas day, clear and crisp, with a crackle of frost and unspoiled fields of snow and caps of lovely white fur on the posts down the lane: but she felt dubious as she took her last look from the kitchen door late on Christmas Eve. She and Judy had stayed up to make the stuffing for "the birds" but Judy was now folding weary hands for slumber in the kitchen chamber and Tillytuck had gone to sleep, perchance to snore, in the granary loft. A snarling, quarrelsome wind was fighting with the white birches and wailing around the barns. It did not sound like a fine day on the morrow but one must hope for the best, as Judy said. Pat shut out the chill of the winter night and paused a moment in the warm old kitchen to gloat over things in general. Everything she loved best was safe under her roof. The house seemed breathing softly and contentedly in its sleep. Life was very sweet.

Pat's hopes for a fine day were vain. Christmas morning dawned on a dreadful combination of fog and rain. Rain by itself, Pat always thought, was an honest thing . . . fog lovely and eerie . . . but together they were horrible. Tillytuck agreed with her.

"It's fogging, Judy," he said dolefully when he came in for breakfast. "Fogging hard. I can put up with a rainy day but I can't come these half-and-halfs, like a woman who never knows her own mind. No, sir."

"Oh, oh, and I'm not knowing what's to be done, wid people tramping all over me clane floor in dirty boots," said Judy viciously.

"We'll just have to do as they do in Nova Scotia, Judy."

Judy bit.

"Oh, oh, and what is it they do in Novy Scoshy, if a body may ask?"

"They do the best they can," said Tillytuck solemnly, as he went out with the milking pails. Tillytuck mostly did the milking now. Judy had surrendered the chore unwillingly. She was afraid, when Long Alec insisted on it, that he thought she was growing too old for it. And she never could be brought to believe that Tillytuck stripped the cows properly. Besides, wasn't he ruining the young barn cats by milking into their mouths? That was no way to be training cats. Ye wudn't be catching Gintleman Tom or Bold-and-Bad or Squedunk at inny such capers.

After breakfast the blue and gold and purple and silver parcels were distributed and every one was pleased. Pat had been afraid Sid might not like the rather gorgeous silk pyjamas she had got him but Sid did.

"They're the very niftiest pyjamas I ever saw in my life," vowed Cuddles.

"And where have you seen so many pyjamas, miss?" demanded Long Alec, thinking to "get a rise" out of Cuddles.

"On the bargain counters," retorted Cuddles . . . and the laugh was on dad. It did not take much to make the Silver Bush people laugh. Laughter came easily to them.

"Isn't she the cliver one," said Judy . . . and then stiffened in horror.

Tillytuck was proudly uncovering his Christmas present for "the missus." A Jerusalem cherry! A pretty thing, to be sure, with its glossy green leaves and ruby red fruit, and mother was delighted with it. But Judy beat a sudden retreat to the kitchen, followed by Pat.

"Judy, what is the matter? You're never going to be sick to-day!"

"Patsy darlint, it's well if there's nothing worse than me being sick happens here this blissed day. Were ye seeing what that Tillytuck did be giving to yer mother? A Jerusalem cherry no less! Sure and didn't I come all out wid gooseflesh whin I saw it."

"But what about it, Judy? It's a pretty thing. I thought it lovely of Tillytuck to remember mother."

"Oh, oh, don't ye be knowing a Jerusalem cherry brings bad luck? There was one brought into this house thirty years ago and yer Uncle Tom slipped on the stairs and bruk three ribs that very night. I'm telling ye. Patsy darlint, can't ye be contriving to set the thing outside somewhere till the dinner be over at laste?"

Pat shook her head.

"We couldn't do that. It would offend Tillytuck. Anyway, I know mother wouldn't hear of it. You mustn't be superstitious, Judy. A pretty thing like a Jerusalem cherry can't bring bad luck."

"I'm hoping ye're right, Patsy, but we'll be seeing what we'll see. 'Fogging, Judy,' sez he. No wonder it do be fogging, and him wid that Jerusalem thing in his granary that blissed minute! But wid all there is to see to I'm not to stand bithering here."

"I'm going to see about the spare room right off so that it will be all in order if any one comes early," said Pat briskly. "May I have that new hooked rug you've got stored away in the attic to lay by the bed . . . the one with the great soft, plushy roses?"

"Av coorse. I mint it for yer hope chist but the way ye're snubbing the min right and lift there'll be lashings av time for *that*. Put plinty av blankets on the bed, Patsy darlint. If the Bay Shore aunts come they may be staying all night. Style widout comfort is not the way av Silver Bush. Yer Aunt Helen at Glenwood now . . . ye do be knowing yersilf what style she puts on . . . silk spreads and liddle lace and ribbing cushions . . . but I've always been hearing that people who slipt there vowed they were cold in bed. The minister slipt there one night and so cold he was he started prowling for a blanket in the night and fell down the back stairs. That was be way av being a disgrace. I'm telling ye."

Cuddles had already made the spare room bed and was infuriated because Pat insisted on making it over again.

"You'll be as bad as Aunt Edith before you're thirty, Pat. She imagines nobody can do anything right but herself. And Judy's no better, no matter what she thinks. She's been teaching me to make gravy for weeks but now when I want to make it to-day she won't let me. You all make me weary."

"Don't be cross, Cuddles. You made the bed as nicely as any one could but the extra blankets have to be put on. Cuddles, do you know I love to make up beds and think of all the tired people who will lie in them. I couldn't bear it if any one should be cold in bed in Silver Bush. Will you get some of the silver polish and do the mirrors? I want them to shine like diamonds . . . especially the one in the hall."

The hall mirror was one that had been brought out from France by Great-great-grandmother, Marie Bonnet. It was a long, softly gleaming thing in a ruddy copper frame and Pat loved it. Cuddles had an affection for it, too, because she thought she looked nicer in it than in any other mirror at Silver Bush.

"Sure and it was always the flattering one," said Judy, as Cuddles rubbed at the frame. "Minny's the pretty face that's looked into it."

"I wonder," said Pat dreamily . . . passing carelessly through the hall just to make sure Cuddles was doing the polishing right . . . "if one came here some moonlit night one couldn't see all the shadowy faces that once looked into it looking out again."

"Oh, oh, ye'd nade the enchanted mirror of Castle McDermott for that," chuckled Judy. "That looking glass wasn't like other looking glasses. There did be a curse on it. I was always afraid av it. Be times it did be saming like a frind and thin again like an inimy. And I was always wanting to look in it, in spite av me fear, jist to be seeing if innything looked out av it."

"And did anything ever, Judy?"

"Niver a bit av it, girl dear. The looking glass wasn't for common folks like mesilf. Niver did I be seeing innything worse than me own frickled face. But there did be thim that did."

"What did they see, Judy?"

"Oh, oh, there's no time for that now. It's me raisin gravy I must be seeing to this blissed minute."

Pat shut the hall door and set her back against it resolutely.

"Judy, not one step do you stir from this hall till you've told us what was seen in the McDermott mirror, if there's no raisin gravy made this Christmas."

"Oh, oh," . . . Judy surrendered . . . "It's mebbe as well to tell it whin Tillytuck can't be claiming to have stipped out av the glass. Did ye be hearing him the other avening whin I was telling av the dance one Saturday night in South Glin that they kipt up too late . . . past the stroke av twilve . . . and the Bad Man Below intered? Sez me Tillytuck solemnly, 'I rimimber it only too well. I was at that dance.' 'Indade,' sez I, sarcastic-like, 'ye must be an aged man, Tillytuck, for the dance was all av eighty years ago.' But he carried it off wid a grin. Ye can't shame that man. But I can't be rimimbering all the tales av the looking glass now. There was a Kathleen McDermott once who was no better than she shud be an me fine lady whips out one night to meet her gintleman lover and run away wid him. But me grand gintleman was killed on his way to her and Kathleen hurried back home thinking no one wud know. But the doors were closed agin her. The McDermott had looked in the glass and seen it all. Bridget McDermott saw *her* soldier husband dying in India the night he was killed. But nobody iver knew what Nora McDermott saw for the pore liddle soul dropped the lamp she was holding and her dress caught fire and she was dead in two hours."

"Oh!" Cuddles shivered deliciously. "Why did they keep such a terrible thing in the castle?"

"Sure, it *belonged* there," said Judy mysteriously. "Ye wudn't have thim move it. And it was be way av being frindly as often as not. Eileen McDermott knew her man was alive, shipwrecked on a South Say island, whin iveryone else was sure for a whole winter that he was drowned. She saw him in the glass. And the McDermott av me own time saw a minuet danced in it one night and niver was inny the worse av it. And now I'm getting back to me kitchen. I've wasted enough time palavering wid ye."

"Half the fun of making preparations for anything is in talking things over," reflected Cuddles, giving the mirror a final whisk. It held no ghosts. But Cuddles felt secretly satisfied with what she saw in it.

6

Eventually everything was in readiness. The table beautifully set . . . Pat made Cuddles take off the tablecloth three times before it was smooth enough to suit her . . . the house full of delicious odours, everybody dressed up except Judy.

"I'm not putting on me dress-up dress till me dinner is out of the way. I'm not wanting spots on it. Whin the last dish is washed I'll slip up and put it on in time for supper. They'll see me in all my grandeur thin. Yer table do be looking lovely, Patsy, but I'm thinking it wud look better if that cherry thing didn't be sitting in the middle av it."

"I thought it would please Tillytuck. He's sensitive, you know. And if it is going to bring us bad luck it will anyhow, so what matter where it sits?"

"Sez she, laughing in her slave at the foolish ould woman. Oh, oh, we'll be seing, Patsy. Joe hasn't come after all and I've me own opinion as to what previnted him."

Pat looked about happily. Everything was just right. She must run and tie Sid's neck-tie for him. She loved to do that . . . nobody else at Silver Bush could suit him. What matter if a cold rain were falling outside? Here it was snug and warm, the smiling rooms full of Christmas magic. Then the old brass knocker on the front door began to go tap-a-tap. The first guests had arrived . . . Uncle Brian and Aunt Jessie, who hadn't been asked at all but had just decided to run down in the free and easy clan fashion and bring rich old Cousin Nicholas Gardiner from New Brunswick, who was visiting them and wanted to see his relatives at Silver Bush. Pat, as she let them in, cast one wild glance through the dining room door to see if three more places could be crowded into the table without spoiling it and knew they couldn't. The Jerusalem cherry had begun its dire work.

Soon everybody had come . . . Frank and Winnie, Aunt Hazel and Uncle Robert Madison and all the little Madisons, the two stately Great-aunts, Frances and Honor from the Bay Shore farm, Uncle Tom and Aunt Barbara and Aunt Edith . . . the latter looking as disapproving as usual.

"Raisin gravy," she sniffed, as she went upstairs. "Judy Plum made that on purpose. She knows I can't eat raisin gravy. It always gives me dyspepsia."

But nobody seemed to have dyspepsia at that Christmas table. At first all went very well. A dear, gentle lady, with golden-brown eyes and silvery hair, sat at the head and her smile made every one feel welcome. Pat had elected to help Judy wait on the table but every one else sat down. The children sat at a special table in the Little Parlour as was the custom of the caste, and the cocktail course passed off without a hitch . . . three extra cocktails having been hurriedly concocted by Cuddles who, however, forgot to put a maraschino cherry on them. Of course Aunt Edith got one of the cherryless ones and blamed Judy Plum for it, and Great-aunt Frances got another and felt slighted. Old Cousin Nicholas got the third and didn't care. He never et the durn things anyhow. Uncle Tom ate his, although Aunt Edith reminded him that maraschino cherries were apt to give old people indigestion. "I'm not so aged yet," said Uncle Tom stiffly. Uncle Tom did look surprisingly young, as Pat and Judy were quick to note. The once flowing, wavy black beard, which had been growing smaller all summer, was by now clipped to quite a smart little point and he had got gold-rimmed eyeglasses in place of the old spectacles. Pat thought of those California letters but put the thought resolutely away. Nothing must mar this Christmas dinner . . . though Winnie was telling a story that would have been much better left untold. Judy almost froze in her tracks with horror as Winnie's clear voice drifted out to the kitchen.

"It was just after Frank and I were married, you know. I hadn't really got settled down. Unexpected company came to supper one night and I sent Frank off to the store to get some sliced ham for an emergency dish. I thought it seemed *rather* pink when I was arranging it on the plate . . . so nicely, with curly little parsley sprays. It *did* look artistic. Frank helped everybody and then took a bite himself. He laid down his fork and looked at me. I knew something was awfully wrong but *what?* I stopped pouring the tea and snatched up a mouthful of ham. What do you think?" Winnie looked impishly around the table. "That ham was *raw!*"

Shouts of laughter filled the dining room. Under cover of the noise Pat dashed out to the kitchen where she and Judy had a silent rage. They had laughed themselves when Winnie had first told the tale at Silver Bush. But to tell it to all the world was a very different thing.

"Oh, oh, the disgrace av having Edith and Mrs. Brian hear av it!" moaned Judy. "But niver be hard on her, Patsy. I do be knowing too

318

well what loosened her tongue. And were ye noticing that Cuddles put the slim grane chair out av the liddle parlour for yer Uncle Brian and it cracked in one leg? Ivery time I've seen the crack widening a bit and the Good Man Above only knows if it'll last out the male. And here's Tillytuck sulking bekase he slipped on the floor and fell on his dog. He's been vowing I spilled a liddle gravy right in his corner, the great clumsy. But it's time to be taking in the soup."

And then, as if it had been waiting for Judy's words as a cue, the Jerusalem cherry showed what it could really do when it gave its mind to it. It seemed as if everything happened at once. Tillytuck, made sulkier still by Judy's speech, opened the door and stalked furiously out into the rain. Uncle Tom's wet, dripping Newfoundland, who had followed the Swallowfield folks over, dashed in. Just Dog simply couldn't stand that, after being fallen on. He flew at the intruder. The two dogs rolled in a furry avalanche right against Pat who had started for the dining room door bearing a trayful of soup plates full of a delicious brew that Judy called chicken broth. Down went poor Pat in a frightful mêlée of dogs, broken plates and spilled soup. Hearing the din, every one, except Cousin Nicholas, rushed out of the dining room. Aunt Hazel's two year old baby began to shriek piercingly. Aunt Edith took a heart attack on the spot. Judy Plum, for the first and only time in her life, lost her head but lost it to good purpose. She grabbed a huge pepper-pot from the dresser and hurled the contents full in the faces of the writhing, snarling dogs. It was effective. The Newfoundland tore loose, dashed wildly through the dining room, ruining Aunt Jessie's new blue georgette dress as he collided with her, tore through the hall, tore upstairs, ran into a delicately papered pastel wall, tore down again, and escaped through the front door which Billy Madison had presence of mind enough to open for him. As for Just Dog, he had bolted through the cellar door, which had been left open, and struck the board shelf across the steps. Just Dog, shelf, three tin pails, two stewpans, and a dozen glass jars of Judy's baked damson preserves all crashed down the cellar steps together!

It seemed that Pandemonium reigned at Silver Bush for the next quarter of an hour. Aunt Edith was gasping for breath and demanding a cold compress. She had to be taken upstairs by Aunt Barbara and ministered to.

"Excitement always brings on that pain in my heart," she murmured piteously. "Judy Plum *knows* that."

Uncle Tom and Uncle Brian were in kinks of laughter. Aunt Frances and Aunt Honor *looked* "This is not how things are done at the Bay Shore." And poor Pat scrambled dizzily up from the floor, dripping with soup, crimson with shame and humiliation. It was Cuddles who saved the situation. Cuddles was superb. She didn't lose her wits for a second.

"Everybody go back and sit down," she ordered. "Buddy, stop yelling . . . stop it, I say! Pat, slip up and get into another dress. Judy, clean up the mess. There is plenty of soup left . . . Pat had only half the servings on the tray and Judy hid a potful away in the pantry. I'll have it ready in a jacksniff. Shut the cellar door and keep that dog down there until he gets the pepper out of his eyes."

Judy always declared she had never been as proud of any one at Silver Bush as she was of Cuddles at that time. But just at the moment poor Judy was feeling nothing but the bitterest humiliation. Never had such a shameful thing happened at Silver Bush. Wait till she got hold of Tillytuck! Wait till she could get her hands on that Jerusalem cherry.

In a surprisingly short time the guests were back at the table, where Cousin Nicholas had been placidly eating crackers through all the hullabaloo. Cuddles and Judy between them served the soup. Pat came down, clothed and in her right mind once more. Two cats, whose nervous systems had been shattered, fled to the peace and calm of Judy's kitchen chamber. The Jerusalem cherry bided its time. The goose-duck-turkey course was a grand success and Judy's raisin gravy was acclaimed the last word in gravies. The dessert was amazing, though Cousin Nicholas did manage to upset a jug of sauce over the tablecloth. Judy came in and calmly mopped it up. Judy had got her second wind now and was prepared for anything.

Pat sat down for the dessert and there was laughter. People were to seek Pat from birth till death because she gave them the gift of laughter. Though she had secret worry gnawing at her heart. Aunt Jessie had eaten only three spoonfuls of her pudding! Wasn't it good? And Winnie . . . somehow . . . wasn't looking just right. She had suddenly become very quiet and rather pale.

To Judy's thankfulness the cracked chair lasted the dinner out, though it creaked alarmingly every time Uncle Brian moved. Then came "the grand dish-washing," as Judy called it, in the kitchen. Judy and Pat and Cuddles tackled it gaily. Things weren't so bad, after all. The guests were enjoying a good clan pi-jaw in the Big Parlour and the children were sitting around Tillytuck in the Little Parlour, looking up fascinated, while he told them stories. "Tarrible lies," Judy vowed they were. But then Tillytuck had once said, "What a dull fellow I'd be if I never told anything but the truth." Anyhow, he was keeping "the young ones" quiet and that was something.

7

The dishes disposed of, Pat and Judy began to think of the supper. Judy determinedly set the Jerusalem cherry on the side-board and hid the slim chair in the hall closet. A fresh cloth . . . the one with daisies woven in it . . . was brought out and Pat began to feel cheered up. After all, the guests were enjoying themselves and that was the main thing. Even Aunt Edith had come down, pale and heroic and forgiving. Just dog crawled out of the cellar and coiled himself up in his own corner. Silver Bush rang with gay voices, firelight shimmered over pretty dishes, delicious things were brought from pantry and cellar: and Pat thought proudly that the supper table, with its lighted candles, looked even prettier than the dinner table. And its circle of faces was happy and wise and kind.

"What's the matter with Win?" asked Cuddles, who had decided to help wait with Judy and Pat and have her supper with them in the kitchen later on. "She's yellow and pea-green . . . is she sick?"

On the very heels of her question Frank came out hurriedly and whispered something to Pat who gave an ejaculation of dismay.

"I didn't think it wise for her to come," said Frank. "But she was so anxious to . . . and you know . . . we didn't expect . . . *this* . . . for two weeks."

Pat pushed him aside and ran to the telephone. Confusion reigned again at Silver Bush. Winnie was being taken upstairs to the Poet's room. Pat and Judy were dashing madly from place to place. Mother couldn't stay at the table. Cuddles was left to wait on it alone and did it well. As Tillytuck was wont to aver, she had her head screwed on right. But it was a rather flat meal. No laughter. And nobody had much appetite now, except Cousin Nicholas. A doctor and a nurse arrived in the pouring rain and as soon as possible the guests departed . . . except Cousin Nicholas, who hadn't caught on to the situation at all and announced his intention of staying a few days at Silver Bush.

As soon as they had gone, Judy, with a set face, marched into the dining room and carried the Jerusalem cherry out to Tillytuck, uncorking the vials of her wrath.

"Take this *thing* out av the house immajetly if not sooner, Josiah Tillytuck. It's done enough harm already and now, wid what's ixpicted upstairs, I'm not having it here one minute longer."

Tillytuck obeyed humbly. What was the use of being peevish with the women?

A strange quiet fell over Silver Bush . . . an expectant quiet. The supper dishes were washed and put away and Judy and Pat and Cuddles sat down before the kitchen fire to wait . . . and eat russet apples in place of their forgotten supper. Their irrepressible gaiety was beginning to bubble up in spite of everything. After all, it *was* something to get a good laugh.

Tillytuck was smoking in his corner with Just Dog at his feet. McGinty was as near Pat as he could get and Bold-and-Bad and Squedunk ventured downstairs. Dad and Cousin Nicholas were raking over clan history in the Little Parlour. Sid was reading a murder mystery in the dining-room. Things seemed quite normal again . . . were it not for muted sounds overhead and the occasional visits of the white-capped nurse to the kitchen.

"Oh, oh, what a day!" sighed Judy.

"It's been dreadful," assented Pat, "but it will be a story to laugh at some day. That is why things don't always go smoothly I suppose. There'd be no interesting history. I only wish Hilary had been here to-day. I must write him a full account of it. What a sight I must have been, drowned in soup and dogs! Well, eight of our good soup plates go to the dump and the slim chair is done for . . . and we'll have no damson preserves till next fall . . . but after all, that's all the real damage."

"I'm hoping it may be," said Judy, with an ear cocked ceilingward. "What did ye do wid yer cherry, Tillytuck? If ye put it in the granary the place'll burn down to-night."

"I hove it into the pig-pen," said Tillytuck sourly.

"Oh, oh, God hilp the poor pigs thin," retorted Judy.

"I'll never forget Aunt Frances' face," giggled Cuddles.

"Oh, oh, Aunt Frances, is it? Niver be minding her, Cuddles dear. Things have happened at the Bay Shore, too. Don't I be minding one time I was over there hilping them out at a big time and whin yer Aunt Frances was jist in the act av setting a big bowl of red currant preserves on the table she did be giving the awfullest yell ye iver heard and falling over backward wid the bowl. Talk av soup! She did be looking as if she was lying murdered in her blood. At first ivery one thought she'd had a fit. But whin they come to find out a wee divil av a b'y had slipped down under the table and grabbed holt av her leg. Oh, oh, minny's the time I've laughed over it. Her dress was clane ruint, and her timper . . . Pasty darlint!"

"Judy . . . What is it?"

"Oh, oh, nothing much," said Judy in a despairing tone. "Only I niver rimimbered to put me dress-up dress on after all! It wint clare out av me head after the dog-fight . . . and me puddling round afore all the company in me old drugget."

"Never mind, Judy," comforted Pat, seeing Judy was really upset. "Nobody would notice it. And you might have got spots on it and then what about Castle McDermott?"

"Yer Aunt Edith wud be thinking I'd nothing but drugget to wear," groaned Judy. "Though she hadn't got all the basting thrids out of her own dress, if ye noticed. It's meself isn't used to dog-fights in me kitchen" . . . with a malevolent glance at Tillytuck. "It's minny a year since I saw one . . . the last was in South Glin church all av tin years ago. Oh, oh, that was a tommyshaw! Billy Gardiner always brought his dog to church. It was be way av being winked at for iverybody knew poor Billy was only half there, and they did be setting in a back pew, the dog behaving himself fine, though he did be giving a tarrible howl whin a lady visitor from town got up one day to sing a solo. Sure, nobody blamed the dog. But this day I'm telling ye av, another dog wandered in, the door being open, and Billy's dog wint for him. The strange dog flew up the aisle wid Billy's dog after him. He was caught jist under the pulpit! Oh, oh!" Judy rocked with laughter at the recollection, forgetful of her unworn splendors.

"What did they do, Judy?"

"Do, is it? Elder Jimmy Gardiner and Elder Tom Robinson aich grabbed a dog and carried it out be the scruff av the neck. Picture to yersilves, girls dear . . . a solemn ould elder wid a long beard and a most unchristian ixpression walking down the aisle, one on one side av the church and one on the other, houlding a dog at arm's length."

"Ah," said Tillytuck, "I was in the church that day. I remember it well."

This was too much for Judy. She got up and went into the pantry. Sid came out to say that Cousin Nicholas wished to go to bed and wanted a hot water bottle to take with him. Pat convoyed him to the spare room. Tillytuck, realising that he was out of favour, went off to the granary.

Pat had just come down when there was a knock at the door. Who on earth could it be at this time of night? Cuddles opened it . . . and in out of the starless dripping night stepped Joe! Captain Joe, tall and bronzed and changed, after years of typhoons on China seas, but unmistakably Joe.

"Flew here," said Joe laconically. "Flew from Halifax. Got into Charlottetown at dusk and hired a motor to bring me out. Thought I'd make it in time for supper anyhow. Everything happened to that car that could happen . . . and finally a broken axle. Nevertheless, here I am . . . and why are you all up as late and looking so solemn?"

Pat told him. Joe whistled.

"Not little Winnie! Why, I always think of her as a kid herself. What a night for the stork to fly! Anything in the pantry, Judy?"

His old grin robbed the question of insult. Joe *knew* there would be something in the pantry. Judy had a whole turkey stowed away, as well as the pot of soup. By the time mother had come down and hugged Joe and hurried anxiously back upstairs Judy had another table spread and they all sat down to it, even forgiven Tillytuck, whom Cuddles haled in from the granary.

"Ah, this is worth coming home for," said Joe. "Cuddles, you're almost grown up. Any beau yet, Pat?"

"Oh, oh, ye'd better be asking her that," said Judy. "Don't ye think it's time we had another widding at Silver Bush? She snubbed Elmer Moody last wake so bad he wint off vowing he'd niver set foot in Silver Bush agin."

"He breathes through his mouth," said Pat airily.

"Listen at her. Some fault to find wid ivery one av the poor b'ys. And what about yersilf, Joe? Do ye be coming home to find a wife?"

Joe blushed surprisingly. Pat only half liked it. She had heard rumours of several girls Captain Joe had been writing to occasionally.

None of them were quite good enough for Joe. But it was the old story . . . change . . . change. Pat hated change so. And little, cool, unexpected breaths of it were always blowing across everything, even the jolliest of times, bringing a chill of foreboding.

"And you're not tattooed after all, Joe," said Cuddles, half disappointedly.

"Only my hands," said Joe, displaying a blue anchor on one and his own initials on the other.

"Will you tattoo mine on mine?" asked Cuddles eagerly.

Before Joe could answer an indignant old man suddenly erupted into the kitchen, wrapped in a dressing gown. It was Cousin Nicholas and Cousin Nicholas was distinctly in a temper.

"Cats!" he snarled. "Cats! I had just fallen into a refreshing slumber when a huge cat jumped on my stomach . . . on my stomach, mark you. I detest cats."

"It . . . must have been Bold-and-Bad," gasped Pat. "He does so love to get into the spare room bed. I'm so sorry, Cousin Nicholas . . ."

"Sorry, miss! I never can get to sleep again after I am once wakened up. Will your sorrow cure that? I came down to ask you to find that cat and secure him. *I* don't know where the beast is . . . probably under the bed, plotting more devilment."

"Peevish . . . very peevish," muttered Tillytuck quite audibly. Cuddles meowed and Cousin Nicholas glared at her.

"The manners of Silver Bush are not what they were in my day," he said crushingly. "I had a very hard time to get to sleep at all. There was too much going and coming upstairs. Is anybody sick?"

"Yes . . . but it don't be catching," said Judy reassuringly.

Pat, trying not to laugh, hurried upstairs and discovered Bold-and-Bad crouching in the corner of the hall, evidently trying to figure out how many lives he had left. For once in his life Bold-and-Bad was cowed. Pat carried him down and shut him up in the back porch, not without a pat or two . . . for she was not overly attracted to Cousin Nicholas.

That irate gentleman was finally persuaded to go back to bed. Evidently some idea of what was going on had filtered through his aged brain, for, as Pat assisted his somewhat shaky steps up the stairs, he whispered,

"Mebbe I shouldn't mention it to a young girl like you . . . but is it a baby?"

Pat nodded.

"Ah, then," said Cousin Nicholas, peering suspiciously about him, "you'd better watch that cat. Cats suck babies' breaths."

"What an opinion our Cousin Nicholas will have of Silver Bush," said Pat, half mournfully, half laughingly, when she returned to the kitchen. "Even our cats and dogs can't behave. And you, Cuddles . . . I'm ashamed of you. Whatever made you meow at him?"

"I wasn't meowing at *him*," said Cuddles gravely. "I was just meowing."

"Oh, oh, ye naden't be worrying over what ould Nicholas Gardiner thinks av our animals," sniffed Judy. "I wasn't saying innything before for he's your cousin and whin all is said and done blood do be thicker than water. But did ye iver hear how me fine Nicholas got his start in life? Whin his liddle baby brother died ould Nicholas . . . only he was jist eliven thin . . . earned fifty cents be letting all the neighbourhood children in to see the wee dead body in the casket for a cint apace. That did be the foundation av *his* fortunes. He turned that fifty cints over and over, it growing wid ivery turn, and niver a bad spec did he make."

"Judy, is that really true? I mean . . . haven't you mixed up Cousin Nicholas with some one else?"

"Niver a bit av it. The Gardiners don't all be angels, me jewel. Sure and that story was laughed over in the clan for years. Aven his mother laughed wid the bist av thim. She was a Bowman and he got his quare ways from her. So he's more to be pitied than laughed at."

"Yes, indeed," agreed Pat. "Think of never knowing the delight of loving a nice, prowly, velvety cat."

"He's awfully rich though, isn't he?" said Cuddles.

"Oh, oh, wid one kind av riches, Cuddles darlint. But it's better to be poor and fale rich than to be rich and fale poor. Hark!"

Judy suddenly held up her hand.

"What's that?"

"Sounds like a cat on the porch roof," said Sid.

Pat dashed upstairs, returning in a few minutes flushed with excitement.

"Come here, *Aunt* Cuddles," she laughed.

8

Joe and Sid and dad went to bed. Tillytuck, mildly remarking that he had had enough passionate scenes for one day, betook himself to the granary. But Pat and Cuddles and Judy decided to make a night of it. It was three now. They sat around the fire and lived over that fateful Christmas Day. They roared with laughter over the look of Cousin Nicholas.

"Sure and he naden't have been making such a fuss over a poor cat," said Judy. "Well do I remimber what happened to a man in Silverbridge years ago. He jumped into his bid one night and found a dead man atwane the shates."

"Judy!"

"I'm telling ye. It was his own brither but if Tillytuck was here he'd be saying he was the dead man. And now let's be having another liddle bite. I'm faling as if I hadn't had a dacent male for wakes, what wid dog-fights and ould cousins and people flying like birds. It's thankful I am that I frog-marched me Tillytuck out wid that Jerusalem cherry afore Joe did be starting from Halyfax."

"To think that mother is a grandmother and we're aunts," said Cuddles. "It makes me feel awfully old. I'm glad it's a girl. You can dress them so cute. They're going to name it Mary Laura Patricia after its two grandmothers and call it Mary. Frank put the Patricia in for you, Pat, because he said if it hadn't been for you that child would never have been born. What did he mean?"

"Just some of his nonsense. He persists in thinking I gave up a career so that Winnie could get married. I'm glad they're calling it mother's name. But I always think a second name seems woeful and reproachful because it is never mentioned often enough to give it personality. As for a third name, it's nothing but a ghost."

"Tillytuck was really quite excited over it, wasn't he?"

"Can you imagine Tillytuck ever being a baby?" said Pat dreamily.

"Oh, oh, he was, and mebbe somebody's pride and joy," sighed Judy sentimentally. "It do be tarrible what we come to wid the years. Sure and another Christmas is over and we can't be denying it was merry in spots."

And then it was morning. The rain was over; the whole world was soaked and sodden but in the east was a primrose brightening and soon the Hill of the Mist was like a bare, brown breast in the pale early sunshine. The house, after all the revel and excitement, had a dishevelled, cynical, ashamed look. Pat longed to fall upon it and restore it to serenity and self-respect.

Winnie, white and sweet, was asking them with her pretty laugh what they thought of her little surprise party. Sid was declaring to indignant Cuddles that the baby had a face like a monkey. Mother was played out and condemned to a day in bed. And Judy stole out to see if the pigs had survived the Jerusalem cherry.

9

"Oh, oh, I do be tasting spring to-day," said Judy one early May morning. It had been a long cold winter, though a pleasant one socially, with dances and doings galore. They had two dances at Silver Bush for Joe . . . one the week after he came home and one on the night before he went away again. Tillytuck had been the fiddler on both occasions and Cuddles had danced several sets and thought she was nearly grown up. It was a family joke that Cuddles had cut Pat out in the good graces of Ned Avery and had been asked to go with him to a dance at South Glen. But mother would not allow this. Cuddles, she said, was far too young. Cuddles was peeved.

"It seems to me you're always too young or too old to do anything you like in this world," she said scornfully. "And you won't let Joe tattoo my initials on my arm. It would be *such* a distinction. Nobody in school is tattooed *anywhere*. Trix Binnie would just be wild with envy."

"Oh, oh, since whin have the Gardiners taken to caring what a Binnie thought av innything?" sniffed Judy.

Spring was late in coming that year. Judy had a saying that "it wudn't be spring till the snow on the Hill av the Mist melted and the snow on the Hill av the Mist wudn't melt till spring." There were fitful promises of it . . . sudden lovely days followed by bitter east winds and grey ghost mists, or icy north-west winds and frosts. But on this particular day it did seem as if it had really come to stay. It was a warm day of entrancing gleams and glooms. Once a silver shower drifted low over the Hill of the Mist . . . over the Long House . . . over the Field of the Pool—over the silver bush . . . and away down to the gulf. Then the day made up its mind to be sunny. The distances were hung with pale blue hazes and there was an emerald mist on the trees everywhere. The world was sweet and the Pool was a great sapphire. Cuddles found some white and purple violets down by the singing waters of Jordan and young ferns were uncoiling along the edge of the birch grove. Pat discovered that the little clump of poet's narcissus on the lawn was peeping above ground. It gave her a pang to remember that she had got it from Bets . . . Bets who had loved the springs so but no longer answered to their call. Pat looked wistfully up the hill to the Long House . . . the Long Lonely House once more, for the people who had moved into it when the Wilcoxes went away had gone again and the house was untenanted, as it had been when Pat was a child and used to wish its windows could be lighted up at night like other houses. Now she no longer felt that way about it, though she still felt a thrill of pleasure when the sunset flame kindled its western windows into a fleeting semblance of life and colour, and still shivered when it looked cold and desolate on moonlit winter nights. She resented the thought of any one living there when Bets, sweet, beloved Bets, had gone, never to return. When it was empty she could pretend Bets was still there and would come running down the hill, as in the old fair and unforgotten days, on some of these spring evenings that seemed able to call anything out of the grave.

When Judy "tasted" spring it was time to begin house-cleaning and as Tillytuck was away for the day on "the other farm" as the "old Adams place" was now called, Judy and Pat took the opportunity to clean the granary chamber . . . a task which Judy performed rather viciously, for Tillytuck was temporarily out of favour with her, partly because Just Dog had killed three of her chickens the day before and chewed up one leg of Siddy's khaki pants, and partly because . . .

"He did be coming home drunk agin last night and slipt in the stable."

Judy's "agin" seemed to imply that Tillytuck came home drunk frequently. As a matter of fact this was only his second offence and Tillytuck was such an excellent worker that Long Alec winked at his very occasional weakness.

"Not that he'd be giving in he was tight . . . Oh, no. He wud only say the moon seemed a bit unsteady-like. And he was after warning me not to be getting inny notion av marrying into me head aven if he did be liking to talk to me. Me! But wud it be inny use getting mad wid

329

the likes av him? It ann'ys him more to be laughing at him. He did be trying to get up the granary stips . . . me watching him through the liddle round windy and having me own fun . . . but he cudn't trust his legs, so he paraded to the stable, walking very stiff and pompous. Oh, oh, the dear knows what we'll be finding in his din . . . a goat's nest, I wudn't be wondering."

"Tillytuck says he's going to get a radio," said Cuddles, who was not in school, as it was Saturday.

"Oh, oh, a radio, is it? I'm relaved to hear it. Mebbe if he gets one he won't be rading such trash as this." Judy indignantly held up a book she had discovered on Tillytuck's table. "Do ye be seeing it . . . *The Mistakes av Moses*. It do be a rank infidel book he borryed off ould Roger Madison av Silverbridge and whin I rated him for rading it he sez, 'I like to see both sides av a question,' sez he. Him and his curiosity!"

Judy tossed the offending volume out of the window into the pig-pen and ostentatiously washed her hands.

"You can't stick Tillytuck on the catechism though," said Pat. "And he really is a great hand to read his Bible."

"But he has his doubts about the story of Jonah and the whale," said Cuddles. "He told me so."

"Does he be talking to children av such things?" Judy was horrified. "It's telling him me opinion av that I'll be. Don't ye be hading him, Cuddles. We've niver hild wid infidelity at Silver Bush and if Moses did be making a mistake or two it's me considered opinion that he knew more about things in gineral than Josiah Tillytuck and ould Roger Madison put together."

"You're just a bit peeved with Tillytuck because he tried to cap your stories," suggested Cuddles slyly. For there had been quite a scene in the kitchen two evenings previously when Judy had told a tale of some lady on the south side who put rat poison by mistake for baking powder in the family pancakes and Tillytuck had said he had eaten one of them.

"It isn't a chanct I do be having wid Tillytuck," said Judy passionately. "I stick to the truth but he do be making things up as he goes along."

"But you made candy for him afterwards, Judy."

"Oh, oh, so I did," admitted Judy with a deprecating grin. "He gets round a body somehow wid his palaver. There do be times whin he cud wheedle the legs off an iron pot. Niver be laughing at an ould woman, Cuddles dear. Tillytuck and I do be understanding each other rale well, for all av our tiffs. If he likes to think I'm dying about him he's welcome to it. He hasn't minny pleasures. And now we've finished the chamber so we'll . . ."

"The pigs are in the graveyard, Judy," cried Cuddles.

"I'll pig thim," ejaculated Judy viciously as she whirled down the granary stairs in horror. But after all cud ye be blaming the poor pigs? They had niver been thimsilves since they et the Jeruselem cherry.

In the afternoon they tackled the garret. Pat always loved cleaning in general and the garret in particular. It was delightful to make Silver Bush as clean and sweet as the spring . . . a new curtain here . . . a new wall-paper there . . . a spot of paint where it would do most good. Little changes that didn't hurt . . . much. Though Pat was always sorry for the old wall-papers and missed them.

When you came to the garret you always found so many things you had almost forgotten and all the family ghosts got a good rummaging.

"Sure, housecleaning and diggin' a well do be the only two things I know av that ye begin at the top and work down wid," said Judy. "Well, the garret do be done and that do be making the fortieth time I've been at the cleaning av it. Forty-one years this very May, Pasty dear, since I tuk up wid Silver Bush, hoping to put the summer in if Long Alec's mother was suited wid me . . . and here I do be still."

"And will be for forty more years I hope," said Pat with a hug. "But we haven't quite finished, Judy. I want to see what's in that old black chest in the corner. It hasn't been turned out properly for years."

"Oh, oh, there's nothing much there but the relics av ould dacency," said Judy.

"We really should examine it. The moths may have got into it."

"Sure and it's always aisy to find an excuse for what ye want to do," said Judy slyly. "But we'll ransack it if ye wait till I get supper. We'll come up here in the dim and see what's in it."

Accordingly, after supper Pat betook herself to the garret, which was growing shadowy, although the outside world was still in the glow of sunset. It was a spring sunset . . . pale golds and soft pinks and ethereal apple greens shading up to silvery blue over the birches. Pat ached with the loveliness of it, being one of those

> "who feel the thrill
> Of beauty like a pang."

Violet mists were veiling the distant hills. The little green-skirted maples over at Swallowfield were dancing girls with the dark spruces behind them, like grim, old-maid duennas. Sid had ploughed the Mince Pie field that day and it lay in beautiful, red, even furrows. From the Field of the Pool there sounded the dreamy trill of a few frogs through the brooding spring evening and there was some indefinable glamour over everything. Things were a little "queer" as they had sometimes seemed in childhood on certain evenings.

"This makes me think of the night you told me Cuddles was coming," she said to Judy, who came up the stairs, panting a little. "Oh, Judy dear, just look at that sunset."

"Innything spacial about it?" asked Judy a little shortly . . . because she didn't like the idea of being out of breath after only two flights of stairs.

"There's something special about every sunset, Judy. I never saw a cloud just that colour and shape before . . . see . . . the one over the tall fir-tree."

"I'm not denying it's handsome. Sure and I wudn't be like ould Rob Pennock at the South Glen. His wife was rale ashamed av his insinsibility. 'He doesn't know there's such a thing as a sunset,'—she sez to me once, impatient-like."

"How terrible it must be not to see and *feel* beauty," said Pat softly. "I'm so glad I can find happiness in all lovely little things . . . like that cloud. It seems to me that every time I look out of a window the world gives me a gift. Look at those old dark firs around the pool. Judy, does it ever seem to you that the Pool is drying up? It seems to me that it isn't as deep as it used to be."

"I'm fearing it is," acknowledged Judy. "It's a way thim pools has. There was one below Swallyfield whin I was here first . . . and now it's nothing but a grane dimple wid some ferns and bracken in it."

"I don't know how I'll bear it if it dries up. I've always loved it so."

"What don't ye be loving around the ould place, Patsy dear?"

"The more things and people you love the more happiness you get, Judy."

"Oh, oh, and the more sorrow too. Now, whativer made me go and say that! It jist slipped out."

"It's true, I suppose," said Pat thoughtfully. "It's the price you pay for loving, I guess. If I hadn't loved Bets so much it wouldn't have hurt me

332

so terribly when she died. But it was worth the hurt, Judy."

"It always do be," said Judy gently. "So niver ye be minding me silly talk av the sorrow."

"Well, how about the black chest, Judy?"

"Cuddles wants us to be waiting till she can come. She said she wudn't be long . . . she had a bit av Lating to look over. She do be getting int'rested in her books at last. Joe did be giving her a bit av advice now and thin."

"I hope we'll be able to afford to give her a real good education, Judy. We never do seem to have much money, I admit."

"Too hospitable, I'm supposing some do be thinking. Mrs. Binnie says we throw out more wid a spoon than the min can bring in wid a shovel . . . Binnie-like. *Our* min like the good living. And what if we don't be having too much money, Patsy dear? Sure and we have lashings av things no money cud be buying. There'll be enough squazed out for Cuddles whin the time comes, niver fear. The Good Man Above will be seeing to that."

The drone of the separator came up from the yard below where Tillytuck was operating under the big maple over the well and singing a Psalm sonorously, with McGinty and some cats for an audience. It struck Pat that Tillytuck had a remarkably good voice. And he was setting the saucer for the fairies, just as Judy always did.

"I used to think the fairies really came and drank it. I wish I could believe things like that now, Judy."

"It do be fun belaving things. I often wonder, Patsy dear, at all the skiptics do be losing. As for the saucer av milk, the dog McGinty gets it now mostly. Look at him sitting there and thumping his bit av a tail ivery time Tillytuck gets to the end av a verse. He may not be having inny great ear for music but he do be knowing how to get round Tillytuck."

"Judy, I'm almost sure dear little dogs like McGinty must have souls."

"A liddle bit av one mebbe," said Judy cautiously. "I niver cud hould wid the verse 'widout are dogs,' Patsy dear, though niver be telling the minister or Tillytuck I said it. Whiniver I see the dog McGinty I think av Jingle. Wasn't it a letter from him ye got to-day? And is there inny word av him coming home this summer?"

"No," Pat sighed. She had been hoping Hilary would come. "He has to work in vacation, Judy."

"I s'pose his mother doesn't be thinking inny more about him than she iver did?"

"I don't know. He never mentions her name now. Of course she is quite willing to send him all the money he needs . . . but he's terribly independent, Judy. He is determined to earn all he can for himself. And as for coming home . . . well, you know, since his uncle died and his aunt went to town he really has no home to come back to. Of course I've told him a dozen times he is to look upon Silver Bush as home. Do you remember how I used to set a light in this very window when I wanted him to come over?"

"And he niver failed to come, did he, Patsy? I'm almost belaving if ye set a light in this windy to-night he'd see it and come. Patsy dear," . . . Judy's voice grew wheedling and confidential . . . "do ye iver be thinking a bit about Jingle . . . ye know . . ."

Pat laughed, her amber eyes full of roguish mirth.

"Judy darling, you've always had great hopes of making a match between Hilary and me but they're doomed to disappointment. Hilary and I are chums but we'll never be anything else. We're *too* good chums to be anything else."

"Ye seen so set on turning ivery one else down," sighed Judy. "And I always did be liking Jingle. It's not a bad thing to be chums wid yer husband, I'm tould."

"*Why* are you so set on my having a 'real' beau, Judy? Any one would think you wanted to get rid of me."

"It's better ye're knowing than that, me jewel. Whin ye lave Silver Bush the light av ould Judy Plum's eyes will go wid ye."

"Then just be glad I mean to stay, Judy. I never want to leave Silver Bush . . . I want to stay here always and grow old with my cats and dogs. I love the very walls of it. Look, Judy, the Virginia creeper has got to the roof. It's lucky we have so many vines here, for the house does need painting terribly and dad says he can't afford it this year."

"Yer Uncle Tom is painting Swallyfield . . . white, wid grane trimmings, it's to be. He started to-day."

"Yes." A shadow fell over Pat's face. Every one in North Glen knew by this time that Tom Gardiner was writing to a lady in California, though not even the keenest of the gossips had found out anything more, not even her name. "Swallowfield really needs painting but it has needed it for years. And now Uncle Tom seems to have a mania for sprucing things up. He's even going to have that dear old red door stained and grained. I've always loved that red door so much. Judy, you don't think there is anything in that story of his going to be married, do you?"

"I wudn't be saying. And me fine Aunt Edith wudn't be liking it," said Judy in a tone which indicated that for her, at least, there would be balm in Gilead if Tom Gardiner really up and married at last. "There do be another story round, Patsy, that Joe do be ingaged to Enid Sutton. Is there inny truth in *it*?"

"I can't say. He saw a good deal of her when he was home. Well, she is a very nice girl and will suit Joe very well."

Pat felt herself very magnanimous in thus according approval to Joe's reputed choice. If it had been Sid . . . Pat shivered a little. But Sid wouldn't be thinking of marrying for years yet.

"Oh, oh, if it iver comes to a widding I hope Enid will be having better luck wid her dress than her mother had. There was a dressmaker in town making it . . . the Suttons houlding thimsilves a bit above the Silverbridge dressmaker . . . and she was sick, but she sint word she'd have the dress ready for the widding day widout fail. Whin the morning come, she did be phoning up she had sint it be the train but whin the train come in niver a widding dress was on it. And, what's more, that dress niver turned up . . . niver, Patsy dear. The poor liddle bride was married in a blue serge suit and tears."

"Whatever became of the dress, Judy?"

"The Good Man Above knows and Him only. It was shipped be the ixpress agent at Charlottetown and that was the last iver seen or heard av it. White sating and lace! But at that I do be thinking she was luckier than the bride at Castle McDermott."

"What happened to her?"

"Oh, oh, it was a hundred years afore me time there but the story was tould me. She wint to the wardrobe and put her hand in to fetch out her widding dress and . . ." Judy leaned forward dramatically in the gathering gloom . . . "*and it was grasped by a bony hand.*"

"Whose?" Pat shivered deliriously.

"Oh, oh, *whose?* That did be the question, Patsy dear. No good Christian, I'm telling ye. The poor bride fainted and the widding had to be put off and the groom was killed on the way home, being thrown from his horse. Minny's the time I did be seeing the wardrobe whin I was working there but niver wud the McDermotts allow that door to be opened agin. The story wint that the widding dress was still hanging there. Oh, oh!" Judy sighed. "I belave I'll have to be paying a visit to ould Ireland this fall. I do be having a hankering for it I haven't had for years."

Cuddles came running up the stairs, preceded by Bold-and-Bad who covered three steps at a leap.

"Oh, I hope I'm in time. I've finished that Latin. No wonder Latin died. *Did* people ever really talk that stuff? Talk it just as you and I do? I can't believe it. Joe made me promise I'd lead my class in it and if I did he'd tattoo my arm next time he came no matter what fuss *you* made. So I'm going to do it or bust."

"The young ladies av Castle McDermott niver did be talking av busting," said Judy reproachfully.

"Oh, I suppose they talked a brogue you could cut with a knife," retorted Cuddles. "Well, let's get at the old chest. It's such fun to rummage through old boxes. You never know what you may come across. It's like living for a while in yesterday."

10

They dragged the old black chest out of its corner to the window. Bold-and-Bad, deciding that it was not a thing likely to do a cat any good, crept off into the darkness under the eaves and imagined himself a Bengal tiger. The black chest was full of the usual miscellany of old garret chests. Ancient lace and velvet and flower-trimmed hats, bundles of banished Christmas cards, limp ostrich feathers, faded family photographs, strings of birds' eggs, discarded dresses with the pointed basques and polonaises and puffed sleeves of other vintages, old school-books, maps the Silver Bush children had drawn, packets of yellow letters, a "rat" worn in the days of pompadours, old faded things once beautiful. They had oceans of fun over them.

"What on earth is this?" demanded Cuddles, holding up an indescribable mass of crushed wire. Judy gave a snort of laughter.

"Oh, oh, that do be yer Aunt Helen's ould bustle. I rimimber how yer dad yelled whin she brought it home. It's the dashing lady she was and always the first in the clan to be out in a new fashion. She wint to a concert that night at the Bridge wid her beau and they say he was crimson to the ears, he was that ashamed av it. But in a few wakes' time iverybody did be wearing thim. He shud have been thankful she didn't wear it like Maggie Jimson at the South Glin did whin her sister as was working up in Bosting sint her one home . . . a rale fancy one all covered wid blue sating."

"How did she wear it, Judy?"

"Outside her dress," said Judy solemly. "They say the folks who were in church that day were niver the same agin. Oh, oh, but the fashions do be changing always. Only kissing stays in. Mebbe this ould bustle will be took down some av these days and displayed on the parlour mantelpiece be way av an heirloom."

"Look at this!" Cuddles held up a huge brown velvet hat with a draggled and enormous shaded-green ostrich feather on it. "Fancy living up to a hat like that!"

"Oh, oh, that was yer Aunt Hazel's hat wid what they called a willow plume and rale nice it did be looking over her pompydore. Though I niver fancied velvet hats mesilf iver since the mouse jumped out av Mrs. Reuben Russell's one Sunday at the Bridge church. *That* was a tommyshaw."

"If Tillytuck was here he'd say he was the mouse," giggled Cuddles.

Pat pounced on an article.

"Judy, if here isn't my old little cheese hoop! I've often wondered where it disappeared to. I wanted to keep it always in remembrance of those dear little cheeses you used to make me in it . . . one for myself every year. You don't remember Judy making cheese, Cuddles, but I do. It was such fun."

"And here do be one av yer Great-grandmother Gardiner's ruffled caps," said Judy. "Minny's the time I've done it up for her . . . she always said that nobody cud be giving the frills the right quirk like young Judy. Oh, oh, I was young Judy thin and I'd larned the trick at Castle McDermott. Ould lady Gardiner always made her caps hersilf . . . it's the beautiful himstitcher she was. She was a rale fine ould lady, if some folks did be thinking her a bit too uppity. Did I iver be telling ye av the night she was knaling be her bed be an open windy, saying her prayers and her thoughts in hiven . . . I'm s'posing . . . and a big cat crawled through the windy and lit on her back suddent-like wid a pair av claws that tuk hold?"

"Oh!" Cuddles shrieked in delight. "What did Great-grand say?"

"Say, is it?" Judy looked cautiously around. "It was thirty-nine years ago and I've niver told a living soul afore. She said a word beginning wid D and inding wid N."

Pat doubled up with laughter. Stately old Great-grandmother Gardiner whose picture hung in the Big Parlour with her white cap encircling her saintly face! Really, the things Judy knew about respectable people were dreadful.

"This ould rag was a dress yer grandmother wore in her day." Judy held up a faded affair with manifold flounces. "Striped silk jist like ribbing grass. Mebbe it's the very one—I'm not saying it is but it might be . . . she wore jist the twicet."

"Why didn't she wear it again?" asked Cuddles.

"Oh, oh, if it's the one . . . mind ye. I'm not saying it is . . . yer grandmother and her cousin, Mrs. Tom Taylor, were great rivals, it did be said, in the matter av dresses and both av thim fond av gay colours. And whin yer grandmother come to church quite gorgeous-like in her striped dress Mrs. Tom turned quite grane and said nothing but wint to town nixt day and bought a dress av the same piece and give it to her ould scrubwoman at the Bridge. The poor ould soul was pleased as Punch and got it made up at oncet and wore it to church the nixt Sunday. Oh, oh, 'twas rale cruel av Mrs. Tom and there was a judgmint on her, for her own father died and she did have to be wearing black for two years. It was rale bitter, for black didn't set her. But niver wud yer grandmother put the striped dress on her back agin."

"How foolish of her," said Cuddles loftily.

"Oh, oh, it's the foolish folks as does all the int'risting things," chuckled Judy. "There'd not be minny stories to tell if ivery one was wise. And if here isn't Siddy's ould Teddy bear! Niver a night wud he go to slape widout it. It's mesilf sewed thim shoe-buttons in for eyes whin Ned Binnie picked the first ones out and poor Siddy's liddle heart was broken."

"They're saying in school Sid has a case on Jenny Madison," said Cuddles.

"Sid has a new 'case' every two months," said Pat lightly. "What a pretty dress this must have been in its time, Judy . . . a sort of silvery stuff with lace frills in the sleeves."

"Silvery, is it? If ye cud see it as I see it! That was a dress yer Aunt Lorraine had for her first liddle party the summer I come here. Ye niver cud imagine innything bluer than her eyes. I can see her dancing in the orchard be moonlight yet to show it off to us afore she wint. She's been churchyard dust for forty years. Her first liddle party was her last. Ye'll rimimber her tombstone av white marble wid a baby's head and wings sticking out behint its ears. Sure I niver thought it suitable for a girl's tombstone but I've been tould it wasn't a baby but a cherub, whativer that may be. I'm not forgetting the day I took Siddy through the South Glin churchyard whin he was six. He did be looking at the cherub and thin at me. 'Where is the rist av it, Judy?' he sez, solemn like."

"Are these her letters?" asked Cuddles, holding up a yellowed packet.

"I'm thinking those are yer Great-aunt Martha's. She did be dying young, too, but she had a beau as was a great letter-writer. Her father didn't hould wid him and some say Martha died av a broken heart and some from wearing too thin stockings in the winter time. Ye can be taking the romantic or the sinsible explanation, whichiver's suiting ye bist."

"Why didn't her father approve of her beau?"

"I'm not thinking he had much agin the young man himself but he was after having an uncle who was hanged for taking part in some rebellion and cut down and recovered. He niver talked agin. Some said his throat had been injured . . . but there was some as thought he'd seen something as scared him out av talking foriver. Anyhow, her father wasn't wanting inny half-hanged person in his fam'ly."

"Now, here's something!" exclaimed Pat, fishing up a silver 'chain' bracelet. "It's a bit black but it could be cleaned."

"The padlock and kay's missing, Patsy dear, so it wudn't be much use. That was yer Aunt Hazel's, too. They did be all the rage thin. I had a hankering after one mesilf but whin I heard the story av Sissy Morgan's chain bracelet up at the Bay Shore it tuk the fascination out av thim for me."

"What was that?"

"Oh, oh, her beau was a capting and afore he wint on the v'yage that proved his last he locked a chain bracelet on her arm . . . a gold one it was, no less . . . and tuk the kay wid him, making her promise she'd niver marry inny one ilse unless he come back and unlocked the bracelet. Sissy promised light enough. The Morgans wud promise innything. But she was pretty, that Sissy, and the capting was crazy about her. He was swept over-board in a storm and the kay wint to the bottom av the Atlantic wid him. Liddle Sissy tuk on a bit but the Morgans soon get over things and in a year she did be wanting rale bad to marry Peter Snowe. But she was scared to bekase av her promise about the bracelet. Her dad wanted the match bekase Peter was rale well to do but Sissy stuck to it she dassn't and siveral tommyshaws they had over it all. Oh, oh, but there was the funny squeal to it."

"What was the sequel?"

"Oh, oh, sequel, is it? Well, Sissy, was slaping sound in her bed one moonlight night and whin she woke the bracelet was unlocked . . . just that. She didn't be seeing nothing or nobody but it was unlocked."

"I don't think that is funny, Judy," said Cuddles with a little shiver. "That was . . . horrible."

"Oh, oh! Sure and it was funny thin whin Peter Snowe wudn't have her after all . . . said he wasn't taking inny ghost's lavings. The rist av the min samed to be having the same faling and she died an ould maid in the ind av it."

"Why, here's Joe's silver spoon," pounced Pat. "This *is* a find. We never knew what became of it. How in the world did it get here? Won't mother be pleased!"

The little silver spoon with the dents where Joe had cut his teeth . . . Joe who was half way to China now. Pat sighed and rose.

"Well, that is all. I wonder if we should burn those old letters. In a way I'd like to read them . . . there's something fascinating in old letters . . . they seem to open ghostly gates . . . but I suppose Aunt Martha wouldn't have liked it."

Pat picked the packet up. An old dim, flattened four-leaved clover slipped from it. Who had found luck with it? Not Aunt Martha at all events. The letters were brittle and yellow . . . full of old words of love written years ago from hearts that were dust . . . full of old joys that had once been raptures and dim old griefs that had once been agonies.

"We must drag the chest back into its corner. Look at Bold-and-Bad peering out of it."

Bold-and-Bad's eyes were glowing in his lair, giving that uncanny expression cats' eyes often do . . . as if they were merely transparent, letting the burning fires behind them become visible.

"They did be saying that Martha's beau's uncle looked like that be times," Judy whispered as she went downstairs.

It was rather too spooky. Cuddles fled in Judy's wake. But Pat still lingered, going back to the window where the full moon was beginning to weave beautiful patterns of vine leaves on the garret floor. The spookier the garret was the more she loved it. The letters in her hands made her think of Hilary's letter that day. Like all his letters it had a certain flavour. It *lived*. You could almost hear Hilary's voice speaking through it . . . see the laughter in his eyes. Every time you re-read one of his letters you found something new in it. To-day's had enclosed a sketch of his prize design for a house on the side of a hill. There was something about it faintly reminiscent of Silver Bush. Pat had one of her moments of wishing passionately that Hilary was somewhere about . . . that they could join hands as of old and run across the old stone bridge over Jordan. Surely they had only to slip over the old bridge to find themselves in the old fairyland. They would go back to Happiness and the Haunted Spring, following the misty little brook through the old fields where the moonlight loved to dream. They would linger there, lapped round by exquisite silence. Shadowy laughter would echo faintly about them. Cool elusive night smells would be all around. Little white sheep would be out on the hills. Surely Happiness kept their old days for them and they would find them there. Pat shivered. The rising wind moaned rather eerily around the lofty window. She felt suddenly, strangely lonely . . . right there in dear Silver Bush she felt lonely . . . *homesick*. It was uncanny. She ran downstairs and left the garret to its ghosts.

11

When Judy read an item from "Events of the Week" in a Charlottetown paper to the Silver Bush girls one evening they were only mildly and pleasantly excited over it. The Countess of Medchester, the paragraph stated, was visiting friends in Ottawa on her way home from Vancouver to England.

"That do be the lady married to the earl as is uncle av yer cousin, Lady Gresham," said Judy proudly. "Oh, oh, it do be giving me a bit av a thrill, as Cuddles says, to rade that item and riflict that we do be in a manner connected wid her."

"Even though she doesn't know of our existence," laughed Pat. "I don't suppose Lady Gresham brags to her friends of her very distant relationship to certain unimportant people on a Canadian farm."

"Likely she thinks we're Indians," grinned Cuddles. "Still, as Judy says, there's a thrill in it."

"Whin ye see May Binnie nixt time ye can be saying . . . to yersilf, av coorse . . . 'Ye don't be having a fourth cousin in the English aristocracy, *Miss* Binnie.' And *that'll* be a satisfaction."

"*I* shall say it to Trix," said Cuddles.

"Indeed, you won't," cried Pat. "Don't make yourself ridiculous, Cuddles. We're of no more importance in the Countess of Medchester's eyes . . . supposing she ever heard of us . . . than the Binnies. And who cares? Look at that froth of cherry bloom behind the turkey house. I'm quite sure there's nothing lovelier on the grounds of Medchester Castle . . . if there is a castle."

"Av coorse there's a castle," said Judy, carefully cutting out the item. "An earl cudn't be living in innything humbler. I'm pinning this up on the wall be me dresser to show Tillytuck. He's niver quate belaved me whin I tould him av yer being third cousin to Lady Gresham . . ."

"Fourth, Judy, fourth."

"Oh, oh, I might have made a bit av a mistake in the figure but does it be mattering? Innyhow, *this* will convince him. He was be way av being a bit cranky this morning whin he come in for breakfast though he cudn't be putting a name to the rason . . . like the cintipede that had rheumatism in one av his legs but cudn't tell which. He was putting on some frills wid me but *this* will be one in the eye for him. A rale countess wid a maid to button her boots! Oh, oh! I had a faling last night there did be something strange in the air."

When the letter came that day . . . being left in the mailbox at the road just like any common epistle and carried up to the house in Tillytuck's none too clean hand . . . Judy felt there was something stranger still in the air. A heavy cream-tinted envelope with a dainty silver crest on the flap, addressed in a black distinctive hand to Mrs. Alex Gardiner, North Glen, P.E. Island, and post-marked Ottawa. The crest and the post-mark had a very queer effect on Judy. She gave a gasp and looked at Gentleman Tom. Gentleman Tom winked knowingly.

"Anybody dead?" said Tillytuck.

Judy ignored him and called for Pat in an agitated voice. Pat came in from the garden, her arms full of the plumes of white lilac, McGinty ambling at her heels. Cuddles came running across the yard, the spring sunlight shining on her golden-brown head. Judy was standing in the middle of the kitchen floor holding the letter at arm's length.

"Judy, what is it?"

"Ye may well ask," said Judy. "Will ye be looking at the crest? And the post-mark?"

Pat took the letter.

"I feel a thrill . . . several thrills," whispered Cuddles.

"Thrills, is it? Sure and ye'll be having thrills wid a vengeance if that do be what I'm thinking it is."

"It's for mother," said Pat slowly. Mother was away for a visit at Glenwood. "I suppose we'd better open it. It may be something requiring prompt attention."

Judy handed Pat the paring knife. She had a presentiment that the letter should not be torn open like an ordinary epistle. Pat slit the envelope, took out the letter . . . likewise crested . . . and glanced over it. She turned red . . . she turned pale . . . she stared at the others in silence.

"What is it?" whispered Cuddles. "Quick . . . I've got such a queer prickly feeling in my spine."

"It's from the Countess of Medchester," said Pat in a hollow voice. "She says she promised Lady Gresham she would see her *cousins* before she returned to England . . . she's coming to Charlottetown to visit friends and she wants to come out here . . . here . . . next Saturday. Saturday!"

Poor Pat repeated the word as if Saturday meant the end of the world.

For a moment nobody spoke . . . could speak. Even Tillytuck seemed to have passed into a state of coma. In the silence Gentleman Tom reached over and dug a claw into his leg but Tillytuck did not even wince.

Cuddles was the first to recover.

"Have the Countess of Medchester *here*," she gasped. "We *can't*."

But Judy had got her second wind. She was an expert in dealing with situations without precedent.

"Oh, oh, mebbe we can't . . . but we will. What's a countess whin all is said and done? Sure, she'll ate and drink and wash behind her ears like inny common person. What time av day will she be here, Patsy?"

"The forenoon . . . she's leaving on the night boat. That means she'll be here for dinner, Judy!"

"She will be in a good place for the same thin, I'm telling ye. It will be a proud day for Silver Bush and no countess was iver ating a better male than we can be putting up. But 'twill take some planning, so kape up yer pecker, Patsy, and let's be getting down to brass tacks. We've no time for blithering. Sure and yer countesses can't be ating lilac blossoms."

Pat came up gasping. She felt ashamed of herself. It was positively Binnie-like to be flabbergasted like this.

"You're right, of course, Judy. Let me see . . . this is Tuesday. The floors in the dining room and the Big Parlour *must* be done over . . . they're simply terrible. I'll paint them to-day and stain them to-morrow. I wish I could do something to the front door. The paint is all peeling off. But I daren't meddle with it. We must just leave it open and trust she won't notice it. Then, Cuddles, we have to go to Winnie's one day this week to help her get her sewing done. We should have gone last week but I wanted to wait till this week to see their big crab-apple tree in bloom. We'll go Thursday. That will give us Friday to prepare. We must take her to the Poet's room because the ceiling isn't cracked there as it is in the spare room and we must put the spread mother embroidered on the bed. Sid can go for mother Friday evening. It *is* a shame to have her visit cut short when it's her first for years . . . but of course she'd like to be here."

"Oh, oh, and there'll be two great ladies together thin," said Judy. "I'll match yer mother agin inny countess in the world. Sure and a Bay Shore Selby cud hould up her hid wid inny av the quality."

Pat was herself again. Tillytuck was lost in admiration of her. From that moment Silver Bush was a place of excited but careful planning and overhauling and cleaning and decorating and discussing. Even Tillytuck had his say.

"The dinner's the thing," he told them. "A good meal is never to be sneezed at, speaking symbolically."

Every one agreed with this. The dinner must be such as even the wife of a belted earl could not turn up her nose at. Pat did endless research work among all her recipe books. Cuddles cut school to help. What was Latin and the chance of tattooing compared to this?

It was decided to have fried chicken for dinner . . . Judy's fried chicken was something to dream about.

"Wid sparrow grass. Sure and sparrow grass is a sort av lordly vegetable. Ye'll be making the sauce ye larned at the Short Coorse, Patsy dear. And will ye be having time to hemstitch the new napkins?"

"Cuddles and I are going to sit up all night to do them. I think we'll have iced melon balls and ice-cream for dessert and a lemon cocoanut cake. We mustn't attempt too much."

"Not to be ostentatious," agreed Judy who dearly loved a big word now and then.

"And, after all, she may be on a diet," grinned Cuddles. Cuddles had regained all her insouciance. Trix Binnie would be sunk when she heard of it all, positively sunk.

"I hope she'll think Silver Bush nice," breathed Pat. That was all she really cared about.

"She cudn't be hilping it," said Judy. "Let's be hoping it will be fine on Saturday. If it rains . . ."

Judy left it to the imagination what it would be like to entertain a countess in a rainstorm.

"It *must* be fine," was Pat's ultimatum.

"Do you think it wouldn't be a good thing to . . . to pray for fine weather?" suggested Cuddles, who felt that no chances should be taken. Judy shook her head solemnly.

"Girls dear, I wudn't. Ye can niver be telling what comes av such praying. Well do I rimimber the day in South Glen church whin the minister, ould Mr. McCary, did be praying for rain wid all his might and main. Whin the people were going home from church down comes a thunderstorm and drinches iverybody to the skin. Ould James Martin and ould Thomas Urquhart were together and Thomas sez, sez he, 'I do be wishing he hadn't prayed till we got home. Thim McCarys niver cud be moderate,' sez he. So ye'd better be laving it to nature, girls dear. And thank the Good Man Above there'll be no Jerusalem cherries around. Whin she comes, Patsy dear, av coorse I'll kape in the background but don't ye be thinking I'd better have me dress-up dress on, in case she might catch a glimpse av me coming or going?"

"Of course, Judy. And oh, Judy, do you think you could coax Tillytuck to leave off that terrible old fur cap of his for one day? If she saw him going through the yard!"

"Niver be worrying over Tillytuck. He'll be away to town that day wid the calves yer dad sold. And none too well plazed about it. Him thinking he wanted a glimpse av a countess! And trying to be sarcastic. He sez to me, sez he, 'Kape a stiff upper lip, Judy. After all, yer grandmother was a witch and that's sort of aristocracy, symbolically spaking.' 'I'm not nading to stiffen me upper lip,' sez I. 'I do be knowing me place and kaping it, spaking the plain truth and no symbols.' Tillytuck do be getting a bit out av hand. He was after smoking his pipe in the graveyard today, setting on Waping Willy's tombstone as bould as brass."

"Aunt Edith and Aunt Barbara are terribly excited," said Pat. "I wanted them to come over for dinner but they wouldn't. Aunt Edith vetoed it. However, she very kindly offered to lend us her silver soup spoons. She said a countess could tell at a glance if the spoons were solid or only plated. I'm so glad our teaspoons are solid . . . only they're so old and thin."

"Oh, oh, they do be all the more aristocratic for that," comforted Judy. "The countess will be saying to hersilf, 'There's *fam'ly* behind *thim*. Nothing av the mushroom in *thim*,' she'll be saying. And spaking av the Swallowfield folks, have ye noticed innything odd about yer Uncle Tom's beard?"

"Yes . . . it has almost disappeared," sighed Pat. "It's nothing more than an imperial now."

"Whin it disappears altogether we'll be hearing some news," said Judy with a mysterious nod.

But Pat had no time just then to be worrying over Uncle Tom's vanishing whiskers. By Wednesday night Silver Bush was ready for the countess . . . or for royalty itself. On Thursday Sid took Pat and Cuddles over to the Bay Shore to help Winnie with her spring sewing. They really sewed all the forenoon. In the afternoon Winnie said, "Never mind any more for a while. Come out in the wind and sun. We don't often have such an afternoon to spend together."

They prowled about the garden, picking flowers, drinking in the crab-apple blossoms, watching the harbour and making nonsense rhymes. In the midst of their fun they heard the telephone ring in the house.

12

Pat went in to answer it, as Winnie had her Christmas baby in her arms. When Pat heard Judy's voice she knew that something tremendous had occurred for Judy never used the telephone if she could help it.

"Patsy dear, is it yersilf? I do be having a word for you. *She's here.*"

"Judy! Who? Not the countess?"

"I'm telling ye. But I can't be ixplaining over the phone. Only come as quick as ye can, darlint. Siddy and yer dad have gone to town."

"We'll be right over," gasped Pat.

But how to get right over? Frank was away with the car. There was nothing for it but the old buggy and the old grey mare. It would take them an hour to get to Silver Bush. And Uncle Brian must be 'phoned to and asked to bring mother right home. Between them Pat and Cuddles got the mare harnessed and after several hundred years . . . or what seemed like it . . . they found themselves alighting in the yard of Silver Bush . . . which looked as quiet and peaceful as usual with Just Dog sleeping on the door-stone and three kittens curled up in a ball on the well platform.

"I suppose the countess is in the Big Parlour," said Pat. "Let's slip into the kitchen and find out everything from Judy first."

"How do you talk to countesses?" gasped Cuddles. "Pat, I think I'll go and hide in the barn loft."

"Indeed you won't! You're not a Binnie! We'll see Judy and then we'll slip upstairs and get some decent clothes on before we beard the lion in her den."

Pat had on her blue linen afternoon dress . . . which, incidentally, was the most becoming thing she owned. Cuddles wore her pretty green sweater with its little white embroidered linen collar, above which her wind-tossed hair gleamed, the colour of sunlight on October beeches. Both girls ran, giggling with nervousness, up the herringbone brick walk to the kitchen door and rushed in unceremoniously. Then they both stopped in their tracks. Cuddles' eyes wirelessed to Pat, "Do you really live through things like this or do you just die?"

Judy Plum and the Countess of Medchester were sitting by the table, whereon were the remnants of a platterful of baked sausages and potatoes. At the very moment of the girls' entry Judy was pouring cream from her "cream cow" into her ladyship's cup and the latter was helping herself to a piece of the delightful thing Judy called "Bishop's bread." Gentleman Tom was attending meticulously to his toilet in the centre of the floor and Bold-and-Bad was coiled on the countess' lap, while McGinty was squatted by the legs of her chair. Tillytuck was sitting in his corner . . . fortunately minus the fur cap, which, however, hung on his chair back. Judy was in her striped drugget but with a beautiful white apron starched stiff as a board. She was as completely at her ease as if the countess had been a scrubwoman. As for Lady Medchester, Pat, amid all her dumfounderment, instantly got the impression that she was enjoying herself hugely.

"And here," said Judy, with incredible nonchalance, "are the girls I've been telling ye av . . . Mrs. Long Alec's daughters. Patricia and Rachel."

The countess instantly got up and shook hands with Patricia and Rachel. She had mouse-coloured hair and a square, reddish face, but the smile on her wide mouth was charming.

"I'm so glad you've come before I have to go," she said. "It would have been dreadful to go back home and have to tell Clara that I hadn't seen any of her cousins at all. She has always had such a dear recollection of some wonderful days she spent on Prince Edward Island when a child. It was too bad to come down on you like this. But I got a cable from England last night which made it imperative I should leave to-night, so I had to come this afternoon. Your Judy . . ." she flashed a smile at Judy . . . "made me delightfully welcome and showed me around your lovely home . . . and, last but not least, has given me a most delicious meal. I was so hungry."

Somehow they found themselves all sitting around the table. Pat realized thankfully that Judy had had sense enough to put the best tablecloth on it and the silver spoons. But why on earth hadn't she got supper in the dining room? And what was the silver teapot doing on the dresser while the old brown crockery one graced the table?

And there was Tillytuck sitting in his shirt sleeves! Was there really anything to do but die? What was one to say? Pat wildly thought of an article in a recent magazine on "How to Start a Conversation With People You Have Just Met," but none of the gambits seemed to fit in here exactly. However, they were not necessary. The countess kept on talking in a frank, friendly, charming way that somehow included everybody, even Tillytuck. Pat, with a reckless feeling that nothing mattered now anyhow, flung conventionality to the winds. Cuddles was never long rattled by anything and in a surprisingly short time they were all chatting gaily and merrily. The countess insisted on their having some tea and Bishop's Bread with her . . . she was on her third cup herself, she said. Judy trotted to the pantry and brought back some forgotten orange biscuits. Lady Medchester wanted to hear all about mother and was only sorry she couldn't see her way clear to taking a Silver Bush kitten back with her to England.

"You see one of your cats has already quite made up his mind to like me," she laughed, looking down at the placidly heaving, furry flanks of Bold-and-Bad.

"And that cat don't condescend to every one, speaking symbolically, ma'am," said Tillytuck.

Pat had a confused impression that it was quite proper to say "ma'am" to a queen but hardly the way to address a countess. A countess! *Was* this stout, comfortable lady, in the plain, rather sloppy tweed suit, really a countess? Why . . . why . . . she seemed just like anybody else. She had the oddest resemblance to Mrs. Snuffy Madison of South Glen! Only Mrs. Snuffy was the better looking!

And there was no mistaking it . . . she was enjoying the bread and biscuits.

"Cats don't," said Lady Medchester, smiling at Tillytuck out of her hazel eyes and giving the wistful McGinty a nip of sausage. "That is why their approval, when they do bestow it, is really so much more of a compliment than a dog's. Dogs are so much easier pleased, don't you think?"

"You've said a mouthful, ma'am," said Tillytuck admiringly.

Cuddles, who, up to now, had contrived to keep a perfectly demure face, narrowly escaped choking to death over a gulp of tea. Pat, glancing wildly around, suddenly encountered Lady Medchester's eyes. Something passed between them . . . understanding . . . comradeship . . . a delicious enjoyment of the situation. After that Pat didn't care what anybody did or said . . . which was rather fortunate, for a few minutes later, when Lady Medchester happened to remark that she had had friends on the *Titanic,* Tillytuck said sympathetically, "Ah, so had I, ma'am . . . so had I."

"The ould liar!" said Judy under her breath. But everybody heard her. This time it was Lady Medchester who narrowly escaped disaster over a bit of biscuit. And again her twinkling eyes sought Pat's.

"Couldn't you stay till mother comes?" asked Pat, as the countess rose, gently and regretfully displacing her lapful of silken cat.

"I'm so sorry I can't. I've really stayed too long as it is. I have to catch that boat train. But it has been delightful. And I can tell Clara that at least I've seen Mary's dear girls. You'll be coming to England some day

I'm sure, and when you do you must look me up. I'm so sorry to put this beautiful cat down."

"You've got hairs all over your stomach, ma'am," said Tillytuck. "Dogs ain't like that now."

If looks could have slain Judy would have been a murderess. But the countess put her hands on Pat's shoulders, kissed her cheek and bowed her head, shaking with laughter.

"He's priceless," she whispered. "Priceless. And so is your Judy. Darlings, I only wish I could have stayed longer."

The countess picked up a little squashy hat with a gold and brown feather on it that looked like a hand-me-down from the Silverbridge store, adjusted a silver fox stole which Pat knew must have cost a small fortune, kissed Cuddles, made a mysterious visit into the pantry with Judy, donned a pair of antiquated gauntlets and went out to her car. Before she got in she looked around her. Silver Bush had cast over her the spell it cast over all.

"A quiet, beautiful place where there is time to live," she said, as if speaking to herself. Then she waved her hand to Judy . . . "We had such a pleasant little chat, hadn't we?" . . . and was gone.

"Oh, oh, but Silver Bush has been honoured this day," said Judy as they went back in.

"Judy, tell us everything . . . I'm simply bursting. And how did you come to have supper in the kitchen?"

"Oh, oh, don't be blaming me," entreated Judy. "It do be a long story that'll take some telling. Niver did I live through such an afternoon in me life. Tillytuck, do ye be wanting a liddle bite? Not that ye desarve it . . . but there's some av the pittaties and sausages lift if ye care for them."

"What's good enough for a countess is good enough for me," said Tillytuck, sitting down to the table with avidity. "She's a fine figure of a woman that, though maybe a bit broader in the beam than you'd expect of a countess, symbolically speaking. I found something alluring about her."

"Come out to the graveyard," whispered Judy to the girls. "We won't be disturbed there and I can be telling ye the tale. Sure and 'twill be one for the annals of Silver Bush."

"Uncle Brian has just phoned that mother was away to a picnic with some friends of Aunt Helen's and he couldn't locate her."

"It doesn't matter now," sighed Pat. "Why, oh, why, do things never happen as you plan? But I don't care . . . she was lovely . . . and she enjoyed herself. . . ."

"Oh, oh, that she did," agreed Judy, settling herself on Weeping Willy's tombstone, while Pat and Cuddles and McGinty squatted on Wild Dick's, "and nothing could or magnificent about her. But whin she drove in, girls dear, I didn't be knowing for a minute whither I stud on me heels or me hid. I did be taking her up to the Poet's room to wash her hands . . . oh, oh, I did all the honours, aven to slipping in that extry nice cake av soap ye brought home the other day, the one wrapped up in shiny paper . . . and the bist av the embridered towels. I cudn't manage the new sprid but if ye'd heard her ladyship rave over the beautiful patchwork quilt! Thin I dashed up to me room for a squint in me book av Useful Knowledge. But niver a word cud I find about intertaining the nobility so I had to be falling back on what I cud rimimber av the doings at Castle McDermott. It do be a pity I niver thought av slipping into me dress-up dress. But I was a bit excited-like. Whin I'd finished ixplaining to her that I'd phoned for ye nothing wud do her but I must show her all round the place. She said she wanted to see a rale Canadian farm at close range. It did be suiting me for I didn't be knowing if it was manners to lave her all alone and to sit wid a countess in the Big Parlour was a fearsome thought. I did be taking her all through the orchard and the silver bush and the cats' burying ground. And thin all through the graveyard and telling her all the ould stories . . . and didn't she laugh over Waping Willy! Thin whin we wint back to the house she wanted to see me kitchen . . . and me not knowing how Just Dog wud behave. Whin we got in it she sez to me, just like one old frind to another, 'Cud ye let me have a cup av tay, Judy . . . and what is that delicious odour I smell?' Well, girls dear, ye know just what it was . . . me bit av baked sausage and pittaties I had in the oven for Tillytuck and mesilf, ivery one ilse being away. 'Will ye be giving me a taste av it?' she sez, wheedling-like. 'Right here in the kitchen, Judy, where the scint av lilacs is coming in through that windy, Judy,' sez she, 'and the very same white kittens that hung on me nursery wall more years ago than I'll admit aven to you, Judy,' sez she. Sure and I cudn't stand up to a countess so she had her way. I got out the bist silver taypot and one av the parlour chairs for her. But she plunked hersilf down on ould Nehemiah's and sez, sez she, 'I want me tay right out av that ould brown pot. There's nothing like it for flavour,' sez she. And nothing wud do but I must sit down wid her

351

and take a share av the sausages and pittaties. But I wasn't after ating minny, girls dear . . . me appetite wasn't wid me. Siven av thim sausages disappeared and I et only the one av thim. Think av it, me drinking tay wid a countess, and crooking me liddle finger rale illigant whin I happened to think av it! Madam Binnie'll niver be belaving it. And wud ye be belaving it, girls dear? She was at Castle McDermott hersilf whin she was a girleen and tould me all about the ould place. It did be making me fale I must be going to see it afore long. Prisently Bold-and-Bad comes along asking 'have ye room for a cat?' and jumps up in her lap. Oh, oh, ye saw for yersilves she was a different brade from Cousin Nicholas. Well, we did be sitting there colloguing, her and me and the cats, rale cosy and frindly, whin I heard a tarrible noise in the back porch. It didn't sound like innything on earth but I did be knowing it was Tillytuck gargling his throat, him thinking it was a bit sore this morning. I did be glancing at the countess a bit apprehensive-like but she was admiring me crame cow and taking no notice apparently. I was fearing whin he finished wid his throat he'd be breaking out into a Psalm but niver did I think he'd have the presumption to come in. I was clane flabbergasted whin I saw him standing in the dureway. I did be giving him the high sign to take himsilf off but he paid no attintion and was all for setting down on her ladyship's hat which she had tossed on a chair careless-like. I got it away just in time, girls dear, and down he plumped. Wud ye belave it, her ladyship smiled at him in that nice way she has and passed a remark about the weather. And didn't Tillytuck tell her rain was coming bekase he had rheumatism in his arms! And thin tilting back on the hind-legs av his chair, wid his thumbs tucked into his bilt, casual-like, he wint on to tell her one av his 'traggedies' . . . how the lion had got out av his cage and clawed him. 'It was a lippard last time,' I cudn't hilp saying, sarcastic-like. But her ladyship tuk his measure and I cud see she was lading him on, and him thinking he was showing me how to hobnob wid the quality. Thin Just Dog started to throw one av his fits but Tillytuck whisked him out so quick I'm not thinking her ladyship tuk it in. What wid it all, me nerves were getting a bit jumpy and niver was there a more welcome sound to me ears than the ould Russell mare's trot up the lane."

"Did you give the countess a swig out of your black bottle, Judy?" asked Sid, who had arrived home and come to find out why nobody had got supper ready for him. "If she left anything in the pantry I'd be glad of a bite."

"Why did you take her into the pantry just as she was leaving, Judy?" asked Pat.

"Oh, oh, I'd promised to give her a jar av me strawberry jam. But she'll niver be getting it home safe . . . there do be something in an ocean v'yage it can't be standing . . . she'll be firing it overboard afore she's half way across. She said to me in the pantry, Patsy dear, that ye did be having a lovely smile and a grand sinse av fun. Sure and I'm putting that bit av biscuit she lift on her plate in me glory box for a kapesake. It was her third so there did be no insult in her laving it. Well, it do be all over and whether I'll slape a wink to-night or not the Good Man Above only knows."

Judy was snoring soundly enough in the kitchen chamber when Pat and Cuddles went to bed. Young Joe Merritt had been around Silver Bush that night, wanting Pat to go to a picture with him but Pat had refused. Judy, as usual, wanted to know why poor Joe was always being snubbed. Wasn't he be way av being a rale nice young man and a cousin av the Charlottetown Merritts at that?

"I haven't a fault to find with him, Judy," said Pat gravely, "but our taste in jokes is entirely different."

"Oh, oh, that's sarious," agreed Judy . . . and crossed Joe Merritt's name from her list of possibles.

"Pull up the blind and let the night in, Cuddles. And don't light the lamp yet. When you light it you make an enemy of the dark. It stares in at you resentfully. Just now it's kind and friendly. Let's sit here at the window and talk it all over. It would be wicked to go to sleep too soon on such a night."

"Sleep! I'll never sleep again in this world," sighed Cuddles luxuriously, squatting on the floor and snuggling against Pat's knee while she proceeded to devour some water-cress sandwiches. They were getting in the habit of these delightful little gossips by their window, with only the trees and the stars to listen. To-night the scent of lilacs drifted in and the night was like a cup of fragrance that had spilled over. A wind was waking far off in the spruces on the hill. The robins were still whistling and the silver bush was an elusive, shadowy world breathing mystery. Bold-and-Bad padded in and insinuated himself into Cuddles' lap, where he lay and purred, tensing and flexing his claws happily. One lap was quite as good as another to Bold-and-Bad.

"I've had too many thrills to-day to be sleepy . . . some just awful and some wonderful. Wasn't Lady Medchester lovely, Pat? And *not* because she was a countess. She had such a finished air somehow. She wasn't a bit handsome . . . did you notice how much she looked like Mrs. Snuffy Madison? . . . and her clothes were really shabby. Except the fox stole of course. But her hat . . . well, it looked as if Tillytuck *had* sat on it. But for all that there was something about her that we can't ever get, Pat, in a hundred years."

"*She* wouldn't care what the Binnies thought," said Pat mischievously.

"Don't . . . I'm blushing. And I'm never going even to mention it to Trix. Have a sandwich, Pat? You must be empty. We neither of us had anything since dinner but a biscuit and a scrap of Bishop's bread. I was only pretending to eat under Lady Medchester's eyes. Puss, do stop digging your claws into me. I'm sure Lady Medchester will have an amusing tale to tell when she gets home. The stately halls of England will resound to mirth over Judy and Tillytuck."

"Tillytuck perhaps . . . but not Judy. People laugh *with* Judy, not *at* her. Our countess liked Judy. Did you notice what a lovely voice she had? It somehow made me think of old mellow things that had been loved for centuries . . . after I got capable of thinking at all, that is. Cuddles, I'll never forget the sight as we bounced into the kitchen . . . Judy Plum and the Countess of Medchester *tête-à-tête* at our kitchen table, with Tillytuck for audience. Nobody will ever believe it. It *will* be something to tell our grandchildren . . . if we ever have any."

"*I* mean to have some," said Cuddles coolly.

"Well," said Pat, leaning out of the window to catch a glimpse of that loveliest of created things . . . a young moon in an evening sky . . . "there's one thing the Countess of Medchester will never know she missed . . . my lemon cocoanut cake and Judy's fried chicken. I must write Hilary an account of this."

THE SECOND YEAR

1

Pat never could discover how Lady Medchester's visit to Silver Bush got into the Charlottetown papers. But there it was in "Happenings of the Week." "The Countess of Medchester, who has been spending a few days with friends in Charlottetown, was a visitor at Silver Bush, North Glen, on Thursday last. Lady Medchester is a distant connection of Mr. and Mrs. Alexander Gardiner. Her Ladyship is delighted with our beautiful Island and says that it resembles the old country more than any place she has yet seen in Canada."

The Silver Bush people did not like the item. It savoured too much of a certain publicity they scorned . . . "putting on dog," as Sid slangily expressed it. No doubt it reduced the Binnies to speechless impotence for a time and everybody in South Glen church the next Sunday gazed at the Gardiner family with almost the awe they would have accorded to royalty itself. But that did not atone for what Pat felt was a breach of good taste. Even Tillytuck thought it "rather crude, symbolically speaking." Nobody happened to notice that Judy, who might have been expected to be the most indignant of all, had very little to say and fought shy of the subject. Eventually it was forgotten. After all, there were much more important things to think of at Silver Bush. Countesses might come and countesses might go but wandering turkeys had to be reclaimed at night and Madonna lilies divided and perennial seeds sown, and a new border of delphiniums planned for down the front walk. Lady Medchester's visit slipped into its proper place in the Silver Bush perspective . . . a gay memory to be talked and laughed over on winter nights before the fire.

Meantime, Uncle Tom had stained and grained his once red front door and had painted his apple house sage green with maroon trim. And everybody in Silver Bush and Swallowfield was wondering more or less uneasily why he had done it. Not but what both needed attention. The apple house had long been a faded affair and the red of the door was badly peeled. Nevertheless they had been that way for years and Uncle

Tom had not bothered about them. And now, right in the pinch of hard times, when the hay crop was poor and the potato bugs unusually rampant and the turnips practically non-existent, Uncle Tom was spending good money in this unnecessary fashion.

"He do be getting younger every day," said Judy. "Oh, oh, it's suspicious, I'm telling ye."

"I opine there's a female in the wind, speaking symbolically,'" said Tillytuck.

It was the one cloud on Pat's horizon that summer. Some change was brewing and change at Swallowfield was nearly as bad as change at Silver Bush. Everything had been the same there for years. Aunt Edith and Aunt Barbara had held sway in the house, agreeing quite amicably in the main, and both bossing Uncle Tom for his soul's and body's good. And now both were uneasy. Tom was getting out of hand.

"It has to do with those California letters . . . I'm sure it has," Aunt Barbara told Pat unhappily. "We know he gets them . . . the post-office people have told it . . . but we've never seen one of them. We don't know where on earth he keeps them . . . we've looked everywhere. Edith says if she can find them she'll burn them to ashes but I don't see what good that would do. We haven't an idea who she is . . . Tom must mail his answers in town."

"If Tom brings a . . . a wife in here . . ." Aunt Edith choked over the word . . . "you and I will have to go, Barbara."

"Oh, don't say that, Edith." Aunt Barbara was on the verge of tears. She loved Swallowfield almost as much as Pat loved Silver Bush.

"I will say it and I do say it," repeated Aunt Edith inflexibly. "Can you think for one minute of us staying here, under the thumb of a new mistress? We can get a little house at the Bridge, I suppose."

"I can't believe Uncle Tom will really be so foolish at his age," said Pat.

"I have never been a man," said Aunt Barbara somewhat superfluously, "but this I do know . . . a man can be a fool at *any* age. And you know the old proverb. Tom is fifty-nine."

"I sometimes think," said Aunt Barbara slowly, "that you . . . that we . . . didn't do quite right when we broke off Tom's affair with Merle Henderson, long ago, Edith."

"Nonsense! What was there to break off?" demanded Aunt Edith crisply. "They weren't engaged. He had a school-boy's fancy for her . . .

but you know as well as I do, Barbara, that it would never have done for him to have married a Henderson."

"She was a clever, pretty little thing," protested Aunt Barbara.

"Her tongue was hung in the middle and her grandmother was insane," said Aunt Edith.

"Well, Dr. Bentley says everybody is a little insane on some points. I do think we shouldn't have meddled, Edith."

Aunt Barbara's "we" was a concession to peace. Both of them knew it had been Edith's doings alone.

Pat sympathised with them and her heart hardened against Uncle Tom when she found him waiting for her at the old stile, half way along the Whispering Lane, where the trees screened them from the sight of both Swallowfield and Silver Bush. Pat was all for sailing on with a frosty nod but Uncle Tom put a shy hand on her shoulder.

"Pat," he said slowly, "I'd . . . I'd like to have a little talk with you. It's . . . it's not often I have the chance to see you alone."

Pat sat down on the stile ungraciously. She had a horrible presentiment of what Uncle Tom wanted to tell her. And she wasn't going to help him out . . . not she! With his vanishing beard and his front doors and his apple barns he had kept everybody on the two farms jittery all summer.

"It's . . . it's a little hard to begin," said Uncle Tom hesitatingly.

Pat wouldn't make it any easier. She gazed uncompromisingly through the birches to a field where winds were weaving patterns in the ripening wheat and making sinuous shadows like flowing amber wine. But for once in her life Pat was blind to beauty.

Poor Uncle Tom took off his straw hat and mopped a brow that had not been so high some thirty-odd years back.

"I don't know if you ever heard of a . . . a . . . a lady by the name of Merle Henderson," he said desperately.

Pat never had until Aunt Edith had mentioned her that day but . . .

"I have," she said drily.

Uncle Tom looked relieved.

"Then . . . then perhaps you know that once . . . long ago . . . when I was young . . . ahem, younger . . . I . . . I . . . in short . . . Merle and I were . . . were . . . in short . . ." Uncle Tom burst out with the truth explosively . . . "I was desperately in love with her."

Pat was furious to find her heart softening. She had always loved

357

Uncle Tom . . . he had always been good to her . . . and he did look so pathetic.

"Why didn't you marry her?" she asked gently.

"She . . . she wouldn't have me," said Uncle Tom, with a sheepish smile. Now that the plunge was over he found himself swimming. "Oh, I know Edith thinks *she* put the kibosh on it. But not by a jugful. If Merle would have married me a regiment of Ediths wouldn't have mattered. I don't wonder Merle turned me down. It would have been a miracle if she had cared for me . . . then. I was nothing but a raw boy and she . . . she was the most beautiful little creature, Pat. I'm not romantic . . . but she always seemed like a . . . like an ethereal being to me, Pat . . . a . . . a fairy, in short."

Pat had a sudden glimpse of understanding. To Uncle Tom his vanished Merle was not only Merle . . . she was youth, beauty, mystery, romance . . . everything that was lacking in the life of a rather bald, more than middle-aged farmer, domineered over by two maiden sisters.

"She had soft, curly, red-brown hair . . . and soft, sweet red-brown eyes . . . and such a sweet little red mouth. If you could have heard her laugh, Pat . . . I've never forgotten that laugh of hers. We used to dance together at parties . . . she was as light as a feather. She was as slim and lovely as . . . as that young white birch in moonlight, Pat. She walked like . . . like spring. I've never cared for anybody else . . . I've loved her all my life."

"What became of her?"

"She went out to California . . . she had an aunt there . . . and married there. But she is a widow now, Pat. Two years ago . . . you remember? . . . the Streeters came home from California for a visit. George Streeter was an old pal of mine. He told me all about Merle . . . she wasn't left well off and she's had to earn her own living. She's a public speaker . . . a lecturer . . . oh, she's very clever, Pat. Her letters are wonderful. I . . . I couldn't get her out of my head after what George told me. And so . . . I . . . well, I wrote her. And we've been corresponding ever since. I've asked her to marry me, Pat."

"And will she?" Pat asked the question kindly. She couldn't hurt Uncle Tom's feelings . . . poor old Uncle Tom who had loved and lost and went on faithfully loving still. It *was* romantic.

"Ah, that's the question, Pat," said Uncle Tom mysteriously. "She hasn't decided . . . but I think she's inclined to, Pat . . . I think she's inclined to. I think she's very tired of facing the world alone, poor little thing. And this is where I want you to help me out, Patsy."

"Me!" said Pat in amazement.

"Yes. You see, she's in New Brunswick now, visiting friends there. And she thinks it would be a good idea for her to run across to the Island and . . . and . . . sorter see how the land lays, I guess. Find out maybe if I'm the kind of man she could be happy with. She wanted me to go over to New Brunswick but it's hard for me to get away just now with harvest coming on and only a half-grown boy to help. Read what she says, Patsy."

Pat took the letter a bit reluctantly. It was written on thick, pale-blue paper and a rather heavy perfume exhaled from it. But the paragraph in reference to her visit was sensibly expressed.

"We have probably both changed a good deal, honey boy, and perhaps we'd better see each other before coming to a decision."

Pat with difficulty repressed a grin over the "honey boy."

"I still don't quite see where I come in, Uncle Tom."

"I . . . I want you to invite her to spend a few days at Silver Bush," said Uncle Tom eagerly. "I can't invite her to Swallowfield . . . Edith would—would have a conniption . . . and anyhow she wouldn't come there. But if you'd write her a nice little note . . . Mrs. Merle Merridew . . . and ask her to Silver Bush . . . she went to school with Alec . . . do, now, Patsy."

Pat knew she would be letting herself in for awful trouble. Certainly Aunt Edith would never forgive her. Judy would think she had gone clean crazy and Cuddles would think it a huge joke. But it was impossible to refuse poor Uncle Tom, pleading for what he believed his chance for happiness again. Pat did not yield at once but after a consultation with mother she told Uncle Tom she would do it. The letter of invitation was written and sent the very next day and during the following week Pat was in swithers of alternate regret, apprehension, and a determination to stand by Uncle Tom at all costs.

There was a good deal of consternation at Silver Bush when the rest of the family heard what she had done. Dad was dubious . . . but after all it was Tom's business, not his. Sid and Cuddles, as Pat had foreseen, considered it a joke. Tillytuck stubbornly refused to express any opinion. It was a man's own concern, symbolically speaking, and wimmen critters had no right to interfere. Judy, after her first horrified, "God give ye some sinse, Patsy!" was just a bit intrigued with the romance of it . . . and a secret desire to see how me fine Edith wud be after taking it.

Edith did not take it very well. She descended on Pat, dragging in her wake poor Aunt Barbara who had been weeping all over the house but still thought they ought not to meddle in the matter. Pat had a bad quarter of an hour.

"How *could* you do such a thing, Pat?"

"I couldn't refuse Uncle Tom," said Pat. "And it doesn't really make any difference, Aunt Edith. If I hadn't asked her to come here he would have gone to New Brunswick to see her. And she may not marry him after all."

"Oh, don't try to be comforting," groaned Aunt Edith.

"Marry him! Of course she'll marry him. And she is a *grandmother*. George Streeter said so . . . and thinks she is still a girl. It's simply terrible to think of it. I don't see how I'm going to stand it. Excitement always brings on a pain in my heart. Everybody knows that. *You* know it, Pat."

Pat did know it. What if it all killed Aunt Edith? But it was too late now. Uncle Tom was quite out of hand. He felt that the situation was delicious. Life had suddenly become romantic again. Nothing that Edith could and did say bothered him in the least. He had even begun negotiating for the purchase of a trim little bungalow at Silverbridge for "the girls" to retire to.

"Him and his bungalow!" said Aunt Edith in a contempt too vast to be expressed in words. "Pat, you're the only one who seems to have any influence . . . *any* influence . . . over that infatuated man now. Can't you put him off this notion in some way? At least, you can try."

Pat promised to try, by way of preventing Aunt Edith from having a heart attack, and went up to the spare room to put a great bowl of yellow mums on the brown bureau. If she were to have a new aunt she must be friends with her. Alienation from Swallowfield was unthinkable. Pat sighed. What a pity it all was! They had been so happy and contented there for years. She hated change more than ever.

2

Mrs. Merridew was coming on the afternoon train and Uncle Tom was going to meet her with the span.

"I suppose I ought to have an automobile, Pat. She'll think this turn-out very old-fashioned."

"She won't see prettier horses anywhere," Pat encouraged. And Uncle Tom drove away with what he hoped was a careless and romantic air. Outwardly he really looked as solemn as his photograph in the family album but at heart he was a boy of twenty again, keeping tryst with an old dream that was to him as of yesterday.

Tillytuck persisted in hanging around although Judy hinted that there was work waiting on the other place. Tillytuck took no hints. "I'm always interested in courtings," he averred shamelessly.

It seemed an endless time after they heard the train blow at Silverbridge before Uncle Tom returned. Sid unromantically proffered the opinion that Uncle Tom had died of fright. Then they heard the span pausing by the gate.

"Here comes the bride," grunted Tillytuck, slipping out by the kitchen door.

Pat and Cuddles ran out to the lawn. Judy peered from the porch window. Tillytuck had secreted himself behind a lilac bush. Even mother, who had one of her bad days and was in bed, raised herself on her pillows to look down through the vines.

They saw Uncle Tom helping out of the phaeton a vast lady who seemed even vaster in a white dress and a large, white, floppy hat. A pair of very fat legs bore her up the walk to the door where the girls awaited her. Pat stared unbelievingly. Could this woman, with feet that bulged over her high-heeled shoes, be the light-footed fairy of Uncle Tom's old dancing dreams?

"And this is Pat? How *are* you, sugar-pie?" Mrs. Merridew gave Pat a hearty hug. "And Cuddles . . . darling!" Cuddles was likewise engulfed. Pat found her voice and asked the guest to come upstairs. Uncle Tom had spoken no word. It was Cuddles' private opinion that his vocal cords had been paralysed by shock.

"Can that be all one woman?" Tillytuck asked the lilac bush. "I don't like 'em skinny . . . but . . ."

"Think av *that* in Swallowfield," Judy said to Gentleman Tom. "Oh, oh, it's widening his front dure as well as painting it Tom Gardiner shud have done."

Gentleman Tom said nothing, as was his habit, but McGinty crawled under the kitchen lounge. And upstairs mother was lying back on her pillows shaking with laughter. "Poor Tom!" she said. "Oh, poor Tom!"

Mrs. Merridew talked and laughed all the way upstairs. She lifted her awful fat arms and removed her hat, showing snow-white hair lying in sleek moulded waves around a face that might once have been pretty but whose red-brown eyes were lost in pockets of flesh. The red sweet mouth was red still . . . rather too red. Lipstick was not in vogue at Silver Bush . . . but the lavish gleam of gold in the teeth inside detracted from its sweetness. As for the laugh that Uncle Tom had remembered, it was merely a fat rumble . . . yet with something good-natured about it, too.

"Oh, honey, let's sit outside," exclaimed Mrs. Merridew, after she had got downstairs again. They trailed out to the garden after her. Uncle Tom, still voiceless, brought up the rear. Pat did not dare look at him. What on earth was going on in his mind? Mrs. Merridew lowered herself into a rustic chair, that creaked ominously, and beamed about her.

"I love to sit and watch the golden bees plundering the sweets of the clover," she announced. "I adore the country. The city is so artificial. Don't you truly think the city is so artificial, sugar-pie? There can be no real interchange of souls in the city. Here in the beautiful country, under God's blue sky" . . . Mrs. Merridew raised fat be-ringed hands to it . . . "human beings can be their real and highest selves. I am sure you agree with me, angel."

"Of course," said Pat stupidly. She couldn't think of an earthly thing to say. Not that it mattered. Mrs. Merridew could and did talk for them all. She babbled on as if she were on the lecture platform and all her audience needed to do was sit and listen. "Are you interested in psychoanalysis?" she asked Pat but waited for no answer. When Judy announced supper Pat asked Uncle Tom to stay and share it with them. But Uncle Tom managed to get out a refusal. He said he must go home and see to the chores.

"Mind, you promised to take me for a drive this evening," said Mrs. Merridew coquettishly. "And, oh, girls, he didn't know me when I got off the train. Fancy that . . . when we were sweethearts in the long ago."

"You were . . . thinner . . . then," said Uncle Tom slowly. Mrs. Merridew shook a pudgy finger at him.

"We've both changed. You look a good bit older, Tom. But never mind . . . at heart we're just as young as ever, aren't we, honey boy?"

Honey boy departed. Pat and Cuddles and Mrs. Merridew went in to supper. Mrs. Merridew wanted to sit where she could see the beauty of the delphiniums down the garden walk. Her life, she said, was a continual search for beauty.

They put her where she could see the delphiniums and listened in fascinated silence while she talked. Never had any one just like this come to Silver Bush. Fat ladies had been there . . . talkative ladies had been there . . . beaming, good-natured ladies had been there. But never any one half so fat and talkative and beaming and good-natured as Mrs. Merridew. Pat and Cuddles dared not look at each other. Only when Mrs. Merridew gave utterance to the phrase, "a heterogeneous mass of potentiality," as airily as if she had said "the blue of delphiniums" Cuddles kicked Pat under the table and Judy, in the kitchen, said piteously to Tillytuck, "Sure and I used to be able to understand the English language."

The next morning Mrs. Merridew came down to breakfast, looking simply enormous in a blue kimono. She talked all through breakfast and all through the forenoon and all through dinner. In the afternoon she was away driving with Uncle Tom but she talked all through supper. During the early evening she stopped talking, probably through sheer exhaustion, and sat on the rustic chair on the lawn, her hands folded across her satin stomach. When Uncle Tom came over she began talking again and talked through the evening, with the exception of a few moments when she went to the piano and sang, *Once in the Dear Dead Days Beyond Recall.* She sang beautifully and if she had been invisible they would all have enjoyed it. Tillytuck, who was in the kitchen and couldn't see her, declared he was enraptured. But Judy could only wonder if the piano bench would ever be the same again.

"She simply can't forget she isn't on the lecture platform," said Pat.

There was no subject Mrs. Merridew couldn't talk about. She discoursed on Christian Science and vitamines, on Bolshevism and little theatres, on Japan's designs in Manchuria and television, on theosophy and bi-metallism, on the colour of your aura and the value of constructive thinking in contrast to negative thinking, on the theory of re-incarnation and the Higher Criticism, on the planetesimal hypothesis and the trend of modern fiction, on the best way to preserve your furs from moths and how to give a cat castor oil. She reminded Pat of a random verse conned in schooldays and she wrote it of her in her descriptive letter to Hilary.

"Her talk was like a stream that runs
With rapid flow from rocks to roses,
She passed from parrakeets to puns,
She leaped from Mahomet to Moses."

"I do be thinking she ain't mentally sound," groaned Judy. "There was a quare streak in the Hindersons I do be rimimbering. Her grandmother was off be spells and her Great-uncle had his coffin made years afore he died and kipt it under the spare-room bed. Oh, oh, the talk it made."

"I knew the man when I was a boy," said Tillytuck. "His wife kept her fruit cake and the good sheets in it."

Judy went on as if there had been no interruption.

"And yet, in spite av iverything, girls dear, I do be kind av liking her."

In truth, they all "kind of liked" her . . . even mother, who, nevertheless, was compelled by Pat to stay in bed most of the time that she might not be talked to death. Mrs. Merridew was so entirely good-natured and her smile *was* charming. The floors might creak as she walked over them but her spirit was feather-light. She might have a liking for snacks of bread and butter with an inch of brown sugar spread on top of it but there wasn't a scrap of malice in her heart. Judy might speculate pessimistically on what would happen if she fell downstairs but she adored McGinty and was hail-fellow-well-met with all the cats. Even Gentleman Tom succumbed to her spell and waved his thin, stiff tail when she tickled him behind the ears. Judy, who had implicit confidence in Gentleman Tom's insight into human nature, admitted that maybe Tom Gardiner wasn't quite the fool she had been thinking him. For Mrs. Merridew, in spite of her avoirdupois, was "rale cliver round the house." She insisted on helping with the chores and washed dishes and polished silver and swept floors with astonishing deftness, talking ceaselessly and effortlessly all the time. In the evenings she went driving with Uncle Tom or sat with him in the moonlight garden. Nobody could tell what Uncle Tom was thinking, not even Pat. But the aunts had subsided into the calm of despair. They had not called on Mrs. Merridew . . . they would not countenance her in any way . . . but it was their opinion that she had Tom hypnotised.

Pat was sitting on a log in the silver bush one evening . . . her own dear, dim silver bush, full of moon-patterned shadows . . . having crept away to be by herself for a little while. Mrs. Merridew was in the kitchen eating doughnuts, telling Judy how travel broadened the mind, and encouraging her to take her trip to Ireland. Judy's kitchen was certainly not what it used to be just now and Pat was secretly relieved to feel that Mrs. Merridew's visit was drawing to a close. Even if she came back to North Glen it would be to Swallowfield, not to Silver Bush.

Some one came along the path and sat down beside her with a heavy sigh. Uncle Tom! Somehow Pat understood what was in his heart without words . . . that "all that was left of his bright, bright dream" was dust and ashes. Poor mistaken Uncle Tom, who had imagined that the old magic could be recaptured.

"She's expecting me to propose to her again, Patsy," he said, after a long silence.

"Must you?" asked Pat.

"As a man of honour I must . . . and that to-night," said Uncle Tom solemnly . . . and said no more.

Pat decided that silence was golden. After a time they got up and went back to the house. As they emerged from the bush the shadow of a fat woman was silhouetted on the kitchen blind.

"Look at it," said Uncle Tom, with a hollow groan. "I never imagined any one could change so much, Patsy. Patsy . . ." there was a break in Uncle Tom's voice . . . "I . . . I . . . wish I had never seen her *old,* Patsy."

When they went in Mrs. Merridew whisked Uncle Tom off to the Little Parlour. But the next day something rather mysterious happened. Mrs. Merridew announced at breakfast that she must catch the ten-fifteen train to town and would Sid be kind enough to drive her down to Silverbridge? She bade them all good-bye cheerily and drew Pat aside for a few whispered sentences.

"Don't blame me, sugar-pie. He told me you knew all about it . . . and I really did intend to take him before I came, darling. But when I saw him . . . well, I knew right off I simply couldn't. Of course it's rotten to let any one down like that but I'm so terribly sensitive in regard to beauty. He was so old-looking and changed. He wasn't a bit the Tom Gardiner I knew. I want you to be specially good to him and cheer him up until he is once more able to tune his spirit into the rhythm of the happiness vibrations that are all around us. He didn't say much but I knew he was feeling my decision very deeply. Still, after a little he'll see for himself that it is all for the best."

She climbed into the waiting car, waved a chubby, dimpled hand at them and departed.

"I hope the springs av that car will be lasting till they get to the station," said Judy. "And whin's the widding to be, Patsy?"

"Never at all," smiled Pat. "It's all off."

"Thank the Good Man Above for that," said Judy devoutly. "Oh, oh, it was a rale noble act av ye to ask her here, Patsy, and ye've had yer reward. If yer Uncle Tom had got ingaged to her be letter he'd have had to have stuck to it, no matter what he filt like whin he saw her. And it isn't but what I liked her, Patsy, and it's sorry for her disappointmint I am . . . but she wud niver have done for a wife for Tom Gardiner. It's well he had the sinse to see it, aven at the last momint."

Pat said nothing. Uncle Tom said nothing . . . neither then nor at any other time. His little flyer in romance was over. The negotiations for the Silverbridge bungalow were abruptly dropped. The aunts both persisted in thinking that Pat had "influenced" Uncle Tom and were overwhelmingly grateful to her. In vain Pat assured them she had done nothing.

"Don't tell *me*," said Aunt Edith. "He was simply *fascinated* from the moment she came. He went around like a man in a dream. But *something* held him back from the last fatal step and that something was *you*, Pat. She'll be furious that he's slipped through her fingers again of course."

Still Pat held her tongue. They would never believe Mrs. Merridew had actually refused Tom and that he thanked heaven for his escape.

Life at Swallowfield and Silver Bush settled back into its customary tranquillity.

"I must write all about it to Hilary," said Pat, sitting down at her window in the afterglow. The world was afloat in primrose light, pale and exquisite. The garden below was alive with robins, and swallows were skimming low across the meadows. The hill field was a sea of wheaten gold and beyond it velvety dark spruces were caressing crystal air. How lovely everything was! How everything seemed to beckon to her! What a *friendly* farm Silver Bush was! And how beautiful it was to have a quiet evening again, with a "liddle bite" and a glorious gab-fest with Judy later on in prospect. And oh, how glad she was that there was to be no change at Swallowfield. Hilary would be glad to hear it, too.

"I wish I could slip that sunset into the letter and send it to him," she thought. "I remember when I was about six saying to Judy, 'Oh, Judy, isn't it lovely to live in a world where there are sunsets?' I still think it is."

3

During the autumn and winter after the shadow of a new bride at Swallowfield had vanished from Pat's sky life went on at Silver Bush delightfully. It was a very cold winter . . . so cold that there was not only frost but feathers on the windows most of the time . . . and there was much snow and wild wind in birch and spruce. And never a thaw, not even in January, although Tillytuck was loath to give up hope of one.

"I've never seen a January without a thaw yet and I've seen hundreds of them," he asserted . . . and wondered grumpily why everybody laughed. But he saw one that year. The cold continued unbroken. The stones around Judy's flower beds always wore white snow caps and looked like humpy little gnomes. Pat was glad the garden was covered up. It always hurt her to see her beautiful garden in winters when there was little snow . . . so forsaken looking, with mournful bare flower stalks sticking up out of the hard frozen earth and bare, writhing shrubs that you never could believe could be mounds of rosy blossoms in June. It was nice to think of it sleeping under a spotless coverlet, dreaming of the time when the first daffodil would usher in spring's age of gold.

And there was beauty, too, everywhere. Sometimes Pat thought the winter woods with their white reserve and fearlessly displayed nakedness seemed the rarest and finest of all. You never knew how beautiful a tree really was until you saw it leafless against a pearl-grey winter sky. And was there ever anything quite so perfect as the birch grove in a pale-rose twilight after a fine calm fall of snow?

In the stormy evenings Silver Bush, snug and sheltered, holding love, laughed defiance through its lighted windows at the grey night full of driving snow. They all crowded into Judy's kitchen and ate apples and candy, while happy cats purred and a wheezy little dog who, alas, was growing old and a bit deaf, snored at Pat's feet. Wild and weird or gay and thrilling were the tales told by Judy and Tillytuck in a rivalry that sometimes convulsed the Silver Bush folks. Judy had taken to locating most of her yarns in Ireland and when she told a gruesome tale of the man who had made a bargain with the Bad Man Below and broke it Tillytuck could not possibly claim to have known or been the man.

"What was the bargain, Judy?"

"Oh, oh, it was for his wife's life. She was to live as long as he niver prayed to God. But if he prayed to God she wud die and *he* was to belong to Ould Satan foriver. Sure and she lived for minny a year. And thin me fine man got a bit forgetful-like and one day whin the pig bruk its leg he sez, sez he, in a tragic tone, 'Oh God!' sez he. And his wife did be dying that very night."

"But that wasn't a prayer, Judy."

"Oh, oh, but it was. Whin ye cry on God like that in inny trouble it do be a prayer. The Bad Man Below knew it well."

"What became of the husband, Judy?"

"Oh, oh, he was *taken away*," said Judy, contriving to convey a suggestion of indescribable eeriness that sent a shiver down everybody's back. Satisfied with the effect she remarked deprecatingly,

"But listen to me prating av ould days. I'd be better imployed setting me bread."

And while Judy set the bread Tillytuck would spin a yarn of being chased by wolves one moonlit night while skating and told it so well that every one shuddered pleasantly. But Judy said coldly,

"I did be rading that very story, Tillytuck, in Long Alec's ould Royal Rader in me blue chist."

"I daresay you read something like it," retorted Tillytuck unabashed. "I never claimed to be the only man chased by wolves."

Then they all had "a liddle bite" and went to bed, snuggled warm and cosy while the winds ravened outside.

Dwight Madison took to haunting Silver Bush that winter and it was quite plain that he had, as Sid said, "a terrible ailment called serious intentions." Pat tried to snub him. Dwight wouldn't *be* snubbed. It never occurred to Dwight that any girl would want to snub him. Aunt Hazel was hot in his favour but Judy, for a wonder, was not. He was a too deadly serious, solemn, in-earnest young man for Judy.

"De ye be calling *that* a beau?" she demanded after his first visit in a tone that implied she would rather call it something the cats had brought in. Pat said she thought he snored and Cuddles remarked that he looked like spinach. After that, there was no more to be said and

Long Alec, who rather favoured Dwight because he had prospects from a bachelor uncle, concluded that modern girls were hard to please. Aunt Hazel was quite cool to Pat for a time.

Bold-and-Bad had pneumonia in March but got over it, thanks, it was believed, to Tillytuck's ministrations. Tillytuck sat up with him two whole nights in the granary chamber, keeping him covered with a blanket in a box by the open window. Twice during each night Judy ploughed out to him through the snow to carry him a hot cup of tea and "a liddle bite." Gentleman Tom did not have pneumonia but he had a narrow escape of his own, which Judy related with gusto.

"Girls dear, niver did I be hearing av such a thing. Ye'll be remembering that whin we had the rolled roast for dinner Sunday I did be taking out the string afore I tuk it to the table and throwing it into the wood-box? Oh, oh, and this afternoon whin I come in didn't Gentleman Tom be sitting there be the stove, wid something hanging from his mouth like a rat's tail. Whin I looked closer I saw it was a bit av string and I tuk hould av it and pulled it. I did be pulling out over a yard av it. The baste had swallied it till he was full av it and cudn't quite manage the last two inches and it did be that saved his life for niver cud he have digested it. But, girls dear, if ye cud have seen the look on his face whin I was pulling at the string! And from this out it's burning ivery roast string at once I'll be doing for we don't want inny more av our cats committing suicide in that fashion."

"Another joke for you to write to Hilary, Pat," said Cuddles slyly.

But at last they were throwing open the windows to let in the spring and Pat learned all over again how lovely young cherry trees were, waving whitely in green twilights, and the scent of apple blossoms in moonlight, and the colonies of blue grape-hyacinths under the dining-room windows. But there were some clouds on her horizon, no bigger than a man's hand yet fraught with worrisome possibilities. She could not settle down in perfect peace, even after housecleaning was, as Tillytuck said, "all done though not quite finished." There was a lick of paint to be administered here and there, some curtains to be mended, the early carrots to be thinned out and dozens of delightful little things like that to be attended to. But ever and anon what Hawthorne calls "a dreary presentiment of impending change" crept across her happiness like a hint of September coolness stealing athwart the languor of an August afternoon. For one thing, trees were dying everywhere as a result of the bitter winter or because of some disease. The cross little spruce tree at the garden gate, which had grown up into a cross big tree, died, and although Pat had liked it the least of all the trees she grieved over its death. It was heartrending to walk through the woods at the back and see a friend here and there turning brown or failing to leaf out. Even the huge spruce in Happiness was dying and one of Hilary's "twin spires."

For another thing, Judy was by now quite keen on going to Ireland for a visit in the fall. Pat hated the very thought but she knew she must not be selfish and horrid. Judy had served Silver Bush long and faithfully and deserved a holiday if any one ever did. Pat choked down her dismay and talked encouragingly. Of course Judy must go. There was nothing in the world to prevent her. Cuddles was going to try the Entrance in July and if she passed would likely be away at Queen's next year, but somebody could be got in to help Pat during Judy's absence. Judy would stay all winter of course. It would not be worth going for less and a winter crossing of the Atlantic was not advisable. The Atlantic! When Pat thought of the Atlantic rolling between her and Judy she felt absolutely sick. But Cuddles was "thrilled" about it all.

"Thrilled, is it?" said Judy rather sourly. "Ye'll be having thrills wid a vengeance if ould Mrs. Bob Robinson comes here in me place. She's the only one we can be getting, it sames. Oh, oh, what'll me poor kitchen be in her rajame?"

"But think of all the fun you'll have when you come back, putting it to rights, Judy."

"Oh, oh, ye've got the right philosophy av it," agreed Judy brightening up. "Did I be telling ye I had a letter from me cousin in Ireland to-day?"

They had been very curious about that letter. A letter for Judy was a phenomenon at Silver Bush. And Judy had been curiously affected by it. If it had been possible for her to turn pale she would have done so. She had taken the letter and stalked off to the graveyard to read it. All the rest of the day she had been strangely quiet.

"I sint her a scratch av me pin back a bit. I hadn't been hearing from her for over twinty years and thinks I to mesilf, 'Maybe she's dead but at innyrate I'll find out.' And to-day along comes her answer. Living and flourishing and that glad to think av me visiting her. And me ould Uncle Michael Plum do be living yet at ninety-five and calling his son av sivinty a saucy young felly whiniver he conterdicts him! It did be giving me a quare faling, Patsy. I'm thinking I know what it's going to be like on the resurrection day, no less."

"Hilary is going across this month," said Pat. "He has won the Bannister scholarship and is going to spend the summer in France, sketching French country houses."

Pat did not tell them everything about the matter. She did not tell them that Hilary had asked her a certain question again. If she could answer it as he wished he would spend the summer in P.E. Island instead of in France. But Pat was sure she couldn't answer it as he wished. She loved him so dearly as a friend but that was all.

"I'm putting into this letter," she concluded, "a little corner of the orchard, a young fir all overgrown with green tassel tips, that moonlit curve you remember in Jordan . . . a bit of wild plum spray . . . a wind that has blown over spice ferns . . . the purr of a little cat and the bark of a little dog who desires to be remembered to you . . . and always my best *friendly* love. Isn't that enough, Hilary, darling? Come home and enjoy these things and let us have one more summer of our old jolly companionship."

Her heart glowed with the thought of it. There never was such a chum and playfellow in the whole world as Hilary. But Hilary couldn't see it that way: and so he was going to France. Perhaps Hilary knew more about some things than Pat ever told him. Cuddles wrote to him occasionally and told him more of Pat's goings-on than Pat ever dreamed of. Hilary knew of all the would-be's who came to Silver Bush and it may be that Cuddles coloured her accounts a trifle highly. Certainly Hilary somehow got the impression that Pat had developed into a notable flirt, with no end of desperate lovers at her feet. Even when Cuddles wrote about Dwight Madison she did not mention his goggling eyes or the fact that he was an agent on commission for farm implements. Instead she said he was President of the Young Men's Bible Class and that dad thought him a very sensible young man who would have oodles of money when his bachelor uncle died. If it had not been for that dramatic epistle of Cuddles . . . who honestly thought she was doing Pat a good turn by trying to make Hilary jealous . . . Hilary might have come to the Island that summer after all. He was too used to being turned down by Pat as a lover to be discouraged by that alone.

Then there was the rumour that Sid was engaged to Dorothy Milton. Jealousy went through Pat like a needle whenever she heard it. Vainly she tried to comfort herself by thinking that, at any rate, Sid could not marry until the other place was paid for and a new house built on it. The old house had been torn down and the lumber in it used to build a new stable. Pat had felt sad over that, too. It had been Hilary's home and they had signalled back and forth on cool blue summer nights. As for Dorothy Milton, she was a nice girl undoubtedly and would be a very suitable wife for Sid if he had to marry some day. Pat told herself this a hundred times without making much impression on something that would not be reconciled. She was hurt, too, that, if it were true, Sid had not told her. They were such chums in everything else. He consulted her in everything else. Sid was taking over the running of the farm more and more, as Long Alec devoted himself to stock-raising on the other place. Every Sunday evening Pat and Sid would walk over the entire farm and note the crops and fences and plan for the future. It was Sid's ambition to make Silver Bush the best farm in North Glen and Pat was with him heart and soul. If only things could go on forever like this! When Pat read her Bible chapter one night she found the verse, "Meddle not with them that are given to change," and underscored it three times. Solomon, she felt, had gone to the root of things.

Cuddles was another of Pat's problems . . . or rather Rae, as she must henceforth be called. On her birthday she had gathered all the family around her and told them without circumlocution that they were not to call her Cuddles any more. She would simply not take any notice of anything that was said to her unless she was called Rae. And she stuck to it. It was hard at first. They all hated to give up the dear, absurd old name that was linked with so many sweet memories of Cuddles when she was an adorable baby, when she was a new school-girl, when she was in her arms-and-legs stage, when she was just stepping daintily into her teens. But Cuddles stood to her guns and they got into the new habit sooner than they would have thought possible . . . all except Judy. Judy did try her best but she could never do better than "Cud-Rae," which was so ridiculous that Rae eventually yielded a point and let Judy revert to the old name.

The Silver Bush folks had suspected for some time that Rae was going to be the beauty of the family and at last they were sure of it. Martin Madison, who had three ugly daughters, said contemptuously that Rae Gardiner was only two dimples and a smile. But there was more to her than that. Tillytuck considered that he had put it in a nutshell when he said she had all the other North Glen girls skinned a mile. There was some "glamour" about her that they didn't have. She really had a headful of brains and talked of being a doctor . . . more to horrify Judy than anything else since she had really no especial hankering for a "career." And she was clever enough to conceal her cleverness, especially from the youths who began to come to Silver Bush . . . boys of the generation after Pat, whom they regarded as quite elderly. Rae was very popular with them: she had a come-and-find out air about her that intrigued them and she had practised a faraway, mysterious smile so faithfully before her mirror that it drove them quite crazy guessing what she was thinking of. None of them interested her at all, not being in the least like the pictures of the movie stars she kept pinned on the wall at the head of her bed. But, she coolly told Pat, they would do for getting your hand in.

Rae was full of life. Her every step was a dance, her every gesture full of grace and virility. She went about looking for thrills and always found them. Pat, looking at the exquisite oval of her little unwritten face, sighed and wondered what life had for this dear sister. She was far more worried over Rae's future than her own and mothered her to what Rae considered an absurd degree. It *was* provoking when you were feeling romantic and ethereal to be cautioned to put on your overshoes! And to be told you were a snob because you complained of Tillytuck saying queer things in the kitchen when you were entertaining a Charlottetown boy and his sister in the Little Parlour.

"I'm *not* a snob, Pat. You know very well Tillytuck is always saying odd things. Of course they're great fun and *we* laugh at them but *strangers* don't understand. And that Little Parlour door *won't* stay shut. I'll *never* forget the look on Jerry Arnold's face last night when he heard Judy and Tillytuck in one of their arguments."

Rae came to an end of breath and italics which gave Pat a chance to say bitingly,

"Jerry Arnold's father was a junk man twenty years ago."

"Who is being the snob now?" retorted Rae. "Jerry is going to have money. Oh, you needn't look at me like that, Pat. I've no notion of ever marrying Jerry Arnold . . . he isn't my style" . . . (was this . . . could this, be little Cuddles who was a baby day before yesterday?) . . . "but when I *do* marry I'm going to marry a rich man. I admit I'm worldly. I like money. And you know, Pat, we've never had quite enough of that at

Silver Bush."

"But think of the other things we've had," said Pat softly. Rae, sweet, absurd little Rae, was not to be taken too seriously. "Not much money I admit but everything else that matters. And besides we've always got tomorrow."

"That sounds very fine but what does it mean?" Rae had taken up a pose of being hard-boiled this spring. "No, my Patricia, one has to be practical in this kind of a world. I've thought it all over carefully and I've decided that I'll marry money . . . and have a good time the rest of my life."

"Have you any one in mind?" enquired Pat sarcastically.

Rae's blue, black-lashed eyes filled with laughter.

"No, darling. There's really plenty of time. Though Trix Binnie is married . . . married at seventeen. Just think of it . . . only two years older than I am. Her face while she was being married was simply a scream. Jerry Arnold says she looked exactly like a kitten that had caught its first mouse."

"Well, we had an excellent view of May's shoulder blades for the space of a quarter of an hour," said Pat, who had been so furious over the Binnies presuming to invite the Gardiners to the wedding that it took Rae a whole evening to persuade her to go to church.

"Those raw-boned girls certainly shouldn't wear backless dresses," said Rae, with a complacent glance over her own shoulder. "Trix really didn't care a bit for Nels Royce, but when she failed in the Entrance last year there was really nothing else for her. It was so funny to hear Mrs. Binnie pretending Trix wouldn't have gone to Queen's even if she had passed. 'I wouldn't have Trix teaching school. I ain't going to have *my* daughter a slave to the public.'"

Pat howled. Rae's mimicry of Mrs. Binnie was inimitable.

"I'm sure May is furious because Trix is married before her," continued Rae. "I suppose she has finally given up hope of Sid, now that he is really engaged to Dorothy Milton."

"Do you suppose . . . he really is?" asked Pat.

"Oh, yes. She's got her ring. I noticed it last night at choir practice. I wonder when they'll be married."

Pat shivered. She suddenly felt like a very small cat in a very big world. The gold was fading out of the evening sky. A great white moth flew by in the dusk. The spruce wood on the hill had turned black. The moon was rising over the Hill of the Mist. Far down the sea shivered in silver ecstasy. Everything was beautiful but there was something in the air . . . another chill of change. Rae had suddenly grown up and Sid belonged to them no longer. Then one of her April changes came over her. After all, the world was full of June and Silver Bush was still the same. She sprang up.

"It's a waste of time to go to bed too early on moonlight nights. And all the wealth of June is ours, no matter how poor we may be according to your worldly standards, darling. Let's get out the car and run over to Winnie's."

Pat had learned to run the car that spring. Judy had been much upset about it and talked gloomily of a girl at the Bridge who had tried to run her father's car, put her foot on the accelerator instead of the brake and had gone clean through a haystack . . . or so Judy had heard. Pat managed to acquire the knack without any such disaster, although Tillytuck averred that on one occasion he saved his life only by jumping over the dog-house, and Judy still came out in goose-flesh when she saw Pat backing the car out of the garage.

"Times do be changed," she remarked to Gentleman Tom. "Here's Patsy and Cuddles dashing off in the car whin they shud be thinking av their bed. Cat dear, is it that I do be getting ould whin I can't get used to it?"

Gentleman Tom put a leg rather stiffly over his shoulder. Perhaps he, too, felt that he was getting old.

4

They heard about the Long House at Winnie's. It was to have new tenants. They had rented the house for the summer . . . not the farm, which was still to be farmed by John Hammond, the owner, who had bought it from the successor of the Wilcoxes.

Pat heard the news with a feeling of distaste. The Long House had been vacant almost ever since Bets had died. A couple had bought the farm, lived there for a few months, then sold out to John Hammond. Pat had been glad of this. It was easier to fancy that Bets was still there when it was empty. In childhood she had resented it being empty and lonely, and had wanted to see it occupied and warmed and lighted. But it was different now. She preferred to think of it as tenanted only by the fragrance of old years and the little spectral joys of the past. Somehow, it seemed to belong to her as long as it was

"Abandoned to the lonely peace
Of bygone ghostly things."

Judy had more news the next morning. The newcomers were a man and his sister. Kirk was their name. He was a widower and had been until recently the editor of a paper in Halifax. And they had bought the house, not rented it. "Wid the garden and the spruce bush thrown in," said Judy. "John Hammond do be still houlding to the farm. He was here last night, after ye wint away, complaining tarrible about the cost av his wife's operation. 'Oh, oh, what a pity,' sez I, sympathetic-like. 'Sure and a funeral wud have come chaper,' sez I. Patsy dear, did ye be hearing Lester Conway was married?"

"Somebody sent me a paper with the notice marked," laughed Pat. "I'm sure it was May Binnie. Fancy any one supposing it mattered to me."

It seemed a lifetime since she had been so wildly in love with Lester Conway. Why was it she never fell in love like that nowadays? Not that she wanted to . . . but *why?* Was she getting too old? Nonsense!

She knew her clan was beginning to say she didn't know what she wanted but she knew quite well and couldn't find it in any of the men who wooed her. As far as they were concerned, she seemed possessed by a spirit of contrariness. No matter how nice they seemed while they were merely friends or acquaintances she could not bear them when they showed signs of developing into lovers. Silver Bush had no rival in her heart.

In the evening she stood in the garden and looked up at the Long House . . . it was suddenly a delicate, aerial pink in the sunset light. Pat had never been near it since the day of Bets' funeral. Now she had a strange whim to visit it once more before the strangers came and took it from her forever . . . to go and keep a tryst with old, sacred memories.

Pat slipped into the house and flung a bright-hued scarf over her brown dress with its neck-frill of pleated pink chiffon. She always thought she looked nicer in that dress than any other. Somehow people seldom wondered whether Pat Gardiner was pretty or not . . . she was so vital, so wholesome, so joyous, that nothing else mattered. Yet her dark-brown hair was wavy and lustrous, her golden-brown eyes held challenging lights and the corners of her mouth had such a jolly quirk. She was looking her best to-night with a little flush of excitement staining her round, creamy cheeks. She felt as if she were slipping back into the past.

Judy was in the kitchen, telling stories to a couple of Aunt Hazel's small fry who were visiting at Silver Bush. Pat caught a sentence or two as she went out. "Oh, oh, the ears av him, children dear! He cud hear the softest wind walking over the hills and what the grasses used to say to aich other at the sunrising." Dear old Judy! What a matchless story-teller she was!

"I remember how Joe and Win and Sid and I used to sit on the backdoor steps and listen to her telling fairy tales by moonlight," thought Pat, "and whatever she told you you felt had happened . . . *must* have happened. That is the difference between her yarns and Tillytuck's. Oh, it is really awful to think of her going away in the fall for a whole winter."

Pat went up to the Long House by the old delightful short cut past Swallowfield and over the brook and up the hill fields. It was a long time since she had trodden that fairy path but it had not changed. The fields on the hill still looked as if they loved each other. The big silver birch still hung over the log bridge across the brook. The damp mint, crushed under her feet, still gave out its old haunting aroma, and all kinds of wild blossom filled the crevices of the stone dyke where she and Bets had picked wild strawberries. Its base was still lost in a wave of fern and bayberry. And on the hill the Watching Pine still watched and seemed to shake a hand meaningly at her. At the top was the old gate, fallen into ruin, and beyond it the path through the spruce bush where silence seemed to kneel like a grey nun and she felt that Bets must come to meet her, walking through the dusk with dreams in her eyes.

Past the bush she came out on the garden with the house in the midst. Pat stopped and gazed around her. Everything she looked on had some memory of pleasure or pain. The old garden was very eloquent . . . that old garden that had once been so beloved by Bets. She seemed to come back again in the flowers she had tended and loved. The whole place was full of her. She had planted that row of lilies . . . she had trained that vine over the trellis . . . she had set out that rose-bush by the porch step. But most of it was now a festering mass of weeds and in its midst was the sad, empty house, with the little dormer window in its spruce-shadowed roof . . . the window of the room where she had seen the sunrise light falling over Bets' dead face. A dreadful pang of loneliness tore her soul.

"I hate those people who are going to live in you," she told the house. "I daresay they'll tear you up and turn you inside out. That will break my heart. You won't be *you* then."

She went across the garden, along an old mossy walk where the unpruned rosebushes caught at her dress as if they wanted to hold her. Across the lawn, overgrown with grass, to the cherry orchard and around its curve. Then she stopped short in amazed embarrassment.

In a little semicircle of young spruces was a fire of applewood, like a vivid rose of night. Two people were squatted on the grass before it . . . two people and a dog and a cat. The dog, a splendid white and gold creature, who looked as if he could understand a joke, sat beside the man, and the cat, black, bigger than any cat had a right to be, with pale-green moonlike eyes, was snuggled down beside the girl, his beautiful white paws folded under his snowy breast. Pat, in a surge of unreasonable indignation . . . Bets had set out that semicircle of trees . . . muttered a curt "Pardon me . . . I didn't mean to . . . intrude."

She, Pat, an *intruder* here! It was bitter.

But before she could turn and vanish the girl had sprung to her feet, run across the intervening space and caught Pat's arm.

"Don't go," she said imploringly. "Oh, don't go. Stop and get acquainted. You must be one of the Gardiner girls from Silver Bush. I've been hearing about you."

"I'm Pat Gardiner," said Pat curtly. She knew she was being silly and bitter but for the moment she could not help it. She almost hated this girl: and yet there was something undeniably attractive about her. You felt that from the very first. She was a little taller than Pat and she wore knickerbockers and a khaki shirt. She had long, slanted, grey-green eyes with long fair lashes that should have gone with fair hair. But her hair was sloe-black, worn in a glossy braid around her head and waving back from her forehead in a peculiarly virile way. Her skin was creamy with a few freckles . . . delicious freckles, as if they had been shaken out of a pepper-pot over nose and tips of cheeks. She had a crooked clever mouth with a mutinous tilt. Pat didn't think her a bit pretty but she felt drawn to that face in spite of herself.

"And I'm Suzanne Kirk. Really Suzanne. Christened so. Not Susan putting on frills. Now we know each other . . . or rather we've known each other for hundreds of years. I recognised you as soon as I saw you. Come and squat with us."

Pat, still a little stiff, let herself be pulled over to the fire. She wanted to be friendly . . . and yet she didn't.

"This is my brother, David, Miss Gardiner."

David Kirk got up and put out a long lean brown hand. He was quite old . . . forty, if a day, Pat thought mercilessly . . . and there were grey dabs in the dark hair over his ears. He was not handsome, yet he was certainly what Judy would have called "a bit distinguished-like." There was a good deal of his sister's charm in his face and though his eyes were grey-blue instead of grey-green, there was the same tilt to his mouth . . . perhaps a little more decided . . . a little cynical. And when he spoke, although he said only, "I am glad to meet you, Miss Gardiner," there was something in his voice that made everything he said seem significant.

"And this is Ichabod," said Suzanne, waving her hand to the dog, who thumped his tail ingratiatingly. "Of course it's an absurd name for a lordly creature like him but David wanted to give him a name no dog had ever had before. I'm *sure* no dog was ever called Ichabod before, aren't you?"

"I never heard of one." Pat felt that she was yielding in spite of herself. It *did* seem as if she had known them before.

"Our cat is called Alphonso-of-the-emerald-eyes. Alphonso, meet Miss Gardiner."

Alphonso did not wave his tail. He merely blinked a disdainful eye and went on being Alphonso-of-the-emerald-eyes. Suzanne whispered to Pat,

"He is a haughty cat of ancient lineage but he likes being tickled under the ear just as well as if he were a cat who didn't know who his grandfather was. He understands every word we say but he never gossips. Pick out a soft spot of ground, Miss Gardiner, and we'll have a nice do-nothing time."

For a moment Pat hesitated. Then she curled up beside Alphonso.

"I suppose I've been trespassing," she said, "but I didn't know you'd come yet. So I wanted to come up and say good-bye to the Long House.

I . . . I used to come here a great deal. I have very dear memories of it."

"But you are not going to say good-bye to it . . . and you are going to come here a great deal again. I know we are going to be good friends," said Suzanne. "David and I want neighbours . . . want them terribly. And we're not really moved in yet . . . we're going to sleep in the hay-loft to-night . . . but our furniture is all in there higgledy-piggledy. The only thing in place is that old iron lantern over the front door. I *had* to hang that up and put a candle in it. It's our beacon star . . . we'll light it every night. Isn't it lovely? We picked it up one time we were over in France . . . in an old château some king had built for his beloved. David went for his paper and I mortgaged my future for years and went with him. I've never regretted it. It's funny . . . but all the things I do regret were prudent things . . . or what seemed so at the time. David and I have just been prowling about this evening. We arrived two hours ago in a terrible old rattling, banging, squeaking car . . . a second-hand which we bought last week. It took all our spare cash to buy the house but we don't grudge it. The minute we saw that house I knew we must have it. It is a house of delightful personality, don't you think?"

"I've always loved it," said Pat softly.

"Oh, I knew it had been loved the moment I saw it. I think you can always tell when a house has been loved. But it's been asleep for so long. And lonely. It always hurts me to see a house lonely. I felt that I must bring it back to life and chum with it. I *know* it feels happy because we are going to fix it up."

Pat felt the cockles of her heart warming. Houses meant to this girl what they meant to herself . . . creatures, not things.

"We found this pile of apple boughs here and couldn't resist the temptation to light it. There is no wood makes such a lovely fire as applewood. And we're so happy tonight. We've just been hungry for a home . . . with trees and flowers and a cat or two to do our purring for us. We haven't had a home since we were children . . . not even when David was married. He and his wife lived in a little apartment for the short time the poor darling did live. We're short on relations so we'll have to depend on neighbours. It doesn't take much to make us laugh and although we're quite clever we're not so clever that anybody need be scared of us. We can't be very wild . . . David here was shell-shocked somewhere in France when he was twenty and has to live quietly . . . but we do mean to be good friends with life."

"I was bad friends with it when I came up here," said Pat frankly, letting herself thaw a little more. "You see, I really did resent you . . . anybody . . . coming in here. It seemed to belong to a dear friend of mine who used to live here . . . and died six years ago."

"But you don't resent us any longer, do you? Because now you know we love this place, too. We'll be good to your ghosts and your memories, Miss Gardiner."

"I'm just Pat," . . . letting herself go completely.

"Just as I'm Suzanne."

Suddenly they all felt comfortable and congenial. Ichabod lay down . . . Alphonso really went to sleep. The applewood fire crackled and sputtered companionably. About them was the velvet and shadow of the oncoming night with dreaming moonlit trees beyond. In the spruces little winds were gossiping and far below the river gleamed like a blue ribbon tied around its green hill.

"I'm so glad the view goes with the house," said Suzanne. "You don't know how rich it makes me feel just to look at it. And that old garden is one I've always dreamed. I knew I had to have wistaria and larkspur and fox-gloves and canterbury-bells and hollyhocks and here they all are. It's uncanny. We're going to build a stone fireplace here in this crescent of trees. It just wants it."

"Bets . . . my friend . . . planted those trees. They're hers . . . really . . . but she won't mind lending them to you."

Suzanne reached across Alphonso and squeezed Pat's hand.

"It's nice of you to say that. No, she won't mind, because we love them. You never mind letting people have things when you know they love them. And she won't mind our making an iris glade in the spruce bush. That is another thing I've always dreamed of . . . hundreds of iris with spruce trees around them . . . all around them, so the glade will never be seen save by those you want to see it. And we can go there when we want to be alone. One needs a little solitude in life."

They sat and talked for what might have been an hour or a century. The talk had colour . . . Pat recognised that fact instantly. Everything they talked of was interesting the moment they touched it. Occasionally there was a flavour of mockery in David Kirk's laughter and a somewhat mordant edge to his wit. Pat thought he was a little bitter but there was something stimulating and pungent about his bitterness and she found herself liking that lean, dark face of his, with its quick smiles. He had a way of saying things that gave them poignancy and Pat loved the fashion in which he and Suzanne could toss a ball of conversation back and forth, always keeping it in the air.

"The moon is going behind a cloud . . . a silvery white cloud," said Suzanne. "I love a cloud like that."

"There are so many things of that sort to give pleasure," said Pat dreamily. "Such *little* things . . . and yet so much pleasure."

"I know . . . like the heart of an unblown rose," murmured Suzanne.

"Or the tang of a fir wood," said David.

"Let's each give a list of loveliest things," said Suzanne. "The things that please us most, just as they come into our heads, no matter what they are. *I* love the strange deep shadows that come just before sunset . . . June bugs thudding against the windows . . . a bite of home-made bread . . . a hot water bottle on a cold winter night . . . wet mossy stones in a brook . . . the song of wind in the top of an old pine. Now, Pat?"

"The way a cat folds its paws under its breast . . . blue smoke rising in the air on a frosty winter morning. . . the way my little niece Mary laughs, crinkling up her eyes . . . old fields dreaming in moonlight . . . the scrunch of dry leaves under your feet in the silver bush in November . . . a baby's toes . . . the smell of clean clothes as you take them off the line."

"David?"

"The cold of ice," said David slowly. "Alphonso's eyes . . . the smell of rain after burning drought . . . water at night . . . a leaping flame . . . the strange dark whiteness of a winter night . . . brook-brown eyes in a girl."

It never occurred to Pat that David Kirk was trying to pay her a compliment. She thought her eyes were yellow . . . "cat's eyes," May Binnie had said. She wondered if David Kirk's dead young wife had had brook-brown eyes.

The Kirks walked down the hill with her and she made them go into the kitchen and have some of Judy's orange biscuits with a glass of milk. There was no place else to take them for Rae had callers in the Big Parlour and mother had an old friend in the Little Parlour and Long Alec was colloguing with the minister in the dining-room. But the Kirks were people you'd just as soon take into the kitchen as not. Judy was excessively polite, in spite of Suzanne's shirt and knickerbockers . . . too polite, really. Judy didn't know what to make of this sudden intimacy.

"I want to see lots of you . . . I'm sure we are going to be good friends."

Sid coming in, spoke to them on the doorstep.

"Do you know them?" asked Pat in surprise.

"Met them in the Silverbridge store this afternoon. The girl asked me if I knew who lived in the queer old-fashioned place at the foot of the hill."

Pat, who had been feeling very rich, suddenly felt poor . . . horribly poor. She went out into the garden and looked at Silver Bush . . . friendly Silver Bush with its lights welcoming all the world. Blossoms cool with night were around her but they meant nothing to her. Squedunk slithered through the delphiniums to rub against her leg and she never even noticed him. The colour had gone out of everything.

"She dared to laugh at you . . . she dared to call you old-fashioned," she whispered to the house. She shook her brown fist at the darkness. She had never been able to hear Silver Bush disparaged in any way. She had hated Uncle Brian last week because he had said that Silver Bush was settling on its foundations and getting a slant to its floors. And now she hated Suzanne Kirk. Suzanne, indeed! No more of Suzanne for her. To think she had been ready to accept her as a friend . . . to put her in Bets' place! To think she had hob-nobbed with her around the applewood fire and told her sacred things! But never again.

"I . . . I feel just like a caterpillar somebody had stepped on," said Pat chokily.

In the kitchen the genius of prophecy had descended upon Tillytuck.

"That'll be a match some day, mark my words, Judy Plum."

"Ye wud better go out and look at the moon," scoffed Judy. "Beaus don't be so scarce at Silver Bush that Patsy nades to take up wid *that*. He do be old enough to be her father. We'll have to be rale civil to him though, for they tell me he do be writing a book and if we offind him he might be putting us into it."

Up at the Long House David Kirk was saying to Suzanne,

"She makes me think of a woodland brook."

5

Pat snubbed Suzanne when the latter telephoned down to ask her and Sid to their house-warming. She could not go because she had another engagement for the evening . . . which was quite true, for, knowing that the house-warming was coming off, she had promised to go to a dance in South Glen. And when Suzanne and David came down the hill path one evening on their way to a moonlit concert which the boarders at the Bay Shore hotel were giving on the North Glen sandshore, and asked Pat to go with them she was entirely gracious and aloof and very sorry she couldn't possibly go . . . with no more excuse than that. Though in her heart she wanted to go. But something in her had been hurt too deeply. She could never forgive a jibe at Silver Bush, as unlucky Lester Conway had discovered years ago, and she took a bitter delight in refusing very sweetly . . . "oh, oh, tarrible polite she was," Judy reported to Tillytuck. Judy was just as well pleased that this threatened friendship with the Long House people seemed unlikely to materialise. "Widowers do be sly . . . tarrible sly," she reflected.

Suzanne was not one of those who could not take a hint and Pat was troubled with no more invitations. The lights gleamed in the Long House at evening but Pat resolutely turned her eyes away from them. Music drifted down the hill when Suzanne played on her violin in the garden under the stars but Pat shut her ears to it.

And yet she felt by times a strange hint of loneliness. Just now and then came a queer, hitherto unknown feeling, expressed by the deadly word "drab" . . . as if life were made of grey flannel. Then she felt guilty. Life at Silver Bush could never be *that*. She wanted nothing but Silver Bush and her own family . . . nothing!

Rae contributed a bit to the comedy of living that summer by having a frightful attack of school-girl veal love, the object of which was a young evangelist who was holding revival meetings in Mr. Jonas Monkman's big barn. He did not approve of "organised churches" and these services were in the nature of a free-for-all and, being very lively of their kind, attracted crowds, some of whom came to scoff and remained to pray. For it could not be denied that the young preacher had a very marked power for stirring the emotions of his hearers to concert pitch. He had an exceedingly handsome, marble-white face with rather too large, too soft, too satiny brown eyes and long, crinkly, mahogany-hued hair, sweeping back in a mane from what Rae once incautiously said was "a noble brow," and a remarkably caressing, wooing voice, expressive of everything. The teen-ages went down like ninepins before him. A choir was collected, consisting of everybody in the two Glens who could be persuaded to function. Rae, who sang sweetly, was leading soprano, looking like the very rose of song as she carolled with her eyes turned heavenward ... or at least towards the banners of cobwebs hanging from the roof of the barn. She went every night, gave up teasing to be allowed to wear knickerbockers around home, and discarded costume earrings because the evangelist referred to jewelry as "gauds ... all gauds." She was tormented terribly because of her "case" on the preacher, but she gave as good as she got and nobody except Pat thought it was anything but a passing crush. For that matter, all the girls were more or less in love with him and it was difficult to tell where love left off and religion began, as Elder Robinson remarked sarcastically. But Elder Robinson did not approve of the revivals conducted by itinerant evangelists ... "go-preachers" he called them. And Rae and her ilk considered Elder Robinson a hidebound old fossil. Even when Jedidiah Madison of Silverbridge, who hadn't been inside of a church for years, wandered into the barn one night and was saved in three minutes Elder Robinson was still incredulous of any good thing. "Let us see if it lasts," he was reported to have said ... and added that he had just been reading of a very successful evangelist who had turned out to be a bank bandit. Pat had no fear that Mr. Wheeler was a bandit but she detested him and was as puzzled as alarmed over Rae's infatuation.

Tillytuck was likewise hard-boiled and said that the meetings were merely a form of religious dissipation. Judy went one night out of curiosity but could never be prevailed on to go again. Mr. Wheeler played a violin solo that night and she was horrified. No matter if the meeting was held in a barn. It was, or purported to be, Divine Service and fiddles had no place in such. Neither had she any exalted opinion of the sermon. "Oh, oh, not much av a pracher that! Sure and I cud understand ivery word he said." So Pat and Rae were the only ones who went regularly ... Pat going because Rae was so set on it ... and very soon it was bruited abroad in the Glens that the Gardiner girls meant to leave the Presbyterian church and join the go-preachers. It blistered Pat's pride to hear it and she was less than civil to Mr. Wheeler when he walked home with them after the meeting. To be sure it was on the way to his boarding house and he always walked by Pat and not by Rae, but Pat was the suspicious older guardian sister to the backbone. It was all very well to laugh at calf love but Rae must be protected. It was a real relief to Pat's mind when, after six hectic weeks, Mr. Wheeler departed for pastures new and Mr. Monkman's barn reverted to rats and silence.

Rae continued to blush furiously for several weeks when Sid teased her about her boy-friend . . . Mr. Wheeler had said that he was glad to find there were still girls in the world who *could* blush . . . but nothing more came of it and Pat's alarm subsided. Rae was asked to sing in the South Glen choir . . . began to experiment with the effect of her eye-lashes on the tenor and wear "gauds" again . . . and everything blew over, save for a little knot of faithful disciples who continued to hold services of their own in their homes and would have nothing further to do with churches of any description.

6

Pat was in a store in town one evening when Suzanne Kirk came up to her and, in spite of Pat's frigid bow, said smilingly,

"May I have a chance home with you, Miss Gardiner? David was to have run in for me but something must have gone wrong with our Lizzie."

"Oh, certainly," said Pat graciously.

"You are sure it won't crowd you?"

"Not in the least," said Pat more graciously still. Inwardly she was furious. She had promised herself a pleasant leisurely drive home through the golden August evening, over a certain little back road where nobody ever went and where there were such delicious things to see. Pat knew all the roads home from town and liked each for some peculiar charm. But now everything was spoiled. Well, she would go by the regular road and get home as soon as she could. She made the car screech violently as she rounded the first corner. It seemed to express her feelings.

"Don't let's go home by this road," said Suzanne softly. "There's so much traffic . . . and it's so straight. A straight road is an abomination, don't you think? I like lovely turns around curves of ferns and spruce . . . and little dips into brooky hollows . . . and the things the car lights pick up as you turn corners, starting out at you in the undergrowth like fairy folk taken by surprise."

"A thunderstorm is coming up," said Pat, more graciously every time she spoke.

"Oh, we'll out-race it. Let us take the road out from that street. David and I went by that last week . . . it's a dear, lost, bewitching road."

Oh, didn't she know it! Pat turned the car so abruptly in the direction of the back road that she narrowly avoided a collision. How dare Suzanne Kirk, who had called Silver Bush queer, like that road? It was an insult. She hated to have Suzanne Kirk like anything she liked. Well, the road was rough and rutty . . . and the thunderstorm was an excuse for driving fast. Suzanne Kirk should have a good bumpy drive that would cure her of her liking for back roads.

Pat did not talk or try to talk. Neither, after a few futile attempts, did Suzanne. They were about half way home when the latter said, with a tinge of alarm in her voice,

"The storm is coming up rather quickly, isn't it?"

Pat had been grimly aware of that for some time. It was growing dark. Huge menacing black masses were piling up in the northwest in the teeth of a rapidly rising wind. This was a frightful road to be on in a rain . . . narrow and twisting with reedy ditches on either side. Curves and dips and startled fairy folk were all very well in fine weather, but in wind and rain and darkness . . . and all three seemed to envelop them at once . . . a wall of black . . . an ocean of driving rain . . . a howl of tempest . . . a blue-white flare of lightning . . . a deafening crash of thunder . . . and then disaster. The car had swerved on the suddenly greasy road and the next moment they were in the ditch.

Well, it might have been worse. The car was right-side up and the ditch was not deep. But it was full of soft mud under its bracken and Pat knew she could never get the car back to the road.

"There's nothing to do but stay here till the storm is over and some one comes along," she said. "I'm . . . I'm sorry I've ditched you, Miss Kirk."

"Never be sorry. This is an adventure. What a storm! It's been brewing all day but I really didn't expect it so soon. What time is it?"

"Eight-thirty. The trouble is this is *such* a back road. Very few people travel on it at any time. And houses are few and far between. But I think that last glare of lightning showed one off to the right. As soon as the rain stops I'll go to it and see if I can get somebody to haul us out . . . or at least phone for help."

It was an hour before the storm passed. It was pitch dark by now and the ditch in which they sat so snugly was a rushing river.

"I'm going to try to make that house," said Pat resolutely.

"I'll go with you," said Suzanne. "I won't stay here alone. And I've got a flashlight in my bag."

They managed to get out of the car and out of the ditch. There was no use in hunting for the gate, if there was a gate, but when Suzanne's flashlight showed a place where it was possible to scramble over the fence they scrambled over it and through a wilderness of raspberry canes. Beyond this a barn loomed up and they had to circumnavigate it in mud. Finally they reached the house.

"No lights," said Pat as they mounted the crazy steps to a dilapidated veranda. "I'm afraid nobody lives here. There are several old uninhabited houses along this road and it's just our luck to strike one."

"What a queer, old-fashioned place!" said Suzanne, playing her flashlight over it. She couldn't have said anything more unfortunate. Pat, who had thawed out a trifle, froze up again.

She knocked on the door . . . knocked again . . . took up a board lying near and pounded vigorously . . . called aloud . . . finally yelled. There was no response.

"Let us see if it is locked," said Suzanne, trying the latch. It wasn't. They stepped in. The flashlight revealed a kitchen that did not seem to have been lived in for many a day. There was an old rusty stove, a trestle table, several dilapidated chairs, and a still more dilapidated couch.

"Any port in a storm," said Suzanne cheerfully. "I suggest, Miss Gardiner, that we camp here for the night. It's beginning to rain again . . . listen . . . and we may be miles from an inhabited house. We can bring in the rugs. You take the couch and I'll pick out the softest spot on the floor. We'll be dry at least and in the morning we can more easily get assistance."

Pat agreed that it was the only thing to do. They would probably not worry at Silver Bush. It had not been certain that she would return home that night . . . an old Queen's classmate had asked her to visit her. They went back to the car, got the rugs and locked it up. Pat insisted that Suzanne should take the couch and Suzanne was determined Pat should have it. They solved it by flipping a coin.

Pat wrapped a rug around her and curled up on the couch. Suzanne lay down on the floor with a cushion under her head. Neither expected to sleep. Who could sleep with a sploshy thud of rain falling regularly near one and rats scurrying overhead. After what seemed hours Suzanne called softly across the room,

"Are you asleep, Miss Gardiner?"

"No . . . I feel as if I could never sleep again."

Suzanne sat up.

"Then for heaven's sake let's talk. This is ghastly. I've a mortal horror of rats. There seem to be simply swarms of them in this house. Talk . . . talk. You needn't pretend to like me if you don't. And for the matter of that, as one woman to another, why don't you like me, Pat Gardiner? Why *won't* you like me? I thought you did that night by the fire. And we liked you . . . we thought there was something simply dear about you. And then when we called on our way to the concert . . . why, we seemed to be looking at you through glass! We couldn't get near you at all. David was hurt but I was furious . . . simply furious. I'm sure my blood boiled. I could hear it bubbling in my veins. Oh, how I hoped your husband would beat you! And yet, every night since, I've been watching your kitchen light and wondering what was going on in it and wishing we could drop in and fraternise. I can't imagine you and I not being friends . . . *real* friends. We were made for it. Isn't it Kipling who says, 'There is no gift like friendship'?"

"Yes . . . *Parnesius* in *Puck*," said Pat.

"Oh, you know *Puck* too? Now, why can't we give that gift to each other?"

"Did you think," said Pat in a choked voice, "that I could be friends with any one who . . . who laughed at Silver Bush?"

"Laugh at Silver Bush! Pat Gardiner, I never did. How could I? I've loved it from the first moment David and I looked down on it."

Pat sat up on the creaking couch.

"You . . . you asked in the Silverbridge store who lived in that *queer* old-fashioned place. Sid heard you."

"Pat! Let me think. Why, I remember . . . I *didn't* say 'queer.' I said, 'Who lives in that dear, quaint, old-fashioned house at the foot of the hill?' Sid forgot one of the adjectives and was mistaken in one of the others. Pat, I couldn't call Silver Bush 'queer.' You don't know how much I admire it. And I admire it all the more because it *is* old-fashioned. That is why I loved the Long House at first sight."

Pat felt the ice round her heart thawing rapidly. "Quaint" was complimentary rather than not and she didn't mind the "old-fashioned." And she did want to be friends with Suzanne. Perhaps Suzanne was prose where Bets had been poetry. But such prose!

"I'm sorry I froze up," she said frankly. "But I'm such a thin-skinned creature where Silver Bush is concerned. I couldn't bear to hear it called queer."

"I don't blame you. And now everything is going to be all right. We just *belong* somehow. Don't you feel it? You're all so nice. I love Judy . . . the wit and sympathy and blarney of her. And that wonderful old, wise, humorous face of hers. She's really a museum piece . . . there's nothing like her anywhere else in the world. You'll like us, too. I'm decent in spots and David is nice . . . sometimes he's very nice. One day he is a philosopher . . . the next day he is a child."

"Aren't all men?" said Pat, tremendously wise.

"David more than most, I think. He's had a rotten life, Pat. He was years getting over his shell-shock. It simply blotted out his career. He was so ambitious once. When he got better it was too late. He has been sub-editor of a Halifax paper for years . . . and hating it. His bit of a wife died, too, just a few months after their marriage. And I taught school . . . and hated it. Then old Uncle Murray died out west and left us some money . . . not a fortune but enough to live on. And so we became free. Free! Oh, Pat, you've never known what slavery meant so you don't know what freedom is. I *love* keeping house . . . it's really a lovely phrase, isn't it? Keeping it . . . holding it fast against the world . . . against all the forces trying to tear it open. And David has time to write his war book at last . . . he's always longed to. We are so happy . . . and we'll be happier still to have you as a friend. I don't believe you've any idea how nice you are, Pat. And now let's just talk all night."

They talked for a good part of it. And then Suzanne fell suddenly silent. Pat rather envied her the floor. It was level, at least . . . not all bumps and hollows, like the couch. Would it ever stop raining? How the windows rattled! Great heavens, what was that? Oh, only a brick blowing off the chimney and thumping down over the roof. Those rats! Oh for an hour of Gentleman Tom! It was . . . so nice . . . to be friends . . . with Suzanne . . . she hoped . . . a great wave of sleep rolled over Pat and engulfed her.

When she wakened the rain had ceased and the outside world was lying in the strange timeless light of early dawn. Pat raised herself on her elbow and looked out. Some squirrels were scolding and chattering in an old apple tree. A little pond at the foot of the slope was softly clear and pellucid, with spruce trees dark and soft beyond it. An old crone of a hemlock was shaking her head rebukingly at some giddy young saplings on the hill. Gossamer clouds were floating in a clear silvery eastern sky that looked as if it had not known a thunderstorm in a hundred years. And a huge black dog was sitting on the doorstep. This was like a place Judy used to tell of in Ireland that was haunted by the ghost of a black dog who bayed at the door before a death. However, this dog didn't look exactly like a ghost!

Suzanne was still asleep. Pat looked around and saw something that gave her an idea. She got to her feet cautiously.

7

When Suzanne wakened half an hour later she sat up and gazed around her in amazement. A most delectable odour came from a sizzling frying pan on the stove in which crisp bacon slices could be discerned. On the hearth was a plateful of golden-brown triangles of toast and Pat was putting a spoonful of tea in a battered old granite teapot.

The table was set with dishes and in the centre was a bouquet of ferns and meadow-queen in an old pickle jar.

"Pat, what magic is this? Are you a witch?"

"Not a bit of it. When I woke up I saw a pile of firewood behind the stove and a frying pan on a nail. I found plates and cups and knives and forks in the pantry. Evidently this house is occupied by times. The owner probably lives on some other farm and camps here for haying and harvest and things like that. I lit the fire and went out to the car. Took a chance with the dog . . . there *is* a dog . . . but he paid no attention to me. I had a package of bacon in the car and a couple of loaves of bread. Mother likes baker's toast, you know. I found some tea in the pantry . . . and so breakfast is served, madam."

"You're a born home-maker, Pat. This awful place actually looks quite homey and pleasant. I never thought a pickle jar bouquet could be so charming. And I'm hungry . . . I'm positively starving. Let's eat. Our first meal together . . . our first breaking of bread. I like that phrase . . . breaking bread together . . . don't you? Who is it speaks of 'bread of friendship'?"

"Carman," said Pat, dishing up her bacon.

"What a lovely *clean* morning it is!" said Suzanne, scrambling up. "Look, Pat, there's a big pine down by that pond. I love pines so much it hurts me. And I love crisp bacon and crisper toast. Thank heaven there is plenty of it. I never was so hungry in my life."

They were half through their breakfast when a queer strangled noise behind them startled them. They turned around . . . and stiffened with horror. In the hall doorway a man was standing . . . a tall, gaunt, unshaven creature in a motley collection of garments, with an extraordinarily long grey moustache, which didn't seem to belong to his lean, lantern-jawed face at all, hanging down on either side of his chin. This apparition was staring at them, apparently as much taken aback as they were.

"I thought I was over it," he said mournfully, shaking a grizzled head. "I mostly sleeps it off."

Pat rose and stammered out an explanation. The gentleman waved a hand at her.

"It's all right. Sorry you had to sleep on the floor. If I'd been awake I'd have give you my bed."

"We knocked . . . and called . . ."

"Just so. Old Gabe's trump couldn't have roused me last night. I was a bit lit up, to state facts. You did right to make yourselves at home. But it's a wonder the dog didn't tear you to pieces. He's a savage brute."

"He wasn't here when we came . . . and he seemed quite quiet this morning."

"'Zat a fact? Then I've been fooled. Bought him on the grounds that he was a tartar. I keep him here for tramps. My name is Nathaniel Butterbloom and I'm just sorter camping here while I take off the harvest. I live down at Three Corners."

"Won't you sit down and share our breakfast?" said Pat lamely.

"Don't care if I do," said Mr. Butterbloom and sat down without more ado. "Sorry there ain't no table-cloth. I had one but the rats et it."

Pat, exchanging a grin with Suzanne, poured him a cup of tea and helped him liberally to bacon and toast.

"This *is* a pleasant surprise and that's a fact. I've been scraping up my own meals. When I run out of provisions I fry a kitten," he added mournfully. "That barn out there is overrun with cats. I started out with three cats two years ago but there must be hundreds now."

"It's a wonder they don't keep the rats down," said Suzanne

mischievously. "And your roof leaks very badly, Mr. Butterbloom."

"Well," said Mr. Butterbloom placidly, "when it rains I can't get up on the roof to work, can I? And when it's fine it doesn't leak."

"I'm sorry there is no milk for your tea," said Pat.

"There's some in the pantry if the spiders haven't got into it."

"They have," said Pat briefly.

Mr. Butterbloom drank his cup of tea and champed his bacon in silence. Suzanne had just whispered solemnly to Pat, "A strong silent man," when he wiped his moustache with the back of his hand and spoke again. "What mought your names be?"

"This is Miss Kirk . . . and I'm one of the Gardiner girls from North Glen."

"Pleased to meet you both. And so you ain't married women?"

"No . . . no." Suzanne shook her head in demure sadness.

"Neither am I. I've a widder woman keeping house for me at Three Corners. She isn't much of a cook but she rubs my back for me. I have to have my back rubbed for half an hour every night before I can sleep . . . unless I'm lit up. I've heard of the Gardiners. Very genteel. I've never been in North Glen but I courted an old maid in South Glen for a while. I was younger then. She kept me dangling for a year and then up and married a widower. Since then I've sorter lost my enthusiasm for marriage."

He relapsed into silence while he polished off another helping. When the platter was empty he sighed deeply.

"Miss, that *was* a breakfast. After all, I may have made a mistake in not getting married." He fixed a fishy, speculative eye on Suzanne. "I haven't much book-larning but I've a couple of farms, nearly paid for."

Suzanne did not rise to this but she and Pat offered to wash the dishes before leaving.

"Never mind," said Mr. Butterbloom gloomily. "I don't wash dishes. The dog licks 'em clean. If you must be going I'll get out the hosses and haul your buzz-wagon out of the ditch."

He refused an offer of payment sadly.

"Didn't you cook my breakfast? But could you do with a kitten? There's several around just the right age."

Pat explained politely that they had all the cats needful at Silver Bush.

"It's of no consequence. I s'pose" . . . with a sigh . . . "it'll come in handy sometime when the cupboard is bare."

When they got out of sight of the house Pat stopped the car so that they might have a laugh. When two people have laughed . . . really laughed . . . together they are friends for life.

"Two unchaperoned females spending the night in a house with a drunken man," gasped Suzanne. "Let's pray the writer of 'North Glen Notes' never finds it out."

Nobody but Judy ever knew the whole story. Judy, of course, knew all about Nathaniel Butterbloom.

"A bit av a divil in his day," she said, "but he's too old now to cut up much. Innyhow, ye can be thankful he didn't ask ye to rub his back for him."

8

Pat had gone to her Secret Field, seeking the refreshment of soul she always found there. It was as beautiful and remote and mystic as ever, full of the sunshine of uncounted summers. The trees about it welcomed her and Pat flung herself down among the feathery bent grasses and listened to the silence until she felt at one with it and certain problems that had rather worried her of late dropped into proper focus as they always did in that sweet place, where the fairies still surely lingered if they lingered in the world at all. Under the ancient spell of the Secret Field Pat became a child again and could believe anything.

She went from it to Happiness by a narrow wood lane where ferns grew waist-high on either side. Pat knew all the little lanes in the woods and was known of them. They had their moods and their whims. One always seemed full of hidden laughter and furtive feet. One never seemed to know just where it wanted to go. In this one it always seemed as if you were in a temple. Overhead in the young, resinous fir boughs a wind was crooning a processional. The aroma drifting under the arches from old sunny hollows and lurking nooks was as the incense of worship, the exquisite shadows that filled the woods were acolytes, and the thoughts that came to her were like prayers.

"If one could only feel always like this," Pat had said once to Judy. "All the little worries swallowed up . . . all the petty spites and fears and disappointments forgotten . . . just love and peace and beauty."

"Oh, oh, but what wud there be lift for heaven, girl dear?" asked Judy.

The lane finally led out to the back fields of the other place and Pat found her way to Happiness and sat down near the Haunted Spring in a little hollow among the ferny cradle-hills. Far down before her, beyond the still, golden pastures, was the sapphire of the gulf. Over the westering hill of spruce a sunset of crimson and warm gold was fading out into apple green. And all this beauty was hers just for the looking. In these silent and remembered places she could think of old, beloved things . . . of sunsets she and Hilary had watched there together . . . Hilary, who at this very moment would be somewhere on the ocean on his way back from his summer in Europe. He had written her most delightful letters but she was glad he would soon be back in Canada. It would be pleasant to think that the Atlantic no longer rolled between them. She wondered a little wistfully why he couldn't have planned to stop off for a few days on the Island on his way to Toronto. She had asked him to. And he had never even referred to the invitation, although he had wound up his letter by saying "my love to Silver Bush." She could see from where she sat her name and his cut on a maple tree and overgrown with lichen. Pat sighed sentimentally. She wished she could be a child again with no worries. To be sure she had thought she had worries then . . . father going west and thinking you were ugly and Joe running away to sea and things like that. But there had been no men then . . . no question of beaus and people who persisted in turning into lovers when all you wanted of them was to be friends. Jim Mallory was in love with her now. She had met him at a dance in Silverbridge and, as Rae told Hilary in her next letter to him, he fell for her with a crash that could be heard for miles. He was a really fine fellow . . . "oh, oh, that's something like now," Judy said, the first evening he came to Silver Bush. Pat liked him terribly . . . almost as much as she liked Hilary and David. Rae told Judy she believed Pat was really in love but Judy had grown pessimistic under repeated disappointments.

"I've no great faith in it lasting," she said.

Pat, when she left home that night, hardly knew herself whether she wasn't a little bit in love or not. Certainly . . . the look in his eyes . . . the touch of his fingers when he lingered to say good-night under enchanted moons . . . she hadn't felt like that since the days of Lester Conway. But her hour in the Secret Field and Happiness cleared the matter up for her. No, liking wasn't enough . . . little thrills and raptures weren't enough.

There must be something more before she could dream of leaving Silver Bush. Poor Jim Mallory never had a chance after that and in a week or two Long Alec was to ask his wife in a mildly exasperated tone what the dickens the girl wanted anyways. Was nobody good enough for her?

"No," said Mother softly, "just as nobody was good enough for me till you came, Alec."

"Fiddlesticks!" said Long Alec. But he said it gently. After all, he was in no hurry to lose Pat.

Rae was another of Pat's little problems. She had passed her Entrance and wanted to go to Queen's. But just where was the money to come from? The crop was only fair: there had been some heavy losses in cattle: it was just barely possible to pay the interest on the mortgage this year. Dad wanted Rae to wait for another year and Rae was taking it hard. But in Happiness Pat decided that Rae must go. They would borrow the money from Uncle Tom who would be quite willing to lend it. Long Alec had a horror of borrowing. It had robbed him of many a night's sleep when he mortgaged Silver Bush to buy the Adams place. But Pat thought she could bring him round. Rae could pay back the loan in a year of teaching if she were lucky enough to get the home school. If not, in two. Everything seemed feasible in Happiness.

If only Judy were not going to Ireland! But Judy was so set on it now that nothing could turn her from it, even if anybody could have been selfish enough to try. She meant to sail in November and was already talking of passports and a new trunk.

"Sure and I cudn't be taking my old blue chist. It's a bit ould-fashioned. I tuk it to Australy wid me and thin to Canady but the times have changed since thin and a body must kape up wid thim. And I'll have to be getting a negleege, too, it's like. There do be a pink silk one wid white cherry blossoms all over it, marked down at Brennan's. Do ye be thinking I'm too old for it, girls dear?"

The idea of Judy, in a pink, cherry-blossomed "negleege" was something nobody at Silver Bush could contemplate with equanimity. But not a word was said to dissuade her. Pat assured her there was no longer any age in fashions.

Yes, Judy was going. The fact must be faced. But it no longer blocked up the future. The winter would pass . . . the spring would come . . . and Judy would come with it. Meanwhile, she was not taking Silver Bush to Ireland in her pocket. It would stay where it was, under its sheltering trees, with its fields lying cool and quiet around it. Pat, on her way home, stopped as ever at the top of the hill to gloat over it—this house where her dear ones were lying asleep.

For she had lingered long in Happiness and Silver Bush had gone to bed. There was still a light in Judy's kitchen chamber. Judy was probably hunting through her book of useful knowledge for remedies for seasickness. Though Uncle Tom had slyly suggested that her black bottle was as good an old reliable as any.

Pat was happy. In spite of everything the autumn world was beautiful. Some of its days might bring purple gifts . . . some might bring peace . . . all would bring loveliness.

"Darling Silver Bush!" said Pat. "How could anybody ever think of leaving you if she could help it?"

She remembered how sorry she had been in childhood for the Jamesons of Silverbridge . . . a family who were always moving round. To be sure, they seemed to like it . . . but the very thought of such an existence made Pat shiver.

Long Alec was horrified at first when Pat broached the idea of borrowing the money for Rae's year at Queen's. But she talked him round. It was beginning to be suspected at Silver Bush that Pat could twist dad around her little finger. Rae averred she did it by flattering him but Pat indignantly denied it.

"It would be of no use to try to flatter dad. You know as well as I do, Rae, that dad is impervious to flattery."

"Oh, oh, there do be no such man," muttered Judy with a grin. Flattery or not, Long Alec yielded and everything was soon arranged. Rae was wild with delight.

"If I'd had to wait till next year I'd have gone straight to the end of the world and jumped off. Emmy's going this year and Dot Robinson and you know we've always been such pals. And I'm going to study, Pat . . . oh, am I going to study? I know everybody says the Silver Bush girls are lookers and popular with the boys but have no brains. I mean to show them. Aunt Barbara says a girl doesn't need brains if she's pretty but that's an idea left over from the Victorians. Nowadays you've got to have brains to capitalise your good looks."

"Did ye be thinking that out for yersilf, darlint?" asked Judy.

"No," said Rae, one of whose charms was honesty, "I saw it in a magazine. Oh, but I'm happy! Pat darling, the world is only sixteen years old to-day. And can't we have a party before I go?"

"Of course, I've got that all planned out."

Pat loved to give parties and welcomed any excuse for one. And this one, being a sort of send-off for Rae, must be a special one.

"We'll have it a week from Friday night. We'll have a platform built in the silver bush for dancing and Chinese lanterns hung on the trees."

"Pat, how lovely! It will be like fairyland. Will there be a moon?"

"There will. I'll see to that," promised Pat.

"Don't make too many fine plans," said Sid warningly. "Remember when you do some of them always go agley."

Pat tossed a defiant brown head.

"What matter? I love making plans. I'll be making plans when I'm eighty. Let's get right to work, Rae, planning out the eats. We'll have some of those new ribbon sandwiches Norma had at her tea last week. They're so pretty."

Brown and golden heads bent together over recipe books. Delicious excitement began to pervade everything. Pat and Rae talked so much about the affair that Long Alec, who was taking a jaundiced view of things just then, growled to Judy that the fools of the world weren't all dead yet.

"Oh, oh, and don't ye think it'll be a rale dull place whin they are?" demanded Judy. "Do ye be thinking . . ." in a soothing whisper . . . "ye'd like a bacon-and-pittatie pie for supper?"

Long Alec brightened. After all, crops might be poor and you might be beginning to suspect that you had paid too much for the old Adams place but Judy's bacon-and-potato pies were something to live for. And girls were only young once.

9

Uncle Horace's letter added to the pleasant excitement. Uncle Horace, who had been living as a retired sea-captain in Vancouver, was coming home for a visit for the first time in twenty years. The older folk were naturally the more deeply stirred by this. Judy for a little while was neither to hold nor bind. But Pat and Rae were intrigued, too, at the thought of this mysterious, romantic uncle they had never seen, about whom Judy had told so many yarns . . . the Horace of the black-ink fruitcake and the monkey and the mutiny off Bombay. The man who, so Judy had said, kept the winds in jars. They *had* believed that once and the charm of it still hung around their thoughts of him.

He had mentioned Wednesday as the probable day of his arrival and on Tuesday Pat subjected Silver Bush to such a furbishing up that Sid asked sarcastically if Uncle Horace were coming to see them or their furniture.

"It's what we are to do wid thim blessed cats do be puzzling me," worried Judy. "Yer Uncle Horace hates cats as bad as ould Cousin Nicholas himsilf cud do."

"Oh, *do* you remember Cousin Nicholas coming downstairs that rainy Christmas night little Mary was born?" giggled Rae.

"Rimimber, is it? Oh, oh, cud I iver be forgetting him, standing there looking like the wrath av God. And now we do be having three to kape out av Horace's way. To be sure, Gintleman Tom won't be bothering him much but Bold-and-Bad and that Squedunk are so frindly. We'll just have to see that the dure av the Poet's room is kipt tight shut and trust the rist to the Good Man Above. It's the lucky thing we've got rid av Popka."

Pat did not know if it were so lucky. It had half-broken her heart to give Popka away to the distant cousin down at East Point. He was such a beautiful cat with his fluffy Maltese coat and white paws, and so affectionate. Why he used to go over the house at night, visit all the bedrooms and kiss all the sleepers. And the purrs of him! He could out-purr Bold-and-Bad and Squedunk together. It was a shame to give him away. But Long Alec was adamant. Three cats were enough . . . more than enough . . . for any house. He would really like to be sure of an unoccupied chair once in a while. Popka must go . . . and Popka went. Pat and Rae both cried when his new owner bore him away, shrieking piteously in a basket.

Uncle Horace did not come Wednesday, nor on Thursday or Friday. Long Alec shrugged disappointedly. Likely he had changed his mind at the last minute and wouldn't come at all. That was Horace all over.

"But if he does come I want all you folks to mind your p's and q's," said Long Alec warningly. "Horace is a bit peculiar in some ways. He was a regular martinet on board ship I understand. Everything had to be just so, running smooth as oil. And he was just the same about a house. That's why he never married, he told us the last time he was home. Couldn't find a wife neat enough. It's all very well to listen to Judy's yarns of his pranks. He used to be a rip for them, I admit, but nobody else was to play them and accidents had no place in his scheme of things. I don't know what he'll think of your dance. The last time he was home he was badly down on dancing."

"And him the liveliest dancer on the Island forty years ago," marvelled Judy.

"He's reformed since then . . . and the reformed ones are generally the stiffest. Anyhow, all of you do your best to keep things moving smoothly. I don't want Horace to go away thinking things not lawful to be uttered of my household."

Pat and Rae promised, and then forgot all about him in the excitement of the party preparations. Hundreds of last minute things to do. Cream to be whipped . . . floors and furniture to be polished . . . at the very last an extra cake to be made because Pat was afraid they mightn't have enough. Judy declared that the queen's pantry couldn't be better stocked but gave in when Pat insisted.

"Oh, oh, ye do be the mistress here," she said with a touch of grandeur. Pat made an old-fashioned jelly roll that would cut into golden coils with ruby jelly between them. A pretty cake . . . just as pretty as any new-fangled thing. Where on earth was Rae? Prinking in her room of course . . . fussing over her hair. And so much yet to be seen to! Pat had always been conscious of a sneaking sympathy with Martha. But she was very happy. Silver Bush looked beautiful. She loved the shining surfaces . . . the flowers in bowls all over the house . . . the glitter of glass and silver in the dining-room . . . everything in the best Gardiner tradition. Sid had strung Chinese lanterns on the trees all around the platform and Tillytuck was to be fiddler, with old Matt Corcoran from the Bridge to spell him. The day of gold would be followed by a night of silver, for the weather was behaving perfectly. And at dusk, pretty girls and girls not so pretty were gazing into mirrors all over the two Glens and Silverbridge and Bay Shore. Judy, with groans that could not be uttered, was donning her wine-hued dress and Tillytuck was struggling into a white collar in the granary loft. Even the cats were giving their flanks a few extra licks. For the party at Silver Bush was easily the event of the season.

Pat, hurrying into a frock of daffodil chiffon, fluffed out her dark-brown cloud of hair and looked in her mirror with pleasure. She was feeling a trifle tired but her reflection heartened her up wonderfully. She had forgotten that she was really rather pretty. "Nae beauty" of course . . . Pat had never forgotten Great-great-Aunt Hannah's dictum . . . but quite pleasant to look upon.

And Rae, in her dress of delphinium blue, was a dream.

"Blue is really the loveliest colour in the world," thought Pat. "I'm sorry I can never wear it."

The dress suited Rae. But for that matter any dress did. Rae's clothes always seemed to *belong* to her. You could never imagine any one else wearing them. Once she slipped a dress over that rippling gold-brown head you thought she must have been born in it. Pat reflected with a thrill of pride that she had never seen this darling sister looking so lovely. Her eyes had such starry lights in them behind her long lashes . . . eyes that were as full of charm as wood violets. To be sure, Rae wouldn't have wanted her eyes compared to wood violets . . . or forget-me-nots either. That was Victorian. Cornflower blue, now . . . that sounded so much more up to date. Don Robinson had told her at the last club dance that her eyes were cornflower blue.

The Binnies were the first to come . . . "spying out the land," Judy vowed. They heard May's laughter far down the lane. "Ye always hear her afore ye see her, that one," sniffed Judy. May was very gorgeous in a gown of cheap, mail-order radium lace that broke in billows around her feet and afforded a wonderful view of most of the bones in her spine. She tapped Pat condescendingly on the shoulder and said,

"You look dragged to death, darling. If I were you I'd stay in bed all day to-morrow. Ma always makes me do that after a spree."

Pat shrugged away from that hateful, fat, dimpled hand with its nails stained coral. What an intolerable phrase . . . "if I were you"! As if a Binnie ever could be a Gardiner! She was thankful that the arrival of the Russells and Uncle Brian's girls saved her from the necessity of replying. Winnie was looking like a girl again to-night, in spite of her two children. For there was a new baby at the Bay Shore and Judy was going to take care of it during the evening, as she loved to do.

Pat did not dance till late. There were too many things to see to. And even when she was free she liked better to stand a little in the background, where a clump of stately white fox-glove spikes glimmered against the edge of the birches, and gloat over the whole scene. Everything was going beautifully. The dreamy August night seemed like a cup of fragrance that had spilled over. The gay lilt of Tillytuck's fiddle rippled through the moonlight to die away magically, through green, enchanted boughs, into the beautiful silences of the silver bush and the misty, glimmering fields beyond. It was really a wonder that Wild Dick didn't rise up out of his grave to dance to it.

The platform, full of flower-like faces and flower-like dresses, looked so pretty. Everybody seemed happy. How sweet darling mother looked, sitting among the young folks like a fine white queen, her gold-brown eyes shining with pleasure. Uncle Tom was as young as anybody, dancing as blithely as if he had never heard of Mrs. Merridew. His beard had grown out in all its old magnificence and the streaks of grey in it did not show in that mellow light. What a lovely dress Suzanne was wearing . . . green crêpe and green lace swirling about her feet. Suzanne was not really pretty . . . she said herself that she had a mouth like a gargoyle . . . but she was distinguished looking . . . a friend to be proud of. May Binnie, with all her flashing, full-blown beauty, looked almost comical beside her. Poor Rex Miller was not there. At home, sulking, Pat thought with a regretful shrug. She had not exactly refused him two evenings before . . . Pat did not often actually have to refuse her lovers . . . she was, as Judy would have said, too diplomatic-like . . . but she had the knack of delicately making them understand a certain thing and thus avoiding for herself and them the awkwardness of a blunt "no."

Where was Sid's Dorothy, with her sweet dark face? She had not come either. Pat wondered why. She hated herself for half hoping Sid and Dorothy had quarrelled. But if that were the reason Sid was dancing so often with May Binnie Pat felt she was already punished for her selfish hope. Of course May was a good dancer . . . of her kind. At any rate, the boys all liked to dance with her. May was never in any danger of being a wallflower.

Amy's new ring flashed on the shoulder of her partner as she drifted by. Amy was engaged. Another change. What a pity people had to grow up . . . and get married . . . and go away. She had always liked Amy much better than Norma. She recalled with considerable relish the time she had slapped Norma's face for making fun of Silver Bush. Norma never dared to do it again.

What an exquisite profile Rae had as she lifted her face to her partner . . . a tall Silverbridge boy. Rae had no lack of partners either. And the way she had of looking at them! Really, the child was getting to be quite a handful. Was there actually anybody standing back in the shadows behind Tillytuck? Pat had fancied several times there was but could never be quite sure. Probably Uncle Tom's hired man.

David hunted her out and insisted on her dancing . . . and sitting out in the silver bush with him afterwards . . . just far enough away from the dancers to make Tillytuck's fiddling sound like fairy music. Pat liked both. David was a capital dancer and she loved to talk with him. He had such a charming voice. Sometimes he was a little bitter but there was such a stimulating pungency about his bitterness. Like choke cherries. They puckered your mouth horribly but still you hankered after them. She would far rather sit here and talk to David than dance with boys who held you closer than you liked and paid you silly compliments, most of which they had picked up from the talkies.

Then a run into the house to see the baby. It was so heavenly to watch a baby asleep, with Judy crooning over it like an old weather-beaten Madonna. Judy was a bit upset on several counts.

"Patsy darlint, there do be some couples spooning on the flat monnymints in the graveyard. Do ye be thinking that dacent now?"

"It's not in the best of taste but we can hardly turn them out of it, Judy. It's only on Wild Dick's and Weeping Willy's. Wild Dick would sympathise with them and as for Weeping Willy . . . who cares for his feelings? We don't count *him* among our glorious dead . . . sitting down and crying instead of going bravely to work. Is that all that's worrying you, Judy?"

"It's not worrying I am but there's been a mysterious disappearance. The roll-jelly cake has gone out av the pantry and the bowl av whipped crame in the ice-house is gone. Siddy forgot to lock it. Bold-and-Bad do be licking his chops very suspicious-like but he'd have been laving the bowl at laste. Of coorse I can be whipping up more crame in a brace av shakes. But who cud have took the cake, Patsy? Niver did the like happen before."

"I suppose some of the boys have been playing tricks. Never mind, Judy, there's plenty of cake . . . you said so yourself."

"But the impidence av thim . . . coming into me pantry like that. Likely enough it was Sam Binnie. Patsy darlint, Rex Miller isn't here. Ye haven't been quarrelling wid him, have ye now?"

"No, Judy darling. But he won't be coming around any more. I couldn't help it. He was nice . . . I liked him but . . . Judy, don't be looking like that. When I asked him a question . . . any question . . . I always knew exactly what he'd answer. And he never . . . really never, Judy . . . laughs in the right place."

"Mebbe ye cud have taught him to laugh in the right place," said Judy sarcastically.

"I don't think I could. One has to be born knowing that. So I had to wave him gently away . . . . 'symbolically speaking.'"

"Oh, oh, ye'll be doing that once too often, me jewel," predicted Judy darkly.

"Judy, this love business is no end of a bother. 'In life's morning march when my bosom was young' I thought it must be tremendously romantic. But it's just a nuisance. Life would be much simpler if there were nothing of the sort."

"Oh, oh, simple, is it? A bit dull, I'm thinking. I've niver had inny love affairs mesilf to spake av but oh, the fun I've had watching other people's!"

Pat had been able to sidetrack Rex Miller "diplomatically" but she was not so fortunate with Samuel MacLeod . . . probably because it had never occurred to her that he had any "intentions" regarding her. Samuel . . . nobody ever called him Sam . . . it simply couldn't be done . . . came now and again to Silver Bush to confer with Pat and Rae on the programs of the Young People's Society, of which he was president, but no one, not even Judy, ever looked upon him as a possible beau. And now after supper, having asked Pat to dance . . . Rae said that dancing with Samuel was almost as solemn a performance as leading the Young People's . . . he followed it up by asking her to go for a walk in the garden. Pat steered him past the graveyard, which he seemed to mistake for the garden, and got him into the delphinium walk. And, standing there, even more dreadfully conscious of hands and feet than usual, he told her that his heart had chosen her for the supreme object of its love and that if she would like to be Mrs. Samuel MacLeod she had only to say the word.

Pat was so dumbfounded that she couldn't speak at all at first and it was not till Samuel, taking her silence for maidenly consent began gingerly to put a long arm around her, that she came to the surface and managed to gasp out,

"Oh, no . . . no . . . I don't think I can . . . I mean, I'm sure I can't. Oh, it's utterly impossible."

As she spoke there was a smothered giggle on the other side of the delphiniums and Emmy Madison and Dot Robinson scuttled away across the lawn.

"Oh, I'm so sorry," cried Pat. "I never thought anybody was there."

"It doesn't matter," said Samuel, with a dignity that somehow did not misbecome him. "I am not ashamed to have people know that I aspired to you."

In spite of his absurd Victorian phrases Pat found herself for the first time rather liking him. He couldn't help being a South Glen MacLeod. They were all like that. And she made up her mind that she would never entertain Judy or Suzanne by an account of this proposal . . . though to be sure that wretched Emmy and Dot would spread it all over the clan.

All in all, Pat drew a breath of relief when the last guest had gone and the last lantern candle expired, leaving the silver bush to its dreams and its moonlight. The party had been a tremendous success . . . "the nicest party I've ever been to," Suzanne whispered before she took the hill road. "And that supper! Come up to-morrow night and we'll have a good pi-jaw about everything."

But when you were hostess there was, as Judy said, "a bit av a strain," especially with the proposal of Samuel thrown in. She turned from the gate and ran up the back walk, crushing the damp mint as she ran. The late August night had grown a bit chilly and Judy's kitchen, where a fire had been lit to brew the coffee, seemed attractive.

Pat halted in the doorway in amazement. There were Uncle Tom and the aunts . . . mother . . . Rae . . . Judy . . . Tillytuck . . . dad . . . and Uncle Horace! For of course the stranger could be nobody else.

Pat felt a little bit dazed as he rose to shake hands with her. This was not the Uncle Horace she had pictured . . . neither the genial old rascal of Judy's yarns nor the typical tar of dad's reminiscences. He was tall and thin and saturnine, with hair of pepper and salt. With his long lean face and shell-rimmed spectacles he looked more like a somewhat dyspeptic minister than a retired sea-captain. To be sure, there was something about his mouth . . . and his keen blue eyes . . . Pat felt that she wouldn't have liked to head that mutiny against him.

"This is Pat," said Long Alec.

"Humph! I've been hearing things about you," grunted Uncle Horace as he shook hands.

Pat hadn't a glimmer whether the things were complimentary or the reverse and retreated into herself. Uncle Horace, it seemed, had arrived unexpectedly, walking up from Silverbridge. Finding a party in full swing he had decided not to show himself until it was over.

"Had some fun watching the dance from the bush," he said. "Some pretty girls clothed in smiles . . . and not much else. I never expected to see P.E. Island girls at a dance with no clothes on."

"No clothes," said Aunt Edith, rather staggered. She had not graced the party but had come over to find out what was keeping Tom so late.

"Well, none to speak of. There were three girls there with no back at all to their frocks. Times have changed since we were young, Alec."

"For the better I should think," said Rae pertly. "It must have been awful . . . dresses lined and re-lined, sleeves as big as balloons, and rats in your hair."

Uncle Horace looked at her meditatively, as if wondering what kind of an insect she was, fitted his finger-tips carefully together, and went on with his tale. For the first time in her life Rae Gardiner felt squelched.

"When I felt that I needed a little sustenance I slipped into the pantry when the coast was clear and got me a cake. A real good cake . . . roll-jelly . . . I didn't think they made them now. Then I scouted around for some milk and found a bowl of whipped cream in the ice-house. 'Plenty more where that came from,' thought I. Made a pretty decent meal."

"And me blaming Sam Binnie," said Judy. "Oh, oh, I'll be begging his pardon, Binnie and all as he is."

"I kept back in the bush . . . had to," said Uncle Horace. "If I moved I fell over some canoodling couple. There were people in love all over the place."

"Love is in the air at Silver Bush, symbolically speaking," said Tillytuck. "I find it rather pleasant. The little girls' love affairs give a flavour to life."

"But Judy here isn't married yet," said Uncle Horace gravely.

"Oh, oh, I cudn't support a husband," sighed Judy.

"Don't you think it's time?" said Uncle Horace gravely. "We're none of us getting younger, you know, Judy."

"But I'm hoping some av us do be getting a liddle wiser," retorted Judy witheringly.

But she was plainly in high cockalorum. Horace had always had a warm spot in her heart and in her eyes he was still a boy.

"I got a drink of the old well while you were at supper," said Uncle

Horace in a different tone. "There's none like it the world over. I've always understood David and his craving for a drink from the well at Bethlehem. And the ferns along the road from Silverbridge. I've smelled smells all the world over, east and west, and there's no perfume like the fragrance of spice ferns as you walk along a P.E. Island road on a summer evening. Well, young folks like your girls and Judy mayn't mind staying up all night, Alec, but I'm not equal to it any longer. Judy, do you suppose it's possible to have fried chicken for breakfast?"

"How like a man!" Rae telegraphed in disgust to Pat. Expecting to have fried chicken for breakfast when it was four o'clock after a party! But Judy was actually looking pleased.

"There do be a pair av young roosters out there just asking for it," she said meditatively.

Judy and Pat and Rae had a last word when everybody had gone.

"Oh, oh, but I'm faling like a bit av chewed string," sighed Judy. "Howiver, the party was a grand success and aven Tillytuck sitting down on a shate av fly-paper in the pantry where he did have no business to be and thin strutting pompous-like across the platform wid it stuck to his pants cudn't be called inny refliction on Silver Bush. He did be purtinding to be mad about it but I'm belaving he did it on purpose to make a sinsation. Oh, oh, ye cud have knocked me down wid a feather whin I was after clearing up the supper dishes. I did be hearing a thud . . . and there was me fine Horace full lingth on the floor ye rubbed up so well, Patsy. 'Tarrible slippy floor ye've got, woman,' was all he said. Ye niver cud be telling if Horace was mad or if he wasn't."

"I like him," said Pat, who had made up her mind about him when he talked of the well and the ferns.

"Pat, what on earth were you and Samuel MacLeod doing in the garden?" asked Rae.

"Oh, just moonlighting," answered Pat, demure as an owl.

"I never saw anything so funny as the two of you dancing together. He looked like a windmill in a fit."

"Don't ye be making fun av the poor boy," said Judy. "He can't be hilping his long arms and legs. At that, it do be better than being sawed off. And while he cudn't be said to talk he does be managing to get things said."

"He gets them said all right," thought Pat. But she heroically contented herself with thinking of it.

10

Uncle Horace did not prove hard to entertain. When he was not talking over old times with dad or Uncle Tom or Judy he was reading sentimental novels . . . the more sentimental the better. When he had exhausted the Silver Bush library he borrowed from the neighbours. But the book David Kirk lent him did not please him at all.

"They don't get married at the last," he grumbled. "I don't care a hoot for a book where they don't get properly married . . . or hanged . . . at the last. These modern novels that leave everything unfinished annoy me. And the heroines are all too old. I don't like 'em a day over sixteen."

"But things are often unfinished in real life," said Pat, who had picked up the idea from David.

"All the more reason why they should come right in books," said Uncle Horace testily. "Real life! We get enough real life living. *I* like fairy tales. I like a nice snug tidy ending in a book with all the loose ends tucked in. Judy's yarns never left things in the air. That's why she's always been such a corking success as a story-teller."

Uncle Horace was no mean story-teller himself when they could get him going . . . which wasn't always. Around Judy's kitchen fire in the cool evenings he would loosen up. They heard the tale of his being wrecked on the Magdalens on his first voyage . . . of the shark crashing through the glass roof of his cabin and landing on the dinner table . . . of the ghost of the black dog that haunted one of his ships and foreboded misfortune.

"Did you ever see it yourself?" asked David Kirk with a sceptical twist to his lips.

Uncle Horace looked at him witheringly.

"Yes . . . once," he said. "Before the mutiny off Bombay."

His listeners shivered. When Tillytuck and Judy told tales of seeing ghosts nobody minded or believed it. But it was different with Uncle Horace someway. Still, David stuck to his guns. Sailors were always superstitious.

"You don't mean to say that you really believe in ghosts, Captain Gardiner?"

Uncle Horace looked through David and far away.

"I believe what I see, sir. It may be that my eyes deceived me. Not everybody can see ghosts. It is a gift."

"A gift I wasn't dowered with," said Suzanne, a trifle too complacently. Uncle Horace demolished her with one of those rare looks of his. Suzanne afterwards told Pat that she felt as if that look had bored a hole clean through her and shown her to be hollow and empty.

The next excitement was Amy's wedding to which everyone at Silver Bush and Swallowfield went through a pouring rain, except Judy and mother. Uncle Horace would not go in the car. It transpired that he had never been in a car and was determined he never would be. So he went with Uncle Tom in the phaeton and got well drenched for his prejudices. It rained all day. But Uncle Horace came back in high good humour.

"Thank goodness there's a bride or two left in the world yet," he said as he came dripping into the kitchen where Rae, who had reached home before him, was describing to a greedy Judy how Amy's bridal veil of tulle was held to her head in the latest fashion by a triple strand of pearls, with white gardenias at the back. Judy didn't feel that what-do-you-call-'ems could be so lucky as orange blossoms but she knew without asking that the wedding feast would have been more fashionable than filling and she had a "liddle bite" ready for everybody as they came in. Pat was last of all, having lingered to help Aunt Jessie and Norma. She looked around at the bright, homely picture with satisfaction. It was dismal to start anywhere in rain: but to come home in rain was pleasant . . . to step from cold and wet into warmth and welcome. The only thing she missed was the cats. Since Uncle Horace's coming they had been religiously banished. Gentleman Tom spent his leisure in the kitchen chamber, Tillytuck kept a disgruntled Bold-and-Bad in the granary and Squedunk was a patient prisoner in the church barn. Only when Uncle Horace was away were they allowed to sneak back into the kitchen.

But that night, while everybody slumbered in the comfort of Silver Bush a poor, foot-sore, half-dead little cat came crawling up the lane. It was Popka, cold, tired, hungry on the last lap of his hundred mile journey from East Point. When he reached the well-remembered doorstone he paused and tried to lick his wet fur into some semblance of decency before meowing faintly and pitifully for admittance. But the door of Silver Bush remained cruelly closed. Not even Judy in the kitchen chamber heard that feeble cry. Poor Popka dragged himself around to the back and there discovered the broken pane in the cellar window which Judy had been lamenting for a week. In the kitchen he found a saucer of milk under the table which an overstuffed Bold-and-Bad had left when Judy had smuggled him in for his supper. Heartened by this Popka looked happily about him. It was home. The kitchen was warm and cosy . . . there were several inviting cushions. But Popka craved the comfort of contact with some of his human friends. On four weary legs he climbed the stairs. Alas, every door but one was closed to him. The door of the Poet's room was half open. Popka slipped in. Ah, here was companionship. Popka jumped on the bed.

Pat, going downstairs before any one else, saw a sight through the door of the Poet's room that both horrified and delighted her. Popka, her dear, lamented Popka, was curled into a placid vibrant ball on Uncle Horace's stomach. Pat slipped in, gently lifted Popka and gently departed, leaving Uncle Horace apparently undisturbed. But when Uncle Horace came down to breakfast his first words were,

"Who came in and took my cat?"

"I did," confessed Pat. "I thought you hated cats."

"Used to," said Uncle Horace. "Couldn't bear 'em years ago. Wiser now. Found out they made life worth living. Been wondering why you didn't have any round. Used to be too much cat here if anything. Missed 'em. Tell you tonight how I come to make friends with the tribe."

That night around the kitchen fire, while Popka purred on his knee and Bold-and-Bad winked at him from the lounge, Uncle Horace told of the mystery of the black cat with the bows of ribbon in its ears.

"It was the last voyage I made on this side of the world. We sailed from Halifax for China and the first mate had his young brother with him . . . a lad of seventeen. He'd fetched his favourite cat along with him . . . Pills was his name. The cat's I mean, not the boy's. The boy's name was Geordie. Pills was black . . . the blackest thing you ever saw, with one white shoe, and cute as a pet fox. Both the cat's ears had been punched and he was togged out with little bows of red ribbon tied in 'em. That proud he was of them, too! Once when Geordie took them out to put fresh ones in and didn't do it for a day Pills just sulked till he had his ribbons back. Every one on board made a pet of him, except Cannibal Jim . . ."

"Cannibal Jim? Why was he called that?" asked Rae.

Uncle Horace frowned at her. He did not like interruptions.

"Don't know, miss. Never asked him. It was his own business. I'd

410

never liked cats before myself but I couldn't help liking Pills. I got just as fond of him as the others and felt as tickled as could be when he favoured me by coming to sleep in my cabin at night. 'Twasn't everybody he'd sleep with. No, sir! That cat picked his bedfellows. There were only three people he'd sleep with . . . Geordie and me and the cook. Turn and turn about. He never got mixed up. One night the cook took him when it was my turn but that cat threw fits till the cook let him go and in less than a minute he was kneading his paws on my stomach. Next night was the cook's regular turn but Pills punished him by acting up again and went and slept in a coil of rope on deck. He wouldn't sleep with Geordie or me out of our turn but the cook had to be dealt with. Well, right in the middle of the Indian Ocean Pills disappeared . . . clean disappeared. We kept hoping for days he'd turn up but he never did. I'd hard work to keep the crew from mobbing Cannibal Jim, for every one believed he'd thrown Pills overboard, though he swore till all was blue he'd never touched him. And now for the part you won't believe. Six months later that cat walks into his own old home in Halifax and curled up on his own special cushion. That's a fact, explain it as you like. He was mighty thin and his feet were bleeding but Geordie's mother knew him at once by the bows in his ears. She took it into her head the ship was lost and that somehow the cat had survived and got home. She nearly went crazy till she found out different. I went to see Pills when I got back and he knew me right off . . . draped himself around my legs and purred like mad. There wasn't any doubt in the world that it was Pills."

"But, Uncle Horace, how *could* he have got home?"

"Well, the only explanation I could figure out was this. The day before we missed Pills we'd been hailed by a ship, the *Alice Lee* bound for Boston, U. S. A. They had sickness on board and had run out of some drug, I forget what, and the captain wanted to know if we could let him have some. We could, so he sent a boat across with two men in it. I concluded that one of them swiped the cat. Afterwards Geordie recalled that Pills had been sitting, perky and impudent, on a coil of rope as the men came over the side. He was never seen again but he wasn't missed till the next day. It was Geordie's turn for him that night but Geordie thought cook had him and being sorry for cook, who was looking like a lopsided squirrel with toothache, made no fuss. He didn't get worried till the next afternoon. The men all maintained that no sailor would ever steal another ship's cat, especially a black one, and blamed Cannibal Jim, as I've said. But I never believed even Cannibal Jim would play fast and loose with luck that way. We certainly had nothing but squalls and typhoons the rest of the voyage and finally a man overboard. But the most puzzling thing was that Pills took six months to get home. I went west that year and took to voyaging the Pacific so I never fell in with any of the *Alice Lee's* crew again but I did find out that she got to Boston two months after she'd passed us. Suppose Pills was on her. That left four months to be accounted for. Where was he? I'll tell you where he was. Travelling the miles between Boston and Halifax on his own black legs."

Tillytuck snorted incredulously.

"Either that or he swum it," said Uncle Horace sternly. "I find it easier to believe he walked. Don't ask me how he knew the road. I tell you that I saw, then and there, that cats had forgotten more than human beings ever knew and I made up my mind to cultivate their society. When this little fellow hopped up on me last night I just told him to pick out a soft spot on my old carcase and snuggle down."

By the time Uncle Horace's visit drew near its close they had all decided that they liked him tremendously, even if he did disapprove of their clothes and avert his eyes in horror from the pale green and pink and orchid silk panties on the line Monday mornings. They thought, too, that Uncle Horace liked them, though they couldn't feel sure of it. Pat was sure, however, that he must approve of Silver Bush. Everything went smoothly until the very last day . . . and *it* was really dreadful. In the first place Sid upset Judy's bowl of breakfast pancake batter on the floor and Winnie's baby crawled into it. Of course Uncle Horace had to appear at the very worst moment before the baby could be even picked up, and probably thought that was how they amused babies at Silver Bush. Then Rae put an unopened can of peas on the stove to heat for dinner. The can exploded with a bang, the kitchen was full of steam and particles of peas, and Uncle Horace got a burn on the cheek where the can struck him. To crown all, Rae dared him to go to Silverbridge in the car with her after supper and Uncle Horace, though he had never been in a car, vowed no girl should stump him and got in. Nobody knew what went wrong . . . Rae was considered a good driver . . . but the car, instead of going down the lane dashed through the paling fence, struck the church barn, and finished up against a tree. No harm was done except a bent bumper and Rae and Uncle Horace proceeded on their way. Uncle Horace did not seem disturbed. He said when he came home he had supposed it was just Rae's way of starting and he thought he'd get a car of his own when he went back to the coast.

"Sure and some av ye must have seen a fairy, wid all the bad luck we've had today," gasped Judy when he was safely off to bed.

"Today simply hasn't happened. I cut it out of the week," said Pat ruefully. "After all our efforts to make a good impression! But did you ever see anything funnier than his expression when that can hit him?"

"Yes . . . his expression when I sideswiped the church barn," said Rae.

They both shrieked with laughter.

"I am afraid Uncle Horace will think we are all terrible and you in particular, Rae."

But Uncle Horace did not think so. That evening he told Long Alec he wanted to pay the expenses of Rae's year at Queen's.

"She's a gallant girl and easy on the eye," he said. "I've neither chick nor child of my own. I like your girls, Alec. They can laugh when things go wrong and I like that. Any one can laugh when it's all smooth sailing. I'll not be east again, Alec, but I'm glad I came for once. It's been good to see old Judy again. Those plum tarts of hers with whipped cream! My stomach will never be the same again but it was worth it. I'm glad you keep up all the old traditions here."

"One does one's best," said Long Alec modestly.

But Judy in the kitchen was shaking her grey bob sorrowfully at Gentleman Tom.

"Young Horace don't be young inny longer. All the divilment has gone out av him. And looking so solemn! There was a time the solemner he looked the more mischief he was plotting. Oh, oh!" Judy sighed. "I'm fearing we do all be getting a bit ould, cat dear."

THE THIRD YEAR

1

Rae was off to Queen's and Pat was very lonely. Of course Rae came home every Friday night, just as Pat had done in her Queen's year, and they had hilarious week ends. But the rest of the time was hard to endure. No Rae to laugh and gossip with . . . no Rae to talk over the day with at bedtime . . . no Rae to sleep in the little white bed beside her own. Pat cried herself to sleep for several nights, and then devoted herself to Silver Bush more passionately than ever.

Rae, after her first homesick week, liked town and college very much, though she was sometimes cold in her boarding house bed and the only window of her room looked out on the blank brick wall of the next house instead of a flower garden and green fields and misty hills.

And Judy was getting ready for her trip to Ireland. She was to go in November with the Patterson family from Summerside, who were revisiting the old sod, and all through October little else was talked of at Silver Bush. Pat, though she hated the thought of Judy going, threw herself heart and soul into the preparations. Judy must and should have this wonderful trip to her old home after her life of hard work. Everybody was interested. Long Alec went to town and got Judy her steamer trunk. Judy looked a bit strange when he dumped it on the walk.

"Oh, oh, I *know* I do be going . . . but I can't belave it, Patsy. That trunk there . . . I can't fale it belongs to me. If it was the old blue chist now . . ."

But of course the old blue chest couldn't be taken to Ireland. And Judy at last believed she was going when a paragraph in the "North Glen Notes" announced that Miss Judy Plum of Silver Bush would spend the winter with her relatives in Ireland. Judy looked queerer than ever when she saw it. It seemed to make everything so irrevocable.

"Patsy darlint, it must be the will av the Good Man Above that I'm to go," she said when she read it.

"Nothing like a change, as old Murdoch MacGonigal said when he turned over in his grave," remarked Tillytuck cheerfully.

Everybody gave Judy something. Uncle Tom gave a leather suit-case and mother a beautiful brush and comb and hand mirror.

"Oh, oh, niver did I be thinking I'd have a t'ilet set av me own," said Judy. "Talk av the silver backed ones the Bishop stole! And wid me monnygram on the back av the looking glass! I do be hoping me ould uncle will have sinse enough lift to take in the grandeur av it."

Pat gave her a "negleege" and Aunt Barbara gave her a crinkly scarf of cardinal crêpe which she had worn only once and which Judy had greatly admired. Even Aunt Edith gave her a grey hug-me-tight with a purple border. Pat nearly went into kinks at the thought of Judy in such a thing but Judy was rather touched.

"Sure and it was rale kind av Edith. I hadn't ixpicted it for we've niver been what ye might call cronies. Mebbe I'll see some poor ould lady in Ireland that it'll set."

Judy's travelling dress exercised them all but one was finally got that pleased her. Also a grey felt hat with a smart, tiny scarlet feather in it. Judy tried the whole outfit on one night in the kitchen chamber and was so scared by her stylish reflection in the cracked mirror that she was for tearing everything off immediately.

"Oh, oh, it doesn't look like *me* Patsy. It does be frightening me. Will I iver get back into mesilf?"

But Pat made her go down to the kitchen and show herself to everybody. And everybody felt that this hatted and coated and scarlet-feathered Judy *was* a stranger but everybody paid her compliments and Tillytuck said if he'd ever suspected what a fine-looking woman she really was there was no knowing what might have happened.

"I hope nothing will prevent Judy from going," said Rae. "It would break her heart to be disappointed now. But when I think of coming home Friday nights and Judy not here! And that horrid old Mrs. Bob Robinson, with her pussy cat face!" Rae blinked her eyes fiercely.

"Mrs. Robinson isn't really so bad, Rae," protested Pat half-heartedly. "At any rate she is the best we can get and it's only for the winter."

"I tell you she's an inquisitive, snooping old thing," snapped Rae. "*You* didn't see her going down the walk after you'd hired her, giving her chops a sly lick of self-satisfaction every three steps. I did. And I know she was thinking, '*I'll* show them what proper housekeeping is at Silver Bush.'"

One burning question had been . . . who was to be got in to help Pat for the winter? From several candidates Mrs. Bob Robinson of Silverbridge was finally chosen, as the least objectionable. Tillytuck didn't take to her and nicknamed her Mrs. Puddleduck at sight. It was not hard to imagine why for Mrs. Robinson was very short and very plump and very waddly. The Silver Bush family could never again think of her as anything but Mrs. Puddleduck. Tillytuck's nicknames had a habit of sticking.

To Judy, of course, Mrs. Puddleduck was nothing but a necessary evil.

"She do be more up to date than mesilf I'm not doubting" . . . with a toss of her grey head. "They do be saying she took that domestic short course last year. But will she be kaping our cats continted I'm asking ye?"

"They say she's a very careful, saving woman," said Long Alec.

"Oh, oh, careful, is it? I'm not doubting it." Judy waxed very sarcastic. "She do be getting that from no stranger. Her grandfather did be putting a sun-dial in his garden and thin built a canopy over it to pertect it from the sun. Oh, oh, careful! Ye've said it!"

"She'll never make such apple fritters as yours, Judy, if she took fifty short courses," said Sid, passing his plate up for a second helping.

Then there was the matter of the passport. They had quite a time convincing Judy that she must have a photograph taken for it.

"Sure an' wud ye want to be photygraphed if ye had a face like that, Rae, darlint," she would demand, pointing to the kitchen mirror which never paid any one compliments. But when the picture came home Judy, in her new hat, with the crinkled crêpe scarf about her throat looked so surprisingly handsome that she was delighted. She kept the passport in the drawer of the kitchen cupboard and took frequent peeps at it when nobody was about.

"Did I iver be thinking a hat cud make such a difference? I can't be seeing but that I do be ivery bit as good-looking as Lady Medchester, and her a blue-blood aristocrat!"

Had it not been for Judy's going that October would have been a perfectly happy month for Pat. It was a golden, frostless autumn and when the high winds blew it fairly rained apples in the orchards and the ferns along the Whispering Lane were brown and spicy. There were gay evenings up at the Long House with Suzanne and David . . . hours of good gab-fest by the light of their leaping fire. David developed a habit of walking down the hill with Pat which Judy did not think at all necessary. Pat had come down that hill many a night alone.

"Thim widowers," she muttered viciously . . . but took care that Pat did not hear her. Judy had soon discovered that Pat resented any criticism of David Kirk.

Then McGinty died. They had long expected it. The little dog had been feeble all summer: he had grown deaf and very wistful. It broke Pat's heart when she met his pleading eyes. But to the very last he tried to wag his tail when she came to him. He died with his golden brown head pillowed on her hand. Judy cried like a child and even Tillytuck and Long Alec blew their noses. McGinty was buried beside Snicklefritz in the old graveyard and Pat had to write and tell Hilary that he was gone.

"I feel as if I could never love a dog again," she wrote. "I miss him so. It is so hard to remember that he is dead. I'm always looking for him. Hilary, just before he died he suddenly lifted his head and pricked his ears just as he used to do when he heard your step. I think he *did* hear something because all at once that heart-breaking look of longing went out of his eyes and he gave such a happy little sigh and cuddled his head down in my hand and . . . it seems too harsh to say he died. He just ceased to be. I wish you had come home, Hilary. I'm sure it was you his eyes were always asking for. Do you remember how he always came to meet us those Friday evenings when we came home from college? And he was with you that night so long ago when you saved me from dying of sheer terror on the base-line road. He was only a little, loving-hearted dog but his going has made a terrible hole in my life. It's another change . . . and Rae is gone . . . and Judy is going. Oh, Hilary, life seems to be just change . . . change . . . change. Everything changes but Silver Bush. It is always the same and I love it more every day of my life."

Hilary Gordon frowned a bit when he read this. And he frowned still more over a certain paragraph in a letter Rae had written.

"I do wish you'd come home this summer, Jingle. If you don't soon come Pat will up and marry that horrid David Kirk. I know she will. It's really mysterious the influence that man has gained over her. It's David this and David that . . . she's always quoting him. So far as I can see he doesn't do anything but talk to her . . . and he *can* talk. The creature is abominably clever."

Hilary sighed. Perhaps he should have gone to the Island last summer. But he was working his way through college . . . for accept help from the mother who had neglected him all his life he would not . . . and summer visits home . . . to Hilary "home" meant Silver Bush . . . could not be squeezed into his budget.

2

The first day of November came when Judy must pack. It was mild and calm and sunny but there had been hard frost the night before, for the first time, and the garden had suffered. Pat hated to look at her flowers. The nasturtiums were positively indecent. She realised that the summer was over at last.

Judy's trunk was in the middle of the kitchen floor. Pat helped her pack. "Don't forget the black bottle, Judy," Sid said slyly as he passed. Judy ignored this but she brought down her book of Useful Knowledge.

"I must be taking this, Patsy. There do be a lot av ettiket hints in it. Or do ye be thinking they're a trifle out av date? The book is by way av being a bit ouldish. I wudn't want me cousins in Ireland to be thinking I didn't know the latest rules. And, Patsy darlint, I'm taking me ould dress-up dress as well as the new one. I did be always loving that dress. The new one is rale fine but I haven't been wearing it long enough to fale acquainted wid it. Do ye rimimber how ye always hated to give up any av yer ould clothes, Patsy? And, Patsy dear, here's the kay av me blue chist. I'm wanting ye to kape it for me whin I'm gone and if innything but good shud be happening to me over there . . . not that I'm thinking it will . . . ye'll be finding me bit av a will in the baking powder can in the till."

"Judy, just imagine it . . . this time next week you'll be in the middle of the Atlantic."

"Patsy dear," said Judy soberly, "there's a favour I'd be asking ye. Will ye be saying that liddle hymn ivery night whin ye say yer prayers . . . the one where it does be mintioning 'those in peril on the say.' It'd be a rale comfort to me on the bounding dape. Well, me trunk's packed, thank the Good Man Above. Sure and I knew a woman that tuk four trunks wid her whin she wint to the Ould Country. I'm not knowing how she stud it. Iverything do be ready but what if something'll be previnting me from going at the last minute, Patsy? I'm that built up on it I cudn't be standing it."

"Nothing will happen to prevent you, Judy. You'll have a splendid trip and a lovely visit with all your cousins."

"I'm hoping it, girl dear. But I've been seeing so minny disappointmints in life. And, Patsy dear, kape an eye on Gintleman Tom, will ye and see that Mrs. Puddleduck don't be imposing on him.

I'm not knowing how the poor baste will be doing widout me."

"Don't worry, Judy. I'll look after him . . . if he doesn't go and disappear as he did the last time you were away from home."

Pat lingered a little while that evening on the back-stair landing looking out of the round window. There was a promise of gathering storm. A peevish wind was tormenting the boughs of the aspen poplar. Scudding clouds seemed to sweep the tips of the silver birches. Soon the rain would be falling on the dark autumn fields. But even a wild wet night like this would have been delightful at Silver Bush if her heart had been lighter. Judy would be gone by this time tomorrow night and Mrs. Puddleduck would be reigning in her stead. No Judy to come home to . . . no Judy to give you "liddle bites" . . . no Judy to stir pea soup . . . no Judy to slip in on cold nights with the eiderdown puff off the Poet's bed.

"And what," said Gentleman Tom on the step above, "is a poor cat to do?"

Long Alec took Judy to the station next morning through a drizzling rain. She was going to Summerside to spend the night at Uncle Brian's and take the boat train with the Pattersons the next day. Everybody stood at the gate and waved her off, smiling gallantly till the car was out of sight. Pat turned back to the kitchen where Mrs. Puddleduck was already making a cake and looking quite at home.

"I hate her," thought Pat, wildly and unjustly.

Dinner . . . the first meal without Judy . . . was a sorry affair. The soup of Mrs. Puddleduck was not the soup of Judy Plum.

"She doesn't know how to stir the brew," Tillytuck whispered to Pat.

Rae came home that night but supper was a gloomy affair. Mrs. Puddleduck's cake, in spite of her domestic short course, rather looked as if somebody had sat down on it: Long Alec was very silent: Tillytuck went straight to his granary roost as soon as the meal was over. Nothing pleased him and he did not pretend to be pleased.

"I feel old, Pat . . . as old as Methuselah," said Rae drearily, as they peeped into the kitchen before going to bed.

"I feel middle-aged, which is far worse," moaned Pat.

Mrs. Puddleduck was sitting there, knitting complacently at a sweater. No cat was in sight, not even Gentleman Tom.

"I wish I could be a cat for a little while, just to bite you," whispered Rae to the fat back of the unconscious Mrs. Puddleduck, who really was quite undeserving of all this hatred and, in fact, thought quite highly of herself for "helping the Gardiners out" while Judy Plum was gallivanting off to Ireland.

Saturday was dark and dour but a pleasant letter from Hilary helped Pat through the forenoon. Dear Hilary! What letters he could write! Hilary as a friend, even in faraway Toronto, was worth all the beaus in the Maritimes.

In mid-afternoon it began to rain again, battering everything down in the desolate garden. Tillytuck and Mrs. Puddleduck were already at loggerheads because when she complained that Just Dog had barked all night he had indulged in one of his silent fits of laughter and said blandly, "If you'd told me he'd purred I'd have been more surprised."

Sid took the girls over to the Bay Shore to help Winnie paper a room. The air was as full of flying leaves as of rain, and floods ran muddily down the gutters of the road. It was just as bad when they returned at night.

"I suppose Judy is on board ship now. They were to sail from Halifax at five o'clock," sighed Rae. "There's Tillytuck playing his fiddle. How can he have the heart? But I suppose he's trying to get on the good side of Mrs. Puddleduck. That man has no soul above snacks."

"I don't know how we'll ever get through the winter," said Pat.

They ran up the wet walk and opened the kitchen door . . . then stood on the threshold literally paralysed with amazement. Tillytuck's fiddle was purring under his hands. Mother was mending by the table whereon was a huge platterful of fat doughnuts. Long Alec lay on the sofa, snoozing blissfully with Squedunk on his chest and Bold-and-Bad and Popka curled up at his feet. Gentleman Tom, with the air of a cat making up his mind to forgive somebody, was sitting on the rug, with his tail stretched out uncompromisingly behind him.

And Judy . . . *Judy* . . . in her old drugget dress was sitting beside the stove stirring the contents of a savoury pot! Her knitting was on her lap and she looked like anything but a heart-broken woman.

For a moment the girls stared at her unbelievingly. Then with a shriek of "Judy!!!" they hurled themselves upon her. Wet as they were she hugged them with a fierce tenderness.

"Judy . . . Judy . . . *darling* . . . but why . . . why . . .?"

"I just cudn't be going, that do be all, me jewels. I was knowing it in me heart as soon as I lift. Poor Alec hadn't a word to throw to a dog. Ye cud have been scraping the blue mould off av him be the time we got to the station. But thinks I to mesilf, 'I'd look like a nice fool backing out now, after all thim prisents,' thinks I. So I did be sticking it out till I got into me bed at yer Uncle Brian's that night . . . the second bist spare room it was . . . oh, oh, they trated me fine, I'll be saying that for thim. But niver the wink wud I be slaping. I kipt thinking av me kitchen here, wid Mrs. Puddleduck reigning in me stid . . . and of all the things that might be happening to me, roaming abroad. Running inty an iceberg maybe . . . or maybe dying over there. Not that I'd be minding the dying so much but being buried among strangers. And thin if innything but good shud be happening to some av ye here! Thinks I, 'Perhaps they'll be larning to like Mrs. Puddleduck better'n me and her as smooth as crame.' I cud see ye all, snug and cosy, wid the beaus slipping along in the dim. Thinks I, 'There do be all the turkeys to be fattened for Christmas and the winter hooking to be done and mebbe Joe coming home to be married,' . . . and I cudn't be standing it. So at breakfast I up and told Brian I'd been after changing me mind and I'd just be going back to Silver Bush instead av to Ireland wid the Pattersons."

"Judy, you said the other day it would break your heart if anything prevented you from going . . ."

"Oh, oh, yisterday and to-day do be two different things," said Judy complacently. "Whin ye thought I was all ixcited over me trip I was just talking to kape me spirits up. It's the happy woman I am to think I'll slape in me own snug bed to-night wid Gintleman Tom curled up at me fate. Brian brought me home this afternoon and whin I stepped over the threshold of me kitchen I wudn't have called the quane me cousin. Oh, oh, ye shud have been seeing Madam Puddleduck's face! 'I thought this was how it wud be,' sez she, as spiteful as a fairy that had just got a spanking."

"Judy, where *is* Mrs. Puddleduck?"

"Safe back at the bridge where she belongs. Sure and she wasn't for staying long whin she saw me back. Oh, oh, she'll be saying plinty besides her prayers to-night. I wint inty me pantry thinking I'd see fine things in the ways av Sunday baking, what wid her domestic short course and all. But all I did be seeing was a cake looking like nothing on earth and a pie wid a lot of hen tracks on it. Tillytuck tells me he did be ating a pace av it and niver will his stomach be the same agin. Oh, oh, domestic science, sez I! I did be putting it in the pig's pail and frying up a big batch av doughnuts."

"Praise the sea but keep on land is a good proverb, symbolically speaking," said Tillytuck. After which he ate nine doughnuts.

Everybody was shamelessly glad and showed it, much to Judy's secret delight and relief. They shut out the rain and the cold wind. Never had the old kitchen held a more contented, more congenial bunch of people. Grief and loneliness had gone where old moons go and even King William looked jubilant in his never-ending passage of the Boyne. Outside it might be a dank and streaming November night but here was the eternal summer of the heart.

"Isn't it nice to look *out* into a storm?" said Rae. "Listen to that wind roaring. I love it. Judy, I'm glad you're not on the Atlantic."

"I do be just where I want to be, Cuddles darlint, and faling rale high and hilarious. Sure and I do be good frinds wid Silver Bush agin. It's been looking at me reproachful-like for a long time. I'm knowing now I cud niver be laving it. It's got into the marrow av me. So here I am, wid enough fine clothes to do me for the rist av me life and all the fun av getting ready. Oh, oh, 'twill be a stirring tale . . . the story av how Judy Plum wint to Ireland and got back so quick she met hersilf going. And now we'll begin planning a bit for Christmas."

Judy crept in that night to see if the girls were warm . . . the darling, thoughtful old thing.

"You're such a *dependable* old sport, Judy," said a drowsy Pat, sitting up and hugging her. "It seems unbelievably lovely that you're here . . . here . . . and not far away on the billow."

Judy was not acquainted with Wilson Macdonald's couplet,

"For this is wealth to know my foot's returning
Is always music to a friend of mine,"

but she felt that she was a very rich woman with only one small cloud on her perfect joy.

"Patsy darlint, do ye think I ought to be giving thim back . . . the prisents, I mane?"

"Certainly not, Judy. They were given to you and they are yours."

Judy gave a sigh of relief.

"It's rale glad I am to hear ye say so, Patsy. It wud have been bitter hard to give up that illigant t'ilet set. But I'm thinking I'll give yer Aunt Edith's hug-me-tight back to her. Niver will I let her be saying I come be it under false pretences."

Just as a great wave of sleep was breaking over Pat a sad premonitory thought drifted across her mind.

"And yet . . . for all she didn't go . . . I feel as if things were going to change."

3

When Rae came home from Queen's in the spring, the happy possessor of a teacher's license, she got the home school and settled down for a summer of good fun before school should open. "Fun" to Rae at this stage meant beaus and, as Judy said, they were standing in line. Pat couldn't quite get used to the idea of "little Cuddles" being really old enough to have beaus but Rae herself had no doubts on that point. And she admitted quite candidly that she liked having them. Not that she ever flirted, in spite of the Binnies. "College has improved Rae Gardiner some," Mrs. Binnie was reported to have said, "but it ain't cured her of being boy-crazy."

Rae just *looked*. "Come," said that look. "I know a secret you would like to know and no one can tell it to you but me."

She was not really as pretty as Winnie or as witty as Pat but there was magic in her . . . what Tillytuck called "glamour, symbolically speaking." "The little monkey has a way with her," said Uncle Tom. And the youth of both Glens knew it. It did not matter how much or how severely she snubbed them, this creature of cruelty and loveliness held them in thrall. Long Alec complained that Silver Bush was literally overrun and that they never had a quiet Sunday any more. But Judy would listen to no such growling.

"Wud ye be wanting yer girls to be like John B. Madison's," she enquired sarcastically. "Six av thim there and niver a beau to divide between them."

"There's reason in all things," protested Long Alec, who liked to have an undisturbed Sunday afternoon nap.

"Not in beaus," said Judy shrewdly. "And I'm minding that the yard at the Bay Shore used to be full of rigs on Sunday afternoons, young Alec Gardiner's among them. Don't be forgetting you were once young, Long Alec. We'll all have a bit av quiet fun be times watching the antics.

Were ye hearing what happened to Just Dog last Sunday afternoon whin one av the young Shortreed sprouts . . . Lloyd I'm thinking his name was . . . was sitting on the front porch steps, looking kind av holy and solemn, for all the world like his ould Grandfather Shortreed at prayer mating. Sure and the poor baste . . . not maning Lloyd . . . met up wid a rat in the stone dyke behind the church barn and cornered it. But me Mr. Rat put up a fight and clamped his teeth in Just Dog's jaw. Such howling ye niver did be hearing as he tore across the yard and through me kitchen and the hall and out past the young fry on the steps and through me bed av petunias. Roaring down the lane he wint, the rat still houlding on tight. The girls wint into kinks and Tillytuck come bucketing out, rale indignant, and saying, the divil himself must have got inty the modern rats. 'Oh, oh,' sez I, 'don't be spaking so flippant av the divil, *Mr.* Tillytuck. He's an ancient ould lad and shud be rispicted,' sez I. Lloyd Shortreed looked rale shocked."

"And no wonder. I don't hold with such goings-on in my house on Sunday."

"Sure and who cud be hilping it?" protested Judy. "It was Just Dog's doings intirely, going rat-hunting on Sunday. Before that the young fry were all quiet and sober-like. As for Tillytuck and his langwidge, iverybody do be knowing him. It's well known he didn't larn it at Silver Bush. Just Dog did be coming back later on wid no rat attached, rale meek and chastened-like. Lloyd hasn't been back since and good riddance. The Shortreeds do be having no sinse av humour."

"Lloyd's a very decent fellow," said Long Alec shortly.

"And that cliver wid his needle," added Judy slyly. "He did be piecing a whole quilt whin he was but four years ould and he's niver been able to live it down. His mother brings it out and shows it round whiniver company comes."

Long Alec got up and went out. He knew he was no match for Judy.

They celebrated Rae's home-coming by another party to which all Rae's college friends came. Rae loved dancing. Her very slippers, if left to themselves, would have danced the whole night through. But Pat's feet were not as light as they had been at the last party. Sid was not there. Sid was a very remote and unhappy boy. There had been a social sensation in North Glen early in the winter. Dorothy Milton, who had been engaged to Sid for two years, ran away with and married her cousin from Halifax, a dissipated, fascinating youth who "travelled" for a Halifax firm. Sid would have nothing of sympathy from his family. He would not talk of the matter at all. But he had been hard and bitter and defiant ever since and Pat felt hopelessly cut off from him. He worked feverishly but he came and went among his own like a stranger.

"Patience," said mother. "It will wear away in time. Poor Dorothy! I'm sorrier for her than for Sid."

"I'm not," sobbed Pat fiercely. "I hate her . . . for breaking Sid's heart."

"Oh, oh, iverybody's heart gets a bit av a crack at one time or another," said Judy. "Siddy isn't the first b'y to be jilted and he won't be the last, as long as the poor girls haven't got the sinse God gave geese."

But Judy didn't like to look at Sid's eyes herself.

When the party was over Pat and Rae went by a mossy, velvety path to their tent in the bush, amid a growth of young white, wild cherry trees. They had achieved their long-cherished dream of sleeping out in the silver bush and the reality was more beautiful than the dream, even when the wind blew the tent down on them one night and Little Mary was half smothered before they could find her. There was another new baby at the Bay Shore and Little Mary had been committed to the care of Aunt Pat until her mother should be about. They all loved Little Mary but Aunt Pat adored and spoiled her. To see Little Mary running about the garden on her dear chubby legs, pausing now and then to lift a flower to her small nose, or following Judy out to feed the chickens, or chasing kittens in the old barns, where generations of furry things had frisked their little lives and ceased to be, gave Pat never-ending thrills. And the questions she would ask . . . "Aunt Pat, why weren't ears made plain?" . . . "Aunt Pat, have flowers little souls?" . . . "Where do the days go, Aunt Pat. Dey mus' go *somewhere*" . . . "Does God live in Judy's blue chest, Aunt Pat?" Once or twice the thought came to Pat that to marry and have a dimpled question mark like this of your very own might even make up for the loss of Silver Bush.

Judy came through the scented darkness to see if they were all right and gossip a little about various things. Judy had been to a funeral that day . . . a very unusual dissipation for her. But old William Madison at the Bridge had died and Judy had worked a few months for his mother before coming to Silver Bush.

"Sure and iverything wint off very well. It was the grand funeral he had and he'd have been rale well plazed if he cud have seen it. He had great fun arranging it all, I'm told. Oh, oh, and he died very politely, asking thim all to ixcuse him for the bother he was putting thim to. His ould Aunt Polly was rale vexed because she didn't be getting the sate at the funeral she thought she shud have but nobody else had inny fault to find wid the programme. It do be hard to plaze ivery one. Polly Madison is one av the Holy Christians . . . holier than inny av thim, I'm hearing."

For the "go-preacher's" disciples had formed themselves into a "Holy Christian church" and were cruelly referred to in the Glen as the Holy Christians.

"I hear they're going to build a church," said Pat.

"That they are . . . but they're not calling it a church. It do be 'a place av meeting.' The same Aunt Polly do be giving the land for it. And Mr. Wheeler is coming back to be their minister . . . or their shepherd as they do be saying, not approving av ministers or av paying thim salaries ather. He'll be living on air no doubt. Aunt Polly says he is very spiritual but I'm thinking it's only the way he was av lifting his eyes and taffying her up. Innyway her husband don't be houlding wid new-fangled religions. 'Are ye prepared to die?' the go-preacher asked him rale solemn-like, I'm tould. But ould Jim Polly was always a hard nut to crack. 'Better be asking if I'm prepared to live,' sez he. 'Living comes first,' sez he."

Pat had detected a sudden movement of Rae's when Judy mentioned Mr. Wheeler's name, and felt her worry increase. Suppose he made up to Rae again!

4

Mr. Wheeler did return and did "make up to" Rae. That is, he fairly haunted Silver Bush and made himself quite agreeable socially . . . or tried to. The Gardiners no longer went to any of his services and the Holy Christians thought he might find more spiritual ways of spending his time than playing violin duets with Rae Gardiner and mooning about the garden with Pat until the very cats were bored. For Pat decidedly put herself forward to entertain him when he came and contrived to be present during most of the duets. To be sure, Rae laughed at and made constant fun of him. But she never seemed her usual saucy, indifferent self in his presence. She was quiet and subdued, with never a coquettish look, and Pat was not exactly easy. The creature *was* handsome in his way, with his dark eyes and crinkly sweep of hair, and his voice in which there were echoes of everything. Aunt Polly's daughter, who taught in South Glen, was reputed to have said that he had a certain Byronic charm. Byronic charm or not Pat wasn't going to have any nonsense and she played gooseberry with amiable persistence whenever he appeared. He looked a great deal at Rae and dropped his voice tenderly when he spoke to her: but he showed no aversion to talking with Pat . . . "currying favour," Tillytuck said.

Judy teased Rae sometimes about him.

"Sure and he'd be easy to cook for, Cuddles darlint. They're telling me he niver ates innything but nuts and bran biscuits. No wonder he's not nading a salary. But how about kaping a wife?"

"You do say such ridiculous things," said Rae rather snappishly. "What is it to me whether he can keep a wife or not?"

Tillytuck was not quite easy in his mind about it. He considered Mr. Wheeler a dangerous creature and wondered why Long Alec tolerated his presence at all. As he entirely disapproved of the Holy Christians he decided he would take up with church-going again as a token of his disapproval. He took several weeks to accumulate enough courage to go, being afraid, as he told Judy, of making too much of a sensation. But when he finally did go and nobody took any particular notice of it he was secretly furious.

"There wasn't a good-looking woman in church," he grumbled, "and no great shakes of a minister. He runs to words and I don't believe his views on the devil are sound. Sort of flabby. I like a devil with some backbone."

"Suppose you do be going to the Holy Christians," said Judy disdainfully, as she sliced up her red cabbage for pickling. "I'm hearing they have wrestling matches wid That Person quite frequent."

"The people of this place are having too much truck with Holy Christians as it is," said Tillytuck sourly, "and the time will come when they'll see it."

"There'll no harm come to Silver Bush from that poor lad," said Judy. "And ye'll all be getting a rale surprise some day."

"You've got wheels in your head," scoffed Tillytuck.

Pat, at that moment, was working in the garden, at peace with herself and all the world. Somehow, she always felt safe from change in that garden. Just now it seemed to be taking pleasure in itself. Its flowers were guests not prisoners . . . its blue delphiniums, its frail fleeting loveliness of poppies, its Canterbury bells, delicious mauve flecked with purple, its roses of gold and snow, its lilies of milk and wine.

Westward the sun was sinking low over a far land of shining hills. The air was sweet with a certain blended fragrance that only the Silver Bush garden knew. The whole lovesome place was full of soft amethyst shadows.

What fairy things the seeds of immortelles were! What a lovely name "bee balm" was! It was on evenings like this long ago she had listened for Joe's whistle as he came home from work. There was never any whistle now . . . Sid never whistled. Poor Sid! Would he never get over fretting for that hateful Dorothy? He was running around, here, there and everywhere, with all kinds of girls, rumour said. They saw very little of him at Silver Bush. At work all day . . . and off in the evening till late. Mother's eyes were very sad sometimes. Judy advised patience . . . he would come back to himself yet. Pat found it hard to be patient. At times she felt like shaking Sid. Why should he shut her out of his life as he did? That was always one of the little shadows in the background.

There was a hint of September coolness blowing across August's languor . . . another summer almost gone. The years were certainly beginning to spin past rather quickly. Well, to grow old with Silver Bush would not be hard, Pat reflected, with the philosophy of one who is as yet very far from age.

Suddenly Pat scowled. There was that wretched Mr. Wheeler coming up the lane. Thank goodness, Rae had gone to Winnie's. Now for another evening of boredom. When would he take the hint that his attentions to Rae weren't welcome to her or anybody else? Her lovely garden evening would be quite spoiled. And he had been here only last night. Really, he was becoming an intolerable nuisance.

Would it be violating Silver Bush traditions too flagrantly to give him a hint of it?

Pat's greeting was a trifle distant and she went on coolly snipping off delphinium seeds. Bold-and-Bad, who had been prowling among the shrubs, made a few spiteful remarks. You couldn't hoodwink Bold-and-Bad.

Mr. Wheeler stood looking down at her. Pat had an old sunburned felt hat of Sid's on her head which she would not have thought . . . if she had thought about it at all . . . likely to attract masculine admiration. And she wore an ancient brown crêpe dress which burrs and stick-tights could no longer injure. She did not know how its warm hues brought out the creaminess of her skin . . . the gloss of her hair . . . the fire of her amber eyes. She was really looking her best and when, after a rather overlong silence, she raised her eyes to her caller's she found his dark, soulful orbs . . . the adjectives were Aunt Polly's daughter's . . . gazing down at her with a strange expression in their depths. An incredible idea came to Pat . . . and was instantly dismissed. Nonsense! She wished he wouldn't stand so close to her. She knew at once what he had for supper. How overfull his red lips were! And when had his finger-nails been cleaned last? *Why* didn't somebody come along? People were always somewhere else when you wanted them and when you didn't you simply fell over them.

"You are smiling . . . you have such a fascinating smile. What are you thinking of, Patricia," he said in a low, caressing tone.

Merciful goodness, suppose she told him what she was thinking! Pat had hard work to avert a grin. And then the bolt fell, straight out of the blue.

Mr. Wheeler helped himself to one of her hands and looked at it.

"Little white hand," he murmured. "Little white hand that holds my heart."

Pat's hands were brown and not particularly little. She tried to pull it away. But he held on and put his arm around her. Worse and more of it, as Tillytuck would say. Suppose Judy were looking out of the kitchen window!

"Please, don't be so . . . foolish," said Pat coldly.

"I'm not foolish. I am wise . . . very wise . . . wise with the wisdom of countless ages." His voice was getting lower and tenderer with every word. "I've been wanting this opportunity for weeks. It has been so hard to find you alone. Dearest, sweetest of angels, have you any idea how much I love you . . . have loved you for a thousand lives?"

"I never thought of such a thing . . . I always thought it was Rae," was all poor Pat could gasp.

Mr. Wheeler smiled patronisingly.

"You couldn't have thought that, my darling. Miss Rachel is a charming child. But it is you, my sweet . . . and always has been since the first moment I drowned my soul in your beautiful eyes. I think I must have dreamed you all my life . . . and now my dream has come true." He tried to draw her closer. "You belong to me . . . you know you do. We will have such a wonderful life together, my queen."

Pat recovered herself. She wrested her hand from his clasp, feeling quite furious over her ridiculous position.

"You must forget all this nonsense, Mr. Wheeler," she said decisively. "I hadn't the slightest idea you felt that way about me. And . . ." Pat was growing angry, "just how did you come to imagine that I would marry *you*?"

Mr. Wheeler dropped her hand and looked down at her, with something rather unpleasant in his eyes.

"You have encouraged me to think so." His voice had lost a good deal of its smooth oiliness. "I cannot believe you do not care for me."

"Please try," said Pat in a dangerous tone. It flicked on the raw. A dark flush spread over Mr. Wheeler's face. He seemed all at once to be quite a different person.

"You have shown me very plainly that you liked my society, Miss Gardiner . . . almost *too* plainly. I consider that I had every right to suppose that my proposal would be welcome . . . very welcome. You have flirted with me shamelessly . . . you have lured me on, for your own amusement I must now suppose. I should have known it . . . I was well warned . . . I was told what you were . . ."

Pat, looking into his angry eyes, felt as she had felt one day when she had turned over an old, beautiful mossy stone in the Whispering Lane and seen what was underneath.

"I think you had better go, Mr. Wheeler," she said icily.

"Oh, I'm going . . . I'm going . . . and rest assured I shall never darken the doors of this place again."

Mr. Wheeler stalked off, his conceit considerably slimmed down, and Pat, still in a swither of various emotions, rushed into the kitchen, displaced a chairful of indignant cats, and gave tongue.

"Oh, oh, and what were you and His Riverince colloguing in the garden about that sint him down the lane at the rate av no man's business?" demanded Judy.

"Judy, I'm feeling so many different things I don't know which I'm feeling most. That horrible creature actually asked me . . . *me*, Pat Gardiner . . . to marry him! And he'd been eating onions, Judy!"

"Sure and weren't ye by way av knowing he was a vegetarian," said

430

Judy coolly. "I've been ixpicting this for some time . . ."

"Judy! What made you expect it?"

"The way he had av looking at ye, whin ye weren't looking at him."

"Oh, Judy . . . the worst of it is . . . he thinks I encouraged him! I feel I'm disgraced. And when he found I wouldn't marry him . . . he was horrid. He hasn't *any* manners, not even bad ones."

"The higher a monkey climbs the more he shows his tail," quoted Judy. "Niver be taking it to heart, Patsy. Ye're rid av him now for good."

"I really think so, Judy. I've an idea he meant it when he said he would never darken our doors again."

"Sure now and that will be our loss," said Judy sarcastically. "He's kipt out considerable av the sunshine this summer. And . . . I'm not sticking up for him, Patsy . . . I did always be thinking he was no rale gintleman under the skin . . . but you *did* be always sticking round . . ."

"I did it to keep him away from Rae. I . . . I . . . thought he'd take the hint. I never dreamed he'd think I was in love with him . . . *him!* Judy, it's really a ridiculous and tiresome world by spells. I'm going up to the Long House . . . I've got to have something to take the taste of the Reverend Wheeler out of my soul and to talk nice scandal with David and Suzanne may do it."

"I'm wondering how Cuddles will be taking this," muttered Judy after Pat had gone out. "I'm thinking iverybody but ould Judy Plum is blind as a bat round here. Well, we're rid av the go-pracher, glory be. But I'm not knowing if I like that Kirk man much better. He's got his eye on her. He's not hurrying . . . whin it's yer second you do be more careful-like. But I do be knowing the signs. Oh, oh, it's a wonder me bit av corned ham wasn't being biled too much whin I was listening to Patsy's troubles. But it's done to the quane's taste and I'm setting it in the ice-house to cool. Beaus may come and beaus may go but we must be having our liddle comforts."

Pat, up at the Long House, soon forgot her anger and humiliation in the company of David and Suzanne. They talked and laughed together around the fireplace the Kirks had built in Bet's crescent of trees while Ichabod sat close to David and Alphonso shared his favours between the girls and the evening star looked over cloudy purple ramparts in the west. It seemed to Pat that every evening she spent there she grew wiser and maturer in some mysterious way. Their talk was so different . . . so rich . . . so stimulating . . . so brimming over with ideas. The ghosts of the past were laid. She had begun to think of the Long House as the home of Suzanne and David rather than as the home of Bets.

"She is growing older and I'm growing younger. Perhaps we'll meet," David was thinking.

"Their souls are the same age," Suzanne was thinking.

But nobody knew what Alphonso-of-the-emerald-eyes or Ichabod thought.

THE FOURTH YEAR

1

Pat looked out of the Little Parlour window a bit wistfully one evening in late November. Another summer was ended. How quickly summers passed now! There was a hard grey twilight after a little snow and there was a threat of still more snow in the dour air. The shadows . . . chilly, hostile shadows . . . seemed to be raining out of the silver bush. A biting wind was lashing everything as if determined to take its ill-temper out on the world. A few forlorn yellow leaves blew crazily over the lawn. An empty nest swung lonesomely in the wind from a bough of the big apple tree on which the pale yellow-green apples always stayed so long after the leaves were gone. The apples were no good and were never picked but the tree always looked so exquisite in its spring blossom that Pat wouldn't have it cut down. It had been what Pat called a peevish day and even the loveliness of a tall, dark spruce tree near the dyke, powdered with feathers of snow, did not give her the shiver of delight such things usually did. She thought it was the kind of a day that would make people quarrel if people ever quarrelled at Silver Bush. But November had been a vexing month all through . . . one day glorious . . . the next day savage. You never knew just where you were with it. And Pat did not like this evening . . . she felt as if some long finger of change which was always reaching out to her was at last just on the point of touching her.

She was restless. She would have liked to go up to the Long House but the Kirks were away. She wished Rae would come home . . . Rae must have called somewhere after school. Though Rae hadn't been exactly the same for the past two months. Pat couldn't lay her finger just on the point of difference but she felt it in her sensitive soul. Rae sometimes snapped now . . . she who had always been so sunshiny. And sometimes Pat thought that when she looked meaningly at Rae in the presence of others, to share the savour of some subtle joke, Rae averted her eyes without any answering twinkle. And at times it almost seemed as if she had taken up a pose of being misunderstood. What was wrong? Weren't things going well in school? From all Pat could find out they were but she couldn't rid herself of the feeling that Rae had some secret trouble . . . for the first time an unshared trouble. Nothing was really changed . . . and yet Pat had moments of feeling that everything was changed. Once she asked Rae if anything was worrying her and Rae snapped out so savage a "Nonsense!" that Pat held her peace. Surely it couldn't be the fact that Mr. Wheeler had suddenly stopped coming to Silver Bush and was reputed to have a wild case on a visiting girl from New Brunswick that accounted for the mournful mauve smudges under Rae's blue eyes some mornings.

Pat reassured herself by reflecting that this would pass. And meanwhile Silver Bush made everything bearable. Pat loved it more with every passing year and all the little household rites that meant so much to her. Always when she came home to Silver Bush its peace and dignity and beauty seemed to envelop her like a charm. Nothing very terrible could happen there.

Judy's cheery philosophy never failed, but Pat could not mention even to Judy the vague chill of change between herself and Rae. In the evenings when they foregathered in the kitchen and Tillytuck played on his fiddle she sometimes felt that she must only have imagined it. Rae was the gayest of them all then . . . "a bit too gay," Judy thought, though she never said so. Things did be often arranging themselves if you just let them alone. Judy was more worried over a reckless look she sometimes caught in Sid's brown eyes and over certain bits of gossip that came her way occasionally.

Pat lighted the lamp as Sid and Rae came in. Rae flung her school-books on a chair and said nothing. But Sid had a chuckle and a bit of news.

"Your go-preacher has gone, Pat. The Holy C's are blaming you for it. They say you flirted with him and made a fool of him and he can't stand the place now. Aunt Polly is especially down on you. She adores

433

that shepherd."

Sid spoke banteringly and Pat had some laughing rejoinder ready when a smothered sound, between a gasp and a cry, made them look at Rae.

"Great Scott, sis, you'll singe your eyelashes if you let your eyes blaze like that," said Sid.

Rae took no notice of him. She was looking at Pat.

"So this is your doing . . . you have driven him away," she said in a low, tense tone . . . such a tone as Pat had never heard Rae use before . . . seventeen-year-old Rae whom Pat still thought of as a child. Pat almost laughed . . . but laughter suddenly fell dead on her lips. Why, the poor darling was in earnest! And how pretty she looked in her golden-brown dress with her flushed cheeks and over-bright eyes! Her head positively shone like a lamp in the dark corner. She was so sweet . . . and absurd . . . and deadly serious. This last realization should have warned Pat but didn't.

"Rae, dearest, don't be foolish," she said gently.

"Oh, don't be foolish," mocked Rae furiously. "That's *your* attitude I know . . . has been right along. *I* am a mere baby of course . . . *I* have no rights . . . no feelings . . . no feelings *at all* . . . no claim to be considered a human being. 'Don't be foolish,' says the wise Patricia. That really *is* a clever idea!"

Rae's voice trembled with passion. She rushed out of the Little Parlour and up the stairs like a golden whirlwind. There were three doors on the way to her room and she banged them all.

"Whew!" whistled Sid. "I always knew she had a bad case on Wheeler but I didn't think it went that deep."

"Sid . . . you don't think she cared really!"

"Oh, calf love no doubt. We all survive it. But it hurts at the time." Sid laughed a bit bitterly.

Pat went up to her room. Rae was pacing up and down it like a caged animal. She turned a stormy young face on her sister.

"Leave me alone, can't you? You've done me enough harm, haven't you? You took him from me . . . deliberately. I saw you trying to attract him. What chance had I? Well, I forgave you. But now he's gone . . . he's gone . . . and I'll never see him again . . . and I can't stand it. I hate you . . . I hate you . . . I hate everything."

"Please don't let's quarrel," said Pat helplessly. In a desperate effort to be calm she picked up her best pair of silk stockings and began to polish the mirror with them, not in the least knowing what she held in her hand. It was the last straw for Rae.

"Who is quarrelling? Don't try to put the blame on me."

"Oh, Rae, Rae . . . don't twist everything I say to mean something else."

"Oh, don't try to twist things, she says. Who twisted things this summer . . . all summer . . . to make him think me a child? It's *such* an interesting thing to watch the man you love making love to another woman and that woman your own sister who is deliberately trying to attract him, just for her own amusement!"

"Rae . . . never . . . never! I *did* try to save you from . . . from . . ."

"Save me! From what? You may well hesitate. You know you made him think I cared for Jerry Arnold. Jerry Arnold! A pipsqueak like that! It was Lawrence Wheeler I loved all the time and you knew it. He loved me, too, till you came between us. Yes, he did. The first time we met we felt . . . we *knew* . . . we had loved each other in a thousand former lives."

For the life of her Pat couldn't help smiling. She recognized the phrase. Hadn't Lawrence Wheeler of the soulful eyes said it to *her*?

"Suppose we talk . . . or try to . . . as if we were grown up," she suggested kindly.

"Oh, but I'm not grown up . . . I'm only a child." Rae was pacing feverishly up and down the room. "A child can't see . . . can't love . . . . can't suffer. *Can't suffer!* Oh, what I've gone through these past two months! And nobody saw . . . nobody understood . . . nobody has ever tried to understand me. *You* didn't. *You* care for nothing but Silver Bush. You acted as you did just because you're so crazy to keep Silver Bush always the same. My own sister to use me like that!"

Pat lost her patience and her temper, too. The idea of a scene like this over a creature like Larry Wheeler!

"This has gone far enough," she said frostily.

"I agree with you," Rae was frost instantly also.

"When you come to your senses," said Pat, "you'll realise perhaps just what a goose you've made of yourself over a go-preacher with cow's eyes."

"Don't you think you're really being a little vulgar, my dear Patricia?" said Rae, with eyes of blue ice. "*I* am of no consequence of course . . . but there is such a thing as good taste. You seem to have forgotten that, along with several other things. *Never mention Lawrence Wheeler's name to me again.*"

Pat clamped her teeth together to keep from saying things she would have been terribly sorry for afterwards. The urge to say them passed.

"We've both lost our tempers, Rae, and said foolish things. We'll feel differently in the morning."

"Oh, will we? I'll never feel differently . . . and I'll never forgive you, Pat Gardiner . . . never. You and that old widower of yours!"

"Who is being vulgar now?" Pat was furious again. "At least Mr. Kirk is a gentleman!"

"And Lawrence Wheeler isn't, I suppose?"

"You can suppose what you like. You've dragged his name up again. He was simply too sloppy for anything. I never dreamed that *you* . . . Rae Gardiner of Silver Bush . . . could take him seriously. And he'd been eating onions before he proposed to me."

"Oh, so he proposed to you. I didn't know you had lured him on that far. I thought even you had enough self-respect to stop short of that."

"We have had enough of this," said Pat, her voice trembling.

"I think so, too. But let me tell you this, Pat Gardiner. Since you are so bent on 'saving' people you'd better look after Sid a bit. He's dangling around May Binnie again. I've known it for weeks but I didn't say anything about it because I knew it would worry you. I had a little consideration for *you*. But you've been so intent on running my life that it has ceased to matter to you what Sid does, I suppose."

"Rae dearest . . . we're both upset . . . we're both saying things we shouldn't . . . let's forget this. We mustn't let any one know we've quarrelled . . ."

"I don't care if all the world knows it." Rae marched out of the room. She did not come back. That night she slept in the Poet's room . . . if she slept at all. Pat didn't. It was the first time since the night before mother's operation that she had lain awake all night. Surely she and Rae couldn't have quarrelled . . . after all their years of comradeship and love . . . all their secrets kept and shared together. It must be a horrid dream. The Binnie girls were always quarrelling . . . one expected nothing better of them. But such things simply couldn't happen at Silver Bush. Was there any truth in what Rae had said about Sid and May? There couldn't be. It was nothing but idle gossip. She knew Sid better than that. Of course May Binnie was pretty, with the obvious, indisputable prettiness of rich black hair, vivid colour, laughing, brilliant, bold eyes. But Sid could never care for her after Bets . . . or even after sweet foolish mistaken Dorothy. Pat brushed the teasing thought away. It was so easy to start gossip in the Glens. Nothing mattered just now but the quarrel with Rae.

Then it was dawn. Very early dawn is a dreary thing. Nothing is quite human. The world is "fey." And there was no Rae in the little bed beside hers. Pat had always loved to watch Rae waking up . . . she had such a pretty way of doing it. And the morning sunshine always poured in on her head, making it like a warm pool of gold on the pillow. But there was no Rae this morning . . . no sunshine. Pat sat up and looked out of the window. The different farmsteads were beginning to take form in the pale grey light on the thin snow. The little row of sheep tracks leading from the church barn across the Mince Pie field might have been made by Pan. A chilly foolish little wind of dawn was sighing around the eaves. A flock of tiny snowbirds settled on the roof of the granary. The haystacks in the Field of Farewell Summers looked gnome-like in the pale greyness. Pat gazed drearily at the blown clouds and the wide white fields and the lonely star of morning.

Everything seemed so much the same . . . and everything was so horribly changed.

Pat looked like the ghost of herself at breakfast but Rae came down, cool, gay, smiling, her face apparently as blithe as the day. She tossed an airy word to Pat, bantered Sid, complimented Judy on her muffins and went off to school with a parting pat for Bold-and-Bad.

Pat tried to feel relieved. It had blown over. Rae was ashamed of her outburst and wanted to ignore it. She was just going to act as if nothing had happened.

"I won't remember it either," vowed Pat. But there was a sore spot in her heart, even after she had talked it all over with Judy . . . Judy who had suspected all along that Rae was nursing some secret sorrow that loomed large in the eyes of seventeen.

"Judy, it was dreadful. We both lost our tempers and said blistering things . . . things that can never be forgotten."

"Oh, oh, it do be amazing how much we can be forgetting in life," said Judy.

"But it was so . . . so ugly, Judy. There has never been a quarrel at Silver Bush before."

"Oh, oh, hasn't there been now, darlint? Sure there was lashings av thim whin yer dad and his gang were growing up. The rafters would ring wid their shouting at each other . . . and Edith giving her opinion av iverybody ivery once in so long. This will be passing away just as they did. Did ye iver be hearing the rason ould Angus MacLeod av the South Glin didn't hang himsilf? He made up his mind to, all bekase life did be getting too tejus. And thin he had a fight wid his wife . . . the first one they'd iver had. It livened him up so he wint out and used the rope to tie up a calf and niver was timpted agin. As for poor liddle Cuddles, that sore and hurt and thinking it do be going to hurt foriver . . . just ye be taking no notice, Patsy . . . be yersilf and iverything will be just the same only more so."

"Mother must know nothing of it . . . I won't have mother hurt," said Pat firmly.

"If she can be kaping it from her she do be cliverer than I'm thinking," Judy told Gentleman Tom when Pat had gone out. "And I'm fearing this quarrel do be a bit more sarious than I've been pretinding. Whin two people don't be caring overmuch for aich other a quarrel niver amounts to much betwane thim. It's soon made up. But whin they love aich other like Patsy and Cuddles it do be going so dape it's rale hard to be forgetting it. I'm wishing Long Alec had chased that go-pracher off Silver Bush wid a shotgun the first time he iver showed his cow-eyes here. Whativer cud inny girl be seeing in him? Didn't he nearly sit down on Gintleman Tom the first time he called!"

2

December was a hard month for Pat. Life seemed to drag itself along like a wounded animal. Winter set in early. It snowed continuously for three weeks. Little storm demons danced in the yard and whirled along the lanes. Everywhere were huge banks of snow, white in the sun, pale blue in the shadows. There were quaint caps of it on the unused chimneys. It was piled deep in the Secret Field when Pat went to it on snowshoes. One felt that spring could never come again, either to Silver Bush or one's heart. On a rare fine day the world seemed made of diamond dust, cold, dazzling, splendid, heartless. There was the beauty of winter moonlight on frosted panes and chill harpings of wind beneath cold, unfriendly stars. At least, Pat felt they were unfriendly. Things were *not* the same. Always between her and Rae was the coldness and shadow of a thing that must not be spoken of . . . that must be forgotten. Rae chattered continuously of surface things but in regard to everything else she preserved a silence more dreadful than anger. There was always that false gaiety, good-humoured and polite! To Pat that politeness of Rae's was a terrible thing. They might have been strangers . . . they *were* strangers. Rae seemed to have locked her heart against her sister forever.

Just before Christmas Rae announced carelessly that she had been awarded a scholarship . . . a three months' course in nature study at the O.A.C. in Guelph and meant to take advantage of it. The trustees had granted her leave of absence and Molly MacLeod of South Glen was to take the school for the three months.

"That is splendid," said Pat, who knew Rae must have been aware of the possibility of this for weeks and had never said a word about it.

"Isn't it?" Rae was brightly enthusiastic. She was very busy during the following days preparing for her going and talking casually of plans. She was all radiance and sparkle and teased mercilessly because Judy was afraid she would learn to smoke cigarettes at Guelph. But she never consulted Pat about anything and when Pat, at Christmas, gave her a crimson kimono with darker crimson 'mums embroidered on it, remarking that she thought it would be nice for Guelph, Rae merely said, "How ripping of you! It's perfectly gorgeous." But she never told Pat that Uncle Horace had sent a check for a new coat and when she bought a stunning one of natural leopard with cuffs and collar of seal, she showed it to Judy and mother and the aunts but not to Pat . . . merely left it lying on her bed where Pat could see it if she chose. Pat was too hurt to mention it.

When Rae went away, looking very smart and grownup in her leopard coat and a little green hat tipped provocatively over one eye, she kissed Pat good-bye as she did the others but her lips merely brushed Pat's cheek and most of the kiss was expended on air. Pat watched her out of sight with a breaking heart and cried herself to sleep that night. The loneliness was hideous. She couldn't bear to look at the bed where Rae had slept or the little old bronze slippers Rae had danced in so often but thought too worn to take to Guelph. One of them was lying forlornly under the bureau, the other under the bed. Pat got up and put them together. They did not look quite so forlorn and discarded then.

True, there had been no real comradeship between her and Rae for weeks, though they had shared the same room and sat at the same table. But now that Rae was gone it seemed as if hope had gone with her. Pat was too proud and hurt even to talk it over with Judy. It was the first time she had not been able to talk a thing over with Judy.

That cold, indifferent good-bye kiss of Rae's! Little Cuddles who used to put her chubby arms about her neck and love her "so hard!" Pat couldn't bear to think of it. She looked at her new calendar hanging on the wall . . . a very elaborate affair which Tillytuck had given her. She had always thought a new calendar a fascinating thing, yet with something a little terrible about it. It was rather fun to flip over the leaves and wonder just what would be happening on this or that day. Now she hated to see it. There were three months to be lived through before Rae would come back. And when she did come would things be any better?

Bold-and-Bad padded into the room and jumped on the bed. Pat gathered him into her arms. Dear old cat, he was still left to her anyhow. And Silver Bush! Whatever came and went, whoever loved or did not love her, there was still Silver Bush.

Nevertheless Pat looked so haggard and woe-begone at breakfast that Judy wished things not lawful to be uttered concerning go-preachers.

During that dreary winter Pat's only real pleasures were her evenings at the Long House—Suzanne and David were so kind and understanding . . . especially David. "I always feel so comfortable with him," thought Pat . . . and her letters from Hilary. One of his stimulating epistles always heartened her up. She saved them up to read in the little violet-blue hour before night came . . . the hour she and Rae had been used to spend in their room, talking and joking. She always slept better after a letter from Hilary. And very poorly after a letter from Rae. For Rae wrote Pat in regular turn . . . flippant little notes, each seeming just like another turn of the screw. They were full of college news and jokes, such as she might have written to any one. But never a word about Silver Bush affairs . . . no reference to home jokes. Rae kept all that for her letters to mother and Judy. "When I see the evening star over the trees on the campus I always think of Silver Bush," Rae wrote Judy. If Rae had only written that to her, thought Pat.

Pat sent Rae a box of goodies and Rae was quite effusive.

"No doubt it's a youthful taste to be thinking of things to eat," she wrote back, "but how the girls did appreciate your box. It was really awfully kind of you to think of sending it," . . . "as if I were some outsider who couldn't be expected to send her a box," thought Pat . . . "I hear that Uncle Tom has had the mumps and that Tillytuck is still howling hymns to the moon in the granary. Also that Sid is still dancing attendance on May Binnie. She'll get him yet. The Binnies never let go. Do you suppose North Glen will faint if I appear out in a bright yellow rain coat when I come home? Or one of those long slinky sophisticated evening dresses? Silver Bush must really wake up to the fact that fashions change. I had a letter from Hilary last night. It's odd to think this is his last year in college. He has won another architectural scholarship and is going to locate in British Columbia when he is through. He thinks he will be able to get out here to see me before I leave."

Hilary had not told Pat about any of his plans.

The announcement of Mr. Wheeler's marriage was in the paper that day. Judy viciously poked the sheet that bore it into the fire and held it down with the poker.

Two weeks later it was the end of March and Judy was getting her dye-pot ready. And Rae was coming home. Pat found herself dreading it . . . and broken-hearted because she was dreading it.

"What is the matter with Pat this spring?" Long Alec asked Judy. "She hasn't seemed like herself all winter . . . and now she's positively moping. Is she in love with anybody?"

Judy snorted.

"Well then, does she need a tonic? I remember you used to dose us all with sulphur and molasses every spring, Judy. Perhaps it might do her good."

Judy did not think sulphur and molasses would help Pat much.

3

It was a mild day when Rae came home . . . a day full of the soft languor of early spring when nature is still tired after her wrestle with winter. There had been a light, misty snowfall in the night and Pat went for a walk to the Secret Field in the afternoon to see if she could win from it a little courage to face Rae's return. It was very lovely in those silent woods with their white-mossed trees. Every step she took revealed some new enchantment as if some ambitious elfin artificer were striving to show just how much could be done with nothing but the white mystery of snow in hands that knew how to make use of it. Such a snowfall, thought Pat, was the finest test of beauty. Whenever there was any ugliness or distortion it showed it mercilessly: but beauty and grace were added unto beauty and grace even as unto him that hath shall be given more abundantly. She wished she had some one to enjoy the loveliness with her . . . Hilary . . . Suzanne . . . David . . . Rae. Rae! But Rae would be coming home in a few hours' time, artificially cordial, looking at her with bright, indifferent eyes.

"I just can't bear it," thought Pat miserably.

When Pat heard the jingle of sleigh-bells coming up the lane in the "dim" she fled to her room. Every one else was in the kitchen waiting for Rae . . . mother and Sid and Judy and Tillytuck and the cats. Pat felt she had no part or lot among them.

It had turned colder. There was a thin green sky behind the snowy trees and the silver gladness of an evening star over the birches. Pat heard the noise of laughter and greeting in the kitchen. Well, she supposed she must go down.

There was a sound of flying feet on the stairs. Suddenly it seemed to Pat that there was no air in the room. Rae burst in . . . a rosy, radiant Rae, her eyes as blue as ever, her mouth like a kissed flower. She engulfed Pat in a fierce leopard-skin hug.

"Patsy darling . . . why weren't you down? Oh, but it's good to see you again!"

This was the old Rae. Pat was afraid she was going to howl. All at once life was beautiful again. It was as if she had wakened up from a horrible dream and seen a starlit sky. "Pat, haven't you a word to say to me? You aren't sore at me still, are you? Oh, I wouldn't blame you if you were. I was the world's prize idiot. I realised that very soon after we quarrelled but I was too proud to admit it. And you wrote me such icy, stiff letters while I was away."

"Oh!" Pat began to laugh and cry at once. They got their arms around each other. Everything was all right . . . beautifully all right again.

It was a wonderful evening. Every one enjoyed Judy's superlative supper, with Rae feeding the cats tid-bits and Tillytuck and Judy outdoing themselves telling stories. Again and again Rae's eyes met

Pat's over the table in the old camaraderie. Even King William looked as if sometime he might really get across the Boyne. But the best of all came at bedtime when they settled down for the old delight of talking things over with Bold-and-Bad tensing and flexing his claws on Pat's bed and Popka blinking goldenly on Rae's.

"Isn't it jolly to be good sisters again?" exclaimed Rae. "I feel like that verse in the Bible where all the morning stars sang together. It's just been horrid . . . horrid. How could I have been such a little fool? I just wallowed in self-pity all the fall and then it seemed as if that outburst had to come. And all over that . . . that creature! I'm so ashamed of ever dreaming I cared for him. I can't understand how I could have been so . . . so fantastic. And yet I really did have a terrible case. Of course I knew perfectly well in my heart it could never come to anything. At the very worst of my infatuation . . . when I was trying to pretend to every one I didn't care a speck . . . I knew no Silver Bush girl could ever marry a go-preacher. But that didn't prevent me from being crazy about him. It seemed so romantic . . . a hopeless love, you know. Two found souls forever sundered by family pride and all that, you know. I just revelled in it . . . I can see that now. The way he used to look at me across that barn! And once, when he read his text . . . 'Behold thou art fair, my love, behold thou art fair. Thou hast dove's eyes' . . . he looked right at me and I nearly died of rapture. He really was in love with me then. You never saw the poem he wrote me, Pat. He was jealous of everything, it seemed . . . of 'the wind that whispered in my ear' . . . of 'the sunshine that played on my hair' . . . of 'the moonbeam that lay on my pillow.' The lines didn't scan very well and the rhymes limped but I thought it was a masterpiece. Can you wonder I was furious when you just stepped in and lifted him under my very nose? By the way, he's married, did you know, Pat?"

"Yes. I saw it in the paper."

"Oh, he sent *me* an announcement," giggled Rae. "You should have seen it. With scrolls of forget-me-nots around the border! If I hadn't been cured before that would have cured me. Pat, why is it written in the stars that girls have to make fools of themselves."

"We were both geese," said Pat.

"Let's blame it all on the moon," said Rae.

They felt very near to each other. And then Judy came in with cups of delicious hot cocoa for them and a "liddle bite" of Bishop's bread and a handful of raisins as if they were children again.

"Just think," said Pat, "to other people this day has been only Wednesday. To me it's the day you came home . . . home to me . . . back into my life. It may be March still by the calendar but it's April in my heart . . . April full of spring song."

"Here's to my having more sense in all the years to come," said Rae, waving her cup of cocoa.

"To *our* having more sense," corrected Pat.

"It's lovely to be home again," sighed Rae. "I had a splendid time at Guelph . . . and I really did learn lots . . . much more than just nature study. The social side was all right, too. There were some nice boys. We had a gorgeous trip to Niagara. But I am half inclined to agree with you that there is no place like Silver Bush. It must do something to people who live in it. Those darling cats! I really haven't seen a decent cat since I left the Island, Pat . . . no cat who looked as if he really enjoyed being a cat, you know. I wish we could do some crazy thing to celebrate. Sleep out in the moonlight or something like that. But it's too Marchy. So we must just have a good pi-jaw. Tell me *everything* that has happened since I went away. Your letters were so . . . so *charitable*. There was no kick in them. Let me tell you once for all, Pat, that a person who always speaks well of every one is a most uninteresting correspondent. I'm sure you must be boiling over with gossip. Have there been any nice juicy scandals? Who has been born . . . married . . . engaged? Not you, I hope. Pat, don't go and get married to David. He's far too old for you, darling . . . he really is."

"Don't be silly, sweetheart. I just want David as a friend."

"The darlints," said Judy happily, as she went downstairs. "I was knowing the good ould Gardiner sinse wud come out on top."

It was wonderful to be too happy to sleep. The very sky through the window looked glad. And when Pat wakened a verse she had heard David read a few days before . . . a verse which had hurt her at the time but now seemed like a friend . . . came to her mind.

> "Whoever wakens on a day,
> Happy to know and be,
> To enjoy the air, to love his kind,
> To labour and be free,

Already his enraptured soul
Lives in Eternity."

She repeated the lines to herself as she stood by her window. Rae
slipped out of bed and joined her. Judy was crossing the yard, carrying
something for the comfort of her hens.

"Pat," said Rae a bit soberly, "does it ever strike you that Judy is
growing old?"

"Don't!" Pat winced. "I don't want to think of anything to spoil this
happy morning."

But she did know that Judy was growing old, shut her eyes to it as she
might. And hadn't Judy said to her rather solemnly one day,

"Patsy darlint, there do be a nightdress wid a croshay yoke all riddy
in the top right hand till av me blue chist if I iver tuk ill suddent-like."

"Judy . . . don't you feel well?" Pat had cried in alarm.

"Oh, oh, niver be worrying, darlint. I'm fit as a fiddle. Only I did
be rading in the dead list av the paper this morning that ould Maggie
Patterson had died in Charlottetown. We were cronies whin I did be
coming to the Island at first and she do be only a year older than mesilf.
So I just thought I'd mintion the nightdress to ye. The ould lady in
Castle McDermott had one av lace and sating she always put on whin
she had the doctor."

"I'm so glad you and Rae are as you used to be, Pat," said mother
when Pat took her breakfast into her. Pat looked at mother.

"I didn't think you knew we weren't," she said slowly.

Mother smiled.

"You can't hide such things from mothers, darling. We always know.
And I think a little wise forgetfulness is indicated."

Pat stooped and kissed her.

"Mr precious dear, wasn't it lucky father fell in love with *you*," she
breathed.

Rae was in kinks in the hall when Pat went out.

"Oh, Pat, Pat, life *is* worth living. I've just seen Judy making Tillytuck
take a dose of castor oil. You'll never know what you've missed."

Yes, life was worth living again. And now Pat felt that she could throw
herself into housecleaning plans and spring renovating with a heart at
leisure from itself. The days that had seemed so endless wouldn't be half
long enough now for all she wanted to crowd into them.

445

4

David and Suzanne went to England for a trip that spring and the Long House was closed for the summer. Pat missed them terribly but Judy and Rae were consolable.

"That Suzanne has been trying iver since she come to make a match betwane her brother and Patsy," Judy told Cuddles. "I've been fearing lately she'd manage it. And him as'll soon be using hair tonics! Patsy hasn't inny other beau after her just now. The min do be getting discouraged. Somehow the word do be going round she thinks nobody good enough for her."

"And there really isn't a man in the Glens she couldn't have by just crooking her finger," said Rae thoughtfully. "I think it's just that way she has of saying 'I know' sympathetically. And she doesn't mean a thing by it."

"Do ye be thinking, Cuddles, that there is inny chance av Jingle coming home this summer now?"

Rae shook her head.

"I'm afraid not, Judy. He's got a big contract for building a mountain inn in B.C. . . . a splendid chance for a young architect. Besides . . . I think he has grown away from us now. He and Pat will never be anything but good friends. You can't make him jealous . . . I know for I've tried . . . so I'm sure he doesn't care for her except just as she cares for him. Do you know, Judy, I think it would be better if the uncles and aunts . . . and perhaps all of us . . . would stop teasing Pat about beaus or their absence. She thinks the whole clan is bent on marrying her off . . . and it rouses the Gardiner obstinacy. There's a streak of it in us all. If you all hadn't been so contemptuous of poor Larry Wheeler I don't believe I'd ever have given him a second thought."

"Girls do be like that, I'm knowing. But I'd like to see both you and Patsy snug and safe, wid some one to care for ye, afore I die, Cuddles darlint."

Rae laughed.

"Judy, I'm only seventeen. Hardly on the shelf yet. And don't you talk of dying . . . you'll live to see our grandchildren."

Judy shook her head.

"I can't be polishing off a day's work like I used to, Cuddles dear. Oh, oh, we all have to grow old and ye haven't larned yet how quick time do be passing."

"As for Pat," resumed Rae, "I think perhaps she'll never marry. She loves Silver Bush too much to leave it for any man. The best chance David has is that the Long House is so near Silver Bush that she could still keep an eye on it. Do you know that Norma is to be married this summer?"

"I've been hearing it. Mrs. Brian will be rale aisy in her mind now wid both of her girls well settled. Norma'll niver have to lift a hand. Not that I do be thinking her beau is inny great shakes av a man wid all his money though he comes of a rale aristocratic family. His mother now . . . she was one av the Summerside MacMillans and niver did she be letting her husband forget it. She kipt up all the MacMillan traditions . . . niver wore the same pair av silk stockings twice and her maid had to be saying, 'Dinner is served, madam,' just like that, afore she cud ate a bite, wid service plates and all the flat silver matching. And in sason and out av sason she did be reminding her husband she was a MacMillan along wid iverybody av inny importance on the Island. It was lucky he had a bit av humour in him or it might have been after being a trifle monotonous. Will I iver be forgetting the story I heard him tell on the madam one cillebration at the Bay Shore? It was whin his b'ys, Jim and Davy, were two liddle chaps and Jim did be coming home from church one day rale earnest and sez he to Davy, 'The minister did be talking av Jesus all the time but he didn't be saying who Jesus was.' 'Why, Jesus MacMillan av coorse,' sez Norma's beau, in just the tone av his mother. Mr. MacMillan did be roaring at it, but yer Aunt Honor thought it was tarrible irriverint. Innyway, a Gardiner is as good as a MacMillan inny day. And now I must be making a few cookies, Liddle Mary will be coming over for a wake. She do be so like Patsy whin she was small. Sometimes I'm wondering if the clock has turned back. She do be always saying good-night to the wind like Patsy did . . . and the quistions av her! 'Have I *got* to be good, Judy? Can't I be a liddle bad sometimes whin I'm alone wid you?' And, 'What's the use av washing me face after dark, Judy?' Sure and it's a bit av sunshine whin she comes and I'm thinking the very smallest flower in the garden do be glad, niver to mintion the cats."

Pat was really far more interested in Rae's matrimonial prospects than her own. For Rae seemed to be "swithering," as Judy put it, between two very nice young men. Bruce Madison of South Glen and

Peter Alward of Charlottetown were both camping on the doorstep, and were frightfully and romantically jealous of each other, turning, so it was said, quite pale when they met. Life, as Tillytuck said, was dramatic because of it.

Pat had nothing against either of them . . . except that they meant change . . . and sometimes it was thought that Rae favoured one and then the other. She discussed them as flippantly as usual with Pat and Judy but both Pat and Judy were agreed that it was highly probable she would eventually decide on one of them. Pat hated the thought, of course. But if Rae had to marry some day . . . of course it wouldn't be for years yet . . . it *must* be somebody living near. Pat inclined to like Peter best but Judy favoured Bruce.

"We *would* make an awfully good-looking couple," agreed Rae. "I really like Bruce best in summer but I have a rankling suspicion that Peter would be the best for winter. And he always makes me *feel* beautiful . . . that's a knack some men never have, you may have noticed. But then . . . his nose! Have you noticed his nose, Pat? It's not so bad now but in a few years it will be very bony and aristocratic. I can't exactly see myself eating breakfast every morning of my life with it opposite me. And it's terrible to think that my daughters might inherit it. It wouldn't matter so much about the boys . . . a boy can get away with any kind of a nose because few girls are as sensitive to noses as I am. But the poor girls!"

Judy was horrified but she had no great liking for Peter's nose herself. So Silver Bush had its own fun out of the haunting suitors and the Golden Age seemed to have returned and nobody took anything very seriously until Pat went to a dance at the Bay Shore Hotel and Donald Holmes, as Rae announced at the breakfast table next morning, fell for her with a crash that could be heard for miles. What was more, Pat blushed, actually blushed, when Rae said this. Everybody drew the same conclusion from that blush. Pat had met her fate.

At once everybody in the Gardiner clan sat up and took notice. For the rest of the summer Donald Holmes was a constant visitor at Silver Bush. Rae and her two jealous suitors no longer held the centre of the stage. Everybody approved. The Holmes family had the proper social and political traditions, and Donald himself was the junior partner in a prosperous firm of chartered accountants.

"Oh, oh, that do be something like now," Judy told Tillytuck delightedly. "There's brading there. And he'll wear well. Patsy was in the right be waiting."

"Methinks I smell the fragrance of orange blossoms, symbolically speaking," Tillytuck remarked to Uncle Tom.

"Well, it's about time," said Uncle Tom, who was not given to symbols.

"It's really better luck than she deserves after all her flirtations," said Aunt Edith rather sourly.

Pat herself believed she was in love . . . really in love. There were weeks of pretty speeches and prettier silences and enchanted moons and stars and kittens . . . though in her secret soul she suspected him of not caring overmuch about cats. But at least he pretended to like the kittens. One couldn't have everything. He was well-born, well-bred, good-looking and charming, and for the first time since the days of Lester Conway Pat felt thrills and queer sensations generally.

"I thought I'd left all that behind with seventeen," she told Rae, "but it really seems to have come back."

Rae, who was expecting "one of the men she's engaged to . . ." *à la* May Binnie . . . carefully perfumed her throat.

"A plain answer to a plain question, Pat. Do you mean to marry him?"

"I'm not Betty Baxter," said Pat with a twinkle.

"Don't be exasperating. Every one knows he means to ask you. Candidly, Pat, I'd like him very much for a brother-in-law."

Pat looked sober. In imagination she saw the paragraph in the Charlottetown papers announcing her engagement.

"I blush when I hear his step at the door," she said meditatively.

"I've noticed that myself," grinned Rae.

"And I suffer agonies of jealousy if he says a word of admiration for any other girl. On the whole . . . I haven't quite made up my mind . . . not quite . . . but I *think*, Rae, when *he* says, 'Will you please?' *I'll* say, 'Yes, thank you.'"

Rae got up and hugged Pat chokily.

"I'm glad . . . I'm glad. And yet I'm on the point of howling."

"Confidence for confidence, Rae. Which, if either, of your young men do you intend to marry?"

Rae pulled an ear of Squedunk, who was sitting on his haunches on her bed, gazing at the girls with his usual limpid, round-eyed look. Gentleman Tom looked as if all the wisdom of the ages was his, Bold-

and-Bad looked as if life was one amusing adventure, but Squedunk always looked as if he could be a kitten forever if he wanted to.

"Pat, I wish I knew. I've been horribly flippant about it but that was just to cover up. I really don't know. I do like them both so much . . . Pat, is it ever possible to be in love with two men? It isn't in books, I know . . . but in life? Because I *do* love them both. They're both darlings. But, Pat, honestly, the minute I decide I like Bruce best I find I have a mind to Peter. And *vice versa*. That's all I can say yet. Well, Norma's wedding comes off next week. Judy is furious because they are going to rehearse the whole ceremony in the church the night before. 'Nixt thing they'll be rehearsing the funerals,' she says. Judy will be simply mad with delight if you marry Donald. And yet she'll die of sorrow when you go. *When you go* . . . that turns me cold. Oh, Pat, wouldn't life be nice and simple if people never fell in love? I wish I *could* make up my mind between Bruce and Peter. But I just can't. If I could only marry them both."

The shrieks of an anguished car resounded from the yard and Rae ran down to welcome Bruce . . . or it may have been Peter.

The next afternoon Pat, as she expressed it, "put off Martha and put on Mary," and hied herself to her Secret Field, although there was apple jelly to make and cucumbers to pickle. She went through the mysterious emerald light of the maple woods, where it seemed as if there must have been silence for a hundred years, and sat down on an old log covered with a mat of green moss in the corner of her field. It had changed so little in all the years. It was still her own and it still held secret understanding with her. But to-day something came between her soul and it. In spite of everything something touched her with unrest . . . the certainty of coming change, perhaps.

She looked up at a splash of crimson in the maple above her head. Another summer almost gone. There was a hint of autumn and decay and change in the air, even the air of the Secret Field, with the purples of its bent grasses. Yes, she would marry Donald Holmes. She was quite sure she loved him. Pat stood up and waved a kiss to the Secret Field. When she next saw it she would belong to Donald Holmes.

She had intended to call at Happiness on her way home . . . she had not been there all summer . . . but she did not. Happiness belonged to things that were . . . things that had passed . . . things that could never return.

She was in the birch grove when Donald came to her the next evening. Donald Holmes was really a fine chap and deeply in love with Pat. To him she looked like love incarnate. She had a kitten on her shoulder and her dress was a young leaf green with a scarlet girdle. There was something about her face that made him think of pine woods and upland meadows and gulf breezes. He had come to ask her a certain question and he asked it, simply and confidently, as he had a right to ask it . . . for if any girl had ever encouraged a man Pat had encouraged Donald Holmes that summer.

Pat turned a little away from his flushed, eager face. Through a gap in the trees she saw the dark purple of the woods on Robinson's hill . . . the blue sheen of the gulf . . . the green of the clover aftermath in the Field of the Pool . . . the misty opal sky . . . and Silver Bush!

She turned to Donald and opened her lips to say, "yes." She found herself trembling.

"I'm . . . I'm terribly sorry," was what she said. "I can't marry you. I thought I could but I can't."

5

"I rather think I hope there'll be an earthquake before to-morrow morning," thought Pat when she went to bed that night. The whole world had gone very stale and life seemed greyer than ashes. In a way she was actually disappointed. She would miss Donald horribly. But leave Silver Bush for him? Impossible!

She knew she was in for a terrible time with her clan and she was not mistaken. By the time they got through with her she felt, as she confided to the not overly sympathetic Rae, "like a bargain counter of soiled rayon." Even mother was a little disappointed.

"*Couldn't* you have cared for him, darling?"

"I thought I could . . . I thought I did . . . mother, I just can't explain. I'm dreadfully sorry . . . I'm so ashamed of myself . . . I deserve everything that is being said of me . . . but I couldn't."

Everybody was saying plenty. All her relatives took turns heckling her about it. Long Alec gave her a piece of his mind.

"But I didn't love him, father . . . I really didn't," said poor Pat miserably.

451

"It's a pity you didn't find that out a little sooner," said Long Alec sourly. "I don't like hearing my daughter called a jilt. No, don't smile at me like that, miss. Let me tell you you trade too much on that smile. *This* is past being a joke."

"You'll go through the woods and pick up a crooked stick yet," warned Aunt Edith darkly.

"There's really been too much of this, Aunt Edith," protested Pat, feeling that any self-respecting worm had to turn sometime. "I'm not going to marry anybody just to please the clan."

"What *can* she be wanting in the way of a husband?" moaned Aunt Barbara.

"Heaven knows," said Aunt Edith . . . but in a tone that sounded very dubious of heaven's knowledge. "She'll never have such a chance again."

"You know you aren't getting any younger, Pat," Uncle Tom objected mildly. "Why couldn't you have cottoned to him?"

Pat was flippant to hide her feelings.

"My English and Scotch blood liked him, Uncle Tom, but the French didn't and I was none too sure about the Irish."

Uncle Tom shook his head.

"If you don't watch out all the men will be grabbed," he said gloomily. "Beaus aren't found hanging on bushes, you know."

"If they were it would be all right," said Pat, more flippantly than ever. "One needn't pick them then. Just let them hang."

Uncle Tom gave it up. What could you do with a she like that?

Aunt Jessie said that the Selbys were always changeable and Uncle Brian said he could always have told her that Pat was only making a fool of young Holmes for her own amusement and Aunt Helen said Pat had always been different from anybody else.

"A girl who would rather ramble in the woods than go to a dance. Don't tell me she's normal."

Most odious of all was the sympathetic Mrs. Binnie who said when she met her,

"You seem to have bad luck with your beaus, Pat dearie. But never be cast down even if he has slipped through your fingers. There's as good fish in the sea as ever come out of it. And you know, dearie, even if you can't git a husband there's lots of careers open to gals nowadays."

It was hard to take that from a Binnie. As if Donald Holmes had jilted her! And harder still to hear that Donald Holmes' mother was saying that that Gardiner girl had deliberately led her son on . . . kept him dangling all summer and then threw him over.

"But I deserve it, I suppose," thought poor Pat bitterly.

The only person who was not reported as saying anything was Donald Holmes himself, who preserved an unbroken silence and behaved, as Aunt Edith averred, in the most gentlemanly fashion about everything connected with the whole pitiable affair.

Judy was upset at first but soon came round when every one else was blaming her darling and recollected that Donald Holmes had had a very quare sort of great-uncle.

"A bit av a miser and always wint about as shabby as a singed cat. Aven the dogs stopped to look at him, him being that peculiar. And I'm minding there did be a cousin somewhere on the mother's side dressed up in weeds and wint to the church widding av a man who had jilted her. Oh, oh, and it's liable to crop out inny time and that I will declare and maintain."

Sid, too, to Pat's surprise, stood up for her.

"Let her alone. If she doesn't want to marry Donald Holmes she doesn't have to."

Pat lingered late in the garden one night. There was a mirth of windy trees all about Silver Bush and a misty, cloud-blown new moon hanging over it. First the twilight was golden-green, then emerald. Afar off the evening hills were drawing purple hoods about them. In spite of everything Pat felt at peace with her own soul as she had not done for a long time.

"If it's foolish to love Silver Bush better than any man I'll always be a fool," she said to herself. "Why, I *belong* here. What an unbelievable thing that I was just on the point of saying something to Donald that would have cut me off from it forever."

As she turned to leave the garden she said passionately and quite sincerely,

"I hope nobody will ever ask me to marry him again." And then a thought darted quite unbidden into her mind.

"I'm glad I don't have to tell Hilary I'm engaged."

6

There came a grim day in November with nothing at first to distinguish it from other days. But in mid-afternoon Gentleman Tom gravely got down from the cushion of Great Grandfather Nehemiah's chair and looked all about him. Judy and Pat watched him as they made the cranberry pies and turkey dressing for Thanksgiving. He gave one long look at Judy, as she recalled afterwards, then walked out of the house, across the yard and along the Whispering Lane, with his thin black tail held gallantly in air. They watched him out of sight but did not attach much importance to his going. He often went on such expeditions, returning at nightfall. But the dim changed into darkness on this particular night and Gentleman Tom had not returned. Gentleman Tom never did return. It seemed a positive calamity to the folks at Silver Bush. Many beloved cats of old days had long been hunting mice in the Elysian fields but their places had soon been filled by other small tigerlings. None, it was felt, could fill Gentleman Tom's place. He had been there so long he seemed like one of the family. They really felt that he must go on living forever.

No light was ever thrown on his fate. All enquiries were vain. Apparently no mortal eye had seen Gentleman Tom after he had gone from Silver Bush. Pat and Rae were mournfully certain that some dire fate had overtaken him but Judy would not have it.

"Gintleman Tom has got the sign and gone to his own place," she said mysteriously. "Don't be asking me where it might be . . . Gintleman Tom did be always one to kape his own counsel. Do ye be minding the night we all thought ye were dying, Patsy dear? I'm not denying I'll miss him. A discrate, well-behaved baste he was. All he iver wanted was his own cushion and a bit av mate or a sup av milk betwane times. Gintleman Tom was niver one to cry over spilt milk, was he now?"

Philosophically as Judy tried to take it she was very lonely when she climbed into her bed at nights, with no black guardian at its foot.

"Changes do be coming," she whispered sadly. "Gintleman Tom *knew*. That do be why he wint. He niver liked to be upset. And I'm fearing the luck av Silver Bush do be gone wid him."

THE FIFTH YEAR

1

Pat, coming home from the Long House, where she and David and Suzanne had been reading poetry before the fire all the evening, paused for a moment to gloat over Silver Bush before going in. She always did that when coming home from anywhere. And to-night it seemed especially beautiful, making an incredibly delicate picture with its dark background of silver birches and dim, dreaming winter fields. There were the white, sparkling snows of a recent storm on its roof. Two lace-like powdered firs, that had grown tall in the last few years, were reaching up to the west of it. To the south were two leafless birches and directly between them the round pearl of the moon. A warm golden light was gleaming out of the kitchen window . . . the light of home. It was fascinating to look at the door and realise that by just opening it one could step into beauty and light and love.

The world seemed all moonlight and silver bush, faintly broken by the music of a wind so uncertain that you hardly knew whether there really was a wind or not. The trees along the Whispering Lane looked as if they had been woven on fairy looms and a beloved pussy cat was stepping daintily through the snow to her.

Pat was very happy. It had been a beautiful winter . . . one of the happiest winters of her life. None of the changes Judy had foreboded upon the departure of Gentleman Tom had so far come to pass. Winnie and her twinkling children came over often and Little Mary stayed for weeks at a time, though her mother complained that Pat spoiled her so outrageously that there was no doing anything with her when she went home. Mary had once said,

"I wish I was an orphan and then I could come and live with Aunt Pat. She lets me do *everysing* I want to."

The only time Mary ever found Aunt Pat cross with her was the day she had taken Tillytuck's hatchet and cut down a little poplar that was just beginning life behind the turkey house. Aunt Pat's eyes did flash then. Mary was packed off home in disgrace and made to feel that if

Aunt Pat ever forgave her it would be more than she deserved. Mary really couldn't understand it. It had been such a *little* tree. Aunt Pat hadn't been half so cross when she, Little Mary, had spilled a whole can of molasses on the Little Parlour rug or upset the jug of water on the floor in the Poet's room.

But everybody at Silver Bush spoiled Little Mary because they loved her. She had such a delightful little face. Everything about it laughed . . . her eyes . . . her mouth . . . the corners of her nose . . . the dimples in her cheeks . . . the little curl in front of her ears. Judy vowed she was "the spit and image" of Pat in childhood but she was far prettier than Pat had ever been. Yet she lacked the elfin charm that had been Pat's and sometimes Judy thought it was just as well. Perhaps it was not a good thing to have that strange little spark of difference that set you off by yourself and made a barrier, however slight and airy it might be, between you and your kind. It is quite likely that this lurking idea of Judy's was born of the fact that Pat's beaus no longer came to Silver Bush. Ever since the affair of Donald Holmes the youth of the Glens had left Pat severely alone. To be sure, when Tillytuck commented on this, Judy scornfully remarked that Pat had had them all tied up by the ears at one time or another and no more men were left. But in secret it worried her. It made Judy quite wild to think of Pat ever being an old maid. Even David Kirk didn't seem to be getting anywhere with what the clan persisted in thinking his wooing. When Judy heard that Mrs. Binnie had said that Pat Gardiner was pretty well on the shelf she trembled with wrath.

"Oh, oh, there do be just this difference betwane Madam Binnie and a rattlesnake, Tillytuck . . . the snake can't be talking."

Pat was not worrying over the absence of the men.

"I fall in love but it doesn't last," she told Judy philosophically. "It never has lasted . . . you know that, Judy. I'm constitutionally fickle and that being the case I'm never going to trust my emotions again. It wouldn't matter if it hurt only me . . . but it hurts other people. There's only one real love in my life, Judy . . . Silver Bush. I'll always be true to *it*. It satisfies me. Nothing else does. Even when I was craziest about Harris Hynes and Lester Conway and . . . and Donald Holmes, I always felt there was something wanting. I couldn't tell what but I knew it. So don't worry over me, Judy."

Judy's only comfort was that Hilary's letters still came regularly.

Pat had had a book from him that day . . . a lovely book in a dull green leather binding with a golden spider-web over it . . . a book that *belonged* to Pat. Hilary's gifts were like that . . . something that must have made him say, whenever his eyes lighted on it, "That is Pat's. It couldn't be anybody else's."

If life could just go on forever like this . . . at least for years, "safe from corroding change." In childhood you thought it would but now you knew it couldn't. Something was always coming up . . . something you never expected. Only that day she had overheard Judy saying to Tillytuck, "Oh, oh, things do be going too well. We do be going to have an awful wallop before long." Tillytuck had told Judy she needed a liver pill but Pat was afraid there was something in it.

At Silver Bush Rae's love affairs had usurped the place that Pat's used to hold. Rae discussed her two suitors very frankly with Pat and Judy in the talks around the kitchen fire o'nights, often to the unromantic accompaniment of butter-fried eggs or turkey bones. Rae was never of the same heart two nights in succession.

"Don't change your mind so often," Pat said once in exasperation.

"Oh, but it's glorious," laughed Rae. "Think how deadly monotonous it would be to be in love with the same man week in and week out. Of course I mean to make up my mind permanently some day. I feel sure I'll marry one of those boys. They are both good matches."

"Rae! That sounds hatefully mercenary."

"Sister dear, I finished with romance when Larry Wheeler sent me a flower-wreathed announcement of his bridals. That cured me forever. And I'm not mercenary . . . I'm only through with being a sentimentalist. It's just that I find it hard to decide between two equally nice boys."

"It's hardly fair to them," protested Pat. "And people are talking. They say you're more or less engaged to both of them."

"Well, you know I'm not. Neither of them is by way of being a bit deceived. And, in spite of their jealousy, they're such good sports over it all, too. They are so fearfully polite to each other outwardly. No fear of a duel there even if it wasn't out of date."

"You wouldn't want a man to risk his life for you, would you?" demanded Pat.

"No . . . no." For a moment Rae looked serious. "But I think I'd like to have him *willing* to risk it. I wonder if either Bruce or Peter would be that. However, they are getting no end of thrills out of it. It's a kind of race, you know, and men enjoy that ever so much more than a tame courtship. Sometimes I think I'll decide it by lot . . . I really do. They seem so evenly balanced. If Peter's nose is not all I would fondly dream neither are Bruce's ears. And their names are nice. That's *something*. How awful it would be to marry a man who had one of those terrible names in Dickens! Judy, do you think Bruce will be fat by the time he is forty? I'm afraid I wouldn't love him then. There is no danger of that with Peter. He'll always be thin as a snipe. But he has rosy cheeks. I don't like rosy cheeks in men. I prefer them pale and interesting. And will his mother like me?"

"It wudn't be inny great odds if she didn't, Cuddles dear," said Judy, who was enjoying Rae's "nonsense" immensely. "The woman has no great gumption. I used to be hearing she was one to give her fam'ly b'iling hot soup on a dog-day. Peter do be getting his sinse from his father's side."

"Last night I *almost* told him I'd marry him. But I had sense enough to know it was just the moon. I could be in love with anybody when the moon is just right. Pat, don't look so disapproving. You've no right to. *You've* been known to change your mind. I wish I could make up my mind . . . I really do. It's so wearing. I never thought I could be in such a predicament."

"I don't believe you care a pin for either of them," said Pat impatiently.

"Pat, I do . . . I really do. That is the exasperating part of it . . . the part that doesn't square with books."

"Why not send them both packing and go on with your college course? You used to want to be a doctor."

Rae sighed.

"It costs too much. And besides . . . my ambition seems to have petered out . . . no, that isn't a pun, really it isn't. We're like that at Silver Bush, it seems, Pat. We're just domestic girls after all and want a home to potter over, with a nice husband and a few nice babies."

"Oh, oh, that's the only sinsible word ye've said to-night, Cuddles darlint," grinned Judy. She knew her Cuddles and did not take her dilemma very seriously. It was all the darlint's fun and added to the gaiety of life at Silver Bush. Some fine day Cuddles would find out which of those nice lads she liked best and there would be a fine wedding and Cuddles would settle down not far from home, as Winnie had done. So Judy hoped in her inveterate match-making old heart. It was only Pat who worried over it. Somehow she could not picture Rae either as Mrs. Bruce Madison or Mrs. Peter Alward. But she asked herself honestly was it because she thought Rae did not care enough for either of them or was it because she hated the change another marriage would bring to Silver Bush?

"Just be letting it alone, Patsy dear," advised Judy. "The Good Man Above do be having things in hand, I'm belaving."

2

It was spring . . . it was summer . . . it was September . . . it was almost another autumn. Pat had come home from a three weeks' visit in Summerside, where Aunt Jessie had been ill and Pat had been keeping house for Uncle Brian. Now she was home again and oh, it was good! Was the sunshine amber or was it gold? How gallant the late hollyhocks looked along the dyke! How alive the air was! What a delightful smell the apple orchard had in September! How adorable were two fat pussy cats rolling in the sun! And the garden welcomed her . . . *wanted* her.

"Any news, Judy? Tell me everything that's happened while I've been away. Letters never tell half enough . . . and Rae's have really been sketchy."

"Oh, oh, Rae!" Judy looked rather as if the world were on its last legs, but Pat was too absorbed in Silver Bush generally to notice it. Tillytuck coughed significantly behind his hand and remarked that Cupid had as usual been busy at Silver Bush.

"Oh, Peter and Bruce, I suppose," laughed Pat. "Is Rae going to keep those poor wretches dangling forever? It's really getting past a joke. Where is she by the way?"

"She did be climbing the haystack in the Mince Pie Field half an hour ago, just after she did be getting home from school," said Judy, frowning at Tillytuck.

Pat betook herself to the Mince Pie Field where a splotch of colour on a half-used haystack betrayed Rae's whereabouts. Pat scrambled up the ladder and Rae grabbed her.

"Darling, I'm so glad you're back. It seems like a hundred years since you went to Summerside. I've just been lying here, letting my thoughts ripen and grow mellow. I think there's a caterpillar on my neck, but it doesn't matter. Even caterpillars have rights."

Pat slipped down beside Rae with a sigh of enjoyment. How blue the sky was, with those great banks of golden cloud in the south! Pat didn't like a cloudless sky . . . it always seemed to her hard and remote. A few clouds made it friendly . . . humanised it. How cool and delicious was the gulf breeze blowing round them, bringing with it all kinds of elusive whiffs from all the little dells and slopes of the old farm. The Buttercup Field was a pasture this year. Pat remembered how she and Sid used to play in that field when the buttercup glory came up to their heads.

"Isn't it heavenly just to lie quiet like this and soak yourself in the beauty of the world?" she said dreamily.

Rae did not answer. Pat turned her head and looked at her sister lying in her lithe young slimness on the hay. How very soft and radiant Rae's eyes were! There was something about her . . .

"Pat darling," said Rae, "I'm engaged."

Pat felt as if a thunderbolt had hit her.

"Rae . . . let me see your tongue."

"No, I'm not feverish, beloved . . . really, I'm not."

"Are you serious, Rae?"

"Absolutely. Oh, Pat, I'm just weak and trembly with happiness. I never knew any one could be so happy. It's only three weeks since you went away but everything has changed. Pat, life has just seemed like a story-book these three weeks, and every day an exciting chapter."

Pat had got her second wind but she, too, felt weak and trembly with something that was not exactly happiness.

"Which is it . . . Bruce or Peter?" she asked a bit drily.

Rae gave a young, delightful laugh.

"Oh, Pat, it's neither of them. It's Brook Hamilton."

Pat felt stunned.

"*Who* is Brook Hamilton?"

Rae laughed again.

"Fancy any one not knowing who Brook Hamilton is. I can't believe I didn't know him myself three weeks ago. I met him the first night you went away at Dot's dance . . ."

"Rae Gardiner, you don't mean to tell me you're engaged to a man you've known only three weeks!"

"Don't go off the deep end, darling. We're not to be married till he's through college so we'll have lots of time to get acquainted. And he's my man . . . there's no mistake about that. At nine o'clock that evening I had never seen him. At ten I loved him. Judy says it happens like that once in a thousand years. I never believed in love at first sight before . . . but now I know it's the only kind."

"Rae . . . Rae . . . *I* thought that once, too . . . I was sure I was madly in love with Lester Conway . . . and it was nothing but the moon . . ."

"There wasn't any moon the night of Dot's party, so you can't blame this on the moon."

"I suppose," said Pat sarcastically, "he's extremely handsome and you've fallen for . . ."

"But he isn't. I think he's ugly really, when I think of his face at all. But it's such a delightful ugliness. And he has such steady blue eyes and such dependable broad shoulders, and such thick black hair . . . though it always looks as if he'd combed it with a rake. But I like that, too. He wouldn't be Brook if he had sleek hair. Dearest, it's all right . . . it really is. Mother and Dad like him and even Judy approves of him. We're to be married when he's through college and go to China."

"China!"

"Yes. He's going to take charge of the Chinese branch of his father's business there . . . I forgot to tell you he's one of the Halifax Hamiltons and Dot's cousin."

"But . . . China!"

"It *does* sound like a long hop. But, really, darling, nothing matters . . . Indian plains or Lapland snows . . . so long as I'm with him. I don't talk like this to the others, Pat . . . but with you I've just got to let myself go."

"And what about Bruce and Peter?" asked Pat, with a faint smile.

"Pat, it was really comical. Oh, there's so much to tell you. You see, they didn't know anything about Brook, but they told me two weeks ago that I had to make up my mind between them. And I just told them I was engaged to Brook. You should have seen their faces. Then they just faded out of the picture. I don't think they ever really existed."

"And were you engaged *then* . . . a week after you'd met him?"

"Darling, we were engaged three days after we met. I couldn't help it. What would *you* do if Sir Launcelot just rode into your back yard and told you you had to marry him? Because Brook didn't *ask* me, you know . . . he just told me I had to. There wasn't the least use objecting even if I'd wanted to. And . . . oh, Pat, I . . . I *cried*. That's the shameful

461

truth. I haven't the least idea why I did, but I simply howled. It was such a relief . . . I'd been thinking I was just one of the crowd to him . . . and Dot was trying to hint he was after Lenore Madison . . . that freckled, snub-nosed thing. You may be sure I didn't ask for any time to consider. Pat, you're not going to cry!"

"No . . . no . . . but this is really a little unexpected, Rae."

For one awful moment Pat had felt as if Rae . . . this Rae . . . were a stranger to her. She had been away from Silver Bush for only three weeks and *this* had happened.

"I know." Rae squeezed Pat's hand. "And I know it must all seem like indecent haste to you. But if you count time by heart-throbs as somebody says you should, it's been a century since I met him. He *isn't* a stranger. He's one of our kind . . . like Hilary . . . knows all our quacks, really he does. You'll understand when you meet him, Pat."

Pat did understand. She couldn't find a single fault with Brook Hamilton. As a brother-in-law he was everything that could be desired. Tall, lean, with intensely blue eyes and straight black brows. Certainly he and Rae made a wonderful-looking young pair in spite of his "rather ugly" face. She couldn't hate him as she had hated Frank, even if he were going to take her sister away. But, mercifully, not for a long time yet. And there was no doubt that Rae loved him.

"I wish I could love somebody like that," said Pat, with a little pang of envy. She sat alone for a long time in her room that evening while the robins whistled outside and the purple night sky looked down on her. So, in the years to come, she would always have to sit alone. For the first time in her life Pat felt *old* . . . for the first time a little chill of fear for her own future touched her. She almost hated Bold-and-Bad for purring so loudly on the bed. It was outrageous that a cat should be so blatantly happy. Really Bold-and-Bad had no tact.

"I suppose," thought Pat dolefully, "the time will come when I'll have nothing left but a cat." Then she brightened up. "And Silver Bush. That will be enough," she added softly.

At bedtime she knelt by Rae's bed and put her arm across Rae's shoulders.

"Cuddles dear," she said, slipping back to the old nickname, "Brook is a dear . . . and I think you're both lucky . . . and I love you . . . love you . . . love you."

"Pat, you're the dearest thing in the world. And why didn't you cast the Reverend Wheeler of happy memory up to me and remind me of the time I thought I was in love with him? I really expected you to do it . . . I don't know how any human being could have resisted doing it."

Judy was only moderately pleased over the engagement because of the prospect of China.

"Oh, oh, I've great opinions of haythens, Patsy dear. They do be all right to sind missionaries to, but not to be living among. And her wid thim looks av hers to go to Chiny! Sure and some ugly girl wud have done for him I'm thinking, since he can't be continted in a civilised country. But I'm not denying he's a fine lad and he can't be hilping his uncle."

"Now, Judy, what about his uncle?"

"Oh, oh, it's an ould tale and better not raked up maybe. Well, if ye will be having it. The Hamiltons may be av Halifax now but the grandfather av thim lived in Charlottetown whin his lads were small. And Brook's uncle was the black shape . . . if it don't be insulting shape to call him so. Crooked he was as a dog's hind leg. He wint out wist after quarrelling wid his dad and what did he do but write a long account av his being killed whin a train struck his horse and buggy at a crossing and got it published in a liddle newspaper there, one av his wild cronies being editor av it, and sint a marked copy home to the ould folks. It just about broke his poor mother's heart . . . I'm not saying his dad tuk it so hard and small blame to him . . . and they had a lot av worry tilligraphing to have the body sint home. And whin they wint to the station wid the hearse and undertaker and all to mate the corpse didn't me fine Dicky Hamilton stip off the train laughing at the joke he'd played on thim!"

"How horrible! But don't tell Rae that, Judy."

"Oh, oh, it's not likely . . . nor the squeal to it ather. For what do you think, Patsy dear? The young scallywag did be killed the nixt wake in the very same way he'd writ av . . . he was driving along one avening reckless-like and the train struck him on that crossing on the wist road and that was the ind av him. Niver be telling me it wasn't jidgmint. But there do be no doubting that Cuddles is over head and heels in love wid Brook. 'Sure and there do be other min in the world, Cuddles darlint,' I sez, be way av tazing her a bit. 'There aren't,' she sez, solemn-like. 'There's simply nobody else in the world, Judy,' sez she. And that being the case we must just be making the bist av it, uncle or no uncle. After all, there do be something rale glamorous about it as Tillytuck wud say."

As a matter of fact, all Tillytuck said was, "Engaged, by gosh!" Such a whirlwind courtship was entirely too much for Tillytuck. He relieved his feeling by playing on his fiddle in the graveyard, seated on Wild Dick's tombstone, much to Judy's horror.

"How do you know Wild Dick doesn't still like to hear the fiddle, Judy?" asked Sid audaciously.

"If Wild Dick do be in heaven he has the angels to be listening to . . . and if he isn't he do be having other things to think av," was Judy's indignant reply. Tillytuck had to give her his old red flannel shirt for the rose-buds in her new hooked rug before he could make his peace with her. And then nearly wrecked it again by solemnly telling Little Mary, to whom Judy had just been relating a story of some naughty children who had been turned into brooms by a witch . . . "I was one of them brooms!"

THE SIXTH YEAR

1

For a year things went beautifully at Silver Bush. Everybody was happy. Mother was better than she had been for a long time. Sid seemed to have recovered his good spirits and was taking a keen interest in everything again. Gossip no longer coupled his name with any girl's and Pat saw her old dream of living always at Silver Bush with Sid taking vague shape again. It was just like it used to be. They planned and joked and walked in faint blue twilights and Sid told her everything, and together they bullied Long Alec and Tillytuck when any difference of opinion came up. Between them they managed to get Silver Bush repainted, although Long Alec hated any extra expense as long as there was a mortgage on it. But Silver Bush looked beautiful . . . so white and trig and prosperous with its green shutters and trim. It warmed the cockles of Pat's heart just to look at it. And to hear Sid say once, gruffly, on their return one winter evening from a long prowl back to their Secret Field,

"You're a good old scout, Pat. I don't know what I'd have done without you these past two years."

"Oh, Sid!" Pat could only say that as she rubbed her face against his shoulder. This was one of life's good moments. They had had such a wonderful walk. It had been lovely back in the woods. It was after the first snowfall and the woods were at peace in a white transfiguration, placidly still and calm, where the thick ranks of the young saplings were snow-laden and an occasional warm golden shaft of light from the low-hanging sun pierced through, tingeing the dark bronze-green of the spruces and the greyish-green streams of moss with vivid beauty. They had come home by way of Happiness, where Jordan was crooning to itself under the ice. The old pastures, which had been so beautiful and flowery in June, were cold and white now, but Pat loved them, as she loved them in all moods.

She lingered at the gate to taste her happiness after Sid had gone on to the barn. It was going to be a night of frost and silver. To her right the garden was hooding itself in the shadows of dusk. Pat loved to think of all her staunch old flowers under the banks of snow, waiting for spring. Far away a dim hill came out darkly against a winter sunset. Beyond the dyke was a group of old spruces which Long Alec often said should be cut down. But Pat pleaded for them. Seen in daylight they *were* old and uncomely, dead almost to the top, with withered branches. But seen in this enchanted light, against a sky that began by being rosy-saffron and continued in silver green, and ended in crystal blue, they were like tall, slender witch women weaving spells of necromancy in a rune of olden days. Pat felt a stirring of her childish desire to share in their gramarye . . . to have fellowship in their twilight sorceries.

Off to her left the orchard was white and still, heaped with drifts along the fences. Over it all was a delicate tracery of shadow where the trees stood up lifeless in seeming death and sorrow. But it was only seeming. The life-blood was in their hearts and by and by it would stir and they would clothe themselves in bridal garments of young green leaves and pink blossoms, and lush grass would wave where the snow was now lying and golden buttercups dance among it. Spring always came again . . . she must never forget that.

Silver Bush looked very beautiful in the faint beginning moonlight . . . her own dear Silver Bush. It still welcomed her . . . it was still hers, no matter what changes came and went. Life seemed to have put on a new meaning now that Sid had come back to her in their old companionship. She pulled his love about her like a cloak and felt warm and satisfied.

Rae had settled down to filling a hope chest and writing daily letters of portentous length to Brook Hamilton. She was changed . . . more gentle, thoughtful, womanly. There was no more pretending to be hard-boiled. Love, Sid told her teasingly, did mellow people remarkably. The old flippancy was gone, though she laughed as much as ever and never had her laughter, thought adoring Pat, been so exquisite.

Pat had resigned herself to the fact of Rae's engagement. But she would not be getting married for at least three years. They had those years to look forward to . . . years, dreamed Pat, of companionship and plans and all the dear intimacies of home.

Winter slipped away . . . spring and summer passed. September wore a golden moon like a ring and again autumn brewed a cup of magic and held it to your lips. Only Tillytuck secretly thought it rather slow. The beaus came no longer, since Rae was known to be bespoken and Pat, so it was said, thought no one good enough for her.

"Life is getting a bit tedious here, Judy," he said, mournfully. "There doesn't seem to be as much glamour, romantically speaking."

Perhaps Judy thought so, too. She sighed . . . it was not like Judy to sigh. Pat would have another birthday in a week . . . and not a beau in sight. Even David, Judy had decided, had really no serious intentions, and she hated him for it as sincerely as if she had never disapproved of him. She did not want Pat to marry him, but that was for Pat to decide, not for him. As for Jingle, there never was any word of his coming home for a visit.

"He's grown away from us, Judy. We're only memories to him now. He has his own work and his own ambitions. Even his letters aren't just what they used to be."

Pat hadn't seemed to care. She was more taken up with Silver Bush than ever and she and Sid were "thick as thieves" again. Which was all to the good, as far as it went. To be sure, of late weeks, Sid had taken to gallivanting again. Nobody could find out where he was going although Judy had certain uneasy suspicions she never breathed to any one. Judy sighed again as she clapped her baked beans and bacon in the oven. Then she brightened up. Every one needed a liddle bite once in so often and as long as she, Judy Plum, could provide it there was balm in Gilead.

A week later Judy looked back to that day and wondered if what had happened had been a judgment on her for thinking life had got a bit dull. For Pat's birthday had come and that evening Sid had brought May Binnie in and announced, curtly and defiantly, and yet with such a pitiful, beaten look on his face, that they had been married that day in Charlottetown.

"We thought we'd surprise you," said May, glancing archly about her out of bold, brilliant eyes. "Birthday surprise for you, Pat."

2

Pat sat up all that night, looking out over the quiet, unchanged fields of the farm, trying to look this hideous fact in the face. She was in the Poet's room and she had locked the door. She would not even have Rae with her.

She could not yet believe that this had happened. At first one cannot believe in a monstrous thing. Can one ever believe it? It was a dream . . . a nightmare. She would waken presently. She must . . . or go mad.

She had been so happy that evening at twilight . . . so unusually, inexplicably happy, as if the gods were going to give her some wonderful gift . . . and now she would never be happy again. Pat was still young enough to think that when a thing like this happened you could never be happy again. Everything . . . *everything* . . . had changed in the twinkling of an eye. Sid was lost to her forever. The very fields she had loved now looked strange and hostile as she gazed on them. "Our inheritance is turned to strangers and our house to aliens." She had read that verse in her Bible chapter two nights ago and shivered over the picture of desolation it presented. And now it had come true in her own life . . . her life that a few hours ago had seemed so full and beautiful and was now so ugly and empty.

It had been such a ghastly hour. Nobody knew what to say or do. Pat's face seemed to wither as she looked at them . . . at May, flushed and triumphant under all her uneasiness, at Sid, sullen and defiant. May tried to carry the situation off brazenly, after the true Binnie fashion.

"Come, Pat, don't look so snooty. *I'm* willing to let bygones be bygones, even if you and I *have* hated each other all our lives."

This was only too true but it was terrible to have the feeling dragged into light as nakedly as this. Pat could not answer. She turned away as if she had neither seen nor heard May and walked blindly out of the room. The only feeling she was keenly conscious of just then was a sick desire to get away from the light into a dark place where no one could see her . . . where she could hide like a wounded animal.

May looked after her and her bold handsome face flushed crimson under Pat's utter disregard. Her black eyes held a flame that was not good to see. But she laughed as she turned to Sid.

"She'll get over it, honey-boy. I never expected a warm welcome from Pat, you know."

Rae alone kept her head. Neither mother nor father must be told till morning, she reflected. As for Judy and Tillytuck, they seemed stricken dumb. Tillytuck slipped off to his granary shaking his head and Judy climbed to her kitchen chamber, feeling, for the time at least, more crushed and cowed than ever in her life before.

"I've felt it coming," she muttered, as she crept into bed forlornly. "I've been hearing he was going wid the bold young hussy. And Gintleman Tom knew it was coming, that he did. That was why he lit out like the knowing baste he was. He knew he cud niver be standing a Binnie. Oh, oh, if I did be knowing as much av magic as me grandmother I'd change her into a toad that I wud. What'll be coming av it the Good Man Above only knows. One does be thinking the world cud be run a bit better. I'm fearing this will break Patsy's heart."

3

All the rest of her life Pat knew she had left girlhood behind her on that dreadful night. Hope seemed to be blotted out entirely. Already the hours that had passed seemed like an eternity and to-morrow . . . all the tomorrows . . . would be just as bad. Her mind went round and round in a miserable circle and got nowhere. May Binnie living at Silver Bush . . . Silver Bush overrun with Binnies . . . they were a clannish crew in their way. Old Mr. Binnie who ate peas with his knife and old Mrs. Binnie who always sopped her bread in her gravy. And all the slangy, loud-voiced crew of them, the kind of people before whom you must always say everything over to yourself beforehand to be sure it was safe. What a crowd for Sid to have got himself mixed up with! No, it could not be faced.

Pat wouldn't go down when morning came . . . couldn't. For the first time in her life she was a shirker. She could hear them talking beneath her at the breakfast-table. She could hear May's desecrating laugh. She clenched her hands in fury and wretchedness. She pulled down the blind and shut out a world that was too glad with its early sunshine and its purple mists.

Presently Rae came in . . . trim, alert, competent. Her blue eyes showed no traces of the tears she had shed in the night.

"Pat, I left you alone last night because I realised that a thing like this had much better be talked over in the morning."

"What is the use of talking it over any time?" asked Pat listlessly.

"We must talk it over because we have to face the situation, Pat. There is no use in turning our back on it or squinting at it out of the corners of our eyes . . . or ignoring it. Let's just get down to real things and look to the future."

"But I can't face it . . . Rae, I *can't*," cried poor Pat desperately. "Talk about the future! There isn't any future! If it had been anybody but May Binnie! I'm not the little fool I once was. I've known for long that Sid would marry sometime. Even when I couldn't help hoping he wouldn't I knew he would. But May Binnie!"

"I know. I know as well as you do that Sid has made a dreadful mistake and will realise it all too clearly some day. I know May is cheap and common and has no background . . . kitchen-bred, as Judy would say . . . but . . ."

"How could he do it? How could he like *her* . . . after Bets . . . even after poor Dorothy?"

"May is alluring in her own way, Pat. *We* can't see it but the men do. And she has always meant to get Sid. We've just got to make the best of it and take things as they come."

"I won't," said Pat rebelliously. "They may *have* to come but I haven't got to take them without protest. I'll never reconcile myself to this . . . never."

"'To-day that seems so long, so strange, so bitter
Will soon be some forgotten yesterday,'"

quoted Rae softly.

"It won't," said Pat dismally.

469

"I've been doing some talking already this morning," went on Rae. "For one thing I broke the news to dad."

"And he . . . what did he . . ."

"Oh, there were fireworks. The Gardiner temper flared up. But I know how to manage dad. I told him he had to take a reasonable view of it for mother's sake. When he calmed down he and I worked it out. Sid and May will have to live here for a year or two, until the mortgage is cleared. Then dad will build a house for them on the other place and they can live there."

"And in the meantime," said Pat passionately, "life will be unlivable at Silver Bush . . . you know it will."

"I don't know anything of the sort. Of course it won't be as pleasant as it has been. But, Pat, you know as well as I do that we've got to make the best of it for mother's sake."

"Does she know?"

"Yes. Dad told her. I funked *that.*"

"And how . . . how did she take it?"

"How does mother take anything? Just like the gallant lady she is! We mustn't fail her, Pat."

Pat groped out a hand, found Rae's and squeezed it. Somehow their ages seemed reversed. It was as if Rae were the older sister.

"I'll do my best," she choked. "There's a verse in the Bible somewhere . . . 'be of good courage' . . . I've always thought it a wonderful phrase. I suppose it was meant just for times like this. But oh, Rae, how *can* we live with May? Her habits . . . her ideals . . . her point of view about everything . . . are so different from ours."

"She must have some good points," said Rae reasonably. "She's really popular in her own set. Everybody says she is a good worker."

"We have no work for her to do here," said Pat bitterly.

"You know, Pat, nothing is ever quite so dreadful in reality as in anticipation. We must just look *around* this. It's blocking up our view at present because we are too close to it."

"We can never be ourselves . . . our real selves . . . when she is about, Rae."

"Perhaps not. But she won't be always around. And she isn't going to rule here whatever she may think. 'I'm master here,' said dad, at the end of our talk, 'and your mother is mistress of Silver Bush and will remain so.' So that's that. I must be off to school now. You won't have to face

470

May this morning. Sid has taken her home for the day."

Judy, who, for the first time in her life, had been a coward, crept in now and Pat flew to her old arms.

"Judy . . . Judy . . . help me to bear it."

"Oh, oh, bearing is it? We'll bear it together, Patsy darling, to the last turn av the screw, wid a grin for the honour av Silver Bush. And just be remimbering, Patsy, what the Good Book says . . . about happiness being inside av ye and not outside. Thim mayn't just be the words but it's what I'm belaving it manes."

"All very well if things outside would stop poking at you," said Pat, rather less forlornly.

"We've got to be saving Silver Bush from her," said Judy slyly. "She'll be trying to spile it while she do be here and we'll have our liddle bit av fun heading her off, Patsy darlint . . . diplomatic-like and widout ructions for the honour av the fam'ly. Ye'd have had a laugh this morning if ye'd been down, Patsy, to see Bould-and-Bad turning his back on her, aven if she did be making a fuss over him. She's rale fond av the animiles so we nadn't worry over that."

To Pat it was almost another count against May that she was fond of cats. She hated to admit a good point in her.

"How was Sid, Judy?"

"Oh, oh, looking like innything but a happy bridegroom. And just a bit under her thumb already, as I cud be seeing. Her wid her 'honey-boy' and telling av the way his hair curled over his forrid! As if I hadn't been knowing it all his life. But I was as smooth as crame, darlint, and that rispictful ye'd have died and niver did I be aven glancing at her stockings all in rolls round her ankles. Sure and it was a comfort to me to be knowing Long Alec wasn't intinding to hand Silver Bush over to Sid, as the Binnies hoped. Long Alec's not taking off his boots afore he goes to bed. 'You and yer wife can stay here till I can afford to build a house for ye,' sez he . . . and me fine May wasn't liking it. She's been telling round what she would do when she got to Silver Bush. 'I can be getting Sid Gardiner back whin I crook me finger,' sez she. Oh, oh, she's got him, worse luck, but she hasn't got Silver Bush and niver will. A year or two will soon pass, Patsy dear, and thin we'll be free av her. Maybe aven sooner wid a bit av luck."

"She has gone home for the day," Rae said.

"To be getting her boxes and breaking the news to the Binnies. I'm thinking they'll bear up well under it. She did be insisting on washing the dishes first and I did be letting her for pace' sake. She did be making as much commotion as a cat in a fit, finding where iverything shud go, and smashed the ould blue plate be way av showing what she cud do. But I'll not be denying she washed thim clane and didn't be laving a grasey sink."

Pat had always washed the dishes. She began to be sorry she hadn't gone down for breakfast after all. It would have been more dignified . . . more Silver Bushish.

"Now, come ye down, Patsy darlint, and have a liddle bite," said Judy wheedlingly. "I've been after frying a bit av the new ham and an egg in butter. A cup av tay will restore yer balance like. And we'll be having our liddle laugh now and agin behind her back, Patsy."

Pat pulled up the blind again. There was a little chill at her heart which had never been there before and which she felt would always be there henceforth. But afar the Hill of the Mist was lovely in the September sunshine. When she looked at it it gave her some of its own pride and calm and faint austerity.

She went up to see mother after she had had her breakfast and found her, as always, serene and clear and pale, like a star seen through the rifts of storm-cloud.

"Darling, it's hard, I know. I'm sorry for Sid . . . he *has* made a great mistake, poor boy. But if we all do our best things will work out somehow. They always do."

Poor brave darling mother!

"We'll be all right when we get our second wind," said Pat staunchly. "I'm going to be decent to May, mother, and there won't be any bickering . . . I won't have that here. But Silver Bush is going to be saved from the Binnies, mother, and no mistake about it."

Mother laughed.

"Trust you for that, Pat."

THE SEVENTH YEAR

1

Pat and Rae felt, in the months of that following winter, that they needed every ounce of philosophy and "diplomacy" that they possessed. The first weeks were very hard. At times adjustment seemed almost impossible. May's quick temper increased the difficulty. Some of the scenes she made always remained in Pat's memory like degrading, vulgar things. Yet her spasms of rage were not so bad, the girls thought, as her little smiles and innuendoes about everything. "I think I have *some* rights surely," she would say to Sid, with a toss of her sleek head. "It's hard to do anything with somebody watching and criticising all the time, isn't it now, honey-boy?" And Sid would look at Pat with defiant and yet appealing eyes that nearly broke her heart.

When May could not get her way she sulked and went round for a day or two "wid a puss on her mouth," according to Judy. Then, finding that nobody paid any attention to her sulks, she would become amiable again. Pat set her teeth and kept her head.

"I *won't* have quarrels at Silver Bush," she said. "Whatever she does or says I won't quarrel with her." And even when May cried passionately, "You've *always* tried to make trouble between me and Sid," Pat would smile and say, "Come, May, be reasonable. We're not children now, you know." Then go up to her room and writhe in secret over the torment and ugliness of it all.

In the long run May succumbed to the inevitable, compromises were made on both sides, and life settled once more into outward calmness at Silver Bush. One thing nobody could deny was that May was a worker; and fortunately she liked outside work better than inside. She took over the care of milk and poultry, Judy making a virtue out of necessity in yielding it to her and never denying that the separator was thoroughly cleaned. "May," Mrs. Binnie said superfluously, "is not a soulless sassiety woman. I brought all *my* gals up to work."

To be sure, May made a frightful racket in everything she did and at Silver Bush, where household ritual had always been performed

473

without noise, this was something of a domestic crime. Pat, suffering too much to be just, told Rae that May made more fuss in ten minutes than any one else could make in a year.

Judy and May had one battle royal as to who was to scrub the kitchen. Judy won. May never attempted to usurp Judy's kitchen privileges again.

Pat found she could get used to being unhappy . . . and then that she could even be happy again, between the spasms of unhappiness. Of course there were changes everywhere . . . little irritating changes which were perhaps harder to bear than some greater dislocation. For one thing, May's friends gave her a "shower," after which Silver Bush was cluttered up with gim-cracks. Pat's especial hatred was a dreadful onyx-topped table. May put it in the hall under the heirloom mirror. It was a desecration. And May's new gay cushions, which made everything else seem faded, were scattered everywhere. But May did not get her own way when it came to moving furniture about.

She learned that things were to be left as they were and that a large engraving of Landseer's stag, framed in crimson plush and gilt a foot wide, was *not* going to be hung in the dining room. May, after a scene, carried it off to her own room, where nobody interfered with her arrangements.

"I suppose your ladyship doesn't object to *that*," she remarked to Pat.

"Of course you can do as you like in your own room," said Pat wearily.

Would this petty bickering go on forever? And that very afternoon May had broken the old Bristol-ware vase by stuffing a huge bouquet of 'mums into it. Of course it was cracked . . . always had been cracked. May said she didn't hold with having cracked things around. She had her own room re-papered . . . blue roses on a bright pink ground. "So cheerful," Mrs. Binnie said admiringly. "That grey paper in what they call the Pote's room gives me the willies, May dearie."

May brought her dog with her, an animal known by the time-tested name of Rover. He killed the chickens, dug up Pat's bulbs, chewed the clothes on the line . . . Tillytuck had a pitched battle with May because his best shirt was mangled . . . and chased the cats in his spare time. Eventually Just Dog gave him a drubbing which chastened him and Rae, in May's absences, used to spank him so soundly with a stiff folded newspaper that he learned manners after a sort. There were even times when Pat was afraid she was learning to like him. It was hard for Pat not to like a dog if he had any decency at all.

As Pat had foreseen Silver Bush was overrun with the Binnie tribe. May's brothers flicked cigarette ashes all over the house. Her sisters and cousins came in what Judy called "droves," filled the house with shrieks, and listened behind doors. Judy caught them at it. And they were always more or less offended no matter how they were treated. If you were nice to them you were patronising them; if you left them alone you were snubbing them. Olive would bring her whole family. Olive did not believe in punishing children. "They're going to enjoy their childhood," she said. Perhaps they enjoyed it but nobody else did. They were what Judy called "holy terrors." Judy found a dirty grey velvet elephant in her soup pot one day. Olive's six-year-old had slipped it in "for fun."

Mrs. Binnie came over frequently and spent the afternoon in Judy's kitchen, proclaiming to the world that as far as she was concerned all was peace and good-will. She rocked fiercely on the golden-oak rocker May had introduced into the kitchen . . . rather fortunately, Judy thought, for certainly no Silver Bush chair could be counted on to bear up under the strain of Mrs. Binnie's two hundred and thirty-three pounds.

"No, no, two hundred and thirty-six, ma," May would argue.

"I guess I know my own weight, child," Mrs. Binnie would retort breezily. "And I ain't ashamed of it. 'Why don't you diet?' my sister Josephine keeps telling me. 'Not for mine,' I tell her, 'I'm contented to be as God made me!'"

"Oh, oh, I do be thinking God had precious little to do wid it," said Judy to Tillytuck.

Mrs. Binnie had a little button nose and yellowish-white hair screwed up in a tight knot on the crown of her head. Gossip was her mother-tongue and grammar was her servant, not her master. Also, her "infernal organs" gave her a good deal of trouble. Pat used to wonder how Sid could bear to look at her and think that May would be like her when she was sixty.

"I'd like to give that hair of hers a bluing rinse," Rae would whisper maliciously to Pat, when Mrs. Binnie was laying down the law about something and nodding her head until a hairpin invariably slipped out.

Mrs. Binnie, unlike May, "couldn't abide" cats. They gave her asthma and, as May said, she started gasping if a cat was parked within a mile

475

of her. So when Mrs. Binnie came out went the cats. Even Bold-and-Bad was no exception. Bold-and-Bad, however, did not hold with self-pity and made himself at home in Tillytuck's granary.

"But I'd like to have seen ye try it on Gintleman Tom," Judy used to think malevolently.

Generally one or more of "thim rampageous Binnie girls" came with her and they and May talked and argued without cessation. The Binnies were a family with no idea of reticence. Everybody told everything to everybody else . . . "talking it over," they called it. None of them could ever understand why everything that was thought about couldn't be talked about. They had no comprehension whatever of people who did not think at the tops of their voices and empty out their feelings to the dregs. There were times when the unceasing clack of their tongues drove Tillytuck to the granary even on the coldest winter afternoons for escape and Pat longed despairingly for the beautiful old silences.

There was at least one consolation for Pat and Rae . . . they still had their evenings undisturbed. May thought it quite awful to sit in the kitchen, "with the servants." Generally she carried Sid off to a dance or show and when they were home they had company of their own in the Little Parlour . . . which had been tacitly handed over to May and which she called the "living room," much to Judy's amusement.

"Oh, oh, we've only the one living room at Silver Bush and that's me kitchen," she would remark to Tillytuck with a wink. "There do be more living done here than in all the other rooms put together."

"You've said a mouthful," said Tillytuck, just as he had said it to Lady Medchester.

So Pat and Rae and Judy and Tillytuck foregathered as of old in the kitchen of evenings and forgot for a few hours the shadow that was over Silver Bush. They always had some special little jamboree to take the taste of some particularly hard day out of their mouths . . . as, for instance, the one on which Pat found May prying into her bureau drawers . . . or the one when May, who had a trick of acting hostess, assured a fastidious visiting clergyman who had declined a second helping that there was plenty more in the kitchen.

They could even laugh over Mrs. Binnie's malapropisms. It was so delicious when she asked Rae gravely whether "phobias" were annuals or perennials. To be sure, neither Judy not Tillytuck was very sure just where the point of the joke was but it was heartening to see the girls laughing again as of old. Those evenings were almost the only time it was safe to laugh. If May heard laughter she took it into her head that they were laughing at her and sulked. Once in a while, when May had gone for one of her frequent visits home, Sid would creep in, too, for a bit of the old-time fun and one of Judy's liddle bites. Sid and Pat had had their hour of reconciliation long ere this: Pat couldn't endure to be "out" with Sid. But there were no more rambles and talks and plans together. May resented any such thing. She went with him now on his walks about the farm and expounded her ideas as to what changes should be made. She also aired her views to the whole family. A lot of trees should be cut down . . . there were entirely too many . . . it was "messy," especially that aspen poplar by the steps. And the Old Part of the orchard ought to be cleaned out entirely; it was a sheer waste of good ground. She did not go so far as to suggest ploughing up the graveyard though she said it was horrid having a place like that so near the house and having to pass it every time you went to the barn or the hen-house. When she went to either of these places after dark she averred it made her flesh creep.

"If I were you," she would remark airily to Pat, "I'd make a few changes round here. A front porch is so out of date. And there really should be a wall or two knocked out. The Poet's room and our room together would just make one real nice-sized room. You don't need two spare rooms any more'n a frog needs trousers."

"Silver Bush suits us as it is," said Pat stiffly.

"Don't get so excited, child," said May provokingly . . . and how provoking May could be! "I was only making a suggestion. Surely you needn't throw a fit over that."

"She would do nothing but patch and change and tear up if she could have her way here," Pat told Rae viciously.

"Oh, oh, just like her ould grandad," said Judy. "He did be having a mania for tearing down and rebuilding. Innything for a change was *his* motto."

"Judy, last night as I passed the Little Parlour I heard May say to Sid, 'Anyway you'll have Silver Bush when your father dies.' Judy, she did! *When your father dies.*"

Judy chuckled.

"It do be ill waiting for dead men's shoes. Yer dad is good for twenty years yet at the laste. But it's like a Binnie to be saying that same."

2

Sometimes Pat would escape from it all to her fields and woods, at peace in their white loveliness. It carried her through many hard hours to remember that in ten minutes she could, if she must, be in that meadow solitude of her Secret Field, far from babble and confusion. There were yet wonderful ethereal dawns which she and Rae shared together . . . there were yet full moons rising behind snowy hills . . . rose tints over sunset dells . . . slender birches and shadowy nooks . . . winds calling to each other at night . . . apple-green "dims" . . . starry quietudes that soothed your pain . . . April buds in happiness . . . "Thank God, April still comes to the world" . . . and Silver Bush to be loved and protected and cherished.

And with the spring Joe came home, to be married at last; after every one had concluded, so Mrs. Binnie said, that poor Enid Sutton was never going to get him.

"Many's the time I've said to her, 'Don't be too sure of him. A sailor has a sweetheart in every port. It isn't as if you was still a girl. You never can depend on them sailors. Take Mrs. Rory MacPherson at the Bridge . . . a disappointed woman if ever there was one. *Her* husband was a sailor and she thought he was dead and was going to get married again when he turned up alive and well.'"

There was a big gay wedding at the Suttons and every one thought bronzed Joe remarkably handsome. Pat thought so, too, and was proud of him; but he seemed a stranger now . . . Joe, whose going had once been such a tragedy. She was even a little glad when all the fuss was over and Joe and his bride were gone on a wonderful bridal trip around the world in Joe's new vessel. She could settle down to housecleaning and gardening now . . . at least, after Mrs. Binnie had had her say about the event.

"A grand wedding. Some people don't see how old Charlie Sutton could afford it but I always say most folks is only married once and why not make a splurge. I always did like a wedding. Wasn't May the naughty thing to run off the way she did, so sly-like? I'll bet you folks here wasn't a bit more flabbergasted than I was when I heard it. And maybe I didn't feel upset about her coming in here with you all. But I always believed it would work out in time and it has. People said May could never live in peace here, Pat was such a crank. But I said, 'No,

Pat isn't a crank. It's just that you have to understand her.' And I was right, wasn't I, dearie? May made up her mind when she come here that she'd get along with you. 'It takes two to make a quarrel, ma, you know,' she said. And I said, 'That's the right spirit, dearie. Behave like a lady whatever you do. You're a Gardiner now and must live up to their traditions. And you must make allowances.' That's what I said to her. 'You must make allowances. And don't be scared. I hope *my* daughter isn't a coward,' I said. It's a real joy to me to see how well you've got on together, though I don't deny that Judy Plum has been a hard nut to crack. May has felt certain things . . . May always did feel things so deeply. But she just made allowances as I advised her. 'Judy Plum has been spoiled as every one knows,' I told her, 'but she's old and breaking up fast and you can afford to humour her a bit, dearie.' 'Oh, I'm not going to stoop to argue with a servant,' May says. 'I'm above that.' May always was so sensible. Well, I'm glad poor Enid Sutton has got married at last . . . she's gone off terrible these past three years waiting for Joe and not knowing if he'd ever come. And what about you, Pat dearie? I can't imagine what the men are thinking of. Isn't your widower a bit slow?" . . . with a smirk that had the same effect on Pat as a dig in the ribs . . . "Folks think he's trying to back out of it but I tell them, 'no, that'll be a match yet.' Just you encourage him a little more, dearie . . . that's all he needs. To be sure, May said to me the other day, *I* wouldn't take another woman's leavings, ma.' But you're not getting any younger, Pat, if you'll excuse my saying so. *I* was married when I was eighteen and I could have been married when I was seventeen. My dress was of red velvet and my hat was of black velvet with a green plume. Every one thought it elegant but I was disappointed. I'd always wanted to be wedded in a sky-blue gown, the hue of God's own heaven."

"Once of her poetical flights," whispered Tillytuck to Judy. But Pat and Rae both heard him and almost choked trying not to laugh. Mrs. Binnie, who never dreamed any one could be laughing at her, kept on.

"Is it true the Kirks are putting up a sun-dial in the Long House garden?"

"Yes," said Pat shortly.

"Well now, I never did hold with them modern inventions," said Mrs. Binnie complacently. "An old-fashioned clock is good enough for *me*."

"Never mind," said Rae, when Mrs. Binnie had finally waddled off to the "living room," "it will soon be lilac time."

"With white apple boughs framing a moon," said Pat.

"And violets in the silver bush," said Rae.

"And a new row of lilies to be planted along the dyke," said Pat.

"And great crimson clovers in the Mince Pie Field."

"And blue-eyed grass around the Pool . . ."

"And pussy-willows in Happiness . . ."

"And a dance of daisies along Jordan."

"Oh, we've heaps of precious things left yet, Pat—things nobody, not even a Binnie can spoil." Were the days when she could wash her being in the sunrise and feel as blithe as a bird gone forever? Perhaps they would come back when the new house would be built and Silver Bush was all their own again. But that was as yet far in the future. There was Judy coming across the yard, bringing in some drenched little chickens May had forgotten to put in. Was Judy getting bent? Pat shivered.

But still life seemed sadly out of tune, struggle as bravely as one might.

3

"I'll have nothing to do with anything to-day but spring," said Pat . . . even gaily. For May had gone home that morning and they had a whole day to be alone . . . three delightful meals to eat alone when they could sit around the table and talk as long as they liked in the old way. Sometimes Pat and Judy thought those frequent visits of May home were all that saved their reason. Everything seemed different. Judy vowed that the very washing machine ran easier when she was away. Even the house seemed to draw a breath of relief. It had never got used to May.

It had not been an easy spring at Silver Bush despite its beauty. House-cleaning with May was rather a heartbreaking business. She was so full of suggestions.

"Why not do away with that messy old front garden, Pat and make a real lawn?" . . . or, "I'd have a window cut there, Pat. This hall is really awfully dark in the afternoons." . . . or, "The orchard is really trying to get into the house, Pat. Why not have that tree cut down?"

May simply could not or would not get it into her head that Pat was not having trees cut down. In regard to this particular tree, May was not, perhaps, so far wrong as in some of her suggestions. It really was too close to the house . . . a young apple tree that had started up of itself and grew so slyly that it was a tree before any one took much notice of it. Now it was pushing its boughs into the very window of the Big Parlour. When May spoke it was a thing of beauty, all starred with tiny red buds just on the point of bursting.

"I think it's lovely having the orchard coming right into the house like this," said Pat.

"You would," said May. It was a favourite retort with her and she always contrived to put a vast amount of contempt into it.

None of her suggestions were adopted and May tearfully told her mother, in Judy's hearing, that she "simply couldn't do a thing in her husband's house." She was determined to have a "herbaceous border" and nagged at Sid until he interceded with Pat and it was decided that it might be made across the bottom of the little lawn, where hitherto nothing but lilies of the valley had grown wildly and thickly. There were plenty of other lilies of the valley about but Pat hated to see those ploughed up and May's iris and delphiniums and what Mrs. Binnie called "concubines," set in their place. Because May really did not care a bit for flowers. She wanted her herbaceous border because Olive had told her they were all the fashion now and every one in town was making one.

"Do you know that May badgered Sid at last into taking her back and showing her the Secret Field?" asked Rae.

Yes, Pat knew it. May had laughed on her return.

"I've seen your famous field, Pat . . . nothing but a little hole in the woods. And you've been making such a fuss over it all these years."

To Pat it was the ultimate treason that Sid should have showed May the Secret Field . . . *their* Secret Field. But she could not blame him. He had to do it for peace' sake.

"You love your sister better than your wife," May told him passionately, whenever he refused to do anything Pat didn't want done. He and May had begun to quarrel violently and life at Silver Bush was made bitter all that summer by it. Meal times were the worst. The bickering between them was almost incessant.

"Oh, do let us have one meal without a fight," Long Alec remarked in exasperation one day. Pat, who had been listening in silence to May's sarcasm and Sid's sulky replies, rose and went to her room.

"I can't bear it any longer . . . I can't," she said wildly. She twitched the shade to pull it down and shut out the insulting sunlight. It escaped her and whizzed wildly to the top, thereby nearly scaring to death Bold-and-Bad, asleep on Rae's bed.

"You don't deserve a cat," said Bold-and-Bad, or words to that effect. Pat glared at him.

"To think that it has come to this at Silver Bush!"

Rae, coming in a little later with the mail and an armful of blossom, turned the key in the door. That was necessary now. There was no longer the old-time privacy at Silver Bush. May might bounce in on them at any time without the pretence of knocking. She merely laughed at the idea of knocking and called it "Silver Bush airs."

"Pat, darling, don't take it so to heart. I admit there's a time every day when May makes me yearn for the good old days when you could pull peoples' wigs off. But when I feel that way I just reflect what Brook's eyes would make of her . . . can't you see the twinkle in them? . . . and she shrinks to her proper perspective. It isn't going to last forever."

"It is . . . it is," cried Pat wildly. "Rae, May doesn't *want* to have a house built on the other place . . . she wants to have Silver Bush. I've heard her talking to Sid . . . I couldn't help hearing . . . you know what her voice is like when she's angry. 'I'll never go to live on the Adams' place . . . it would be so far out of the world . . . you can't move all them barns. You told me when you persuaded me to marry you that we would live at Silver Bush. And I'm going to . . . and it won't be under the thumb of your old-maid sister either. She's nothing but a parasite . . . living off your father when there's nothing now to prevent her from going away and earning her own living when I'm here to run things.' She's doing her best to set Sid against us all . . . you know she is. And she attributes some petty motive to everything we do or say . . . or *don't* say. Remember the scene she made last week because I hadn't taken any notice of her new dress . . . that awful concoction of cheap radium lace over that sleazy bright blue silk. I thought the kindest thing I could do was *not* to take notice of it. I was ashamed to think any one at Silver Bush could wear such a thing. And she tells Sid we're always laughing at her."

"Well, you *did* laugh last night when she said that thing about the moon," grinned Rae.

"Who could help it? I forgot myself in the delight of seeing that new moon over the crest of that fir in the silver bush and I pointed it out to May. 'How cute!' remarks my sister-in-law. And that creature is . . . by law . . . a Gardiner of Silver Bush!"

"Still, the new moon over the fir tree is just as exquisite as it ever was," said Rae softly.

But Pat would listen just then to no comforting.

"Think of dinner. At the best now we never have any real conversation at our meals . . . and at the worst it is like it was to-day. Rae, at times it simply seems to me that everything sane and sweet and happy has vanished from Silver Bush and only returns for a little while when she is away. Why, she listens on the 'phone . . . fancy any one at Silver Bush listening on the 'phone! . . . and gossips over what she hears. I feel dragged in the dust when I hear her. Do you know that she took that gang of her Summerside cousins into our room yesterday . . . our room! . . . and showed it to them?"

"Well, she wouldn't find it littered with hair-pins and face powder as hers is," said Rae, looking fondly around at their little immaculate room, engoldened by the light of the new corn-coloured curtains she and Pat had selected that spring. Here, at least, were yet stillness and peace and refreshment whatever might be the state of things elsewhere. "And as for her setting Sid against us, she can't do that, Pat. Sid knows what she is now. And dad will remain master of Silver Bush. Let's just sit tight and wait. Here's a letter from Hilary I've just brought in from the box. It will cheer you up."

But it hardly did, though Pat wistfully read it over three times in the hope of finding that elusive something Hilary's letters used to possess. It was nice, like all Hilary's letters. But it was the first for quite a long time . . . and it was a little remote, somehow . . . as if he were thinking of something else all the time he was writing it. He was going to Italy and then to the east . . . Egypt . . . India . . . to study architecture. He would be away for a year.

"I want to see the whole world," he wrote. Pat shivered. The "whole world" had a cold, huge sound to her. Yet for the first time the idea came into her head that it might be rather nice to see the world with Hilary or some such congenial companion. Philae against a desert sunset . . . the storied Alhambra . . . the pearl-white wonder of the Taj Mahal by moonlight . . . Petra, that "rose-red city half as old as Time," as Hilary had quoted. It would be wonderful to see them. But it would be more wonderful still to look at Silver Bush and know it for her own again . . . as she was afraid it never would be. Perhaps May was there to stay. She wanted to and she always got what she wanted. She had wanted Sid and she had got him. She would get Silver Bush by hook or crook. Already at times she assumed sly airs of mistress-ship and did the honours of the garden on the strength of her "herbaceous border," explaining ungraciously that the stones around the beds were a whim of old Judy Plum's. "We humour her."

And the place was over-run by her family. Judy used to tell Tillytuck that Silver Bush was crawling wid thim. Sure and wasn't all the Binnie clan that prolific!

That hateful young brother of May's with the weasel eyes was there more than half his time, "helping" Sid and making fun of Judy who revenged herself by hiding tidbits he coveted away in the pantry and blandly knowing nothing about them.

"Poor old Judy is failing fast," said May. "She puts things away and forgets where she puts them."

May was much in the kitchen now, cooking up what Judy called "messes" for her own friends and leaving all the greasy or doughy pots and pans for Judy to wash. Judy couldn't have told you whether she disliked May more in good humour or in "the sulks." When she was sulky she banged and slammed but her tongue was still; when she was in good humour she never stopped talking. There were few quiet moments at Silver Bush now. Judy in despair took to sitting and knitting on Wild Dick's tombstone. Tillytuck sat there, too, on Weeping Willy's, smoking his pipe. "I like company but not too much," was all he would say. It was all great fun for May. She persisted in assuming that Tillytuck and Judy were "courting" in the graveyard.

"Will I be caring what she says?" said Judy bitterly to Pat. "Oh, oh, she can't run me kitchen. She was be way av hanging up a calendar on me wall yesterday right below King William and Quane Victoria . . . a picture av a big fat girl wid no clothes at all on. I did be taking it down and throwing it in the fire. 'Sure,' sez I to her, 'that hussy is no fit company for ather a king or a quane,' sez I. And nather was that cousin av hers she had here yesterday in a bathing suit. She come in as bould as brass wid her great bare fat legs and did be setting on yer Great-grandfather Nehemiah's chair, wid thim crossed. And thim not aven a dacent white . . . sun-tan she did be calling it . . . more like the colour av skim milk cheese. Tillytuck just took one look and flid to the granary. I cudn't be trating her as I did the calendar but I sez, 'People that fond av showing their legs ought to be dieting a bit,' sez I. 'You quaint thing!' sez she. Oh, oh, it's thanking the Good Man Above I am she didn't call me priceless. It do be her fav'rite ajective. But whin May did be saying that one-pace bathing suits were all the fashion now and did I ixpict people to go bathing in long dresses and crinolines, I sez, 'Oh, oh, far be it from me to be like yer Aunt Ellice, May,' sez I. 'Whin her nace sint her a statue av the Venus av Mily for a Christmas prisent she did be putting a dress on it, rale tasty, afore she showed it to her frinds. I'm not objicting to legs as legs,' sez I, 'spacially at the shore where they do be plinty av background for thim, but whin they're as big and fat as yer lady cousin's,' sez I, 'they do be a bit overpowering in me kitchen.' 'Ivery one thinks that Emma looks stunning in her suit,' sez May. 'Stunning do be the right word,' sez I. 'Ye saw the iffict she had on Tillytuck and he's not a man asily upset,' sez I. 'As for the fashion,' sez I, 'av coorse what one monkey does all the other monkeys will be doing,' sez I. Me fine May sez that I'd insulted her frind and hadn't a word to throw to a dog all day but I'm liking her far better whin she's sulky than whin she's frindly. She did be trying to pump me about Cleaver this morning but I wasn't knowing innything. Do there be innything to know, Patsy dear?"

"Not a thing," said Pat with a smile.

"Oh, oh, I wasn't ixpicting it," said Judy with no smile. She did not know whether to feel relieved or disappointed. She did not quite like Cleaver, who was an honour graduate of McGill and was spending his summer doing research work at the Silverbridge harbour. Pat had got acquainted with him at the Long House and he had dangled a bit round Silver Bush. He was enormously clever and his researches into various elusive bacilli had already put him in the limelight. But poor Cleaver looked rather like a magnified bacillus himself and Judy, try as she would, could not see him as a husband for Pat.

"It'll be the widower yet, I'm fearing," she told Tillytuck in the graveyard. "Spacially if this news we're hearing about Jingle is true. I've always had me own ideas . . . but I do be only an ould fool and getting no younger, as Mrs. Binnie do be saying ivery once in so long."

"Old Matilda Binnie has a new set of teeth and a new fur coat," said Tillytuck. "Now, if she could get a new set of brains she might do very well for a while." He took a few whiffs at his pipe and then added gravely, "Symbolically speaking."

4

Aunt Edith died very suddenly in August. They all felt the shock of it. None of them had ever loved Aunt Edith very much . . . she was not a lovable person. But she was part of the established order of things and her passing meant another change. Oddly enough, Judy, who had had a life-long vendetta with her, seemed to mourn and miss her most. Judy thought life would be almost stodgy when there was no Aunt Edith to horrify and exchange polite, barbed jabs with.

"Whin I think I'll niver see her in me kitchen agin, insulting me, I do be having a very quare faling, Patsy dear."

It was of course May who told Pat, with much relish, that Hilary Gordon was engaged. Some Binnie had had a letter from another Binnie who lived in Vancouver and knew the girl. She and Hilary were to be married when he returned from his year abroad and he was to be taken into the noted firm of architects in which her father was the senior partner.

"He was a beau of yours long ago, wasn't he, when you were a young girl?" asked May in a malicious drawl.

"I think it's true," Rae told Pat that night. "I heard it some time ago. Dot has friends in Vancouver and they wrote it to her. I . . . I didn't know whether to tell you or not."

"Why on earth shouldn't you tell me?" said Pat very coldly.

"Well . . ." Rae hesitated . . . "you and Hilary were always such friends . . ."

"Exactly!" Pat bit the word off and her brook-brown eyes were full of a rather dangerous fire. "We have always been good friends and so I would naturally be interested in hearing any good news about him. All that . . . that hurts me is that he should have left me to hear it from others. Rae Gardiner, what are you looking at me like that for?"

"I've always thought," said Rae, taking her life in her hands, "that you . . . that you cared much more for Hilary than you ever suspected yourself, Pat."

486

Pat laughed a little unsteadily.

"Rae, don't be a goose. You and Judy have always been a little delirious on the subject of Hilary. I've always loved Hilary and always will. He's just like a dear brother to me. Do you realise how many years it is since I've seen him? Of course we've drifted apart even as friends. It was inevitable. Even our correspondence is dying a natural death. I haven't had a letter from him since he went abroad."

"I was only a child when he went away but I remember how I liked him," said Rae. "I used to think he was the nicest boy in the world."

"So he was," said Pat. "And I hope he's going to marry some one who is nice enough for him."

"He really was in love with you, wasn't he, Pat?"

"He thought he was. I knew he would get over that."

"Well..." Rae had been irradiated all day with some secret happiness and now it came out... "Brook is coming over for a week before college opens. I do hope Miss Macauly will have my blue georgette done by that time. And I think I'll have a little jacket of that lovely transparent blue velvet we saw in town to go with it. I feel sure Brook will love me in that dress."

"I thought he loved you in any dress," teased Pat.

"Oh, he does. But there are degrees, Pat."

"And no one," thought Pat a little drearily, "cares how I'm dressed."

She looked out of the window and saw a rising moon . . . and remembered old moonrises she had watched with Hilary . . . "when she was a girl." That phrase of May's rankled. And Mrs. Binnie had been rather odious the other day, assuring her again there were as good fish in the sea as ever came out of it . . . apropos of the announcement of the engagement of a South Glen girl to Donald Holmes.

"You're young enough yet," said Mrs. Binnie soothingly. "And when people say you're beginning to look a bit old-maidish I always tell them, 'Is it any wonder? Think of the responsibility Pat has had for years, with her mother ill and so much on her shoulders. No wonder she's getting old-looking afore her time.'"

Pat had got pretty well into the habit of ignoring Mrs. Binnie but that phrase "young yet" haunted her. She went to the mirror and looked dispassionately at herself. She really did not think she looked old. Her dark brown hair was as glossy as ever . . . her amber eyes as bright . . . her cheeks as smooth and rounded. Perhaps there were a few tiny lines in the corners of her eyes and . . . *what was that?* Pat leaned nearer, her eyes dilating a little. Was it . . . could it be . . . yes, it was! A grey hair!

5

Pat went up to the Long House that night. She walked blithely and springily. She was not going to worry over that grey hair. She would not even pull it out. The Selbys all turned grey young. What did it matter? She would not grow old in heart, no matter what she did in head. She would always keep her banner of youth flying gallantly. Wrinkles might come on her face but there should never be any on her soul. And yet there had been a moment that day when Pat had felt as if she didn't want to be young any longer. Things hurt you too much when you were young. Surely they wouldn't hurt so much when you got old. You wouldn't care so much then . . . things would be settled . . . there wouldn't be so many changes. People you knew wouldn't always be running off to far lands . . . or getting married. Your hair would be *all* grey and it wouldn't matter. You wouldn't be eating your heart out longing for a lost paradise.

Altogether it had not been a pleasant day. May had had a fit of the sulks and had taken it out slamming doors . . . Rover had eaten a plateful of fudge Pat had set outside to cool . . . Judy had seemed down-hearted about something . . . perhaps the news about Hilary though she never referred to it but only muttered occasionally to herself about "strange going-ons." Pat decided that she felt a trifle stodgy and needed something to pep her up a bit. She would find it at the Long House . . . she always did. Whenever life seemed a bit grey . . . whenever she felt a passing pang of loneliness over the changes that had been and . . . worse still . . . would be, she went up the hill to David and Suzanne. Whenever the door of the Long House clanged behind her it seemed to shut out the world, with its corroding discontents and vexations. Once, Pat thought with a stab of pain, she had felt that way when she went into Silver Bush. That she couldn't feel so any longer was a very bitter thing . . . a thing she couldn't get used to. But to-night as she and David and Suzanne sat around the fire—it was a cool September night and any excuse served when they wanted to light that fire . . . and cracked nuts and talked . . . or didn't talk . . . the bitterness faded out of Pat's heart as it always did in their company. Suzanne was rather quiet, sitting with Alphonso curled up in her lap: but Pat and David never found themselves lacking for something to say. Pat looked at the motto that ran in quaint, irregular letters around the fireplace.

"There be three gentle and goodlie things,
To be here,
To be together,
And to think well of one another."

That was true: and while it remained true one could bear anything else, no matter what sort of a hole it left in your life. What a dear Suzanne was! And what nice eyes David had . . . very whimsical when they were not tender and very tender when they were not whimsical. And his voice . . . what did his voice always remind her of? She could never tell but she knew it was something that always tugged at her heart. And she knew he liked her very much. It was nice to be liked . . . nice to have such friends to come to whenever you wanted to.

David walked home with her as he always did. Pat had never until to-night stopped to think how very pleasant those walks home were. To-night the hills were dreamy under a harvest moon. They went through the close-set spruce grove that always seemed to be guarding so many secrets . . . down the field path under the Watching Pine that still watched . . . for what? . . . over the brook and along the Whispering Lane. At the gate where they always parted they stood in silence for a little while, lost in the beauty of the night. Faint music came to them. It was only Tillytuck playing in his lair but, muted by the distance, it sounded like some fairy melody under a haunted moon. Beyond the trees were great quietudes of sky where burned the stars that never changed . . . the only things that never changed.

David was thinking that silence with Pat was more eloquent than talk with any other woman. He was also wondering what Pat would do or say if he suddenly did what he had always wanted to do . . . put his arm about her and said, "darling." What he did say was almost as shattering to Pat's new-found mood of contentment.

"Has Suzanne told you her little secret yet?"

Suzanne? A secret? There was only one kind of a secret people spoke about in that tone. Pat involuntarily put up her hand as if warding off

489

a blow.

"No ... o ... o," she said faintly.

"She probably would have if you had been alone with her to-night. She's very happy. She has made up a quarrel she had before we came here with an old lover ... and they are engaged."

It was too much ... it really was. So Suzanne was to be lost to her, too! And she had to be polite and say something nice.

"I ... I ... hope she will always be very happy," she gasped.

"I think she will," said David quietly. "She has loved him for years .. . I never knew just what the trouble was. We're a secretive lot, we Kirks. Of course they won't be married till he has finished college. He has had to work his way through. And then ... what am I to do, Pat?"

"You ... you'll miss her," said Pat. She knew she was being incredibly stupid.

"You'll have to tell me what to do, Pat," David said, bending a little nearer, his voice taking on a very significant tone.

Was David by any chance proposing to her? And if he were what on earth could she say? She wasn't going to say anything! She had had enough shocks for one day ... Hilary engaged ... grey hair ... Suzanne engaged! Oh, why must life be such an uncertain thing? You never knew where you were ... you never had security ... you never knew when there might not be some dreadful bolt from the blue. She would just pretend she hadn't heard David's question and go in. Which she did.

But that night she sat in the moonlight in her room for a long while and looked at the two paths she might take in life. Rae was away and the house was silent ... and, so it seemed to Pat, lonely. Silver Bush always seemed when night fell to be mourning for its ravished peace. The sky outside was cloudless but a brisk wind was blowing past. "What is the wind in such a hurry for, Aunt Pat?" Little Mary had asked wistfully not long ago. Everything seemed in a hurry ... life was in a hurry ... it couldn't let you be ... it swept you on with it as if you were a leaf in the wind.

Which path should she take? David was going to ask her to marry him ... she had known for a long time in the back of her mind that he would ask her if she ever let him. She was terribly fond of David. Life with him would be a very pleasant pilgrimage. Even a grey day was full of colour when David was around. She was always contented in his company. And his eyes were sometimes so sad. She wanted to make

490

them happy. Was that reason enough for marrying a man, even one as nice as David? If she didn't marry him she would lose him out of her life. He would never stay at the Long House after Suzanne had gone. And she couldn't lose any more friends . . . she just couldn't.

Suppose she didn't take that path? Suppose she just went on living here at Silver Bush . . . growing into being "Aunt Pat" . . . helping plan the clan weddings and funerals . . . her brown hair turning pepper-and-salt. That grey hair popped into her mind. It seemed as if age had just tapped her on the shoulder. But it would be all right if only Silver Bush might be hers to love and plan for and live for, free from all outsiders and intruders. She wouldn't hesitate a second then. But would it be? Would it ever be hers again? She knew what May's designs were. And she knew Sid didn't want to leave Silver Bush for the other place. Would dad stand out against them . . . could he? No, it would end in May being mistress of Silver Bush some day. That was the secret dread that always haunted Pat. And if it ever came about . . .

A few weeks later David said quietly to her in the garden of the Long House . . . the garden where Bet's ghost sometimes walked even yet for Pat . . .

"Do you think you could marry me, Pat?"

Pat looked afar for a moment of silence to the firry rim of an eastern hill. Then she said just as quietly, "I think I could."

6

Mother was told first. Mother's face was always serene but it changed a little when Pat told her.

"Darling, do you really love him?"

Pat looked out of the window. There had been a frost the night before and the garden had a blighted look. She had been hoping mother wouldn't ask that question.

"I do really, mother, but perhaps not in just the way you mean."

"There's only the one way," said mother softly.

"Then I'm one of the kind of people who can't love that way. I've tried . . . and I can't."

"It doesn't come by trying either," said mother.

"Mother dear, I'm terribly fond of David. We suit each other . . . our minds click. He loves the same things I do. I'm always happy with him . . . we'll always be good chums."

Mother said no more. She picked up something she was making for Rae's hope chest and went on putting tiny invisible stitches in it. After all perhaps it would work out. It was not what she had wanted for Pat but the child must make her own choices. David Kirk was a nice fellow . . . mother had always liked him. And Pat would not be far from her.

Judy came next and, for one who had always been anxious to see Pat "settled", betrayed no great delight. But she wished Pat well and was careful to say that *Mr.* Kirk had rale brading. Since the engagement was an accomplished fact Judy was not going to say anything against a future member of the family.

"The poor darlint, she don't be as happy as she thinks hersilf," Judy told Bold-and-Bad, regarding him as the only safe confidant. Only she felt that Bold-and-Bad never understood her quite so well as Gentleman Tom had done. "And after all the min she might have had! But I'm hoping the Good Man Above knows what's bist for us all."

To Rae Pat talked more frankly than to any one.

"Pat dear, if you love him . . ."

"Not as you love Brook, Rae. I'm just not capable of that sort of loving . . . or it doesn't last. David *needs* me . . . or will need me when Suzanne goes. We're not going to be married until she is . . . for two years at the least. I wouldn't marry him, Rae . . . I wouldn't marry anybody . . . if I knew I could go on living at Silver Bush. But if May stays here . . . and she means to . . . I can't, especially when you are gone to China. I've always loved the Long House next to Silver Bush. I'll be *near* Silver Bush . . . I can always look down on it and watch over it."

"I believe that's the real reason you're going to marry David Kirk," thought Rae. She looked at the shadow of the vine leaves on the bedroom floor. It looked like a dancing faun. Rae blinked to hide sudden foolish tears. Pat was going to miss something. But aloud she said only,

"I hope you'll be happy, Pat. You deserve to be. You've always been a darling."

Father took it philosophically. He would have liked some one a bit younger. But Kirk was a nice chap and seemed to have enough money to live on. There was something distinguished about him. His war book had been acclaimed by the critics and he was working on a "History of the Maritimes" of which, Long Alec had been told, great things were expected. Pat had always liked those brainy fellows. She had a right to please herself.

The rest of the clan were surprised and amused. Pat sensed that none of them quite approved. Winnie and the Bay Shore aunts said absolutely nothing, but silence can say a great deal sometimes. Only Aunt Barbara said deprecatingly,

"But, Pat, he's *grey*."

"So am I," said Pat, flaunting her one grey hair.

"Let's hope it lasts this time," said Uncle Tom. Pat thought he might have been nicer after the way she had stood by him in the affair of Mrs. Merridew.

May was frankly delighted, though her delight faded a little when she learned that there was no prospect of an immediate marriage. Mrs. Binnie, rocking fiercely, had her say-so as well.

"So you've hooked the widower at last, Pat? What did I tell you . . . never give up. I've never understood how a gal could bring herself to marry a widower . . . but then any port in a storm. Of course, as I said to Olive, he's a bit on the old side . . ."

"I don't like boys," said Pat coolly. "I get on better with men. And you must admit, Mrs. Binnie, that his ears don't stick out."

"*I* call that flippant, Pat. Marriage is a very serious thing. As I was saying, when I said that to Olive she sez, 'I s'pose it's better to be an old man's darling than a young man's slave. Pat isn't so young as she used to be herself, ma. She'll make a very good wife for David Kirk.' Olive always kind of liked you, Pat. She always said you meant well."

"That was very kind of her."

Pat's amused, remote smile offended Mrs. Binnie. That was the worst of Pat. Always laughing at you in her sleeve. Mebbe she'd find out marrying an old widower was no laughing matter.

Suzanne was wild with delight.

"I've been hoping for it from the first, Pat. You're made for each other. David worries a bit because he's so much older. I tell him he's growing younger every day and you're growing older so you'll soon meet. He's a darling if he is my brother. He never dared to hope . . . till lately. He always said he had two rivals."

"Two?"

"Silver Bush . . . and Hilary Gordon."

Pat smiled.

"Silver Bush *was* his rival, I'll admit. But Hilary . . . he might as well call Sid a rival."

Yet her face had changed subtly. Some of the laughter went out of it. She was wondering why there was such a distinct relief in the thought that, since her correspondence with Hilary seemed to have died a natural death, she would not have to write him that she was going to marry David Kirk.

THE EIGHTH YEAR

1

It rained Thursday and Friday and then for a change, as Tillytuck said, it rained Saturday. Not the romping, rollicking, laughter-filled rain of spring but the sad, hopeless rain of autumn that seemed like the tears of old sorrows on the window-panes of Silver Bush.

"I love some kinds of rain," said Rae, "but not this kind. Doesn't the garden look forlorn? Nothing but the ghosts of flowers left in it . . . and such unkempt ghosts at that. And we had such good times all summer working in that garden, hadn't we, Pat? I wonder if it will be the same next summer? I've a nasty, going-to-happeny feeling this morning that I don't like."

Judy, too, had had some kind of a "sign" in the night and was pessimistic. But nobody at first sight connected these forewarnings with the tall, thin lady who drove up the lane late in the afternoon and tied a spiritless grey nag to the paling of the graveyard.

"One more av thim agents," said Judy, watching her from the kitchen window, as she stalked up the wet walk, a suit-case dangling from the end of one of her long arms.

"Sure and I've been pestered wid half a dozen of thim this wake. She don't be looking as if business was inny too prosperous."

"She looks like an angleworm on end," giggled Rae.

"I wouldn't let her in if I was you," said Mrs. Binnie, who seldom let a Saturday afternoon pass without a call at Silver Bush.

Judy had had some such idea herself but that speech of Mrs. Binnie's banished it.

"Oh, oh, we do be more mannerly than that at Silver Bush," she said loftily, and invited the stranger in cordially, offering her a chair near the fire. No Binnie was going to tell Judy who was to be let in or out of *her* kitchen!

"It's a wet day," sighed the caller, as she sank into the chair and let the suit-case drop on the floor with an air of relief. She was remarkably tall and very slight, dressed in shabby black, and with enormous pale blue eyes. They positively drowned out her face and gave you the uncanny impression that she hadn't any features but eyes. Otherwise you might have noticed that her cheek-bones were a shade too high and her thin mouth rather long and new-moonish. She gave Squedunk such a look of disapproval that that astute cat remarked that he would go out and have a look at the weather and stood not upon the order of his going.

"It's a wet day for travelling but I've allowed myself just ten days to do the Island and time is getting on."

"You don't belong to the Island?" said Rae . . . quite superfluously, Judy thought. Sure and cudn't ye be telling *that* niver belonged to the Island!

"No." Another long sigh. "My home is in Novy Scoshy. I've seen better days. But when you haven't a husband to support you you've got to make a living somehow. I was an agent before I was married and so I just took to the road again. Every little helps."

"Sure and it do be hard lines to be a widdy in this could world," said Judy, instantly sympathetic, and hauling forward her pot of soup.

"Oh, I ain't a widdy woman, worse luck." Another sigh. "My husband left me years ago."

"Oh, oh!" Judy pushed the pot back again. If your husband left you there was something wrong somewhere. "And what might ye be selling?"

"All kinds of pills and liniments, tonics and perfumes, face creams and powders," said the caller, opening her suit-case and preparing to display her wares. But at this juncture the porch door opened and Tillytuck appeared in the doorway. He got no further, being apparently frozen in his tracks. As for the lady of the eyes, she clasped her hands and opened and shut her mouth twice. The third time she managed to ejaculate,

"Josiah!"

Tillytuck said something like "Good gosh!" He gazed helplessly around him. "I'm sober . . . I'm sober . . . I can't hope I'm drunk now."

"Oh, oh, so this lady is no stranger to you I'm thinking?" said Judy.

"Stranger!" The lady in question rolled her eyes rapidly, making Rae think of the dogs in the old fairy tale. "He is . . . he was . . . he is my husband."

Judy looked at Tillytuck.

"Is it the truth she do be spaking, *Mr.* Tillytuck?"

Tillytuck tried to brazen it out. He nodded and grinned.

"Oh, oh," said Judy sarcastically, "and isn't the truth refreshing after all the lies we've been hearing!"

"I've always felt," said Tillytuck mournfully, "that you never really believed anything I said. But if this . . . person has been telling you I left her she's been speaking symbolically. I was druv to it. She told me to go."

"Because he didn't . . . and wouldn't . . . believe in predestination," said Mrs. Tillytuck. "He was no better than a modernist. I couldn't live with a man who didn't believe in predestination. Could you?"

"Sure and I've niver tried," said Judy, to whom Mrs. Tillytuck had seemed to appeal. Mrs. Binnie asked what predestination was but nobody answered her.

"She told me to go," repeated Tillytuck, "and I took her at her word. 'There's really been too much of this,' I said . . . and it was all I did say. I appeal to you, Jane Maria, wasn't it all I did say?"

Tears filled Mrs. Tillytuck's eyes. You really felt afraid of drowning in them.

"You're welcome back any time, Josiah," she sobbed. "Any time you believe in predestination you can come home."

Tillytuck said nothing. He turned and went out. Mrs. Tillytuck wiped her eyes while Judy regarded her rather stonily and Pat and Rae tried to keep their faces straight.

"This . . . this has upset me a little," said Mrs. Tillytuck apologetically. "I hope you'll excuse me. I hadn't laid eyes on Josiah for fifteen years. He hasn't changed a particle. Has he been here all that time?"

"No," said Judy shortly. "Only seven years."

"Then you know him pretty well I daresay. Always telling wonderful stories of his adventures I suppose? The yarns I've listened to! And every last one of them crazier than the others."

"Was his grandfather really a pirate?" asked Rae. She had always been curious on that point.

"Listen to her now. His grandfather a pirate! Why, he was only a minister. But isn't that like Josiah? Him and his romances and 'traggedies'! He always had a wild desire for notoriety . . . always had a craze to be mixed up with any scandal or catastrophe he heard of. Why, that man didn't like funerals because he couldn't pretend to be the corpse. But it wasn't that I minded. After all, his lies were interesting and I like a little frivolous conversation once in a while. He was easy enough to live with, I'll say that for him. And I didn't mind his sly orgies so much though I warned him what happened to my Uncle Asa. Uncle Asa threw himself into a full bath-tub when *he* was full, mistaking it for his bed. He broke his neck first and then he drowned. No, it was Josiah's theology. At first I thought it was just indigestion but when I realized he meant it my conscience wouldn't stand for it. He said there never was an Adam or Eve and he said the doctrine of predestination was blasphemous and abominable. So I told him he had to choose between me and modernism. But I suffered. I loved that man with all his faults. It has preyed on my mind all these years. What is going to become of his immortal soul?"

Nobody, not even Mrs. Binnie, tried to answer this question.

"Well," resumed Mrs. Tillytuck more briskly, "this isn't business. I dunno as I feel very business-like just now. My heart don't feel just right. This has been a shock to it. I suffer greatly from a tired heart."

Nobody knew whether this was a physical or an emotional ailment. Mrs. Binnie understood it to be the former and asked quite sympathetically, "Did you ever try a mustard plaster at the pit of your stomach, Mrs. Tillytuck?"

"I fear that wouldn't benefit a weary heart," said Mrs. Tillytuck pathetically. "Possibly, madam, you have never suffered as I have from a weary wounded heart?"

"No, thank goodness my heart is all right," said Mrs. Binnie. "My only trouble is rheumatism in the knee j'ints."

"I have the very thing for that here," said Mrs. Tillytuck briskly. "You try this liniment."

Mrs. Binnie bought the liniment and Mrs. Tillytuck looked appealingly at the others. But Judy said darkly they didn't be wanting inny beautifying messes.

"We do all be handsome enough here widout thim."

"I've never seen anybody so handsome she couldn't be handsomer," said Mrs. Tillytuck with another sigh as she closed her bag. At the door she turned.

"I s'pose you don't happen to know if Josiah has saved up any money these fifteen years?"

Nobody happened to know.

"Ah well, it isn't likely. A rolling stone gathers no moss. Though he wasn't lazy . . . I'll say that for him. And you can tell him my parting word was . . . believe in predestination Josiah, and you'll be welcome home at any time."

Mrs. Tillytuck was gone. The echo of her steps died away down the walk. Pat and Rae went into their long repressed spasm. Mrs. Binnie said there was always something about Tillytuck that made her think he was married.

Judy was very silent, her only remark being, as she watched Mrs. Tillytuck driving out of the yard,

"A bean-pole like that!"

2

Tillytuck did not show up for supper, having gone on an errand, real or pretended, to Silverbridge. But he slipped into the kitchen at night, when Judy and Rae and Pat were roasting apples around the fire, and slid into his own corner. Judy bustled about to get him a liddle bite and was markedly cordial. Sure and couldn't she be as civil to Tillytuck now as she pleased when nobody could ever again be thinking she was setting her cap for him!

"I suppose you were all a bit surprised to learn I was a family man?" he said, in a tone of mingled sheepishness and bravado.

"Tillytuck, tell us all about it," pleaded Rae. "We're dying of curiosity."

Tillytuck fitted his finger-tips carefully together. "There ain't much to tell," he said . . . and proceeded to tell it, punctuated by gentle snorts from Judy.

"I've often wondered how I came to do it. It all begun with a moon. You can never trust a moon."

"Oh, oh, we must have something to blame our mistakes on," said

Judy, good-humouredly, as she set a large plateful of his favourite cinnamon buns beside him on the corner of the table.

"I'd known her for some time in a kind of a way, but the first time I really met her was at a friend's house and we sot out on the porch and talked. She was a fine figger of a woman then . . . some meat on her bones . . . and them eyes of hers was kind of devastating by moonlight. I won't deny there was a touch of glamour about it. But I didn't really mean to propose to her . . . honest, I didn't. It *wasn't* a proposal . . . just a kind of a hint. Partly out of sympathy and partly because of the moon. But she snapped me up so quick I was an engaged man before I knew what had happened to me. Hog-tied, that's what I was. Well, we was married and went to live in her house. It was rather prosy for a man of my romantic temperament but we was well enough for a spell, though the boys called us the long and short of it. I was devoted to that woman, Judy. (Snort.) Many a time I've got up in the middle of the night and made a cup of tea for her. She always liked a cup of tea when she got up in the night. Claimed it was good for her heart. And she was the best wife in the world except for a few things. She sighed too much and she used to get hopping mad if I hung my cap on the wrong hook. Likewise she had an edge to her tongue if I went in without scraping my boots. I ain't denying we had a few surface quarrels but no more than enough to spice life up a bit. It was her theology we went to the mat about finally. I couldn't stomach it and I told her so. She was a fundamentalist . . . oh, was she a fundamentalist? I was one myself but I wouldn't give her the satisfaction of admitting it, and anyhow I stopped short at predestination. As for my saying there was no Adam or Eve I was only talking poetically but when I saw how she got her dander up over it I pretended to be in earnest. From that on there was no living with her and when she up and told me to go I went as quick as I could get. I was tired of her lumpy gravy anyhow, and the dishwater she called soup. If she'd been a cook like you, Judy, I could have believed in anything."

Tillytuck rumbled and took a large bite out of a cinnamon bun.

"Life would be dull if we hadn't a few traggedies to look back on," he said philosophically.

But three days later the world of Silver Bush temporarily toppled into chaos. Tillytuck had given warning.

Everybody went into a state of consternation. Long Alec and Sid, because they were losing a good man, Judy and Rae and Pat, because they were losing Tillytuck. It did not seem possible. He had been a part of their life so long that it was unthinkable that he could cease to be such. Another change, thought Pat sadly.

"It's just that he feels he's lost face," said Rae. "He would never have thought of going if that horrid woman hadn't come here and given him away. That is his real reason for going, whatever he may say. I'm just going to sit here and hate her hard."

"It do be too bad ye can't be putting up wid us inny longer," said Judy bitterly to him that evening.

"You know it ain't that, Judy. I've stayed longer here than any place I've been in. But I'm getting too contented here. It's always been my motto to move on if I got too contented anywhere. And I'll admit there's been too much Binnie around here of late for my liking. Besides, I'm getting on in years. You can't escape Anno Domini. Farm work on a place like this is a bit hard on me now. I've saved up a little money and me and a friend on the South shore are going to start up a fox ranch of our own. But I'll never forget you folks here. I'll miss your soup, Judy."

There was a tremble in Tillytuck's voice. Judy was setting the supper-table and trying to make an obstreperous saltcellar shake. Suddenly she snatched it up and hurled it through the open window.

"I've put up wid that thing for twinty years," she said savagely, "but I'll not be putting up wid it another day."

Tillytuck went away one bleak November evening. He turned in the doorway for a last word.

"May the years be kind to ye all, speaking poetically," he said. "You are as fine a bunch of folks as I ever had the good luck to live among. You understand a man of my calibre. It's a great thing to be understood. Long Alec is the right kind of a man to work for and your mother is a saint if ever there was one. I haven't cried since I was a child but I come near it when she told me good-bye before she went up to bed. If that wild woman of mine ever pays you another call, Judy, for pity's sake don't tell her I believe in predestination now. If she knew it she'd drag me back by hook or crook. I'll send for my radio when I get settled. Ajoo."

He waved his hand with a courtly air, sniffed sadly the aroma of Judy's beans and onions, and turned his back on her cheery domain. They watched him going down the lane in the dim, with his stuffed owl under his arm and the same old fur cap on his head that he had worn upon his arrival. Just Dog walked close beside him, with a tail that had apparently no wag left in it. A weird moon with a cloud-ribbed face was rising over the Hill of the Mist. The surging of wind in the tree branches was very mournful.

Rae's face crumpled up.

"I . . . I . . . think I'd like to cry," she said chokily. "Do you remember the night he came? You sent me to show him the way to the granary and he said 'Good-night, little Cuddles,' as he went up the stair. I felt he was an old friend then."

"Sure and I wish I'd niver found fault wid him for playing his fiddle in the graveyard," said Judy. "Maybe the poor soul will niver get a taste av dape apple pie again. That wife av his was wondering what wud become av his soul but I'm wondering what's going to happen to his poor body."

"He was a genial old soul," said Mrs. Binnie.

"There was something so quaint about him," whimpered May.

Pat wanted to cry but wouldn't because May was doing it. She slipped an arm about Judy, who, somehow, was looking strangely old.

"Anyway, we've got Silver Bush and you left," she whispered.

Judy poked the fire fiercely.

"Sure and it's a could world and we must all do our bist to bring a liddle warmth into it," she said briskly.

And so passed Josiah Tillytuck from the annals of Silver Bush.

3

Life seemed to change somehow at Silver Bush after Tillytuck's going though it was hard just to put your finger on the change. The evenings in the kitchen didn't seem half so jolly for one thing, lacking the rivalry in tale-telling between Judy and Tillytuck. Tillytuck's place had been taken by young Jim Macaulay from Silverbridge who was efficient as a worker but was only "young Jim Macaulay." He occupied the granary chamber but when evening came he departed on his own social pursuits. He never went on "sprees" and was more amenable to suggestion than Tillytuck had been, so that Long Alec liked him. But Judy said the pinch av salt had been left out of him. Pat was just as well pleased; nobody could ever take Tillytuck's place and it was as well there was nobody to try. She spent more evenings at the Long House that winter than ever before. David sometimes came down but he was always rather a misfit in Judy's kitchen. She Mr. Kirked him so politely and always shut up like a clam. He and Pat were, as Pat frequently told herself, very happy in their engagement. They had such a nice friendly understanding. No nonsense. Just good comradeship and quiet laughter and a kiss or two. Pat did not mind David's kisses at all.

So another winter slipped away . . . another miracle of spring was worked . . . another summer brought its treasures to Silver Bush. And one evening Pat read in the paper that the *Ausonia* had arrived at Halifax. The next day the wire came from Hilary. He was coming to the Island for just a day.

Rae found Pat in a kind of trance in their room.

"Rae . . . Hilary is coming . . . Hilary! He will be here tomorrow night."

"How jolly!" gasped Rae. "I was just a kid when he went away but I remember him well. Pat, you look funny. Won't you be glad to see him?"

"I would be glad to see the Hilary who went away," said Pat restlessly. "But will he be? He must have changed. We've all changed. Will he think I've got terribly old?"

"Pat, you goose! When you laugh you look about seventeen. Remember he has grown older himself."

But Pat couldn't sleep that night. She re-read the telegram before she went to bed. It meant Hilary . . . Hilary and the fir-scented Silver Bush . . . Hilary and the water laughing over the rocks in happiness . . . Hilary and snacks in Judy's kitchen. But did it . . . could it? Could the gulf of years be bridged so easily?

"Of course we'll be strangers," thought Pat miserably. But no . . . no. Hilary and she could never be strangers. To see him again . . . to hear his voice . . . she had not been thrilled like this for years. Did his eyes still laugh when they looked at you? With that hint of wistful appeal back of their laughter? And in the back of her mind, thrust out of sight, was a queer relief that David was away. He and Suzanne had gone for a visit to Nova Scotia. Pat would not acknowledge the relief or look at it.

Judy was almost tremulous over the news. She spent the next day making all the things she knew Hilary had liked in the old days and polished everything in the kitchen till it shone. Even the white kittens and King William and Queen Victoria all had their faces washed. May said you would have thought the Prince of Wales was coming.

"I suppose he'll be married as soon as he gets back to Vancouver," she said.

"Oh, oh, that's as the Good Man Above wills," said Judy, "and neither you nor I do be having innything to do wid it."

"Pat always wanted him, didn't she?" said May. "She never took up with David Kirk until she heard Hilary was engaged."

"Pat niver 'wanted' him," retorted Judy. "The shoe was on the other foot intirely. But ye cudn't be understanding."

She muttered under her breath as she went into the pantry, "'Spake not in the ears av a fool.'" May overheard it and shrugged. Who cared what Judy said!

There was a whispering of rain in the air and a growl of thunder when Pat went up to dress for Hilary's coming. She tried on three dresses and tore them off in despair. Finally she slipped on her old marigold chiffon. After all, yellow was her colour. She fluffed out her brown hair and looked at herself with a little bit of exultation such as she had not felt for a long while. The mirror was still a friend. She was flushed with excitement . . . her gold-brown eyes were starry . . . surely Hilary would not think her so very much changed.

She moved restlessly about the room, changing things aimlessly, then changing them back again. What was it David had read to her from a poem the night before he went away?

"Nothing in earth or heaven
Comes as it came before."

It couldn't be the old Hilary who was coming.

"And I can't bear it if he is a stranger . . . I *can't*," she thought passionately. "It would be better if he never came back if he comes as a stranger."

All at once she did something she couldn't account for. She pulled David's diamond and sapphire ring off her finger and dropped it in a tray on her table. She felt a thrill of shame as she did it . . . but she *had* to do it. There was some inner compulsion that would not be disobeyed.

Rae came running up.

"Pat, he's here . . . he's getting out of a car in the yard."

"I simply can't go down to see him," gasped Pat, going momentarily to pieces. "He'll be so changed . . ."

"Nonsense. There is Judy letting him in. He'll be in the Big Parlour . . . hurry."

Pat ran blindly downstairs. She collided with somebody in the hall . . . she never knew who it was. She stood in the doorway for a moment. It was a very poignant moment. Afterwards Pat was sure she had never experienced anything like it. She always maintained she knew exactly what she would feel like on the resurrection morning.

"Jingle!" The old name came spontaneously to her lips. It *was* Jingle . . . Jingle and no stranger. How could she ever have feared he would be a stranger? He was holding her hands.

"Pat . . . Pat . . . I've years of things to say to you . . . but I'll say them all in one sentence . . . you haven't changed. Pat, I've been so terribly afraid you would have changed. But it was only yesterday we parted at the bridge over Jordan. But why aren't you laughing, Pat? I've always seen you laughing."

Pat couldn't laugh just then. Next day . . . next hour she might laugh. But now at this longed-for meeting after so many years she must be quiet for a space.

Yet they had a wonderful evening . . . just she and Hilary and a rejuvenated Judy . . . and of course the cats . . . in the old kitchen. May was luckily away and Rae considerately effaced herself. Outside the whole world might be a welter of wind and flame and water but here was calm and beauty and old delight. It was so enchanting to be shut away from the storm with Hilary . . . just as of yore . . . to be drinking amber tea and eating Judy's apple-cake with him and talking of old days and fun and dreams.

He *had* changed a little after all. His delicately cut face was more mature and had lost its boyish curves. His slim figure . . . so nicely lean . . . had an added distinction and poise. But his eyes still laughed wistfully and his thin, sensitive lips still parted in the old intriguing smile. She suddenly knew what it was she had always liked in David's smile. It was a little like Hilary's.

Hilary, looking at Pat, saw, as he had always seen, all his fancies, hopes, dreams in a human shape. She, too, had changed a little. More womanly . . . even more desirable. Her sweet brown face . . . her quick twisted smile . . . the witchery of her brown eyes . . . they were all as he had remembered them. How lovely was the curve of her chin and neck melting into the glow of mellow lamplight behind her! She looked all gold and rose and laughter. And she had the same trick of lifting her eyes which had been wont to set his head spinning long ago . . . a trick all the more effective because it was so wholly unconscious.

How much like old times it was . . . and was not! Time had been kind to the old place. But Gentleman Tom and McGinty had gone and Judy had grown old. She looked at him with all her old affection in her grey-green eyes but the eyes were more sunken than he remembered them and the hair more grizzled. Yet she could still tell a story and she could still produce a gorgeous "liddle bite." Through years of boarding houses Hilary had always remembered Judy's "liddle bites."

"Judy, will you leave me that picture of the white kittens when . . . a hundred years from now I hope . . . you are finished with the things of this planet?"

"Oh, oh, but I will that," Judy promised. "It do be the only picture I've iver owned. I did be bringing it wid me from the ould sod and I wudn't know me kitchen widout it."

"I'll hang it in my study," said Hilary.

"In one of thim wonderful new houses ye'll be building," said Judy slyly. "Sure and ye've got on a bit, haven't ye, Jingle? Oh, oh, will ye be excusing me? I'm knowing I shud be saying Mr. Gordon."

"Don't you know what would happen to you if you called me that, Judy? I love to hear the old nickname. As for getting on . . . yes, I suppose I have. I've got about everything I ever wanted" . . . "except," he added, but only in thought, "the one thing that mattered."

Judy caught his look at Pat and went into the pantry, ostensibly to bring out some new dainty but really to shut the door and relieve her feelings.

"Oh, oh, I'm not wishing *Mr.* Kirk innything but good," she told the soup tureen, "but if he'd just vanish inty thin air I'd be taking it as a kind act av the Good Man Above."

The glow at Pat's heart when she went to sleep was with her when she woke and went with her through the day . . . an exquisite day of sunshine when beauty seemed veritably to shimmer over fields and woods and sea . . . when there were great creamy cloud-mountains with amber valleys beyond the hills . . . when the air was full of the sweet smell of young grasses in early morning. Pat and Hilary went back into the past. Its iridescence was over everything they looked at. They went to the well down which Hilary had once gone to rescue a small cat . . . and Pat, looking down it as she had not looked for a long time, saw the old Pat-of-the-Well with Hilary's face beside her in its calm, fern-fringed depths. They made pilgrimages to the Field of the Pool and the Mince Pie Field and the Buttercup Field and the Field of Farewell Summers. They went to the orchard and saw the little glade among the spruces of the Old Part where all the Silver Bush cats were buried.

"I wonder if the spirits of all the pussy folk and the doggy folk I've loved will meet me with purrs and yaps of gladness at the pearly gates," said Pat whimsically, as they went through the graveyard to McGinty's grave. "We buried him right here, Hilary. He was such a dear little dog. I've never had the heart for a dog since. Dogs come and go . . . Sid always has one for the cows . . . and May's dog isn't so bad as dogs go . . . but I can never let myself really love a dog again."

"I've never had one either. Of course I've never had a place I could keep a dog and do justice to him. Some day . . . perhaps . . ." Hilary stopped and looked at Judy's whitewashed stones along the graveyard paths and around her "bed" of perennials . . . Judy did not hold with herbaceous borders . . . by the turkey house, where bloomed gallant delphiniums higher than your head. May could never understand why her delphiniums didn't flourish the way Judy's did.

"It's jolly to see these again. I'll have some whitewashed stones . . ." Hilary checked himself again. He gazed about him greedily. "I've seen many wonderful abodes since I went away, Pat . . . palaces and castles galore . . . but I've never seen any place so absolutely *right* as Silver Bush. It's good to be here again and find it so unchanged."

"I've tried to keep it so," said Pat warmly.

"To see the Swallowfield chimney over there" . . . Hilary seemed to be speaking to himself . . . "and the delphiniums . . . and the Field of the Pool . . . and those lombardies far away on that purple hill. Only there used to be three of them. Even McGinty must be somewhere round, I think. I'm expecting to feel his warm, rough little tongue on my hand any moment. Do you remember the time we lost McGinty and Mary Ann McClenahan found him for us? I really believed she was a witch that night."

Their conversation was punctuated with "do you remembers." "Do you remember the night you found me lost on the Base Line road?" .

506

.. "Do you remember how you used to signal to me from the garret window?" ... "Do you remember the time we were so afraid your father was going out west?" ... "Do you remember the time the tide caught us in Tiny Cove?" ... "Do you remember the time you almost died of scarlet fever?" ... "Do you remember" ... this was Pat's question, very tender and gentle ... "do you remember Bets?"

"It seems as if your coming had brought her back, too ... I feel that she *must* be up there at the Long House and might come lilting down the hill at any moment."

"Yes, I remember her. She was a sweet thing. Who is living in the Long House now?"

"David and Suzanne Kirk ... brother and sister ... friends of mine ... they're away just now." Pat spoke rather jerkily. "Shall we have our walk back to Happiness now, Hilary?"

Our walk back to Happiness! Was it possible to walk back to happiness? At all events they tried it. They went through a golden summer world ... through the eternal green twilight of the silver bush ... through the field beyond ... over the old stone bridge across Jordan.

"We made a good job of that, didn't we?" said Hilary. "There isn't a stone out of place after all these years."

It was all so like the old days. They were boy and girl again. The wind companioned them gallantly and feathery bent-grasses bathed their feet in coolness. On every hand were little green valleys full of loveliness. Everything was wrapped in the light of other days. The dance of sunbeams in the brook shallows was just as it had been so many years ago. And so they came to Happiness and the Haunted Spring again.

"I haven't been here for years," said Pat under her breath. "I couldn't bear to come ... alone ... somehow. It's as lovely as ever, isn't it?"

"Do you remember," said Hilary slowly, "the day ... my mother came ... and you burned my letters?"

Pat nodded. She felt like slipping her hand into Hilary's and giving him the old sympathetic squeeze. Something in his tone told her that the pain and disillusionment of that memory was still keen.

"She is dead," said Hilary. "She died last year. She left me ... some money. At first I didn't think I could take it. Then ... I thought ... perhaps it would be a slap in her dead face if I didn't. So I took it ... and had my year in the East. After all ... I think she loved me once .. . when I was her little Jingle-baby. Afterwards ... she forgot. *He* made her forget. I mean to try to think of her without bitterness, Pat."

"It doesn't do to hold bitterness," said Pat slowly. "Judy always says that. It . . . it poisons life. I know. I'm trying to put a certain bitterness out of my own life. Oh, Hilary . . . I know it is babyish to long as I do for the old happy days . . . they can never come back, although, now that you are here, they seem to be just around the corner."

In the evening they went through the woods to the Secret Field. Hilary had always understood her love of that field. The woods had a beautiful mood on that evening . . . a friendly mood. They didn't always have it. Sometimes they were aloof . . . wrapped up in their own concerns. Sometimes they even frowned. But she and Hilary were two children again and the woods took them to their heart. They were full of little pockets of sunshine and ferny paths and whispers and clumps of birches that the winds loved . . . wild growths and colours and scents in sweet procession . . . a sunset seen through fir tops . . . great rosy clouds over the Secret Field . . . all the old magic and witchery had come back.

"If this could last," thought Pat.

It was raining moonlight through the poplars when they got back. They went into the old garden, lying fragrant and velvety under the moon. White roses glimmered mysteriously here and there. A little wind brought them the spice of the ferns along the Whispering Lane. Pat was silent. Talk was a commonplace which did not belong to this enchanted hour. It was one of the moments when beauty seemed to flow through her like a river. She surrendered herself utterly to the charm of the time and place. There was no past—no future—nothing but this exquisite present.

Hilary looked at the moonlit brilliance of her eyes and bent a little nearer . . . his lips opened to speak. But a car came whirling into the yard and May got out of it, amid a chorus of howls without words from its other occupants. Pat shivered. May was back. The day of enchantment was over.

May saw them in the garden and came to them. Scent of honeysuckle . . . fragrance of fern . . . breath of tea-roses, were all drowned in the wave of cheap perfume that preceded her. She greeted Hilary very gushingly and looked vicious over his cool courtesy. Hilary had never liked May and he was not going to pretend pleasure over meeting her again. May gave one of her nasty little laughs.

"I suppose I'm a crowd," she remarked. "Isn't it . . . lucky . . . David isn't home, Pat?"

"I don't know what you mean," said Pat icily . . . knowing perfectly.

"Of course Pat has told you of her engagement to David Kirk," May said maliciously, turning to Hilary. "He's really quite a nice old chap, you know. Such a pity you couldn't have met him."

Nobody spoke. May, having gratified her spite, went into the house. Pat shivered again. Everything was spoiled. Suddenly Hilary seemed very remote . . . as remote as those dark firs spiring above the silver birches.

"Is this true, Pat?" he asked in a low tone.

Pat nodded. She could not speak.

Hilary took her hand.

"As an old friend there is no happiness I don't wish you, dear. You know that, don't you?"

"Of course." Pat tried to speak lightly . . . airily. "And I return your good wishes, Hilary. We . . . we heard of your engagement last year."

She thought miserably, "I'm simply not going to let him off with it. I would have told him about David . . . if he had told me . . ."

"My engagement?" Hilary laughed slightly. "I'm not engaged. Oh, I know there was some silly gossip about me and Anna Loveday. Her brother is a great friend of mine and I'm going into his firm when I go back. Anna's a sweet thing and has her own 'beau' as Judy would say. There's only one girl in my life . . . and you know who she is, Pat. I didn't think there was any hope for me but I felt I must come and see."

"You'll find . . . some one yet . . ."

"No . . . you've spoiled me for loving any one else. There's only one *you*."

Pat said nothing more . . . there did not seem anything she could say.

They went into the kitchen for a parting hour before Hilary must leave for the boat train. They were all there . . . Judy, Rae, Sid, and Long Alec. Even mother had stayed up late to say good-bye. It should have been a merry evening. Judy was in great fettle and told some of her inimitable tales. Hilary laughed with the others but there was no mirth in his laughter. Pat had one of her dismal moments of feeling that she would never laugh again.

She and Judy stood together at the door and watched Hilary go across the yard to his waiting car.

"Oh, oh, it's a sorryful thing to watch inny one going away by moonlight," said Judy. "I'm thinking, Patsy, I'll never be seeing Jingle again, the dear lad."

"I don't think he will ever come again to Silver Bush," said Pat. Her voice was quiet but her very words seemed tears. "Judy, why must there be so much bitterness in everything . . . even in what should be a beautiful friendship?"

"I'm not knowing," admitted Judy.

"The scissors are lost *again*," May told them as they re-entered the kitchen, her tone implying that every one at Silver Bush was responsible for their disappearance.

"Oh, oh, if that was all that did be lost!" Judy sighed dismally, as she climbed to her kitchen chamber. Judy was quite unacquainted with Tennyson but she would wholeheartedly have agreed with him that there was something in the world amiss . . . oh, oh, very much amiss. And she was far from being sure . . . now . . . that it would ever be unriddled.

THE NINTH YEAR

1

Hilary wrote just once to Pat after he went away . . . one of his old delightful letters, full of beautiful little pencil sketches of the houses he was going to design. Just at the last he wrote:

"Don't feel badly, Pat, dear, because I love you and you can't love me. I've always loved you. I can't help it and I wouldn't if I could. If the choice had been mine I would still have chosen to love you. There are people who try to forget a hopeless love. I'm not one of them, Pat. To me the greatest misfortune life could bring would be that I should forget you. I want to remember and love you always. That will be unspeakably better than any happiness that could come through forgetting. My love for you is the best thing . . . always has been the best thing . . . in my life. It hasn't made me poorer. On the contrary it has enriched my whole existence and given me the gift of clear vision for the things that matter; it has been a lamp held before my feet whereby I have avoided many pitfalls of baser passions and unworthy dreams. It will always be so. Therefore don't pity me and don't feel unhappy about me."

But Pat did feel unhappy and the feeling persisted more or less under all the outward happiness of the autumn and winter. For it did seem to be a happy time. Long Alec had definitely stated that in a year from the next spring he hoped to build on the other farm for Sid and May. Every one knew this was final and May, with much pouting and sulking, had to reconcile herself to the fact that she would never be mistress of Silver Bush.

Mother, too, was stronger and better than she had been for years. She said with a laugh that she was having a second youth. She was able to join in the family life again and go about seeing her friends. It seemed like a miracle for they had all accepted the fact for years that mother would always be an invalid, with a "good day" once in a while. Now the good days were the rule rather than the exception. So in spite of May that year was the pleasantest Pat had known for a long time . . . except for that odd persistent little ache of indefinable longing under everything. It never exactly ceased . . . though she forgot about it often . . . when she was gardening . . . sewing . . . planning . . . when Little Mary came to Silver Bush and wanted some of Judy's "malicious toast" . . . when Bold-and-Bad trounced some upstart kitten for its own good . . . when she and Suzanne and David sat by the Long House fire . . . when she and Rae took sweet counsel together over plans and problems . . . when she wakened early to revel in Silver Bush lying in its misty morning silence . . . *her* home . . . her dear, beloved, all-sufficing home . . . when Winnie came to Silver Bush, purring over her golden babies. For Winnie had twins . . . Winnie and Rachel . . . babies that looked as if they had been lifted bodily out of a magazine advertisement. When Pat looked at the two absurd, darling, round-faced, blue-eyed mites on the same pillow she always swallowed a little choke of longing.

Rae expected to be married in another year. Her hope chest was full to overflowing and she and Pat were already planning the details of the wedding . . . a regular clan wedding, of course.

"The last big wedding at Silver Bush," said Pat.

"What about your own?" asked Rae.

"Oh, mine. It won't be a smart event. David and I will just slip away some day and be married. There isn't going to be any fuss," said Pat hurriedly . . . and turned the conversation to something else. She was very, very fond of David but things were nice just as they were. She did not want to think of marrying at all. The thought of leaving Silver Bush was not bearable.

Rae looked at her curiously but said nothing. Rae was very wise in her generation.

"It doesn't do to meddle," she reflected sagely. "I sometimes wish I'd never written Hilary about Pat's various beaus. Perhaps it did more harm than good . . . if he had come sooner . . ."

Well, life was full of "ifs." For instance *if* she had not gone to the dance where she met Brook? She had been within an inch of *not* going. Rae shuddered.

"When Rae is married," Pat told Judy, "I want her to have the loveliest wedding we've ever had at Silver Bush."

"Oh, oh, it ought to be wid a whole year to get riddy in," agreed Judy.

But nothing ever happens just as you imagine it will, as Pat had many times discovered. A week later came the bolt from the blue. Brook wrote that the manager of the Chinese branch had suddenly died. It had become absolutely necessary for him to start for China at once instead of next year. Would Rae go with him?

Of course Rae would go with him. It meant a marriage at three day's notice, but what of that?

"You . . . can't," gasped Pat.

They were sitting in the hay-mow of the church barn, having discovered that it was about the only place where they were safe from May or some prowling Binnie coming down on them. The fragrance of dried clover was around them and an arrogant orange-gold barn cat sat on a rafter and looked at them out of mysterious jewel-like eyes.

"I can and will," said Rae resolutely. "Lily Robinson will take the school and be thankful to get it. We won't bother with a wedding cake . . ."

"Rae, do you want Judy to drop dead! Of course we'll have a wedding cake. It won't have time to ripen as good wedding cake should but in all else it shall be the weddingest cake ever seen. But what about your dress?"

"Will it be possible to have a white dress, Pat . . . a white satin dress? I'm old-fashioned . . . I'm Victorian . . . I want to be married in a white satin dress. I love satin."

"We'll make it possible," said Pat. Forthwith she and Rae and Judy and mother went into committee on the subject. Pat and Rae hustled off to town for the dress . . . Inez Macaulay came to make it and sewed for dear life. Mother, who hadn't done such a thing for years, declared she would make the cake.

"Oh, oh, and she do be the lady as can do it," said Judy. "All the Bay Shore girls cud make fruit-cake to the quane's taste."

Judy pleaded for "just a liddle wedding." They could have the aunts and uncles and cousins surely. But nobody agreed with her.

"We can't have all the two clans, and since we can't have all we must have none. No, Judy, Brook and I are just going to be married here with you home folks looking on."

Judy had to reconcile herself. But she shook her grizzled head. Times indeed were changed at Silver Bush when one of its daughters could be married off like this.

"Sure and I fale ould and done," said Judy . . . looking cautiously about, however, to make sure nobody heard her.

"You've taken your own time about telling me," said May with a toss of her head when Pat informed her that Rae was to be married.

"We've only known it for twenty-four hours ourselves," said Pat. May, however, was determined to be sulky. Nevertheless, there were times when Judy surprised a smug look on her face.

"She do be thinking there'll be one more out av her way," reflected Judy scornfully.

"I'm glad to hear you're getting another of your gals married off," Mrs. Binnie told mother patronisingly. "You'll soon be like myself . . . only one left." A sentimental sigh. "What about you, Pat? Isn't it time you were thinking of leaping the ditch? The men don't seem to be what they were in *my* young days."

Pat fled to her room where Rae had piled all her belongings on the bed.

"Forget Mother Binnie, Pat, and help me pack. I never was any good at packing. Tell me what to take or leave."

The yawning trunk gave Pat a stab. Rae was really going away . . . going to China! Why couldn't it have been Rae's fortune to settle down near home like Winnie? Yet she remembered that she had thought Winnie's going a tragedy. How life grew around changes until they became a part of it and were changes no more! Winnie coming home with her babies . . . Winnie's home to visit . . . why, it was all delightful.

But China! And yet Rae was serenely happy over it all. A line of some old-fashioned song Aunt Hazel used to sing long ago came back to Pat, as she folded and packed. *"The one who goes is happier far than the one that's left behind."*

Perhaps it was true. She almost envied Rae her happiness. And yet she felt sorry for her . . . for Rae, who was leaving Silver Bush. How *could* any one be happy, leaving Silver Bush?

"This time to-morrow I'll be an old married woman," said Rae, scrutinising herself in the mirror. "I believe it's high time I was married, Pat. It seems to me that I'm getting a certain school-teacherish look already. Do you know Brook is having the wedding ring specially made. No hand-me-downs for him, he says. I hope I'll get through the ceremony respectably. Mother Binnie will be there, watching me."

"She isn't coming, Rae!"

"She is. May asked me if her mother couldn't come to see me married? I really couldn't say no. So I want everything to go nicely. I'm *not* going to look up at Brook when I'm uttering the final vow. That has got so common . . . Mrs. Binnie said Olive did it and every one thought it 'so touching.' Anyway, I'd be sure to laugh. Listen to that bluebird out in the orchard, Pat. I suppose they don't have bluebirds in China . . . or do they? But there'll be cats . . . surely there'll be cats in China . . . cats guarding mysterious secrets . . . cats furry and contented. Only . . . will they mew in Chinese? If they do! And then, of course, after a while there'll be my children. I want ten."

"Ten? Why stop short of the dozen?" giggled Pat.

"Oh, I'm not greedy. One must leave a few for other people."

"If Aunt Barbara heard you!" said Pat, as she tucked a bag of dried lavender into Rae's trunk . . . lavender from the Silver Bush garden to sweeten sheets in China.

"But she doesn't. I don't say these things to anybody but you. We've been such chums, haven't we, Pat? We've laughed and cried together . . . we're *friends* as well as sisters . . . only for those horrid weeks we never really spoke to each other. That's the memory I'm ashamed of. But I've so many beautiful memories . . . of home and you and mother and Judy. They'll always light life like a lamp. Can you quote that verse we found the other night and thought so lovely?"

"'What Love anticipates may die in flower,
What Love possesses may be thine an hour,
But redly gleams in Life's unlit Decembers
What Love remembers.'"

"It's true, isn't it, dear? We'll always have our lovely memories even in our 'late Decembers.' Oh, I'm going to miss you all. I'll often be hungry for Silver Bush. Don't think I don't feel leaving it and you all, Pat. I do. But . . . but . . ."

"There's Brook Hamilton," smiled Pat.

"Yes." Rae was very thoughtful. "But the old life I'm leaving will always be very dear to me. And you've been the dearest sister."

"Just don't," said Pat. "You'll have me breaking down and howling. I've made up my mind I won't spoil your wedding with tears."

"And please, darling, don't cry after I'm gone. I can't bear to think of you here, in tears, after I'm gone."

"I'll likely have a little weep," said Pat frankly. "I don't think I can escape that. But I never give way to despair as I used to long ago. Rae, I've learned to accept change even though I can never help dreading it . . . never can understand people who actually seem to like it. There's Lily calling you for your last fitting."

The day before the wedding there was hope at Silver Bush that Mrs. Binnie wouldn't be able to come after all. Her first cousin, old Samuel Cobbledick, had died and the funeral was to be an hour before the time fixed for the ceremony.

"It's a real apostrophe to have him dying at this particular time," Mrs. Binnie grumbled to May. "He's been suffering from general ability for years but he needn't of died till after the wedding. He was always a very tiresome man. It was an infernal hemmeridge finished him off. I'm awful disappointed. I'd set my heart on seeing darling Rae married."

"Oh, oh, I do be hoping the funeral will go off more harmonious than his brother John's did," said Judy. "John did be wanting to make all the arrangements for the funeral himself before he died . . . wanting things done rale stylish and having no confidence in his wife, her being av the second skimmings brand. They did be fighting all their lives but the biggest row they iver had was over his funeral. She didn't be spaking to him agin while he was alive and she wudn't sit among the mourners at all, nor have innything to do wid the doings. It did be kind av spiling

515

the occasion."

"All fam'lies have their little differences," said Mrs. Binnie stiffly. "Poor Sam's widow is feeling blue enough. I've been there all the afternoon condoning with her."

"Ye'll be maning 'condole,'" said Judy innocently. It was not often she bothered correcting Madam Binnie but there were times and seasons.

"I meant what I said," returned Mrs. Binnie, "and I'll thank you, Miss Plum, not to be putting words in my mouth."

Pat and Rae found it hard to win sleep that last night together. Half a dozen times one of them would say, "Well, let's turn over and go to sleep." They would turn over but they wouldn't go to sleep. Soon they would be talking again.

"I hope it will be fine to-morrow," said Rae. "I want to leave Silver Bush with my last sight of it bathed in sunshine."

"To-morrow?" said Pat. *"Today!* The clock in the Little Parlour has just struck twelve. It's your wedding day, Cuddles."

"Time I was taking the bridal jitters," laughed Rae. "I don't believe I'll have them at all. It all seems so—so *natural* to be marrying Brook, you know."

They must have slept a little for presently Pat was surprised to find herself sitting up in bed looking through the window at a world that lay in a clear, pale, thin dawnlight. It was Rae's wedding day and hereafter when she wakened she must waken alone.

A beautiful sunshiny day as Rae had desired, with mad, happy crickets singing everywhere and sinuous winds making golden shivers in the wheat-fields.

"Really," said Rae, "the weather at Silver Bush isn't like the weather anywhere else, even over at Swallowfield. I've teased you so often, Pat, for thinking things here were different from anywhere else . . . but in my heart I've always known it, too."

"Isn't it a *wonderful* day!" gushed May when they went down.

May rather spoiled the weather for Pat. But then with May everything was always either "wonderful" or "priceless." Those were her pet adjectives. Pat felt that she didn't want May to have anything to do with Rae's wedding day, even to the extent of approving it.

It was a busy morning. Brook arrived at noon. Pat laid and decorated the wedding table. May, too, by way of asserting her rights, set a huge hodge-podge from her herbaceous border in the centre of it after Pat had gone up to dress. Judy carried it ostentatiously out to the kitchen.

"Always taking a bit too much on hersilf," she muttered.

May got square by saying, when Judy appeared in her wine-coloured dress-up dress,

"How well that dress has kept its looks, Judy. It doesn't really look very old-fashioned at all."

2

Upstairs a bride was being dressed.

"Here's a blue garter for luck," whispered Pat.

Rae stood, looking rather wraith-like in her shimmer of satin and tulle. She wore mother's old veil . . . a bit creamy and a bit old-fashioned . . . high on the head instead of the modern mob-cap . . . but Rae's young beauty shone radiantly among its folds. She was so full of happiness that it seemed to spill over and make everything lovely.

"Doesn't she look cute?" said May, who had pushed herself in.

Pat and Rae's eyes met in the last of their many amused, secret exchanges of looks. Pat knew it would be the last . . . at least for many years.

"I won't . . . I *won't* cry," she said grimly to herself. "At least not now."

As Rae gathered up her dress to go downstairs Bold-and-Bad saw his opportunity. He had been sitting at the head of the stairs, very sulky and offended because he had been shut out of Pat's room. He pounced and bit . . . bit Rae right in the fleshy part of her slender leg. Rae gave a little squeal . . . Bold-and-Bad fled . . . and Pat examined the damage.

"He hasn't broken the skin . . . but, darling, the beast has started a run in your stocking. What on earth got into him?"

"It can't be helped now," said Rae, stifling a laugh. "Thank heaven skirts are long. I deserve it . . . it was I who shut the door in his face. I was afraid he'd get tangled up in my veil. It was no way to treat an old family cat. He did perfectly right to bite me."

The rest all seemed rather dream-like to Pat. The ceremony went off beautifully . . . though Rae afterwards said she could think of nothing but that run in her stocking the whole time. It would be so awful if Mrs. Binnie caught a glimpse of it somehow in spite of long skirts . . . for Mrs. Binnie was there after all, having rushed madly away as soon as dear Samuel's funeral was over. She reached Silver Bush just as the bride came down the stairs.

Mother was pale and sweet and composed and dad, dreaming of youth and his own bridal day, looked very tenderly at this baby of his who had so swiftly and unaccountably grown up and was being married before he had realised that she was out of her cradle.

Just as Brook took his bride in his arms to kiss her Bold-and-Bad stalked in . . . a repentant Bold-and-Bad, carrying a large and juicy rat in his mouth which he laid down at Rae's feet, with an air of atonement. A moment before everybody had been on the point of tears . . . but the tension dissolved in a burst of laughter and Rae's wedding feast was as jolly as she had wanted it to be.

Nevertheless she found it hard to keep back her own tears when she turned at the door of her room for a farewell look. She recalled all the times she had left home before . . . but always to come back. Now she was going, never to come back . . . at least as Rae Gardiner. She would go out and shut the door and never open it again. She had finished with it and the happy, laughter-filled past that was linked with it. She clung to Pat.

"Darling, you'll write me every week, won't you? And I'm sure we'll be home for a visit in three years at the latest."

They were gone.

"I never saw Rae look so sweet and lovely," sobbed Mrs. Binnie, her fat figure shaking. May was trying to squeeze out a few tears but Pat did not feel in the least like crying, though she thought her face would crack if she went on smiling any longer. She and Judy cleared up the rooms and washed the dishes and put things away. When Pat crept into the kitchen at dusk she found Judy sitting by a fire she had kindled.

"Oh, oh, I thought a bit av a fire wudn't be amiss a could avening like this. The cats do be liking it. Ye know, Patsy, I've just been wishing poor ould Tillytuck was here, there in his corner, smoking his pipe. It . . . it wudn't same so lonesome-like."

It was odd to hear Judy talking of being lonesome. Pat sat down beside her on the floor, resting her head in Judy's lap and pulling Judy's arm around her. They sat so in silence for a long time, listening to the pleasant snap of the starting fire and the vociferous purring of the kitten Judy had snuggled at her side. Judy had always known how to make little creatures happy.

518

"Judy, this is the third time we've kept vigil in this old kitchen after we've seen a bride drive away. Do you remember Aunt Hazel's . . . and Winnie's? . . . how we sat here and you told me stories to cheer me up? I don't want stories to-night, Judy. I just want to be quiet . . . and have you baby me a bit. I'm . . . tired."

When Pat had risen and gone to the porch door to let in a pleading Popka Judy signed and whispered to herself.

"Oh, oh, I'm thinking all me stories do be told. Sure and I'm nothing but a guttering candle now." But she did not let Pat hear her. And before long, when she had been thinking of Mrs. Binnie tearing in red-faced from the funeral, she began to chuckle.

"What is it, Judy?"

"Oh, oh, I didn't mane to be laughing, Patsy, but it did be just coming inty me head what they did be telling once av ould Sam Cobbledick. He was fond av a drop whin he was younger but what wid his wife watching him he niver got much ava chanct to one. He was rale sick wid the flu one time and the doctor lift a liddle whiskey in a bottle for him. Mrs. Cobbledick thought it was only midicine and wint out to church. Thin in drops a neighbour man, ould Lem Morrison, and *he* brings a liddle drop in a bottle, too, sly-like. But ould Sam looks at it in dape disappointment. 'There isn't enough to make us both drunk,' sez he. 'Let's put it together and make one av us drunk,' sez he. 'And let's draw lots to see which'll it be,' sez he. So the lot fell to ould Sam. But ye did be saying ye weren't wanting inny stories to-night."

"I want to hear this one. What happened to old Sam, Judy?"

"Oh, oh, whin Sarah Coddledick came home her sick man was dancing and singing in the middle av the floor and niver a bit av flu left in him. She didn't be guessing inny av the truth but she tould the doctor his midicines were entirely too strong for a sick man, aven if it cured him that quick. And now, Pasty, darlint, we'll be having a liddle bite. I was noticing ye didn't be ating much supper."

Pat found the night bitter. There seemed such an unearthly stillness over the whole house. She sat at her window for a long time in the darkness. Below in the garden the white phlox glimmered . . . one of the many flowers Bets had given her . . . that sweet-lipped friend of long ago. The pain of Bets' passing had faded out with time as gently as an old, old moon fades out into the sunrise, but it always came back at moments like this. She remembered how she used to lie awake,

519

especially on stormy nights, after Winnie and Joe had gone. She could not bear to look at Rae's little white bed.

But there was a wonderful sunrise the next morning . . . crimson and warm gold flushing up into the blue. A bird was singing somewhere in the orchard and the borders of the hill field were aflame with golden rod. Dawn still came beautifully . . . and she still had Silver Bush. Little Mary would often come to occupy Rae's bed. Her spun-gold hair would gleam on that lonely pillow.

And, of course, there was always David . . . dear old dependable David. She must not forget him.

THE TENTH YEAR

1

It took Pat a long while to get used to Rae's absence. Sometimes she thought she would never get used to it. The autumn weeks were very hard. Every place . . . every room . . . seemed so full of Rae . . . even more so than when she had been home. Pat was, somehow, always expecting to see her . . . glimmering through the birches on moonlit nights . . . lilting along the Whispering Lane . . . coming home from school laughing over some jest of the day . . . wearing her youth like a golden rose. And then the renewed sadness of the realisation that she would not come. For a time it really seemed that Rae had taken the laughter of Silver Bush with her. Then it crept back; again there were jokes and talks in the kitchen o'nights.

Two things helped Pat through the fall and winter . . . Silver Bush and her evenings with David and Suzanne. Her love for Silver Bush had suffered no abatement . . . nay, it had seemed to deepen and intensify with the years, as other loves passed out of her life, as other changes came . . . or threatened to come. For Uncle Tom's big black beard was quite grey now and dad was getting bald and Winnie's gold hair was fading to drab. And . . . though Pat put the thought fiercely away whenever it came to her . . . Judy was getting old. It was not all May's malice.

But then mother was so much better . . . almost well . . . beginning to take her place in the family life again. It was like a miracle, everybody said. So Pat was happy and contented in spite of certain passing aches of loneliness which made themselves felt on wakeful nights when a grief-possessed wind wailed around the eaves.

Then it seemed that spring touched Silver Bush in the night and winter was over. Drifts of rain softened over the hills that were not yet green . . . it was more as if a faint green shadow had fallen over them. Warm, wet winds blew through the awakening silver bush. Faint mists curled and uncurled in the Field of the Pool. Then came the snow of cherry petals on the walks and the wind in the grasses at morning and the delight of seeing young shoots pop up in the garden.

"I have nothing to do with anything in the world today but spring," vowed Pat, the morning after housecleaning was finished. She refused to be cast down even by the fact that the building of the new house on the other place had to be postponed again for financial reasons. She spent the whole day in the garden, planning, discovering, exulting. Judy's clump of bleeding-heart was in bloom. Nothing could be so lovely. But then, to Pat, one flower from the garden of Silver Bush would always be sweeter than a whole florist's window.

"Let's have supper in the orchard to-night, Judy."

They had it . . . just she and mother and Judy and Little Mary, for the men were all away and May had gone home to help her mother houseclean. The Binnies generally got around to housecleaning when every one else was finishing.

Supper under hanging white boughs . . . apple blossoms dropping into your cream-pitcher . . . a dear, gentle evening with the "ancient lyric madness" Carman speaks of loose in the air. A meal like this was a sacrament. Pat was happy . . . mother was happy . . . Little Mary was happy because she was always happy where Aunt Pat was . . . even though the sky was so terribly big. It was one of the secret fears of Little Mary's life, which she had never yet whispered to any one, that the sky was too big. Even Judy, who had been mourning all day because a brood of young turkeys had got their feet wet and died, took heart of grace and thought maybe she was good for many a year yet.

"Life is sweet," thought Pat, looking about her with a gaze of dreamy delight.

A few hours later life handed her one of its surprises.

She went up to the Long House in the twilight . . . past the velvety green of the hill field, through the spruce bush. The perfume of lilacs had not changed and the robins still sang vespers in some lost sweet language of elder days. She found David in the garden by the stone fireplace, where he had kindled a fire … "for company," he said. Suzanne had gone to town but Ichabod and Alphonso were sitting beside him. Pat sat down on the bench.

"Any news?" she asked idly.

"Yes. The wild cherry at the south-east corner of the spruce bush is coming into bloom," said David … and said nothing more for a long time. Pat did not mind. She liked their long, frequent, friendly silences when you could think of anything you liked.

"Suzanne is going to be married next month," said David suddenly.

Pat lifted a startled face. She had not thought it would be before the fall. And … if Suzanne were to be married … what about David? He couldn't stay on at the Long House alone. Would his next words say something of the sort? Pat felt her lips and mouth go curiously dry. But of course …

What *was* David saying?

"Do you really want to marry me, Pat?"

What an extraordinary question! Hadn't she promised to marry him? Hadn't they been engaged … happily, contentedly, engaged, for years?

"David! What *do* you mean? Of course …"

"Wait." David bent forward and looked her squarely in the face.

"Look into my eyes, Pat … don't turn your face away. Tell me the truth."

Under his compelling gaze Pat gasped out,

"I … I can't … I don't know it. But I think I do, David … oh, I really think I do."

"*I* think, dear," said David slowly, "that your attitude, whether you realise it or not, is, 'I'd just as soon be married to you as any one, if I have to be married.' That isn't enough for me, Pat. No, you don't love me, though you've pretended you have . . . pretended beautifully, to yourself as well as me. I won't have you on those terms, Pat."

The garden whirled around Pat … jigged up and down … steadied itself.

"I … I meant to make you happy, David," she said piteously.

"I know. And I don't mind taking chances with my own life … but with yours . . . no, I can't risk it."

"You seem to have made up your mind to jilt me, David." Pat was between tears and something like hysterical laughter. "And I do . . . I really do . . . like you so much."

"That isn't enough. I'm not blaming you. I took a chance. I thought I could teach you to love me. I've failed. I'm the kind of man all women like . . . and none love. It . . . it was that way before. I will not have it so again . . . it's too bitter. There's an old couplet—

"'There's always one who kisses
And one who turns the cheek.'"

"Not always," murmured Pat.

"No, not always. But often . . . and it's not going to be that way with me a second time. We'll always be good friends, Pat . . . and nothing more."

"You *need* me," said Pat desperately again. After all . . . though she knew in her heart he was right . . . knew he had never been anything but a way out . . . knew that sometimes at three o'clock of night she had wakened and felt that she was a prisoner . . . she could not bear to lose him out of her life.

"Yes, I need you . . . but I can never have *you*. I've known that ever since Hilary Gordon's visit last summer."

"David, what nonsense have you got into your head? Hilary has always been like a dear brother to me . . ."

"He's twined with the roots of your life, Pat . . . in some way I can never be. I can't brook such a rival."

Pat couldn't have told what she felt like . . . on the surface. The whole experience seemed unreal. Had David really told her he couldn't marry her? But away down under everything she knew she felt *free* . . . curiously free. She was almost a little dizzy with the thought of freedom . . . as if she had drunk some heady, potent wine. Mechanically she began to take his ring off her finger.

"No." David lifted his hand. "Keep it, Pat . . . wear it on some other finger. We've had a wonderful . . . friendship. It was only my blindness that I hoped for more. And don't worry over me. I've been offered the head editorship of the *Weekly Review*. When Suzanne marries I'll take it."

So he would go, too, out of her life. Pat never remembered quite how she got home. But Judy was knitting in the kitchen and Pat sat down opposite her rather grimly.

"Judy . . . I've been jilted."

"Jilted, is it?" Judy said no more. She was suddenly like a watchful terrier.

"Yes . . . in the most bare-faced manner. David Kirk told me to-night that he wouldn't marry me" . . . Pat contrived to give her voice a plaintive twist . . . "that nothing on earth would induce him to marry me."

"Oh, oh, ye didn't be asking him to marry ye, I'm thinking. Did he be giving his rasons?" Judy was still watchful.

"He said I didn't love him . . . enough."

"Oh, oh, and do ye?"

"No," said Pat in a low tone. "No. I've tried, Judy . . . I've tried . . . but I think I've always known. And so have you."

"I'm not be way av being sorry it's all off," said Judy. She went on knitting quietly.

"What will the Binnies say?" said Pat whimsically.

"Oh, oh, I don't think ye've come down to minding what the Binnies say, me jewel."

"No, I don't care a rap what they say. But others . . . oh well, they are used to me by this time. And this is the last of my broken-backed love affairs they'll ever have to worry over. I'll never have any more, Judy."

"Niver do be a long day," said Judy sceptically. Then she added,

"Ye'll be getting the one ye *are* to get. A thing like that don't be left to chance, Patsy."

"Anyway, Judy, we won't talk of this any more. It . . . it isn't pleasant. I'm free once more . . . free to love and live for Silver Bush. That's all that matters. Free! It's a wonderful word."

When Pat had gone out Judy knitted inscrutably for a while. Then she remarked to Bold-and-Bad, "So that do be the last av the widower, thank the Good Man Above."

2

The breaking of Pat's engagement made but little flurry in the clan. They had given up expecting anything else of this fickle wayward girl. May said she had always looked for it . . . she knew David wasn't really the marrying kind. Dad said nothing . . . what was there to say? Mother understood, as always. In her heart mother was relieved. Suzanne understood, too.

"I'm sorry . . . terribly sorry . . . and bitterly disappointed. But it was just one of the things that had to be."

"It's nice to be able to lay the blame of everything on predestination," said Pat ruefully. "I feel I've failed you . . . and David . . . and I'm ever so fond of him . . ."

"That might be enough for some men, but not David," said Suzanne quietly. "I wish it could have been different, Pat dear . . . but it can't be, so we must just put it behind us and go on."

When Suzanne was married and David had gone the Long House was closed and lightless once more. Again it was the Long Lonely House. Some houses are like that . . . they have a doom on them which they can never long escape.

Pat took stock of things. She was at peace. Her whole world had been temporarily wrecked . . . ruined . . . turned upside down, but nothing had really changed in Silver Bush. There was no longer anything to come between her and it . . . never would be again. She was through with love and all its counterfeits. Henceforth Silver Bush would have no rival in her heart. She could live for it alone. There might be some hours of loneliness. But there was something wonderful even in loneliness. At least you belonged to yourself when you were lonely.

Pat flung back her brown head and her brown eyes kindled.

"Freedom is a glad thing," she said.

3

One smoky October evening they found Judy lying unconscious in the stable beside the old white cow. She had not been allowed to do any milking for a long time but she had slipped out in the dim to do it that night, since May was away and she knew "the min" would be tired when they came home from the other place.

They carried her to her bed in the kitchen chamber and sent for Dr. Bentley. Under his ministrations she recovered consciousness but he looked very grave when he came down to the kitchen.

"Her heart is in a very bad condition. I can't understand how she kept up so long."

"Judy hasn't felt well all summer," said Pat heavily. "I've known it . . . though she wouldn't give in that there was anything the matter with her or let me call you. 'Can he be curing old age?' she would say. I know I should have insisted . . . I knew she was old but I think I never realised it . . . never believed Judy *could* be ill . . ."

"It wouldn't have mattered. I could have done nothing," said Dr. Bentley. "It's only a question of a week or two."

Pat hated him for his casualness. To him Judy was nothing but an old, worn-out servant. When he had gone she went up to the kitchen chamber where Judy was lying. Pale rays slanted through the clouds above the silver bush and gleamed athwart all Judy's little treasured possessions.

Judy turned her dim old eyes lovingly on Pat's face.

"Don't be faling down, Patsy darlint. I've been sure iver since Gintleman Tom wint away that me own time wasn't far off. And of late I've been faling it drawing nigh just as ye fale snow in the air before it comes. Oh, oh, I'm glad I won't be a bother to inny one long or make inny one much trouble dying."

"Judy . . . Judy . . ."

"Oh, oh, I'm knowing ye wudn't think innything ye cud do for ould Judy a trouble, darlint. But I've always asked the Good Man Above that I wudn't be bed-rid long whin me time came and I've always been hoping I cud die at Silver Bush. It's been me home for long, long years. I've had a happy life here, Patsy, and now death seems rale frindly."

Pat wondered how many people would think that Judy had had a happy life . . . a life spent in what they would think the monotonous drudgery of service on a little farm. Ah well, "the kingdom of heaven is within you," Pat knew Judy had been happy . . . that she asked for nothing but that people should turn to her for help . . . should "want" her. Nothing so dreadful could happen to Judy as not to be wanted.

But was it . . . could it be . . . Judy who was talking so calmly of dying? Judy!

Dr. Bentley had given Judy two weeks but she lived for four. She was very happy and contented. Life, she felt, was ending beautifully for her, here where her heart had always been. There would be no going away from Silver Bush . . . no long lingering in uselessness until people came in time to hate her because she was so helpless and in their way. Everything was just as she would have wished it.

Pat was her constant attendant. May would have nothing to do with waiting on her . . . "I hate sick people," she announced airily . . . but nobody wanted her to.

"Oh, oh, it's rale nice to be looked after," Judy told Pat with her old smile.

"You've looked after us all long enough, Judy. It's your turn to be waited on now."

"Patsy darlint, if I cud just be having you and nobody else to do for me!"

"I'm with you to the last, dearest Judy."

"I'm knowing ye'll come as far as ye can wid me but ye mustn't be tiring yersilf out, Patsy."

"It doesn't tire me. I'm just going to do nothing for a while but look after you. May is doing the work . . . to give her her due, Judy, she isn't lazy."

"Oh, oh, but she'll never have the luck wid the young turkeys that I've had," said Judy in a tone of satisfaction.

Bold-and-Bad seldom left Judy. He curled up on the bed beside her where she could stroke him if she wanted to and always purred when she did so. "Looking at me wid his big round eyes, Patsy, as much as to say, 'I cud spare a life or two, Judy, if ye wanted one.' Sure and he's far better company than inny av the Binnies," she added with a grin. Mrs. Binnie thought it her duty to "sit by" Judy frequently and Judy endured it courteously. She wasn't going to forget her pretty manners even on her dying bed. But she always sighed with relief when Mrs. Binnie trundled downstairs.

Yes, it was pleasant to lie easily and think over old days and jokes and triumphs . . . all the tears and joys of forgotten years . . . all the pain and beauty of life. "Oh, oh, we've had our frolics," she would think with a little chuckle. Nothing worried her any more.

Pat always sat and talked with her in "the dim." Sometimes Judy seemed so well and natural that wild hopes would spring up in Pat's heart.

"I've been minding mesilf a bit av the ould days, Patsy. It's me way av passing the time. De ye be rimimbering the night yer Aunt Edith caught ye dancing naked in Silver Bush and they sint ye to Coventry? And the time Long Alec shaved his moustache off and bruk yer liddle heart? And the night Pepper fell into the well? Do ye be rimimbering whin liddle Jingle and his dog wud be hanging round? There was something in his face I always did be liking. He had a way wid him. And how ye did be hating to hear him called yer beau! 'That isn't a beau,' sez she, indignant, 'That was just Jingle.' And the two av ye slipping in to ask me for a handful av raisins. Oh, oh, thim was the good ould days. But I'm thinking these days be good, too. There do be always new good coming up to take the place av the old that goes, Patsy. There's liddle Mary now . . . she was here this afternoon wid her liddle buttercup head shining like a star in me ould room, and her liddle tongue going nineteen to the dozen. The questions she do be asking. 'Isn't there inny Mrs. God, Judy?' And whin I sez 'no' she did just be looking a look at me, and sez she solemn-like, 'Then is God an ould bachelor, Judy?' Sure and maybe I shudn't have laughed, Patsy, but the darlint wasn't maning inny irriverince and ye'll be knowing I niver cud miss a joke. I'm thinking God himsilf wud have laughed at the face av her. He must be liking a bit av fun, too, Patsy, whin he made us so fond av it. I've been having a long life, Patsy, and minny things to be thankful for but for nothing more than me liddle gift av seeing something to laugh at in almost iverything. And that do be minding me . . . whin Dr. Bentley was here today he did be taking me timperature and I did be thinking av the scare yer Aunt Hazel did be giving us once. She had a rale bad spell av flu and yer Aunt Edith was bound to take her timperature wid her funny liddle thermometer. It didn't suit yer Aunt Hazel to be fussed over so whiniver me fine Edith's back was turned Hazel whips the thermometer out av her mouth and sticks it in her hot cup av tay. Whin she heard Edith coming back she sticks it in her mouth again. And poor Edith just about died av fright whin she looked at it and saw what it rigistered. She flew downstairs and sint Long Alec for the doctor at the rate av no man's business, being sure Hazel had pewmonia wid a timperature like that. Oh, oh, but we had the laugh on her whin the truth come out. Niver cud ye be saying 'timperature' to Edith agin, poor soul. Her and me niver were be way av being cronies but I'll niver deny she had the bist blood av P. E. Island in her veins."

"Are you sure you're not tiring yourself, Judy?"

"Talking so much, sez she. Oh, oh, Patsy darlint, it rists me . . . and what do a few hours one way or another be mattering whin ye've come to journey's ind?"

One night Judy talked of the disposal of her few treasures.

"There'll be a bit av money in the bank after me funeral ixpinses do be paid. I've lift it to be divided betwane Winnie and Cuddles and yersilf. Winnie is to hev me autygraph quilt and I promised me blue chist to Siddy years ago. There do be some mats in the garret I put away for ye, Patsy, and me Book av Useful Knowledge and all the liddle things in me glory box. And the book wid all me resates in it. Ye'll sind Hilary the white kittens, darlint. I'll be giving me bead pincushion to yer Aunt Barbara for a liddle rimimberance. Her and me always did be hitting it off rale well. And ye'll see that the ould black bottle is destroyed afore inny one sees it. Folks might be misunderstanding it."

"I'll . . . I'll see to everything, Judy."

"And, Patsy darlint, ye'll see that they bury me out there in the ould graveyard where I won't be far from Silver Bush? There do be a liddle place betwane Waping Willy and the fince where ye can be squazing me in wid a slip av white lilac at me hid. And I'd like a slab on me grave, too, in place av a standing-up tombstone, so the cats can slape on it. It wud be company-like. And ye'll dress me in me ould dress-up dress . . . the blue one. I always did be liking it. It won't be as tight as it was at Winnie's widding. Do ye be minding?"

"Judy" . . . Pat did not often break down but there were times when she could not help it . . . "however can I . . . however can Silver Bush get along without you?"

"There'll be a way," said Judy gently. "There always do be a way. There do be only one thing . . . I'm wondering who'll white-wash the stones and the posts nixt spring. Me fine May won't . . . she niver hild be it."

"I'll see to that, Judy. Everything is going to be kept at Silver Bush just as you left it."

"It'll be too hard on yer hands, Patsy dear." But Judy was not really worried. She knew the Good Man Above would attend to things.

But it seemed there were one or two things on Judy's conscience.

"Patsy darlint, do ye be minding whin that bit av news about the countess visiting at Silver Bush was put in the paper and ye niver cud find out who did be doing it? Darlint, it was be way av being mesilf. I've been often thinking av owning up to it but niver cud I get up me courage. I did be wanting all the folks to know av it so I 'phoned it in. The editor, he did be touching it up a bit though. Can ye be forgiving me, Patsy?"

"Forgive? Oh, Judy! Why . . . that was . . . nothing."

"It wasn't in kaping wid the traditions av Silver Bush and well I knew it. And, Patsy darlint, all thim stories av mine . . . most av thim happened but maybe I did touch thim up a bit, dramatic-like, now and agin. Me grandmother niver was a witch . . . but she *cud* see things other folks cudn't. One day I do be minding I was walking wid her, me being a slip av tin or twilve . . . and we met a man there was talk av. He was alone, saming-like, but me grandmother sez to him, sez she, 'Good day to you and *yer company*.' I've niver forgot his face but whin I asked her what she mint she said to thank God I didn't be knowing and not another word wud she say. He did be hanging himself not long after on his verandah, deliberate-like. And now I've tould ye this I'm not worrying over innything. All will be coming right . . . I'm knowing it somehow, being death-wise. Love doesn't iver be dying, Patsy. I'd like to have seen ye a bride, darlint. But it's glad I am I'll niver have to live at Silver Bush wid ye gone."

One afternoon Judy wandered a little. She thought she heard Joe's whistle and Rae's laugh. "The Silver Bush girls always had the pretty way av laughing," she murmured. She raked down some one who "didn't be washing the butter properly." Once she said, "If ye'd set a light in the windy, Patsy." Again she was hunting through an imaginary parsley bed for something she couldn't find. "I'm fearing I've lost the knack av finding thim," she sighed.

But when Pat went up to her in the dim she was lying peacefully. Mrs. Binnie had just gone down and had passed Pat on the stairs with an ominous moan.

"Thank the Good Man Above I've seen the last av the Binnie gang," said Judy. "I heard her groaning to you on the stairs. It's bad luck to mate on the stairs as the mouse said whin the cat caught him half way down, but the luck'll be on her. She's been talking av funerals be way av cheering me up. 'Whin me father died,' sez she, 'he had a wonderful funeral. The flowers were grand! And the crowds!' Ye cud be seeing it was a great comfort to the fam'ly."

"Are you feeling any worse, Judy?"

"I niver felt better in me life, darlint. I haven't an ache or a pain. Wud ye be propping me up a bit? I'd like to have a look at the ould silver bush and the clouds having their fun wid the wind over it."

"Can you guess who's been here inquiring for you, Judy? Tillytuck, no less. He came all the way from the South shore to ask after you."

"Oh, oh, that was very affable av him," said Judy in a gratified tone.

Judy's bed had been moved so that she could see out of the window when propped up. Pat raised her on her pillows and she looked out with a relish on a scene that was for her full of memories. The owls were calling in the silver bush. The patient acres of the old farm were lying in the fitful light of a windy sunset. But the twilight shadows were falling peacefully over the sheltered kitchen garden where Long Alec was burning weeds. Tillytuck, who had asked Long Alec if he might have a few parsnips, was squatted down on his haunches, busily digging, while a stick of some kind which he had thrust into his pants pocket stuck up behind him with a grotesque resemblance to a forked tail.

Judy reached out and clutched Pat's hand.

> "'Did ye iver see the devil
> Wid his liddle wooden shovel
> Digging pittaties in the garden
> Wid his tail cocked up?'"

she quoted, laughing, and fell back on her pillows. Her kind loving eyes closed. Judy, who had laughed so bravely, gaily, gallantly all her life, had died laughing.

4

Silver Bush was made ready to receive death. Judy lay in state in the Big Parlour . . . Pat had a queer feeling that it should really have been in the kitchen . . . while outside great flakes of the first snowfall were coming down. Her busy hands were still, quite still, at last. Beautiful flowers had been sent in, but Pat searched her garden and found a few late 'mums and some crimson leaves and berries to put in Judy's hands, folded on the breast of her blue dress-up dress. Judy's face took on a beauty and dignity in death it had never known in life. The funeral was largely attended . . . Pat couldn't help feeling that Judy would have been proud of it. And then it was over . . . the house, so terribly still, to be put in order and no Judy to talk it over with in the kitchen afterwards! Pat reflected, with a horrible choke, how Judy would have enjoyed talking over her own funeral . . . how she would have chuckled over the jokes. For there had been jokes . . . it seemed that there were jokes everywhere, even at funerals. Old Malcolm Anderson making one of his rare remarks as he looked down on Judy's dead face, "Poor woman, I hope you're as happy as you look," . . . mournfully, as if he rather doubted it; and Olive's son yowling because his sisters pushed him away from the window and he couldn't see the flowers being carried out . . . "Never mind," one of his sisters comforting him, "you'll see the flowers at mother's funeral."

When all was done, Pat, wondering how she could bear the dull, dead ache in her heart, averted her eyes from the spectral winter landscape and went to the kitchen expecting to find it a tragedy of emptiness. But mother was there in Judy's place, with a chairful of cats beside her. Pat buried her head in mother's lap and cried out all the tears she had wanted to cry out since Judy was stricken down.

"Oh, mother . . . mother . . . I've nothing but you and Silver Bush left now."

THE ELEVENTH YEAR

1

There were many times in the year following Judy's death when cold waves of pain went over Pat. At first it seemed literally impossible to carry on without Judy. Life seemed very savourless now that Judy's tales were all told. But Pat found, as others have done, that "we forget because we must." Life began to be livable again and then sweet. Silver Bush seemed to cry to her, "Make me home-like again . . . keep my rooms lighted . . . my heart warmed. Bring young laughter here to keep me from growing old."

Almost every one she had loved was changed or gone . . . the old voices of gladness sounded no more . . . but Silver Bush was still the same.

That first Christmas without Judy was bitter. Winnie wanted them all to go to the Bay Shore for the day but Pat wouldn't hear of it. Leave Silver Bush alone for Christmas? Not she! Every tradition was scrupulously carried out. It was easier because mother could share in things now, and they had a good Christmas Day after all. Uncle Tom and Aunt Barbara and Winnie and Frank and their children came. May went home for the day, so there was no jarring presence. A letter came from Rae with the good news that in two years' time she and Brook would be coming "home" to take charge of the Vancouver branch. Compared to China Vancouver seemed next door. As Judy used to say, there was always something to take the edge off. Nevertheless Pat was glad when the day was over. The first Christmas above a grave can never be a wholly joyous thing. She and mother talked it over in the kitchen afterwards and laughed a little over certain things. The cats purred around them and Uncle Tom and dad played checkers. But once or twice Pat caught herself listening for Judy's step on the back stairs.

By spring hope was her friend again and her delight in Silver Bush was keen and vivid once more. Her love for it kept her young. To be sure, often now came little needle-like reminders of the passing years. Now and again there was another grey hair and she knew the quirk at the corner of her mouth was getting a little more pronounced. "We're all growing old," she thought with a pang. But she really didn't mind it so much for herself. It was the change in others she hated to see. Winnie was getting matronly and Frank . . . who had just been elected to membership in the Provincial House . . . was grey above the ears. If other people would only stay young, Pat thought, she wouldn't mind growing old herself. Though it was rather horrid to be told you "looked young," as Uncle Brian once did. She knew the Binnies regarded her as definitely "on the shelf" and that they were calling her among themselves "the single perennial." Even Little Mary once gravely asked her, "Aunt Pat, did *you* ever have any beaus?" It sometimes amused her to reflect that she was really quite a different person to different people. To the Binnies she was a disappointed spinster who had been "crossed in love" . . . to the Great-aunts at the Bay Shore she was an inexperienced child . . . to Lester Conway she was a divine, alluring, unobtainable creature. For Lester, who was now a young widower, had

533

tried vainly to warm up the cold soup. Pat would none of him. The time when she had been so wildly in love with him in her Queen's days seemed as far away and unreal as the days of immemorial antiquity. To be sure, he had been slim and romantic and dashing then, whereas he was stout and plump-faced now. And he had once laughed at Silver Bush. Pat had never forgiven him for that . . . never would forgive him.

In the spring Long Alec again announced that the next year the new house would be built. It had been postponed twice but the mortgage was paid at last and there would be no more postponements. Pat lived on this through the summer. Nevertheless, when the autumn came again it was not just a wholesome time for Pat. Sometimes mother watched her a little anxiously. Pat seemed to have an attack of nerves now and then. She developed a taste for taking lonely walks by herself among the twilight shadows. They seemed to be better company than she found in the sunlight. She came back from them looking as if she were of the band of grey shadows herself. Mother didn't like it. It seemed to her that the child, on those lone rambles, was trying to warm herself by some fire that had died out years ago. She had that look on her face when she came in. Mother wanted Pat to go away for a visit somewhere but Pat only laughed.

"There is nowhere I could go where I would be half as happy as I am at Silver Bush. You know I've died several times of homesickness when I was away. Don't worry over me, sweetheart. I'm fine and dandy . . . and next year Silver Bush will be *ours* again . . . and I've a hundred plans for it."

A night came when Pat found herself alone at Silver Bush . . . absolutely alone for the first time, in that old house where there had been always so many. Mother and father were over at the Bay Shore and would not be back till late. It was wonderful that mother could gad about like that again. Pat thought she wouldn't mind being alone . . . *could* she be alone with dear Silver Bush? . . . but some restlessness drove her outside. There was a moan of the autumn wind in the leafless birches and a wonderful display of northern lights. Pat recalled that Judy had always been superstitious about northern lights. They were a "sign." How Judy seemed to come back on a night like this! Dead and gone years seemed to be whispering to themselves all about her. The crisp leaves rustled under her feet as she went along the path to the orchard. She recalled old autumns when she and Sid had raced through the fallen leaves. There were voices in the wind, calling to her out of the past. Many things came back to her . . . bitter, beautiful, sad, joyous things . . . crises that had seemed to wreck life and were only dim memories now. She was haunted. This would not do. She must shake this off. She would go in and light up the house. It did not like to be dark and silent. Yet she paused for a moment on the door-step, the prey of a sudden fancy. That shut door was a door of dreams through which she might slip into the Silver Bush of long ago. For a fleeting space she had a curious feeling that Judy and Tillytuck and Hilary and Rae and Winnie and Joe were all in there and if she could only go in quickly and silently enough she would find them. A world utterly passed away might be her universe once more.

"This is nonsense," said Pat, giving herself a shake. "This won't do. These moods are coming too often now."

She flung open the door and went in . . . lighted a lamp. There was nobody there except Bold-and-Bad. But Pat could have sworn that Judy had been there a moment before.

She did not sleep for a long time that night. She felt vaguely apprehensive, although she could assign no reason for it. As she said afterwards her soul knew something she did not. Late in the night she fell into a troubled slumber. Thus was passed her last night in that beloved old room where she had dreamed her dreams of girlhood and suffered the heartaches of womanhood, where she had endured her defeats and exulted over her victories. Never again was she to lay her head on its pillow . . . never again waken to see the morning sunshine gleaming in at her vine-hung window. She had looked from that window on spring blossom and summer greenness, on autumn fields and winter snows. She had seen star-shine and sunrise from it. She had knelt there in keen happiness and bitter sorrow. And now that was all finished. The Angel of the Years turned the page whereon it was writ while she lay in that uneasy slumber . . . and she knew it not.

It was Sunday and everybody went to church. Pat remembered as she went out of the door that when she was a child she had always been so sorry for Silver Bush when everybody went to church. It must feel lonely. She had always been glad when she was left home because she would be company for it.

Something made her turn her head as the car went down the lane. Silver Bush looked beautiful, even on that dour November day, against its sheltering trees. She felt her heart go out to it as they turned the corner and it was hidden from her sight.

The minister had just announced his text . . . it was always remarked as a curious coincidence that it was, "Thy house shall become a desolation" . . . when young Corey Robinson entered the church, hurried up the aisle and whispered a word to Long Alec. Pat heard it . . . every one in the church heard it in a few moments.

Silver Bush was burning!

Pat seemed to die a thousand deaths on that ride home. Yet when she got there she was curiously numb . . . terror seemed to have washed her being clean of everything. Even when she saw that terrible fire blazing against the grey November hillside she gave no sign . . . made no sound.

It seemed as if everybody in both the Glens and Silverbridge and Bay Shore were there . . . but nothing could be done . . . nothing but stand helplessly and see a home that had been a home for generations wiped out. That night Silver Bush, with all its memories, all its possessions, was in ashes!

2

They all went to Swallowfield until things could be settled. Pat took no part in the settling. Life had suddenly become for her like a landscape on the moon. She had the odd feeling of not belonging to this or any world that she had felt once or twice after a bad attack of flu. Only . . . this feeling would never pass. Mother, who bore up wonderfully, watched her anxiously.

It turned out that May had left the oil stove in the porch burning when she went to church. It was supposed to have exploded. Pat was not in the least interested in *how* it had happened. She was not interested in anything . . . not even in the finding of Judy's "cream cow" quite unharmed amid the ashes in the cellar and the old front door with its knocker, lying on the lawn. Somebody had wrenched it off in a first vain attempt to enter the blazing house. She did not care when it was discovered that all the hooked rugs Judy had stored in the garret for her were safe, Aunt Barbara having borrowed them to copy the patterns the day before the fire. When you are horribly, hopelessly tired you can't care about anything.

The only thing that seemed to be the least bit of comfort to her was that the white kittens had not been burned. She had packed the picture up after Judy's death and sent it to Hilary. He had never even acknowledged it . . . that hurt her . . . but as she had sent it to his office she felt quite sure he must have received it. Yes, she was faintly glad Judy's kittens had not been burned.

At first Long Alec talked of rebuilding Silver Bush. It was insured. Everybody seemed very pleased about the insurance . . . but no insurance could restore the old heirlooms . . . the old associations. And then, four days after the fire, Great-Aunt Frances at the Bay Shore died and it was found that she had left the Bay Shore farm to mother.

"It's strange how things work out," said Aunt Barbara.

"Very strange," agreed Pat bitterly.

The kaleidoscope shifted again. Long Alec and mother and Pat would go to live at the Bay Shore. And the new house for Sid and May . . . a house without memories . . . would be built on the old foundation of Silver Bush. It would not be like the old Silver Bush. That was gone and the place thereof would know it no more.

May was openly triumphant. A new house, with all the bay windows she wanted and a colour-scheme kitchen like Olive's! Lovely!

Mother was really pleased at the thought of going back to her old home to live.

"Mother is younger than I am," thought Pat drearily.

She felt horribly old. Her love for Silver Bush had kept her young . . . and now it was gone. Nothing was left . . . there was only a dreadful, unbearable emptiness.

"Life has beaten me," she told herself. She had had enough grief in her life to know that in time even the bitterest fades out into a not unpleasing dearness and sweetness of recollection. But this heart-break could never fade. Everything had fallen into ruins around her. She could never fit into the life at the Bay Shore. She had a terrible feeling that she did not belong anywhere . . . or to anybody . . . in this new sad lonely world.

"I think . . . if I could ever be glad of anything again . . . I'd be glad that Judy died before this happened," she thought. She did not say these things to anybody. Nobody but mother would have understood and she was not going to make things harder for mother. But her heart was like an unlighted room and nothing, she thought she knew, could ever illumine it again.

3

One evening two weeks later Pat slipped away in the twilight and went along the Whispering Lane like a ghost, to where home had been. She had never dared to go before. But something drew her now.

Where Silver Bush had been was only a yawning cellar full of ashes and charred beams. Pat leaned on the old yard gate . . . which had not burned because the wind had blown the flames back against the bush . . . and looked long and quietly about her. She wore her long blue coat and the little dress of crinkled red crepe she had worn to church . . . the only clothes she owned just now. Her head was bare and her face was very pale.

The evening was soft and gentle and almost windless. No living thing stirred near her except a lean adventurous barn cat that picked its way gingerly through the yard. Bold-and-Bad and Popka had been transferred to Swallowfield and Winnie had taken Squedunk.

It hurt Pat worse than anything else to see the dead stark trees of the birch grove. She shuddered as she recalled standing there that fatal Sunday and seeing the flames ravage them. It had seemed to hurt her even more than seeing her home burn . . . those trees she had always loved . . . trees that had been akin to her. More than half the bush was killed. The old aspen by the kitchen door was only a charred stump and the maple over the well was an indecency. The hood of the well was burned. May would have a pump put in now. But that didn't matter. Nothing mattered.

All the flower clumps near the house had been burned . . . Judy's bleeding-heart . . . the southernwood . . . the white lilac. The lawn itself looked like an old yellow blanket. Beyond stretched a russet land of shadows and lonely furrows and woods that stirred faintly in their dreams. Far away, in the direction of Silverbridge, Angus Macaulay must have been working in his forge for she could hear the ring of his anvil, faintly clear, as if some goblin forger were at work among the hills.

"I suppose I can teach," thought Pat. "I have my old licence. They won't need me at the Bay Shore . . . they've had Anna Palmer there for years to help and she'll stay on. But I can't build up a new life . . . I'm too tired. I'll just go on existing . . . withering into unimportance . . . drifting from one place to another . . . rootless . . . living in houses I hate . . . oh, can it be I standing here looking at the place where Silver Bush was? . . . that old Bible verse . . . 'it shall be a heap forever . . . it shall not be built again' . . . I wish that were true . . . I wish no house could ever be built here again . . . it will be a desecration. Oh, if I could only wake up and find it all a dream!"

"Pat, darling," said a voice from the shadows around her.

She turned . . . incredulous . . . amazed . . .

"Jingle!"

The old name sprang to her lips. The autumn dusk was no longer cold and loveless over the remote hills. Something seemed to have come with him . . . courage . . . hope . . . inspiration . . . that same dear sense of protection and understanding that had come to her that evening of long ago when he had found her lost in the dark on the Base Line road. She held out both her hands but he caught her in his arms . . . his lips were seeking hers . . . a tremor half fear, half delight, shook her. And then that old, old unacknowledged ache of loneliness she had tried to stifle with Silver Bush vanished forever. His lips were on hers . . . and she *knew*. It was like a tide turning home.

"I've made you mine forever with that kiss," he said triumphantly. "You can never belong to anyone else. And I've waited long enough for it," he added with his old laugh.

Pat stood quivering with his arms about her. Life was not over after all . . . it was only beginning.

"I . . . I don't deserve you, Hilary," she whispered humbly. "It seems . . . it seems . . . oh, are you *really* here? I'm not dreaming it, am I?"

"I'm real, sweetheart . . . joy . . . delight . . . wonder! I started as soon as I saw the account of the fire in an Island paper. But I was coming anyway . . . I had only been waiting to finish our house. I know what this tragedy of Silver Bush must have meant to you . . . but I've a home for you by another sea, Pat. And in it we'll build up a new life and the old will become just a treasury of dear and sacred memories . . . of things time cannot destroy. Will you come to it with me?"

"I'll go to the end of the world and back with you, Hilary. I can't understand my not knowing all these years that it was you I loved. Those other men . . . some of them were so nice . . . I thought I couldn't marry them because I couldn't leave Silver Bush . . . but I know now it was because they weren't *you* . . ."

"Are you really my girl . . . *my* girl at last, Pat? You remember how furiously you used to deny it? And your eyes are as brown as ever, Pat. I can't see in the dimness but I'm sure they are. And I know you look just as much as ever like a creamy rose with gold in its heart. Do you know, Pat, I never got your letter or Judy's kittens till two months ago? I've been in Japan for over a year, studying Japanese architecture. Letters were forwarded but parcels weren't. And you broke the postal laws shamelessly by tucking your letter inside the parcel. Dearest, let's go into the old graveyard and sit on a slab. I want to have you wholly to myself for an hour before we go back to Swallowfield. There's going to be a moonrise to-night . . . how long is it since we watched a moonrise together?"

"A moonrise tonight." That was always a magical phrase. Pat was in a maze of happiness as they walked to the old graveyard and sat on Weeping Willy's flat tombstone. She hadn't felt like this for years . . . had believed she could never feel like this again . . . as if some supernal musician had swept her very soul with his fingers and evolved some ethereal harmony. Was it possible life could always be so rich . . . so poignant . . . so *significant* as this?

"I want to tell you all about the home I have ready for you," said Hilary. "When I came back from Japan and found the picture and your letter I wanted to come east at once. But that very day when I was prowling on the heights above the city I found a spot . . . a spot I *recognized*, although I had never seen it before . . . a spot that *wanted* me. There was a spring in the corner with a little brook trickling out . . . four darling little apple trees in another corner . . . and a hill of pines behind it, with a river and a mountain within neighborly distance . . . a faint blue mountain. I don't know its name but we'll call it the Hill of the Mist. That spot was just crying for a house to be built on it. So . . . I built one. It's waiting for you. It's a dear house, Pat . . . fat red chimneys . . . sharp little gables on the side of the roof . . . a door that says 'come in' and another one that says, 'stay out.' It's painted white and has bottlegreen shutters like Silver Bush."

"It sounds heavenly, Hilary . . . but I'd live in an igloo in Greenland if you were there."

"There's a lovely jam closet," said Hilary slyly. "I thought you'd want one."

Pat's eyes flickered.

"Of course I want one. While I live and move and have my being I'll want a jam closet," she said decidedly. "And we'll have Judy's rugs on the floor and the old Silver Bush knocker on the door that says 'come in'."

"The dining-room has a wide, low window opening into the pine wood at the back. We can eat with the sound of the pines in our ears. And from the other window we can see the sunset while we eat our supper. I've built the house, Pat . . . I've provided the body but you must provide the soul. There's a lovely big fireplace that can hold real logs . . . I left it all laid ready for lighting . . . you will light the fire and make the room live."

"Like the old kitchen at Silver Bush. It *will* be homelike."

"You could make any place home-like, Pat. We'll sit there caring only when we want to care for what is outside . . . wind or rain, mist or moonshine. We'll have a dog that wags his tail when he sees us . . . more than one. Lots of jolly little dogs and furry kittens. And a Silver Bush cat. I suppose Bold-and-Bad is too old to endure emigration to a far land."

"Yes, he must end his days at Swallowfield. Aunt Barbara loves him. But I'm sure it will be possible to send a kitten by express—it has been done. Hilary, why did you give up writing to me?"

"I thought it wasn't any use. I thought the only decent thing to do was to leave you in peace. Besides, you *were* taking me too much for granted, Pat. You were blinded by our years of friendship. When can we be married, Pat?"

"As soon as you like," said Pat shamelessly. "At least . . . when I've had time to get a few clothes. I haven't a rag but what I'm wearing."

"We'll spend our honeymoon in a chalet in the Austrian Tyrol, Pat. I picked it out years ago. Then we'll go home . . . *home*. Listen to me rolling the word under my tongue. I've never had a home, you know. Oh, how tired I am of living in other people's houses! Pat, there is water in the house, of course, but I've made a little well out of the spring in the corner and stoned it up . . . a delightful little well where we can dip up water under the ferns. And we'll put a saucer of milk there every night for the fairies. Judy's white kittens are already hanging on the wall of our living room and that old china dog with the blue eyes you gave me years ago is squatting on the mantelpiece."

"Hilary, you don't mean to say you've got that yet?"

"Haven't I! It has gone everywhere with me . . . it's been my mascot. We'll make it a family heirloom. And I have a few things picked up in my wanderings you'll love, Pat."

"Is there a good place for a garden?"

"The best. We'll have a garden, my very own dear . . . with columbine for the fairies and poppies for dancing shadows and marigolds for laughter. And we'll have the walks picked off with whitewashed stones. Slugs and spiders and blight and mildew will never infest it, I feel sure. You've always been a sort of half-cousin to the fairies and you ought to be able to keep such plagues away."

Delightful nonsense! Was it she, Pat, who was laughing at it . . . she, who had been in such despair an hour ago? Miracles *did* happen. And it was so easy to laugh when Hilary was about. That new, far, unseen home would be as full of laughter as Silver Bush had been.

"And Rae will be somewhere near after two years," thought Pat.

They sat in a trance of happiness, savouring "the unspent joy of all the unborn years" in the moonlight and waving shadows of the ancient graveyard where so many kind old hearts rested. They had been dust for many years but their love lived on. Judy had been right. Love did not . . . could not die.

The moon had risen. The sky was like a great silver bowl pouring down light over the world. A little wind raised and swayed the long hair-like grass growing around the slab on Judy's grave, giving the curious suggestion of something prisoned under it trying to draw a long breath and float upward.

"I wish Judy could have known of this," said Pat softly. "Dear old Judy . . . she always wanted it."

"Judy knew it would come to pass. She sent me this. I got it in Japan after months of delay. I would have started for Silver Bush at the moment if I could have, but it was impossible to arrange. And anyway . . . I thought I might have a better chance if I waited a decent interval."

Hilary had taken a cheap crumpled envelope from his pocket book and extracted a sheet of bluelined paper.

"Dear Jingle," Judy had printed on it in faint, straggling letters, "She has give David Kirk the air. I'm thinking youd have a good chance if youd come back.

Judy Plum."

"Dear, dear old Judy," said Pat. "She must have written that on her dying bed . . . look how feeble some of the letters are . . . and got somebody to smuggle it out to the mail-box for her."

"Judy knew that would bring me back from the dead," said Hilary with pardonable exaggeration. "She died knowing it. And, Pat," he added quickly, sensing that she was too near tears for a betrothal hour, "will you make soup for me like Judy's when we're married?"

Just as they had admitted they must really return to Swallowfield a grey shadow leaped over the paling, poised for a moment on Judy's slab and then skimmed away.

"Oh, there's Bold-and-Bad," cried Pat. "I must catch him and take him back. He's too old to be left out o'nights."

"This evening belongs to me," said Hilary firmly. "I won't let you go chasing cats . . . not even Bold-and-Bad. He'll follow us back without any chasing. I've found something I once thought I'd lost forever and I won't be cheated out of a single moment."

The old graveyard heard the most charming sound in the world . . . the low yielding laugh of a girl held prisoner by her lover.

THE END

OTHER BOOKS TO EXPLORE BY
L. M. MONTGOMERY

THE ANNE OF GREEN GABLES SERIES
Anne of Green Gables
Anne of Avonlea
Anne of the Island
Anne's House of Dreams
Rainbow Valley
Rilla of Ingleside
Anne of Windy Poplars
Anne of Ingleside
Chronicles of Avonlea
Further Chronicles of Avonlea
The Anne of Green Gables Poetry Book - Selected Poems from
   Anne and Her Friends

THE STORY GIRL SERIES
The Story Girl
The Golden Road

THE EMILY STARR SERIES
Emily of New Moon
Emily Climbs
Emily's Quest

PAT OF SILVER BUSH SERIES
Pat of Silver Bush
Mistress Pat

OTHER BOOKS TO EXPLORE BY
L. M. MONTGOMERY

NOVELS
Kilmeny of the Orchard
The Blue Castle
A Tangled Web
Magic for Marigold
Jane of Lantern Hill

POETRY
The Watchman & Other Poems

AUTOBIOGRAPHY
The Alpine Path: The Story of My Career

COLLECTIONS
The Anne of Green Gables Collection - Volumes 1-3
   (Anne of Green Gables, Anne of Avonlea and Anne of the Island)
The Emily Starr Series
   (Emily of New Moon, Emily Climbs and Emily's Quest)
The Story Girl & The Golden Road
Pat of Silver Bush & Mistress Pat
The Blue Castle & A Tangled Web
Magic for Marigold & Jane of Lantern Hill
Lucy Maud Montgomery Short Stories, 1896 to 1901
Lucy Maud Montgomery Short Stories, 1902 to 1903
Lucy Maud Montgomery Short Stories, 1904
Lucy Maud Montgomery Short Stories, 1905 to 1906
Lucy Maud Montgomery Short Stories, 1907 to 1908
Lucy Maud Montgomery Short Stories, 1909 to 1922